Heroines of Film and Television

Heroines of Film and Television

Portrayals in Popular Culture

Edited by
Norma Jones, Maja Bajac-Carter,
and Bob Batchelor

ROWMAN & LITTLEFIELD
Lanham • Boulder • New York • Toronto • Plymouth, UK

Published by Rowman & Littlefield
4501 Forbes Boulevard, Suite 200, Lanham, Maryland 20706
www.rowman.com

Unit A, Whitacre Mews, 26-34 Stannary Street, London SE11 4AB

Copyright © 2014 by Rowman & Littlefield
First paperback edition 2016

British Library Cataloguing in Publication Information Available

Library of Congress Cataloging-in-Publication Data
The hardback edition of this book was previously catalogued by the Library of Congress as follows:

Heroines of film and television : portrayals in popular culture / edited by Norma Jones, Maja Bajac-Carter, and Bob Batchelor.
pages cm
Includes index.
1. Women in motion pictures. 2. Women on television. 3. Heroines in motion pictures. 4. Heroines on television. I. Jones, Norma, 1972– editor of compilation. II. Bajac-Carter, Maja, 1979– editor of compilation. III. Batchelor, Bob, editor of compilation.
PN1995.9.W6H465 2014
791.43'6522—dc23
2013040492

ISBN 978-1-4422-3149-8 (cloth : alk. paper)
ISBN 978-1-4422-7564-5 (pbk. : alk. paper)
ISBN 978-1-4422-3150-4 (electronic)

♾ ™ The paper used in this publication meets the minimum requirements of American National Standard for Information Sciences Permanence of Paper for Printed Library Materials, ANSI/NISO Z39.48-1992.

Printed in the United States of America

Contents

Acknowledgments

Heroines of Film and Television: Portrayals in Popular Culture would not have been possible without the support of Stephen Ryan at Rowman & Littlefield. As editors, we would also like to thank our contributors for being integral parts of this book. As a whole, your essays are creative and timely, and they allow for richer explorations of heroines in popular culture. We appreciate your works and contributions to further the understandings and readings of these heroic women.

Norma and Maja would like to thank Bob for giving us the encouragement and support to pursue this book project. We realize that as doctoral students, we are often more limited in our autonomy to initiate and then manage a book-length project such as this one. Bob, we would like to express our deep gratitude for your trust and guidance. You knew when to step in and when to let us go, and for this we thank you. We would also like to acknowledge our mutual advisor, George Cheney, in the College of Communication and Information at Kent State. We appreciate you trusting your advisees with the space to take on a book project while we were still in your classes. Thank you for being a fantastic mentor, teacher, and advisor.

Bob would like to acknowledge his colleagues at Thiel College, including department mates Victor Evans and Laurie Moroco. He would also like to thank Dean Lynn Franken and President Troy VanAken for their support and encouragement. Finally, it is a great honor to hold the James Pedas Professor of Communication position—many thanks to James Pedas and his family for their continued support of Thiel College, including providing the funding for the James Pedas Communication Center.

We also have some individual acknowledgments:

Norma: I would like to thank my family—the Chus, Murphrees, Joneses, Rayburns, Yaghmaeis, Yangs, Chens, and Lipscombs. To my wonderful

Brent, I am deeply grateful for you, and everything I do is only possible with you. I also want to thank Maja who is my wonderfully awesome friend.

Maja: I would like to thank my family—my mother Lidija who is an endless inspiration in my life, and my brother Vojislav—my friends, and Norma, my great friend and academic accomplice.

Bob: My family is incredibly supportive and kind, considering the fact that writing books necessitates long hours of writing and thinking time in virtual solitary. Thanks to my parents, Jon and Linda Bowen, for everything they do to make our lives infinitely better. My daughter Kassie's bright smile and the love in her eyes brings laughter and joy into every moment. My wife Kathy is my pillar of strength and soul mate.

Introduction

What is popular culture? Is it culture left over from higher forms of art? Is it culture that most people understand and enjoy? Is it a space to interact and create shared meanings as we conduct our everyday lives? Or is popular culture a gravitational center that pulls, drags, and attracts people to interact with it, and perhaps, also to create it? In this book, we consider heroines in popular culture as the portrayals/representations of heroic women as influential in how we think about, interact with, and even conduct our lives. What are our boundaries and limitations? What can we achieve? And at the most basic level of identity, who are we?

By conceptualizing it as a gravitational force, and by interacting with popular culture as a constellation of meaning, we have opportunities to navigate and "change our stars," so to speak, it in order to challenge and resist representations. Instead of relying on traditional forms of media production, and by using emergent technology, we have unprecedented access to interact with, read, and interpret these representations and then help others to re/imagine possibilities for social betterment. The stories we see, hear, feel, and interact with in popular culture oftentimes show us existing norms and values in our society. They can also mark shifting values and norms as our societies experience economic, social, and other changes. In that sense exploring heroines in popular culture allows understandings of women in traditional and resistant roles.

Heroines are becoming more prevalent with more varied representations/portrayals in films, television shows, and video games. Heroines are sometimes simultaneously worshipped as goddesses, reviled as villainesses, raped and beaten as victims, lusted after as sex objects, placed on pedestals as positive role models, and of course rescued as damsels. Some fight with brute strength and weapons, while others seduce, love, lead, and resist domination. As women were excluded from the hero's journey, their roles and embodied meanings are, at times, traditional, ambiguous, contested, and even controversial. Thus, in this book, we offer spaces for contributors to highlight, critically interrogate, and share re/imagined heroines.

We arranged the chapters in four thematic, but also overlapping, sections. We start with heroines on television, move on to heroines on film, discuss diversity concerns, and then conclude with heroines that cross media boundaries. We start our exploration of heroines with female heroes on television. Suzy D'Enbeau and Patrice M. Buzzanell consider Joan Harris as an erotic heroine in *Mad Men*. Katie Snyder offers Nancy Botwin as a symbol to fight against domination in her reading of *Weeds*. Jennifer K. Stuller describes a lineage of heroines that is not derived from male heroes in her reading of *Lost Girl*. From the small screen, we move on to heroines on film.

Jeffrey A. Brown challenges the ideological linkages between femininity and being a powerless victim in *The Girl with the Dragon Tattoo*. Maura Grady analyzes the Bride and two volumes of *Kill Bill* to understand a heroine's claim to masculine power. Ryan Castillo and Katie Gibson offer a subversive rereading of *Sin City* to allow for spaces of female audience empowerment. Pedro Ponce reviews *27 Dresses* and reads Jane Nichols as a Paranoid Heroine. Cassandra Bausman challenges understandings of the Sorsha in *Willow*. She argues that the warrior princess serves as a significant keystone in the quest for alternative heroic models. Cynthia J. Miller closes out the section with her analysis of *Cowboys and Aliens* and offers a new transcendent heroine to Western lore. Next, we consider diversity issues.

Catherine Bailey Kyle articulates criteria for a more inclusive feminist hero/ine's journey with her reading of *Final Fantasy X* and *Revolutionary Girl Utena*. Rekha Sharma and Carol A. Savery explore Bollywood to offer insight into how readings of heroines may serve to transcend social boundaries. Robin R. Means Coleman offers us a lone black heroine fighting against Jim Crow domination in her reading of *Chloe, Love Is Calling You*. Lien Fan Shen rounds out this section with her reading of Japanese cuteness in *Puella Magi Madoka Magica*. Lastly, we conclude with heroines that span media boundaries.

A. Bowdoin Van Riper reaches back to review the emergence of female captains in the 1990s to offer an exploration of transcendent feminine authority. Norma Jones reads Harry Potter not as a hero, but as a heroine who is loving and sacrificial. Then Carolyn Cocca analyzes the tensions of constraint/resistance of *Wonder Woman* and *Buffy the Vampire Slayer*.

Our goal is that these chapters influence the conversations around identity and the role of female heroes in popular culture, specifically in films, television shows, and video games. We also hope that these readings of heroines and their heroic narratives allow for spaces of imagination and might influence future scholarship on gender, hero/ines, and popular culture.

Part I

Heroines on Television

Chapter One

The Erotic Heroine and the Politics of Gender at Work

A Feminist Reading of Mad Men's *Joan Harris*

Suzy D'Enbeau and Patrice M. Buzzanell

How female characters are portrayed in popular culture has fascinated communication, gender, and media scholars because media has the power to both perpetuate and challenge dominant gender norms and expectations.[1] Indeed, many of the key assumptions that scholars and workers hold about gender, sexuality, power, and workplace relations are socially constructed within lived and mediated contexts.[2] In movies, viewers watch a single mother who works her way up in a law firm and reveals a pollution cover-up by a national energy company (*Erin Brockovich*); an ill-treated maid in the segregated South who becomes a civil rights activist, mobilizing her community and changing her life (*The Help*); a young woman with a penchant for Goth who tracks down and punishes men who abuse women (*The Girl with the Dragon Tattoo*); and a teenage girl who sacrifices herself for her sister and prepares to fight to the death (*The Hunger Games*). Each of these powerful female popular-culture heroines displays resilience and perseverance and works to transform her own life and the lives of those around her. Through popular culture, audiences learn that there is much to discover about gender, sexuality, and power in work and career contexts.[3]

Feminist popular-cultural analyses have focused on how gender norms and power are (re)produced, normalized, and resisted in a variety of contexts, including the workplace.[4] Scholars have also explored the emancipatory potential of workplace representations in popular culture, inviting viewers to consider how asymmetrical gender relations can be transformed.[5] We take this research as our starting point to explore popular-cultural heroines because heroines have the capacity to both reinforce and resist asymmetrical gender workplace relations. Referred to as the "paragon of paradoxes," heroines are unlike other women in their agentic characteristics but are also "quintessentially feminine."[6] In other words, part of the appeal of heroines in popular culture may result from their ability to navigate the tensions between unique and familiar, individual and collective, erotic and chaste, masculine and feminine, work and family, and public and private. They do what "ordinary" women perceive that they cannot do easily or at all. The specific tactics and strategies that heroines employ to navigate these tensions can inform intersections of gender, sexuality, and power in the workplace and the extent to which gendered inequities are sustained or transformed.

In this chapter, we critically analyze one popular-cultural heroine, *Mad Men*'s Joan (Holloway) Harris. Currently in its sixth season, *Mad Men* follows the lives of the men (and women) working in the Madison Avenue advertising agencies in 1960s New York. The series revolves around Don Draper, the most successful creative director in advertising, and his colleagues at Sterling Cooper Draper and Pryce (SCDP). Joan begins her nearly ten-year tenure with SCDP as the office manager, responsible for the secretarial pool, taking care of the agency executives, and coordinating work events. She also attends partner meetings, taking notes and ensuring that the meetings stay on track, and gently reminds the male partners of their roles and responsibilities. By season 5, she is the agency's first female partner. *Mad Men* viewers see how and where work takes place, from SCDP boardroom and offices to after-work cocktails and late nights in the office. Viewers also get a glimpse of what it was like for women to work in this context, including the juxtaposition of individual career dreams and aspirations with the everyday realities and constraints of occupational and gendered norms.

Mad Men offers a compelling case to explore the emergence of Joan as an unlikely heroine and how she navigates the tensions of workplace power and sexuality. First, *Mad Men* has received critical acclaim for its historical depiction of gender and workplace processes, garnering numerous awards and recognition. Second, show commentary and critique suggest that *Mad Men* offers an accurate picture of women's roles in the advertising industry during this time.[7] Third, *Mad Men* entices viewers with nostalgic appeals for life during presumably simpler times. The word *nostalgia* comes from the Greek words for *home* and *pain* and can be described as an emotional longing for a better place and time.[8] Indeed, "feelings of joy, pleasure, and security can be elicited by images that relate to historic events or times that are socially or collectively held to be of value."[9] However, by peeling back the guise of 1960s traditional family values, the show ironically critiques this nostalgia by tracing and exposing systematic instances and structures of sexism that permeated 1960s culture.[10] Fourth, *Mad Men* provides a telling exemplar of popular-cultural portrayals of meaningful work, work–life intersections, and how characters navigate attendant moral dilemmas.[11] Last, Joan Harris has become somewhat of a cultural icon as demonstrated by references to her characteristics, her appearance, her voluptuous body, and her relationships in news reports, magazine features, websites, and blogs.[12]

Our feminist reading of Joan Harris proposes that she is an erotic heroine who merges gender, sexuality, and power to advance within a patriarchal system that is premised upon asymmetrical gender relations. As an erotic heroine, Joan provides a counterexample to conventional heroine stories premised either on romantic love or on single-minded devotion to career or "calling." As such, she presents possibilities for audience members to envision different gender and workplace dynamics than they have viewed or experienced prior to *Mad Men* and/or provides a space in which they can come into contact vicariously with portrayed interactions and their outcomes; much as television viewers can learn how to resist and subvert workplace injustice through characters on other programs.[13] In the following sections, we theorize the heroine and elaborate on popular-cultural representations of gendered workplace processes that offer sites of continuity and change.

THEORIZING THE HEROINE

In popular culture, heroism is arguably a masculine affair, underscoring gender archetypes that emphasize a man's linear, rational-logical trajectory toward a noble goal and self-fulfillment.[14] In other words, most popular-cultural portrayals of heroism highlight a lone man's journey to stop injustices and develop a deeper understanding of himself in the process. For example, Peter Parker is the orphaned adolescent who is obsessed with loneliness, rejection, and inadequacy but transforms into the powerful hero Spider-Man, learning that with power and fame comes responsibility. In these tales of heroism, women are often overlooked, silent, victimized, passive, or rescued. In this way, hero archetypes presumably reveal what is quintessentially inherent in men and women.[15] Masculine ideals hinged on competitiveness, cause-and-effect thinking, and the individual are privileged, whereas feminine ideals that highlight community, integrative thinking, and connection are devalued.[16] As a result, feminist scholars contend that many archetypal heroic myths have been manipulated in a way to solidify gender inequities and patriarchal power.[17]

Furthermore, two cultural myths encapsulate the heroine. The first myth highlights our culture's emphasis on romantic love, including the tension of interdependence and antagonism between the sexes.[18] This myth is the basis for many romantic comedies in which the heroine eventually falls in love with the man whom she originally found unappealing or problematic (e.g., *The Ugly Truth* and *Knocked Up*). In these stories, the heroine realizes that her initial inclinations about her eventual love were wrong and that the two were intended to be together all along. The second myth is based on the quest form of romance "which puts at its center the development of a single, individual hero, and which rests on strongly end-oriented, rationally ordered, monolinear chains of cause and effect, and provides the conceptual form in which history is thought to happen."[19] This framing of romance as a quest is a linear, masculine orientation that, in popular culture, usually ends in marriage. For example, Kelley's critique of *Pretty Woman* articulates how this highly successful movie reproduces a Prince Charming story line in which the heroine is rescued by her hero after he confronts and comes to terms with her stigmatized occupation as a hooker.[20] Taken together, these myths construct and add intrigue and suspense (entertainment value) to the heroine's journey as a reflection of the hero's journey.

However, some stories privilege a feminist understanding of the heroine. From this perspective, heroines are paradoxical, their goals move beyond self-fulfillment, and their trajectory is not linear. Indeed, "to want to be a heroine is to want to be something special, something else, to want to change, to be changed, and also to want to stay the same."[21] Accordingly, heroines are also unlike other women but feminine so as to be representative of women.[22] Heroines are embedded within their community, connected to others, and confronted by the constraints of "the gender that delimits her life."[23] Like heroes, heroines have a similar goal of self-fulfillment and a realized identity. However, contemporary heroines are no longer exclusively focused on love and marriage but instead struggle to gain access to power, recognition as unique individuals, success in a man's world, and an improved life within the dominant social structure coupled with the desire to change that social structure.[24] Goal attainment is embedded within familial and community contexts in which connection, relationships, and the collective are privileged over the individual. Thus, where the hero's development is treated as unified, singular, and linear, explication of how a heroine develops reveals the complex, multiple, and contradictory ways in which feminine characters progress and toward what ends, much as men's and women's career stories occur in the workplace.[25]

Consequently, alternative readings of mythic archetypes that reclaim and privilege the feminine can illuminate our understanding of contemporary heroines. Indeed, Rushing links the mythic aspects of popular-culture artifacts to ordinary gender relations under the banner of the erotic.[26] Myths of gods and goddesses such as the Mistress, the Siren, and the Amazon offer insight into the processes whereby individuals respond to, reinforce, and problematize gendered relationships. These myths often serve as templates that shape and guide behaviors and interactions but also offer opportunities for transformation. That is, Rushing argues that "myths should help us, then, not only as ways into our individual and collective dilemmas . . . but in lighting pathways out of them."[27]

POPULAR-CULTURE REPRESENTATIONS OF GENDER IN THE WORKPLACE

Gender norms shape expectations for appropriate behaviors in communicative interactions and expectations for how the work gets done.[28] In the workplace, gender expectations implicate cultural norms around, for instance, superior–subordinate relationships, cross-sex mentoring, after-work interactions, sexual appearance, and so on. Women are expected to be passive, cooperative, emotional, and caring. Men are rewarded for their initiative, competitive spirit, and rational-logical decision making.[29] The feminine attributes are devalued while masculine characteristics are privileged.[30] Accordingly, gendered contradictions emerge when women attempt to assert organizational power because qualities associated with leading and managing are not stereotypically feminine.[31] Popular-culture representations can reinforce these problematic constructions. For example, Höpfl critiques *G. I. Jane*, which starred Demi Moore as a female solider in the hypermasculine military, for claiming that women could not succeed in the military if they maintained their femininity.[32] In another example, Buzzanell and D'Enbeau explain how female mentees on *Mad Men* are the recipients of paradoxical gender communication in which they believe they are being groomed for leadership but then are repeatedly undermined by organizational structures that perpetuate gender inequities.[33] These critiques suggest how popular-cultural representations can privilege a "fix-the-woman" approach in which the woman is to blame for her inability to think, behave, and communicate like a man.[34]

Sexuality also is insinuated in gendered occupational expectations. Indeed, Gherardi contends that the employment contract implicitly "grants command over a body, which is utilized according to the times and in the manner stipulated; and bodies are sexually differentiated."[35] That is, gender norms influence what the work should look like, and these expectations vary according to sex. Even if a man and woman hold the same position, gender norms command that they do the work differently, and sexuality is often incorporated into a woman's organizational role.[36] For instance, work that is typically delegated to women may require or at least benefit from an attractive appearance. In other cases, there is the expectation that women must (at least pretend to) be sexy when interacting with the public.[37] For example, Phillips and Knowles consider how the novel *Chocolat* conflates female entrepreneurial success with sexuality.[38] In this way, sexuality becomes a commodity that "colours the service that the organization delivers to its clientele."[39]

However, there are also popular-cultural representations of gender that suggest possibilities for change. Pullens and Rhodes consider the malleability of gender and the use of parody to critique dominant constructions of gender through an examination of the television show *Futurama*.[40] In her reading of HBO's *Cathouse*, Dunn explicates how the show offers a counter-discourse to typical constructions of prostitution by representing the women as sex workers who are independent and empowered by their work.[41] Zayer et al. examine how the women on *Sex and the City* vacillate between restrictive and contemporary gender norms around sexuality, domesticity, and authenticity, employing consumption to push gender boundaries.[42] Non-Western cultures are not immune to sexuality, idealized femininity, and consumption tensions produced, promoted, and usurped by popular culture. For instance, Luo portrays how consumerism and subordination is promoted and inscribed on contemporary Chinese women through widely circulated bridal magazines.[43] However, Chinese women resist Westernized gendered depictions by integrating Western with traditional Chinese values, artifacts, and practices to create culturally unique women's roles and ceremonies. These examples problematize gender inequities, explore the transformative potential of popular-culture representations of gender, and provide a starting point to consider how a popular-culture heroine can navigate the tension between the gendered status quo and change. We turn to *Mad Men* to elucidate our reading of Joan Harris as an erotic heroine.

JOAN AS THE SIREN, THE MISTRESS, AND THE AMAZON

Our reading of Joan suggests that she is an erotic heroine who embodies Rushing's archetypal Mistress and Siren, and then evolves into the Amazon. These different archetypal combinations are what make Joan so interesting. Our reading illustrates how she is a complex, paradoxical, nuanced character who transcends but also fulfills each of these archetypes and the conundrums they pose for everyday life. In displaying these different archetypal roles, we offer a complex reading of Joan that emphasizes transformative possibilities for gender change in popular culture.

Joan as the Siren

The first way to consider Joan is as the Siren. According to Rushing, "the Siren possesses her own body, which she freely employs to gain power over a man."[44] That is, the Siren utilizes her own corporeality for personal gain. At around five feet six inches and 150 pounds, Joan's body is full of voluminous curves. She has bright red hair, full lips, and large breasts. Her beauty and sensuality are showcased on the series. For example, during the second season when the agency was working on the Playtex account, the creative team came up with an advertisement that suggested every woman was either a Marilyn Monroe or a Jackie Kennedy. The campaign was premised on the possibility of categorizing women as exclusively one of two types. When the men label each secretary in the office as a Marilyn or a Jackie, a copywriter explains that Marilyn is really a Joan and not the other way around. There are at least two ways to read this scene. First, this commentary suggests that Joan is more sensual and has more sex appeal than Marilyn Monroe, one of the most famous sex symbols of all time. Second, the foundation of this advertising campaign, which Playtex eventually turned down in favor of a more conservative angle, is based on a problematic and patriarchal approach that forces women into opposing archetypal roles as either a sex symbol or a mother figure. Joan is categorized as a sex symbol, as a Siren.

The Siren is also "a manifestation of men's worst fears about women . . . just as surely to bring about their demise by drowning them in a sea of sensuality."[45] For example, Joan led a focus group for women to try on different shades of lipstick. During the group, Joan knowingly put her body on display for the creative team whose members were covertly observing this focus group through the double-sided mirror. As such, it may be that the embodiment of the Siren persona prevented Joan from being appreciated for her workplace and professional skills. That is, because many of the men in power at SCDP were so transfixed by Joan's body—an archetypal male fear of being consumed by feminine allure—they often failed to recognize or sufficiently value the professional and occupational contributions that she made to the agency. For instance, Joan designed office space insofar as she directed the placement of new technologies (e.g., a Xerox photocopier and IBM Selectric typewriters), secretarial rotations, and focus group participants. She organized meetings and agendas. She directed others in emergencies, calling ambulances and applying tourniquets when a man's foot was run over by a John Deere tractor during the British headquarters' inspection of the agency. Joan took care of the office and its members, even to the point that she was the only one who knew where records were kept and how to run the agency. She is the soul of SCDP.

Just as Joan received attention from the men in the office because of her appearance, it was her appearance that distracted many of them from giving her the tangible rewards that her good work for the agency deserved. To be sure, some partners who knew her also as a hugely competent individual fought for her inclusion in business practices and took her advice to heart. In these cases, she is able to collaboratively circumvent disadvantageous archetypes and associated double binds of attractiveness-competence to be sponsored for organizational positions.[46] In brief, the Siren is faced with a paradox of attraction and revulsion.[47] Exposing this mythic archetype reveals that

Joan has use value as a Siren. Even when she is promoted at the end of season 4, she is reminded of her place. Although she was named a director, her job responsibilities remained the same, and there was no celebration of her promotion. Joan may know everything in the office and have great networks, but she cannot truly be promoted in anything but name because of gender inequity regimes within which she fulfills these archetypal functions.[48]

Joan as the Mistress

Although in some ways Joan embodies the Siren who has more control over her own sexuality, in other instances, Joan is the Mistress who is used by men because of her sexuality. Rushing explains that "a woman becomes Mistress when her utility to the man shifts from soul to spirit to body."[49] Moreover, regardless of whether a woman is a willing partner or not, she is likely to suffer a loss in her own self-worth and to experience despair as the Mistress.[50]

Take, for example, the longtime affair between Joan and Roger Sterling. Roger is a senior partner at SCDP. In terms of mythic archetypes, Roger Sterling takes on the role of the Trickster.[51] Roger maintained his childishness, petulance, lack of foresight, arrogance, and self-centeredness despite heart attacks, feedback from others, and unfulfilled opportunities to assist the agency. These qualities extended to his relationship with Joan. Roger embodied a Trickster who disobeyed normal rules. He refused to take blame for his misdeeds, and he also took no responsibility for the SCDP agency's financial woes. His cleverness was most evident in his constant verbal quips. Joan recognized these characteristics and traits in Roger and often attempted to provide guidance and support. Although their relationship included an extramarital affair, Joan received developmental benefits in terms of her workplace role and eventual promotion as a result of her relationship with Roger. At first, it appeared that Joan was in a relationship with Roger for these material gifts. But she was careful not to devote herself only to this particular relationship but to also nurture friendships, so she turned Roger down for long weekends and marriage. When he had a heart attack, it became obvious that she cared deeply for him and expressed these feelings. True to the Trickster, Roger's expression of gratitude to her upon his second heart attack and wait for the ambulance let her know that he viewed her mainly as a means for sex, as his mistress.

A second example concerns Joan's relationship with Dr. Greg Harris. Following Joan's affair with Roger, she becomes engaged to Greg. Joan never tells Greg about her affair with Roger. However, upon a visit to the office, Greg becomes suspicious of Roger because he seems to know a lot about Joan's likes and dislikes. As Joan locks up another executive's office,

Greg follows her, forces her to the floor, and rapes her. Rushing argues that "men get tired of their Mistresses" once they become "used goods."[52] In this case, Greg was jealous of Roger and viewed Joan as his property. He exerted his power over his Mistress through sexual violence. Perhaps seeing no other way of achieving her goal of being married to a man in a prominent role (doctor), Joan moved forward with wedding plans despite tears in her eyes.

A final example is from an episode titled "The Other Woman." During contract discussions with Jaguar, the member of the Jaguar selection committee, Herb Rennet, indicates that SCDP might improve their competitiveness if they arrange an evening for Herb with Joan. When this idea is presented at a partners' meeting, Don Draper leaves in disgust, but the rest of the partners remain and decide to propose the idea to Joan for $50,000. Following some advice from another partner, Joan makes a counteroffer, demanding a 5 percent partnership for her night with Herb. Don learns that the proposal negotiations have progressed and rushes to Joan's apartment. Viewers see Joan taking off her necklace and putting on her bathrobe as she greets Don at the door. He attempts to dissuade Joan from going through with the meeting with Herb and believes that he has succeeded. The next day, Don presents what he feels is a very strong creative idea to Jaguar and believes that he has secured the account. However, he is surprised when Joan turns up at the next SCDP partners' meeting. At that time, he realizes that Joan had sex with Herb to secure the account and that it was not his own "magical" creative touch.[53] As the Mistress, Joan's utility for SCDP was her sexuality and her body.

However, Rushing warns that "if a woman is valuable for her sexuality, what becomes of her when she is 'used'?"[54] Indeed, men have a difficult time relating to women who attempt to move beyond the Mistress role.[55] For example, during season 6, Harry Crane, the head of the media department, becomes upset with Joan because she fired Harry's secretary for lying about her time sheet. Harry sees Joan in a partners' meeting and storms in to brag about landing Dow Chemical as a sponsor for an upcoming television special. Harry adamantly declares, "I'm sorry my accomplishments happened in broad daylight. The next time this group is called to order, I expect to be sitting at this table." Harry's aggressive lines work to undermine Joan's position at the table and reinforce the perception that she is the Mistress of the agency, valued for her body and her sexuality instead of her professional accomplishments. Indeed, despite her qualifications, work tenure, competence, and dedication, she still had to use her body to advance within SCDP. Harry was arguing that the system is not fair, but he failed to see that he has the advantage within the current system (as a legitimate member by being male and by being situated within the profit or line hierarchy) and that Joan has the disadvantage.

Joan as the Amazon

The final way in which we can view Joan is as an Amazon. The Amazon is an archetype that, unlike the Siren or the Mistress, stands apart from men and embodies strength, independence, and courage.[56] As Rushing explains, "When they do wield intellectual power, often in service of a cause, they are 'skilled in battle' and thus forces to be reckoned with."[57] Moreover, original conceptualizations of the Amazon focused on collaboration, connectedness, and the pursuit of social change.

Our reading of Joan highlights these pursuits. During season 4 while her husband Greg was in Vietnam, Joan and Roger go out for a friendly dinner but are mugged on the way home. The event prompts them to have a one-night stand, a momentary departure from their nonsexual relationship, which leaves Joan pregnant. She decides to keep the baby and leads Greg to believe that he is the father. Then, over the course of season 5, Joan seems to be becoming the Amazon mother who would do anything to fiercely protect her young, and who must balance independence–connectedness tensions, for instance, when she must rely on her mother for help in caring for her son, Kevin. Joan also struggles with her desire for independence and her desire to have fulfilling relationships with men. This complexity comes out in full force in season 5 when she rejects Greg during his furlough from Vietnam because he lied to her about his voluntary reenlistment. He insists that he is a good man, but Joan counters that he has never been a good man, alluding to the rape. At this point, it is clear that Joan would rather maintain her independence than be connected to a man like Greg, and eventually the two divorce. Indeed, she would rather be potentially stigmatized as a divorcee than maintain a marriage that outwardly seems respectable.

Our reading of Joan as the Amazon also highlights her courage as she first refuses then accepts a way to secure her own partnership and her child's future through the use of her body. She strategically made the decision to sleep with Herb from Jaguar to enhance her financial and occupational stability over the long run. Although the partners at SCDP framed Joan as their Mistress when they came to her with this proposal, from Joan's perspective, her decision to go through with it may be more in line with the Amazon archetype. Indeed, agency men are preoccupied with power, sex, and the individual. But it seems as if Joan would prefer to separate herself from that world so that she can focus on her connections in other life aspects, like to her child. Thus she engages in highly rational-logical decision making processes to ensure that autonomy.

As the Amazon, Joan knows who she (and others) is (are); she is straightforward in what she says, and she is intensely loyal to those who deserve such loyalty. For instance, her baby deserves her loyalty and sacrifice of self, whereas Greg has broken the trust bond one too many times to deserve such loyalty. Joan makes the most of the positions in which she finds, or creates for, herself. She sees life as it is and doesn't waver in life's pursuits. Indeed, our reading suggests that Joan embodies resilience and the notions that women can advance through their brains, feminine bodies, and communal (and competitive) natures.

THEORIZING THE EROTIC HEROINE

In this chapter, we considered *Mad Men*'s Joan Harris as an erotic heroine through the mythic archetypes of the Siren, the Mistress, and the Amazon. In this section, we pull together several theoretical contributions to the construction of an erotic heroine. First, we elucidate archetypal functions and behaviors of a heroine and highlight points of connection between sexuality, history, and language. That is, our reading indicates how mythic stories are (re)produced over time and shows how popular culture can both collude in and contest gendered norms, constraints, and prescriptions by drawing upon these archetypes.

Second, our multifaceted reading articulates how Joan asserts her own agency throughout *Mad Men*. Constructing Joan as the Siren, the Mistress, and the Amazon offers a complex rendering of a very complex character. Examining Joan through a singular archetype ignores this complexity and perpetuates a patriarchal tendency to force women into restrictive categories. In contrast, our reading explores how Joan takes advantage of the contexts in which she is embedded, how she forges her own path, and how she strategically pursues a life that will offer her the most transformative possibilities. Her actions problematize the dominant gender perspectives within SCDP. In doing so, our reading offers a counternarrative to dominant understandings of gender relations in popular culture in which viewers are potentially seduced into a limited interpretation of the narrator that is based upon internalized gendered codes and ideologies that appear natural and taken for granted.[58] In other words, looking at Joan through these different mythic lenses highlights the ways in which motives shift over time and context, and that attitudes, behaviors, and assumptions regarding gender are not always what they appear to be on the surface.

Third, our reading of Joan as an erotic heroine problematizes dominant heroine myths that privilege a romantic, linear quest with an end goal of marriage. Indeed, instead of seeking totality and a realized identity like the hero, the erotic heroine seeks "connection between the fragments into which a rationalist social order has divided the organic network of lived experience."[59] Joan's development is not linear, and her goals are not only rooted in a better understanding of her own self-identity. Rather, her goal is to forge a new path that will secure her future and that of her family. Her choices may seem problematic to some, but that is because her goals are in contradiction to the primary interests of patriarchy. In short, Joan is a heroine because she is a threat to patriarchy, because she is unpredictable, and because she transcends polarities. With our reading, we do not seek to resolve the contradictions that surface, such as that between independence and connection, but instead our goal is to offer an entry point for the perspective of the heroine to be displayed. We all too often critique women's actions through the eyes of men, but our reading indicates how Joan's actions make sense given the structural gendered constraints in which her decision making must happen.

In terms of future research, as women like Joan move up the hierarchy and out of the secretarial pool, African American women are entering the lowest-level jobs. Indeed, season 6 begins to explore the perspectives of African American women. This transition is ripe for an analysis of how gender, race, and power intersect and the heroines that emerge in this evolving context.

In closing, there is much to learn from popular culture about how gender and sexuality are constructed, enacted, controlled, and resisted in workplace contexts. How heroines are portrayed offers a fruitful opportunity to explore the transformative possibilities of gender change through popular culture.

NOTES

1. Bonnie J. Dow, "Gender and Communication in Mediated Contexts: Introduction," in *The Sage Handbook of Gender and Communication*, ed. Bonnie J. Dow et al. (Thousand Oaks, CA: Sage, 2006), 264. See also Katie Milestone and Anneke Meyer, *Gender and Popular Culture* (Cambridge, UK: Polity Press, 2011).

2. George Cheney and Karen L. Ashcraft, "Considering 'The Professional' in Communication Studies: Implications for Theory and Research within and beyond the Boundaries of Organizational Communication," *Communication Theory* 17, no. 2 (2007): 160–61.

3. John Hassard and Ruth Holliday, *Organization-Representation: Work and Organization in Popular Culture* (London: Sage, 1998), 7–8.

4. Jessica Birthisel and Jason A. Martin, "'That's What She Said': Gender, Satire, and the American Workplace on the Sitcom *The Office*," *Journal of Communication Inquiry* 37, no. 1 (2013).

5. Emma Bell, *Reading Management and Organization in Film* (Hampshire, England: Palgrave Macmillan, 2008), 4.

6. Rachel Brownstein, *Becoming a Heroine: Reading about Women in Novels* (New York: Columbia University Press, 1994), xxi.

7. Erin DeJesus, "Mad Women," *Bust*, December/January 2009, 50–52.

8. Lynette S. Unger, Diane M. McConocha, and John A. Faier, "The Use of Nostalgia in Television Advertising: A Content Analysis," *Journalism Quarterly* 63, no. 3 (1991): 346.

9. Unger et al., "Use of Nostalgia," 346.

10. Patrice M. Buzzanell and Suzy D'Enbeau, "Intimate, Ambivalent, and Erotic Mentoring: Popular Culture and Mentor–Mentee Relational Processes in *Mad Men*," in progress.

11. Patrice M. Buzzanell and Suzy D'Enbeau, "Explicating Creativity and Design: The Nature and Meaningfulness of Work in *Mad Men*," *Western Journal of Communication* 77, no. 1 (2013): 55.

12. Kelley L. Carter, "The Women of *Mad Men* Evolve," *USA Today*, October 23, 2008, http://usatoday30.usatoday.com/life/television/news/2008-10-23-women-of-mad-men_N.htm.

13. Robert Westwood and Allanah Johnston, "Reclaiming Authentic Selves: Control, Resistive Humour and Identity Work in *The Office*," *Organization* 19, no. 6 (2012).

14. Meredith A. Powers, *The Heroine in Western Literature: The Archetype and Her Reemergence in Modern Prose* (Jefferson, NC: McFarland, 1991), 3.

15. Ibid., 5.

16. Patrice M. Buzzanell, "Gaining a Voice: Feminist Organizational Communication Theorizing," *Management Communication Quarterly* 7, no. 4 (1994): 344.

17. Powers, *The Heroine in Western Literature*, 6.

18. Leslie W. Rabine, *Reading the Romantic Heroine: Text, History, Ideology* (Ann Arbor: University of Michigan Press, 1985), 2.

19. Ibid.

20. Karol Kelley, "A Modern Cinderella," *Journal of American Culture* 17, no. 1 (1994): 88.

21. Brownstein, *Becoming a Heroine*, xv.

22. Ibid., xxi.

23. Ibid., xix.

24. Rabine, *Reading the Romantic Heroine*, 166.

25. Patrice M. Buzzanell and Kristen Lucas, "Gendered Stories of Career: Unfolding Discourses of Time, Space, and Identity," in *The Sage Handbook of Gender and Communication*, ed. Bonnie J. Dow et al. (Thousand Oaks, CA: Sage, 2006), 161–78.

26. Janice H. Rushing, *Erotic Mentoring: Women's Transformations in the University* (Walnut Creek, CA: Left Coast Press, 2006).

27. Ibid., 15.

28. Joan Acker, "Inequality Regimes: Gender, Class, and Race in Organizations," *Gender & Society* 20, no. 4 (2006): 443.

29. Buzzanell, "Gaining a Voice," 344.

30. Marta B. Calás and Linda Smircich, "From the 'Woman Point of View' Ten Years Later: Towards a Feminist Organization Studies," in *The Sage Handbook of Organization Studies*, ed. Stewart R. Clegg et al. (London: Sage, 2006), 285.

31. Acker, "Inequality Regimes," 444.

32. Heather Höpfl, "Becoming a (Virile) Member: Women and the Military Body," *Body and Society* 9, no. 4 (2003).

33. Buzzanell and D'Enbeau, "Intimate, Ambivalent," 24.

34. Robin J. Ely and Debra E. Meyerson, "Theories of Gender in Organizations: A New Approach to Organizational Analysis and Change," *Research in Organizational Behavior* 22 (2000): 106.

35. Silvia Gherardi, *Gender, Symbolism and Organizational Cultures* (London: Sage, 1995), 42.

36. Angela Trethewey, Cliff Scott, and Marianne LeGreco, "Constructing Embodied Organizational Identities: Commodifying, Securing, and Servicing Professional Bodies," in *The Sage Handbook of Gender and Communication*, ed. Bonnie J. Dow et al. (Thousand Oaks, CA: Sage, 2006), 129.

37. Gherardi, *Gender*, 43.

38. Mary Phillips and Deborah Knowles, "Performance and Performativity: Undoing Fictions of Women Business Owners," *Gender, Work and Organization* 19, no. 4 (2012): 424–26.

39. Gherardi, *Gender*, 43.

40. Alison Pullens and Carl Rhodes, "Parody, Subversion and the Politics of Gender at Work: The Case of *Futurama*'s 'Raging Bender,'" *Organization* 20, no. 4 (2012): 3.

41. Jennifer Dunn, "HBO's *Cathouse*: Problematizing Representations of Sex Workers and Sexual Women," *Feminist Media Studies* 10, no. 1 (2010): 105.

42. Linda T. Zayer, Katherine Sredl, Marie-Agnès Parmentier, and Catherine Coleman, "Consumption and Gender Identity in Popular Media: Discourses of Domesticity, Authenticity, and Sexuality," *Consumption Markets & Culture* 15, no. 4 (2012): 352.

43. Wei Luo, "Packaged Glamour: Constructing the Modern Bride in China's Bridal Media," *Asian Women* 28, no. 4 (2012).

44. Rushing, *Erotic Mentoring*, 111.

45. Ibid.

46. Herminia Ibarra, Nancy M. Carter, and Christine Silva, "Why Men Still Get More Promotions than Women: Your High-Potential Females Need More than Just Well-Meaning Mentors," *Harvard Business Review* 88, no. 9 (2010): 80–85.

47. Rushing, *Erotic Mentoring*, 114.

48. Acker, "Inequality Regimes," 443.

49. Rushing, *Erotic Mentoring*, 53.

50. Ibid., 54.

51. Carmen Robertson, "Trickster in the Press: Kainai Editorial Cartoonist Everett Soop's Framing of Canada's 1969 White Paper Events," *Media History* 14, no. 1 (2008): 74.

52. Rushing, *Erotic Mentoring*, 62.

53. Patrice M. Buzzanell, Suzy D'Enbeau, and Stacey Connaughton, "Fascinated, Repulsed, & Bewitched: Framing Creative Directors' Work in *Mad Men*," in *Global Cities in eTimes: Communication, Design & Creativity* (Shanghai, China: Shanghai People's Publishing House, 2012), 176–94.

54. Rushing, *Erotic Mentoring*, 65.

55. Ibid., 68.

56. Ibid., 165.

57. Ibid., 169.

58. Rabine, *Reading the Romantic Heroine*, 18.

59. Ibid., 188.

Chapter Two

Burn One Down

Nancy Botwin as (Post)Feminist (Anti)Heroine

Katie Snyder

IN THE WEEDS

Showtime's *Weeds* emerged to critical acclaim in 2005 as a dark comedy offering a not-so-subtle critique of upper-middle-class suburbia. Over eight seasons, viewers followed the exploits of recently widowed housewife and marijuana dealer Nancy Botwin (Mary-Louise Parker). Despite its irreverent approach, *Weeds* received multiple awards and high viewer ratings, particularly through its first four seasons.[1] Some reviewers have suggested that *Weeds* ushered in a new type of programming—"high television"—featuring story lines and characters that were desirably gritty and subversive.[2] Critical analyses of *Weeds* have pointed to its "libertarian escapism,"[3] its treatment of drug culture,[4] beauty,[5] and race.[6] Questions about motherhood, sexuality, and identity are at the forefront of most episodes, along with concerns about how to balance work and play with the obligations of family life. These topics are approached with a kind of sardonic humor that is both disarming and alarming. In more than one episode, for example, parents admit they wish they had aborted their children, rather than face the mire and sacrifice of parenthood. Other episodes show Nancy being raped, or seeking out and engaging in very violent sex. The show doesn't valorize rape or abortion as much as it complicates our understandings of these issues. In many ways, its bitter humor is representative of postfeminist assertions that we have moved beyond the era of male domination.[7] At the same time, female characters regularly question the idea that feminism's work is done. At one point Nancy asks an Arab American drug dealer, "Why do you do that—that whole sexist thing—that whole oppression thing—why do you do that?" He replies, "You guys scare the shit out of us."[8]

Strong female characters are the norm in *Weeds*, but these women struggle dramatically in the face of patriarchal constraints and social norms, and they often willingly participate in their own exploitation in order to get ahead (or just get by). This assertion is most true for Nancy, who dresses provocatively, occasionally adopts a submissive persona during her interactions with men, and regularly engages in sex as part of her business strategy. *Weeds* episodes play out like comic book narratives to the extent that the impossible happens on a regular basis, and Nancy usually makes it so. There is no denying that her power is derived from her sexuality. Of course, this power has limits, given that patriarchy is still the dominant structure for her field of play. The thread that runs through *Weeds*, however, is the problematization of Nancy's identity. Not unlike Diana Prince or Selina Kyle, the question of identity becomes complex for those with "great power." Certainly *Weeds* plays up the power and danger of Nancy's secret identity—Nancy's power is grounded, and often imploded, by the secrecy of her alter ego. The difficulty, for Nancy, is how to reconcile her many conflicting selves—the conflict between public and private self, but also between oppositional social roles such as mother and drug dealer or loving wife and femme fatale. Nancy must create a conception of self that has few, if any, role models to emulate. In this way, her struggle is similar to current feminist efforts to understand and redefine feminine identities. Questions of motherhood and sexuality, for example, have long been near the top of feminist agendas. In feminism's Second Wave, Adrienne Rich wrote about motherhood, drawing on extensive research and personal experience to illustrate its dichotomous "anger and tenderness."[9] While some feminists argue that women should avoid pregnancy and/or motherhood in order to build an equitable society,[10] others, like Rich, argue that we need not relinquish motherhood, but we do need to rethink it. The feminist debate about sexuality is similar in that some activists argue for a sex-positive feminism that advocates use of pornographic material and prostitution as valid sexual practices,[11] while others argue that sex is oppression of women and violence against women, and there is no way to conceive of prostitution as a liberating profession.[12] These debates, including subsequent efforts to critique and reimagine feminine identities, are evident in Nancy's life and in the characters she confronts. Thus, I argue that *Weeds* provides a forum to reconsider feminine identities, particularly in the context of sexuality, motherhood, and the interplay between them. Further, I argue that Nancy's struggle provides a clear example of why we still need feminism today.

MOMMY DEALER IN THE BURBS

Nancy's saga begins in Agrestic, a fictional suburb of Los Angeles where she decides to support her sons by selling marijuana to upstanding community members—as the theme song suggests, she sells to "doctors and lawyers and business executives."[13] During the first season she carries a beeper and responds to calls from customers between PTA meetings (where she's head of the "healthy kids committee") and at soccer games. Nancy gets into the business because she has no marketable skills but feels she can capitalize on the heavy flow of marijuana through her community. Initially, Nancy is quite successful at dealing, though she rejects the idea that she is a "dealer." In terms of personal identity, she understands herself to be a mom, though she openly questions modern motherhood as embodied in her fellow PTA members and their obsession with controlling every aspect of their children's education and life experiences. Nancy rationalizes her drug dealing as necessary to care for her sons, to maintain their lifestyle and return some sense of security after her husband's tragic heart attack while he was out running with ten-year-old Shane (Alexander Gould). Very quickly, however, Nancy realizes that she enjoys dealing, taking pleasure in its quick financial rewards, along with its inherent risk and danger.

Admittedly, Nancy is both savior and persecutor of the men in her life. As her business success peaks and plummets, Nancy's character develops along an uncomfortable arc where she flies ever further from "the cool mom,"[14] willing to talk with her son's girlfriend about sex, to the neglectful mom who abdicates the everydayness of parenting to brother-in-law Andy Botwin (Justin Kirk), to family friend and tagalong Doug Wilson (Kevin Nealon), and to her oldest son, Silas (Hunter Parrish). Despite much rebellion and frustration, Nancy's boys continue to look to her for approval and direction. Further, Shane feels that his mother is in need of *his* protection after his father Judah's (Jeffery Dean Morgan) death. Nancy repeatedly asserts to Shane that she is the protector of the family and that he should worry about "kid things." But Shane sees her protection as reckless and speculates that her success is born mostly of luck. The boys suffer for her recklessness, as Silas is beaten by a competing drug dealer[15] and Shane takes a bullet in the arm.[16] Both boys also agree to morally questionable and emotionally disruptive behavior for the sake of the family business.

IS SHE A HERO?

If we define a heroine as a central female character who acts courageously for the sake of others,[17] Nancy fits the bill—she faces guns and gangsters to save her sons on a regular basis. If we include the addendum that she must exhibit "noble qualities,"[18] then it may be easier to locate Nancy in the realm of antiheroine—one who acts courageously but lacks nobility.[19] In the blogosphere, there has been much debate about Nancy's moral character, particularly after she burns down her house, pursues a violent affair with a leader of the Mexican mafia, and travels ever deeper into the world of the illegal drug trade. Online reviewers have voiced their disapproval, calling her selfish, with a penchant for danger, and unwilling to rectify her sons' burgeoning criminal behavior (Silas grows and distributes his own marijuana strain, Shane deals marijuana at school).[20] But to call Nancy an antiheroine ignores the subtlety and depth of her love in action. She is not a typical mother, but there is no fifth act of *Medea* here. Nancy burns down her house because she wants to start over; she wants to protect her children and herself from a lifestyle that had gotten out of hand. Her pursuit of drug kingpin Esteban Reyes (Demian Bichir) is largely selfish, but her drug dealing is simply "the family business." Certainly Nancy is unorthodox, and her life is an exaggeration of reality. But her exploits raise real questions about the difference between a heroine and an antiheroine—and how and why we distinguish between the two, particularly in the context of feminist analyses which suggest that traditional heroic qualities are not always transferrable to women's lives and circumstances. For example, one analysis of "(super)heroism" suggests that a heroine's agency is often limited and she frequently must defer to authority. A hero, in contrast, is typically self-determined and lauded for his agential courage.[21] Nancy is heroic in this latter masculine sense, as she defers to no one and takes charge of difficult situations where others (mostly men) fail to act.

TAPPING INTO HER HIGHER POWER

If Nancy were a superhero, her superpower would be sex. Early in the series, in fact, when Nancy is still mourning the loss of her husband, she has a dream that is sexually arousing. She tries to "get herself off" but is unable. She alludes to this problem in conversation with Andy when he tells her to "tap into her higher power" to find a solution to a separate problem she is facing. Nancy replies, "If I could tap into my higher power, my fingers wouldn't be numb."[22] Nancy finds her power later in season 1 when she goes after competing dealer Alejandro (Vincent Laresca), who throws pennies at Nancy's car and stakes out her house. Nancy follows him into an abandoned alley where the confrontation is heated and quickly escalates into sex. Nancy is clearly the aggressor and finishes the encounter by pointing Shane's BB gun at Alejandro's jeans and saying, "This dick does nice work. I'd hate to see it full of holes. It's nothing personal. This was unexpected, but it's never going to happen again. Okay, Menudo? Stay away from my family. You stay away from my house, and you quit with the fuckin' pennies. Okay?"[23] This encounter is the first of many where Nancy uses sex, both for her own pleasure and as a power play to secure her business. She acts as a stereotypical male predator in that she does not want a relationship with her sexual partner and she does not know or even care what his name is—in fact, calling him "Menudo" can be read as a racial slur meant to further humiliate him. In line with Foucauldian analysis, Nancy's sexuality proves "an especially dense transfer point for relations of power."[24] In this case, theorist Michel Foucault argues that sex is not all powerful, but it is an extremely useful "maneuver" in power relations. Further, he suggests that no version of sexuality or sexual practice is natural or unnatural—rather, sexuality is socially constructed according to structures of power (including taboo) and the lines along which that power is transferred.[25] Nancy is, from a feminist standpoint, outside of many power lines. Still she has a sexual appetite that always works to her advantage because she does not easily become emotionally attached to her partners. Instead, she has a long history of sleeping with men who become obsessed with her, while she repeatedly finds reasons to move on. Alejandro, for example, sends her lingerie and shows up at her bakery to ask her out. There are few people in her life, in fact, who are not obsessed with her, including her two sons who make their own way through the Oedipal complex in season 4.[26]

Indeed, there is much about Nancy's sexuality that defies easy categorization—just as her drug business takes her back and forth across borders, Nancy plays across the line that separates masculine from feminine. Feminist theorist Catharine MacKinnon expands on Foucault's analysis above, arguing that sexuality is "a social construct of male power: defined by men, forced on women, and constitutive in the meaning of gender."[27] It is true that Nancy works within a patriarchal field of play, but she usually defines her terms of engagement. Notably, her terms are not exclusively heterosexual. In season 1, Nancy tells friend Celia Hodes (Elizabeth Perkins) that she slept with a woman in college,[28] and in season 7 we learn that Nancy took a lover, Zoya (Olga Sosnovska), during her three years in prison. The fluidity of Nancy's sexuality works counter to traditional sex/gender constructs. It calls into question what is appropriate sexual behavior for women, particularly for a middle-aged mother of three sons. Not surprisingly, Nancy is regularly teased and ridiculed by Andy and her sons for behaving and dressing like a "whore." Early in the first season, as Nancy heads out to a club with Celia, Andy comments that it looks like she is not just dealing drugs, but also "turnin' tricks." Nancy responds to Andy's characterization of her attire by turning attention to the fact that he has no job, that she is providing a place for him to live and supporting him financially.[29] Importantly, Nancy does not reject the term *whore*, nor does she openly engage with it. Rather, she characterizes her dress and sexual exploits as necessary to earn a living. In this way, she represents a facet of Third Wave feminist thought that seeks to embrace and/or rehabilitate "whoring." This group seeks to affirm careers that make use of sex for pleasure and profit.[30] They also advocate for more discussion of women's sexual fantasies and preferences, even if those fantasies are violent and exploitative. In fact, MacKinnon argues that the majority of women do not enjoy sex because sex *is* violence against women.[31]

As mentioned above, many of Nancy's sexual encounters are violent. A dramatic example appears in season 5 where Esteban rapes Nancy after learning that she has put their unborn child in danger. Quite literally, he tells her that she no longer dictates the terms of their relationship, and he uses violent penetration to make his point. This scene is extremely disturbing, but it is not without some sense of ambiguity given that Nancy is shown to have a history of enjoying violent sex, and in this particular scene it is not clear whether she is enjoying herself or whether she feels she is being violated. In at least two other scenes, in seasons 3[32] and 6,[33] Nancy takes pleasure in provoking men into having angry, violent sex with her. She laughs at their anger and takes pleasure in their inability to control their emotions. In addition, the rape event nearly backfires against Esteban as, shortly after the incident, Nancy starts to bleed and must make an emergency doctor visit. As it turns out, the baby's health was not in jeopardy, but Nancy jokes bitterly to the doctor (who is a Mexican doctor under Esteban's thumb) that it must be "all that rough sex" she has been having that caused the bleeding.

MOMMY DEAREST

Given that we understand mothers to be "pure" and "nurturing,"[34] Nancy continually fails to meet this standard. One recent analysis of television moms suggests that Nancy's nonconformity pokes much-needed holes in the "shroud of motherhood," under which most women are still heavily encumbered.[35] Indeed, Nancy is a mother who cannot abide by the scripts and tenets of patriarchal motherhood. But, as Adrienne Rich argued decades ago, there is a significant difference between *motherhood* and *mothering*. Motherhood is a patriarchal institution that limits women's power and assigns them a particular role that is as maligned as it is revered. Mothering is a practice wherein one loves and protects her children within the bounds of her own values, abilities, and weaknesses.[36] Nancy's mothering is no different—passionate, impulsive, and sometimes deeply flawed. Her love for her sons is profound but also difficult for her to express. An example of her struggle comes when she tries to compose a birthday card for Silas. When Silas turns eighteen, Nancy has to drive to meet Esteban in Tijuana. Nancy orders a gift basket for Silas while on the road, and after composing several rambling apologies and excuses for her absence, she finally decides on a note that says simply, "Silas, You are loved. Me. Mom."[37]

Nancy asks just about everyone in her line of work how to balance family and dealing. Heylia James (Tonye Patano) provides the most advice, advocating family dinners, spanking, and fear. Conrad (Romany Malco) advises Nancy to keep her product as far from her family as possible. Esteban and local big shot Tusk (Keith Diamond) move their children overseas and across the country, respectively. When Nancy asks Tusk if he misses his kids, he replies that he would miss them more "if they were dead."[38] Somehow Nancy and her sons cannot bring themselves to separate, at least not until it is forced upon them by her incarceration. With great consistency, she enacts "[t]hat curious primitive reaction of protectiveness, the beast defending her cub, when anyone attacks or criticizes him—and yet no one more hard on him than I!"[39] Nancy's mothering is messy and inconsistent, but she never gives up on her kids. For example, when it would have been easier, and likely safer for almost everyone, to return her youngest son Stevie to Esteban, Nancy goes to jail to protect and save them all.

HER MILD-MANNERED ALTER EGOS

Nancy survives jail, along with a host of other traumas. In the series' final episode we find her as a successful businesswoman and mother, hosting a party for Stevie's (Mateus Ward) Bar Mitzvah. At one point someone draws Nancy's attention to a statue in her living room. The statue is of Kali, the Hindu goddess of death, sex, and violence, but also the goddess of motherly love.[40] This eight-limbed figure is symbolic of Nancy and provides a visualization of the many identities she embodies. While it may seem ironic to associate the same goddess with these disparate characteristics, the linkages become clearer in the context of Nancy's experience. Kali is part of a patriarchal religion that has constructed women as dichotomously "pure" and "impure," "dangerous" and life giving, "moral" and "corrupt,"[41] leaving no room to inhabit the vast gray area in between these extremes. Nancy lives through these dichotomies as much as they are embodied in her—at the same time, she seems always in a process of sorting them, discarding them, and negotiating new terrain.

One of the most conflicted of Nancy's identities is that of wife, and with good reason. Despite her frequent partnering (for sex and for business), Nancy is a lone wolf. She has no female friends and spends most of her time with her family. Feminists have long argued that marriage is an arrangement in which a married woman is constrained as literally belonging to her husband. This is still the case in many countries around the world. Given her sexual prowess, Nancy could have found another wealthy husband in short order and maintained her suburban wife/mommy identity—DEA agent and second husband Peter Scottson (Martin Donovan) proposes as much as a way to encourage Nancy to get out of the drug business altogether. Nancy never takes Scottson's name, as their marriage was a sham, meant to protect their burgeoning relationship and inoculate each other from the harms of their adversarial vocations. When Nancy agrees to marry Esteban, she tells him that she is afraid Mrs. Esteban Reyes (her married identity) is going to kill Nancy Botwin. He tells her she does not need to change her name after their marriage.[42] Her choice to maintain her original married name, Botwin, seems a tribute to Judah—an indication of her love for him and affinity for the identity she cultivated when they were together. All of which is not to say that that identity was unproblematic. Her choice to sell marijuana reveals both her tolerance for risk and her desire to take control of her life in a way that was not available to her when Judah was alive. Nancy wants to solve her problem (lack of funds to support her family) on her own terms. But she has to reinvent herself in order to accomplish that goal.

But Nancy's terms are not easy to define, particularly her perceptions of masculinity and femininity. As mentioned above, her sexuality is not easily located along traditional gender lines—this may be due in part to her frustration with men and male behavior more broadly. With the exception of Andy, the adult men in Nancy's life have access to political and economic power—but they tend to look to Nancy for direction and support, often acting like wayward children. Doug Wilson, a gifted CPA and corporate executive, is an excellent example of this tendency, as he expends most of his energy on getting high and watching porn. Nancy provides him with a place to live, a sense of purpose, and a family of support. She does the same for Andy. In both cases, masculinity is repeatedly enacted as weak, needy, and childish. We can see a slightly different characterization in her relationship with Esteban. Esteban is the epitome of masculine leadership and counterculture machismo, but he is also a parent and Nancy finds in him a persona she can emulate. While he is unwilling to share power with Nancy, he admits that she makes him do things he wouldn't normally do.[43] She leaves him later because she must—as Shane murders Esteban's ally and Mexican politician, Pilar Zuazo (Kate del Castillo)—but also because his masculinity begins to seem childish and weak. It is childish in that he forbids her from wearing his deodorant because he does not want her to smell like a man,[44] and weak because he continually agrees to remake himself according to Pilar's will. Shortly before Nancy leaves Esteban, she tells her massage therapist that men are weak, women are strong—she makes the same assertion to Andy later and admits that she can no longer depend on men.[45]

Through it all, her identity as a drug dealer is never concealed for long. Nancy is continually amazed when people find out what she is up to: Andy, her sons, Celia, DEA captain Roy Till (Jack Stehlin)—just to name a few.

Certainly this failure is what leads her to pursue legitimate work. For a short time at least, she inhabits an acceptable, well-defined social identity—the working mother. But this "fitting in" does not last long. Seven years after she launches her legal weed empire, we learn that she has married a fourth husband, Rabbi David Bloom (David Julian Hirsh). David adopts Stevie, and the three of them live happily until David is tragically killed in a car accident. Stevie then decides to go to boarding school and develop his soccer skills. In contrast to Shane and Silas, Stevie has a good relationship with his mom and thanks her for always being there for him. Nancy tears up at his words, as they remind her of what she tried and failed to do for Silas and Shane. Faced with the prospect of being alone, Nancy tries to salvage her relationship with Andy, which ended badly seven years prior. Andy tells her that she saved him, gave him purpose and direction, and he will always love her—but that he cannot be around her. For the first time since the births of her children, Nancy is left to consider how she wants to define herself moving forward.

IT'S TIME TO FACE YOURSELF

Nancy Botwin embodies feminist struggle, past and current. She shows us what feminism has wrought to date, in all its incompleteness and fragmentary glory. Yes, women are free to make choices not imaginable even twenty years ago. But who do we mean when we say *women*, and how are women allowed to behave in this new world feminism is still creating? In terms of Nancy's life, she is able to pursue her own goals and is beholden to no one, but she also assents to marriage (repeatedly) and spends at least fifteen years as a housewife. She is a femme fatale in that all four of her husbands end up dead, but she is not above putting on a demure persona if it suits her purpose. Nancy is sex-positive and saves video of herself and Judah making love. She repeatedly sleeps with strangers and business partners—both for pleasure and for strategic purposes. We can also assume, based on a scene where Silas seeks to hide an issue of *Penthouse* that's arrived for Judah after his death, that Nancy is not in support of pornography. But she solicits violent sex on multiple occasions—Andy describes her preference as "rapey."[46] She takes pleasure in gentler entanglements, at least with men with whom she is willing to engage emotionally. And she sleeps with women—whether for companionship or other purposes is not clear. Thus, her sexuality is fluid and defies heterosexist claims on what counts as normal desire and behavior.

Nancy is also affluent, white, long-haired, long-legged, and thin, with curves and cleavage—all of the qualities patriarchy has suggested are most indicative of femininity—a body type that feminists often identify as unrealistic and problematic for women who cannot, or chose not to, adopt it. In short, her appearance provides recourse to power that many women cannot access. Her whiteness certainly provides an advantage, and Nancy's engagement with race is complex. While she befriends, marries, and even births outside her race, she also counts racist rich guy Doug among her inner circle. Her marijuana business team is multiracial, and she later makes millionaires of former partners Conrad, Guillermo (Guillermo Diaz), and Sanjay (Maulik Pancholy), along with a host of characters she variously chafed and cajoled over the years. She counts African American dealer Heylia as a wiser and better mother than herself and comments in the first season that every time she leaves Heylia's house she feels like "such an asshole" because of her ignorance on how to manage her business and her family safely and successfully.[47]

Of course, Nancy's mothering is always in question. She is driven to provide for her boys and protect them. It is true they sometimes need as much protection from the fallout of her efforts as not, but still, like Rich, she leads with what she identifies as "the mother lion" intention. "I'm a mother lion, and you can't beat a mother lion when you threaten her cubs," she tells Esteban, after escaping his thugs and retrieving her boys from their clutches. "You might think it's the same with a papa lion, but it's not. It's not the same thing at all."[48] And here she taps into the motherhood debate that continues to plague feminists—we do not want mothers on a pedestal, but neither do we want to deny their unique power. We want a different understanding of motherhood that is more fluid and realistic. As mentioned earlier, some have argued that Nancy's character works toward that new understanding. I tend to agree.

It is critical to consider all of these components in the context of Nancy's shifting identity—she is a mother, not a dealer; she is a businesswoman, not a criminal—until she *is* a criminal, convicted and serving time in prison. Her name is always in question, and depending on whom you ask, she is Nancy, Nance, Pants, Barbie, Snowflake, Blanca, MILF, Pot Mommy, Lacie La-Plante, Not-Franzi, Nathlie Newman, Nancy Price, Mrs. B., Mrs. Judah Botwin, Mrs. Peter Scottson, Mrs. Esteban Reyes, or Mrs. David Bloom. But in the closing minutes of the final episode she admits that she does not know who she is—and Andy convinces her that the next chapter of her life is about figuring that out. "You're so strong," he tells her. "It's time to face yourself."[49]

Nancy's struggle is emblematic of the situation Rich identified decades ago—that we now inhabit a unique, "transitory" period in history when "global domination of women by men can no longer be either denied or defended."[50] While many have argued that we are in a postfeminist era, that sexism has been resolved and we are now nearing "the end of men,"[51] the fact remains that power still tends to transfer along patriarchal lines. Women are still given away in marriage, men are still leaders of most governments and corporations, women's bodies are still heavily trafficked and exploited in flesh and in print. Rich argues that this point of transition means a tearing apart of "power relationships" such that we are left to sort through "a tangle of lust, violence, possession, fear, conscious longing, unconscious hostility, sentiment, rationalization: the sexual understructure of social and political forms."[52] And so it is in Nancy's world, where she must break her own path because there is no one for her to follow. Certainly, her path-breaking is an act of courage that also calls into question available gender constructs, social mores, and maternal identities. At the same time, it calls attention to Nancy's persistent inability to make friends with other women. She is a "lone wolf," and women have as much difficulty coming to terms with her as Nancy has in revealing herself to anyone completely. The fact that Nancy has no female allies is indicative of the hostility that continues to divide women against one another. Further, it should serve as a message to feminist activists that community building remains a serious concern, as much as it is a message to lone wolves that they should continue to fight the good fight.

NOTES

1. Academy of Television Arts and Sciences, "Weeds/Emmys.com," http://www.emmys.com/shows/weeds (accessed July 20, 2013).

2. Ben Hourigan, "Libertarian Escapism," *IPA Review*, September 2011, 23–26.

3. Ibid.

4. Deborah Jaramillo, "Narcocorridos and Newbie Drug Dealers: The Changing Image of the Mexican Narco on US Television," *Ethnic and Racial Studies*, 2013.

5. Johnanna J. Ganz, "'The Bigger, the Better': Challenges in Portraying a Positive Fat Character in *Weeds*," *Fat Studies* 1, no 2 (2012): 960–78.

6. David Gillota, "'People of Color': Multiethnic Humor in *Harold and Kumar Go to White Castle* and *Weeds*," *Journal of Popular Culture* 55, no. 5 (2012): 960–78.

7. Hanna Rosin, *The End of Men: And the Rise of Women*. New York: Riverhead Books, 2012.

8. "Viking Pride," *Weeds*, season 6, episode 11, written by Brendan Kelly and Tara Herrmann, directed by Michael Trim, aired on Showtime, November 1, 2010.

9. Adrienne Rich, *Of Woman Born: Motherhood as Experience and Institution* (New York: Norton, 1976).

10. Fhulamith Firestone, *The Dialectic of Sex: The Case for Feminist Revolution* (New York: Morrow, 1970).

11. Merri Lisa Johnson, ed., *Jane Sexes It Up: True Confessions of Feminist Desire* (New York: Thunder's Mouth Press, 2002).

12. Catharine A. MacKinnon, *Women's Lives, Men's Laws* (Cambridge, MA: Belknap Press, 2005).

13. Genius Media Group, "Malvina Reynolds—'Little Boxes (*Weeds* Theme Song)' Lyrics," last modified 2013, http://rapgenius.com/Malvina-reynolds-little-boxes-weeds-theme-song-lyrics (accessed July 1, 2013).

14. "Don't Miss the Bear," *Weeds*, season 1, episode 1, written by Jenji Kohan, directed by Brian Dannell, aired on Showtime, August 8, 2005.

15. "Risk," *Weeds*, season 3, episode 13, written by Roberto Benabib, Rolin Jones, and Matthew Salsberg, directed by Paul Feig, aired on Showtime, November 5, 2007.

16. "Suck n Spit," *Weeds*, season 5, episode 9, written by Chris Offutt, directed by Scott Ellis, aired on Showtime, August 3, 2009.

17. "Heroine," Merriam-Webster.com, http://www.merriam-webster.com/dictionary/heroine (accessed July 31, 2013).

18. "Hero," Merriam-Webster.com, http://www.merriam-webster.com/dictionary/hero (accessed July 31, 2013).

19. Mary-Louise Parker has appeared on Comic-Con Panels for television antiheroes, and Nancy Botwin is regularly described as such in the popular press.

20. Dee Doyle, "*Weeds* Recap: Nancy Botwin Is the Worst Mom Ever," *Star Pulse*, August 4, 2009, http://www.starpulse.com/news/Dee_Doyle/2009/08/04/weeds_recap_nancy_botwin_is_the_worst_mo (accessed July 8, 2013); "Drug Dealing Mommy: *Weeds'* Nancy Botwin," *The Lilith Effect* (blog), April 10, 2011, http://blogs.cofc.edu/thelilitheffect/2011/04/10/drug-dealing-mommy-weeds'-nancy-botwin; Drew Grant, "Nancy Botwin, TV's Worst Mom?," *Salon*, July 19, 2011, http://www.salon.com/2011/07/19/nancy_botwin_weeds (accessed July 8, 2013); "Mama Grizzly and Medea: Nancy Botwin as a Post-Feminist Icon," *Discipline and Anarchy* (blog), January 16, 2011, http://disciplineandanarchy.wordpress.com/2011/01/16/mama-grizzly-and-medea-nancy-botwin-as-a-feminist-icon-for-postmodern-america; "Nancy Botwin a Feminist," *Heartsheaux* (blog), November 29, 2012, http://heartsheaux.tumblr.com/post/36829853983/nancybotwinfeminist; Laura Sundstrom, "What Happened to *Weeds*?," *Adventures of a Young Feminist* (blog), June 27, 2009, http://youngfeministadventures.blogspot.com/2009/06/what-happened-to-weeds.html.

21. Julie O'Reilly, "The Wonder Woman Precedent: Female (Super)Heroism on Trial," *Journal of American Culture* 28, no. 3 (2005): 273–83.

22. "Dead in the Nethers," *Weeds*, season 1, episode 6, written by Michael Platt and Barry Safchik, directed by Arlene Sanford, aired on Showtime, September 12, 2005.

23. "The Punishment Light," *Weeds*, season 1, episode 8, written by Rolin Jones, directed by Robert Berlinger, aired on Showtime, September 26, 2005.

24. Michel Foucault, *The History of Sexuality: An Introduction*, vol. 1 (New York: Vintage, 1988), 103.

25. Ibid.

26. "Little Boats," *Weeds*, season 4, episode 9, written by Ron Fitzgerald, directed by Craig Zisk, aired on Showtime, August 11, 2008.

27. Catharine A. MacKinnon, "Sexuality, Pornography, and Method: 'Pleasure under Patriarchy,'" *Ethics* 99, no. 2 (1989): 135.

28. "Good Shit Lollipop," *Weeds*, season 1, episode 3, written by Roberto Benabib, directed by Craig Zisk, aired on Showtime, August 22, 2005.

29. "Dead in the Nethers," *Weeds*.

30. Kirsten Pullen, "Co-Ed Call Girls: The Whore Stigma Is Alive & Well in Madison, Wisconsin," in *Jane Sexes It Up: True Confessions of Feminist Desire*, ed. Meri Lisa Johnson (New York: Thunder's Mouth Press, 2002).

31. MacKinnon, "Sexuality, Pornography, and Method," 135.

32. "Roy Till Called," *Weeds*, season 3, episode 10, written by Victoria Morrow, directed by Craig Zisk, aired on Showtime, October 15, 2007.

33. "Gentle Puppies," *Weeds*, season 6, episode 8, written by Victoria Morrow, directed by Scott Ellis, aired on Showtime, October 11, 2010.

34. Rich, *Of Woman Born*, 34.

35. Suzanna Danuta Walters and Laura Harrison, "Not Ready to Make Nice: Aberrant Mothers in Contemporary Culture," *Feminist Media Studies*, ahead of print (2012): 1–18.

36. Rich, *Of Woman Born*, 13.

37. "If You Work for a Living, Why Do You Kill Yourself Working?," *Weeds*, season 4, episode 13, written by Jenji Kohan, directed by Craig Zisk, aired on Showtime, September 15, 2008.

38. "Dead in the Nethers," *Weeds*.

39. Ibid., 22.

40. Encyclopedia Britannica Online, s.v. "Kali," http://www.britannica.com/EBchecked/topic/310141/Kali (accessed July 2, 2013).

41. Rich, *Of Woman Born*, 34.

42. "A Modest Proposal," *Weeds*, season 5, episode 6, written by Vanessa Reisen, directed by Michael Trim, aired on Showtime, July 13, 2009.

43. "Till We Meet Again," *Weeds*, season 4, episode 12, written by Roberto Benabib, Rolin Jones, and Matthew Salsberg, directed by Michael Trim, aired on Showtime, September 8, 2008.

44. "All About My Mom," *Weeds*, season 5, episode 13, written by Jenji Kohan, directed by Scott Ellis, aired on Showtime, August 31, 2009.

45. Ibid.

46. "Where the Sidewalk Ends," *Weeds*, season 5, episode 7, written by Roberto Benabib and Matthew Salsberg, directed by Jeremy Podeswa, aired on Showtime, July 20, 2009.

47. "Higher Education," *Weeds*, season 1, episode 7, written by Shawn Schepps, directed by Tucker Gates, aired on Showtime, September 19, 2005.

48. "A Shoe for a Shoe," *Weeds*, season 6, episode 6, written by David Holstein, directed by Michael Trim, aired on Showtime, September 27, 2010.

49. "It's Time: Part 2," *Weeds*, season 8, episode 13, written by Jenji Kohan, directed by Michael Trim, aired on Showtime, September 16, 2012.

50. Rich, *Of Woman Born*, 56.

51. Rosin, *The End of Men*.

52. Rich, *Of Woman Born*, 56.

Chapter Three

Choosing Her "Fae"te

Subversive Sexuality and Lost Girl's *Re/evolutionary Female Hero*

Jennifer K. Stuller

Make your choice. Are you ready to be strong? —Buffy Summers, *Buffy the Vampire Slayer*

I will live the life I choose! —Bo Dennis, *Lost Girl*

The most intriguing, complex, and subversive female heroes come out of genre storytelling—particularly through the serialized medium of television, itself a format traditionally marketed to female viewers. For example, Joss Whedon's seminal *Buffy the Vampire Slayer* (1997–2003) challenged viewer expectations by having the previously doomed "girl in the dark alley" emerge as the hero instead. In doing so, he forever changed the way we think about female identity and heroism.[1] *Xena, Warrior Princess* (1995–2001), presented in lead characters Xena and Gabrielle the rare example of two female companions on a hero journey together as they supported, loved, and challenged one another to be better people.

They existed during a landmark era of strong female characters on American television during the mid- to late 1990s and early aughts that included *The X-Files'* (1993—2002) Dana Scully and *Alias*'s (2001–2006) Sydney Bristow and inspired a subsequent wave of heroic female characters that was as unprecedented as it seemed unstoppable. But suddenly they disappeared. Or, rather, they existed as supporting players in ensemble—and often cult or genre—shows. There was Kara Thrace on *Battlestar Galactica* (2004–2009); Rose Tyler, Martha Jones, Donna Noble, Amy Pond, Sarah Jane Smith, and River Song on the British export *Doctor Who* (2005–); and

31

others on *Heroes* (2006–2010), *Eureka* (2006–2012), and *Lost* (2004–2010)—but rarely were they the center of the narrative, or if they were, like the *Bionic Woman* (2007) or Diana in David E. Kelley's unaired *Wonder Woman* pilot (2011), they were tone-deaf failures. Some, like *Nikita* (2010–2013), existed in relative quiet on the CW network, while others, such as *True Blood*'s (2008–2014) Sookie Stackhouse, were damsels to be rescued by sexy supernatural men.

That is, until 2010, when word of mouth popularized a supernatural show featuring one of the most unique female heroes to grace the small screen in more recent years. *Lost Girl*—a Canadian series created by Michelle Lovretta with explicitly feminist intent—was, like the shows that inspired it, a revolutionary exploration of heroic female identity and an evolution in representations of the female hero and her journey.[2]

Lost Girl is the story of a bisexual succubus private detective, named Ysabeau "Bo" Dennis, exploring her identity as a supernatural being and sexual female as she navigates the light and dark worlds of the Fae. But like other serials with silly-sounding premises (such as a high school cheerleader who slays vampires in Southern California or a warrior princess forged in the heat of battle), this show is much smarter than it might initially seem, and its protagonist is an original consideration of female agency and heroism.

The series builds on the best modern televisual representations of female heroism that use genre and serial storytelling to explore the female hero quest (discovery, identity, parents, redemption, community, created family, and how rejection of the lone wolf model of heroism leads to a stronger hero), most notably *Buffy the Vampire Slayer*, with a healthy dose of *Xena, Warrior Princess*.[3] While these shows were groundbreaking in that they addressed the hero quest from a female perspective, foregrounded the importance of female companionship, and created icons of its female heroes, *Lost Girl* excels in providing a much more complex look at female sexuality, friendship, and relationships than *Buffy* and earlier shows were able to achieve.

While rooted in familiar tropes including global mythology and folklore, urban fantasy storytelling, and the archetype of the femme fatale, *Lost Girl*, like the aforementioned *Buffy* and *Xena*, challenges our relationship to these topoi, simultaneously subverting and reinventing archetypes through clever narrative and playful characterization. Yet *Lost Girl* has the rare and modern opportunity to reference female hero–oriented shows rather than using male hero source material as a baseline from which to build. The series is influenced by, and draws reference from, a relatively new, female-defined, if not *feminine*, tradition. In other words, we're seeing, for perhaps the first time on television, the creation of a complex, fully adult, fully modern, female hero that emerges from a female heroic tradition.

A GOOFY-ASS SHOW

It's a goofy-ass show and I say that with love. —Michelle Lovretta[4]

When executive producer Jay Firestone (*La Femme Nikita*, *Relic Hunter*) tasked writer Michelle Lovretta (*Mutant X*) with creating a strong female character that embraced sexuality, one who was a bisexual superhero and used sex as part of her arsenal, Lovretta's initial excitement was soon followed by trepidation and concerns that the result would be misogynistic, exploitative, and homophobic on the one hand, or overtly "PC" on the other. As she told *The Watercooler*,

> The challenge was to create a fun, sex-positive world that celebrates provocative cheesecake for everyone, without falling into base stereotypes or misogynistic (or misandristic) exploitation along the way. I also really wanted to defend the bisexual community and counter some sad tropes out there (bisexuals are sluts, can't commit, are just afraid to be gay, yadda yadda) while also valuing and representing female friendships that have nothing sexualized about them at all.[5]

The result is a refreshing—landmark, even—look at female sexuality that dares to suggest that sex is a superpower. But above all, *Lost Girl* is not, in fact, a show "about" sex—even as it explicitly deals with issues of female sexuality. Rather, it's a show about female friendship framed by the female hero journey.

Bo (Anna Silk) had been raised by adoptive human parents in a small country town, with no knowledge of her true heritage or the magnitude of her power, and was taught to believe that her sexuality was shameful. At eighteen years old, filled with an adolescent combination of lust and love, she had sex with her high school sweetheart, Kyle. The enormity of her innate, and seemingly uncontrollable, desires resulted in his accidental death. She confessed to her parents, who reinforced her fear that she was a monster and that sexuality itself is monstrous. Bo also learned that she was adopted, ran away from home, and was "lost" for ten years, moving from place to place, running and hiding when her desires killed, as she searched for knowledge about who and what she is.

Bo's lonely search ends when she saves a petite twenty-something goth pickpocket named Kenzi (Ksenia Solo) from a sexual predator by draining him of his life force—setting off a chain of events that connects her to her true identity. Her encounter with Kenzi leads to the discovery that Bo is "Fae"—a species of supernatural beings found in myth and folklore and an evolutionary branch that predates humans.[6] Separated into two factions—Light and Dark—with various subclans and families, the Fae feed off of human energy systems. While there isn't a lot of moral difference between

Light and Dark (i.e., not all Light Fae are "good" and not all Dark "bad"), the Light generally do not kill their feeds.

She also, after years of solitude, gains a new created family: Dyson (Kris Holden-Ried), a centuries-old wolf-shifter and police detective; Dr. Lauren Lewis (Zoie Palmer), a human doctor and scientist working for the Light; Hale (K. C. Collins), a siren and Dyson's colleague; and Fitzpatrick "Trick" McCoreighan (Rick Howland), a blood sage later revealed to be "the Blood King" who long ago used his powers, at great cost, to force a truce and write the laws that keep peace (albeit tenuously) between Light and Dark Fae. Trick, kindly and wise, owns and operates the Dál Riata, a gastropub that provides neutral territory for Light and Dark Fae to comingle, sanctuary if needed, and a waypoint for traveling Fae.

As Bo is introduced to this secret world, she learns that all Fae are required to undergo a rite of passage that aligns them to the Light or the Dark. She also discovers, with the help of Lauren, that she's a succubus—a creature that feeds off of sexual energy. Had she not been hidden from the Fae (for reasons yet to be revealed) and adopted by a human family, Bo would have grown up learning how to control and use her power. When Bo is forced to choose a side, she refuses, instead forging her own path, even in a sea of unknowns. Like Buffy, Bo refuses to let those who control information to maintain their own power guide her future; and in controlling her destiny, she inspires others to do the same. As the "unaligned succubus"—a phrase repeated in nearly every episode—Bo is treated with reverence, and often envy, by others wishing they could reject or subvert the system instead of continuing to reinforce it. As she learns more about herself, and the politics of the Fae world, Bo teams up with Kenzi to form "Bo's Private Investigation Service" which helps Light and Dark Fae, as well as humans.

A story about a bisexual-sex-chi-eater-cum-supernatural-private-detective certainly has a lot of potential to be visually exploitative and narratively nonfeminist. According to an interview with Syfy's *Blastr*, when actress Anna Silk first heard about a new Canadian series called *Lost Girl*, her initial reaction was, "This is totally written by a guy. Bisexual succubus who has to have sex to heal? Oh, my God. I just thought, 'What is this?'"[7] What it is, is an international hit that strongly resonates with female viewers.

PROVOCATIVE CHEESECAKE

> You can say a lot of things about sex with a series like this. —Michelle Lovretta[8]

Like *Lost Girl*, *Xena* was a cult hit with a vocal lesbian and bisexual fan base who lauded the relationship of Xena and Gabrielle—reading it as romantic and committed. Series creators subtly fed that interpretation both narratively and visually. As openly gay *Xena* producer Liz Friedman has said of what fans call "the subtext," she's "always been a big believer in the power of popular culture. The best way to convey more challenging ideas is to make something that functions on a mainstream level but that has a subtext people can pick up on—or not."[9]

According to scholar Lorna Jowett, in cult fandom, "viewers may develop subtextual or resistant readings that actively queer characters or relationships, as an abundance of slash fan fiction testifies," adding that "more self-conscious shows encourage such readings."[10]

On *Lost Girl* there are plenty of opportunities for shipping[11]—facilitated by Bo's nature, as well as the recurring question of whether a succubus can truly be monogamous. (Spoiler alert: Yes!) But Lovretta encourages fans to ship various character pairings, noting that she herself is a big shipper: "[A]nd I've already shipped the hell out of every possible relationship dynamic on this show in my head for hours of my own enjoyment, and i [*sic*] hope our viewers feel that drive as well. That's not just half the fun of watching a show like this, it's half the fun of writing it."[12] Therefore, with *Lost Girl*, there is no need for resistant readings or subtext because it is already queered in its very premise.

Xena and *Buffy* helped normalize "alternative" sexualities and thus paved the way for a show like *Lost Girl*. Consider that *Buffy the Vampire Slayer* and *Xena, Warrior Princess* existed in an era of "Don't Ask, Don't Tell" (DADT) and the Defense of Marriage Act (DOMA). *Xena* courted viewers with subtextual, and subversive, references to its lead characters' bisexuality and committed partnership. *Buffy* pushed the envelope further by having a lesbian relationship in the core group of protagonists, and later, by featuring the first lesbian sex scene on network television. They broke ground that enabled *Lost Girl* to be free to explore the healthy normalcy of LGBTQ relationships—monogamous, polyamorous, or otherwise—always without judgment. Just fifteen or so years later, *Lost Girl* exists in a world where gay marriage is being legalized, DADT has been repealed, and DOMA ruled unconstitutional.[13]

Lovretta, who notes that because Bo is a succubus, a grown woman, and bisexual, says that

> you can say a lot of things about sex with a series like this. And what's a little intimidating is that people can also read whatever they want into it. The one thing I hope is clear is that, in our Lost Girl world, healthy consensual sex is good, and repression and shame can be dangerous. Part of Bo's problem is that she's been denying herself sex until the hunger builds into something ugly, and she loses control of it.[14]

Although *Buffy* broke ground in terms of showing healthy and loving lesbian relationships, Buffy herself rarely embraced sex. Consider this exchange from the first appearance of Faith (Eliza Dushku), her sister slayer, rival, shadow self, and Sunnydale's resident "Bad Girl"/"slut":

> Faith: I could eat a horse. Ain't it crazy how slaying just always makes you hungry and horny?
>
> (*Xander, Cordy, Willow, and Oz all look at Buffy for confirmation.*)
>
> Buffy: Well . . . sometimes I—I crave a nonfat yogurt after. [15]

Buffy's concern for her reputation—both sexual and dietary—belie restraint (possibly prudishness) as well as self-deprivation underscored by her fears of judgment. Bo, on the other hand, indulges in chocolate, ice cream, recreational drinking, and other guilt-free pleasures after her epic sexcapades—a far cry from a nonfat yogurt. [16] Sexuality is expressed much more openly on *Lost Girl*—partly because of the premise, but also because it's presented as matter of fact, healthy, natural, necessary, and enjoyable.

By presenting a female protagonist who while conventionally sexy is not overtly sexualized, series creators manage to explore Bo's sexuality without objectifying it or her (at least in ways that are exploitative)—a fine line to walk, but for the most part one navigated with laudable success. Rather than perpetuating the notion of a femme fatale—a woman whose sexuality is so dangerous that it will bring men to their destruction—*Lost Girl* revisits, and subverts, the archetype by making sexuality a superpower.

It was Lovretta who came up with the idea of Bo being a succubus—a female creature, usually a demon, that seduces men and causes their death or destruction. [17] The succubus has historically been imagined as a femme fatale, an irresistible, insatiable, deadly female, usually revealed to be a monster—the very thing Bo spent a decade believing she was.

Taking a typically demonized, if not even outright demonic, creature and making her heroic has the potential to change negative cultural messages about female sexuality as dangerous, evil, shameful, and, of course, threatening to men, as well as to challenge larger hegemonic patriarchal systems of power—both within the series, as well as in the real world. Lorna Jowett asks, "How realistic is it to expect cult television, something many consider a niche market, to impact perceptions of sex, gender, or race?" Noting that television fiction reflects societal changes, Jowett argues that "television's popular nature makes these negotiations influential." [18]

Viewers applaud that throughout *Lost Girl*'s run, at least so far, Bo's sexual appetites are normalized, as well as encouraged and supported by her loved ones, who recognize—often more so than Bo herself (who still struggles with internalized negative messaging)—that she needs sex to survive. [19]

As she marvels in an early episode, while eating an apple no less—an iconic symbol of the biblical Eve—"For me sexual healing is *a literal thing.*"[20]

Themes of slut shaming and misogyny—especially with regard to sexual women—parallel Bo's own navigation of her sexuality and the healing of her damaged relationship to her true nature. In the first season episode "Raging Fae," Bo tells Kenzi of her continuing struggle with her past (particularly her guilt over Kyle's death) and her identity as Fae:

Bo: I grew up on a farm. I thought I was a regular girl. I went to church with my parents.

Kenzi: What happened?

Bo: When I hit puberty . . . I started to feel different.

Kenzi: Your powers kicked in.

Bo: I didn't know how dangerous I was. My parents taught me that sex was evil, and I found out just how right they were. I found out how evil I was. I had the devil inside of me, Kenzi.

Kenzi: You really thought that?

Bo: I am so tired of my life being dictated by something I didn't choose. I am done being Fae![21]

This is complicated by the opposing ideologies of Bo's adoptive mother (who proclaimed Bo was deviant) and her biological mother, Aife, who is also a succubus—and an evil one at that—who encourages the femme fatale path. Bo, who refuses to choose sides or absolutes (Light or Dark, mother or whore, straight or gay), chooses to exist in a liminal space as she searches for her identity—making liminality itself a place of empowerment. She didn't *choose* to be "special," but she is choosing how to exist, and on her own terms. The narrative intro to each episode—"I will live the life I choose"— can't help but feel like a response echoing back to Buffy Summers' question to potential slayers in the series finale of *BtVS*: "Make your choice. Are you ready to be strong?" Bo answers, "Yes."

As Anna Silk has noted of Bo's reconciliation with her past and her nature, "She's had to learn to be really strong. Her past is rather shameful to her, but her greatest source of shame became her power. And that's been the growth for Bo."[22]

Maureen Ryan wrote for the *Huffington Post* of Michelle Lovretta's extraordinary female hero, "She's created a Hero's Journey with a self-confident woman—a succubus, no less—at the center of it," adding,

> Succubi have generally terrible P.R.—find a positive depiction of a woman
> who takes the sexual life force from frequently male victims and I'll give you a
> shiny new quarter—but Lovretta has done something subversively impressive
> with "Lost Girl." She's built a whole show around the idea of a woman who is
> learning just how much she can or should take from others, and how much she
> can rely on herself.[23]

For a woman to have her sexuality—her individual needs and desires (however complicated they may or may not be) honored, respected, and encouraged—is relatively unprecedented in popular culture. And as a creature that
requires sex to survive, those around Bo make sure that her needs are met,
without judgment. Ever.

Much of this is achieved by using what Michelle Lovretta jokingly referred to at San Diego Comic-Con as the three Fs of what they try and put in
the show: "Fun, Friendship, and Fornication" (noting that they "reorder them
each episode").[24] *Lost Girl* also makes good use of internal rules created by
Lovretta for navigating a balance between socially conscious empowerment
and good, silly fun:

1. sexual orientation is not discussed, and never an issue;
2. no slut shaming—Bo is allowed to have sex outside of relationships;
3. Bo's male and female partners are equally viable;
4. Bo is capable of monogamy, when desired;
5. both genders are to be (adoringly!) objectified—equal opportunity eye
   candy FTW.[25]

Sex on the show is usually character driven rather than exploitative (in
contrast to other genre shows such as *Game of Thrones* or *True Blood*), nor is
it overly risqué. Male- and female-identified bodies are ("adoringly!") objectified playfully and self-consciously. *AfterEllen*—a site that provides reviews
and commentary on media representations of lesbians and bisexual women—
includes a screen shot with each *Lost Girl* episode recap called "Boobs o'
Clock o' the Week" because, as they remind us, "you can't spell 'Boobs'
without 'Bo.'"

> You can always count on Bo to give us a glimpse of the girls. In fact, I'm
> pretty sure besides her succubus chi-draining skills, her second strongest
> superpower is cleavage. Also, someone needs to send the *Lost Girl* costumer
> department a muffin basket for the copious low-cut tank tops and assorted
> tight leather ensembles they've put Bo in so far this season. Keep it up—or
> low, as the case may be.[26]

Even with this objectification, it's still subversive in that it's directed to the
lesbian gaze, rather than the typically heterosexual "male gaze" of cinema.

Lost Girl also provides "man candy" (most often courtesy of a frequently shirtless, abtastic Dyson). As Jowett notes, "Television as a medium seems to lend itself to queering or otherwise disrupting the supposed 'male gaze' of cinema. The male in cult shows, as in current television, is just as likely to be displayed openly as an object for the gaze as the female, whether this is via Clark Kent's too-tight shirts in *Smallville* or Angel's torture scenes in *Buffy*."[27] Equal opportunity eye candy FTW, indeed.

"Hopefully viewers will get that we're taking the piss more often than not," Lovretta told *RGBfilter*. "I mean: hello, monsters and secret societies and a sassy sex predator: you can't be too precious about that! We aim to entertain, to make people laugh and give them a world to get lost in and characters to care about, should they choose."[28]

PLATONIC-YET-EPIC BFFNESS

> I think friendship is the fifth element. . . . So, hidden in amongst all the romance and cleavage and threesomes, the Lost Girl Bo and Kenzi relationship is my own little love poem to all the BFFs out there who do it right.
> —Michelle Lovretta[29]

For all its subversive sexuality, clever *Buffy*-inspired pop-culture-laden dialogue, imaginative references to myth, and strong commitment to diversity (sexual, racial, and physical), perhaps *Lost Girl*'s greatest achievement is its emphasis on female friendship.

To proactively curb any chance of sexualizing the relationship between Bo and Kenzi, and to demonstrate that sexuality can be complicated while simultaneously celebrating committed platonic relationships, Lovretta made sure the "Platonic-yet-epic" central friendship was written into the script of the first episode so it would be canon.[30]

> I have no doubt that Kenzi and Bo would kill or die for one another, although there's nothing sexual between them to be gained. I love that about them, and that platonic loyalty was very important for me to protect throughout the development process: that Bo and Kenzi are sisters, not love interests. I didn't want to feed into the stereotype that because someone is bisexual (as Bo is) that they're sexually available to, or interested in, everyone. I love me my Bo—so, I don't want to paint her as a Walking Hungry Crotch, or someone's fantasy fulfillment.[31]

Lovretta was inspired by the friendships in her own life, and this, combined with the focus on how female friendships can be transformative in ways that differ from romantic or sexual ones, makes *Lost Girl* an example of the unique perspective offered by women-created and/or run series. Lovretta was particularly committed to honoring the concept of the "Bechdel test"—a commonly referred to litmus test for the representation of women in movies, television, and comics that originated in Alison Bechdel's *Dykes to Watch Out For* and which suggests that a movie should have two women who talk to each other about something other than men. Lovretta notes that Bo is strong and kick-ass, and that when she saved Kenzi, the two of them saved each other. As Kenzi herself says to Bo in the very first episode, "Mama always said find the toughest kid on the playground and make friends with them. You are definitely the toughest kid on this playground, and it would kick ass to be your friend. . . . Come on. Every superhero needs a partner. Let me be your Robin." For Lovretta, this relationship forms the very core of *Lost Girl*:

> So much of the heart [of the series] is about continually saving each other. Through all their screw-ups, through all the dangers—and that they become sisters. It was very important for me that the sexuality didn't bleed into that relationship as well. . . . You can say "that's enough on its own." It doesn't always have to end up in bed. It can just be the fact that you have chosen somebody to be one of the most important people in your life—and that's your best friend.[32]

FAETASTIC TELEVISION AND THE
FEMALE HERO JOURNEY AT ITS BEST

Lost Girl, like the very best of modern female hero myths, is about relationships and community, the search for identity in a patriarchal or similarly oppressive social structure, and what it means to choose your own heroic path with the love of supportive outsiders who band together to create family. As Anna Silk has noted, Bo has a "goofy sweetness" and a lot of heart: "She *loves* her friends. She *loves* her lovers. She's very protective of this instant family she has, this instant, weird, family that she now has."[33]

The focus on interpersonal relationships, the combination of genre storytelling, budget constraints that force creative solutions and inspire earnestness, and the more relaxed mores of its Canadian, rather than American, production, enables fun, yet subversive, representations regarding gender roles, sexuality, female agency, and heroism. *Lost Girl* is groundbreaking in its honest and nonexploitative presentation of female sexuality—all the more notable in that it rejects and subverts the culturally damaging femme fatale narrative and refuses to shame its protagonist for being actively sexual. *Lost Girl* presents expressions of female sexual pleasure with nonjudgment and normalizes LGBTQ lifestyles.[34] The show has a diverse cast, including persons of color as both peers and leaders (these are not the nameless and quickly dusted vampires of *Buffy*), and a main character with dwarfism, whose physical stature is never a plot point, and who himself is presented as having a healthy sex life. Gender roles are subverted; women and men un-apologetically assume both masculine and feminine characteristics.[35] And it's all tempered with a playfulness that's been adopted by fans and encouraged by show-runners.

It's imperfect—as is all popular culture.[36] There is sometimes cultural ignorance in its loose adaptations of world myth. Plot points are dropped, overlooked, or resolved quickly, and it definitely lacks the depth and plotting of *Buffy the Vampire Slayer*—even as it draws from its tradition.

But it doesn't need to be *Buffy*, and *Lost Girl* has secured its own place in the canon of female heroes in modern mythology. As Alyssa Rosenberg wrote for *Think Progress*, "*Buffy* laid a foundation on which *Lost Girl*'s building a somewhat more sexually progressive and more diverse universe . . . [and] it's laying down a marker for fantasy, reminding us in a world where we have diversity in our monsters and myths, it's not so strange to have a true diversity of people."[37] Most important, *Lost Girl* offers us a glimpse of how we can imagine female heroes whose spiritual genealogy is female rather than male.

Bo is multifaceted—a complex character in a self-consciously silly show. She's independent, strong, smart, compassionate, and imperfect. As she continues to answer Buffy's call to be strong and forges her own path to live a life of her choosing, she uses her superpowers—a curse that became a gift—to help those around her. And that's Faetastic.

NOTES

1. *Buffy the Vampire Slayer* famously came out of Joss Whedon's desire to create a strong female protagonist to counter the lack of empowered women in popular culture. Buffy's influence cannot be underestimated—she has been a point of reference for nearly every "strong female character" that came after her. She resonated because, as Whedon himself told the *Los Angeles Times* in 2003, "she fulfilled a need for a female hero, which is distinctly different from a heroine. While a heroine is the protagonist, generally speaking, somebody swoops in and saves her. A hero is a more complex figure and has to deal with all the traditional rites of passage. Everything Luke Skywalker had to go through, Buffy had to go through, and then some." ("R.I.P. 'Buffy': You Drove a Stake through Convention," May 20).

2. Shot in Toronto, *Lost Girl* was the most successful premiere in Showcase history when it debuted in 2010. The series was developed by Prodigy Pictures, in association with Shaw Media and Showcase. Executive producers are Jay Firestone and Emily Andras. *Lost Girl* is broadcast in the United States on the Syfy network.

3. See Jennifer K. Stuller, *Ink-Stained Amazons and Cinematic Warriors: Superwomen in Modern Mythology* (London: I. B. Tauris, 2010) for more.

4. Katie Bailey, "In the Writer's Room with Not-So-Lost Girl Michelle Lovretta," January 13, 2012, http://playbackonline.ca/2012/01/13/in-the-writers-room-with-not-so-lost-girl-michelle-lovretta/#ixzz2YaghZsXc.

5. Helena Vann, "An Interview with Michelle Lovretta," *The Watercooler*, publication date unknown, http://watercoolerjournal.com/?page_id=3077 (accessed August 11, 2013).

6. "Fae" serves as a broad term for characters and archetypes from myth, culture, and folklore from around the world—though much like *Xena*, the depictions are not deeply reverent or exact.

42   *Jennifer K. Stuller*

7. Kathie Huddleston, "Meet Anna Silk, Sexy Succubus of Lost Girl, Syfy's Newest Series," *Blastr*, January 10, 2012, http://www.blastr.com/2012/01/syfys_sexy_lost_girl_bo_a.php.

8. drsquid,"Nine Questions with Lost Girl Creator and Writer Michelle Lovretta," September 30, 2010, http://www.rgbfilter.com/?p=10538.

9. M. Flaherty, "Xenaphilia," *Entertainment Weekly*, March 7, 1997, 1–6, http://www.ew.com/ew/article/0,,287017,00.html.

10. Lorna Jowett, "Representation: Exploring Issues of Sex, Gender, and Race in Cult Television," in *The Cult TV Book: From* Star Trek *to* Dexter, *New Approaches to TV outside the Box*, ed. Stacey Abbott (Berkeley, CA: Soft Skull Press, 2010), 111.

11. A term from fandom that relates to fans' preference for relationship pairings within a series.

12. drsquid, "Nine Questions."

13. That, and it's produced in Canada—lending it a freedom in terms of storytelling and casting that arguably wouldn't be possible in the United States.

14. drsquid, "Nine Questions."

15. "Faith, Hope, and Trick," *Buffy the Vampire Slayer*, season 3, episode 3, written by David Greenwalt, directed by James A. Contner, aired October 13, 1998.

16. Some critics have also argued that Buffy was "punished" for her sexuality: Angel turns evil, Parker rejects her after a one-night stand, Riley cheats on her, and Spike is a toxic distraction who attempts to rape her.

17. Lilith, the first wife of Adam in Hebrew myth, who refused to lie below him during intercourse as she considered them equal, became a succubus. The archetype is prevalent throughout myth and popular culture, in myriad forms (though not always labeled "succubi," and symbolically connected to the vampire), from Ampata, the "Inca Mummy Girl" on an early episode of *Buffy the Vampire Slayer*, to Rogue of Marvel Comics, whose succubus-like power allows her to absorb energy from others, with the unfortunate side effect of draining their life force (and who, like Bo, had a traumatic first sexual encounter as a result), to the vampire goddess, and aptly named, Lilith, on *True Blood*.

18. Jowett, "Representation," 107.

19. Female fans of *Lost Girl* have said that what they appreciate most about the series is that there is no fuss made over different sorts of relationships; that it's refreshing to see unapologetic bisexual characters accompanied by a loving, unjudging community capable of witty banter and humor; that the protagonist is in charge of her sexuality and relationships, and not at the mercy of them; that her sexuality doesn't rule her, even though it's an essential part of who she is and what she needs as sustenance; that the depiction of lesbian relationships is truly loving and not just about sex between two women, catered to the male gaze; and that though there are times when the sex depicted on the show is there for titillation, you still get to see emotional growth in many of the recurring characters and how their relationships evolve past the physical, into genuinely intimate exchanges. (Thanks to the following for sharing what they love and/or appreciate about *Lost Girl*: Emily Beckley, Alyson Buckman, Jamala Henderson, Katherine Hunnicutt, Michele Jenkins, Allexa Lee Laycock, Al Lyka, Jessica Obrist, Kris Panchyk, Amy Peloff, and Stephanie Zimmerman.)

20. "Faetal Attraction," *Lost Girl*, season 1, episode 4, written by Jeremy Boxen, directed by David Greene, aired October 3, 2010.

21. "Raging Fae," *Lost Girl*, season 2, episode 10, written by Jeremy Boxen, directed by Steve DiMarco, aired November 27, 2011.

22. Huddleston, "Meet Anna Silk."

23. Maureen Ryan, "*Lost Girl*: The Best Show You're Not Watching Plus Exclusive Video," *Huffington Post*, February 2, 2012, http://www.huffingtonpost.com/maureen-ryan/lost-girl-syfy_b_1249995.html.

24. Michelle Lovretta at the *Lost Girl* panel at San Diego Comic-Con International 2011.

25. Vann, "Interview with Michelle Lovretta."

26. Dorothy Snarker, "'Lost Girl' SnapCap (2.01–2.02): The Story So Far," *AfterEllen*, September 16, 2011, http://www.afterellen.com/lost-girl-snapcap-201-202-the-story-so-far/09/2011.

27. Jowett, "Representation," 111–12.

28. drsquid, "Nine Questions."

29. Vann, "Interview with Michelle Lovretta."

30. Lovretta has noted that in production some directors predictably wanted to sexualize the dynamic between Bo and Kenzi, to make the show "hotter."

31. drsquid, "Nine Questions."

32. Michelle Lovretta at the *Lost Girl* panel at San Diego Comic-Con International 2011.

33. Anna Silk at the *Lost Girl* panel at San Diego Comic-Con International 2011.

34. *Lost Girl* was voted by fans to be Favorite TV Drama, Favorite Actress (Anna Silk), Hottest Hookup, and Favorite Fictional Couple in *AfterEllen*'s 2012 Visibility Awards.

35. For example, one storyline involves Hale's father's disappointment at Hale having in-herited the Siren, and thus inherently feminine, powers of his mother.

36. *Lost Girl* has been criticized on *Racialicious* for its fading representations of diversity and cultural ignorance in its loose adaptations of world myth. It also faced criticism for its treatment of transwomen in the season 3 premiere, "Caged Fae."

37. Alyssa Rosenberg, "*Lost Girl* Isn't *Buffy the Vampire Slayer*—and That's Okay," *Think Progress*, April 3, 2012, http://thinkprogress.org/alyssa/2012/04/03/457055/lost-girl-isnt-buffy-the-vampire-slayerand-thats-okay.

Part II

Heroines on Film

.

Chapter Four

Torture, Rape, Action Heroines, and *The Girl with the Dragon Tattoo*

Jeffrey A. Brown

One of the most important motifs for male characters in action films is the convention of torture, and the hero's ability to withstand it. Torture is also a key component for action heroines, but the often brutal on-screen torture of female characters foregrounds issues of sexualized violence, rape, power, and gender in a manner very different than with male characters. Heroes can triumphantly turn the tables on their torturers and thus prove their superior manliness. But when heroines are victimized in torture scenes, often to the point of actual rape, the films risk eroticizing images of violence against women, even if the women do eventually triumph over their torturers. The pivotal rape scene in Stieg Larsson's controversial, but incredibly popular, novel *The Girl with the Dragon Tattoo*[1] (henceforth *Dragon Tattoo*) was cause for a great deal of debate among critics and many of the book's readers. Was the graphic and prolonged description of the heroine Lisbeth Salander's horrific anal rape misogynistic? Or was it necessary to reveal the brutality and inhumanity of the act and to justify her violent revenge? The debates were renewed when both the Swedish version of the film (2009) and the subsequent Hollywood version (2011) each depicted the rape in graphic detail. When considered within the larger context of torture in recent Hollywood film and television action genres, the torture and rape of Lisbeth Salander in all three versions of *Dragon Tattoo* reveal a complex understanding of victimization and redemption that cuts across traditional gender boundaries. Unlike earlier action movies or rape-revenge films, contemporary depictions of torture and rape lay bare the tenuous links assumed in our patriarchal culture between notions of power and powerlessness, masculinity and femininity.

TORTURE AND THE MALE ACTION HERO

Torture has always been a concise and effective means to establish both the heroism and the unassailable masculinity of characters. The primary function of male torture at the narrative level is to demonstrate the exceptional strength, nobility, and endurance of the protagonist. Yet, as critics like Steve Neale,[2] Kaja Silverman,[3] Susan Jeffords,[4] and David Savran[5] have argued, the incessant and spectacular depiction of male torture in action movies functions to both eroticize the male body and to deny that very eroticism. Ever since Laura Mulvey[6] first identified the dichotomous ways that gender is represented in cinema with the dominant gaze coded as masculine and the object of that fetishizing gaze being feminine, it has been commonplace to understand prolonged looking at male bodies as a potentially feminizing erotic act. In visual forms of media, men are coded as voyeurs and women as exhibitionists, thus any time the male gaze of the camera dwells on a male body, there is a symbolic risk of emasculation. Torture is one of the most common of conventions that have developed to compensate for the fetishization of male bodies in the media. Neale argues that "male heroes can at times be marked as the object of an erotic gaze"; thus "it is not surprising that 'male' genres and films constantly involve sado-masochistic themes, scenes, and phantasies."[7] Building on these theories in her analysis of 1980s action movies, Susan Jeffords argues that "the chief mechanism in mainstream cinema for deferring eroticism in the heterosexual male body is through establishing that body as an object of violence, so that erotic desire can be displaced as sadomasochism."[8] The torture of male action heroes allows the camera to appreciate the shirtless and bound bodies of male ideals as they valiantly writhe in pain without any feminizing or homoerotic implications. The tortured male body is not a passive and inviting spectacle; it is a body that demonstrates strength and resilience even when it is at its most vulnerable point.

The tortured male body in film is a way to display and to deny feminization of the body. Its resistance to torture demonstrates not just the heroism of the character and his strength but also that the body is not passive or penetrable. To be penetrable and passive is to be coded as feminine, and the suffering of male heroes carefully denies feminization. So common is the depiction of male heroes being tortured and subjected to prolonged suffering that it seems willfully masochistic. In fact the extensive suffering that seems to be embraced by heroes like Rambo, Bond, and any character played by Mel Gibson can be understood as a form of reflexive masochism. Others may be the actual agents of the hero's physical torment, but the persistent spectacle of heroic suffering suggests that it is ultimately a willful form of self-punishment undertaken to solidify a masculine position and eradicate any hint of passivity or feminization. According to Kaja Silverman, "because reflexive masochism does not demand the renunciation of activity, it is ideally suited for negotiating the contradictions inherent in masculinity. The male subject can indulge his appetite for pain without at the same time calling into question . . . his virility."[9] For example, in his analysis of the Rambo films, David Savran argues, "These ordeals [Rambo's exaggerated sufferings] must be seen as self-willed, as being the product of his need to prove his masculinity the only way he can, by allowing his sadistic, masculinized half to kick his masochistic, feminized flesh 'to shit.'"[10] Any hint of feminization is symbolically eradicated through a momentary embrace of masochism and the hero's ability to overcome whatever tortures are heaped upon him.

For some critics, masochism is as fundamental to filmic depictions of masculinity as are displays of strength, intelligence, and sexual conquest. Gaylyn Studlar[11] argues that the central appeal of visual pleasure in cinema for male spectators may not be rooted in identification with control and power but in an alignment with masochistic fantasies. Studlar claims that masculine pleasure "contains passive elements and can signify *submission to* rather than *possession of* the female"[12] (italics in original). Tim Edwards convincingly argues that Hollywood movies from *Spartacus* (1960) and *Ben-Hur* (1959), to *The Terminator* (1984) and *Die Hard* (1988), to *Fight Club* (1999) and *Casino Royale*, "centrally and fundamentally construct masculinity around *heroism* which is then in turn dependent upon suffering, endurance and the spectacle of masochism for its resolution into happiness"[13] (italics in original). While Studlar sees erotic identificatory possibilities in the masochistic submission to females as key to visual pleasure, Edwards argues that masochism is fundamental to our basic understanding of heroic masculinity because it confirms the hero's strength, fortitude, and commitment to an ideal. Whether erotic, or heroic, or a combination of both, torture and other forms of masochistic suffering are an integral part of filmic depictions of masculinity. Within the overall context of the films, the masochistic moment of torture does not subvert or undermine cultural standards of masculinity. Instead, these masochistic moments reinforce the perception of hegemonic masculinity as invincible precisely because they are endured and because the hero always manages to reestablish the prevailing status quo.

TORTURE AND THE FEMALE ACTION HEROINE

While the torture of male heroes, and their subsequent victories, has long been a staple of action and adventure films, women have typically been relegated to the damsel-in-distress role with merely the threat of bodily violation. But as action heroines have come to prominence as leading characters in their own right, torture has become an increasingly common trope for heroines as well. In *The Long Kiss Goodnight* (1996), the amnesiac spy Samantha/Charly (Geena Davis) is tied to a mill wheel and repeatedly lowered into freezing water while being interrogated. The opening scenes of *Salt* (2010) depict CIA agent Evelyn Salt (Angelina Jolie) being bound, beaten, and water-boarded in a North Korean prison. The first time we see the Black Widow (Scarlett Johansson) in *The Avengers* (2012) she is tied to a chair as several generic European bad guys punch and slap her. On television, Sydney Bristow (Jennifer Garner) of *Alias* (2001–2006) was often captured and tortured in various ways, including teeth pulling, water-boarding, and electrocution. Likewise the two heroines of the most recent TV version of *Nikita* (2010 to present), Nikita (Maggie Q) and Alex (Lyndsy Fonseca), have each been subjected to multiple torture scenes. In fact, by the second season of *Nikita*, the CW Network lured audiences with advertisements featuring the heroine bound to a metal chair while her nemesis points a gun at her, with the tagline, "Nikita: Discovered. Tortured. Betrayed." And while Lisbeth Salander's rape in all the versions of *Dragon Tattoo* is not torture in the sense of pain inflicted for the sole purpose of deriving information, it is still clearly presented as a torturous experience as she is bound, gagged, and raped. For the purposes of this chapter, "torture" incorporates scenes that dwell on the hero's or heroine's physical and emotional pain for prolonged periods when the character is bound or helpless and cannot resist being victimized by the villain. Scenes like the lengthy black-and-white opening sequence of *Kill Bill* (2003) featuring an extreme close-up of the Bride's (Uma Thurman) bruised, bloody, and tear-stained face as she is taunted by Bill is no less a torture scene than clichéd portrayals of violent military interrogations.

Fictional film and television depictions of torture often share many of the same conventions and serve similar narrative goals whether the protagonist being tortured is male or female. Where they do differ greatly, depending on the gender of the sufferer, is in relation to issues of eroticization. While the torture of action heroes strives to offset or negate the sexualization of the male body, the torture of action heroines risks eroticizing the victimized female body. Because women are already so heavily coded as sexual objects in the media, female torture scenes can be understood as more overtly erotic. Women in Hollywood films are so thoroughly eroticized and objectified that it becomes difficult to present them, or read them, through any other perspective. From the very start of many movies certain female characters are marked as undeniable sexual spectacles. In this context it is easy to see the initial introduction of Black Widow in the blockbuster movie *The Avengers* as an eroticized torture scene. Black Widow is dressed in a revealing little black dress and nylons, with her arms bound behind the back of a chair so that her chest is thrust out, her hair carefully tousled. Black Widow is roughed up by the men interrogating her, but she remains beautiful and confidently flirtatious during the beating, demurely asking her captors, "Do you think I'm pretty?" She eventually beats all of the bad guys to a pulp (while still tied to the chair, no less), but the scene is designed to eroticize her more than it is about her endurance of torture. That the establishing scene for Black Widow in a family friendly movie like *The Avengers* is so thoroughly fetishistic reveals just how much our society is accustomed to objectifying women in ways that overlap sex with violence. The consistent problem in popular culture is that female vulnerability and sexuality are yoked together.

The current popularity of "torture porn" horror films explicitly links together the premise of torturous violence with the exploitative erotic thrills of pornography. It is no surprise that the majority of victims in torture porn are women, their beauty and pain spectacularized for viewers.[14] Less extreme than torture porn, but perhaps more influential, is the kinky erotic symbolism of BDSM that originated in fetish subcultures and has achieved mainstream acceptability. Contemporary Western culture is flooded with images of women enjoying sadomasochistic play. Films like *Secretary* (2002), *Unfaithful* (2002), and *Kinky Boots* (2005) offer explorations of submissiveness. Likewise, mild bondage commonly appears on television, and sexy sadomasochistic scenarios are common in advertising for everything from cars to shoes. To promote voter registration, young sex symbols like Jessica Alba and Christina Aguilera appeared in print advertisements bound by black duct tape and wearing fetish muzzles. Turn on the radio and you can hear Rihanna singing, "Sticks and stones may break my bones, but chains and whips excite me," in her song "S/M." E. L. James' book trilogy *Fifty Shades of Grey* (2012) has become a best seller chronicling the heroine's increasing submissiveness to her sadistic lover and includes numerous erotic scenes of bondage. Charting the mainstreaming of sadomasochism, Eleanor Wilkinson argues, "Since the 1990s we have seen a proliferation of SM images in western cultures, leading some to claim that representations of BDSM are everywhere."[15] Specifically, these images of female sexuality in the media routinely combine objectification with the symbols of sadomasochism. Brian McNair refers to the increased commonness of this fetishistic type of images as "porno-chic."[16] These mainstream images, McNair argues, are "not porn, then, but the *representation* of porn in non-pornographic art and culture,"[17] and "porno-chic replaced the traditional demonization of porn with, if not always approval or celebration, a spirit of excited inquiry into its nature, appeal and musings."[18] Similarly, these common glossy, often sanitized, images of fetishism and sadomasochistic play can be understood as "bondage chic" or "torture chic." They represent the trappings of bondage and torture in a highly stylized and unthreatening manner that flirts with fantasies of domination and submission but always with a message that it is good sexy fun, and implies that women are always aroused by these scenarios. The omnipresence of BDSM imagery in the media is presented as postmodern playfulness and minimizes any threat of real violence. "Ultimately," Wilkinson points out, "there is no escaping the fact that SM has been made 'safe,' toned down and commodified."[19]

In a culture that normalizes female sexuality as submissive, filmic torture scenarios with victimized women are likely to eroticize them as much as, or more than, to validate their strength. For male action heroes, torture can deny their feminization, but for female action heroines, torture confirms femininity. The long-standing cultural assumption that masculinity is active and powerful, while femininity is passive and powerless, extends to a belief that male sexuality is naturally sadistic and female sexuality is naturally masochistic. Masochism is only pathological for men because it renounces subjectivity and control and is feminizing (hence all of the filmic strategies to deny the hero's feminization), while masochism is natural for women. In her thorough discussion of masochism, Kaja Silverman points out that this gendered way of thinking assumes that masochism "is an accepted—indeed a requisite—element of 'normal' female subjectivity, providing a crucial mechanism for eroticizing lack and subordination."[20] This binary logic that assumes masochism is a natural or normal condition of femininity means that when strong women are tortured in the media it is not a transgression but a reaffirmation of their inherent femininity. That so many of these scenes are eroticized, like the torture of Black Widow described above, only reinforces the objectification of women and its association with violence. Torture and rape are, at their core, more about power than about sex, but because torture is so heavily laden with sexuality in filmic representations, it is usually far more disturbing when the victim is female.

Like the male hero, action heroines usually endure the pain with only grimaces of discomfort, lots of brave wisecracks, and promises to exact revenge. Ultimately the heroines prove their superiority by escaping and killing or wounding their torturers. When Charly/Samantha is strapped to the mill wheel in freezing water in *The Long Kiss Goodnight*, she refuses to give up information and instead says, "I feel dirty; time for a bath." When she is lowered into the water again she frees her hand and retrieves a gun from a corpse; then she kills her captor. The pilot of *Alias* is structured around Sydney Bristow's torture at the hands of foreign terrorists. Sydney is bound to a chair as they beat her and pull her teeth out. Her torturer taunts her by calling her just a "pretty, pretty girl," but Sydney taunts him right back before freeing herself and subduing dozens of armed men. In the first season of *Nikita*, the heroine has been captured and is suspended by her arms in a barren room, chained to the concrete ceiling. Nikita is promised impending torture by knives, needles, and electricity. Though visibly distraught, Nikita responds with, "You should be wondering who is going to save you," just before her preplanted bomb explodes. Nikita pulls herself up on the chains and rips them from the ceiling before assaulting her captors and escaping. And in a revealing example, when Jordan (Demi Moore) in *G. I. Jane* (1997) is bound, beaten, and nearly raped after her squad has been captured during a training exercise, she ends up beating her assailant to the ground and then galvanizes her unit by taunting him with a chant of "Suck my dick!" In cases like these, as the *G. I. Jane* example makes abundantly clear, the torture scene serves the same function as for male heroes. It proves that the heroine is the toughest, the most resilient, the most resourceful . . . the one who wields the phallus and all of its assumed power. But even in these scenes the threat of sexual violence is closer to the surface than it is when men are tortured. Samantha/Charly is clad only in a flimsy slip that becomes relatively transparent in the water. Sydney wears a tight black sweater, leather pants, and is taunted for her beauty. Nikita is dressed in a tight undershirt and pants that show off her curves. And, of course, the attempted rape of Jordan reveals that sexual assault is always more of an imminent threat to females who have been captured.

THE RAPE OF LISBETH SALANDER

The combination of Hollywood's persistent objectification of women, the implicit eroticization of these types of scenes, the omnipresence of torture chic, and the heroine's physical vulnerability means that the possibility of rape is always an underlying current for action heroines. It is within this context that the rape of Lisbeth Salander in *Dragon Tattoo* is problematic. The story is narratively more of a mystery, a thriller, or even a rape-revenge tale, but the character of Salander is so original, so competent, so intelligent, so strong, and so active that she was quickly categorized as a new type of action heroine. "The success of the heroine Lisbeth Salander suggests a hunger in audiences for an action picture hero," writes Roger Ebert, describing her as "thin, stark, haunted, with a look that crosses goth with S&M, she is fearsomely intelligent and emotionally stranded."[21] A cover story in *Entertainment Weekly* called her "the inscrutable, androgynous, and explosive heroine," a "sleek, spooky avatar of payback," and "a stone-cold female badass."[22] Salander may be understood as an action heroine—she is certainly tough, smart, active, and self-reliant—but her depiction in both film and print is far more realistic than is normal for action heroines. She does not have crazy kung-fu skills or superpowers (though she is unsurpassed in computer hacking), she is not a master of swordplay or archery, and she is not conventionally beautiful with a Hollywood-perfect body slinking around in a tight black leather outfit. Both the character of Salander and the narrative of *Dragon Tattoo* are grounded in realism rather than the fantasy world of unquestionable empowerment offered in action films. Salander's torture and rape is also more disturbingly realistic; there are no witty and confident rejoinders, no feats of remarkable skill to free oneself from chains before sexual assault can take place. She may be a tough action heroine, but the reality of sexual violence and victimization is laid bare rather than glossed over as teasing and stylish torture chic.

The novel and both film versions of *Dragon Tattoo* feature a complicated narrative that weaves together three different stories. The central story deals with disgraced journalist Mikael Blomkvist attempting to solve the mystery of a young woman, Harriet Vanger, who disappeared from her wealthy family's island estate forty years ago. Blomkvist is a skilled researcher, but when he discovers just how complicated the case is, and how it may be intertwined with the rape and murder of dozens of women over several decades, he asks Lisbeth Salander, a formidable investigator in her own right, to help him. Together they solve the mystery and locate the now grown Harriet Vanger who had fled her family home to escape her brother who had been raping and murdering women (including repeatedly raping Harriet) just as their father had been doing before. But it is the character of Salander that really fascinated readers and viewers the world over. Salander is a withdrawn, antisocial, and hostile young woman covered in tattoos and piercings who dresses in an aggressive punk style. Salander has been declared incompetent, spent her youth in a mental institution, and is thus a ward of the state and has to answer to a court-appointed guardian. It is the abuse she suffers from her newly assigned advokat Nils Bjurman that provides most of the controversial points of the story. Bjurman sexually assaults her twice. The first time Salander meets with him in his office, Bjurman forces her to perform oral sex on him. The second time, Bjurman brutally rapes Salander after insisting that she must come to his apartment. But the third time Salander meets with Bjurman, she exacts her revenge by Tasing him, tying him down, and raping him anally with a butt plug. She then tattoos "I am a sadistic pig, a pervert, and a rapist" on Bjurman's stomach and blackmails him into obedience with a video that she had clandestinely recorded when he had raped her previously. It is Salander's story that is at the heart of the narrative and all of the controversy that surrounds *Dragon Tattoo*.

The motivation for Salander's quest is revenge, a common provocation for modern action heroines used explicitly in films like *Enough* (2002), *Kill Bill, Salt* (2010), *Colombiana* (2011), *Haywire* (2011), and television series like *Nikita* and the aptly titled *Revenge* (2011–current). More specifically, Salander's story is about revenge for the sexual abuses she and other women have suffered, and aligns closely with the subgenre of rape-revenge films that emerged in the 1970s and 1980s such as *The Last House on the Left* (1972), *I Spit on Your Grave* (1978), *Ms. 45* (1981), and *Extremities* (1986). During the first wave of rape-revenge films, Pam Cook argued that while these and other exploitation-type films allowed for new representations of women, the "stereotype of the aggressive positive heroine obsessed with revenge,"[23] they undermined feminist messages about rape by framing the assaults with titillating nudity, numerous seduction scenes, and by sexualizing the female victims. The ongoing tendency in Hollywood is to suggest that female victims are somehow complicit in their rape because they have been flirtatious or hypersexual. But Salander is not overtly sexualized, her past abuses have left her seething with animosity, and her unusual appearance is carefully constructed to scare people away.

The controversy in the popular press, and on the Internet, over Salander's rape stems from the assumption that scenes of graphic sexual violence always eroticize the act and perpetuate or normalize violence against women. But Salander's rape scene in the book and both movies is anything but eroticized. By not glossing over the brutality of sexual assault, *Dragon Tattoo* distinguishes itself from making light of the reality of violence against women in torturous scenarios. Moreover, the horrendous nature of the act has to be apparent so that her brutal revenge is justified narratively. Still, the reaction many had to the anal rape scene in the novel reveals the shock that realistic violence contains in a media environment where we have all gotten used to female torture scenes that tease but do not really lead to the logical level of sexual assault. The editorial in *Bitch* magazine argued that the book "dwells on Salander's rape in indulgently gory detail."[24] In fact, in the book, the description of the rape is less than a page long (the earlier oral rape is even shorter). The particulars of Salander's physical and mental pain after the assault and the steps she takes to recover are given more time and detail than the rape. The description of her revenge on Bjurman, on the other hand, is over eight pages long, with far more detail about how she assaults him.

The filmic representations of Salander's rape, in both the Swedish and the American versions of *Dragon Tattoo*, are powerful scenes that carefully avoid eroticizing the assault. They each make it clear that this is a perverse violation of Salander's body, that it is violent, painful, dehumanizing, and a twisted exertion of Bjurman's state institutionalized power over her. The Swedish film directed by Niels Arden Oplev stars Michael Nyqvist as Mikael Blomkvist and Noomi Rapace as Lisbeth Salander. Roger Ebert describes the sexual violence in the Swedish film as "having a ferocious feminist orientation," arguing that "there are scenes involving rape, bondage and assault that are stronger than most of what serves in the movies for sexual violence, but these scenes are not exploitation."[25] When Bjurman (Peter Andersson) rapes Salander in his apartment, there is no hint of titillation, only the pain of her suffering. Salander kicks at Bjurman, she flails and tries to rip the handcuffs from the bed frame, and she screams in anger even after he shoves a rag in her mouth and wraps a belt around it. The review of the Swedish film version in *Ms.* magazine emphasizes the emotional force of the pivotal rape: "While the scene isn't pornographic, the vehemence of her excruciating struggle renders it horrific enough to still set my heart racing. One feels her desperate determination to be angrier than her attacker is strong, and it's stunning that her ferocity fails to save her."[26] The scene is more violently shocking than in the book because we are forced to bear witness to the assault. There is nothing erotic about it. It is filmed from Salander's perspective as Bjurman's deranged face descends on her, intercut with close-ups of her eyes wide in terror, and her desperate cries of anger and then pain. The scene is raw, violent, terrifying, and, as it should be, difficult to watch.

There was concern that the American remake of *Dragon Tattoo* would eroticize the violence and portray Salander as more of a sexpot. Ultimately, the Hollywood version was still a gut-wrenching depiction of violence against women. Peter Bradshaw in the *Guardian* declared that Fincher's take on the story "is sleeker, smoother, sexier than its Swedish predecessors," and that "it is a muscular, overwhelmingly confident movie—and its brutal violence is thus even tougher to take."[27] The rape scene is filmed in a manner very similar to the Swedish version. When Salander (Rooney Mara) visits Bjurman's (Yorick van Wageningen) apartment, he leads her to the bedroom, grabs her hand, and slaps a handcuff on it as she fights to reach the door. Salander wails and thrashes in terror as Bjurman rips her clothes off, asks her if she likes anal sex, and then penetrates her as she screams. There is no hint of titillation, no suggestion that Salander wanted it, deserved it, or enjoyed it. There are no snappy comebacks or eleventh-hour rescue; there is nothing but violence and victimization. Though, ultimately, Salander rejects being victimized.

In all three versions of the story, Salander's rape is difficult for readers/ viewers to experience, precisely because we do "experience" it with her. We identify with her horror and her helplessness. We vicariously empathize with her being exploited just as much as we thrill to her brutal revenge against Bjurman. Salander's rape is undoubtedly one of the most controversial and painful scenes ever to appear in mainstream cinema. The laborious realism of sexual violence in *Dragon Tattoo* sets the story apart from the earlier wave of rape-revenge films, and Salander's gritty appearance and ruthless demeanor distinguish her from the unbelievable stylized glamour of traditional action heroines. The brutality of Salander's rape is jarring because it confronts viewers with the ugly reality of sexual assault rather than glossing over it or fading to black to avoid depicting such upsetting moments. The tone and style of the rape in *Dragon Tattoo* is similar to *Monster* (2003), another progressive film about sexual violence and its consequences. Lisa Purse astutely argues that the vicious rape of Aileen (Charlize Theron) by Corey (Lee Tergesen), which sets her on a murderous path, is filmed in a way that "interrupts" the usual cinematic landscape of sanitized images of female violence played out by beautiful actresses. Purse contends that the rape scene in *Monster* "feels 'too close,' like an invasion of one's personal space. The staging prevents a clear view of what is being done to Aileen's body: we access the violence not through its spectacle (which risks sensationalizing or eroticizing the event) but through glimpses of Corey's instruments of torture and, much more importantly, Aileen's facial reactions; her struggle for comprehension; her silent cry as she experiences the physical and mental agony of the rape."[28] Salander's rape in both movies functions in much the same way, not because it is filmed in an excessively choppy or claustrophobic manner but because we have been situated to identify with Salander. As with Aileen, Salander's rape is not an eroticized spectacle but a horrific event that audiences, both male and female, *experience*.

While every reiteration of *Dragon Tattoo* depicts Salander's rape as a vile and torturous experience perpetrated by a sadist with physical and institutionalized legal power over her, the story ventures into rape-revenge territory because she refuses to define herself as a powerless victim. She carefully plots and prepares for her revenge and makes Bjurman suffer the same physical pains that she endured and sets in place safeguards to protect herself from any retribution he might think of, and to prevent him from assaulting other women. In effect, Salander proves herself a far more successful torturer than Bjurman. She not only turns the tables on him, but she also demonstrates her ability to exert power over him without the aid of physical size or institutional support. Salander shows Bjurman that rape is about power not sex, and that power can be exercised by women as well as by men.

"I WANT YOU TO HELP ME CATCH A KILLER OF WOMEN"

Salander's story is clearly rooted in rape-revenge fantasies, but where earlier films focused entirely on the woman's revenge against her own rapists, Salander ties her personal revenge against men to a larger agenda of retribution against violent misogyny. Salander initially refuses to help Blomkvist with his murder investigation when she first meets him, but as soon as he explains that he is asking her to help catch a rapist and killer of women, she readily agrees. Ultimately she is instrumental in figuring out that Harriet Vanger's brother, Martin, has been torturing, raping, and killing women for decades. In the two subsequent books, Salander's quest continues as she hunts down and kills her villainous father, half brother, and other men involved in a sex-trafficking organization, and she helps expose a clandestine government organization that had aided her father and a psychologist who had tortured her as a child. The stories' project of exposing and dismantling a variety of sexually abusive men struck a chord with audiences worldwide. Hundreds of blogs cheered Salander's emergence as a realistic fantasy of a feminist avenger. FemMagazine.com wrote, "Ms. Salander is a bona-fide badass. I believe she appeals to women because she operates under a code of justice that gains revenge for victimized women everywhere."[29] Zeldalily.com refers to Salander as "a stone cold feminist."[30] Media reviewer Susan Toepfer at TrueSlant.com calls her a "tiny terminator" and declares, "Lisbeth is a super-heroine for our time, a feminist avenger."[31] Likewise, Feminist-ing.com calls her "basically a feminist avenger."[32] Christina Konig at *The Times* argues that the story is "a contemporary feminist polemic with a good old fashioned thriller."[33] Opinionessoftheworld.com says, "Salander is a fe-rocious feminist, crusading for women's empowerment."[34] And Forbes.com claims that "what's significant—and utterly awesome—is that Lisbeth is not a victim. She's a revenger seeking payback and justice."[35]

Because Salander can be so readily understood as a realistic feminist avenger, fighting on behalf of women everywhere who have been victimized by men, she represents a far more radical challenge to misogyny than the standard Hollywood action heroine who may beat up men but always looks like a beauty queen while doing it. David Denby writes in the *New Yorker* that "everything that happens to Lisbeth is a real enough danger in the world—it has happened to many women. She's a genuine possibility, not a cartoon, and therefore far more serious as a pop-culture figure than the super-killers played by Uma Thurman in the *Kill Bill* movies or by pouting, vogue-ing Angelina Jolie in her kick-groin roles."[36] Salander may be the most visible feminist-influenced character in popular film, but she is not complete-ly alone. In an era where female empowerment in the movies is still grounded in an overvaluing of female beauty, when tough women are more likely to look like the sexy fantasy figures embodied by the five young heroines of *Sucker Punch* (2011) than the punkish and antisocial but realistic Salander, there have been a few other exceptions. Most notable is perhaps the character of Hayley Stark (Ellen Page) in the revisionist rape-revenge film *Hard Candy* (2005). In this critically acclaimed film, Hayley is a young teen who tortures and kills suspected pedophile Jeff (Patrick Wilson). *Hard Can-dy* is a rape-revenge film that shockingly does not portray the initial rape, nor does it present any sexualized images of women or victims at all. The film thus manages to avoid any complicity in perpetuating images of sexualized violence against women that might be titillating. In her fascinating analysis of *Hard Candy*, Rebecca Stringer argues that "the character of Hayley Stark is more clearly drawn as a feminist avenger—a vigilante acting directly on the basis of feminist principles."[37] There is no clear connection between Hayley and the girl who was killed, no explanation for why she took it upon herself to hunt down and destroy Jeff for his sexual abuses (she also claims to have killed his accomplice). At the end of the film, when Jeff begs Hayley to tell him who she really is and why she is doing this, she vaguely replies, "I am every girl you ever watched, touched, hurt, screwed, killed." Though she eschews certain feminist principles like nonviolence and collective action, Hayley is, like Salander, an agent of female anger and vengeance against not just specific men but an entire culture that normalizes sexual violence against women.

As powerful and shocking as Salander's revenge on Bjurman is, it is over before the story is even a third of the way completed. The larger project of *Dragon Tattoo* and the entire Millennium Trilogy is her struggle to uncover who has been torturing and raping women for decades, and then to avenge and dismantle the state-sanctioned organization that has been involved in exploiting young women. It is these overarching plots that truly cast Salander as a feminist avenger writ large, rather than just a singular agent of rape revenge. Importantly, Mikael Blomkvist is her partner in vengeance against systemic sexual violence. Blomkvist may sleep with numerous women throughout the stories, including Salander, but he is important because the revulsion he shares with Salander regarding the exploitation of women clarifies that systemic sexual violence is not just an issue for women. Larsson's point is that this is a cultural problem that requires deep structural change and should be addressed by everyone regardless of gender, class, or sexual orientation. In *Dragon Tattoo* Blomkvist's character is also crucial for revealing that torture and sexual violence are not gender specific. Being male or female does not matter when torture and rape are reduced to situations of being in power or being powerless.

Lisbeth Salander is undoubtedly one of the most original and spectacular fictional characters to come along in years and has become the focal point of the Millennium Trilogy phenomenon, but Mikael Blomkvist is a sympathetic male presence that broadens the gender politics of the stories. For all his competencies as an investigator and as a romantic partner, Blomkvist is cast in a melodramatic tradition as a "fallen man," for whom we can feel pathos and cheer for redemption. Whereas the stereotype of the "fallen woman" most commonly found in film noir and melodrama usually arrives at her lowly status due to the misfortunes of love and sex, fallen men lose their way for any number of reasons. Though love and sex are often involved, Janet Staiger argues that "plot devices lure a man into wayward paths because of his lack of control. These lures may be drink or gambling or even blind ambition."[38] The ability to control one's life, to control any situation, is a key feature of our cultural definition of masculinity. To lose control is to lose masculine stature, to lose one's way. Blomkvist is established as a fallen man at the onset of *Dragon Tattoo* through the detailing of his conviction for slander against a corrupt industrialist. As in so many action movies, Blomkvist must redeem his masculine identity, which he does in the end by publishing a damning account of the industrialist's illegal activities. And, like action heroes, part of Blomkvist's redemption is written on his body as he suffers torture at the hands of the story's villain. But unlike the Rambos, John McClanes, and Martin Riggses of action movies, Blomkvist is unable to save himself.

In the novel, Blomkvist is captured almost immediately after he figures out that Martin has been abducting, torturing, and killing young women and is the reason for the disappearance of his sister Harriet. Martin takes Blom-kvist at gunpoint into his personal torture chamber in the basement of his expensive home, handcuffs him, and uses a throat collar attached to an eyelet in the floor to bind Blomkvist while he beats him. Feeling safe in the knowl-edge that he has complete control over Blomkvist, Martin explains the pleas-ure he takes in kidnapping women and then keeping them captive while he tortures and abuses them for days on end, even videotaping the assaults. Then, in between bouts of hysteria and homicidal glee, Martin suspends Blomkvist from the ceiling by a leather noose, rips most of his clothes off, and prepares to rape him. Just before the final violation, as Blomkvist is gasping for a last few breaths of air, Salander arrives. She beats Martin viciously with a golf club, breaking many of his bones, before she takes a moment to free Blomkvist from the noose. Martin makes a desperate run for it, driving off in his car, but Salander pursues him on her motorcycle until he crashes and dies in a fiery explosion. Nor does the American film shy away from Martin's intent to rape Blomkvist. Martin explains that he "feels him-self getting hard," as the hope drains from Blomkvist's face, similar to when he watches his female victims. Then he cuts off Blomkvist's shirt and undoes his pants, relishing having a man as a victim for the first time.

The use of Daniel Craig, the current James Bond, as Mikael Blomkvist in the American adaptation of *Dragon Tattoo* is an especially fortuitous bit of casting. Craig's identification with the role of 007 does risk bringing Bond's famous hypermasculinity, his toughness and his sexual desirability, to the character of Blomkvist. But Craig's version of Bond, especially in the widely praised rebooting of the franchise *Casino Royale* (2006), represents a differ-ent take on ideal masculinity and the vulnerability of the hard male body. "Above all, *Casino Royale* is a story of remasculinization," argue Susanne Kord and Elisabeth Krimmer. "Surprisingly, although the popular notion of Bond suggests otherwise, Craig's Bond is ideally suited for such a narrative. The new Bond is a paradoxical hero who embodies both hypermasculinity and vulnerability."[39] This shift to a more realistic Bond, whose version of masculinity bears the physical and emotional scars of vulnerability, is no-where more evident than in *Casino Royale*'s infamous torture scene. The villain's torture of Bond has long been a convention of the series, from the classic scene of Sean Connery's Bond strapped to a metal table in *Goldfinger* as a laser slowly burns its way toward his groin, to Pierce Brosnan's Bond being tied to an antique strangling chair device in *The World Is Not Enough* (1999). But where Connery's Bond bluffs his way out of the death trap with cool quips, and Brosnan's Bond actually has sex with the villainess while bound, Craig's Bond is tortured in a far more realistic, painful, and emascu-lating way. When Bond is captured by Le Chiffre (Mads Mikkelsen), the evil financial dealer of *Casino Royale*, he is stripped naked and bound to a bot-tomless chair. Le Chiffre proceeds to interrogate and torture Bond by repeatedly pummeling his testicles with a large knotted rope. Unlike earlier Bond tortures that established the hero's superior masculinity, Johnson argues that the scene "brings us up close to the torture of Craig's Bond."[40] As Johnson describes it, "An establishing long shot shows a naked Bond in the bottomless chair, and, as it proceeds, the scene contains close-ups on the expressions of pain on his face throughout. Just as we see the physical presence of Bond, we hear his pain since he does not try to remain stoically silent but instead exhales and howls loudly."[41] Still, in traditional heroic fashion, Bond endures the pain and refuses to divulge any of the information that Le Chiffre is after.

But the scene was shocking to many fans, and painful to watch, because it diverges so much from traditional torture scenes with heroic male ideals. First, Bond is fully naked, not just shirtless, and his genitals are explicitly the location of the torture; in other words, Bond's preeminent phallus is literally being destroyed, and along with it all of the mythos about masculine impermeability. Second, the scene may not be an actual rape, but it is clearly presented as a sexual violation and does not shy away from the threat of male-on-male rape. Le Chiffre touches Bond in a sexual manner, admires his physique, and commends him on the wonderful shape he has kept his body in—before making it clear that none of Bond's physical strength matters now that he has been put in a position of powerlessness. The third, and most realistic, divergence is that Bond is rendered incapable of triumphant self-rescue. He cannot free himself from the bonds; he cannot bluff or fuck his way out of the torture. Indeed he blacks out from the pain and is only saved when an assault team bursts in at the last minute and kills Le Chiffre. Moreover, he does not miraculously recover from the wounds inflicted upon him. Bond spends months confined to a hospital bed and a wheelchair, and it is explained that his penis, his "manhood" itself, may never work again. This infamous torture scene does not employ any of the compensation techniques used in most action films to confirm the hero's masculinity. According to the logic of our cultural perception of gender, this scene feminizes Bond by offering his body as a spectacle and by restricting him to passivity and vulnerability. That *Casino Royale* can do this to Bond himself, and still be a huge critical and commercial success, indicates a significant shift in understanding issues of gender and victimization. That Craig's Bond and his Blomkvist can each embody ideal masculinity and rapeable vulnerability helps to reposition our understanding of torture and rape as undeniably about issues of power rather than just gender.

Salander may be the one who is actually raped in *Dragon Tattoo*, but the story indicates that Blomkvist can also be victimized. Moreover, in the ultimate reversal of the damsel-in-distress trope, Blomkvist is saved by a woman and never achieves his own revenge on Martin Vanger. Likewise, in *Casino Royale*, we find out that Bond's rescue is thanks in large part to information provided by Vesper Lynd (Eva Green), and he is denied the possibility of revenge against Le Chiffre. Throughout the Millennium Trilogy, Salander is accorded the full status of what Carol Clover refers to as the "victim-hero" of rape-revenge films.[42] Salander is sexually victimized, but the larger portion of the story deals with her calculated, lengthy, and violent revenge. Blomkvist, on the other hand, is only victimized. That both Salander and Blomkvist are tortured and sexually victimized suggests that Carol Clover is correct in her assertion that rape-revenge films can facilitate audience identification with the victim-hero regardless of the viewer's gender because the biology of the character is less important than the performance of victimization or revenge. Clover insightfully argues that rape-revenge films "operate on the basis of a one-sex body, the maleness or femaleness of which is performatively determined by the social gender of the acts it undergoes or undertakes."[43] While Clover is talking about rape-revenge films specifically as a horror subgenre, her theory about gender roles being performative based on either the suffering or the retribution they enact is equally applicable to understanding torture in action films.

The slippage between torture as sexual victimization and as potential or actual rape in action movies, regardless of a character's gender, means that these films may be reworking issues of gendered assumptions about power in an increasingly progressive way. That men like Blomkvist and Bond can be depicted as powerless victims of sexual violence, as rapeable, helps to uncouple the ideological link between helpless victim and femininity. That neither of these two male characters is allowed direct revenge, nor a triumphant self-rescue, means that their masculinity is not magically restored through any of the complex compensation techniques that are so commonplace when male heroes are tortured. Blomkvist's and Bond's position as helpless victims of torture and sexual assault casts them not as masculine or feminine but as powerless regardless of gender. Likewise, Salander's rape casts her as a momentarily powerless victim who happens to be a woman. Salander's revenge on Bjurman for her rape can be seen as masculinizing her (she does penetrate him), but it is not a radical shift in her demeanor. She was smart and tough before the rape; the need for vengeance did not transform her from passive femininity to active masculinity. Moreover, Salander's larger revenge against men who torture, rape, and murder women raises the revenge narrative to the level of feminist politics. While popular culture may still be a long way away from truly repositioning violence and sexual assaults as not gender specific, these films are at least grappling with the deeper complexity of the issues.

In addition to revealing that torture and rape are about powerlessness and vulnerability regardless of the victim's gender, *Dragon Tattoo* and the entire Millennium Trilogy also demonstrate that sexual violence against women should be condemned and fought against by both women and men. Blomkvist is an example of appropriate male disgust with sexual violence. Blom-kvist is as invested as Salander in the quest to catch Martin, the serial rapist and murderer, and the organization of men who have been abusing and trafficking in women for years. The stories make it clear that Blomkvist is out to take these men down not because it is his job, not because he was assaulted, not because he has a brief relationship with Salander, but because it is the morally responsible thing to do. Nor does Blomkvist take the lead in the struggle; he and Salander work together. Though Salander is more than capable of handling almost anything on her own, Blomkvist is always ready to assist her because systemic sexual violence against women is something that everyone should rally against. While the central revenge fantasy of the Millennium Trilogy is focused around Salander and her remarkable exploits, her mission is never really a solitary one in the tradition of earlier rape-revenge narratives. In the Millennium Trilogy, Salander does not act entirely alone; nor does Blomkvist act alone on her behalf. They fight systemic misogyny and sexual violence individually and together.

NOTES

1. Stieg Larsson, *The Girl with the Dragon Tattoo* (New York: Vintage, 2005).

2. Steve Neale, "Masculinity as Spectacle: Reflections on Men and Mainstream Cinema," *Screen* 24, no. 6 (1983): 2–16.

3. Kaja Silverman, *Male Subjectivity at the Margins* (New York: Routledge, 1992).

4. Susan Jeffords, *Hard Bodies: Hollywood Masculinity in the Reagan Era* (New Brunswick, NJ: Rutgers University Press, 1994).

5. David Savran, *Taking It Like a Man: White Masculinity, Masochism, and Contemporary American Culture* (Princeton, NJ: Princeton University Press, 1992).

6. Laura Mulvey, "Visual Pleasure and Narrative Cinema," *Screen* 16, no. 3 (1975): 6–18.

7. Neale, "Masculinity as Spectacle," 13.

8. Jeffords, *Hard Bodies*, 51.

9. Silverman, *Male Subjectivity*, 326.

10. Savran, *Taking It Like a Man*, 201.

11. Gaylyn Studlar, "Masochism and the Perverse Pleasures of the Cinema," reprinted in *Film Theory and Criticism: Introductory Readings*, 4th ed., ed. Gerald Mast, Marshall Cohen, and Leo Braudy (New York: Oxford University Press, 1992).

12. Ibid., 783.

13. Tim Edwards, "Spectacular Pain: Masculinity, Masochism and Men in the Movies," in *Sex, Violence and the Body: The Erotics of Wounding*, ed. Viv Burr and Jeff Hearn (New York: Palgrave Macmillan, 2008), 169.

14. See Adam Lowenstein, "Spectacle Horror and *Hostel*: Why 'Torture Porn' Does Not Exist," *Critical Quarterly* 53, no. 1 (2011): 42–60; or Dean Lockwood, "All Stripped Down: The Spectacle of Torture Porn," *Popular Communication* 7 (2009): 40–48.

15. Eleanor Wilkinson, "Perverting Visual Pleasure: Representing Sadomasochism," *Sexualities* 12, no. 2 (2009): 182.

16. Brian McNair, *Striptease Culture: Sex, Media and the Democratisation of Desire* (New York: Routledge, 2002).

17. Ibid., 61.

18. Ibid., 63.

19. Wilkinson, "Perverting Visual Pleasure," 185.

20. Silverman, *Male Subjectivity*, 189.

21. Roger Ebert, *"The Girl with the Dragon Tattoo," Chicago Sun-Times*, December 19, 2011.

22. Mark Harris, "Enter the Dragon," *Entertainment Weekly*, January 6, 2012, 26, 28, 30.

23. Pam Cook, "'Exploitation' Films and Feminism," *Screen* 17, no. 2 (1976): 124.

24. Taraneh Ghajar Jerven, "The Girl Who Doubted Stieg Larsson's Feminism" in *Bitch* 48 (Fall 2010): 9.

25. Ebert, *"The Girl with the Dragon Tattoo,"* 2.

26. http://msmagazine.com/blog/blog/2010/04/14/the-rape-of-the-girl-with-the-dragon-tattoo.

27. Peter Bradshaw, *"The Girl with the Dragon Tattoo"*—Review," *Guardian*, December 22, 2011.

28. Lisa Purse, "Return of the 'Angry Woman': Authenticating Female Physical Action in Contemporary Cinema," in *Women on Screen: Feminism and Femininity in Visual Culture*, ed. Melanie Waters (New York: Palgrave Macmillan, 2011), 192.

29. Admin, "Feminist Fatale: Lisabeth Salander in "The Girl with the Dragon Tattoo," Femmamagzine.com, January 7, 2012, http://femmagazine.com/?p=1460.

30. Katie Loud, "Lisabeth Salander: The Girl Who Was a Feminist," Zeldalily.com, July 11, 2010.

31. Susan Toepfer, "'Girl With the Dragon Tattoo': Lisabeth Salander Makes My Day," Trueslant.com, May 24, 2010.

32. Courtney, "Not Oprah's Book Club: *The Girl with the Dragon Tattoo*," Feministing.com, March 9, 2010.

33. Christina Konig, "The Girl with the Dragon Tattoo," TheTimes.co.uk, March 3, 2010.

34. Amber Leab, "Before Premiere of 'The Girl with the Dragon Tattoo' Remake, Revisit the Original Film and Lisabeth Salander's Badassery," Opinionsoftheworld.com, December 9, 2011.

35. Melissa Silverstein, "Lisabeth Salander, The Girl Who Started a Feminist Franchise," Forbes.com, July 1, 2010.

36. David Denby, "Lisbeth Salander: The Movies Have Never Had a Heroine Quite Like Her," *New Yorker*, December 27, 2011.

37. Rebecca Stringer, "From Victim to Vigilante: Gender, Violence, and Revenge in *The Brave One* (2007) and *Hard Candy* (2005)," in *Feminism at the Movies: Understanding Gender in Contemporary Popular Cinema*, ed. Hilary Radner and Rebecca Stringer (New York: Routledge, 2011), 277.

38. Janet Staiger, "Film Noir as Male Melodrama: The Politics of Film Genre Labeling," in *The Shifting Definitions of Genre: Essays on Labeling Films, Television Shows and Media*, ed. Lincoln Geraghty and Mark Jancovich (Jefferson, NC: McFarland, 2008), 73.

39. Susanne Kord and Elisabeth Krimmer, *Contemporary Hollywood Masculinities: Gender, Genre, and Politics* (New York: Palgrave Macmillan, 2011), 130.

40. Ibid., 119.

41. Ibid.

42. Carol Clover, *Men, Women & Chain Saws: Gender in the Modern Horror Film* (Princeton, NJ: Princeton University Press, 1993).

43. Ibid., 159.

Chapter Five

The Maternal Hero in Tarantino's *Kill Bill*

Maura Grady

In 2003 and 2004, director/screenwriter Quentin Tarantino released the long-awaited follow-up to 1997's *Jackie Brown*—*Kill Bill Vols. 1 and 2*, his homage-fusion of grindhouse, exploitation, revenge, kung fu, samurai, and spaghetti Western films. Uma Thurman previously acted for Tarantino in 1994's *Pulp Fiction* and portrays the lead character here, known in *Vol. 1* only as "the Bride."[1] As with his earlier films, Tarantino tells his story in a nonchronological fashion, and the audience is not given the full backstory until nearly the end of *Vol. 2*. *Vol. 1*, an exposition-free revenge story is a thrill-packed series of episodes featuring the Bride performing what is usually masculine-identified action. Thurman describes the Bride:

> If it's a character, it's a very male character. I mean, the scope of the journey that the character goes through is something that you wouldn't blink twice if you saw Mel Gibson's Mad Max in this position, or Clint Eastwood.[2]

At the time of its release, *Kill Bill* and star Thurman were praised by critics for presenting a strong and powerful female image to movie audiences. Thurman, in the above quote, seems anxious to align her performance with those of male movie heavies such as Gibson and Eastwood, and she is in many ways justified: the Bride is a trained marksman, kung fu fighter, and swordsman; wears the same costume Bruce Lee wore in his last film, 1978's *Game of Death*; performs numerous acts of violence; and is the film's central figure—not the girlfriend or damsel in distress. Her "journey," as Thurman calls it, involves her traveling the globe, mercilessly slaying her enemies, being buried alive, and getting severely wounded, until she at last reclaims her child. She appears bloody, bruised, and dirty throughout most of the two films but is, in the end, victorious—a triumphant hero like Eastwood and Gibson might play. But the Bride's victory—murdering those who wronged her and taking her rightful place as a mother—undermines any subversive content her action-hero posturing would suggest. *Kill Bill* lets the Bride play at the role of a male hero for the bulk of the movie but ultimately denies her the agency that a male hero would have because her biology determines her fate more than her actions. Tarantino creates cinematic worlds that borrow from and fuse together genres, styles, and time periods, and the movie interacts with numerous cultural anxieties surrounding working women, focusing on a woman who decides to leave the masculine working world when she discovers she is pregnant.

Despite an attempt to create a female hero, *Kill Bill* cannot reconcile the masculine action the lead female hero performs with the moments of biological essentialism assigned to her. The audience is continually reminded that the Bride has a female body, however well she may perform masculine heroism, and that her ultimate goal is to reunite with her child and leave her profession. What, then, is the ultimate message about the female hero's claim to masculine power?

The film opens with a scene of the Bride in a weakened, vulnerable position—prone and bloody, and shot from Bill's point of view as he stands over her wounded form and speaks to her before shooting her in the head—but this scene is immediately followed by a knife fight sequence in which we see the Bride challenge and defeat her first opponent, Vernita Green (Vivica A. Fox). Tarantino makes sure to remind us of the particular vulnerability of a beautiful woman in the scene after this one, by showing us that a hospital orderly has been raping the Bride while she lies in a coma and making her available to his friends. Though she gets her revenge on the orderly and an additional rapist, it's difficult to imagine Clint Eastwood standing in for Thurman in this particular scene. Rather than echoing Eastwood films, the segment is instead a homage to such exploitation rape-revenge films as *I Spit on Your Grave* and *Thriller (They Call Her One Eye)*. This genre features women victims of rape exacting brutal revenge on the assailants. When the Bride awakens and overhears the orderly discussing the price for her body, she becomes aware of the violation she has been unknowingly enduring. She symbolically castrates both men, ripping out the tongue of one rapist and smashing the head of the other in a door.

Scenes such as this essentialize the biology of the Bride's female body, and Tarantino further narrows the definition of that female body to a maternal one. The Bride wakes from her coma and, realizing she is no longer pregnant, grabs her stomach and weeps bitterly at the loss of her baby. This is only the first instance where the film assumes a "natural" maternal instinct for its female characters. The Bride's encounter with former DiVA member Vernita takes place in front of the latter's daughter, and the women make a temporary truce not to fight in front of the young girl. The appearance of a school bus outside the window and the arrival of Vernita's daughter causes the women to stop fighting, establishing the idea that these professional assassins will surrender their aggression and what amounts to their "work" (fighting) because it is simply wrong to fight (work) in front of one's child. A later scene reinforces the idea that a mother's only job should be to mother. The Bride speaks to Bill, her former lover, boss, and the head of the Deadly Viper Assassination Squad. She tells him her reasons for quitting the Vipers, a decision made after taking a home pregnancy test:

> Before that strip turned blue, I was a woman. I was your woman. I was a killer who killed for you. I would have jumped a motorcycle onto a speeding train for you. But once that strip turned blue, I could no longer do any of those things. Not anymore. Because I was going to be a mother.

Becoming a mother supersedes everything else. There is even an automatic woman-to-woman understanding that motherhood is sacred, even among assassins. During the conversation with Bill, the film flashes back to the scene in which the Bride finds she is pregnant. Bill has sent her to L.A. on a job, and she is in her hotel room after arriving in the city. Having felt sick on the plane, she thinks she might be pregnant and does a home test, not really believing it will have a positive result. Immediately after taking it, with the little stick in her hand, she is called to the door and nearly killed by a rival assassin, also a woman. The scene is played for humor—as the two assassins have their guns pointed at each other, the Bride asks her opponent to please "look at the stick." The assassin does, sees the Bride is pregnant, and therefore quickly agrees to just walk away and let the Bride go home. The Bride explains, "I'm the deadliest woman in the world, but right now I'm just scared for my baby." The implication that the deadliest woman in the world can be brought to her knees and made so fearful by becoming pregnant grants incredible power to the male phallus—all the patriarch need do is impregnate her to render her completely powerless. Again, this scene is played for humor, but it is certainly unsettling to any female claim to masculine power or other message of female empowerment. This biological essentialism, articulated by the Bride herself in her words to Bill, indicates that she has never been her own person. She *is* determined that her daughter will be *her* own person ("she deserved to be born with a clean slate," says the Bride), so she keeps her pregnancy secret, later explaining to Bill, "Once you knew, you'd claim [the child], and I didn't want that." Bill tells the Bride, "Not your decision to make," and she does not argue with him that she should have been the one to decide what happened to her body and its contents.

Bill's reaction to the Bride's decision was to attempt to murder her. In his justification for his jealous and violent reaction, Bill disputes the Bride's narrow interpretation of her body's ownership, suggesting that her work is simply incompatible with motherhood.

This essentialization is emphasized by having the camera treat the Bride as feminine in moments that concern her biologically female body. One of Carol Clover's assertions about gendered figures on-screen reinforces this idea. In the universe of horror films, "sex . . . proceeds from gender, not the other way around. A figure does not cry and cower because she is a woman; she is a woman because she cries and cowers."[3] In *Kill Bill*, the Bride does cry, but she never cowers. And the moments when she does cry are specifically associated with biological femaleness: when she awakens from her coma and realizes she is no longer pregnant (she assumes the baby is dead); when she is shot with a truth serum by Bill and forced to relive her decisions regarding her pregnancy; and finally after she has killed Bill and escaped to the open road with her child, she lies on the floor of the hotel bathroom and weeps as her daughter watches cartoons in the room outside. The closing-credit sequence of *Vol. 2* shows us all the leading players with their character names and aliases. The last two characters given credit are the young actress playing the Bride's daughter, B. B., and the Bride. Her credit is listed as "Uma Thurman as Beatrix Kiddo AKA the Bride AKA Black Mamba AKA Mommy." Here we have the Bride not as Carol Clover's "final girl" but as "final mommy."

Mulvey's "Visual Pleasure and Narrative Cinema" establishes the phallocentrism of the camera, which almost universally takes the masculine point of view as its own, and that the on-screen woman exists to point to the contrast between the male (who possesses a phallus) and herself (who does not). She notes that "it is [the on-screen female's] lack that produces the phallus as a symbolic presence."[4] In *Kill Bill*, the female hero could be seen as producing the phallus of the absent male (Bill) as symbolic presence. It was, after all, his literal phallus that set the action of the story in motion, since he impregnated the Bride and precipitated her departure from the Deadly Vipers. His revenge on her for this departure is in turn the motive for her revenge. That she chooses to conduct her rampage of revenge with the phallic samurai sword indicates that she desires "to make good the lack of the phallus"[5] by defeating those who have attempted to suppress her. She symbolizes the threat of castration both literally and symbolically by pursuing and defeating the patriarchal male, and she "turns her child into the signifier of her own desire to possess a penis."[6] *Vol. 1* implies that the Bride's motivation is to avenge the attack against her, her fiancé, and her friends and the destruction of her baby. In *Vol. 2*, we discover that the friends and fiancé meant nothing to her, so the revenge is actually on behalf of herself and her child. Mulvey's formulation becomes much more apt, then, with this in mind. The child is the reason for her to wield the phallic weapon, perform these acts of symbolic castration, and destroy the patriarchal figure of Bill, thus establishing a new symbolic order consisting only of herself and her female child.

By positioning herself as "a very male character," Thurman is explicitly asking that her character be identified as a masculine hero. In *Female Masculinity*, Judith Halberstam declares that "what we understand as heroic masculinity has been produced by and across both male and female bodies,"[7] and this production of masculinity by a female body can help to deconstruct the link between biological maleness and masculinity. Halberstam argues that we only truly begin to *see* masculinity "when and where it leaves the white male middle-class body,"[8] and *Kill Bill* offers us several examples of masculinity performed by nonmale and nonwhite bodies. The (female) bodies doing this performing are not "ambiguously gendered bodies"[9]—they are all played by feminine, well-known beauties—but I would argue that their actions within the world of the film are definitely performances of cinematic masculine behaviors. Filmic masculinity is as dictated by industry and cultural tradition as any other film convention insofar as it echoes a limited number of archetypes. Therefore, when a female body performs these actions, even when she is not "ambiguously gendered," I argue she may be identified as masculine. And fluidity of gender identification can, as Halberstam argues, begin to "reorganize masculinity itself" and "assaul[t] dominant gender regimes"[10] by dismantling the link between biology and gender. Seeing this represented in popular-cultural form, such as a film, could in turn help advance the goal of creating or encouraging gender fluidity, thus also dismantling the links between biology and power.

Kill Bill is a film which does help to deconstruct the link between biological maleness and masculinity at certain points, but which also reinforces the biological femaleness of its central character, therefore denying her a total identification with the masculine and undermining the masculine power she claims through her behavior. Moreover, the film maintains that masculine behavior and identification *is* the only way to access power. In the film, all the traditional cultural moments of female triumph—wedding, pregnancy, giving birth, mothering an infant—are denied the Bride. The only avenues of power left available to her are masculine ones.

By creating a movie in which women stand in for male action heroes, Tarantino might be seen as enacting a critique of conventional masculinity, since this is at least an attempt to address and depict the existence of male-identified women in a mainstream popular film. Halberstam states that the insisted linking of maleness and masculinity and "the indifference to female masculinity . . . has clearly ideological motivations and has sustained the complex social structures that wed masculinity to maleness and to power and domination."[11] Therefore Tarantino's use of female masculinity might be seen as a way of deconstructing these "complex social structures" such as patriarchy and the family, and indeed at first the film reinforces the power of these structures by making Bill (the patriarch) such a dominant figure. He robs the Bride of her consciousness, her mobility, and her child. Even though she eventually kills Bill and takes back their daughter, Bill's decisions are the ones that drive the narrative.

Naming her "the Bride" places her squarely within the realm of a generic femininity. Throughout *Vol. 1*, Beatrix Kiddo's name is withheld or bleeped out when uttered by other characters. "The Bride" is how the male sheriff and the deputies who discover the carnage of the slain wedding party refer to her. This is the name she is given in the end credits of *Vol. 1*. Tarantino is likely paying homage to Clint Eastwood's powerful "Man with No Name" character in spaghetti Westerns *A Fistful of Dollars*, *For a Few Dollars More*, and *The Good, the Bad, and the Ugly*. Though this comparison does convey a modicum of power to the Bride, by denying her a name, the film also denies her a degree of subjectivity. The bleeping out of the Bride's name draws attention to the conventions of film—something Tarantino is actively doing throughout both volumes of *Kill Bill* with his postmodern barrage of references to other filmic sources—and places the audience in a position of passivity and powerlessness: everything the audience experiences is controlled by the filmmaker. There is no clear reason within the narrative to withhold her name from the audience, apart from the police at the scene of the massacre being unable to identify her and thus assigning her the pseudonym "the Bride." The use of this particular pseudonym by the police and in the audience's mind is a way to force the audience to experience the paradox of "a bride" performing all of these brutal (masculine) acts.

While it is true that there are several instances of the camera "viewing" the bride as a passive (feminine) figure, there are many more examples that support a reading of her as active (masculine). A key component of Mulvey's distinction between filmic masculine and feminine subjects is that the masculine subject does the seeing, and the feminine object is seen. Says Mulvey, "The determining male gaze projects its phantasy on to the female figure . . . [whose] appearance [is] coded for strong visual and erotic impact so that they can be said to connote *to-be-looked-at-ness*."[12] The first scene of the film, in which the camera is in a tight black-and-white close-up on the Bride's bruised and bloodstained face, helps to reinforce this distinction. We hear Bill's voice off camera and see the effects of his action on the Bride whom he sees (he wipes her bloody face then shoots her), but we are denied the opportunity to see him; in fact we do not see his face clearly at all in *Vol. 1*. We hear his voice and see various parts of his body (his hands, his arms, and his torso), but never his entire person.[13] This visually establishes Bill as a powerful figure, and the story reinforces this—he is the central agent of the story's momentum. It is he who forms the Deadly Viper Squad, trains its workers, and impregnates the Bride, prompting her to run away, which then leads Bill to order the assassination at the wedding chapel,[14] all leading to the central action of the story: the Bride's revenge.

An antecedent to the Bride's story is a revenge film starring and directed by Clint Eastwood, the postmodern Western *High Plains Drifter* (1973). In this film, Eastwood plays a "man with no name," a vengeance-minded drifter who menaces a frontier town. We slowly learn that he is a reincarnation of the town's marshal who was murdered by outlaws, with the complicity of the townspeople. Tarantino echoes the film's visual references in flashback to the scenes of violent and brutal betrayal. In both films, when a protagonist sees one of his/her betrayers, a certain eerie musical motif is heard, and the camera looks up from the bloodied hero's prone point of view at the faces of the betrayers, intercutting between the present and a flashback to that same character at the moment of violence against the hero.

When the Bride awakens from her coma, she begins to take on the masculine role of the seer rather than the seen. After she wakes with a start, we finally get a glimpse of Bill from the Bride's point of view as she has a flashback of the scene at the chapel just before she is shot. The barrel of a gun is in the foreground, and behind it Bill is out of focus, as he would have been through the Bride's swollen eyes. From this point in the story, the camera more often than not takes the Bride's point of view, and she becomes the privileged eye with which the audience identifies.

Especially whenever the Bride performs masculine action, this male/seer, female/seen paradigm is reversed, and the Bride is the one who does the seeing. Even lying prone in her hospital bed, the camera is positioned from her viewpoint once she is awake. At the moments when she spots an aggressor from the chapel massacre episode, the camera takes her point of view, both at the present scene of agency and back at the chapel scene of violence toward her. We see each character through her eyes as they were then and as they appear now. A scene that illustrates this masculine ownership of sight particularly well is the showdown with O-Ren Ishii (Lucy Liu) and her followers at the House of Blue Leaves restaurant in Tokyo. This is chronologically the first stop on the Bride's "death list" of revenge, though it does not occur until the end of *Vol. 1*. The Bride's point of view is almost universally the camera's; she (and we) watches O-Ren and followers enter the restaurant, and observes O-Ren and fellow chapel massacre participant Sofie Fatale through the "revenge" lens of double-seeing (present and flashback). More explicitly, when the Bride is surrounded by O-Ren's bodyguards, "the Crazy 88," she looks into her sword and sees reflected even those opponents that are behind her. Her possession and control of the phallic weapon could be read as what enables her to see.

The power of her sight is further emphasized by her ability to actively rob her opponents of sight. In the House of Blue Leaves, the Bride plucks out the eye of one male opponent and slays, with her sword, all the others who oppose her, thus denying them the right to ever "see" her again. In *Vol. 2*, she also plucks out the remaining eye of Elle Driver (Daryl Hannah), a former member of the Vipers. Preceding the fight between the Bride and Driver, Driver has in turn successfully performed the masculine filmic role herself. She drives up to the trailer of Bill's brother Budd in a Thunderbird convertible (a "penis car") wearing a suit. She then kills him with a phallic instrument of death (a poisonous snake) in order to steal a phallic weapon (a valuable samurai sword), which he had stolen from the Bride. The previous night, Budd had buried the Bride alive and is as of yet unaware that she has escaped. As Budd lies dying, Driver expresses her regret that "the greatest warrior she has ever met"—that is, the Bride—should have met her death "at the hands of a bushwhackin', scrub, alky piece of shit like" Budd. The Bride then returns to defeat Driver, which she does by blinding her and leaving her alone in the trailer with the snake, thereafter repossessing her samurai sword. As well as depriving her opponent of sight, plucking out the eyes is symbolic of castration, so the Bride is the one to remain in possession of both the phallus (sword) as well as the ability to see.

The possession and successful use of this phallic weapon can be viewed as a means by which the Bride, having been weakened by the penetration and impregnation of her body, rejects any further penetration of her own body and instead will penetrate others (both male and female) as she seeks her revenge. The Bride travels with her phallic sword always visible—on the plane it is next to her, and as the plane lands in Tokyo, she even strokes the hilt in a masturbatory manner. In the airport, there is a posterior waist-height shot of her walking, and she holds the sword close to her side. Judith Butler theorizes that a "feminine penetration of the feminine, or a feminine penetration of the masculine" (both of which occur in *Kill Bill*) "could be considered something like a cooptation and displacement of phallic autonomy that would undermine the phallic assurance over its own exclusive rights."[15]

Existing side by side with progressive depictions of powerful women, however, are scenes of victimization. Ben Singer, in *Melodrama and Modernity: Early Sensational Cinema and Its Contexts*, addresses the simultaneous and seemingly contradictory presence in silent serials of scenes of victimization of women, alongside the depiction of women as heroic agents—a pattern replicated in *Kill Bill*. He addresses the "lurid victimization of the heroine by male villains who exploit their greater size, strength and sadistic guile to render [the heroine] powerless and terrified."[16] This suggests that we read *Kill Bill* as a modern-day serial-queen film. The Bride, too, goes through an alternating series of empowering and humiliating scenes. The film begins with a view of her prone, bloody, and helpless and alternates such scenes as her rape, defeat, and live burial at the hands of Bill's brother Budd with scenes of her strong and competent triumph over her adversaries, which also couples, as Singer puts it, "an ideology of female power with an equally vivid exposition of female defenselessness and weakness."[17]

Singer mentions that psychoanalysis offers several explanations for an audience's willingness to view female power and victimization in the same film but does not believe that these explanations alone cover the facts and that the historical context must be taken into account: "The serial-queen's oscillation between agency and vulnerability expressed the paradoxes and ambiguities of women's new situation in urban modernity."[18] My explanation is that a female character performing heroism is distinct from a "heroine" character and can offer the male members of the audience an opportunity to identify with moments of heroic agency but distance themselves from the moments of vulnerability since these moments are specifically female identified.

In this way, the serial-queen genre is also an ancestor of the horror film because it allows the audience to identify with a vulnerable lead character. Clover claims that the horror genre "is far more victim-identified than the standard view would have it."[19] She notes that these films are comfortable with the "possibility that male viewers are quite prepared to identify not just with screen females, but with . . . screen females in fear and pain."[20] She notes that the viewer's first identification is with the camera and then only secondarily with the main character. Since *Kill Bill*'s camera so often privileges the Bride's viewpoint, the viewers are led to identify with her even when her gender does not match theirs, and even when she is a victim.

Ultimately, the Bride may be less in line with Halberstam's ideal performance of the masculine by females and more in line with Mulvey's assessment that she stands in "patriarchal culture as signifier for the male other."[21] Halberstam acknowledges that this has frequently been the role of the masculine female, to show how male masculinity is the real thing, by framing female masculinities as "the rejected scraps of dominant masculinity."[22]

Halberstam says that "not-masculine" is defined through the nonwhite, nonhetero, and nonworker, since white middle-class maleness is seen to stand in for essentialized masculinity.[23] Tarantino's fascination in *Reservoir Dogs* with that white middle-class maleness supports this point. *Kill Bill*'s more ethnically diverse, female-centered cast (especially in *Vol. 1*) might, according to Halberstam, continue to define that same white masculinity by showing us the "not" side of the equation. Thurman's fights with Fox and Liu, though tougher and more down and dirty than women usually get to be, still point the comparison to the male bodies who "normally" perform violent fight scenes. Halberstam says, "We tend to believe that female gender deviance is much more tolerated than male gender deviance,"[24] and this certainly seems true for Tarantino. There are several moments in *Reservoir Dogs* (1992) and *Pulp Fiction* (1994) where suspected homosexuality or other gender deviance is ridiculed and/or reacted against with violence. This preoccupation is evident also in Tarantino's turn as an actor in *Sleep with Me*, in which he muses about the homosexual subtext of super hetero-militaristic *Top Gun*.

Halberstam maintains that heterosexual female masculinity—as we see in *Kill Bill*—"menaces gender conformity in its own way, but all too often it represents an acceptable degree of female masculinity as compared to the excessive masculinity of the dyke."[25] Again, Tarantino does not clearly present a queer sexuality in the film, and in this way he falls short of the truly subversive critique Halberstam envisions. Nor does the film heed Halberstam's warning that "it is important when thinking about gender variations such as male femininity and female masculinity not simply to create another binary in which masculine always signifies power. In alternative models of gender variation, female masculinity is not simply the opposite of female femininity nor is it a female version of male masculinity."[26] *Kill Bill* fails to fully embrace an alternate, female masculinity, but getting the audience to accept Thurman's Bride as "a very male character" points to the constructedness of an essentially male masculine cinematic heroism: if a woman may fulfill the male hero role in a popular film, then the inherent maleness of that masculinity is still in doubt, and while that does help the audience envision possibilities for women fighters in the future, that transgressive future is not realized in *Kill Bill*. Because the Bride is a mother, and rape victim, *Kill Bill* remains a chauvinist fantasy where a woman can play at heroism but is always defeated via her female body. In the end, the Bride becomes defined by her maternity and not her masculine action.

NOTES

1. Although her name is later spoken in *Vol. 2*, I will refer to her only as the Bride throughout.

2. Interview by Stephen Shaefer in the *Boston Herald* ("The Edge" section), April 12, 2004. In another article, the film's producer, Lawrence Bender, describes Thurman as "Clint Eastwood in the body of a beautiful woman" (Jamie Malanowski, "Catching up with Uma Thurman," *USA Today*, October 5, 2003).

3. Carol Clover, *Men, Women & Chain Saws: Gender in the Modern Horror Film* (Princeton, NJ: Princeton University Press, 1993), 13.

4. Laura Mulvey, "Visual Pleasure and Narrative Cinema," in *The Sexual Subject: A Screen Reader in Sexuality*, ed. Mandy Merck (New York: Routledge, 1992), 22.

5. Ibid.

6. Ibid.

7. Judith Halberstam, *Female Masculinity* (Durham, NC: Duke University Press, 1998), 1–2.

8. Ibid., 2.

9. Ibid., 15.

10. Ibid., 29.

11. Ibid., 2.

12. Mulvey, "Visual Pleasure and Narrative Cinema," 27, italics in original.

13. We nearly get a glimpse of him as the Bride awakens from her coma and sees in flashback the moment when he shot her. He is out of focus, but this recreates her point of view.

14. When the sheriff looks at the Bride lying on the floor, his view is clearly prioritized. This is emphasized by shooting her in a green filter to represent the way she appears as he looks through his tinted glasses.

15. Judith Butler, *Bodies That Matter: On the Discursive Limits of "Sex"* (New York: Routledge, 1993), 51.

16. Ben Singer, *Melodrama and Modernity: Early Sensational Cinema and Its Contexts* (New York: Columbia University Press, 2001).

17. Ibid., 255.

18. Ibid., 262.

19. Clover, *Men, Women, & Chain Saws*, 8.

20. Ibid., 5.

21. Mulvey, "Visual Pleasure and Narrative Cinema," 23.

22. Halberstam, *Female Masculinity*, 1.

23. Ibid., 2.

24. Ibid., 5.

25. Ibid., 28.

26. Ibid., 29.

Chapter Six

We've Seen This Deadly Web Before

*Repackaging the Femme Fatale and Representing the
Superhero(ine) as Neo-noir "Black Widow" in* Sin City

Ryan Castillo and Katie Gibson

When director Robert Rodriguez adapted the graphic novel *Sin City* to the Hollywood silver screen, he did so in spectacular and revolutionary style. The 2005 blockbuster came as a fresh and innovative take on the recent explosion of fantastic superheroes in popular culture, a period from 2001 to the present that Shaun Treat deems a *superhero zeitgeist* for how we saw more commercial releases in the superhero genre than all prior years in Hollywood combined.[1] *Sin City* was refreshing for how it broke from traditional Hollywood narrative structure to deliver three nonlinear story lines based on Frank Miller's dark neo-noir comics. One critic deemed the film "hyper-stylized" for how its "raw, simple stories" and "sexually charged, blood-soaked world" heavily appeals to the infantile "desires of the male imagination."[2] For the indie director turned Hollywood visionary, Rodriguez truly understands and respects the artistic allure of comic books for grown men with a predilection for macho fantasy.[3] Countercritics went as far as to label *Sin City* a cheap "multi-million dollar spectacle" whose narratives are more reminiscent of a Hollywood exploitation film by "sinking into brainless violence, gender exploitation . . . and cheap, adolescent nihilism."[4] Roger Ebert received the film as more a representation of style than a narrative in any traditional sense: "[*Sin City*] internalizes the harsh world of the Frank Miller comic books and processes it through computer effects, grotesque makeup, lurid costumes and dialogue that chops at the language of noir."[5] What Rodriguez achieved in visual style was just the piece so many graphic novel adaptations had strived to put together time and again yet had failed to accomplish. In other words, Rodriguez/Miller's creative brainchild captured an aesthetic that paid honest tribute to the graphic, visceral, and hallucinatory highs of its comic book origin. Beyond merely bringing Miller's stories to the moveable screen at twenty-four frames per second, Rodriguez translates them with precise and awe-inspiring fidelity to their source, making each independent frame of the comic medium the practical storyboard for the film. While many lauded Rodriguez/Miller for creating a new artistic style with intertextual appeal and multigenre scope, others have called their finished product a modern-day film noir exemplar for how its dark visuals and dialogue reconstruct the hopeless worlds of *Casablanca* (1942) and *Sunset Boulevard* (1950) with their socially regressive messages and motifs.

Sin City stands as an intriguing rhetorical takeoff point into feminist film criticism. Many have addressed the film's visual style as a historical and aesthetic signifier for classical Hollywood noir films. Jeff Otto argues that the film signals a "neo-noir" narrative for how its constant voice-over monologues and hard-boiled lines remain heavily steeped in the world of 1950s pulp fiction magazines and B-grade detective films.[6] Spicer situates the entire milieu of these types of films into a contemporary genre of "neo-noir" because they draw distinctly on the classical period's (1930s–1950s) signature styles.[7] Rodriguez/Miller's film is styled in the explicit vein of film noir—a term which translates literally from its French coinage as "black film"—and the genre's use of shadow and stark backgrounds, black-white contrasts, and themes of darkness, obsession, and doom.[8] It may not be surprising how and why these themes tend to arise in Hollywood during times of political dismay, especially in response to oppressive practices of monopoly capitalism gone awry.[9] Unlike Hollywood audiences of decades past, we are permitted by modern-day technological/industrial advancements to experience the world of *Sin City* beyond grainy 16 mm black-and-whites through a more futuristic high-definition lens (a shiny and gray look) with the occasional splash of a bright color (a streaking red or yellow) to call attention to a specific character.[10] Given how the characters of *Sin City* act as mirrored archetypes for the psychologically tortured antiprotagonists of noir lore, we inspect supernatural images of hero/heroine as rhetorical neo-noir signifiers for classical Hollywood themes of aesthetic/narrative darkness, obsession, and doom.

From their comic book births into action blockbuster figures, shifting signification processes of the superhero mythos have been common across history. Yet the American superhero has floated across time as a patriarchal image belonging to a predominantly male domain.[11] The recent infiltration of Hollywood superheroes onto our popular-culture landscape has not only made it difficult for scholarship to keep up but has also begun to recreate the screen as an empowering space where super*heroines* are allowed to exist. This chapter seeks a rhetorical engagement with and critical interrogation of supernatural females as they act as signifiers for feminist strength in Rodriguez/Miller's hyperstylized world. To call *Sin City* a neo-noir film foregrounds the similar cultural mood that binds our Bush post-9/11 recession decade to the postdepression, World War II political climate of the 1940s and 1950s. If, as Shugart contends, superheroes act as floating historical signifiers that speak to a particular cultural moment,[12] we wonder whether the fantastic nature of the American superheroine might inspire a playful subversion of gender identity for viewing superhero films through a feminist lens. We approach this fascination with a Foucauldian understanding of power and dominance to utilize the dynamic approach that Raymie McKerrow deems a critical rhetoric. To avoid pursuing a narrow feminist critique, we find it important to discuss signified portrayals of women/femininity conceptually in relation to men/masculinity while paying careful attention to how these interdependent identity factors work with and against one another in ubiquity. We therefore approach gender and sex as independent factors that require detailed and sustained attention to their formation and to the nonsimple ways in which they play out onto one another.[13] This chapter explores the contradictory relationships of dominant social-structural forces and individual subjectivities, surface and substance in texts, gender normative images masked in acts of subversion, and comic book versus motion picture treatments of identity.

GENDERED SIGNIFIERS AND STYLE IN THE NEO-NOIR TEXT

The characters of Miller/Rodriguez's world are fascinating both for how they gender the highly stylized world of Basin City (universally known as Sin City) and signify the superhero film as a neo-noir text. First, the film's five characters are styled for the gender archetypes they contain to give audiences a taste "not so much of their presence as their essence."[14] The three principal narratives tell the stories of five ultraviolent protagonists who remain tied to one another through various degrees of separation and become rotated into a hyperdimension throughout the film's progression[15]: Marv is a towering, seven-foot-tall man of dim intellect with a superhuman appetite for violence, yet one who highly values loyalty and kindness; Dwight McCarthy, a tortured soul with a nihilistic worldview, is a model of chivalry with a bad temper, a passion for romance, and a history of binge drinking and wild love affairs; Gail is a dominatrix, Catwoman type who exists in a love-hate power relationship with Dwight and stands as the authority figure over a community of prostitutes in Old Town; Detective John Hartigan is a muscular, imposing man who gets wrongly convicted of raping eleven-year-old Nancy Callahan; Nancy is a sensitive, caring exotic dancer who develops a love affair with Hartigan after he rescues her from the villainous Yellow Bastard.

We only need a glimpse into how these characters are styled in costume, color, lighting, camera angle, and so on to gain a deeper understanding into the contradictory gendered politics that govern Basin City. Reading characters at the surface level of style does not deemphasize their humanity, for, as Horsley argues, "despite their relentless pulpiness, despite their walking clichés caught inside a demented fantasy of postmodern medievalism, Miller/ Rodriguez's characters develop, improbably, into flesh and blood beings, with hearts that bleed and not just bodies."[16] Style can be crucially important to uncovering the rhetoric of images, for, as Vivian argues, style not only reflects how a director's worldview surfaces in individual aesthetic but offers us an intellectual category for understanding a big-picture social reality beyond the level of artistic form.[17] As rhetorical scholars are coming to recognize the substantive social and political influences of style apart from its traditional connotations of artistic characteristics,[18] we must see style as a kind of ideology or set of ideologies that give it discursive impact.[19] Because style carries with it many ideological beliefs, it is necessarily prone to contradictory interpretations. Just as we can never speak for how another received a film, or how a picture says a thousand words, the rhetoric of style can reveal a whole complex array of competing subjectivities. Therefore, we must take care in piecing together the muted ideologies within style because ideology is itself contradictory.[20]

Second, the characters in *Sin City* represent contradictory beings for how they act in subversion to traditional gender norms inherent within the superhero narrative but remain styled in the aesthetic vein of the film noir genre. The superheroes and superheroines of *Sin City* resonate as gendered signifiers for two classic archetypes in film noir: the morally conflicted *antihero*, doomed to be a victim of his own demise, and the poisonous *Black Widow*, a sultry seductress who leads the antihero protagonist to his inevitable destruction. The neo-noir Black Widow is renegotiated by regressive film noir standards of the femme fatale and, as such, embodies the paradoxical legacies of sexism prominent in classical Hollywood. Goldie, a sex worker who leads Marv to his violent death, provides a shining example in this regard as she floats through Sin City flaunting her sexuality in exchange for physical protection. Goldie is styled in full color with a keen aesthetic focus on her blond curly locks of hair as she radiates the screen when contrasted with the film's stark black-and-white aesthetic. Goldie embodies Hollywood's "continued legacy of sexism in a culture that understands itself as post-feminist, if not post-gender," knowing fully that she can gain power over men by calling attention to her body.[21] Film noir was keen on these lethal female archetypes, whose questionable virtue and mental imbalance were masked by a faux feminine empowerment.[22] Constructed in binary opposition to the Super Antihero, the Black Widow maintains her role as temptress as a "grounds to legitimize [male] acts of torture and extreme violence."[23] Because she has no agency without her male counterpart, her signified image has over time re-vealed her as a disabling figure for women. Indeed, countless scholars have lamented how the Black Widow is granted agency and control only when she administers her lethal dose of femme fatale through sexual prowess.

The male Super Antihero signifies a contemporary archetype of film noir lore because, like these classic "nonheroic heroes," he remains an unstable, ineffectual, flawed, tragic protagonist who suffers from a range of psycho-logical neuroses, and is unable to solve the problems he faces.[24] He is a dystopian figure defined by anarchic violence and the male societal standard of "it's not what you are underneath, but what you do that defines you."[25] He thus remains a morally ambiguous hero who runs the perpetual risk of be-coming Supervillain.[26] Detective Hartigan exemplifies this notion for how he must "wield redemptive violence in outlaw crusades against evil, tacitly flirt-ing with antidemocratic values."[27] As a decorated cop who is made criminal by a faulty judicial system, he represents the typical Super Antihero morality tale and becomes the "secular savior" who ultimately sacrifices himself for his Black Widow, Nancy Callahan, without clearing his own name. His death as Super Antihero is further exaggerated by style when he stands as a black silhouette against a white, snowy backdrop and shoots himself point blank as bright red splatters the landscape. The archetypal characteristics running be-neath surface images of superheroine and superhero make them useful for calling critically on style to interrogate how and why gender-subversive acts become normalized within the morally backward world of Sin City.

Just as superheroes document specific historical moments, these nostalgic neo-noir archetypes are useful signifiers for understanding what it means to be male and female in our post-9/11 era and further offer scholars a rhetorical "springboard for discussing ideological mainstays informing [dominant] nar-ratives of good American citizenship."[28] The commercial signs of Black Widow and Super Antihero are used in style to simplify and smooth over the complexities of identity to inform citizens how to act in and out of accor-dance with one's gender in U.S. culture. Gendered neo-noir images, there-fore, function in popular culture as rhetorical scripts to further streamline the discursive meanings behind being female and acting feminine, being male and acting masculine, being female and acting masculine, acting both mascu-line and feminine, or being both male and female. Privileging style as a sign system of rhetorical meaning provides critics a pathway to comb through the complicated web of possibilities that make up identity and subjectivity. Pay-ing attention to gender in this contradictory signification process allows for a crystallized understanding of why strength, for instance, is inherently con-nected to men in the dominant cultural imagination or why we must remain critically vigilant to the subtle ways that power and virility become reclaimed as feminine qualities in the dominant Hollywood structure. Since Hollywood narrative convention has long dictated that male and female characters cannot exist without the other, we strive toward pinning down how power functions to discursively "naturalize" the social norms that position heroines (and by extension females) beneath males to encourage consent within a dominant order.

STYLE AND POWER ENTANGLED
IN A DENSE WEB OF MEANING

While rhetorical scholars have paid much attention to the role of discourse in addressing gender marginalization since the ideological turn, the coming of a critical rhetoric project has brought about new ways to think of discursive power relations as they create and sustain social norms to control the dominated.[29] Acting on the postmodern tendency of critical rhetoric, McKerrow contends that by "pulling together" discourses as "fragmented, unconnected, even contradictory or momentarily oppositional," we can "illuminate otherwise hidden or taken for granted social practices."[30] Many scholars of critical rhetoric seek to deconstruct texts as a "dense web" of micropolitics, muted discourses, and localized narratives to challenge the upheld social practices we willingly participate in to discipline ourselves.[31] These works call for new understandings of power that complicate already accepted notions of domination and coercion.[32] One could read and watch *Sin City* itself as a critical project for how Rodriguez/Miller make the concerted attempt toward feminine subversion by portraying superheroines who use muscular force to act out of accordance with their gender. The prostitutes of Old Town, in particular, hold on to a feminist commitment to community while adopting the masculine qualities that have traditionally floated around the male Super Antihero: they administer a violent brand of vigilante justice, operate with their own mortality in close hindsight, and violently navigate their deadly neighborhood as bloody dominatrices of anarchy. The film operates as gender subversive in this way to give commercial audiences superheroines of substance who blatantly contradict and upset the dominant male societal standard that situates women as protected beneath men as protectors.

Style works in the critical project as a strong rhetorical basis for confronting dominant ideologies because it attempts to get to structural discourses of power beneath superficial surfaces. Because ideology is deeply embedded within images, we can arrive at its many complexities if we approach ideology as a web of meanings that we generate and piece together through a system of cultural artifacts.[33] Style grants us the ability to draw ideological connections between different historical periods (e.g., classical 1930s–1950s film noir and post-9/11 neo-noir) as well as to construct new rhetorical meanings at the surface level of form and medium (e.g., comic books and blockbuster films) and genre and subgenre (e.g., superhero, neo-noir, and exploitation film). Paying attention to style ought not stop at the surface either, since style, like ideology, runs deeper. Style can help us rearticulate dominant discourses operating beneath commercial images that ideologically inform elements of our identity. Because style is a means by which power is negotiated and struggled over in society,[34] style performs the "demystifying function" of the critical project that uncovers the silent and often overlooked ways in which rhetoric conceals as much as it reveals through its relationship with power.[35] When we look again to the prostitutes of Old Town, they come to gain vast social and political power in Basin City by exemplifying feminine physical strength over men through literal killing acts. Yet these subversive superheroines become undermined by style in their sexualized dominatrix dress that ultimately signifies them alongside the faux feminist empowerment of Third Wave ideology. Style operates here as more than the whips and chains that Old Town prostitutes don on their bodies or the splashes of bright red blood that stain the dark urban streets of their black-and-white world. Style is, for Brummett, a socially embedded symbol system that includes visual discourse and performs powerful rhetorical functions in everyday life.[36] It is at the surface level of style where the Old Town prostitutes' power becomes undermined by overly sexualized dress as they continue to perpetuate the regressive traits of the evil Black Widow archetype. The rhetorical script given to audiences is a gender-normative one when the superheroine sex workers remain disallowed from seeing past their romantic heterosexual compulsion and only spin their sultry webs of seduction with one end goal—to lead men to their eventual doom. We need to look more closely into how the prostitutes' individual acts of gender subversion work within and around style to situate women in subordination to men within the popular imagination. We now interrogate the visual images and discursive messages that float around the Black Widow as they work to constrain and enable the superheroine, Gail, who dominates part 2 of the film narrative.

"THE BIG FAT KILL": GENDERED IMAGES AND DISCURSIVE ARRANGEMENT

Gendered images become a prominent feature in Miller/Rodriguez's world for how the graphic novel medium itself relies more on artistic arrangement and hyperstylized illustrations to tell a story than its emblematic dialogue bubbles. The film's distinct first-person voice-over is one stylistic feature reminiscent of film noir, in which Dwight McCarthy narrates the world of Basin City from the masculine point of view of the Super Antihero as his inner monologues drive the plot progression. Because the combined sexist legacy of the superhero mythos and classical noir privileges male voice, Gail is introduced to the film's second plotline as a neo-noir Black Widow figure who embodies the paradox of "femme fatale as projection of male fears and desires."[37] Gail is a strong, stubborn, overtly sexualized woman depicted in the dominatrix attire of chains, netted stockings, and patent leather dress. She represents symbols of societal anarchy and power as she rules her neighborhood of Old Town with an iron fist. Old Town is a section of Basin City where "the girls get to administer their own brand of justice" through anarchic violence and sexual dexterity. According to Dwight, "the ladies are the law here; beautiful and merciless; if you've got the cash and you play by their rules, they can make all your dreams come true, but if you cross them you're a corpse." Dwight exists in his mind as a protector over the prostitutes of Old Town, though Gail sees him more as a difficult ally she cannot seem to abandon. As a hopeless romantic who always folds under Gail's seductive spell, Dwight possesses the ultraviolent and superhuman qualities of the Super Antihero as he jumps off skyscrapers and flies through car windshields unscathed. He stands as a symbol of bravery and assumes the role of calm, collected alpha male who presents a stoic and confident public self, though he questions himself internally.

Gail stands as a tough female subject within Dwight's morally questionable inner monologue as he follows a group of dangerously intoxicated men driving into the bleak domain of Old Town. Dwight uses his supernatural sense to locate trouble lurking around the group of men's search for sex and stands by to aid the women. The group's ringleader then makes a fatal mistake when he pulls a gun on one of Old Town's sex workers, resulting in a bloody massacre that leads to their brutal deaths. The prostitutes stretch the male corpses out along an alley street to discover that they had murdered a "hero" police officer in cold blood, which violated the prostitutes' volatile agreement with the Basin City authorities. As Dwight tells the audience, "If a cop wanders into the neighborhood and he's not shopping for what the girls are selling, they send him packing. But they send him back alive. That's the rules." Dwight subsequently embarks on a dangerous journey to hide the bodies in order to uphold the prostitutes' unsteady truce and maintain the social order of Sin City. As Dwight finds himself in the inevitability of near-death situations, his internal monologue reveals his insecurity over having failed the women. Yet the hopeless Super Antihero never ceases to be rescued by several supernatural female prostitutes in order to fulfill his duty as protector of Old Town. These acts tend toward the subversive for how the Super Antihero himself becomes reliant on feminine strength for physical protection. In this way, Gail and Dwight operate as subversive reminders that "one is never *only* a woman or *only* a man"[38] as they further work to problematize our "understandings of the male gaze and female spectatorial pleasure."[39] Indeed, many have noted how gender and sexual identity are intersectional insofar as men can take on many feminine characteristics while women may adopt typically masculine ones. Yet the film maintains a dominant discourse of what it means to act female and male in our world in how gender-normative roles are visually reinforced through style.

The Black Widow and Super Antihero figures come to represent a site of tension where woman and man are seen as working together, yet in binary opposition to one another. This power struggle is exemplified through the characters of Gail and Dwight. On one hand, Gail operates under the feminist notion that she and her deadly community of superheroines need no help from a man. Initially, Gail views Dwight's offer to help as trivial and cute, assuring him that she "has it under control." This progressive narrative depiction of the Black Widow becomes problematic when Gail and her band of prostitutes commit the murderous act that threatens their social power (and their very material well-being) in the masculine superhero world of Sin City. Either they must rely on the male Super Antihero for help or become once again subjugated to the rule of the mob and corrupted police force. When Gail sees this dilemma as an ultimatum with no other option but to elicit Dwight's help, she willingly places herself as a subject implicated into the visual aesthetic of the neo-noir superhero mythos. As images of femme fatale, Gail and the sex workers of Old Town accessorize themselves with heavy jewelry, sharp knives and katanas, cigarettes, and machine guns. Yet the superheroine style remains predominantly marked by their scandalous dress, with an overtly sexualized emphasis on their tight, scantily clad, revealing leather costumes complete with whips and chains. Therefore, the prostitutes' sense of style is more an expression of fashion that operates under the distinct superhero male gaze to uphold dominant discourses about females and femininity. Brummett elaborates how "style is not simply a matter of which shirt one puts on but is the transcendent ground in which the social is formed,"[40] where style functions to reveal hidden ideological beliefs operating at the level of the image.

While the prostitutes function autonomously, having transcended the past patriarchal oppression of their pimps, the idea of feminist community becomes undermined when they bend to the dominant tendency to let males lead. Indeed, Gail views Dwight's offer to help as genuine and without personal agenda, which ultimately justifies his masculine imposition onto the collective good of Old Town. Gail thus has trouble existing independently of Dwight and always succumbs to his indelibly masculine demands to lead, thereby reinscribing men as symbols of protection. As Stabile contends, "these narratives are quintessential protection scenarios that indulge in fantasies about the heroes' unlimited ability to protect a silent and largely feminized humanity from that which threatens it."[41] Miller/Rodriguez attempt to resolve this tension through style: the resolution of "The Big Fat Kill" ends in bloody and grandiose fashion with the image of Dwight holding Gail steadily by his side as they, with machine guns in hand, brutally murder the mob and the police against a blood-red backdrop of the sky. After the gory bullet fest, Dwight ultimately has the last say in resolving the superhero plotline as he reverts to his morally questionable inner monologue to refer to Gail. The Super Antihero idolizes his female counterpart in hopeless romanticism: "My warrior woman, my valkyrie, you'll always be mine. Always. And Never." Here, the Black Widow functions beyond regressive film noir standards (e.g., luring the protagonist to his death) and assists the Super Antihero in eliminating a powerful, violent group of men. This is a common staple of the contemporary superhero mythos, one which refers to what Wanzo refers to as the "tension of inclusiveness," which is masked by exclusivity, where the hero is essentially the chosen protector and the female heroine is just "hot."[42] As Stabile argues, "gender is an important rail of superhero narratives and to upset it is to undo the whole edifice of protection upon which the stories are erected."[43] In similar tradition as classical film noir, Miller/Rodriguez portray the Black Widow as ultimately reliant on the Super Antihero, thereby reinforcing their regressive meaning through a seemingly subversive reiteration of gendered superhero(ine) acts. The film's story line may appear on the surface to be subversive inasmuch as it features tough, violent women, but at the end of the day, only white men protect.

POSSIBILITIES OF STYLE: BEYOND BLACK WIDOW AND SUPER ANTIHERO

Unlike the supernatural saviors of the traditional superhero mythos, the flawed characters of *Sin City* are particularly interesting for how they function within their own human morality and challenge societal sex and gender roles on the surface. Indeed, *Sin City* operates in stylistic grandeur and portrays superhuman men and women often acting out of accordance with their gender. Yet it is sometimes at the pinnacle of subversion where archetypes are stereotyped and exploited in the most concealed ways. This chapter sought to interrogate whether individual acts of gender subversion by the characters in Miller/Rodriguez's film actually reinforces a normative script for how to perform one's gender and sex. By examining the figure of the Black Widow and her male counterpart, the Super Antihero, we have attempted to unmask the ways in which *Sin City* operates at the intersection of visual images and rhetorical discourse to situate women in subordination to men within the cultural imagination. It was important to study gendered images as hyperstylized since style is a theoretical instrument to understand market production, consumption, and how they function together in society as rhetorics that strive to maintain a hierarchical discourse of power. We conclude with a consideration of how individual (male) directors operating within the Hollywood structure might fashion gender messages that work with subversive intent yet remain vulnerable to the inevitable process of dominant translation.

Looking to the Super Antihero and the Black Widow as resonant signifiers of 1950s noir archetypal figures reveals much about Rodriguez and Miller's film as a pseudo-feminist text. That is to say that Rodriguez/Miller know the power of floating images in the twenty-first century, and so too must critics. To use rhetoric as a critical practice, we must remain open to being positioned and situated in different ways depending on different historical moments.[44] Using style in one such system can, for instance, reveal how the Black Widow gets depicted as a subversive image who fulfills Third Wave feminist "empowerment" and ultimately reinforces a normative gendered script for what it means to be a woman. We need to engage critical discussions and scholarly critiques of superheroes that recenter the female experience as central to the male-dominated superhero narrative. This project is one such attempt to not only answer McKerrow's call to destabilize the "rational, male voice" that has dominated Western rhetoric but to use feminism as a critical practice that recreates the superhero mythos as a narrative for remembering his-tories as her-stories.

To think about *style as aesthetics* is useful for opening up *Sin City* as a rhetorical text that ventures beyond visual surface into how power relations function inside and beyond the Hollywood commodity. McGee suggests that all commodity exchanges are, in essence, "a fight for control over consciousness" between "human agents who play the role of 'power' and 'people' in a given transaction."[45] Rushing and Frentz have further documented the ways in which films can reveal and repress that which is odious to consciousness.[46] That is to say that Hollywood products like *Sin City* float in popular culture to maintain what Cloud laments is a "rhetoric of control," or a system of persuasion to encourage consent in behavior and belief.[47] Commercial film represents a site of tension and negotiation between a director's attempt at artistic subversion and the Hollywood industry's corporate agenda.[48] Creative works, as Horsley maintains, consequently become commodities to serve the function of propaganda instead of art, and what were once individual forms of expression become corporate means of social indoctrination.[49] The paradox here is that movies become instruments of domination as well as visionary art as they simultaneously reaffirm and subvert the status quo.[50] When social identity becomes learned and fulfilled through consumption patterns, consent is renegotiated into compliance with larger institutions of power. So, the question remains as to how gendered images and messages may be read subversively in small individual "slights" or slip through industrial "cracks," and how those combined "fractures" might be reimagined as a mode of collective female empowerment to reshape popular consciousness. Rodriguez/Miller's portrayal of the Black Widow certainly attempts to "re-spin" a cultural web of meaning in this way, inviting female viewers into a fleeting sense of empowerment, if only for a moment. Yet we need potentialities for lasting social change upon leaving the on-screen world of the superhero(ine) so that we may continue to reorder how we are instructed toward being/becoming women/men in an age of aestheticization where meaning is often manipulated at the level of the sensational image.

NOTES

1. Shaun Treat, "How America Learned to Stop Worrying and Cynically Enjoy! the Post-9/11 Superhero Zeitgeist," *Communication and Critical/Cultural Studies* 6 (2009): 105.

2. Jeff Otto, "Pure Entertainment with Insanely Cool Visuals, *Sin City* Is the Most Faithful Comic Adaptation of All Time," *IGN Movies*, 2005, 2, http://www.ign.com/articles/2005/03/29/sin-city-2 (accessed March 15, 2010).

3. Jake Horsley, *Dogville vs. Hollywood: The War between Independent Film and Mainstream Movies* (London, UK: Marion Boyars, 2005), 229.

4. Ibid., 228.

5. Roger Ebert, "Reviews: *Sin City*," *Chicago Sun-Times*, 2005, 1, http://www.rogerebert.com/reviews/sin-city-2005 (accessed March 31, 2010).

6. Otto, "Pure Entertainment," 2.

7. Andrew Spicer, "Problems of Memory and Identity in Neo-noir's Existentialist Antihero," in *The Philosophy of Neo-noir*, ed. Mark. T. Conrad (Lexington: University of Kentucky Press, 2007); Mantha Diawara, "Noir by Noirs: Toward a New Realism in Black Cinema," in *Shades of Noir*, ed. Joan Copjec (New York: Verso, 1993), 261–78; J. P. Telotte, "Film Noir and the Dangers of Discourse," *Quarterly Review of Film Studies* 9 (1984): 101–12.

8. *Sin City* further resonates a neo-noir sign for how it borrows heavily from classical Hollywood mise-en-scène ("everything in the scene") and their use of bleak urban sceneries, nighttime settings, chiaroscuro camera styles, and low-key lighting.

9. Thomas Elsaesser, "Tales of Sounds and Fury: Observations on the Family Melodrama," *Monogram* 4 (1972): 2–15.

10. Otto, "Pure Entertainment," 3.

11. Carol A. Stabile, "'Sweetheart, This Ain't Gender Studies': Sexism and Superheroes," *Communication and Critical/Cultural Studies* 6 (2009): 86–92; Rebecca Wanzo, "The Superhero: Meditations on Surveillance, Salvation, and Desire," *Communication and Critical/Cultural Studies* 6 (2009): 93–97.

12. Helene Shugart, "Supermarginal," *Communication and Critical/Cultural Studies* 6 (2009): 98.

13. Bonnie Dow and Celeste Condit, "The State of the Art in Feminist Scholarship in Communication," *Journal of Communication* (2005): 448–78.

14. Ebert, "*Sin City*," 3.

15. Ibid.

16. Horsley, *Dogville*, 230.

17. Bradford Vivian, "Style, Rhetoric, and Communication," *Philosophy & Rhetoric* 35 (2002): 224.

18. Robert Hariman, *Political Style: The Artistry of Power* (Chicago: University of Chicago Press, 1994), 8. See also collected essays in *The Politics of Style and the Style of Politics*, ed. Barry Brummett (Lanham, MD: Lexington, 2011).

19. Barry Brummett, *Rhetoric of Style* (Carbondale: University of Southern Illinois Press, 1998), 169–72.

20. Ibid., 169.

21. Stabile, "'Sweetheart,'" 86.

22. Julie Grossman, "Film Noir's 'Femme Fatale' Hard-Boiled Women: Moving beyond Gender Fantasies," *Quarterly Review of Film and Video* 24 (2011): 19–30; Mark Jancovich, "Female Monsters: Horror, Femme Fatale, and World War II," *European Journal of American*

Culture 27 (2008): 133–49; Elizabeth Cowie, "Film Noir and Women," in *Shades of Noir*, ed. Joan Copjec (New York: Verso, 1993), 121–66.

23. Stabile, "'Sweetheart,'" 87.

24. Spicer, "Problems of Memory," 47.

25. Treat, "How America," 230.

26. Peter Coogen, *Superhero: The Secret Origin of a Genre* (Austin, TX: MonkeyBrain, 2006).

27. John Shelton Lawrence and Robert Jewett, *The Myth of the American Superhero* (Grand Rapids, MI: Eerdmans, 2002), 157–73.

28. Wanzo, "The Superhero," 93.

29. Raymie McKerrow, "Critical Rhetoric: Theory and Praxis," *Communication Monographs* 56 (1989): 91–111.

30. Ibid., 101.

31. V. Mosco, "Critical Research and the Role of Labor," *Journal of Communication* 33 (1983): 230; quoted in Lisa Flores, "Rethinking Race, Revealing New Dilemmas: Imagining a New Racial Subject in Race Traitor," *Western Journal of Communication* 66 (2002): 181–207.

32. Lisa Flores, "Rethinking Race," 183–84; see also McKerrow, "Critical Rhetoric," 91–111; Dana L. Cloud, "The Materiality of Discourse as Oxymoron: A Challenge to Critical Rhetoric," *Western Journal of Communication* 58 (1994): 141–63; John Sloop, "'The Parents I Never Had': Contemporary Construction of Alternatives to Incarceration," *Communication Studies* 43 (1992): 1–13.

33. Raymond Williams, *Marxism and Literature* (New York: Oxford University Press, 1977), 155.

34. Brummett, *Rhetoric of Style*, xi.

35. Quoted in McKerrow, "Critical Rhetoric," 91; Cornel West, "Marxist Theory and the Specificity of Afro-American Oppression," in *Marxism and the Interpretation of Culture*, ed. Cary Nelson and Lawrence Grossberg (Urbana: University of Illinois Press, 1998), 18.

36. Brummett, *Rhetoric of Style*, xi.

37. Julie Grossman, "Film Noir's 'Femme Fatale,'" 28–29.

38. Catherine Palczewski, "The Male Madonna and the Feminine Uncle Sam: Visual Argument, Icons, and Ideographs in the 1909 Anti-Woman Suffrage Postcards," *Quarterly Journal of Speech* 4 (2005): 385.

39. Miranda Sherwin, "Deconstructing the Male: Machoism, Female, Spectatorship, and the Femme Fatale in *Fatal Attraction, Body of Evidence*, and *Basic Instinct*," *Journal of Popular Film & Television* 35 (2008): 180.

40. Brummett, *Rhetoric of Style*, 3.

41. Stabile, "'Sweetheart,'" 87.

42. Wanzo, "The Superhero," 95.

43. Stabile, "'Sweetheart,'" 87.

44. Stuart Hall, "Gramsci's Relevance for the Study of Race and Ethnicity," *Journal of Communication Inquiry* 10 (1986): 5–27.

45. Michael McGee, "The 'Ideograph': The Link between Rhetoric and Ideology," *Quarterly Journal of Speech* 66, no. 1 (1980): 5–6.

46. Janice H. Rushing and Thomas S. Frentz, *Projecting the Shadow: The Cyborg Hero in American Film* (Chicago: University of Chicago Press, 1995).

47. Dana L. Cloud, *Control and Consolation in American Culture and Politics* (Thousand Oaks, CA: Sage, 1998).

48. Horsley, *Dogville.*

49. Ibid.

50. Rushing and Frentz, *Projecting the Shadow.*

Chapter Seven

Romance, Comedy, Conspiracy

The Paranoid Heroine in
Contemporary Romantic Comedy

Pedro Ponce

Kevin Doyle has a way with words. As played by James Marsden in *27 Dresses*, Doyle is an ambitious reporter stuck in what he sardonically calls the Taffeta Ghetto, writing wedding announcements for the "Commitments" section of the *New York Journal*.[1] He recovers a day planner misplaced by Jane Nichols (Katherine Heigl) after the two meet cute at a wedding. Jane's gratitude is tempered by Doyle's intrusion into her private and professional life. In order to track her down, he has read her planner, or at least attempted to; Jane's is crammed with scrawled reminders that Kevin describes as "very Unabomber."[2]

The reference to Theodore Kaczynski—who pled guilty in 1998 to killing three people with letter bombs, among other federal charges[3]—seems strikingly out of place, to say the least. Jane is an overextended but self-possessed assistant to an eco-friendly philanthropist; Kaczynski, a former college professor, is a diagnosed paranoid schizophrenic.[4] Jane, an unmarried romantic, collects wedding mementoes crammed between the pages of her busy schedule; Kaczynski authored a thirty-five-thousand-word manifesto on his theory of societal decline, published with the approval of the FBI as part of its ongoing investigation.[5] For a brief moment, we have somehow stumbled into another movie. Soon enough, Jane gets the narrative back on track, rebuffing Kevin's offer of a drink and watching helplessly as her sister, Tess (Malin Akerman), has her own meet cute with Jane's boss and unrequited love, George (Edward Burns).

In *Empire of Conspiracy*, Timothy Melley warns the scholar of paranoia that the line between method and madness is disturbingly thin: "The interpretive drive of the analyst—the desire to find some kind of 'coherent system lying behind' what initially seems to be 'random fancy'—is structurally analogous to the interpretive drive of the paranoiac, whose disorder is characterized by the tendency to locate coherent motives in what others believe to be 'random' or 'chance' events."[6] Bearing this caveat in mind, paranoia and romantic comedy do manage to hook up with surprising frequency in the history of the genre. A prime example is *Annie Hall*, in which comedian Alvy Singer (Woody Allen) recalls loving and losing the title character (played by Diane Keaton). When a "big, tall, blonde, crew-cutted guy" advertises a sale on Wagner records, Alvy hears anti-Semitism, and he neglects his first wife (played by Carol Kane) to mull over inconsistencies in the investigation of the Kennedy assassination.[7] Though played for laughs, Alvy's paranoia resonates with the culture of American anxiety after World War II as delineated by Melley. Late in the film, after Alvy is lured out to California for a television appearance, he starts to feel sick as his friend Rob (Tony Roberts) dubs laughter into an episode of his hit sitcom. Over Alvy's protests, Rob continues to supervise the dubbing, boasting that "this machine is dynamite."[8]

Alvy's subsequent swoon is never explained (physically at least), but Melley might diagnose it as agency panic, "intense anxiety about an apparent loss of autonomy or self-control—the conviction that one's actions are being controlled by someone else, that one has been 'constructed' by powerful external agents."[9] From the very beginning of *Annie Hall*, humor is deployed in anxious defense of individual integrity. Alvy's opening joke—that he would never want admission to a club that would have him as a member[10]—can be read as a manifesto of sorts for the nervous comedy to follow, in which the narrator's individuality will yield to nothing, ultimately not even union with another. Laughter from an intoxicated audience "doesn't count."[11] According to Melley, agency panic "is a fundamentally conservative response—'conservative' in the sense that it conserves a traditional model of the self in spite of the obvious challenges that postwar technologies of communication and social organization pose to that model." Instead of "a long-standing national fantasy of subjectivity," the paranoid postmodern individual is confronted with the prospect that "identity is constructed from without, repeatedly reshaped through performance, and (in extreme accounts) best understood as a schizophrenic and anchorless array of separate components."[12]

The subgenre of "nervous" romantic comedy, as represented by *Annie Hall*, was just the latest genre permutation arising from a context of changing cultural mores. Alfred Kinsey's study of female sexuality, published in 1953, revealed that some women were not willing to wait for marriage to have sex.

Birth control in the mid-1960s separated sex from procreation. The upheaval of civil unrest and assassinations at home, and war abroad, resonated from news reports to cinema aisles.[13] It's not surprising, then, that Alvy's narrative is fraught with so much self-awareness and ambivalence. Notes Claire Mortimer, "These films reflected the angst and world-weariness of the period, where there is no longer any certainty about relationship and identity, and happy endings are rejected in favour of greater realism. . . . Nevertheless there is a powerful sense of nostalgia evoked within these films as characters strive to form meaningful and lasting relationships, which have increasingly come to be regarded as mythical and unrealistic in an ephemeral society."[14]

Melley observes that "conspiracy *theory*—the apprehension of conspiracy by those *not* involved in it—begins with individual self-protection, with an attempt to defend the integrity of the self against the social order"; this assumes, he continues, that personal agency is an all-or-nothing material possession that can either be completely independent or otherwise under control of a malevolent other.[15] The struggle for individuality amid foreign encroachments informs Alvy's relationship with Annie. Annie enjoys sex while high, but Alvy insists on a captive audience in bed as well. He may have Annie's body, but "I want the whole thing."[16] The battle is already lost, however; the quest for an authentic reaction, whether at a comedy club or in the bedroom, already suggests that both are stages on which actors are performing.

Scholars of romantic comedy see a subsequent return to conservatism in films of the 1980s and onward, with more of an attempt to smooth over the rough edges exposed by deconstructions such as *Annie Hall*. Courting exhaustion at a time when questions of the real and virtual are even more fraught, the genre itself seems to suffer from a kind of agency panic disguised by the misdirection of revived conventions and suggestive soundtracks. According to Jeffers McDonald, "the hard work of establishing character traits becomes unnecessary; much more simply a song, a landmark, or a line of dialogue with an already-established emotional resonance can be employed to evoke a feeling which then gets co-opted into the new movie."[17] Audiences are cued by romantic convention in the same way that Rob's machine cues laughter in *Annie Hall*. Claire Mortimer sees such reactionary manipulation in *27 Dresses* when she writes that, ultimately,

> Kevin rescues [Jane] from her Cinderella existence and a life devoted to others, never putting herself first. When she realizes her love for Kevin she immediately quits her job, the only goal being to be with him. Her existence as an independent working woman is represented as superfluous to her real destiny, to be a bride for the right man. Just as in the fairy tales, the modern romantic comedy concludes with a wedding, reinforcing the importance of tradition and conformity.[18]

A paranoid reading of contemporary romantic comedy complements readings such as Mortimer's, exposing the stakes in such a blatant cover-up. Discourse has always been important to the genre, from back in its snappy, screwball days. Discourse continues to be a site of confrontation and compromise in more recent comedies energized by suppressed anxieties. The diagnosis of paranoia is itself a competition between discourses, much more contingent than acknowledged: "Paranoia is an interpretive disorder that revolves around questions of control and manipulation. . . . Understood less judgmentally, it is a condition in which one's interpretations seem unfounded and abnormal *to an interpretive community*."[19] And yet, this is often what romantic comedy asks its audience to do, sorting good from bad decisions on the way to finding one's perfect mate. In reference to a recent spate of male-centered romantic comedies, Jeffers McDonald notes how they posit a set of rules for love that is ultimately abandoned when confronted with love's actual complications. "What this interest in the codes of romance indicates is an overwhelming awareness of the *lack* of rules for love," she observes.[20] A paranoid reading of recent romantic comedies suggests that their heroines, too, tend to operate according to a given set of rules, deployed similarly (and ineffectively) in the service of reasserted conventions.

Someone Like You is narrated by Jane Goodale (Ashley Judd), an amateur sex theorist whose ideas about why men cheat "took over my entire existence."[21] A talent booker for a New York talk show, Jane goes from polished professional to paranoid hermit after her boyfriend Ray (Greg Kinnear) breaks up with her right before they are to move in together. Ignoring what, in retrospect, seem like obvious warning signs of Ray's ambivalence, Jane nevertheless starts to experience a paranoid resonance between inner and outer life. During a television nature documentary on how prey animals evade predators, she is addressed directly by a furry animal on-screen (voiced by Julie Kavner), who asks, "Smell the bacon, Jane?"[22] This happens again after Ray stands her up on what would have been a conciliatory date for New Year's. Watching the news as she waits for Ray's phone call, Hugh Downs updates viewers on Jane's lonely night alone: "The question remains, why hasn't he shown up yet?"[23] (Especially paranoid viewers will notice that as Jane waits for Ray's call, she plays a game of solitaire. The command to play solitaire, conveyed by phone, is the trigger for brainwashed assassin Raymond Shaw in John Frankenheimer's *The Manchurian Candidate*.)

In her grief, Jane develops the "New Cow Theory," inspired by an article on bovine mating in the *New York Times*. The article reports that a bull will not mate more than once with the same cow, even if that cow wears the scent of a different cow.[24] Jane decides to extrapolate the results of this study to human mating behavior, prompting a flurry of research and subsequent notoriety after she writes a sex column under the pseudonym of Dr. Marie Charles. Her dossier of evidence is the film's framing device; above the image of a cow's muzzle Jane has scrawled an epigram by Blaise Pascal: "The heart has its reasons in which reason knows nothing."[25] Left with nowhere to live, she moves in with her womanizing colleague, Eddie Alden (Hugh Jackman), literally occupying a hole in the wall which over time fills with a growing library for her research. Mel Gibson's character in *Conspiracy Theory*, Jerry Fletcher, occupies a similar hovel[26]; like Jerry, Jane will spout her theories about men to whoever will listen.[27]

Unlike Annie Hall, the contemporary romantic heroine is unable to navigate and integrate (however provisionally) the many discourses that impinge on her identity. Annie at first seems like a dabbler, a dilettante in art and life who just wants to have fun; Alvy introduces her to psychoanalysis and serious books about death. Alvy's tutelage in recreating Annie in his own image backfires. Therapy makes her more sensitive to her own needs. She leaves New York for California. When we learn at film's end that Annie has returned to New York, where she is living with a new man in Soho, one does not get the sense of failure in her new life but rather another stage in Annie's ongoing personal development. In order for Alvy to narrate (and thus begin to understand) his relationship to Annie, the narrative itself must constantly reframe itself using the language and conventions of multiple filmic and social discourses. If agency panic "may be understood as a nervous acknowledgment, and rejection, of postmodern subjectivity,"[28] the anxiety that permeates *Annie Hall* acknowledges but does not attempt to simplify the many facets of Annie's identity.

Discourse, for the contemporary heroine, however, is problematic and ultimately dangerous. Jane in *Someone Like You* addresses the viewer like a recovering addict; even in the midst of her paranoid tailspin, she acknowledges to her friend that her research is "a sick, twisted, pathetic little hobby."[29] True love, as represented in the contemporary romantic comedy, is marked by the absence of discourse and theorizing. In the midst of explaining the New Cow Theory to her friend Liz (Marisa Tomei), Jane is surprised to find out that Liz is in love. Otherwise articulate and caustically cynical, love reduces Liz to conversational ellipses: "Just incredible and . . . he's . . . so and . . . I'm so and."[30] When Liz suspects that her new man is cheating on her, she reverts to talkative cynicism, indulging Jane's lecture on the "copulatory imperative" that leads men to cheat.[31] There seems to be no middle ground for the discursive heroine. Either she is constantly theorizing her relations with men, to the point of paralysis if not pathology, or she is silenced by true love, relinquishing the ability to conceive or articulate connections now that the only worthwhile connection has been made. Not surprisingly, the last image in Jane's "New Cow" dossier is of her and Eddie embracing after she discovers the tender side to his inveterate womanizing. The book closes, signaling the end of the film. Case closed—nothing more to read here.[32]

The extent to which a character can understand and control discourse has obvious implications for his or her autonomy. For the romantic heroine, the price of fulfilled silence is fairly steep. Andie (Kate Hudson) and Ben (Matthew McConaughey) are both playing games in *How to Lose a Guy in 10 Days*; Andie has been assigned to find and break up with someone for an article in *Composure* magazine; Ben attempts to seduce a woman in order to secure a lucrative diamond account for his ad agency. Both admit their ulterior motives by the closing credits, but it is Andie who decides to quit her job after confessing her love for Ben in her last article for the magazine. Chased down by Ben on her way to a job interview in D.C.—"the only place I can go and write what I want to write, serious journalism as opposed to fluffy how-to pieces"—she is convinced to stay after Ben assures her she can write from anywhere. As she trades her cab for his motorcycle, Andie baby talks with her "Benny Boo Boo Boo Boo Boo," a reference to the irritating pet name she employs earlier to get Ben to break up with her. The joke implies that the games are over and things from now on will be serious, but the bluff being called here is Andie's. The discursive play is over now that she has found love.[33]

Discourse as a means of control also figures into *Knocked Up*, another Katherine Heigl vehicle. When Alison Scott (Heigl) gets pregnant after a one-night stand with Ben Stone (Seth Rogen), she decides to have the baby. As Alison and Ben drive to a gynecologist appointment, they begin to disagree over, among other things, Ben's seriousness as a father. Alison has good reason to be skeptical of Ben's maturity; he's (barely) self-employed and seems interested in little more than getting stoned with his friends. Alison is also angered that Ben has not read the pregnancy books they have purchased together. This leads to a blowout at the gynecologist's office as Alison is being weighed, in which Ben responds, "What's gonna happen? How did anyone ever give birth without a baby book? . . . Who gives a flying fuck about the baby books?"[34] Ben has previously expressed his commitment to Alison by proposing to her; she has declined. Ben is justifiably hurt, but his anger results from misreading on two levels. First, he assumes that a wedding proposal (without a ring) is enough to bolster his commitment to Alison and their baby, in the absence of any other significant changes to his life.[35] Second, he overlooks the larger limitations that parenting imposes on their relationship. Alison is upset at the gynecologist by the amount of weight she has gained; one of the staff assures her, "Your baby wants you to gain a whole mess of weight."[36] In her angry reaction, Alison expresses paranoia at losing control of her own body as she assumes not only the physiological but also social markings of motherhood. Her tendency to analyze exposes a reality obscured by romantic convention. As Melley observes, "the 'paranoid' tendency to imagine strict boundaries between self and environment is a way of conceptualizing resistance to 'invasive' technologies of femininity—to the idea that one is 'under construction,' subject to what Gayle Rubin once called 'a social apparatus that takes up females as raw materials and fashions domesticated women as products.'"[37]

Jane in *27 Dresses* idealizes weddings partially in response to the death of her mother when she was a child. One of the first family events she attends after her mother's death is a cousin's wedding, when Jane is eight. In her voice-over, Jane recites a list of prodigies who discovered their talents early in life: Mozart, Picasso, Tiger Woods. She herself says she discovered her purpose in life when, using her sister's hair ribbon, she helps mend the bride's torn dress. As for what proclivities this suggests in the younger Jane, she is unclear—or perhaps not: "And that was the moment. That's when I fell in love with weddings. I knew that I had helped someone on the most important day of their life and I couldn't wait for my own special day."[38] From the very beginning of the film, Jane's capacity to help others is portrayed in terms of her progress toward a wedding of her own. To her boss at Urban Everest, she is an invaluable team member; to her family and friends, she is a loyal confidante and wedding planner. To the paranoid viewer, though, she seems like a pushover, whose individual autonomy is oddly connected to a "special day" experienced every day. Our first glimpse of Jane as an adult is in a wedding dress which she is trying on for a friend because they are the same size. In the sequence that follows, set to Michael Jackson's "Don't Stop 'til You Get Enough," Jane attends two weddings at once, one in traditional Western clothes, the other in a sari and bindi. Despite the different clothes, the film is at pains to emphasize how interchangeable these experiences really are. Jane dances to the same song, helps both brides with their dresses as they urinate, and accepts interchangeable thank-you speeches at each reception. The traditional Western wedding is distinguished by Jane's getting knocked unconscious during the bouquet toss. When she opens her eyes, Kevin is standing over her.[39]

As frantic as this sequence might seem to the viewer, for Jane this is normal life. She does not experience romantic paranoia until her sister Tess intrudes on her (strictly professional, at least thus far) relationship with Jane's philanthropist boss. The meeting of Tess and George is a conventional meeting of stares across a crowded room; what makes it disturbing is that the film's actual protagonist is excluded from this staple of romantic comedy. Jane is now the passive audience to a story she believes was meant for her. She registers disbelief as Tess, her younger, less responsible sister, engages in the type of witty banter usually associated with romantic leads. Before Kevin returns her lost day planner, Jane must step outside to curse this disruption of her intimate plot—interrupting a fiftieth-anniversary celebration with her obscenities. Finally, she learns that it is not George but Kevin—a cynic about weddings—who has anonymously delivered Jane flowers at the office.[40] Jane's extreme reactions to these ordinary encounters and misunderstandings is suggestive of the anxiety suppressed by romantic conventions: not only is the "special day" anticipated by Jane not that special, but the intimacy at its core seems arbitrary as well, promoting a secondary character to lead and vice versa based only on who happens to be sitting where at the bar.

Jane learns that the cynical Kevin is actually Malcolm Doyle, her favorite writer for "Commitments." When Tess and George become engaged, Kevin is assigned to cover their wedding and interviews Jane. On his visit to her apartment, he discovers her hoard of bridesmaid dresses—twenty-seven and counting. When he asks her why she is willing to go to so much trouble for so many others, Jane responds, "Someday . . . it'll be my day," and those people she supported will be there for her.[41] Kevin, who mocks her as delusional, decides to use her as a springboard for his journalism career, profiling her eccentric fascination with weddings for "Commitments." By the time the article appears, Kevin and Jane have slept together, and Jane is humiliated by the public attention. After she exposes Tess' lies in convincing George to marry her, Jane confronts Kevin, who apologizes and praises her for finally standing up for herself: "For the first time, you were not the perfect bridesmaid."[42] Kevin adds that Jane also deserves to have others take care of her. And Jane needs a caretaker once she decides to quit her job; she confesses her feelings for George, but when they finally kiss, she feels nothing. "That's not what it's supposed to feel like," Jane muses, "when you're with the person you're meant to be with." Jane's new electronic planner—a gift from Kevin—buzzes; her new planner is programmed to play "Bennie and the Jets," which in an earlier scene served as the prelude to their night together. Recognizing that she is now meant to be with Kevin, she decides to track him down while he covers his last wedding for "Commitments."[43]

The subsequent chase and reunion of Jane and Kevin follows the predictable trajectory of romantic conclusion: Kevin is right about Jane, she admits, and while he has upset her expectations, he has also exceeded them by showing her that love is possible beyond these expectations. The ambivalence elided by convention remains onstage, so to speak; Jane delivers her conciliatory speech on the stage of a wedding reception, complete with spotlight highlighting Kevin's reactions to the audience both on and off screen. Jane's wedding to Kevin the following year includes twenty-seven bridesmaids, each wearing a dress from her collection. In her concluding voiceover, Jane says, "I knew they'd all be there for me someday."[44] With each dress taken in by the camera, Jane's luck at finding Mr. Right seems less like fate and more like a measure of just how deindividualizing Jane's special day really is.

NOTES

An earlier version of this chapter was presented at the 2006 Literature/Film Association Conference in Towson, MD.

1. "Great Story," 27 *Dresses*, directed by Anne Fletcher (2008; Beverly Hills, CA: Twentieth Century Fox Home Entertainment, 2008), DVD.

2. "Kid Sister," *27 Dresses.*

3. "Kaczynski Pleads Guilty, Avoids Death Sentence," CNN.com, last modified January 22, 1998, http://www.cnn.com/US/9801/22/unabomb.wrap.

4. Ibid.

5. "FBI 100: The Unabomber," Federal Bureau of Investigation, last modified April 24, 2008, http://www.fbi.gov/news/stories/2008/april/unabomber_042408.

6. Timothy Melley, *Empire of Conspiracy: The Culture of Paranoia in Postwar America* (Ithaca, NY: Cornell University Press, 2000), 19.

7. "I Wound Up a Comedian" and "Alvy and Allison," *Annie Hall*, directed by Woody Allen (1977; Santa Monica, CA: MGM Home Entertainment, 2005), DVD.

8. "Canned Laughs," *Annie Hall.*

9. Melley, *Empire of Conspiracy*, 12.

10. "There's an Old Joke," *Annie Hall.*

11. "Out to the Hamptons," ibid.

12. Melley, *Empire of Conspiracy*, 15.

13. Tamar Jeffers McDonald, *Romantic Comedy: Boy Meets Girl Meets Genre* (London: Wallflower, 2007), 40–41, 43, 60–61.

14. Claire Mortimer, *Romantic Comedy* (London: Routledge, 2010), 17.

15. Melley, *Empire of Conspiracy*, 10, author's italics.

16. "Out to the Hamptons," *Annie Hall.*

17. Jeffers McDonald, *Romantic Comedy*, 92–93.

18. Mortimer, *Romantic Comedy*, 31.

19. Melley, *Empire of Conspiracy*, 16–17, author's italics.

20. Jeffers McDonald, *Romantic Comedy*, 109.

21. "The Whole Story," *Someone Like You*, directed by Tony Goldwyn (2002; Beverly Hills, CA: Twentieth Century Fox Home Entertainment, 2002), DVD.

22. "Complications," *Someone Like You.*

23. "New Year's Eve," ibid.

24. "The New Cow Theory," ibid.

25. Ibid.

26. "A New Roommate," *Someone Like You*; "The Next Issue," *Conspiracy Theory*, directed by Richard Donner (1997; Burbank, CA: Warner Home Video, 2009), DVD.

27. "A Magazine Column," *Someone Like You*; "Jerry's Theories," *Conspiracy Theory.*

28. Melley, *Empire of Conspiracy*, 15.

29. "A Magazine Column," *Someone Like You.*

30. "Animal Husbandry," ibid.

31. "Unhappy in Love," ibid.

32. "Eddie," ibid.

33. "How to Catch the Girl," *How to Lose a Guy in 10 Days*, directed by Donald Petrie (2003; Hollywood, CA: Paramount Pictures, 2007), DVD.

34. "Get Out," *Knocked Up*, directed by Judd Apatow (2007; Universal City, CA: Universal Studios, 2007), DVD.

35. "Do They Know?," ibid.

36. "Get Out," ibid.

37. Melley, *Empire of Conspiracy*, 125.

38. "Main Titles/Life Purpose," *27 Dresses.*

39. "Double-Booked," ibid.

40. "Kid Sister," ibid.

41. "27 Dresses," ibid.

42. "You Deserve More," ibid.

43. "You're the One," ibid.
44. "That Look/End Titles," ibid.

Chapter Eight

Conflicted Hybridity

Negotiating the Warrior Princess Archetype in Willow

Cassandra Bausman

While women warriors are a familiar presence in fiction, and television screens have been graced with strong heroines since Xena took her place as a small-screen queen, there is a comparative lack of such characters in fantasy film. In most such films, women have often played central roles, but those roles have frequently reinforced gender stereotypes, remained two-dimensional, and been supporting rather than leading. More broadly, women have historically played very limited roles, often restricted to evil (or good) queens and/or sorceresses, beautiful princesses and/or love interests, saucy and buxom wenches or barmaids, or mythical creatures like fairy queens. The warrior princess or "chick in chainmail" is comparatively rare.

However, the classic fantasy adventure film *Willow* (1988) manages to feature *all* of these character types. Criticized by many as a medieval transposition of George Lucas' *Star Wars*, *Willow* features many similar character types and archetypal conflicts. More interesting than the similarities, however, are some of the creative decisions made to introduce variation, especially inasmuch as they concern gender. Indeed, Bob Dolman, the screenwriter chosen to fix Lucas' story to the page, has confessed to just such an agenda, admitting that he "was secretly trying to get more women into the movie and attempting to make it different from all the other movies George had done."[1] The injection of female roles is notable, with the role of eccentric magical teacher (Yoda) and evil ruler (Emperor Palpatine) both made women, and, while there is a feisty princess paralleling the Leia role in Sorsha, the struggle between good and evil, the choice between her mother's rule and the cause of a band of freedom fighters which echoes Luke Skywalker's epic journey, is also, ostensibly, made hers. Indeed, Princess Sorsha, *Willow*'s dominant female character, is an important character in the history of screen heroines, as she, as a sort of archetypal hybrid, represented a kind of heroine not often seen and yet remains one of the most nuanced examples of a warrior princess in a fantasy film.

The possibilities and potential of such a character were not lost on the actress depicting her,[2] and an examination of the making of the film reveals much about what the character could have been and what the finished film shows of her. The discrepancies between these understandings of character are fascinating, and an examination of this difference speaks to a wider conversation about the conventions of gender, their collision with popular culture, and the power of movies to empower but also still constrain and limit women's roles in the heroines they project. As Dolman's comments about the construction of the film's story reveal, *Willow*, and particularly the heroine it gives us in Sorsha, exemplifies an ongoing tension between the ease of adhering to narrative tradition, a simplistic cultural shorthand, and the difficulty of making more interesting or innovative creative choices. For, while Sorsha is an adept swordsman and military commander, compelling in her role as "warrior," she must also live up to the "princess" portion of her double-barreled character description. Thus, while Sorsha flaunts both a wicked serrated sword and a virginal white gown and ringlets with equal appeal, the movie, whatever its successes, does show its faults in its difficulties reconciling Sorsha's warrior identity with what it understands the role of princess to be, a role which is largely governed by stereotypical and conservative traditions which teach that princesses are for rescuing and serve best as rewards for worthy princes.

The labyrinthine narrative particulars of the way in which the film negotiates these two roles and attempts to resolve them into one coherent and still decidedly secondary character offers fascinating terrain for investigation, as in mingling the two archetypes—princess and warrior—despite challenging stereotypes, only one really survives. Furthermore, as there have been shockingly few warrior princesses in the twenty-five years since the release of *Willow*, the complicated legacy of Sorsha, of what *Willow*'s execution did and did not allow her, is especially important in terms of subsequent attempts at depicting similar screen heroines. Thus, this chapter will examine some of the creative decisions made in bringing Sorsha to the screen in order to interrogate the limiting legacy of fantasy film's heroines and the lack of evolution in the kind of storytelling we see committed to a silver screen, which still all too often clings to the tried-and-true formula of the male heroic model.

SORSHA

There can be no denying that Sorsha is, indeed, a compelling and complex character. The film presents her as a combination of capable warrior and beautiful princess, at once a dispassionate military commander and skilled warrior and a vulnerable, emotionally susceptible, physically attractive young woman. Indeed, conceptually she seems intended to be an ideal combination, a union of the taxonomically distant princess and warrior, the best of two seemingly disparate worlds.

Sorsha first appears in the film as a warrior, performing the important task of searching newborn girls for a birthmark that indicates a threat to the reign of her sorceress mother, Bavmorda. Ruthlessly competent and apparently willing to sacrifice the discovered babe to her mother's magical rituals, Sorsha is entrusted with the continued hunt for the child. Her softer princess role emerges in the course of this search, developing through encounters with the gentle farmer and family man Willow, and the rogue swordsman Madmartigan. After several sexually charged exchanges, Madmartigan seduces or at least confuses Sorsha in a confrontation in her tent, professing his love with fairy-dust-induced poetry before escaping with the prophecy's child. Thus torn, Sorsha must choose whether to join the child's protectors and fight against her mother or return to Bavmorda's side. Sorsha eventually decides to assist Willow, Madmartigan, and the good sorceress Fin Raziel in their attempts to stop the evil queen from killing the child. She cements her choice with a passionate kiss with Madmartigan amid the heat of battle. After a climactic castle siege, the film ends happily with Sorsha rather domestically holding the rescued babe in her arms while wrapped in the circle of Madmartigan's arms.

Sorsha is a strong presence in the film, and *Willow*'s structure and moralizing message (as a tale of unconventional heroes uniting to fight for what's right) is clearly played out in her role. Indeed, her character arc, by virtue of a literalized conversion from antagonist to protagonist, is arguably the *most* transformative and significant in the film, perhaps best explicating the themes of the film as a whole. As critics have noted, Sorsha's choice between the cause of the freedom fighters and the mother who raised her and whose approval she clearly seeks[3] is central to the film. When Sorsha eventually and momentously conforms to the common logic of the film, daring to follow where her heart leads, hers is a particularly perilous undertaking, as she abandons a secured future to join the obvious underdogs (indeed, when she makes her decision, she's observing two-against-an-army odds), magnifying the bravery and risk of her decision. Indeed, *The Official* Willow *Movie Magazine* suggests that Sorsha's choice is the very heart of the film, proclaiming that "Sorsha must make a fateful choice," such that "on her decision rests the fate of the world of *Willow*."[4] In a film about surprising heroic transformations and difficult choices, the filmmakers ascribe a tremendous amount of importance to Sorsha and her transformative choice, making her story an especially central thread in the wider thematic tapestry of the film.

However, despite her apparent strength as an active heroine and her importance to the unlikely crusade, elements of her character emerge as particularly confusing and/or problematic given her representation as a nuanced heroine able to participate in an archetypal tradition without, initially, being limited by it. While Sorsha's identity as a warrior comes off rather successfully in the first half of the film, problems with her characterization quickly emerge once the film invokes expectations surrounding the "princess" archetype, and many of the elisions and erasures of her character evident in the film stem from these limitations.

In seeking to maintain a balance between the hybrid aspects of Sorsha's character as both princess and warrior, the film performs a precarious balancing act between the extremities of type, and the difficulty of this continuous negotiation is revealed in its invariable oscillation and ultimate unevenness. Where the film ultimately comes down in its portrayal of Sorsha and its willingness to embrace the complexity of combining these often complicated, conflicting elements tells us much about fantasy storytelling in film, the kinds of stories and characters that audiences are expected to be invested in, the emotional journeys judged to be deserving of time and depth, and the psychologies and relationships of characters deemed worthy of investigation. For, as a finished film, *Willow* argues that we, as audience, should be fine with reducing Sorsha to a simplified, singular type. While the film works to be innovative with familiar fantasy elements (by borrowing and blending traditional elements to create a new take on classic themes and, with it, a differently enabled heroine), the weight of the tradition in which it participates ultimately overbalances the film away from any useful evolution. Much of Sorsha's motivation, as well as her voice and agency, are removed once she can be understood more simply, and more traditionally, as a love interest. In this capacity, the story successfully tracks without the earlier complexity set up for her character, and that the film directs us not to miss such elisions, not to notice or wish to question such erasure, speaks to a significant failing of the kind of brave, unexpected decision making and archetypal negotiation it claims to champion.

For all that the film presents itself[5] as a story about a band of improbable protagonists in the firm plural, one that purports to argue for an enlightened understanding that heroes can come in all shapes, sizes, and guises—including an armor-clad feisty female whose role seems intriguingly uncertain as hero and villain, warrior to be feared and princess to be wooed—Sorsha. However, she is rarely included in critical discussions of unlikely heroism and transformation, for all that her transformation from enemy to friend and her role in the film's resolution as an active hero in her own right would seem to be central. While *Willow*, as director Ron Howard reminds us, "is a character story, about some very unlikely heroes being emotionally involved in an issue, to the point where they're willing to risk their lives," elaboration on his heroes' paths accompanies an interesting omission that effectively removes Sorsha as one of the "unlikely heroes" in question. As Howard finishes his statement, *Willow*'s collection of unlikely heroes devote themselves to the cause "to the point where they're willing to risk their lives and *do something that neither one of them ever would have expected they could do.*"[6] Moving from a generously plural and all-encompassing "they're" to a significantly narrowed and restricted "neither one," this reduction privileges Madmartigan and Willow's roles while shockingly excluding Sorsha, refusing to acknowledge her heroism, her shared difficult and emotional investment, and her transformational journey in the common quest to save the prophesied princess and defeat Bavmorda. Despite Sorsha's role as exemplar of the central conflicts and themes that Howard asserts are central to his film and his understanding of its story, his quote gestures toward Sorsha's erasure as a phenomenon that extends well beyond a simple interview.

Indeed, as the film progresses, both her role and her importance are undercut, underplaying and muddying her character considerably. This disintegration of the integrity of her double-barreled character largely hinges on a key question of motivation, as her decision to change sides invokes both sides of her hybrid archetype. As a warrior in the midst of battle, she seems to evaluate the consequences of her allegiance, judging the actions and motivations of the soldiers around her against the pure and honorable intentions of Madmartigan and Willow; as a woman, she also seems physically drawn to Madmartigan, puzzling over what to make of a somewhat schizophrenic mutual attraction while admiring his impressive physical prowess like a princess dazzled by a knightly suitor's display of astonishing skill and bravery. That both perspectives seem to inform her decision here to the point of being indistinguishable is not necessarily problematic—indeed, it serves to show how successfully intermingled multiple aspects of this kind of character might function. Rather, the problem arises when, at the moment of her decision, all such complexity and multiplicity go out the window. For her decision—that decision on which "the fate of the world of *Willow*" was said to hinge—while represented as important and climatic, is structured so as to seem important only in terms of her relationship with Madmartigan and the resolution of the romantic story line, instead of any sense that she might be useful or necessary as a converted hero in her own right.

Once Sorsha kisses Madmartigan, cementing her conversion and publicly declaring her allegiance beyond question, her decision, for all that it comes laden with complex personal baggage and echoes themes carried through in other aspects of the film, also serves as the turning point the film uses to streamline its story. Able now to read Sorsha comprehensibly and much more simplistically as a typical starry-eyed maiden following her knight, the film instantly strips Sorsha of her intricacy, and then much of her agency, and then seems fully content to exchange complexity of character for efficiency of story for all its claims about the supremacy of characterization.

To be clear, it is not her relationship with Madmartigan that is the problem here; that she joins him, kisses him, or seems to have found love with him and he vice versa, is not the problem. The problem is that her relationship with him, her role as *attached to* him, once confirmed, becomes the filter through which the film directs us to view her. In the eyes of the film, his reasons become hers, his decisions hers. That the two warriors now share a mission, a mission to which she has her own unique skills and perspective to offer in aid, a mission that she committed to only after significant personal struggle and at great personal risk, becomes irrelevant; from what we are shown of her in the film, she's simply following Madmartigan on his. In accepting such a simplified understanding, in allowing the character to be so easily read in this limited way, the film trades complexity in for type, evolution for tradition, and, in so doing, skirts the need to explore the motivation and consequences of her decision, thus reducing Sorsha's role in the final third of the film to a somewhat awkward accessory rather than a primary agent in the coming final battle. This, we find the flagrant erasure of a female character and her experiences and motivations.

Interestingly, this crucial moment in the logic of the film corresponds with a clear reduction of Sorsha's physical role, as if her warrior identity has been forgotten, deemed no longer necessary or interesting against the fulfillment of her function as a more traditional "princess." As a reward for a knight's proven heroism, however willing, Sorsha is required to trade in her own heroism, becoming a passive princess who can then be set aside without complaint or notice, and thus effectively written off for the remainder of the film, for all that its resolution has as much to do with her transformative journey as hero and her emotional investment in the climactic conflict as anyone's.

This elision postswitch was not always so complete, as cuts and changes made to the finished film highlight decisions made in which moments of opportunity to preserve the complexity of her character existed but were abandoned. Indeed, even the moment of Sorsha's conversion was once more complexly figured. While the film focuses on locked gazes and the kiss Sorsha and Madmartigan share, other variants of the *Willow* story retain the extended action drafted in the screenplay, figuring moments which reestablish Sorsha's martial skills and value and thus effectively and interestingly maintain the balance between her two roles as princess and warrior.[7] Similarly, while virtually all of the texts associated with the film provide an additional scene in which Sorsha, after joining the rebels, pursues and defeats a number of enemy soldiers on horseback with a superb demonstration of both her skills as a warrior and her new allegiances, the film does not.[8]

Practical exigencies requiring the streamlining of story may exist,[9] but in these cut scenes, when the action goes missing, Madmartigan gets to demonstrate his prowess, and Sorsha does not. This difference is significant in terms of a movie audience's ability to see the pair as warriors of comparable skill, to understand Sorsha as an equal partner in this battle. Reducing her action in the way the film chooses to do—suggesting that a kiss or romantic attachment is the only change, the only consequence or possible action to come from her momentous decision—not only minimizes her role as a warrior but trades in swordplay for a smooch along a dangerous trajectory which speaks to limitations of character.[10]

Removing Sorsha's physical actions is also problematic in underscoring her intentions, as such deleted opportunities to confirm the continuity of her warrior skill would also provide a rationale to trust her. For indeed, not only is her participation in any pursuit not actively shown in the film, but her part in it is not even questioned, despite being an issue that would seem to require some resolution. In the film, in a version of the story in which Sorsha takes out none of her former troops, it occurs to no one to ask why a woman previously intent on annihilating them now rides alongside them; no one questions her fairly unproven allegiance. As this justification, too, was dealt with in alternative textual versions and, based on available publicity images, likely filmed, such a deletion serves an insidious purpose: if the rebels don't question her, why should we as an audience? If they don't pause to consider her motivation and actions—or, especially, the lack thereof—neither should we notice or object to such an absence. As a further damper on the question of Sorsha's involvement, a lack of curiosity or criticism on the part of her new companions is meant to mirror and direct ours. In these deletions, the film's not-so-subtle request for simplicity, for ignoring Sorsha, rings clear: let the kiss be the end of it.

In short, once Sorsha joins the other heroes, the film no longer needs her to be a warrior; it has other characters, traditional male characters, who fulfill that function, rendering her suddenly secondary rather than necessary in that capacity. As careful as the film seemed to be in initially establishing a respect for her identity as a warrior, its final scenes grant Sorsha little to do.

Perhaps the most damning evidence that the film sees Sorsha differently at the film's end lies in the fact that, when the rebel army moves into position to assault the castle, no one seems to consult Sorsha, let alone give her any authority over the battle plans, despite the fact that she grew up in the castle in question as well as fought and trained with much of the force they are to face. To not use Sorsha as a resource at this point is a missed opportunity for the rebels, as well as for the film to show her contribution and make clear that she is no tagalong; she might be a late addition to the heroic party, but she is invested in its success as a leader and fully committed to its goals. But the film fumbles this gimme, rendering her presence a silent one. And, as other versions of the *Willow* story pick up on the obvious applied purpose of her character in this moment,[11] it seems clear that the film is uninterested in giving Sorsha something to do, and instead ignores her, setting her aside even when her inclusion is both logical and valuable.

Furthermore, while this initial silence is a notable absence, her continued quiet in subsequent scenes as the rebels huddle together to draw up war plans is an especially telling and particularly egregious moment of erasure. While the paratexts surrounding *Willow* present Sorsha's voice as a clear and leading one supporting immediate action and expressing valid and informed concerns about its feasibility in a way which invokes and acknowledges the specialized knowledge she possesses, by contrast, in the film, Sorsha manages only a single half line (in which she notes rather obviously that "Elora Danan will die"). Essentially voiceless, she is shown to do even less, as her scrap of a line comes as the camera pans across soldiers slipping into the tent, then immediately cuts to reaction shots of Willow and the Brownies. Sorsha's perspective, her point of view, is considered fully unimportant, the camera movements figuring it here as secondary at best. Indeed, her silence in this scene is especially problematic, as she does lend her support to the assault, rising alongside Madmartigan as they physically signal their commitment to "stand" against Bavmorda, but, in verbalizing nothing, she seems again to be merely following his lead rather than contributing her own.

Thus removed from consideration as a warrior in the planning stages of the siege of Bavmorda's castle, Sorsha's role is also notably diminished when it comes to the actual battle. While Airk and Madmartigan lead the army into the castle and take charge of the fighting within, Sorsha escorts Willow and Raziel inside, leading them up her mother's tower so that the sorcerers might reach the baby in time to disrupt the ritual ceremony. Originally intercut with the battle raging below, Sorsha's role as guide through the castle was validated by a significant amount of performed defense. The novel tells us that, "grimly, Sorsha had led Willow and Raziel through corridors and up staircases that she knew well. Once she beheaded a troll who leaped snarling from an alcove, and once a Death Dog that came pelting in silence, eyes fixed on her throat."[12] And, later, as "Bavmorda signaled the three priests from the shadows and they slid forward like one body, beginning in unison the Chant of Infinite Diminishment," we witness how "Sorsha cut them down": "She did it cleanly—three strokes of her sword across their necks. She stepped across their bodies toward the altar where Elora Danan lay, whimpering pathetically," proclaiming, "You will not kill this child!"[13] Even in the junior novel, as Bavmorda's druids move to attack the two women, "Sorsha stepped forward to meet them, defended Raziel, and killed them both with her sword."[14] This version, with its curtailed action and number of enemies, most closely echoes the film, which does allow Sorsha to fight and kill the druids—however, as they are unfortunately and anticlimactically embodied by old, bearded men who lurch forward in long robes, her skill is comparably undermined, particularly given the kind of extended action Airk and Madmartigan engage in outside.

But the real clincher is when Sorsha faces her mother. She impressively defies Bavmorda to her face, struggles to cling to her confidence, and holds her ground against her mother's insults that Sorsha is a "traitor child" whom she must now "despise" and "destroy." Sorsha is almost instantly knocked unconscious and is left to spend the final battle in a heap on the floor. The novelization politely summarizes her removal from consideration: "So, she did not see the last battle. Only Willow saw; Willow, quaking in mortal terror but summoning enough courage to creep to the top step and peer over."[15] In this resolution, which amounts to a final removal of Sorsha as warrior, we see the film's shortsightedness in its consideration of her character, its confusion over her contribution, and its lack of certainty regarding her relationships. In the end, she cannot participate as a mere warrior, battling in the contest of physical might with Airk and Madmartigan below, for there are already two swordsmen in which we are invested. Neither can she participate in the magical duel in the tower above, because she, unlike Raziel or Willow (both of whom get their respective chances at Bavmorda), is no sorcerer. The film, it seems, cannot imagine a middle path or conceive of any means to provide her character with an active resolution. Thus, *Willow* does the only thing it can think to do with her: it removes her from the equation by rendering her unconscious and saves itself the chore of finding something useful for her to do by finding a solution that will allow her to (continue to) do nothing.

While she does, at least, get a few moments in which to stand up to her mother, to heap further insult to injury on our warrior who is denied a fight in the best battle of them all, her unconscious state is itself resolved in a manner which undercuts her active presence and warrior potency even more. The film, at least, plays it relatively cool, salvaging what it can of her character's involvement by allowing her to wake in time to witness her mother's end and, as rain batters the tower room, to regain consciousness of her own accord before being raised to her feet by a quite naturally concerned and relieved Madmartigan, who arrives too late to be otherwise helpful. Other versions, however, demonstrate a broader difficulty in representing this dual archetype, playing up the fairy-tale qualities of the tower scene in a way that recalls Sleeping Beauty, that most iconic figure of princess passivity, and capitulate fully to the sort of clichés *Willow* seemed so keen to otherwise avoid. The junior novel refuses to discuss her return to consciousness entirely, but in the adult novelization we are told that "Sorsha revived as Madmartigan rushed in and gathered her into his arms,"[16] and in the storybook that, "with a shout, Madmartigan rammed open the door" and "scooped up the limp Sorsha in his arms and revived her with a kiss."[17] More than simple shared pleasure at their success, relief at finding each other still alive, these versions, in keeping Sorsha unconscious until Madmartigan arrives, not only prevent her from seeing her mother's demise (let alone acting to bring it about), but reinforce the idea that her role, her action—here even more fully literalized as her very consciousness—is dependent on him. With this cap-stone, resolution for Sorsha is found in the arms of Madmartigan more than in facing or defeating her mother, the film's clear endgame. In this, we find a final reminder that the relationship that matters for Sorsha, the journey in which the film most fully invests, is the love story, hers with Madmartigan. Again, directing focus here in its own right is not problematic, as their relationship is a significant and compelling story line deserving of its own happy ending; the problem enters in once it comes at the expense of the importance of providing the same for Sorsha and Bavmorda's. In a last weighing of narrative investment, the final battle reveals a final failure of the film to choose complexly, to embrace multiplicity in its inability or unwill-ingness to imagine a resolution that could more fully, and more complexly, do or be both, and concludes, ultimately, with a Sorsha who is much more passive princess than active warrior.

CONCLUSIONS

For all that *Willow* starts strong, filled with good intentions and the highest of hopes for presenting its heroine as a strong role model, an active, hybridized archetype and antidote to traditionally limited female fantasy characters, it ultimately works its way back into stereotype. This limited rendering of character, this relegation of her potential to something much closer to tradi-tional princess than consistently hybridized warrior princess is important, for it affects the way the film is seen and the way the character is ultimately understood. Reducing Sorsha in this way underlines the creative tension inherent in managing the multiple aspects of her hybrid character, and aban-doning that complexity confirms the limited and limiting legacy of the kinds of narratives pursued in so many films, including this one which seems to have deliberately aimed higher. While *Willow*'s idealistic tagline, "Forget All You Know, or Think You Know," highlights its intended complex relation-ship with narrative tradition and the assumptions of genre, it ultimately does little to challenge easy or familiar narratives or to critically engage fantasy tropes and expectations with respect to its warrior princess.

An elemental quest story at its heart, the story of *Willow*'s creative devel-opment is a story of good intentions and high hopes, a bold quest for a progressive fantasy adventure as much as a cautionary tale which reveals the combined dangers and allures of fixed narratives, those most familiar of narrative paths. As has been said of quests, in an argument which echoes the language of Willow's tagline, "true quest is about agency, and the capacity to be driven past one's limits in pursuit of something greater. It's about a desire that extends beyond what we may know about who we are. It's a test of mettle, a destiny."[18] In this sense, *Willow* remains a valuable quest story, as the construction of Sorsha is, in a way, a quest in itself: a fight for agency, a search to realize her character as an active player in her own story within a larger generic framework. Her story is not only that of plot, that of a significant heroine whose role stands out for its successes more than twenty-five years later, but also a story of the many creative choices made or abandoned—choices which, like the hybrid archetypes whose expectation-laced-baggage she balances, not only support but also undermine the success of the complexity and promise of that role, such that in its failures there remains much to be learned.

Inasmuch as stories tell us who we are and what we are capable of, when we accompany characters on their journeys in quest stories, we are also going in search of ourselves, trying to find an understanding of our own lives and the forces surrounding it. This is especially true of narratives envisioning female characters who seek to challenge or expand an existing narrative tradition, for in examining the shaky pantheon of the warrior princesses in fantasy film, the collective picture that emerges is one of complex, inconsistent, and contradictory messages about a woman's place and potential. Understanding both the potential and limits that these characters reflect is a necessary step if we are to take stock of the current state of the filmic fantasy heroine; and if we are to move forward, if we are to demand and receive more of our screen heroines and seek to open up new narrative horizons for the fantasy genre in film, we must understand clearly where we've been, and how far there is yet to go. We must remember that when narrative attempts at transcendence end in an erasure of character and agency, it is not a single act of erasure, but a wider political one that elides the stories of women and the motives which move them, cutting away their complexity or importance and reducing narrative options for heroines. If quest is about asserting agency, about pushing past limits, about making choices and discovering more than was imagined, *Willow* should inspire us to make more interesting choices. The successes and shortcomings of its efforts with Sorsha should motivate us to quest further, to continue to seek stories that do more than recycle familiar and fixed narratives, that abandon simplistic story lines and truly "forget" to look to expectation and convention, received knowledge and didactic tradition, as guideposts. If questing is foundationally about the desire to extend the parameters of experience, then we are still in search of alternative heroic models, still in need of stories that successfully and fully render strong central heroines, and we are all still commonly engaged in a quest for heroines—

a quest along whose path Sorsha may serve as a keystone in the arch under which we must pass.

NOTES

1. Marc Shapiro, "In the Words of Willow," *Starlog*, no. 139 (February 1989): 68.

2. While actress Joanne Whalley has an appreciation for *Willow* as recognizably conventional, "a classic story" that "has all the right elements in it," she is also well aware of the opportunity the role offered to do something more special or unusual or in embodying "the courageous female warrior heart," something "girls . . . so rarely get an opportunity to do" or see. When interviewed, Whalley makes clear which aspects of Sorsha she found most appealing: "My first impression when I read the script was that we would get to see a young woman who's in control and has a certain amount of power and responsibility and not just some young girl wandering around the castle in a long dress." In describing "the essence of Sorsha," the significance of an active heroine and potential role model offering girls a positive alternative to the more typical passive fantasy heroines is clear: "She's quite fearless, tough, adventurous. She's feminine, too. . . . I hope she represents a positive image, a good role model for girls. Though she never loses her vulnerability, she can still go out on her own and *do* things" ("Sorsha's Cutting Remarks"; "Revealing the Secrets of Sorsha").

3. When Sorsha finally captures the baby, she hands it over to Kael with a telling line, bitterly delivered: "That should make my mother happy" (scene 19, "Betrayed"). Contrasted sharply with Kael's later triumphant howl, "I have the child!" (scene 27, "Elora Abducted"), Sorsha's brief line here may suggest that she takes no joy or personal pride in carrying out her mission. A potential early indicator separating her own sensibilities from those of her Nockmaar allies, this moment clearly indicates that Sorsha's performance is for her mother alone, her participation a matter of loyalty and obedience rather than shared values.

4. Patrick Daniel O'Neil, "Sorsha: Joanne Whalley," *The Official* Willow *Movie Magazine*, 1988, 24.

5. As *Willow*'s creators repeatedly eulogize, character is meant to be the focus. While an epic action-adventure, at its core *Willow* is a movie invested in the personal journeys and transformations of its characters, and the story of its creation is largely a conversation about introducing unexpected and humanizing touches to fantasy set pieces. The first-ever issue of the *Lucasfilm Fan Club Magazine* introduced *Willow* thematically as "a movie with heart," its expectant fans promised a film "about friends, about caring and fighting for what's right against incredible odds," while director Ron Howard glossed the film in a teaser interview as "an adventure story filled with excitement, wonder and danger" that "is also about very unlikely heroes and their efforts—both successful and unsuccessful—in learning to trust themselves, follow their heart, and do what they believe is right." Thus, the magic of the film is that its titular hero isn't the only one with a hero's journey—the theme of the unlikely hero made multiple, encompassing not only Willow but all who join him in his quest. While Willow, a humble farmer and family man, the aspiring magician who's "short, even for a Nelwyn," is an example of someone not typically conventional being given the opportunity to be a hero, so, too, are many of the film's other characters, from Madmartigan, who, once introduced in a filthy prison, moves from total brigandry and irresponsibility to a sense of duty and redemption as an honorable warrior, to Sorsha, the naïve princess and yet hardened warrior who starts out dutifully obeying her mother's orders only to exchange her inherited cruelty for a crusade to save a baby, on down to supporting characters like the Brownies, even shorter than Willow but decidedly intrepid in their conviction to see the quest completed, and Fin Raziel, who aids the cause as a possum, crow, and goat before assuming a more traditional physicality as a venerable old woman and white witch. *Willow*, it seems, can easily claim to be a story which demonstrates that heroes can literally, as well as more broadly metaphorically, come in all shapes and sizes.

6. Adam Pirani, "Ron Howard: Storyteller of Shadow & Magic," *Starlog*, no. 132 (July 1988): 35, emphasis mine.

7. Fascinatingly, the novelization works especially hard to deliberately figure Madmartigan and Sorsha as partners, as they not only battle together as warriors but are united even to the sword stroke in Drew's prose. Indeed, in a notable change in his adaptation, the significant kiss is significantly absent; here it is their blades which join rather than their lips, as if for Drew this is a "warrior princess" version of a kiss as they come together in mirrored motion. Wayland Drew, *Willow* (New York: DelRey, 1988), 239–40.

8. Ironically, in a twist that emphasizes how far distant what is important for Sorsha's character becomes from what is important to the film, this cut scene was not only specifically mentioned as a favorite of Joanne Whalley's, but dubbed unimportant or unnecessary enough to be removed from the finished feature yet important enough to become one of the production stills included in the film's press kit. Thus understood as a particularly legible and saleable moment of the "warrior" part of Sorsha's character, and thus valuable to the "progressive" work being done by the film, this discrepancy in asserting such a moment's iconic importance underscores the divide in Sorsha's hybrid character and the accompanying divide in the film's interests. While this scene is clearly recognized as significant in terms of character as an independent force, in the logic of the film by this point, Sorsha's warrior identity has been rendered less important to the story's coherence, her character now undergoing a transition from an initial understanding as respectable warrior to a resolution along princess/prize lines.

9. As Joanne Whalley has remarked about the loss of some of her favorite action sequences she performed as Sorsha, "it's a shame it's gone, but there's so much action in the film, you can't keep everything. That was just a tiny bit." And while each deletion may be "just a tiny bit" of film, there is a distinction between these significant physical moments for Sorsha and much of the other action in this fairly action-packed film, as Sorsha's are often closely related to an understanding of her character. Thus, such deletions are not as important in terms of quantity (although that, too, is rather startling) as they are with respect to an understanding of how that activity aids character and how its removal hurts it, particularly as many of these cuts repeatedly support her relationship with and value to the heroic forces as a warrior, not just as Madmartigan's converted/romantically captured princess.

10. For, of course, her decision is not only to join Madmartigan, but to turn against her mother and the men she's battled alongside. The extent to which the film ignores the fact that she must essentially be willing to kill her mother, whereas for other characters defeating Bavmorda is more about eliminating the bad guy, and to recognize that her personal connection to the archvillain should *extend* her moment of personal crisis rather than work to suppress or resolve it, is another significant failing of *Willow*'s investment in figuring the complexity of its heroine.

11. In the novelization, amid the action of preparing for an assault, as common troopers run around readying battering rams and assault towers, and Willow and Fin Raziel are discussing magical preparations, Airk and Madmartigan are described as "listening attentively to Sorsha as she drew a plan of the castle" (Drew, *Willow*, 248). Similarly, when "Madmartigan and Sorsha pulled their horses up short at the brink of the moat" and "stared at the castle walls rising above them, huge, dark, powerful—and evil," in the junior novel, the first action of the heroes is the obvious one—to consult Sorsha, a former military commander, about her former home. "Is there any way in there?" Madmartigan asked. "No," Sorsha shook her head. "It's protected on all sides" (Vinge, 106). Indeed, this rendition effectively narrativizes an exchange which seems to come directly from the screenplay: "M: Sorsha! Any way in there? Sorsha rides up to his side. S: No. The fortress is protected on all sides. The Tir Asleen warriors, dwarfed by the huge black wall, look at one another with doubt and worry" (Dolman, 81–82).

12. Drew, *Willow*, 264.

13. Ibid., 266.

14. Vinge, *Willow*, 117.

15. Drew, *Willow*, 266.

16. Ibid., 271.

17. Cathy East Dubowski, *Willow: The Storybook Based on the Movie* (New York: Random House, 1988), 78.

18. Vanessa Veselka, "Green Screen: The Lack of Female Road Narratives and Why It Matters," *American Reader*, February/March 2013, para. 5, 9.

Chapter Nine

The Woman Who Fell from the Sky

Cowboys and Aliens' *Hybrid Heroine*

Cynthia J. Miller

In 1961, John Wayne, with the help of the Texas Rangers, repelled a Comanche raid and then rode off into the sunset in *The Comancheros*. Fifty years later, in 2011, Daniel Craig, with the help of the Apaches, repelled an *alien* invasion and then rode off into the sunset in *Cowboys and Aliens*. On the face of things, the intervening half century did little to alter the traditional frontier narrative. But there is more, as they say, to the story, for without the intervention of the film's heroine, the gunslinger, the townsfolk, and the planet would all have been lost.

The film's departure from archetypal Western characterizations of women nearly goes unnoticed due to its blending of Western and science fiction genres. Beginning as a traditional Western film, its narrative structure appears little affected by the introduction of an extraterrestrial enemy which, as a reviewer for the *New York Times* notes, "might as well be Russians or Nazis" (or marauding Native Americans of cinematic days gone by).[1] It is precisely that hybridity, however, that opens up the story line for the film's shift in portrayals, as its heroine, Ella Swenson (Olivia Wilde), serves as a lightning rod for tropes of both the Western and science fiction genres.

At the time of its release, *Cowboys and Aliens* received significant criticism from critics and audiences alike, largely due to its hybrid status, reading as a failed Western for frontier fans, and paced too slowly for those accustomed to the spectacular interplanetary warfare of the twenty-first century delivered by science fiction blockbusters.[2] With a production budget of $163,000,000 and domestic box office receipts of slightly over $100,000,000, the film may, in fact, be considered a commercial "flop."[3] However, little attention has been paid to the complexities that resulted as characters, eras, gender roles, and genres transformed as a result of the film's hybrid narrative. Each of these transformations has Swenson at its narrative center, as a catalyst and focal point, as she moves across—and intertwines— the archetypes, tropes, and ideologies of the film's source genres. One part Rancher's Daughter, one part Ancient Alien, and one part Mystic Ancestor, Swenson is herself a hybrid character who bridges the gap between self and Other, past and future, wisdom and instinct, faith and action. What follows, then, is a look at the power of Swenson's genre-bending transformation from victim to heroine and its impact on the narrative universe of the film, where, in a Native American–inflected context, she serves as a futuristic spirit guide for those around her, and "saving the Earth" signifies regeneration far more than it does destruction.

THE WEST GETS A LITTLE WILDER

Set in 1873, *Cowboys and Aliens* tells a revisionist Western tale that is at once familiar and utterly strange. It is the latest entry in the decades-long history of hybrid Westerns—an intermittent subgenre of films that merge the classic tropes and icons of the West with elements of the fantastic—that began in 1935 with the movie-house serial *The Phantom Empire*, featuring cowboy crooner Gene Autry. Several generations later, its descendant, *Cowboys and Aliens*, draws on classic Western visual and narrative traditions— evocative southwestern landscapes, a small mining town in need of a savior, a tyrannical cattle baron, and a wandering gunslinger—to stage its own CGI-fueled showdown between the forces of good and evil, as grotesque alien invaders wreak havoc, abducting the townspeople and plundering the West for its deposits of gold, in a futuristic version of the traditional frontier fight for the right to land and resources.

Based on the 2006 graphic novel created by Scott Mitchell Rosenberg, this new spin on the Old West, directed by Jon Favreau, stars Daniel Craig as its disaffected, amnesiac antihero, former outlaw Jake Lonergan. After awakening in the desert, wounded, disoriented, and wearing a metal gauntlet that he cannot disengage, Lonergan makes his way to the town of Absolution— the symbolism here is, of course, telling—where his reluctant intervention between its ineffectual citizenry and the sociopathic son (Paul Dano) of powerful Colonel Woodrow Dolarhyde (Harrison Ford) earns him notice by good and evil alike, and positions him as the pivotal, though ambivalent, figure in the action. A timid saloon owner (Sam Rockwell), a philosophical preacher (Clancy Brown), and an impressionable young boy (Noah Ringer) round out the roster of stock Western personalities that alternately rise and fall in defense of civilization over the course of the tale.

Exotic and mysterious, Ella Swenson is the one character that departs from this archetypal frontier template. Love interest, warrior, and also, incidentally, an alien in human form, she is bent on protecting Earth from suffering the same fate as her own planet at the hands of the forces of the interplanetary menace that has come to strip the planet of precious raw materials. The traditional frontier drama is interrupted when the invaders lay siege to the town in futuristic aircraft, snatching townsfolk into the air and carrying them away, among them Rockwell's wife and Dolarhyde's son. Lonergan's mysterious gauntlet is activated, and it shoots down one of the alien craft, linking him, inextricably, to the town's struggle. A rescue posse is immediately formed, headed by Dolarhyde and the reluctant wanderer, and the group, including Swenson, set off on their quest to track and defeat the aliens and bring their loved ones home.

Midway through the film, Swenson is also abducted by the evil invaders, and though rescued by Lonergan, she dies from wounds she receives in the skirmish—only to be resurrected during a Native American cremation ritual. In a blinding explosion of light, she transforms from victim to aggressor and shifts primary genre orientations as well. Shedding her waifish Western character—vulnerable, fragile, and chafing against the limitations of her gender in a masculine frontier narrative—she reveals and fully inhabits her powerful science fictional identity, with knowledge, confidence, and abilities far exceeding those of Western genre heroines.

Classic Western lore instructs that the frontier is a place of encounters, a space betwixt and between civilization and wildness, where anything can happen. Director Favreau makes full use of that received knowledge, weaving the fantastic into spaces within the film's narrative where dramatic tension would traditionally exist, in the form of romantic encounters, Indian incursions, or melodramatic conflict and death. The boundaries between traditional Western binaries of good and evil lose their meaning as they come into contact with the tropes of science fiction and fantasy: the outlaw Lonergan, although still pursuing his own agenda, becomes a reluctant hero; Dolarhyde is forced to depend on the very townsfolk whom he has cruelly oppressed in order to save his son; the God-fearing and the ruthless, among both settlers and Native Americans, find their differences erased. The new and unpredictable adversary rapidly becomes the focus of all narrative action, forcing lawmen and outlaws alike to leave behind more "human" concerns in favor of the higher-order mandate to save humanity from extinction at the hands of an alien foe that seeks to plunder the Earth in ways reminiscent of the scars wrought upon the land by white settlers during the original conquest of the frontier.

Reminders such as these, of the exploitation of land and subjugation of people in the name of progress and Manifest Destiny, aid in the construction of a new form of revisionist Western that is easily read by contemporary viewers, while scenes of abduction and horrific experimentation add a visceral terror drawn directly from the science fiction canon. The alien invaders do not seek to enslave humans but rather to eradicate them from the land in order to extract its riches. Their mining ship, ripping gold from veins hidden beneath the bleak landscape, is a disturbing presence in the rock-jutted desert canyon, dwarfing—in both size and power—the small band of humans that attempt to thwart its mission.

In the end, however, the film's narrative resolution privileges the mandates of the Western genre, rather than those of science fiction and fantasy. The ragtag band of townsfolk, outlaws, Native Americans, and lone benevolent alien not only drives out the invaders, but destroys them. In the process, those characters who transgressed the usually clear boundaries between statuses—Ella, the alien ally in alluring human form, and Native American Nat Colorado (Adam Beach), who, through his abiding admiration for Dolarhyde, bridged the divide between the settlers and the Apaches—both die noble deaths; Dolarhyde learns compassion and is drawn back into the community; and the volatile Percy is transformed into a dutiful son.

Humanity, the ultimate "good," thus wins the day, and the moral order is restored. Lonergan, having found his personal "absolution" along the way, declines to linger in the small frontier town and rides away, following the well-worn trails of countless Western heroes who have gone before.

HYBRID FILMS/HYBRID HEROINE

In order to understand the significance of Favreau's film, it is important to consider it in relation to its status as a hybrid—a merging of the tropes and conventions of Western and science fiction genres in such a way that the end result is both, and yet neither. The hybrid Western stage was set by films ranging from early fare, beginning with the aforementioned *Phantom Empire*, as well as fantastic mergings with horror, in films such as *Curse of the Undead* (1959) and *Billy the Kid vs. Dracula* (1966), to fantasy and steampunk in more contemporary cinematic offerings, such as *Westworld* (1973), *Wild Wild West* (1999), *Serenity* (2005), and *Jonah Hex* (2010).[4] Because these genre blends often draw on source material such as comics and graphic novels or B-movie tropes, they have often been dismissed as simply absurd, adolescent fare—as was the case when one reviewer quipped that *Billy the Kid vs. Dracula* and its double-bill release, *Jesse James Meets Frankenstein's Daughter*, were nothing more than a "mind boggling fuse" of the "Western and horror genres,"[5] or when Roger Ebert deemed *Cowboys and Aliens* "the most cockamamie plot I've witnessed in many a moon."[6] Conversely, *Cowboys and Aliens* star Brendan Wayne reassured that his grandpa, the iconic John Wayne, would have approved of the film, pointing specifically to its hybridity: "He'd have thought it was great that the film was introducing a whole new generation to Western films, in a visual language that they were already familiar with."[7]

These often-misunderstood or overlooked cinematic texts have taken scholarly discussions of genre in new directions, however, in efforts to understand their impacts on both viewing and the workings of genres themselves. As literary critic Thomas Kent observes, genre in film may usefully be cast on a spectrum, with the "highly formulaic" text at one end, and at the other "a kind of theoretical 'supergenre,'" which is highly unformulaic and unpredictable, "shift[ing] ceaselessly from one set of generic conventions to another."[8] Scattered between these two poles, as Kent observes, would be texts that created varying degrees of generic uncertainty and difficulty in classification—works that "deform" well-known genre conventions[9] —and hybrid cinematic texts, such as *Cowboys and Aliens*, would be among these. While Kent's taxonomy of genre nods in the direction of creativity and innovation, the very language with which it describes hybridity—as a kind of genre deformity—misses the significance of the phenomenon, and the potential for transformation, revitalization, and regeneration that it offers.

In a related discussion of films that blur the boundaries between cinematic genres—and the Western, in particular—Adam Knee suggests that movies such as *Cowboys and Aliens* be viewed as "compound genre" films, a status that signals their ability to "concurrently engage multiple distinct and relatively autonomous horizons of generic expectations."[10] The concept of the compound genre draws attention to the various conventions simultaneously at play in films such as this, creating tension across the text as each vies to define the film's narrative. Within Knee's framework, then, the introduction of the alien invaders, a staple of the science fiction genre, into the midst of conventional Western tropes and characters, would create a cinematic text in which two "quite distinct sets of generic conventions have been pulled together and forced into a showdown."[11] The synergy generated by such pairings, however, is missing from the discussion once again, shortchanging the genre mash-up as a cultural product.

This notion of the compound genre, while useful, also implies that the generic elements present in the film coexist unchanged—in tension, perhaps, but nonetheless intact. *Cowboys and Aliens* moves quickly beyond this format, displaying the traits and characteristics of both genres, while also creating a space for the emergence of elements that are unique results of their mergings and confrontations. In the company of Western films, *Cowboys and Aliens* is a dismal failure; and when compared to the body of science fiction films of the decade, the outcome is similar. But when processed through the imaginative lens of hybrid creativity, the film becomes something more. Its hybridity moves beyond simple surface structure, illustrating a significant degree of unique genre innovation. While the narrative follows a traditional

Western genre template, its collision of characters is far from ordinary, as elements of both science fiction and the Western are adapted for the encounter. While framed as incomprehensible, marauding murderers, the film's alien invaders are not merely extraterrestrial stand-ins for cinematic Native Americans. Rather, they emerge as a constellation of earthly threats to humanity that draw together survival of the species, the environment, and the moral order. They are colonizers, who seek not to convert or enslave humans, but to eradicate them from the face of the Earth in much the same way that Indigenous people were eradicated from the plains, the hills, and the deserts of the West—technologically advanced beings exercising their own notions of intergalactic Manifest Destiny; they are futuristic industrialists, seizing a landscape for which they have no affinity, no rights to place, and stripping it of its resources for their own advancement, merging the rapacious big business of *Pale Rider* with the technologically fueled horrors of *War of the Worlds*; and they are bloodthirsty outlaws, violating the Code of the West, and massacring women, children, the elderly, and the infirm without hesitation, crushing weakness and eliminating resistance. They, like other horrific, fantastic, or supernatural genre trespassers in the American West that have preceded them, are the antithesis of humanity: rational, efficient, interchangeable, and emotionless, standing in opposition to those qualities that have come to be understood as the American character.[12]

And resistance, when it comes, takes the form of their diametric opposites: flawed, angry, fearful, and uncertain archetypal revisionist Western characters, armed with a befuddling element of technology that they can neither understand nor control. The nineteenth-century townsfolk of Absolution are, indeed, childlike in the face of the alien menace. If they are to survive—as individuals, a community, and inhabitants of the planet—Lonergan must, himself, cross the genre divide and master the powerful weapon affixed to his arm, shifting from disaffected antihero to science fictional defender of his race. He cannot accomplish this movement across genres, however, without a guide, and it is here that we see the film's genre mash-up embodied most clearly in the character of Ella Swenson, who not only is, herself, a hybrid heroine with a foot in both genres, but whose transformation from Western damsel in distress to fantastic otherworldly being is the catalyst for multiple narrative shifts in the film.

Resurrection and Regeneration

At the film's outset, Swenson's demeanor is that of a silent stranger. She is visible only in glimpses at first, silent and watching: an outsider. When she is finally featured full screen, she both resonates with and appears transfixed by Lonergan's character. She approaches him in a bar and stares, silently, until he rebuffs her, mistaking her for a harlot: "I'm just here to drink." Her quiet intensity matches his; her composure never falters. She clearly needs his help but resorts to none of the emotional transparency that characterizes archetypal Western heroines, instead bringing an air of mystery to the scene, more typical of science fiction:

Lonergan: Is there something you know about me, lady?

Swenson: You don't remember anything, do you?

Lonergan: What is it you want?

Swenson: I know you're looking for something. So am I.

Several scenes later, when she reveals that "they" (the aliens) have taken her "people," too, he has no interest in coming to her aid, forcing her to align herself with Dolarhyde's newly formed posse as it sets out to find the abducted townspeople. The former general mutters, "We've got a kid and a dog. Why not a woman, too?" Soon, he has Lonergan, and his futuristic weapon as well, as the gunslinger's memory starts to return, giving him personal, rather than communal, motivation for finding the invaders.

As the film's action unfolds, Swenson frequently is among the first to take action—preventing Lonergan from leaving town and abdicating his role as champion of civilization, rescuing young Emmett Taggart when the aliens attack, and leading the response to a bloodcurdling scream as a family is eviscerated by one of the intruders. However, in this first half of the film, which is clearly dominated by traditions drawn from the Western genre, she recedes into the background whenever Lonergan enters the frame.

The chemistry between the two outsiders is clear, evidenced by fixed gazes, closeness in two-shots, and in particular a scene where Swenson, caught voyeuristically observing Lonergan examining a wound on his abdomen that he received from the aliens, does not withdraw in embarrassment but instead closes the physical distance between herself and the gunslinger and intimately lays her hand on his injury. The sexual tension between the pair continues to heighten as the posse gives chase to the alien predators, but the traditional romantic subplot common to both genres is cut short when she is abducted by an alien craft and dies as a result of her injuries. As Lonergan collapses in grief, the group is surrounded by Chiricahua Apache warriors and taken captive—a traditional Western plot point, which, in the context of the film's science fictional elements, seems far less dire—and it is this confrontation that becomes the setting for the most significant narrative moment in the film.

Lonergan, Dolarhyde, and the rest of the posse are dragged into the warriors' camp, and Swenson's lifeless body, now wrapped in strips of linen, is unceremoniously thrown onto the fire. The tension between whites and Natives quickly escalates, amid accusations of murder and pillage on both sides, when the fire engulfing Swenson's body explodes in a brilliant flash of light. The shouting turns to utter silence as she emerges naked from the flames, as if reborn.

This moment is, from an analytical standpoint, perhaps the most signifi-cant scene of the film. Swenson dies a Western character—a central female figure, but also a victim, whose untold story dies with her. She returns from the dead, however, as a quintessential figure of science fiction—an alien from "a place beyond the stars," as she tells the Apache chief—adopting the limitations of the human form, she explains, "so I could walk among you." Speaking the Chiricahua dialect as easily as English, she relates the story of her people, and in finally telling her story, she commands the attention of all. They listen in silence and awe until Dolarhyde, blustering in disbelief, inter-rupts her tale. The chief insists that the mystical Swenson be shown respect from all, including so-called great men, admonishing, "You should not speak."

With Swenson's "resurrection," not only does her character's primary genre orientation move from Western to science fiction, but that shift serves as a pivot point for the genre orientation of the film as well. Standard science fiction tropes dominate the film's second half, as the entire cast unites in a battle to save the planet, guided by her advanced knowledge, Lonergan's futuristic weapon, and the Apache's faith in unexplainable phenomena. The narrative focus also shifts from the cattle baron–versus–gunslinger conflict that previously consumed the two male leads (as well as from the star power of Harrison Ford and Daniel Craig) to the ethereal presence of their soft-spoken female co-star. From the moment of her transformation from a West-ern figure to one of science fiction, it is *her* knowledge and actions that determine the final outcome of the film's tale, rather than the battling of her male companions—carried out in support of her ultimate sacrifice—even though their graphic final battles with the film's alien enemies are granted the lion's share of screen time.

Swenson's resurrection and transformation regenerates the story line of the film, but it also creates the context for the regeneration of individuals, relationships, and community in the larger scope of the film's narrative. Her message, "We have to work together," becomes her legacy. The destruction of the alien mining craft and Swenson's death remove the science fictional elements from the narrative, and the Western genre is restored as the film's guiding force. Lonergan, Dolarhyde, and those around them emerge from their victory over the alien invaders with a renewed sense of frontier values as relationships and bodies are mended and tiny Absolution prepares for its future as a gold rush boomtown.

Ancient Astronauts and Apache Ancestors

It is no accident that Swenson's character undergoes this mystical transformation in an Apache camp, nor is it simply an efficient strategy for concocting an alliance with a requisite tribe in a Western narrative. Her fiery rebirth, regenerating her adopted terrestrial image, hints at ties not only with Native American shamanism, but also with tales of alien visitors that have come before.

Connections between Native American culture and ancient aliens have been pervasive in popular culture for decades, many including speculation about indigenous origins in the stars. Ancient astronaut (paleocontact) theorists contend that visitors from the stars have been traveling to Earth since the beginning of time, influencing cultures, technologies, and religions.[13] Ardy Sixkiller Clarke explains,

> There is a popular belief, sometimes known as the ancient astronaut theory, that aliens walked the Earth in ancient times. Some theorize that ancient aliens are responsible for ancient technological wonders such as Stonehenge, Palenque, Machu Picchu, and the Pyramids of Egypt. Some theorists suggest that the ancient gods were, in fact, aliens.[14]

The Nazca lines, petroglyphs, carvings, megalithic sites, and other ancient art forms are, for these theorists, clear evidence of an alien presence, as is the received lore of stories, myths, and legends. Clarke continues, "To support their claims, they often portray the legends of Native American tribes as proof of human interaction with the Star People."[15] Counterarguments abound, of course,[16] and the topic generally remains relegated to discussions of pseudoscience.

Nonetheless, the connection in popular culture persists between alien astronauts and Native Americans, and it has become a highly recognizable plot device in science fiction film, television, and literature. Ancient aliens appear as wise, infinite, but often fragile beings, periodically intervening in human affairs in order to instruct or protect the much younger, more impulsive and immature inhabitants of Earth.[17] This complex blending of alien and ancestor in relation to Native Americans takes on a mystical, rather than science fictional, tone in the context of traditional Western tales in literature and film, investing Native characters with access to uncanny knowledge and wisdom, the ability to transcend time and space, and often the ability to traverse the boundaries between life and death.

These portrayals form one side of a binary approach to Native Americans, which casts them as spiritual children of nature, while the other portrays them as the bloodthirsty savages featured in countless Western narratives across the decades, such as *Stagecoach* (1939), *The Searchers* (1956), and *Jeremiah Johnson* (1972)—an opposition that is particularly relevant to understanding the context and narrative impact of Swenson's transformation in *Cowboys and Aliens*. Chiricahua Apaches are, perhaps, one of the most often portrayed of the Southern Athapaskan tribes.[18] Beginning in the late nineteenth century, the Chiricahua were featured in newspapers and media coverage across the country as a result of the Apache Wars and the fame—or infamy—of legendary warriors Cochise and Geronimo.[19] Thus, their presence in a Western film signifies a threat to white civilization—a savage impulse to murder and destroy. In the blinding explosion of Swenson's rebirth, however, the Chiricahua are also transformed, shifting to a focus on traditional spirituality and mysticism. The chief is the first to accept Swenson's spectacular reentry into the narrative, affording her respect and offering his allegiance; as Nat translates for Dolarhyde, "He says he will follow *her*." The formerly fearsome warriors, together with Swenson, then gently ease Lonergan into a drug-induced "vision quest" of sorts so that he might regain his memory—something neither Swenson alone nor white medicine could accomplish—enabling the combined search party to locate the alien ship.

In many Native philosophies, transformations such as these—shifts in outlook as the result of experiential learning—are often considered vital to the survival of communities, as Ted Jojola notes, and are implicated in movement toward a higher ideological level of consciousness.[20] The community that cannot change, adapt, and grow as it gains knowledge and experiences from new contacts in the world around it withers and dies.

This view of fluid, experiential change resonates with the Apache worldview, the origins of which are expressed by "a cycle of rich and intricate stories that teach concepts about, and explain, the creation of the universe and the sequences of stages by which it reached its present form."[21] In many of these folktales, women play a key role in the creation, regeneration, and persistence of the world as we know it. There is no single creation story among Native Americans, but women figure prominently in several, often journeying to Earth, like Swenson, from "a place beyond the stars": the Woman Who Fell from the Sky; the Changing Woman; Divine Woman, the Creator; "first woman"; and of course Mother Earth, the core of all life, on which all other beings depend—a living entity that directs the life force that animates the world, sustaining all creations.[22] In each, it is woman who facilitates the existence of life, as it is known, but only with the assistance of other living things already inhabiting the world; the relationship is one of reciprocity and interrelationship.

Generativity, transformation, and interdependence all define the various guises of the "woman" of spiritual lore, and in similar ways, they define Swenson—another mystical Woman Who Fell from the Sky. Like the Apache ancestors, her arrival fosters great change, creativity, and rebirth and has many lessons to teach about traditional Native American values: honor, the responsibility of power, and the importance of community over individuality. Her presence, and the challenges she presents, draw together the most unlikely of collaborators in a Western narrative—lawmen and gunslingers, Indians and townspeople, victims and warriors—and all are transformed. Yet she is also in need; her knowledge of how to save the Earth and its inhabitants from destruction is incomplete without the help of this constellation of characters. And in the process of carrying out her mission, she facilitates experiential learning about interdependence for both groups that leads them to adapt, and in that adaptation, thrive.

CONCLUSION

Swenson's initial appearance as a waifish outsider in need of a gunslinger is both illusion and truth—a difficult combination for the philosophical orientation of most audiences, particularly those accustomed to the clear binary oppositions that traditionally shape Western films. It is not so difficult, however, if her character is considered as inhabiting the worlds of multiple genres, where one's illusion is, in fact, the other's truth.

Within the cinematic context of the Western genre, she is limited to the waifish and vulnerable: on the frontier, traditional, positively coded female roles demand subordination to six-gun patriarchy. Even in revisionist films designed to interrogate and critique those very values, the opportunities for female characters to transgress boundaries established by the genre are limited and carry a high narrative price tag.[23] Within the cultural confines of Absolution (in its role as signifier of the Old West), for example, her budding romance with Lonergan has no future and is subject to the same narrative "resolution" as any other plotline hinting at miscegenation.[24] Her death, albeit noble, was preordained by the genre itself.

Not so in the science fiction universe, where species are continually in contact and things are often not what they seem, and not only gender roles but also the entire notion of gender are more malleable.[25] As a unique product of both narrative contexts, her role is loosened from the moorings of genre, and space is created for her status as a heroic figure that engages with, and upholds, the values of both genres, while at the same time altering their conventions.

As a heroine, then, Ella Swenson is a multifaceted hybrid—not only a female warrior who journeys to Earth to save the planet and its people, but a complex, integrative figure that blurs categories and serves as a catalyst for action, innovation, and change. Her status as the focal point for the film's hybridity makes her critical to the final outcome for all concerned. While overlooked by many as "just the pretty girl" in a male-centered blockbuster,[26] she serves as a unifier and a champion of community—one who brings together disparate factions among the characters who share her struggles;

merges the material and the transcendent; unites the Earth and "places beyond the stars"; turns our gaze, once again, to the question of ancient astronauts and mystical beliefs; and adds another Woman Who Fell from the Sky to the pantheon of Western lore.

NOTES

1. Manohla Dargis, "Extraterrestrials Land at the O.K. Corral," *New York Times*, July 29, 2011, C4.

2. See Dargis, "Extraterrestrials"; also Roger Ebert, "Cowboys and Aliens," July 27, 2011, http://www.rogerebert.com/reviews/cowboys-and-aliens-2011.

3. After fourteen weeks, the film's worldwide gross totaled $174,822,325. *Cowboys and Aliens*, Box Office Mojo, http://www.boxofficemojo.com/movies/?id=cowboysandaliens.htm.

4. Along with their comic and television predecessors: *Wild, Wild West* (1965–1969); *Jonah Hex*, beginning in 1972; and the short-lived *Firefly* series (2002).

5. Dennis Hunt, "Video Log," *Los Angeles Times*, August 22, 1986, D23.

6. Roger Ebert, "Cowboys and Aliens."

7. Brendan Wayne, personal communication, May 13, 2011.

8. Thomas Kent, *Interpretation and Genre: The Role of Generic Perception in the Study of Narrative Texts* (Lewisburg, PA: Bucknell University Press, 1986), 21–22.

9. Ibid., 10.

10. Adam Knee, "The Compound Genre: *Billy the Kid versus Dracula* meets *The Harvey Girls*," in *Intertextuality in Literature and Film: Selected Papers from the Thirteenth Annual Florida State University Conference on Literature and Film*, ed. Elaine D. Cancalon and Antonie Spacagna (Gainesville: University Press of Florida, 1994), 141.

11. Ibid., 143.

12. See Frederick Jackson Turner, *The Frontier in American History* (New York: Holt, 1923).

13. For example, Erich von Däniken's *Chariots of the Gods?: Unsolved Mysteries of the Past* (New York: Putnam, 1968); Robert K. G. Temple's *The Sirius Mystery* (New York: St. Martin's, 1976); and Peter Kolosimo's *Astronavi sulla preistoria*, 1972; translated as *Spaceships in Prehistory* (Berkeley, CA: University Books, 1976) and *Not of This World* (New York: Sphere, 1974).

14. Ardy Sixkiller Clark, *Encounters with Star People: Untold Stories of American Indians* (San Antonio, TX: Anomalist Books, 2012), 97.

15. Clark, *Encounters*, 7; also see the History Channel program *Ancient Aliens*.

16. These criticisms come from the scholarly, Christian, and Indigenous communities alike, though for different reasons. See, for example, Clifford A. Wilson's *Crash Go the Chariots* (Green Forest, AR: Master Books, 1972); Alan F. Alford's "Ancient Astronauts," http://www.eridu.co.uk/Author/human_origins/ancient_astronauts.html; and Chris White's "Ancient Aliens Debunked," http://ancientaliensdebunked.com.

17. Examples may be readily found in numerous episodes of *Star Trek* (1966–1969), *Stargate SGI* (1997–2007), and many science fiction films, such as *The Day the Earth Stood Still* (1951/2008).

18. The Chiricahua traditionally inhabited southwestern New Mexico and southeastern Arizona.

19. Veronica E. Velarde Tiller, *Culture and Customs of the Apache Indians* (Santa Barbara, CA: Greenwood Press, 2011), 3.

20. Ted Jojola, "Notes on Identity, Time, Space, and Place," in *American Indian Thought*, ed. Anne Waters (Oxford, UK: Blackwell Publishing, 2004), 92.

21. Keith Basso, quoted in Tiller, *Culture and Customs*, 22.

22. See Kathleen Dean Moore, Kurt Peters, Ted Jojola, and Amber Lacy's *How It Is: The Native American Philosophy of V. F. Cordova* (Tucson: University of Arizona Press, 2007).

23. For more on women in revisionist Westerns, see M. Elise Marubbio, *Killing the Indian Maiden: Images of Native American Women in Film* (Lexington: University Press of Kentucky, 2009).

24. Although science fiction narratives have their miscegenation issues as well. See Cynthia J. Miller, "Wild Women: Interracial Romance on the Western Frontier," in *Love in Western Film and Television: Lonely Hearts and Happy Trails*, ed. Sue Matheson (New York: Palgrave, 2013), 71–90.

25. See Cynthia J. Miller and A. Bowdoin Van Riper, "The Future in Bed with the Past: Miscegenation in Space," in *The Sex Is Out of This World: Essays on the Carnal Side of Science Fiction*, ed. Sherry Ginn and Michael Cornelius (Jefferson, NC: McFarland, 2012), 17–33.

26. Andy Greenwald and Lane Brown, "Bomb Shelter: Why Did *Cowboys and Aliens* Fail?," *Grantland*, http://www.grantland.com/blog/hollywood-prospectus/post/_/id/31772/ bomb-shelter-why-did-cowboys-aliens-fail.

Part III

Diversity Concerns

Chapter Ten

Her Story, Too

Final Fantasy X, Revolutionary Girl Utena, *and the Feminist Hero's Journey*

Catherine Bailey Kyle

You say it's your story, but it's my story, too. —Yuna, *Final Fantasy X*

Trigger warning: Some of the content here deals with rape and other forms of violence against women.

NO GIRLS ALLOWED: WHY GENDER EQUALITY IN GEEK CULTURE MATTERS

In May 2012, Canadian American feminist media critic Anita Sarkeesian initiated a Kickstarter campaign intended to fund a series of short films analyzing the often-problematic treatment of female characters in video games.[1] The series was called "Tropes vs. Women in Video Games." Supporters rallied behind Sarkeesian's cause, raising her desired goal of $6,000 in under twenty-four hours. By June 30, the project had generated an astounding $158,922 from 6,968 donors, with which Sarkeesian plans to create a set of at least twelve ad-free videos and a classroom curriculum as of this writing.[2]

However, this feat was not achieved without significant backlash. In a TEDxWomen talk, Sarkeesian describes the "cyber mob" that resorted to all manner of vitriolic tactics to shame and silence her, including hacking her social media accounts, vandalizing her Wikipedia page, e-mailing her images of her likeness being sexually assaulted, and even creating a digital "game" where players could "beat the bitch up," depicting an image of the critic's face that became increasingly bloodied with each click of the mouse.[3] The genesis of the attacks? As one antagonist snarled in a Tweet directed at Sarkeesian, "I'll rape you and put your head on a stick if you ever touch my video games."[4]

The problem of misogyny in geek culture—loosely defined here as the social enjoyment of science fiction, fantasy, and/or action-adventure narratives as they appear in literature, film, television, video games, and other media—is widespread and rampant. The online world is rife with sexism, but so too are conventions and other gatherings. One example that garnered media attention was cosplayer Mandy Caruso's experience at New York Comic-Con in 2012 when an interviewer asked her to "spank [him]" and reveal her cup size.[5] Sarkeesian accurately observes that much of geek culture is defined by a sort of "boys' club" mentality,[6] one that seeks to resist alterations to the status quo by creating a toxic environment for females who would dare to participate. Patriarchal attitudes still hold sway over many areas of life, but what, specifically, is at the root of this intense hostility among geeks, a group that has long faced second-class treatment itself?

Patriarchy is a many-headed hydra, so it may be impossible to pin down a single "right" answer. However, one element that undoubtedly contributes to the boys' club mentality Sarkeesian speaks of is the repeated reliance of sci-fi, fantasy, and action-adventure plots on narrative formulas that glorify men and objectify, marginalize, and disempower women. In the first installment of her "Tropes vs. Women in Video Games" series, Sarkeesian points out that the "damsel in distress" cliché frequently seen in games has been continually implemented in storytelling since ancient Greece, citing the myth of Perseus and Andromeda as one well-known example.[7] Joseph Campbell names dozens more in his famous study of world mythology, *The Hero with a Thousand Faces*. From these centuries-old origins, the trope of the damsel in distress bled into European medieval literature, proliferated in early American cinema and pulp fiction, and eventually wormed its way into video games starting in the late 1970s.[8] In her first two videos, Sarkeesian shows clips from over thirty games that have resorted to this hackneyed plot device just since 2001. In many of them, the distressed damsels are shot, stabbed, starved, tortured, struck, or otherwise brutalized.[9] And Sarkeesian is clear on the point that these treatments differ from the struggles Campbell's archetypal hero must face on (usually) his quest:

> [T]he typically male character may occasionally also be harmed, incapacitated or briefly imprisoned at some point during their journey. In these situations, the character relies on their intelligence, cunning, and skill to engineer their own escape. . . . That process of overcoming the ordeal is an important step in the protagonist's transformation into a hero figure.

A Damsel'ed woman on the other hand is shown to be incapable of escaping the predicament on her own and then must wait for a savior to come and do it for her. . . . Consequently, the trope robs women in peril of the opportunity to be the architects of their own escape and therefore prevents them from becoming archetypal heroes themselves.[10]

Indeed, when feminist mythologist Maureen Murdock asked Joseph Campbell about the idea of a female hero's journey, he responded that "all [a woman] has to do is realize that she's the place that people are trying to get to. When a woman realizes what her wonderful character is, she's not going to get messed up with the notion of being pseudo-male."[11] In other words, as Murdock translates, "women don't need to make the journey."[12] While *The Hero with a Thousand Faces* does delve into a few myths centering on female protagonists, such as that of Psyche and Cupid, the vast majority of them star male leads. Moreover, as Sarkeesian suggests, the male hero's emergence into adulthood and hero status not only repeatedly includes, but *hinges* on the rescue of a helpless maiden, bolstering the message again and again that boys save while girls need saving. In short, scores of female characters are habitually denied the complexity of their male saviors, rendered objectified stepping stones on the hero's quest for power and respect.

Of course there are alternative forms of storytelling that more commonly exhibit thoughtfully fleshed-out and psychologically complex female characters. The literary fiction of Jane Austen, George Eliot (also known as Mary Ann Evans), Virginia Woolf, and Toni Morrison, to name only a few, all feature complicated and well-crafted female leads. However, none of these stories fulfill the needs of a reader seeking the epic stakes and otherworldly feel of a high fantasy quest or sci-fi adventure. There is something uniquely alluring about the tales that emerge out of the hero's journey tradition— psychologist Dan P. McAdams even states that epics are one of the four major narrative arcs that can shape people's understanding of what is possible in their own lives[13] —and female fans should not be made to feel alienated from this vital genre as a whole on account of outdated tropes.

Progress is slowly being made on this front: In *Buffy the Vampire Slayer*, *Xena: Warrior Princess*, and other texts, we find strong, confident, and capable female heroes. Feminist critic Jennifer K. Stuller draws important connections between our abiding need for myth and the narratives found in popular culture in *Ink-Stained Amazons and Cinematic Warriors: Superwomen in Modern Mythology*. Fantasy author Valerie Estelle Frankel's *Buffy and the Heroine's Journey: Vampire Slayer and Feminine Chosen One* explores this parallel as well. As is evidenced by the outpouring of support for "Tropes vs. Women in Video Games," the plethora of sites, forums, online communities, and nonprofits committed to improving the representation of women in the media, and the ever-increasing volume of female fans' voices in geek culture, the tide is gradually turning. Still, an examination of the narrative formula that so reflexively and routinely marginalizes female characters—that is, the traditional, archetypal hero's journey—can be a useful tool in the march toward gender equality.

NEW GEAR: TWEAKING THE HERO'S JOURNEY

Frankel, in *From Girl to Goddess: The Heroine's Journey through Myth and Legend*, and Murdock, in *The Heroine's Journey*, offer thoughtful revisions of Campbell's hero's journey that adapt it for a female quester. For instance, Frankel replaces Campbell's "Meeting with the Goddess" stage with "Wedding the Animus," his "Woman as Temptress" stage with "Facing Bluebeard,"[14] his "Atonement with the Father" stage with "Atonement with the Mother," and so on.[15] Murdock includes stages such as "Identification with the masculine" and "Awakening to feelings of spiritual aridity" that are followed by "Urgent yearning to connect with the feminine," "Healing the mother/daughter split," and "Healing the wounded masculine."[16] In both cases, the authors maintain the basic structure of Campbell's model—they even translate some of his stages word for word—but address what they see as the unique needs of female protagonists (and the female audiences who absorb their stories). As to the nature of the fully actualized female hero, Frankel writes that the "archetypal Goddess, or Great Mother . . . was worshiped as the ultimate creator, the vessel of emerging power and source of all life" and that "girls emulate that path on their journeys by forming a family circle that they can rule as supreme nurturer and protector."[17] Murdock puts forth that the purpose of the female hero's journey is to allow women to "fully embrace their feminine nature, learning how to value themselves as women and to heal the deep wound of the feminine."[18] In less direct terms, psychologist Clarissa Pinkola Estés' *Women Who Run with the Wolves: Myths and Stories of the Wild Woman Archetype* suggests that the function of the female hero's journey is to reconnect with "the feminine instinctive nature."[19]

  While I profoundly admire the work of these authors, in this discussion I am going to approach the idea of a revised hero's journey from a slightly different angle. Murdock, Frankel, and Estés—and, of course, Campbell—are all coming at this conversation from the perspective of depth psychology. All draw from Jung's ideas in some way, and Murdock and Estés are even practicing psychoanalysts. Depth psychology deals largely with the unconscious mind and tends to argue in favor of distinct differences between males and females. Contrastingly, in queer theory, which has constituted a large part of my training, gender is seen as a cultural construction, and theorists tend to deal with the conscious mind and society. For the sake of advancing the dialogue surrounding the idea of a female hero's journey, I will offer what I can from this perspective.[20]

In short, rather than essentializing about what makes a "heroine's journey" different from a "hero's journey," I would like to introduce the idea of what I will call the Feminist Hero's Journey. Inspired by the success of the Bechdel test, an increasingly well-known measure of females' representation in film and other media that will be further discussed momentarily, I will offer some criteria that may be applied to the epic narratives found in fantasy, sci-fi, and action-adventure stories to determine their feminist undertones in the hopes of spurring new conversations about the democratization of the Hero's Journey.

To illustrate some of my points, I will use examples from the anime *Revolutionary Girl Utena* (1997),[21] its accompanying film *Revolutionary Girl Utena: The Movie* (1999),[22] and the Japanese role-playing games *Final Fantasy X* (2001)[23] and *Final Fantasy X-2* (2003).[24] While there are other games, TV shows, comics, and films that demonstrate some of my criteria—including other manga, anime, and JRPGs—these are particularly noteworthy due to their global success, their recent resurgence—the *Utena* series, *FFX*, and *FFX-2* were re-released in high definition in 2013—and, on a more personal level, the fact that they deeply inspired me as a young member of geek culture. As an adult, I can honestly say that these narratives shaped my beliefs about what it means to be a confident and determined friend, colleague, life partner, activist, and more. Having experienced firsthand the impact of such Feminist Hero's Journey stories, I believe all the more strongly that these types of narratives are beneficial—even necessary—for young people and adults alike.

One final note about my methodology: in his analysis of individual and collective memory in *Final Fantasy X*, literary critic Dennis Washburn points out that there is some debate in the scholarly community about the ideal method of analyzing video games, as they combine text, image, and interactivity, unlike a conventional book or even a conventional film.[25] Similarly, the editors of *The Superhero Reader* rightly observe that contemporary superhero narratives—along with other "low art" emerging out of fantasy, sci-fi, and so forth—occupy a precarious shelf in academia.[26] Part of this comes, I think, from critics' uncertainty about how best to approach them. Washburn ultimately concludes that the tools supplied by literary criticism and film criticism are appropriate in the discussion of video games where "the unfolding of a narrative is a central component of gameplay,"[27] and as is evidenced by the very existence of a *Superhero Reader*, an increasing number of thinkers feel that the same rule applies to epic narratives found in popular culture. I am an avid believer in the significance of popular culture as a sort of barometer of zeitgeist, so naturally I agree with these interpretations.

In summary, I will utilize literary criticism, film criticism, feminist criticism, and queer theory to theorize a set of "criteria" for a Feminist Hero's Journey, using examples from popular culture. Items will not be listed in order of importance.

I realize, of course, that some of these criteria are more subjective than others and that few stories meet them all. Therefore, rather than a "prescription" to which a narrative must adhere entirely or face total condemnation, I encourage readers to think of this as more of a "checklist." The more "checks" an epic narrative receives, the more feminist it is. Thus, narratives like *Utena* and *FFX* are considered highly feminist heroes' journeys because they fit almost every criterion, but this by no means discounts a narrative like *Sailor Moon*, which features numerous instances of nonviolent problem solving and other feminist features despite its reliance on the "chosen one" trope. Although it may seem counterintuitive, even a narrative like *Harry Potter* earns some credit on this scale; although events largely center on Harry, the books and films depict complicated female characters who engineer their own solutions to problems, and so on.

So as not to set the bar *too* low, I would suggest that a hero's journey be deemed "feminist" if it meets four or more of the following criteria.

Now, on to the list.

LEVELING UP: A FEMINIST HERO'S JOURNEY

Criterion 1: The narrative passes the Bechdel test.

The Bechdel test, a concept birthed from a 1985 strip of Alison Bechdel's comic *Dykes to Watch Out For*, comes from a character's assertion that she will not watch a movie unless it fits three simple criteria: (1) it must have two female characters, (2) who talk to each other, (3) about something other than a male character.[28] This is a very basic criterion, but the abundance of media that cannot meet it is staggering. To convey this, fans have started a site called the "Bechdel Test Movie List" that allows users to rate and discuss any films they wish. Currently, out of the 4,176 movies rated on the site, 44.6 percent fail the test.[29] Of course, this is a self-selected set of participants, so things may be even bleaker in terms of worldwide cinematic female representation, to say nothing of games, comics, and other media.

Utena and *FFX* easily fulfill this criterion. *Utena* tells the story of a young woman (Utena) who becomes involved in a series of cultlike duels in an attempt to protect her friend and eventual lover, Anthy. The two women share an intimate relationship and, over the course of the series, discuss everything from curry recipes and sports to the elusive nature of justice and the arrogance of savior complexes. Furthermore, the multitude of female cast members means that numerous conversations of substance take place, many of which do not even involve the titular hero.

Over the span of her journey, *FFX*'s main protagonist Yuna speaks with multiple women, including her friend Lulu, her cousin Rikku, a rival quester, and a mentor. These conversations help Yuna find her personal resolve, strengthen her compassion, and teach her new skills.

Criterion 2: The narrative includes representations of round, dynamic female characters.

In literary studies, characters are often referred to as either "round or flat" and as either "dynamic or static." A round character is one who is well developed, who has positive as well as negative qualities, and whose motivations are multilateral.[30] A flat character, in contrast, is one who is poorly developed and often compiled of worn-out stereotypes. Sarkeesian identifies the "Helpful Damsel" as one example of a flat character.[31] You've seen her before: the sweet, innocent, supportive healer who carries a magic staff and fights from the back row, if at all. She's often the love interest, and she often gets damsel'ed. These types of characters are predictable, if not boring, and though one could make the case that many male leads are flat characters, too (the sword-swinging macho man, anyone?), it is more typically a problem for female "sidekicks."

Similarly, a dynamic character is one who changes over the course of a narrative, while a static character does not.[32] Dynamic characters learn, change, and grow from their experiences, emerging from their narrative wiser—though not always happier—than before.

Utena and Yuna are both round, dynamic characters. Yuna transforms from a shy, soft-spoken young woman to a confident political leader by the end of *FFX* and again to a free-spirited bounty hunter in *FFX-2*. Her lover Tidus even remarks at the end of the sequel, "You've changed!" Furthermore, she moves from blind religious follower to full-on heretic, though this change is gradual.

Utena, an even more psychologically complex character, shifts from treating Anthy as a generic damsel in distress to recognizing her unique kind of strength and suffering. Moreover, she even realizes that her attempts at playing prince have prevented her from viewing Anthy as a whole human being and struggles to redeem herself. With this, *Utena* confronts conventional narratives head on.

Criterion 3: The narrative positions at least one female character as a heroic agent.

If a story is going to tell the tale of a Feminist Hero's Journey, it should ideally feature as least one female[33] hero. But what exactly *is* a hero? Sarkeesian writes that a character must be the "architect" of her own fate in order to achieve hero status. Additionally, Stuller states that a character must have "a uniquely identifiable skill or power" and "a mission or purpose that benefits the greater good."[34] I would add that a hero should help at least one person on an individual level over the course of her quest to fulfill the greater mission. But, loosely, let us say that a hero is someone who overcomes obstacles and helps others using her own talents and resources.

As has already been stated, Utena's whole raison d'être is the liberation of Anthy from the manipulative cult of duelists. However, she also goes out of her way to stand up for the underdogs of her school. Using her incredible sword-fighting skills and her enigmatic connection to a ghostly prince, Utena battles her way through numerous challenges.

Yuna's quest begins when she decides to become a Summoner, one who can call forth powerful creatures known as Aeons in the hopes of vanquishing Sin, the monster that plagues the world of Spira every ten years. Thus, although she is a healer, she can also deal devastating damage with the help of the Aeons. With the help of her allies, Yuna eventually does save the world (twice, in fact), bringing peace to Spira.

Criterion 4: The narrative includes at least one instance of nonviolent problem solving.

Sarkeesian brings up an important point when she claims that "game developers have backed themselves into a corner" by making violence "the primary way that the player engages with the game-world," stating that "[t]he player is then forced to use violence to deal with almost *all* situations" (italics in original).[35] Indeed, one of the major criticisms of video games has been its glorification of violence. But like the damsel-in-distress trope, the equation of problem solving with aggressive action in epic narratives is not a modern invention. In many (though, to be fair, not all) of the sagas Campbell cites, violence is used before any other tactic. The romanticization of war is classically patriarchal, so on the one hand nonviolent conflict resolution could be seen as a feminist alternative. However, it is equally problematic to conflate femininity with inherent gentleness and pacifism. Therefore, a middle ground must be struck. The hero's journey as a narrative arc demands the surmounting of adversaries, but the protagonist(s) of a Feminist Hero's Journey should rely on more than brutality.

Gloria Steinem praises Wonder Woman for her ability to "conquer with force, but only a force that was tempered by love and justice."[36] Likewise, Stuller devotes a whole chapter of her book to female heroes who incorporate "redemption, collaboration, and compassion" into their foe-confronting tool kits.[37] Feminist heroes do not automatically obliterate their enemies or relish their destruction; they seek to reason with them, win them over to the side of good, or come to a compromise. In this way, they resist the limiting binary of "good" and "evil" that has, for centuries, functioned to unjustly oppress women, sexual minorities, and other marginalized groups.

Again, this is not to express that a feminist hero cannot or should not use violence at any point over the course of the journey—it merely asks that at least one instance of creative, nonviolent problem solving be deployed for the sake of diversifying the concept of justice.

The most obvious example of this comes from Utena's duels. Instead of impaling or even harming one another, fighters win duels by cutting a single rose from the breast of their opponent. In another instance less particular to a preexisting system, Utena opens an enchanted door not with brute force but with a single earnest tear. Timothy Perper and Martha Cornog write that "Utena's gentleness—her noble heart—opens the Way."[38]

Yuna, for her part, uses her power as a Summoner to send wandering spirits of the dead to the afterlife after she and her companions fail to destroy them using conventional swords and sorcery. This not only resolves the conflict, but it frees the lost souls, too.

Criterion 5: The narrative accounts for multiple subjectivities.

Feminist philosopher Hélène Cixous suggests that narrative polyphony, or the revelation of details about the same plot from differing points of view, can translate to a wider social tolerance of dissenting perspectives. Literary critic Marilyn Farwell explains that this is because multiple voices highlight the limited, flawed, and even unreliable subjectivity of any given narrator.[39] By including the traditionally marginalized or discredited voices of so-called minor (often female) characters in the storytelling framework, a text may begin to qualify as feminist on a symbolic level.

FFX and *Utena* exhibit these qualities in fascinating ways. Judging from the opening scene of *FFX*, it appears as if the narrative arc will resemble a prototypical male hero's journey. "Listen to my story," says Tidus, the young male protagonist who serves as the player's avatar during the majority of game play. Immediately, from the very first line, Tidus claims the narrative as his own, establishing himself as both the vocal narrator of the story and the viewpoint through which it will be focalized. Yet this monolithic authority is subverted as the narrative goes on. At one point, after Tidus reiterates, "This is my story. It'll go the way I want, or I'll end it here," Yuna retaliates, "You say it's your story, but it's my story, too." Furthermore, players spend some time navigating through the game using Yuna as their avatar, dismissing the idea that this is, indeed, merely Tidus' story. By shifting the narrative focus to Yuna's experience, *FFX* calls into question the idea of the paternalistic male hero as the center of a compelling story line. Moreover, in *FFX-2*, Yuna serves as the narrator and avatar throughout the entire game, finalizing her shift from silence to audibility.

Utena plays with narration via two recurring shadow puppets who appear for a moment or two midepisode to reinterpret, misinterpret, or allegorize the story. Intentionally absurdist yet occasionally profound, these narrators draw attention to the arbitrariness of any given point of view.

Criterion 6: The narrative does not trap female characters in the marriage/death plot.

Farwell also observes that in countless epic narratives, the female life is seen as a "natural" progression toward marriage and maternity, and that women who resist this trajectory are met with untimely death.[40] Moreover, Carol Pearson and Katherine Pope point out that even in a seemingly happy fairy-tale marriage (of the heterosexual variety, of course—gay and lesbian narratives are virtually invisible in most traditional epics), there is often an "imbalance of power" because the male has quested for the female while the female has "merely wait[ed]."[41] Though Pixar and Disney's *Brave* indicates that attitudes are slowly changing,[42] the idea of a free and autonomous female agent surviving the hero's journey without adhering to one of these endings has traditionally prompted cultural anxiety.

As Baumlin and Baumlin point out in their study of *Jane Eyre* as female hero's journey, marriage does not *have* to signal misery for the protagonist.[43] My intention here is not to condemn marriage, but rather to criticize the disturbing trend of narratives based on the hero's journey that fail to represent alternative futures for females.

Most overtly, there is a scene in *FFX* where Yuna defies both marriage and death. Earlier in the game, the hero horrifies her companions by accepting the marriage proposal of the central villain, a vengeful ghost. At the altar, Yuna turns the tables by revealing that it was all a ruse to send his spirit to the afterlife. When the plan goes awry, she is literally backed into the corner of a balcony, over which she jumps in an apparent act of suicide. Yet Yuna does not die. Using the powers she has mastered, she summons one of the Aeons to catch her and carry her gently to safety. The story ultimately leaves her positioned as a prominent political leader, delivering a speech to her country and planning for her future. Unpartnered but alive, she disrupts common expectations for an adventure story's "happy ending."

Utena carves out a similar fate. Rejecting the advances of a charming but wicked "prince" and his attempts to domesticate her into a quaint, submissive "princess," she refuses to live happily ever after in a (literal) castle in the sky while Anthy remains a pawn of the duelists. Though Utena's fate is left uncertain in the TV series, in the film she and Anthy escape to the world outside the suffocating school.

Criterion 7: The narrative eschews the "chosen one" plot in favor of voluntary heroism.

In his TED talk "The Antidote to Apathy," community organizer Dave Meslin criticizes narratives that center on "chosen ones" who are compelled to complete heroic deeds by external drives, such as a prophesy, rather than their own intrinsic motivation.[44] He argues that one of the key points of heroic leadership is that "it comes from within" and that saturating our culture with narratives in which heroes are appointed relieves "ordinary" viewers from participating in activism. These stories suggest, moreover, that there is one "right" person for certain difficult tasks, a notion that runs counter to the collaborative efforts of social justice movements.

Many "chosen one" stories have significant feminist value. However, in perpetuating the notion that heroes are born and not made, such stories may contribute to the misconception that heroism is a solitary, elite, and even biologically deterministic attribute. In alignment with feminist and queer theory, which advocate a cultural constructivist approach to gender and other aspects of identity, a Feminist Hero's Journey should include a hero who acts out of personal desire instead of foretold destiny.

Both Yuna and Utena choose to set forth on their journeys: Yuna because her father was a Summoner before her and she wants to save Spira from Sin, Utena because she wants to end Anthy's exploitation. Each continues fighting against insurmountable odds because she believes in her mission and in herself, not because her quest is preordained. Also, in Yuna's case, any Summoner can defeat Sin, eliminating the trope that there is one exceptional savior.

Criterion 8: The narrative engages intersectionality.

One of the most important differences between Second and Third Wave feminism is the latter's awareness of intersectionality, or the ways in which various social markers, such as race, class, age, ability, body type, gender identity, and sexuality converge with sex and gender to restrict and police privilege. Intersectionality recognizes that sexism is connected to many other manifestations of prejudice and that the struggles of seemingly disparate groups for fair treatment are actually intertwined. A Feminist Hero's Journey, therefore, should not only grapple with topics relating to sex and gender, but other social hierarchies as well.

Neither narrative does overwhelmingly well on this criterion, but they do fulfill it to some extent. *FFX* tackles topics of racism via the ongoing tensions between the Al-Bhed, Ronso, and Guado peoples. *Utena* includes numerous same-sex and same-gender relationships and casts lesbianism in a positive though not overly sentimental light. The canon also contains numerous interracial relationships, one of which a fan thoughtfully analyzes through the lens of postcolonial feminist theory.[45] So, the narratives have some potential for shedding light on these topics.

Criterion 9: The narrative does not pointlessly sexualize female characters.

If you're reading this book, there's a good chance you've seen it by now: the "broke back" (sometimes "brokeback") pose. Notorious among North American superhero comics, this visual trope depicts female characters contorted in such a way that their breasts and rear ends are gratuitously displayed simultaneously.[46] It is so named because many of the poses would only be possible if the characters' spines were broken. This is an extreme example of sexual objectification in epic narratives that teeters on the absurd, but it is also a microcosm of geek culture's propensity for unnecessarily sexualizing female characters. In her landmark essay "Visual Pleasure and Narrative Cinema," film critic Laura Mulvey writes that women in visual media are frequently "coded for strong visual and erotic impact so that they can be said to connote *to-be-looked-at-ness*."[47] Clearly this is an inappropriate and regressive treatment of female and feminine bodies, both fictional and real.

While this criterion is primarily designed for film, TV shows, games, comics, artwork, and other visual media, it can apply to exclusively textual narratives as well. Traditional fairy tales and modern stories that dwell on female characters' physical "fairness," "beauty," or sex appeal while neglecting all of their other qualities help to promote the message that females are, indeed, only here to be looked at.

This is not to say that female heroes should wear full suits of armor at all times. Sometimes it is appropriate for a character to dress or act sexily or even behave sexually given her personality and her context. That is why this criterion uses the word *pointlessly*. The sexualization of female bodies that is simply intended to titillate readers and serves no narrative purpose is the sort I believe we should try to avoid in the Feminist Hero's Journey.

This is one area where the *FF* series falls down on the job a bit. Though Yuna wears a kimono in *FFX*, in *FFX-2* she is clothed in much more revealing attire, complete with a neckline that reaches halfway down to her navel. Though a few years have passed since the events of *FFX* and Yuna is more outgoing than in the original, it seems out of character for her to be display-ing her body this way.

Neither Utena's school uniform nor her modified dueling costume are too suggestive, though one could argue her shorts are needlessly form fitting and scant. Interestingly, one of the "transformation" animation sequences repeat-ed in the second half of the series depicts Utena in a somewhat erotic manner, but as I have discussed elsewhere, I believe it serves mainly to illustrate the intensifying romantic relationship between her and Anthy.[48] Some of the narrative's promotional artwork, especially that related to the film, is more voyeuristic, though it sexualizes both male and female characters. While this does present some obvious problems, it correlates to some extent with the themes of discomforting, forbidden love that weave throughout Utena's jour-ney.[49]

HER STORY TOO: THE (R)EVOLUTION OF A GENRE

The hero's journey in and of itself can be a thrilling and worthwhile basis for a plot—*Star Wars*, *The Lord of the Rings*, *The Matrix*, and other internation-ally acclaimed tales beloved by people of all genders stem from its basic cycle of departure, trial, and emergence—but we must consider the implica-tions of telling and retelling narratives that dismiss the power and complexity of females and female-coded settings, objects, and actions. Fortunately, al-though popular media does show signs of advancement, we do not have to wait for Hollywood to produce such stories for us—feminist fans are writing their own comics,[50] hacking games to make the "damsel in distress" the star,[51] and using other creative methods to subvert the current saturation of androcentrism in geek culture.

Critics agree that Yuna and Utena are characters who revolutionize their settings. Washburn writes that by the end of *FFX* "the system of belief that has sustained the cultures of Spira is radically undermined,"[52] Mari Kotani states that Utena "unravel[s] the school's mysterious hierarchies,"[53] and Perper and Cornog state that "*Utena* tells of the destruction of one way of life and the beginning of another."[54] In their courage and compassion, they break from the worn-out paradigms of their old worlds to forge something un-charted and new. If more stories begin to reflect some of the suggestions laid out in this model of the Feminist Hero's Journey, perhaps the members of geek culture and beyond can undergo a similar revolution.

NOTES

1. Anita Sarkeesian, "Tropes vs. Women in Video Games," *Kickstarter*, accessed July 15, 2013, http://www.kickstarter.com/projects/566429325/tropes-vs-women-in-video-games.
2. Ibid.

3. Anita Sarkeesian, "Anita Sarkeesian at TEDxWomen 2012," *TEDxWomen* video, 10:30, December 1, 2012, http://tedxwomen.org/speakers/anita-sarkeesian-2.

4. Ibid.

5. Aja Romano, "Black Cat Cosplayer Sexually Harassed at Comic Con Becomes Tumblr Hero," *The Daily Dot*, http://www.dailydot.com/news/black-cat-cosplayer-nycc-harassment-tumblr (accessed July 21, 2013).

6. Sarkeesian, "TEDxWomen."

7. Anita Sarkeesian, "Damsel in Distress: Part 1—Tropes vs. Women in Video Games," *Feminist Frequency* video, 23:35, March 7, 2013, http://www.feministfrequency.com/2013/03/damsel-in-distress-part-1. In this myth, the naked Andromeda is chained to a rock to appease an angry sea monster; Perseus rescues her and takes her as his wife.

8. Ibid.

9. Anita Sarkeesian, "Damsel in Distress: Part 2—Tropes vs. Women in Video Games," *Feminist Frequency* video, 25:41, May 28, 2013, http://www.feministfrequency.com/2013/05/damsel-in-distress-part-2-tropes-vs-women.

10. Sarkeesian, "Damsel in Distress: Part 1."

11. Maureen Murdock, *The Heroine's Journey: Woman's Quest for Wholeness* (Boston: Shambhala, 1990), Kindle edition, loc. 259.

12. Ibid., loc. 259.

13. Dan P. McAdams, *The Stories We Live By: Personal Myths and the Making of the Self* (New York: Morrow, 1993), 50–51. McAdams names comedy, irony, and tragedy as the other major arcs and observes, based on interviews, that people who identify with the "romance" (epic) and comedy narratives tend to have more optimistic outlooks on life. The relationship between a reader/viewer/player's digestion of epic narratives produced by geek culture and her or his sense of personal empowerment and agency is a fascinating topic I strongly believe merits further exploration.

14. Along with "Finding the Sensitive Man" and "Confronting the Powerless Father."

15. Valerie Estelle Frankel, *From Girl to Goddess: The Heroine's Journey through Myth and Legend* (Jefferson, NC: McFarland, 2010), Kindle edition, loc. 104.

16. Murdock, *The Heroine's Journey*, loc. 305.

17. Frankel, *From Girl to Goddess*, loc. 92.

18. Murdock, *The Heroine's Journey*, loc. 272.

19. Clarissa Pinkola Estés, *Women Who Run with the Wolves: Myths and Stories of the Wild Woman Archetype* (New York: Ballantine, 1992), 3.

20. For those who may find this style of argumentation unconventional, please see Catherine E. Lamb, "Other Voices, Different Parties: Feminist Responses to Argument," *Teaching Argument in the Composition Course*, ed. Timothy Barnett (Boston: Bedford/St. Martin's, 2002), 159. Lamb suggests that it is more in line with feminist ideals to see argumentation as a process of "problem solving rather than a contest," with which I agree. Though there are many fundamental differences between depth psychology and queer theory, I believe we can have a productive conversation based on mutual courtesy and respect.

21. *Revolutionary Girl Utena*, directed by Kunihiku Ikuhara (1997; New York: Central Park Media, 1998–2003), DVD.

22. *Revolutionary Girl Utena: The Movie*, directed by Kunihiku Ikuhara (1999; New York: Central Mark Media, 2001), DVD. The original title translates to "The Adolescence of Utena."

23. *Final Fantasy X*, PlayStation 2 version (Square Electronic Arts, 2001).

24. *Final Fantasy X-2*, PlayStation 2 version (Square Enix, 2003).

25. Dennis Washburn, "Imagined History, Fading Memory: Mastering Narrative in *Final Fantasy X*," *Mechademia* 4 (2009): 154–57.

26. Charles Hatfield, Jeet Heer, and Kent Worcester, eds., *The Superhero Reader* (Jackson: University of Mississippi Press, 2013), xv–xvi.

27. Washburn, "Imagined History," 157.

28. "About," *Bechdel Test Movie List*, http://bechdeltest.com (accessed July 16, 2013). In a variation on the test, the women must also have names; however, the original comic strip does not state this.

29. "Statistics," *Bechdel Test Movie List*, http://bechdeltest.com/statistics (accessed July 16, 2013).

30. Laurie G. Kirszner and Stephen R. Mandell, eds., "Character," in *Compact Literature: Reading, Reacting, Writing*, 8th ed. (Boston: Wadsworth, Cengage Learning), 231.

31. Sarkeesian, "Damsel in Distress: Part 1."

32. Kirszner and Mandell, "Character," 232.

33. I realize that sex and gender are not synonymous; thus, I have tried to stay away from terms like *man* and *woman*. By using the term *female* here, I wish to acknowledge that although the representation of biologically sexed female bodies in the media is important, so too is the dissolution of these reductive categories. When I say "female hero," I intend for this to mean any female-sexed or female-gendered individuals.

34. Jennifer K. Stuller, *Ink-Stained Amazons and Cinematic Warriors: Superwomen in Modern Mythology* (New York: I. B. Tauris, 2010), Kindle edition, loc. 219–30.

35. Sarkeesian, "Damsel in Distress—Part 2," italics in original.

36. Gloria Steinem, "Wonder Woman," in *The Superhero Reader*, ed. Charles Hatfield, Jeet Heer, and Kent Worcester (Jackson: University of Mississippi Press, 2013), Kindle edition, loc. 4478–86.

37. Stuller, *Ink-Stained*, starting at loc. 1872.

38. Timothy Perper and Martha Cornog, "In the Sound of the Bells: Freedom and Revolution in *Revolutionary Girl Utena*," *Mechademia* 1 (2006): 185.

39. Marilyn Farwell, *Heterosexual Plots & Lesbian Narratives* (New York: New York University Press, 1996), 62.

40. Farwell, *Heterosexual Plots*, 27.

41. Carol Pearson and Katherine Pope, *The Female Hero in American and British Literature* (New York: R. R. Bowker, 1981), 34.

42. *Brave*, directed by Mark Andrews and Brenda Chapman (2012; Burbank, CA: Walt Disney Studios Motion Pictures, 2012), DVD. In this film, the female protagonist Merida actively resists marriage and embarks on a Feminist Hero's Journey that meets many of my outlined criteria.

43. Tita French Baumlin and James S. Baumlin, "Jane Iterare: *Jane Eyre* as Feminist Revision of the Hero's Journey," in *Post-Jungian Criticism: Theory and Practice*, ed. James S. Baumlin, Tita French Baumlin, and George H. Jensen (Albany: State University of New York Press, 2004), 120.

44. Dave Meslin, "The Antidote to Apathy," *TEDxTorono* video, 7:06, October 2010, http://www.ted.com/talks/dave_meslin_the_antidote_to_apathy.html (accessed October 2, 2011).

45. "The Dark Bride and the Pale Prince," *GAR GAR Stegosaurus*, February 25, 2010, http://gargarstegosaurus.wordpress.com/2010/02/25/the-dark-bride-and-the-pale-prince (accessed November 1, 2011).

46. For a few examples, see Heidi MacDonald, "Fact Check: Can You Really Fight in the Brokeback Pose?," *Comics Beat*, January 3, 2012, http://comicsbeat.com/fact-check-can-you-really-fight-in-the-brokeback-pose (accessed July 25, 2013).

47. Laura Mulvey, "Visual Pleasure and Narrative Cinema," in *Film Theory and Criticism: Introductory Readings*, ed. Leo Braudy and Marshall Cohen (New York: Oxford University Press, 1999), 837, italics in original.

48. See Catherine E. Bailey, "Prince Charming by Day, Superheroine by Night? Subversive Sexualities and Gender Fluidity in *Revolutionary Girl Utena* and *Sailor Moon*," *Colloquy: Text Theory Critique* 24 (2012), 207–22.

49. The tensions created between the show's feminist narrative and its problematic promotional artwork are ones I hope to explore in future writing.

50. See, for example, Will Brooker, Sarah Zaidan, Susan Shore, "About My So-Called Secret Identity," *My So-Called Secret Identity*, http://www.mysocalledsecretidentity.com/aboutcat (accessed July 25, 2013).

51. Ian Sherr, "Fans Take Videogame Damsels Out of Distress, Put Them in Charge," *Wall Street Journal*, July 3, 2013, accessed July 25, 2013.

52. Washburn, "Imagined History," 158.

53. Mari Kotani, "Metamorphosis of the Japanese Girl: The Girl, the Hyper-Girl, and the Battling Beauty," *Mechademia* 1 (2006): 160.

54. Perper and Cornog, "In the Sound," 184.

Chapter Eleven

Bollywood Marriages

Portrayals of Matrimony in Hindi Popular Cinema

Rekha Sharma and Carol A. Savery

Movies may contribute to attitudes about gender because they utilize language as well as nonverbal communication and create a space for expression and debate over values within cultures and across cultural boundaries. "Bollywood" films, originating from the Indian subcontinent, communicate attitudes regarding gender portrayals and cultural mores not only to South Asian viewers but also to audiences around the world. In addition to reflecting aspects of Indian culture, Hindi cinema may also influence attitudes and reshape social structures.[1]

The Indian film industry contains linguistic variations, with five centers of production reflecting eight languages.[2] Commercial movies are nicknamed "Bollywood" films because of their origin in Mumbai, formerly Bombay.[3] The dialogue of Bollywood films combines Hindi and Urdu, which could account for their ability to have reached such a large audience, especially in the northern half of the country.[4] Bollywood has emerged as a unique site of cultural articulation because the movies transcend barriers such as literacy and economic class, serving as a point of mediation for tensions created by capitalistic modernity at all levels of society.[5]

Although scholars have recognized a handful of Indian films deemed to be progressive, artistic, or realistic, the popular Bollywood amalgam of family drama, romance, action, song, and dance[6] was often considered too "lowbrow" a form of entertainment to be worthy of serious study.[7] In recent years, however, Bollywood has proved to be a lucrative, powerful industry. Indian production companies have exported Hindi movies and songs around the world,[8] and Bollywood celebrities have ventured successfully into arenas of politics and social activism.[9]

At their most basic level, Bollywood movies could be characterized as morality plays, pitting good against evil.[10] For Indians living in India as well as in diaspora communities, the conflict is often perceived as one between traditional and Western values. But K. Moti Gokulsing and Wimal Dissanayake[11] argued that the true conflict is between religious and secular values. Viewed in this light, analyzing Bollywood movies could reveal how consumers of these films have come to articulate or balance religious and secular values in their own lives.

This chapter serves as an exploration of cinematic portrayals of marriage in India, paying special attention to portrayals of heroines in the roles of love interests, wives, and mothers as well as what these portrayals convey regarding values and issues such as sacrifice, strength, family, sexuality, and femininity. This analysis addresses the practices of arranged and "love" marriages grounded in Hindu religious archetypes (i.e., Ram-Sita, Radha-Krishna, Shiva-Parvati) as depicted in Bollywood, paying special attention to the characteristics of culturally acceptable relationships and ideal partners. That is, if Bollywood films have showcased the tension between religious and secular values, how have they impacted Indians' notions about matrimony—a societal custom grounded in religion and secular law? Has a change in Bollywood's typical narrative formulas spurred audiences to reexamine notions of marriage, or has it merely reflected a general shift in cultural attitudes?

The analysis will first address gender stereotypes in media. Then we will discuss ideal marriage partners in terms of Hindu archetypes. An examination of depictions in Bollywood will explicate cinematic treatments of premarital cohabitation and extramarital affairs as well as a trend toward depicting characters as imperfect people rather than as "heroes" or "heroines." Ultimately, the analysis will elucidate the potential heuristic value for further research of Bollywood as a site of mediation of cultural values and gender depictions.

GENDER STEREOTYPES IN MEDIA

Becky Michele Mulvaney[12] asserts that communication about gender is a form of intercultural communication, outlining two main assumptions: (1) communication is the medium that most individuals are able to grasp and learn, and (2) language is subjective and value laden, in that all communication imparts a viewpoint. In addition to language, worldview and nonverbal communication are important components of intercultural communication. Worldview has been defined as "a culture's orientation toward such things as God, humanity, nature, the universe, and the other philosophical issues that are concerned with the concept of being."[13] Laurie P. Arliss argues that individuals learn to be male or female through communication.[14] So gender can be considered both an influence on and an outcome of communication.

Gender is a "social symbolic construction that expresses the meanings a society confers on a biological sex."[15] Media reflect and reinforce the dominant ideology of a society, including how women and men are portrayed in films. These portrayals convey complex messages about personality traits, communication patterns, expected behaviors, and social norms via heuristic shortcuts. Such characterizations rely on stereotypes, which are defined as "a broad generalization about an entire class of phenomena, based on some knowledge of limited aspects of certain members of the class."[16] Katy Gilpatric (2010) points out that gender stereotypes can be problematic in research[17] and suggests that the standard used in social science research on stereotypes[18] focuses on gender traits. Masculine stereotype traits include dominant, aggressive, independent, ambitious, self-confident, adventurous, and decisive. Feminine stereotype traits include affectionate, submissive, emotional, sympathetic, talkative, and gentle. Research has also focused on how females are portrayed as passive, sexually subordinate, and dominated.[19]

Gender research has suggested that individuals create a schema about the stereotypes of women in three major subgroups: homemaker, professional, and sex object.[20] These subgroups are often differentiated along two dimensions: agency (power and competence) and virtue (sexual and moral).[21] Moral and sexual virtue seems to be important to perceptions of women. The theory of paternalistic prejudices[22] proposes that negative stereotypes about women's agency (e.g., less power and competence than men) are accepted if accompanied by positive stereotypes (e.g., women are more virtuous than men). These stereotypes may hamper women's equality, as virtue grants some respect but little actual power.[23]

Julia T. Wood (1994) provides insights into how media portray women as either good or bad.[24] Good women are pretty, subordinate, and focused on home, family, and supporting others.[25] Subordinate portrayals show women as victims, angels, martyrs, loyal wives, and helpmates. Bad women are portrayed as witches, bitches, whores, or nonwomen (callous, cold, and aggressive). Media frequently depict men saving women from their own incompetence.[26] Other media themes are women as primary caregivers, passive victims, and sex objects, while men are breadwinners and aggressors in relationships.[27] Wood also suggests cultural themes in how women are stereotyped: they are judged by their appearance (focus on being attractive, thin, and well dressed); are pressured to be nice, sensitive, and helpful; are devalued and mistreated; and are expected to be homemaker, mother, and career woman simultaneously.[28]

In Hindi—and in Bollywood—several terms link religious archetypes with gender norms or ideals. While the Hindi language contains many derogatory terms referencing mothers, sisters, and daughters, there are superlative synonyms for husbands that equate them with the divine.[29] For example, *Patidev* and *Pati-Parmeshwar* convey a "husband as Lord" power dynamic.[30] In *Raavan*,[31] the female protagonist defends her husband as "Godlike" when her abductor tries to cast aspersions on his character. But in *Kabhi Khushi Kabhie Gham*[32] (Sometimes Happy, Sometimes Sad), Nandini (Jaya Bachchan) reprimands her husband for alienating their son. She reminds her husband that she was taught to view him as Pati-Parmeshwar: "Mother always says that a husband is God: Whatever he says, whatever he thinks, is always right." She then recounts how he allowed their family to fall apart, concluding, "God can't do any wrong, can he? My husband is a husband . . . just a husband . . . not God." She challenges the expectations of her role by asserting herself but retains credibility by adhering to her obligations as wife and mother.

THE PERFECT COUPLES: HINDU ARCHETYPES OF HEROES AND HEROINES

Traditional conceptions of matrimony in India frequently center on arranged marriages, often viewed as the antithesis of "love" marriages (i.e., those in which individuals decide to marry after a period of courtship and romance). However, love is also a component of arranged marriages. The difference is said to be that in arranged marriages, love develops between the bride and groom after the wedding as the individuals build their lives together. Research has shown that people in Western, individualistic cultures tend to place more importance on romance, whereas collectivist societies such as India view romance as less imperative to a successful marriage.[33] Rather, arranged marriages are seen as the union of two families, so relationship partners are matched on multiple levels of compatibility; the goals of the families are paramount to personal considerations.[34]

Bollywood has often juxtaposed arranged and romance-based relationships. This is possibly because conflicts of the heart make for interesting plots and character development, but also because viewers are mindful of obligations to their families as well as the temptations of pursuing love on their own terms. Many musical sequences in Bollywood films convey physical attraction, romantic desire, and high emotion in quasi-religious ways tailored to audiences who understand coded meanings that would otherwise be inexpressible under current social norms.[35] Although viewers from many religions watch Bollywood films, the movies tend to reinforce Hindu themes, norms, and ideals. Such meanings are apparent in the relationship models and conceptualizations of ideal wives/husbands in Bollywood movies.

Ram and Sita

In Hinduism, divinity manifests in gods and goddesses who are revered in multiple forms and as various incarnations.[36] Marital dyads of these deities symbolize the duality of the universe as well as complementary forces.[37] One of the most prominent religious archetypal relationships is that of the marriage of Ram and Sita, the principal figures in the *Ramayan*, a Hindu epic. Sita is idealized as the perfect woman, possessing unwavering loyalty, modesty, and devotion.[38] Therefore, the "good wife" in Indian culture should dedicate herself to the welfare of her husband and family, performing religious rituals and household chores, and remaining truthful and virtuous.[39] According to this archetype, a filmic heroine would be defined by her denial of independence in service of her commitment to family.[40] Sita sacrificed comfort and safety for her husband when he was exiled from Ayodhya and stripped of his birthright, and Ram honored and protected the chaste Sita during their banishment. This pairing of an ideal husband and wife is a common underpinning in Bollywood, particularly when characters have an arranged marriage.

The *Ramayan* inspired the allegorical *Hum Saath-Saath Hain*[41] (We Are United). Vivek (Mohnish Behl), the eldest son of a wealthy family, agrees to an arranged marriage with demure Sadhna (Tabu). Sadhna loves her family so much that she only agrees to a honeymoon if her new relatives accompany them. Solidarity is shattered, though, when socialites persuade Vivek's stepmother, Mamta (Reema Lagoo), to safeguard the family assets for her biological son, Prem (Salman Khan). Vivek and Sadhna leave the household to avoid further conflict. Thus, Vivek and Sadhna embody the self-sacrificing nature of Ram and Sita.

Radha and Krishna

A secondary couple in *HSSH*[42] mirrors another Hindu archetypal relationship: Radha and Krishna. Bollywood allusions to this couple represent a permissible form of romantic love: "In classical Indian texts, the love of Radha for Krishna is all-consuming, absolutely pure, and eternal, and this is the kind of romantic love depicted in mainstream Indian films."[43] Krishna is often portrayed as mischievous and flirtatious, yet dutiful. Frequently, fictional couples following the Radha-Krishna motif are temporarily separated or forced to marry other people; in this way, viewers can reconcile the yearning for romance with the pragmatic need to satisfy one's duty to family in a socially acceptable way.

In *HSSH*,[44] Vinod (Saif Ali Khan) and Sapna (Karishma Kapoor) reminisce over home movies, gazing romantically as they see younger versions of themselves singing, dancing, and fighting during a Janmashtami celebration[45] in which they dressed up as Krishna and Radha. Later, Sapna performs the same song, complaining to Krishna's foster mother about his charmingly roguish behavior—clearly poking fun at Vinod. A marriage between Sapna and Vinod is halted, though. When Vivek and Sadhna are forced to leave, Vinod accompanies them, just as Ram's brother Lakshman joined him in exile. But the characterization of Vinod clearly references Krishna as well; both are playful, yet adhere to a dharmic code of duty.

Hum Aapke Hain Koun . . . ![46] (Who Am I to You?) highlights the merits of and tensions between arranged and love marriages via the employment of Ram-Sita and Radha-Krishna archetypes. The first half of the film centers on the arranged marriage of Rajesh (Mohnish Behl) and Pooja (Renuka Shahane), showcasing the engagement planned by their parents, the Hindu marriage rituals, and the birth of their child. Like Ram and Sita, Rajesh and Pooja are dutiful, modest, and focused on the happiness of their families. The corollary to this action is the attraction between Rajesh's younger brother, Prem (Salman Khan), and Pooja's younger sister, Nisha (Madhuri Dixit). Pooja teases Prem about whether she should begin looking for a suitable bride for him or whether he would prefer a "love" marriage. Prem responds that he would want both—a love marriage that his family could arrange— indicating that he wishes to marry Nisha. The relationship between Prem and Nisha, as an expression of the Krishna-Radha archetypes, is the focus of the second half of the film. Their relationship is threatened when Pooja dies and the families expect Nisha to marry Rajesh to help raise his child. Prem and Nisha struggle with their unwillingness to disappoint their families and the norms that inhibit an open declaration of their feelings. Still, *HAHK*[47] represented arranged marriages and extended family in a positive light, and it also aligned romantic love with religious archetypes acceptable to conservative, Hindu audiences.

Shiva and Parvati

Although the Ram-Sita and Krishna-Radha motifs[48] are more apparent in Bollywood, less attention has been paid to the Shiva-Parvati dyad. Shiva is a male deity who represents purity of consciousness and is the divine destroyer.[49] According to many narratives, Shiva lived an ascetic life, resisting obligations of marriage and fatherhood.[50] Eventually, though, he married Parvati.[51] She is the mother of the elephant-headed god, Ganesh, whom she created without Shiva. Shiva and Parvati represent the creative and destructive forces of nature in complementary ways.[52]

In *Rowdy Rathore*,[53] a thief named Shiva (Akshay Kumar) falls in love with Paro (Sonakshi Sinha). But Shiva is forced to care for a police inspector's young daughter, who has mistaken Shiva for her father. To protect his new ward and avenge the inspector, Shiva takes on the persona of Officer

Vikram Rathore[54] and convinces Paro to help him care for the girl. Thus, the man who initially resisted the idea of domestic life as husband and father finds fulfillment in family and in upholding the law rather than skirting it. When criminals kidnap Paro and the child, Paro simultaneously comforts the girl and intimidates their captors. She pins them in an ominous glare and warns them that Shiva will massacre them. Together, Shiva and Paro combat evil,[55] in keeping with their allegorical referents: the destroyer, Shiva, and his consort, Parvati.

Parvati herself has also taken on the role of the eradicator of evil when manifested as Kali or Durga. In these incarnations, she transforms from a beautiful goddess to a fearsome creature able to swallow legions of sinners to purify the world. In the revenge fantasy *Anjaam*[56] (Consequence), Shivani (Madhuri Dixit) is an air hostess victimized by an obsessed admirer, Vijay (Shah Rukh Khan). Vijay stalks her; kills her husband, sister, and daughter; and frames her for attempted murder. After years of torment, Shivani kills a violent prison guard who caused the miscarriage of her second child. She then slaughters her brother-in-law, who had abused her sister. Then she murders the corrupt police inspector who attempted to rape her. In her final attempt to avenge her loved ones and seek retribution for her own suffering, Shivani attacks Vijay. Although Vijay viewed her as an object of desire and servitude, Shivani scorns the system that failed her and delivers justice herself. Just as Parvati manifests as Kali or Durga, Shivani transforms from a happy wife, mother, and sister into a fierce, uncontrollable vindicator.

Mother India[57] contains multiple levels of symbolism, as the heroine stands in for Radha, Sita, and Parvati at various points in her life. The film begins with the wedding of Radha (Nargis), a bride who becomes a dutiful daughter-in-law, mother, and—after a series of tragedies and challenges—the matriarch of the village. After her mother-in-law mortgages their farm to an unscrupulous moneylender to finance Radha's wedding, Radha and her husband, Shyamu,[58] struggle to repay the loan. But an accident disables Shyamu, and he abandons the family out of shame. For the rest of her life, Radha searches and longs for her husband to return.

This separation also underscores Radha's function as a Sita-type heroine. The opening scene of *Mother India*[59] shows an older version of Radha holding a handful of earth to her face as a chorus sings about "Dharti Mata," or Mother Earth. This refers not only to Dharti, the goddess symbolizing Earth as the female half of the Earth-Sky duality, but also to Sita, whose name means "furrow" because she was found by her father when he was plowing a field.[60] Sita raised two sons (Lav and Kush), and *Mother India*[61] focuses on Radha raising her sons, Ramu and Birju. At one point, Radha runs through a blazing field to find Birju (Sunil Dutt), who is hiding from a mob because the moneylender's daughter has falsely accused him of harassment. This mirrors Sita's trial by fire upon her return to Ayodhya.

Despite his righteous fury at the unethical behavior of the moneylender and his daughter, Birju's vengeance drives him to indefensible actions: he murders the moneylender and kidnaps his daughter. Radha, having promised the villagers to defend the honor of herself, her family, and her village, shoots Birju. In killing him to restore order, she symbolizes Parvati, a goddess who embodies the nurturing, protective nature of a mother as well as a purifying, destructive force. The goddess personifies complementary opposites (e.g., virgin/mother, nurturance/destruction, reassurance/terror, life/death), representing the totality of existence.[62]

CHALLENGING AND REINFORCING STEREOTYPES

Characters who deviate from archetypes also fall outside mainstream notions of Bollywood "heroes" and "heroines." For women, "bad" equates to individualism and hedonism, concepts often conveyed symbolically by association with Western decadence: smoking, drinking, dancing in nightclubs, and falling in and out of love quickly.[63] The "dancing girl" character drew upon a story from the *Mahabharat* in which Menaka, a nymph, dances temptingly to test the will of a meditating sage: "This beauty and dancing skill align her with sex rather than love, body rather than emotion, frivolousness and willfulness rather than obedience, creating tearing dichotomies that divide 'independent dancing woman' from 'motherly, domesticated woman.'"[64] The Menaka archetype has been used as a basis for courtesan, vamp, and "item girl" characters, all of whom contrast with Sita-based heroines.

For decades, the Bollywood "vamp" was differentiated from the heroine by the vamp's choice of Westernized, glamorous, and often revealing outfits.[65] This wardrobe symbolized excess, materialism, and sin.[66] However, by the 1980s and 1990s, economic changes such as globalization, a growing middle class, and the cultivation of consumerism blurred boundaries between the vamp and the heroine. Instead, the "college girl" could wear Indian and Western clothing to demonstrate independence and cosmopolitanism,[67] while adhering to moral codes such as safeguarding her virginity and obeying paternal authority.[68]

Antonio Gramsci's critical theories regarding hegemony allowed scholars to view popular film as a venue for trying to resolve contradictory beliefs.[69] The Gramscian conceptualization of hegemony also allowed scholars to view the "Westernized" elements of Bollywood movies not as evidence of cultural imperialism, but as indicative of the complex interaction of global and local forces within societies. This globalization perspective takes into account consumers' interpretation of imported content, highlighting the range of alternative meanings a text can carry when consumed in different cultural contexts.[70]

In recent years, traditional notions about marriage and ideal husbands/wives have been challenged by unorthodox representations of matrimony and romantic relationships that exist outside of the bonds of wedlock. As Amita Nijhawan (2009) explains:

> "Wife" characters (good women) in current-day Bollywood can simply be girlfriends, can dance, can wear revealing clothing, be assertive and independent and can tend toward Menaka archetypes in their bodies, movements and clothing. Sita archetypes, in dress and deportment, and even in narrative and textual elements, are becoming less and less visible in Bollywood as global youth culture in collusion with capitalist consumption is becoming the audience of choice.[71]

Just as Indian audiences are trying to reconcile religious and secular values in their own lives, Bollywood is also attempting to expand the boundaries of expression and convention without offending the sensibilities of Indian audiences. This is perhaps why many Bollywood films send conflicting messages about people who challenge social norms. For example, female characters associated with modernity are often vilified[72] and punished,[73] or else they are reformed and made to appreciate the conventional duties of a wife.

Although Bollywood has increasingly come to rely upon Hollywood for plots and to associate modern, secular values with Western commodities, Indian filmmakers and audiences still create meanings based on *their* cultural experiences as Indians. The tensions created by this interpretive consumption allow for a dialogue about societal institutions. Bollywood hits as well as Indian independent films have dealt with important issues challenging mainstream depictions of women, with varying degrees of acceptance. For instance, *Fire*[74] narrated a lesbian relationship between characters named Sita (Nandita Das) and Radha (Shabana Azmi); protestors decried the film as an attack on Hinduism.[75]

Baabul[76] (Father) and *Water*[77] addressed the ostracism of widows in India, who have been scorned, exploited, and forced to renounce worldly pleasures and colorful adornments. Under Hindu tradition, widows are considered bad luck.[78] In *Water*, director Deepa Mehta highlighted the oppression of widows in 1938 India. Widows had three options after the death of their husbands: burning with their deceased husbands, leading a life of self-denial in an ashram, or marrying their late husband's younger brother.[79] In the film, the women lack control both politically and materially, lacking agency to make decisions or support themselves financially.[80] Hindu fundamentalist groups protested the film and ransacked the set, delaying production for four years and forcing Mehta to shoot under a fake title in another location.[81]

Lajja[82] (Shame) advocated for women's rights by highlighting the unfair treatment of Sita after she and Ram returned to their kingdom in the *Rama-*

yan. Sita endured a literal trial by fire when people speculated that she may not have remained faithful to her husband during her captivity. In the film, Janki (Madhuri Dixit), an actress who had been portraying Sita in a stage dramatization of the *Ramayan*, lambasts Ram's unwillingness to defend his wife against unfounded gossip. Enraged at what they consider to be a bastardization of the religious text, the audience assaults Janki. Other characters[83] suffer abuse, humiliation, demands for dowry, assault, and murder simply due to their status as women in a patriarchal society.

Sita's abduction by the demon king, Raavan, is also a motif for depicting male and female ideals of heroism. In *Khal Nayak*[84] (Villain), a police officer, Ganga (Madhuri Dixit), is kidnapped by a crime boss, Ballu (Sanjay Dutt). She pines for her police inspector boyfriend, Ram (Jackie Shroff), to rescue her. Although Ram does attempt to save Ganga, viewers see Ballu as Ganga's savior when he surrenders to defend her against charges of aiding a criminal.

Raavan[85] also draws upon Sita's captivity. In this film, Ragini (Aishwarya Rai), the wife of police superintendent Dev (Vikram), is kidnapped by Beera (Abhiskek Bachchan), an intrepid outlaw. Beera is attempting to avenge the rape of his sister at the hands of corrupt police, which makes him a sympathetic antihero. But in this film, Dev—whose name comes from the Sanskrit word for "God"—accuses his own wife of infidelity to trick her into revealing Beera's hideout.

Both *Khal Nayak*[86] and *Raavan*[87] rendered the Ram-based character ineffectual or even culpable in the victimization of the Sita-based character. But these films challenge religious narratives by repositioning the villainous character inspired by Raavan as a more complex, redeeming figure. In both films, the heroine is defined by her ability to endure hardship, remain faithful to her husband, and demonstrate her purity in the face of doubt. She is infallible and indefatigable, but her heroism ultimately is proven through her suffering.

With regard to depictions of matrimony, Bollywood seems unwilling to relinquish entirely the traditional religious values in a predominantly Hindu society. While Hindu religious archetypes, narratives, and symbolism remain a vital part of Bollywood films, audiences seem open to examining the struggle to reconcile the religious and secular aspects of life in society.

A Shift toward the Secular

Contemporary movies have suggested that Bollywood is branching out from religion-based characterizations to include diverse representations grounded in secular ways of life. Research regarding Indian attitudes about arranged marriage has indicated that young adults tend to favor arranged marriages over free-choice marriages, believing that their parents would be mindful of their best interests, and that even those young adults who did fall in love still valued their parents' approval of the relationship.[88] Therefore, Bollywood has, in general, reflected audiences' beliefs about the ideal circumstances in which marriages ought to take place.

However, recent Bollywood movies have begun to move away from traditional depictions of marriage and spousal fidelity, touching on controversial themes of premarital sex and infidelity. *Salaam Namaste*[89] (a combination of Muslim and Hindu greetings) carried the tagline, "Let's get to know each other," and dealt with a couple who live together before marriage. Nikhil (Saif Ali Khan), who prefers to be called Nick, and Ambar (Preity Zinta) meet in Australia, where they have moved to distance themselves from parental pressures. Nick suggests they share a house as they pursue their budding romance. Ambar becomes pregnant, and Nick—in an unheroic manner for Bollywood—suggests she "kill" the fetus. He waits in the car outside an abortion clinic and is dismayed when Ambar does not undergo the procedure. Ambar, infuriated and disillusioned at Nick's attitude, refuses to leave the house they shared. During the pregnancy, Nick undergoes a change of heart and proposes to Ambar in the delivery room.

This movie challenged traditional gender roles and notions about marriage on several levels. Ambar has rejected her parents' attempts at arranging her marriage and lives a cosmopolitan, individualistic lifestyle that is nearly nonexistent in Bollywood depictions of femininity.[90] Nick dodges his responsibilities until the very end of the film. Throughout the movie, the characters face the conflict between their cultural upbringing and their rejection of social norms while living abroad. Interestingly, their secular lifestyles are again aligned with Western commodities and locations, since the story takes place in Australia rather than India.

Several filmmakers have released unconventional movies about complicated relationships and flawed protagonists. They include *Omkara*,[91] an adaptation of William Shakespeare's *Othello*; *Nishabd*[92] (No Words), inspired by *American Beauty*; and *Kabhi Alvida Naa Kehna*[93] (Never Say Good-Bye), about infidelity. Of note is that these films provide no reasons for the characters' imperfections. Whereas Bollywood films normally included an explanation for a character's flaws, such as a childhood tragedy or injustice, more recent films let characters' actions speak for themselves. Filmmakers have justified these omissions as realistic depictions of human behavior—it is simply in the characters' nature to err.[94]

CONCLUSION

This analysis describes some of the Bollywood films that have utilized or subverted religious archetypes to convey messages about gender and culture.

Readers should recognize this as an exploration of an influential genre that merits more attention. As more scholars recognize Bollywood films as artifacts worthy of analysis, substantial insights could be revealed about how audiences of various backgrounds and economic classes use the movies to negotiate alternative meanings and articulate cultural values regarding gender. Although attention has been paid to the patriarchal nature of Indian society and the reinforcement of hierarchical power structures in Bollywood films, scholars also need to examine the ways that popular Hindi cinema has allowed diverse groups to transcend social divisions and share a cultural experience.

We encourage educators to include international cinema in the classroom to enhance students' awareness of the nexus of gender and culture. Though undergraduate-level textbooks increase knowledge and sensitivity toward gender, they lack insight into how to understand specific behaviors through the lens of intercultural communication. LaRay M. Barna identified six impediments to intercultural communication that could also apply to gender communication: (1) assumed similarity, (2) language, (3) nonverbal cues, (4) preconceptions and stereotypes, (5) tendency to evaluate, and (6) anxiety.[95] Students could learn to avoid the tendency to evaluate another culture as inferior or to view individuals solely in terms of national identity, improving intercultural communication and fostering respect for diversity.

If all communication is intercultural,[96] then studying portrayals of heroes, heroines, relationships, and matrimony in Hindi popular cinema only suggests the kinds of exploration that scholars or educators could undertake. Given the extensive global diffusion of Bollywood as a form of entertainment and as an educational tool for diasporic audiences, researchers should probe the conventions and beliefs reinforced by these movies—as well as the innovative ways filmmakers and audiences can voice *their* opinions and reshape their societies.

NOTES

1. Sameera Khan Rehmani, "Putting Words in Her Mouth: Gender and Discourse in Contemporary Hindi Cinema," *Amity Journal of Media & Communications Studies* 1 (2011): 24–28.

2. James Chapman, *Cinemas of the World: Film and Society from 1895 to the Present* (London: Reaktion Books, 2003).

3. Tejaswini Ganti, *Bollywood: A Guidebook to Popular Hindi Cinema* (New York: Routledge, 2013).

4. Chapman, *Cinemas of the World*.

5. Veena Naregal, "Bollywood and Indian Cinema: Changing Contexts and Articulations of National Cultural Desire," in *The Sage Handbook of Media Studies*, ed. John D. H. Downing et al. (Thousand Oaks, CA: Sage, 2004), 517–39.

6. Shamita Das Dasgupta, "Feminist Consciousness in Woman-Centered Hindi Films," *Journal of Popular Culture* 30 (1996): 173–89.

7. Naregal, "Bollywood and Indian Cinema."

8. Karim H. Karim, "Mapping Diasporic Mediascapes," in *The Media of Diaspora*, ed. Karim H. Karim (New York: Routledge, 2003), 1–17.

9. Dasgupta, "Feminist Consciousness."

10. K. Moti Gokulsing and Wimal Dissanayake, *Indian Popular Cinema: A Narrative of Cultural Change* (Stoke on Trent, UK: Trentham Books, 2004).

11. Ibid.

12. Becky Michele Mulvaney, "Gender Differences in Communication: An Intercultural Experience," in *Intercultural Communication: A Global Reader*, ed. Fred E. Jandt (Thousand Oaks, CA: Sage, 1994), 221–29.

13. Larry A. Samovar and Richard E. Porter, *Intercultural Communication: A Reader*, 2nd ed. (Belmont, CA: Wadsworth, 1976), 26.

14. Laurie P. Arliss, *Gender Communication* (Englewood Cliffs, NJ: Prentice Hall, 1991).

15. Julia T. Wood, *Gendered Lives: Communication, Gender, and Culture*, 9th ed. (Belmont, CA: Wadsworth, 2011): 320.

16. Ibid., 323.

17. Katy Gilpatric, "Violent Female Action Characters in Contemporary American Cinema," *Sex Roles* 62 (2010): 734–36.

18. Sarah Eschholz and Jana Bufkin, "Crime in the Movies: Investigating the Efficacy of Measures of Both Sex and Gender for Predicting Victimization and Offending in Film," *Sociological Forum* 16 (2001): 655–76.

19. Michael Rich, "Music Videos: Media of the Youth by the Youth, for the Youth," in *The Changing Portrayal of Adolescents in the Media since 1950*, ed. Patrick E. Jamieson and Daniel Romer (New York: Oxford University Press, 2008), 78–102.

20. Kay Deaux, Ward Winton, Maureen Crowley, and Laurie L. Lewis, "Level of Categorization and Content of Gender Stereotypes," *Social Cognition* 3 (1985): 145–67.

21. T. William Altermatt, C. Nathan DeWall, and Emily Leskinen, "Agency and Virtue: Dimensions of Female Stereotypes," *Sex Roles* 49 (2003): 631–41.

22. Peter Glick and Susan T. Fiske, "An Ambivalent Alliance: Hostile and Benevolent Sexism as Complementary Justifications for Gender Inequality," *American Psychologist* 56 (2001): 109–18.

23. C. Nathan DeWall, T. William Altermatt, and Heather Thompson, "Understanding the Structure of Stereotypes of Women: Virtue and Agency as Dimensions Distinguishing Female Subgroups," *Psychology of Women Quarterly* 29 (2005): 296–405.

24. Julia T. Wood, *Communication, Gender, and Culture* (Belmont, CA: Wadsworth, 1994).

25. Ibid.

26. Ibid.

27. Ibid.

28. Wood, *Gendered Lives*.

29. Rehmani, "Putting Words in Her Mouth."

30. Conversely, *Pativrata* denotes a woman who is chaste and faithful to her husband. *Sati Savitri* is another term for such a woman, and it derives from a tale in the *Mahabharat* about a woman who saves her husband from fated death through her cleverness, devotion, persistence, and sacrifice.

31. *Raavan*, directed by Mani Ratnam (India: Madras Talkies, 2010).

32. *Kabhi Khushi Kabhie Gham*, directed by Karan Johar (India: Dharma Productions, 2001).

33. Nilufer P. Medora, "Mate Selection in Contemporary India," in *Mate Selection across Cultures*, ed. Raeann R. Hamon and Bron B. Ingoldsby (Thousand Oaks, CA: Sage, 2003): 209–30.

34. Ibid.

35. Gregory Booth, "Religion, Gossip, Narrative Conventions and the Construction of Meaning in Hindi Film Songs," *Popular Music* 19 (2000): 125–45.

36. Although some Western scholars have described Hinduism as a polytheistic religion, Hindu gods and goddesses may be better understood as manifestations of a supreme divinity. Hinduism is an ancient way of life that encompasses a broad range of beliefs, practices, and

methods of worship combining faith with intellect, philosophy and morality, and respect for other belief systems and religions.

37. Devdutt Pattanaik, *The Goddess in India: The Five Faces of the Eternal Feminine* (Rochester, VT: Inner Traditions, 2000).

38. Gokulsing and Dissanayake, *Indian Popular Cinema*.

39. Carol E. Henderson, *Culture and Customs of India* (Westport, CT: Greenwood Press, 2002).

40. Clare M. Wilkinson-Weber, "Tailoring Expectations: How Film Costumes Became the Audience's Clothes," *South Asian Popular Culture* 3 (2005): 135–59.

41. *Hum Saath-Saath Hain*, directed by Sooraj R. Barjatya (India: Rajshri Productions, 1999).

42. Ibid.

43. Gokulsing and Dissanayake, *Indian Popular Cinema*, 78.

44. *Hum Saath-Saath Hain*.

45. Janmashtami is a Hindu holiday marking the birth of Krishna.

46. *Hum Aapke Hain Koun . . . !*, directed by Sooraj R. Barjatya (India: Rajshri Productions, 1994).

47. Ibid.

48. Ram and Sita are considered avatars of Vishnu and Laxmi, as are Krishna and Radha. Hinduism recognizes the cyclical nature of time as well as reincarnation as part of a birth–life–death cycle, so many of the gods and goddesses in Hindu narratives are incarnations of the divine, manifesting in different forms in different epochs.

49. Brahma, the creator, and Vishnu, the preserver, complete a Hindu trinity, though each male deity has a female consort who serves essential and complementary functions. Brahma's wife is Saraswati, the goddess of wisdom and creativity. Vishnu's wife, Laxmi, is the goddess of prosperity. When a woman marries, she is often referred to as *ghar ki Laxmi* (the Laxmi of the house), as her arrival is thought to bring wealth to the family of the groom in the form of dowry, children, her work in maintaining the household, or by bringing good luck.

50. Pattanaik, *The Goddess in India*.

51. Parvati is also worshipped as Shakti, signifying her power, and as Gauri, referring to her fair complexion.

52. Ibid.

53. *Rowdy Rathore*, directed by Prabhu Deva (India: UTV Motion Pictures, 2012).

54. In an added bit of allegory, the story of the demise of police inspector Vikram Rathore reveals that he was shot during a Dussehra celebration. The Hindu holiday commemorates the victory of Ram over Raavan, the clever demon king. Furthermore, the name *Vikram* refers to Ram, who is an avatar of Vishnu, the preserver/protector. The name may be translated as "brave" or "victorious," and it derives from the Sanskrit words for "victory of Ram," though on a more spiritual level, it may symbolize one who takes purposeful action.

55. The archetypes and religious narratives in Hinduism may be interpreted in several ways, as variations in regional practices of worship or details of plot and characterization influence the meanings of stories that have been transmitted orally or recorded and translated from various epic texts. For example, many of the narratives transcend the simple binaries of good versus evil to address conquering the consciousness, ego, temptation, greed, and other mental vices. As with the narratives of most religions, Hinduism allows for contemplation of these narratives on literal and philosophical levels, so the stories contain multiple levels of meaning.

56. *Anjaam*, directed by Rahul Rawail (India: Shiv-Bharat Films, 1994).

57. *Mother India*, directed by Mehboob Khan (India: Mehboob Productions, 1957).

58. The name of Radha's husband, *Shyamu*, is a variation of *Shyam*, another name for Krishna.

59. *Mother India*.

60. Dharti is the mother goddess, representing the Earth and the literal and symbolic functions of culturing, nurturing, and sustenance. Sita is the daughter of Bhumi (another name for Dharti or Prithvi) as well as an incarnation of Laxmi. Dharti and Laxmi are both depicted as consorts of Vishnu. Thus, *Mother India* shows land and wealth as crucial to the preservation of Radha's life, family, community, and honor.

61. *Mother India*.

62. Joseph Campbell, *The Hero with a Thousand Faces* (Novato, CA: New World Library, 2008).

63. Gokulsing and Dissanayake, *Indian Popular Cinema*.

64. Amita Nijhawan, "Excusing the Female Dancer: Tradition and Transgression in Bollywood Dancing," *South Asian Popular Culture* 7 (2009): 100.

65. Wilkinson-Weber, "Tailoring Expectations."

66. Ibid.

67. Manas Ray, "Nation, Nostalgia, and Bollywood: In the Tracks of a Twice-Displaced Community," in *The Media of Diaspora*, ed. Karim H. Karim (New York: Routledge, 2003), 21–35.

68. Wilkinson-Weber, "Tailoring Expectations."

69. Andrew Willis, "Cultural Studies and Popular Film," in *Approaches to Popular Film*, ed. Joanne Hollows and Mark Jancovich (Manchester, UK: Manchester University Press, 1995), 173–91.

70. John Storey, *Inventing Popular Culture: From Folklore to Globalization* (Melden, MA: Blackwell Publishing, 2006).

71. Nijhawan, "Excusing the Female Dancer," 108.

72. Dasgupta, "Feminist Consciousness."

73. Gokulsing and Dissanayake, *Indian Popular Cinema*.

74. *Fire*, directed by Deepa Mehta (Canada/India: Trial by Fire Films, 1996).

75. Senthoran Raj, "Igniting Desires: Politicising Queer Female Subjectives in *Fire*," *Intersections: Gender and Sexuality in Asia and the Pacific* 28 (2012), http://intersections.anu.edu.au/issue28/raj.htm (accessed May 29, 2013).

76. *Baabul*, directed by Ravi Chopra (India: B. R. Films, 2006).

77. *Water*, directed by Deepa Mehta (Canada/India: Deepa Mehta Films, 2005).

78. Lauren J. DeCarvalho, "Head above *Water*: Applying Nussbaum's 'Capabilities Approach' to Deepa Mehta's 2005 Film," in *Media Depictions of Brides, Wives, and Mothers*, ed. Alena Amato Ruggerio (Lanham, MD: Lexington Books, 2012), 77–89.

79. Ibid.

80. Ibid.

81. Elisabeth Bumiller, "Film Ignites the Wrath of Hindu Fundamentalists," *New York Times*, May 3, 2006, http://www.nytimes.com/2006/05/03/movies/03wate.html?_r=1& (accessed May 31, 2013).

82. *Lajja*, directed by Rajkumar Santoshi (India: Santoshi Productions, 2001).

83. *Janki* is a synonym for *Sita*, as it derives from her father's name, *Janak*. Characters named Maithili, Vaidehi, and Ramdulari were also featured as primary characters, and those names are also synonyms for *Sita*. These names reference the capital city of Sita's father's kingdom (Mithila in Videha) and Sita's status as Ram's beloved.

84. *Khal Nayak*, directed by Subhash Ghai (India: Mukta Arts, 1993).

85. *Raavan*.

86. *Khal Nayak*.

87. *Raavan*.

88. Medora, "Mate Selection."

89. *Salaam Namaste*, directed by Siddharth Anand (India: Yash Raj Films, 2005).

90. Shanti Kumar and Michael Curtin, "'Made in India': In between Music Television and Patriarchy," *Television & New Media* 3 (2002): 345–66.

91. *Omkara*, directed by Vishal Bhardwaj (India: Big Screen Entertainment, 2006).

92. *Nishabd*, directed by Ram Gopal Varma (India: RGV Film Factory, 2007).

93. *Kabhi Alvida Naa Kehna*, directed by Karan Johar (India: Dharma Productions, 2006).

94. Kaveree Bamzai, "In Praise of Imperfection," *India Today International*, July 10, 2006, 46–47.

95. LaRay M. Barna, "Stumbling Blocks in Intercultural Communication," in *Intercultural Communication: A Reader*, 4th ed., ed. Larry A. Samovar and Richard E. Porter (Belmont, CA: Wadsworth, 1985), 330–38.

96. Adrian Holliday, Martin Hyde, and John Kullman, *Intercultural Communication: An Advanced Resource Book* (London: Routledge, 2004), xv.

Chapter Twelve

The Enduring Woman

Race, Revenge, and Self-Determination in Chloe, Love Is Calling You

Robin R. Means Coleman

The 1934 horror film *Chloe, Love Is Calling You* perhaps unintentionally presents its central character Mandy—an aged, Black, Voodoo priestess on a destructive path of revenge against a White family—as a heroine. As is often characteristic of Voodoo-themed horror films (e.g., *Black Moon*, 1934; *Ouanga*, 1936), *Chloe* locates the monstrous within Blackness.[1] In the film, Blacks are "known" to sacrifice their White enemies, "cut[ting] out their hearts." Their sadism, according to the film, is quite literally a recipe for disaster, a soup of "savagery, gin, mumbo jumbo, and drum beats" that, to White observers, sounds like a "menu at Sing Sing [Correctional Facility]." As a result, in such horror films, Whites and Whiteness benefit from being marked against the immoderation of Blacks and Blackness. Whites in these portrayals, then, are to be perceived as beleaguered and long-suffering as they work to shoulder the proverbial White man's burden in the midst of an overprofusion of Black dysfunction. In contrast, all parts of Blackness are represented as wicked. Black men are physically and sexually predatory, Black religions are an abomination, and Black communities are a breeding ground for all manner of cultural deficiency that must be overseen and managed. Even Black music, particularly the use of drums, is terrifying, with the bass of the beat characterized as an ominous signifier of race warfare, thereby striking fear in Whites.[2] However, I suggest that *Chloe*, specifically in its presentation of Mandy, may be read counter to these oft-inscribed horror tropes that inform readings of Blackness. I argue here that the seemingly evil-doing Mandy can be read as working against type, personifying a heroine as she, a lone Black woman, enters into battle against subjugation by White male adherents of Jim Crow.

Released in 1934 during the bloodthirsty Jim Crow era, and distributed largely to Black audiences through neighborhood theaters in predominantly Black communities—even though Blacks were not the imagined target audience—*Chloe* asks viewers to easily interpret race as a function of dramatis personae, with Whites' motivations and actions as virtuous, and Blacks as whole and full embodiments of the flagitious. However, Mandy complicates portrayals of Blacks as antiheroes, as her character can be read against (stereo)type, resulting in a unique set of heroic norms in which vengeance, race pride, and disrupted gender role expectations become new touchstones for courage. This rearticulation of heroism ultimately pushes back against (albeit not entirely successfully) the constraints placed on representational Blackness. Here, I consider horror films' construction of Black heroines, positing that they can be perceived in Mandy, as well as in more contemporary figures such as Sugar of the Voodoo-themed horror film *Sugar Hill* (1974), to illuminate the conditions under which valorous women are born and their motives coerced. Toward this end, I draw on and extend Carol Clover's popular conceptualization of the heroine, the undaunted "Final Girl"—she is the one who does not die, not only surviving a monster's terror, but often defeating the monster herself.[3] I argue that Black women in horror must be much more than "final." Rather, their heroism is tied to their ability to be "enduring"; that is, Black women must be resilient battlers of evil who not only live on, but live on to *continue to fight* monstrous forms of systemic (racial) injustices. As such, I conclude that Black heroines are frequently "Enduring Women" caught in a ceaseless war against commonplace monsters who are frequently tied to symbolic structures of Whiteness and maleness and who threaten these women's self-worth, bodies, relationships, and Blackness.[4]

REFORMING MANDY AS HEROINE

In the film, Mandy (Georgette Harvey, a Black actress) is "mammy" to her young adult, mixed-race daughter Chloe (Olive Borden, a White actress).[5] Mandy and Chloe have led a hardscrabble life in exile, having fled a Louisiana turpentine plantation when Chloe was but an infant in the wake of the lynching of Sam, Mandy's Black husband, after he gets into an altercation with the plantation's owner, the Colonel (Frank Joyner). Mandy and Chloe return to the plantation more than fifteen years later where Mandy revisits the racism-fueled atrocities that savaged her marriage: "Thar' is. Thar' is. That old hangman's tree. Where them White folks killed my Sam and the bloodhounds tore him to pieces." Mandy then talks to her beloved Sam, assuring him that her Voodoo "sure is talking" and that she will avenge his death by using black magic against the Colonel: "Here I is, Sammy. Here is your Mandy come back to put curses on the Colonel and them White folks."

In the film, Mandy is not to be regarded as a sympathetic figure. Rather, she is portrayed as physically and emotionally contemptible—crippled, obese, missing teeth, sexually unappealing, and hardened by hate. By contrast, the vivacious Chloe, who is phenotypically White, is deemed a beautiful "sweet little somebody." Still, Chloe is both loved and scorned for possessing Black blood. A pair of White women, after discerning Chloe's features, reject her in disgust by proclaiming, "She's so dark." A pair of drunken Black men, depicted as carnivorous predators, harass and manhandle Chloe as one of them, armed with a gun, spews at her: "High yellow, they always was my meat." However, things are not entirely desperate for Chloe, as love is indeed "calling" her (as the film's title suggests) in the form of two suitors. The first, whom Chloe does not love, is Jim (Philip Ober, a White actor), a doting "colored" man (his White appearance goes unacknowledged in the film).[6] The second would-be lover, whom Chloe desperately desires, is Wade (Reed Howes), a knightly White man who is newly hired to manage the plantation. Chloe is accused by Jim of loving Wade, whom she has known for only one day, because she is inadvisably listening to her "White blood speaking." Initially winning Wade's love by passing for White, Chloe heartbreakingly finds herself spurning him because of her racial secret and social taboos against racial mongrelization.

The film takes a dramatic turn when Mandy's life story comes into full frame. Sam's murder is but one tragedy that befell Mandy. Around the same time as Sam's lynching, Mandy and Sam's infant daughter also dies. It is in these two temporally connected, cataclysmic events that Mandy makes her monstrous decision—Mandy hides the death of their (Black) baby and steals the Colonel's infant daughter out of revenge for Sam's murder. The Colonel is led to believe that his child, "Betty Ann," died in a drowning accident. Renaming the Colonel's daughter "Chloe," Mandy claims Betty Ann as her own and runs away, only to return years later when the girl is unrecognizable to her family. The story ends gloriously for Chloe who is proven to be neither "so dark" nor "high yellow" but simply, happily White. After her crimes, Mandy, however, is merely lucky to be alive.

While portrayals of heroines in literature and popular culture tend to follow a Proppian-esque narrative structure of overcoming obstacles (tension), sacrifice (intervention), and redemption (transformation) to ultimately emerge as heroic in the salvation of others and/or the self, Mandy can be viewed as complicating this morphology when read against what is seemingly the expected, inscribed meaning in the film. Because the deaths of Sam and the infant at the plantation are in the distant past and are not depicted, and because the inhabitants of the plantation are shown as leading relatively normal lives with Whites and Blacks each in their respective places, the film's narrative asks the viewer to consider that the introduction of conflict comes through the return of Mandy who is enshrouded in criminality and lies. First, Mandy disrupts the idyllic plantation bringing her Voodoo spells to cast on the Colonel. For example, she leaves tree branches and a Voodoo doll on the Colonel's doorstep; the branches, or "switches," mean he is going to "get whipped," while the doll's heart is pierced by a shard of wood, thereby signaling death. Additionally, Mandy's anger and actions function to excite and poison the plantation's Black men who have taken to secretly staying up all night and "Voodooing" in the swamps. And finally, Mandy brings with her the long-deceived Chloe, a tortured young tragic mulatto figure who is pitiable in every sense, from initially suffering from a lack of true romantic love to the denial of an "authentic" racial and familial identity.

Most significantly, the film's narrative asserts that Mandy is stunningly irrational because the Colonel *himself* did not kill Sam. Rather, after the Colonel abruptly fires Sam for some unknown reason—"don't remember what for"—thereby provoking Sam's ire, Sam realizes the trouble he is in (after all, this is a period when Blacks cannot even shake hands with Whites). Sam runs away only to be pursued by a hanging party of Whites. The Colonel breezily reports it was "folks who tracked him down and lynched him." Hence, Mandy's rage is to be seen as misplaced since she would "never listen to any explanation" that Sam was lynched, not by the Colonel, but by his proxies.

Chloe was seen by Black audiences within the 1930s context of a strict, legal U.S. racial caste system (i.e., Jim Crow) often enforced through extralegal deadly violence, as well as during a mainstream media climate that abided by and reflected the separatist racial sentiments of the time. The era of Jim Crow not only legally restricted Blacks' access to public positions such as juries and employment and to public facilities such as transportation and recreation outlets such as movie theaters, but it also controlled the more mundane aspects of Black life such as who Blacks could play games of checkers with (not with Whites) and whose hair they could cut (never a White woman's). Mainstream media reinforced and recirculated the devaluing of Blacks, through films featuring White actors in blackface, press news reports harboring anti-Black sentiments, greeting cards invoking the word *nigger* in their cheery messages, and even school textbooks with anti-Black propaganda. *Chloe* falls in line with this racial milieu, asking viewers to regard Mandy as despicable, anything but heroic or righteous in her quest for justice.

Indeed, Mandy is depicted as part and parcel with the likes of other rogue Blacks in *Chloe* such as Mose (Augustus Smith), a thief and a Voodooist who attacks Chloe. By contrast, Mandy is quite the opposite of Ben (Richard Huey), the Colonel's doting and loyal Black servant who between whipping up the South's "best" mint juleps investigates Mandy, uncovering her Voodoo plot. It is his sleuthing which reveals that Chloe and the Colonel are victims of an abhorrent fraud.

While *Chloe* presents a confining articulation of Blackness that makes it difficult to access alternate, resistant readings of Mandy, those readings are attainable nonetheless. Judith Fetterley, in writing about American fiction, observes that resistant readers may find themselves engaged not with an invitingly open, polysemic text, but with a "closed system [that] cannot be opened up from within but only from without. It must be entered into from a point of view which questions its values and assumptions and which has its investment in making available to consciousness precisely that which the literature wishes to keep hidden."[7] In writing specifically about media images, Liza Bakewell similarly posits that texts inevitably tap and tax our consciousness as "images do things":

> Far from being ineffective and inert, images are powerful tools. We employ them regularly to do many things: to make promises, issue commands, or simply state. We use them to establish group solidarity, give visibility to our opinions, and create boundaries around ourselves and others. We use them in ways that reveal much about who we are: our class, gender, culture, age, personality, temperament, mood, and morals. . . . If images are actions, it follows that images must have an effect on us.[8]

As such, out of the dysfunction and deviance of Blackness that *Chloe* has enveloping Mandy emerges images of a hidden heroism, punctuated by a history and climate of racism. These racialized images "do things," such as providing evidence of a new Black/female visibility that does more than provoke fear, but seeks condonation. To be sure, *Chloe* is a horror film that is steeped in violent themes (though profoundly tame by today's standards). Hence, that Mandy works to terrorize is not outside of the tolerable for the genre.

The depiction of a Black woman as deeply affected by racial injustice, tormented by death, and one who seeks to retaliate against Whites for the purpose of reclaiming her power is striking. To put it another way, Mandy resides at the junction of crushing subjugation and self-determination. Mandy is distinguishable for what compels her to step out and fight back against Jim Crow even at her own great peril. Mandy's quest for retribution begins as personal, but it should also be understood as a horror-style kind of race pride moment. Provisioned with the power of Voodoo, Mandy is engaged in armed defense, battling against racist vigilantes shielded by Jim Crow laws. She is a Stokely Carmichael–esque figure, a sort of Black Power forerunner, in her rhetoric and approach. Mandy is certain that an unmitigated nonviolent response to violent bloodlust is no response at all. Over thirty years after the release of *Chloe* and in the face of still-persistent Jim Crow laws, Carmichael, a Black Power movement leader, posited that a nonviolent approach in the face of racist hate crimes was one "Black people cannot afford and a luxury White people did not deserve."[9] Mandy's race conscious-ness and her view that the placation of attacking Whites is intolerable is not entirely dissimilar. For example, she, with Mose in agreement, concludes that there is no other choice but to strike back after "what they've done to me and mine."

To be sure, the juxtaposition here is predictive, calling attention to the potential readings of *Chloe* and how, even through the imaginative, it can reflect on the United States' past (and present) race problems. It should be made clear that where the fictional Mandy and real-life adherents of Black Power ideologies differ is not only in how they respond to injustice, but when. For those invested in the ideologies of Black Power, self-defense of home and family in the face of attack is prescribed. However, for Mandy it is revenge that is curative. That Mandy acts after the fact, after Sam's death, rather than attempting to stave off his death in the midst of a lynching party and ravenous hounds does not attenuate her response of defending herself against oppression.

In addition to Mandy's enacted race politics, her heroism encompasses her ability to both recoup her desirability and to slip between gender roles. Mandy is desexualized in *Chloe*, reduced simply to a renegade "Voodoo negress" who, though once a doting wife and mother, is tragically denied both identities. Mandy makes clear that she is no bowing mammy, while also working to recover some semblance of her past selfhood. Though robbed of her treasured Sam, she refuses to be entirely divorced of him or their love, thereby reasserting their eternal bond: "Here I is, Sammy. Here is your Mandy." Similarly, the absconding of Chloe functions to allow Mandy to get her daughter back while simultaneously getting back at those who wronged her. With Chloe at her side, and through the return to Sam's grave site, Mandy attempts to re-form herself as wife and mother.

However, as things again fall apart around her, starting with the discovery that Chloe is Betty Ann, Mandy's identity as reluctant and childless widow reemerges. In response, Mandy assumes a new role in the form of the Haitian male *loa* (spirit) Baron Semedi. In Haitian Vodou and folklore, Baron Seme-di (aka Samedi) is an alarming figure dressed in a top hat and tuxedo coat-tails, sometimes fashionably sporting sunglasses. His face is painted in shades of black, white, and gray to create the skeletal look of the dead. He is a keeper of the dead, watching over bodies and cemeteries as well as shep-herding one's death journey, be it down to the underworld or trapped as the undead (a zombie).[10] Mandy's Baron Semedi is a *bocour* (witch doctor), an extension of her initial identification as a Voodoo "negress" who first at-tempts to curse the Colonel with a Voodoo doll. It is in the symbolic form of a powerful, mystical Black man that Mandy seeks to get her revenge against the Colonel once again by attacking Chloe.

When Chloe learns that she is in fact White, she wastes no time dismissing Mandy, donning the finest of attire, gliding easily around the plantation's looming mansion, reestablishing her relationship with Wade, and assuming her place at the top of the racial hierarchy. In her final act of erasing Chloe and separating herself from her "mammy" Mandy, Chloe quickly returns to her birth name, "Betty Ann," proclaiming that she never wants to hear "Chloe" again. Hurt by Chloe's perfunctory rejection, it is Mandy's view that the time for Voodoo dolls is over. As Baron Semedi, Mandy ensnares Chloe yet again, but this time evoking potent black magic in a ritual in which Chloe is to be sacrificed. Bound and laid out on an altar, Chloe is surrounded by hordes of shirtless men whose drumming-induced frenzied dancing is a mix of exuberance and violence as they prance and jump, but also tangle with each other. Finally, one of them, under Mandy's command, emerges from the fray to plunge a knife into Chloe's heart. Of course, Mandy as Baron Semedi is prevented from meting out "his" vengeance against a White woman. Chloe is rescued by Wade. Her plan doomed, Mandy once again loses her selfhood. She is no longer a wounded woman reempowered by capably slipping into the traditionally male role of Baron Semedi. Rather, her passions and the evil of Voodoo have, the viewer is told, literally transformed her into a monstrosity, and ultimately into the newer role of kidnapper, attempted murderer, and felon.

THE MAKING AND RACING OF HEROINES: THE FINAL GIRL VERSUS THE ENDURING WOMAN

"The functions of monster and hero are far more frequently represented by males and the function of the victim far more garishly by females," observes Clover.[11] Increasingly, however, women have taken on more compelling roles in horror films, surmounting narratives of the (sexy) distressed damsel, to intervene in the male character bailiwick. Robin Means Coleman notes that breakthrough roles for women in horror, particularly White women, became a trend in the 1970s as women stepped into the role of heroine and "triumphantly battled against monsters (e.g., Laurie Strode in *Halloween* [1978])," or they daringly took a turn at being "frightening evil (e.g., Pamela Voorhees in *Friday the 13th* [1980])."[12] In examining the generic changes taking place for women during this time, Clover theorizes that the decade saw horror's most innovative heroine (perhaps to date) in the "Final Girl," a portrayal markedly different in form and function from past characterizations. "She alone looks death in the face," explains Clover, "[and] she alone also finds the strength either to stay the killer long enough to be rescued (ending A) or to kill him herself (ending B)." Possessing the qualities of fighter *and* of survivor, the Final Girl is *a* survivor in that she is an adroit combatant in the face of evil. The Final Girl is also *the* survivor, outlasting the monster's attack and being the only one to do so.[13] Final Girls are not only fighters and survivors, but they "do so with ferocity and even kill the killer on their own."[14] Indeed, it is worth highlighting that not only does the Final Girl take down the (male) monster, but she often does so without help from a male savior.

The horror genre has offered up some classic White Final Girls. Teenager Laurie Strode (Jamie Lee Curtis) of *Halloween* evolved from average baby-sitter to heroic Final Girl, displaying her resourceful fighter qualities by, first, leading her charges to safety. Then, when she is pinned down in a closet by the bloodlusting, psychopathic Michael Myers (Tony Moran), she deftly fashions a weapon out of a coat hanger to go head-to-head with the monster. Finally, the teen single-handedly stays the monster until a gun-toting adult arrives. Similarly, Ellen Ripley (Sigourney Weaver) of *Alien* (1979) showed off her survivor abilities through sharp cunning and directorship skill—"Shut up and let me think!"—to single-handedly destroy an unstoppable predator who had annihilated all those around her.[15] Most notably, for the White Final Girl (movie franchises notwithstanding), the end of her showdown with the monster also means the restoration of the ordinary—"When their fight with the monster is over, their lives return to stasis. Ripley sleeps peacefully after she ejects the alien. Laurie Strode's quiet, suburban life can return to nor-mal."[16]

However, Coleman theorizes that the Black Final Girl of the 1970s devi-ates significantly and meaningfully from the Strodes and the Ripleys. White Final Girls are depicted as generally unavailable sexually, representing a significant departure from previous sexy and sexualized treatments of wom-en in horror (e.g., Helen Grosvenor [Zita Johann] in 1932's *The Mummy*, Ann Darrow [Fay Wray] in 1933's *King Kong*). Armed with knives and other weaponry, White Final Girls present a reversal of the symbolic phallus, with them literally and metaphorically sticking it in and to the monster.[17] By contrast, Black women in horror have seduction—lips and hips—as a key component of their arsenal. Black women often lure the monster to its im-pending doom through provocative dress, innuendo, and teasing promises of lust-filled encounters (e.g., *Sugar Hill*, 1974). Markedly, though both the White and Black Final Girl heroically work to defy death, each battles very different monsters. While Whites tend to go up against some sort of supernat-ural boogeyman, Blacks' battle is often with something much closer to home in the form of racism and corruption. "In this regard," writes Coleman, "there is no going to sleep once the 'monster' is defeated as the monster is often amorphously coded as 'Whitey,' and Whitey's oppressions are here to stay."[18] These oppressions are typically a range of discriminations and exploitations, from police brutality; to the corruption of Black communities with an infusion of guns, drugs, and prostitution; to overt racism. With complete freedom from "Whitey" and bigotry out of reach, the Black Final Girl becomes an Enduring Woman as she must be resilient and prepared to fight for autonomy and justice in the long haul. The Enduring Woman must be a durable, persevering soldier in an everlasting battle against persecution and discrimination in which she recognizes that total victory is elusive.

Recalling the significance of a performance of sexuality and sensuality to the identity of the Enduring Woman, her additional hallmark is that she is a woman who not only fights for her survival, but also on behalf of her man. The (always heterosexual) Enduring Woman's male partner is often terrorized, if not slain, by a White male tormentor (monster) for trying to bring an end to oppression or for attempting to start a new, clean life away from criminality. Given these parts of the definition—(1) a defiant warrior in a struggle against inequalities and (2) seeking retribution on behalf of her man—certainly *Chloe*'s Mandy materializes as an early Enduring Woman. More, Mandy's progeny may be seen in Diana "Sugar" Hill (Marki Bey), the quintessential Enduring Woman, as represented in the zombie horror film *Sugar Hill*. In the film, the sexily attired, provocatively named Sugar fights to avenge the death of her boyfriend, Langston (Larry Don Johnson), who is killed by Morgan (Robert Quarry), a "Whitey" head of a criminal syndicate who profits from a vast network of criminal enterprises that exploit and victimize Blacks. Langston is murdered for refusing to pay into Morgan's protection racket.

In the film, Langston is one of many victims. For example, in one scene, Black dockworkers are told that they must pay a kickback to get a job unloading a cargo ship filled with bananas (of course). When the men balk, one is punched, and all are threatened with unemployment and starvation until they pay up. Following in the footsteps of Mandy, Sugar turns to Voodoo, calling upon an army of resurrected slaves-turned-zombies led by none other than Baron Semedi. The zombies rise up to aid Sugar in securing retribution. They kill off everyone in the crime syndicate involved in the death of Sugar's boyfriend and in the exploitation of the Black community. Sugar is present for the killings, even proclaiming to one of her zombies' quarry, "Hey, Whitey, you and your punk friends killed my man. . . . I'm not accusing you, honk, I'm passing sentence. . . . And the sentence is death!"[19]

Sugar Hill's deployment of Voodoo differs from *Chloe*'s. *Chloe* exploited Voodoo by further stoking Whites' repulsion of Blacks during Jim Crow, with the effect of inspiring antebellum nostalgia and fantasy for when "good" Black slaves were mythically viewed as docile, obedient workers laboring under difficult conditions without complaint. By contrast, released in 1974 at the height of the Black Power movement and made with a Black audience in mind, *Sugar Hill* reflects a different, albeit similarly distinct sociopolitical climate. The film responds rebelliously to myths around Black religion and the effects of slavery through depictions of ennobled Black strength and agency. Thanks to Voodoo and an empowered army of undead slaves, Sugar is able to restore equanimity and lawfulness to her Black community even as it is clear that there are still more "Whiteys" out there. In this regard, Sugar and Baron Semedi succeed where Mandy as Baron Semedi fails.

Mandy and Sugar are not unusual. The popular 1970s film actress Pam Grier similarly played an Enduring Woman in the vampire horror film *Scream, Blacula, Scream* (1973) in her role as Lisa. Lisa is reluctantly drawn into battle, again with the help of Voodoo, to fight to save not one, but two Black men from racism-tied vampirism. *Scream* is a sequel to *Blacula* (1972) in which an eighteenth-century African prince, Mamuwalde (William Marshall), is infected with vampirism by a 1780s version of Whitey in Count Dracula. Dracula is depicted as a virulent racist who is amassing enormous wealth through the ultimate Black exploitation—the slave trade. Imprisoned in a coffin, Mamuwalde makes a much-belated twentieth-century journey through the Middle Passage to the United States. *Blacula* and *Scream*, then, function to expose the lingering effects of racism. Through a "sucking the blood out of the Black community" metaphor, *Scream* lays bare how the legacy of slavery continues to victimize Blacks centuries later. In 1974, Pam Grier would again play a kind of Enduring Woman in the nonhorror film *Foxy Brown* in which (the again provocatively named) Foxy exposes herself to all manner of brutality, including beatings and rape, to lure in and kill White male members of a drug syndicate who murdered her good-guy, government-agent boyfriend. This particular form of Enduring Woman outside of horror—a sexy, leading heroine seeking revenge, though on occasion with the support of savior men—can be seen in several films, including *Cleopatra Jones* (1973), *Coffy* (1973), and *Sheba, Baby* (1975).

Yet it is the heroines of horror, as seen in *Chloe, Sugar Hill*, and *Scream, Blacula, Scream*, that are most recognizable as Enduring Women who are not only left to pick up the pieces of their broken personal lives and communities, but must fight twin monsters of racist/misogynist White men and systems of oppression sans saviors. Victory celebrations for the successfully heroic Enduring Woman is fleeting, as her "triumphant walk into the sunset promises to take her, not toward a life of peace, but right back into the midst of rogue police, sexist men, and 'the Man' who is exploiting her Black community."[20]

CONCLUSION

For all of the inroads the Mandys, Sugars, and Lisas made in reimagining the heroine, that progress has not always been pervasive as evidenced by recent horror representations of Black women. Black women have experienced a symbolic annihilation as seen in model-singer Grace Jones' portrayal of the vampire Katrina in 1986's *Vamp*, in which the mute Katrina is quite literally seen (as eye candy) but not heard. Likewise, in *Queen of the Damned* (2002), the powerful vampire Queen Akasha (portrayed by singer Aaliyah) is narrowed to the sexual obsession of the vampire Lestat, a rock singer (Stuart Townsend). These examples represent a general trend in mainstream horror in which Black women tend to be reduced to window dressing. Nevertheless, the trajectory of Black women's contribution to the horror film has slowly continued to evolve into increasingly complex and diverse characterizations. For example, the low-budget, limited-release horror film *Def by Temptation* (1990) witnesses a grandmother coming to the rescue of her grandson whose life is threatened by a demonic temptress. The straight-to-DVD horror film *Holla* (2006) casts women as equally hardy villains and heroes. The big-budget, big-screen projects, too, are catching up as witnessed in *Alien vs. Predator*, aka *AVP* (2004), which features Alexa Woods (Sanaa Lathan) as not only a formidable intellect and resourceful heroine, but also the rare Black Final Girl. Yet it is the 2005 blockbuster British horror film *The Descent* that perhaps more robustly shows what women in complex roles imagined *for women* can bring to horror, rather than women dropped into a man's role. With an all-female, racially and ethnically diverse cast (with the exception of the cannibalistic, cave-dwelling monsters), *The Descent* shows women as strong and weak, hero, antihero, and victim. More, this portrayal was done with purpose, as its director Neil Marshall explains: "Originally the cast was going to be mixed gender, but then it occurred to my business partner that horror films almost never have a female cast. So we made all the cavers women. But, it was important that I didn't make them clichés: either ladettes or victims. I talked to my female friends as I wrote and got advice— basic advice, but it worked."[21] Indeed, from *Chloe* to *The Descent*, horror reveals that women can work effectively and even heroically in the genre.

One hallmark of the horror genre is that it is predicated on pushing boundaries. It challenges our assumptions and plays with taboos. (In)famously, horror has invited its viewers to identify with its monsters, be it a forlorn rampaging giant ape, a man assembled by a mad scientist from the parts of murderers, or a debonair and bloodthirsty aristocrat. In this lineup, there must certainly be room for a Mandy who, unbowed by racism, proclaims, "The thunder's gonna growl and the lightning's gonna rain. And the devil's gonna walk on a White man's grave!" Mandy has wreaked havoc in snatching Betty Ann and trading in Voodoo, but she sees one small victory in living to tell the tale. The film draws to a close with the Colonel ordering that Mandy be arrested and taken to the sheriff, explaining, "We don't want any lynching." While it can be presumed that if Mandy tries to run away like her Sam attempted to do, she too would find herself on the "old hangman's tree," the point is that she is not lynched. Rather, Mandy works to evidence the Final Girl/Enduring Woman continuum—still in mourning, angry, unrepentant, and in possession of her Voodoo power, but facing punishment, she survives her encounter with the monster.

While the Enduring Woman finds her most provocative treatment in the genre of horror, she need not be confined there. Unlike the Final Girl whose primary goal is to survive the monster, for the Enduring Woman such a showdown is only half the battle. Indeed, her battle is only just beginning as her existence is overtly political, directing our attention to complex structural and systemic injustices that plague societies and can frustrate us all. Even as debates are ongoing about whether U.S. society is turning toward a post–civil rights, postfeminist, postracial, and postidentity one in which larger structural and legal problems have been knocked back,[22] the Enduring Woman is evidence that claims of "post" eras are premature.

Race in media, observes Daniel Bernardi, is "neither fictional nor illusion."[23] In this regard, if the dictum of the synergistic relationship between art and life holds some measure of verity, then there will continue to be ample opportunity to identify heroines at the intersections of mythical/popular culture and the social/mediated world. More, it can be expected that Blackness, specifically, will continue to be an excessive signifier through which Whiteness, the cultural dynamics of oppression, and even, ultimately, self-determination and agency are understood. With this in mind, the Enduring Woman will find that she is not in a "post" moment, free of oppressions plaguing her communities. Rather, her actions will continue to be attention-getting, promising to find space in the fictional/popular, and nonfictional public, spheres for decades to come.

NOTES

1. *Chloe, Love Is Calling You,* directed by Marshall Neilan (1934; Narbeth, PA: Alpha Video Distributors, 2005), DVD. Gary D. Rhodes, *White Zombie: Anatomy of a Horror Film* (Jefferson, NC: McFarland, 2001). See also Peter Noble, *The Negro in Films* (New York: Arno Press and the *New York Times*, 1970), 8. In the United States, the spelling of the Haitian religion Vodou was vulgarized, becoming "Voodoo." Here, I use the spelling "Voodoo" just as the films discussed in this chapter do. In doing so, I work to distinguish between popular culture's fictional depiction of the (evil) rituals performed by Blacks as informed by Haitian Vodou or the West African form Vodun. American horror films typically depict Louisiana as the wellspring of the religion in the United States, calling it "Voodoo."

2. R. J. Smith, *The One: The Life and Music of James Brown* (New York: Gotham Books, 2012). Smith writes of the fear of Blacks' drumming: eighteenth-century South Carolina colonial legislators "frantically pass the Slave Code of 1740, banning chattel from using or even owning drums. The overall law forbade drums and swords alike, making clear how South Carolina viewed the instrument: as a weapon." (p. 2).

3. Carol Clover, *Men, Women, and Chainsaws: Gender in the Modern Horror Film* (Princeton, NJ: Princeton University Press, 1992).

4. For the original conceptualization and discussion of the Final Girl versus the Enduring Woman, see Robin Means Coleman, *Horror Noire: Blacks in American Horror Films from the*

1890s to Present (New York: Routledge, 2011), 131–42. See also Clover, *Men, Women, and Chainsaws*.

5. It is not explained in the film how Mandy accounted for Chloe's biracial identity.

6. The race casting of the actors is important here as the Motion Picture Production Code or "Hays Code" governing film's moral content prohibited on-screen romantic race mixing—miscegenation—between White women and Black men. As such, the White actress Borden shared scenes with the White actors Ober and Howes. As a result, Ober's light skin color had to be explained away as "colored."

7. Judith Fetterley, *The Resisting Reader: A Feminist Approach to American Fiction* (Bloomington: Indiana University Press, 1978), xx.

8. Liza Bakewell, "Image Acts," *American Anthropologist* 100 (1998): 22–32.

9. Kwame Ture and Charles Hamilton, *Black Power: The Politics of Liberation in America* (New York: Vintage, 1992).

10. Paul Christopher Johnson, "Secretism and the Apotheosis of Duvalier," *Journal of the American Academies of Religion* 74 (2006): 420–45.

11. Clover, *Men, Women, and Chainsaws*, 12.

12. Coleman, *Horror Noire*, 131.

13. See Clover, *Men, Women, and Chainsaws*, 39; and Coleman, *Horror Noire*, 131.

14. Clover, *Men, Women, and Chainsaws*, 37.

15. *Alien*, directed by Ridley Scott (USA, 1979).

16. Coleman, *Horror Noire*, 131.

17. Ibid., 132.

18. Ibid.

19. *Sugar Hill*, directed by Paul Maslansky (USA, 1974).

20. Coleman, *Horror Noire*, 132.

21. Donald Clarke, "Subterranean Sick Blues," *Irish Times*, July 9, 2005, http://search.proquest.com/docview/309909336?accountid=14667 (accessed July 9, 2005).

22. See Jasmine Nichole Cobb, "No We Can't!: Postracialism and the Popular Appearance of a Rhetorical Fiction," *Communication Studies* 62 (2011): 406–21.

23. Daniel Bernardi, *The Persistence of Whiteness: Race and Contemporary Hollywood Cinema* (New York: Routledge, 2008), xvi.

Chapter Thirteen

The Dark, Twisted Magical Girls

Shōjo *Heroines in* Puella Magi Madoka Magica

Lien Fan Shen

> Although there is nothing special per se about being shōjo, the ability to view the world with the eye of shōjo positions the person involved outside accepted gender categories . . . and through her consciousness of this, she will be astounded to discover a world that permits anything imaginable. —Takahara Eiri [1]

In 2009, Tsutomu Nakagawa, the head of the cultural affairs division at the Japanese Ministry of Foreign Affairs, launched a "cultural ambassadors" program, exploiting the popularity of Japan's cute culture overseas. In addition to the two anime ambassadors appointed in the previous year—Hello Kitty and Doraemon—three young girls, one school uniform girl, one street-fashion style, and one Lolita-style girl, were appointed as cultural envoys to present Japan. Nakagawa said, "We want people abroad to know these kinds of people exist in Japan and to feel close to them." [2] The three girls looked younger than their actual age; one of the outfits was a miniskirt with school uniform, and one was a polka-dot shirt highlighted with ribbons and pink color. The last one, the Lolita-style girl, dressed like a Victorian doll in voluminous frilly skirts, was Misako Aoki. While addressing the Japanese Lolita style as "princess-like," she said, "When the girls were in our childhood, most of us wanted to be a princess, and I am trying to keep that heart forever." [3]

Although the girl ambassadors may not be referred to as *shōjo* since they are in their twenties, they certainly look like they are in their teens. *Shōjo* literally means a girl or girls' flavor in Japanese, and signifies women between seven and eighteen years old. This diplomatic effort employs *shōjo* to promote Japan's cuteness in the global consumer society. Christine Yano pinpoints that cuteness and *shōjo* have been increasingly interconnected, and the characteristics of both are almost interchangeable in the Japanese public's mind.[4] The three girls, rather than being subjects of *shōjo*, are diplomatic symbols presenting qualities of innocence, sweetness, adorable imperfection, and bright and cheerful spirits to stimulate global consumption of Japanese cute products. While Nakagawa ironically asserts that these cute ambassadors are real people in Japan, the most significant quality of *shōjo* is its disconnection from reality.

With the aesthetic qualities of cuteness, *shōjo* has played important roles in the symbolic system of anime since the 1960s. *Shōjo* is an anime genre, a variety of representation in narratives, a targeted group of consumers and viewers, and a particular way of seeing and thinking. Almost every popular anime has a few *shōjo* heroines. For example, the prominent anime directors Hayao Miyazaki and Satoshi Kon, whose works are widely analyzed and discussed in scholarly writings and by fans, often use *shōjo* heroines to lead stories. While anime's Western counterpart, Disney, reaffirms gender norms through its female characters, scholars argue that anime's representation of *shōjo* heroines empowers female viewers to challenge these norms.[5] This chapter examines the portrayals of *shōjo* heroines in the magical girl anime *Puella Magi Madoka Magica*, paying attention not only to *shōjo* heroines' roles in destabilizing gender norms but also to the self-reflective subject of *shōjo*, who fully recognizes her subject self as an object in the masculine order. Constantly questing after "who am I to others?" the dark and twisted *shōjo* heroines are self-reflective in understanding their subject as one among many represented objects in the world, acknowledging the fundamental misrecognition of self-autonomy. The *shōjo* heroines in *Puella Magi Madoka Magica* may show us a way in which female subjects speak an alternative language *with* and *for* herself/itself, complicating *shōjo* subjectivity in the masculine order.

WHAT IS *SHŌJO*?

The modern concept of *shōjo* emerged in late nineteenth- and early twentieth-century Japan, when rapid economic change produced a social utility for "adolescence," a period between childhood and adulthood during which labor was trained for its role in industrial culture.[6] Originating in the Meiji period, single-sex girls' schools were established for this purpose, and they fostered high literacy among girls. The homogenous school space and the development of female readerships, including illustrative magazines and fiction specifically for female readers, constructed an identity of *shōjo* during Japan's modernization.[7]

However, such definition was rearticulated as a significant phenomenon of Japanese consumer culture in the late twentieth century. *Shōjo* plays an important role for fetishism and consumption in Japan's postmodernity. Cute but sexually appealing *shōjo* is consumed as a desirable object toward erotic purity, virginity, and innocence—the qualities revolving around nonthreatening schoolgirls and Lolita girls. Rather than being a subject or an identity, *shōjo* becomes a mass-produced commodity for the male gaze in which the subject does not exist but only functions as a ritualized sign of male fetishism.

On the other hand, *shōjo* with excess cuteness also functions as a surplus, an embodiment of female subjects' constant lack, which drives consumption of cute products in Japan. With the notions of innocent, sweet, adorably imperfect, emotional, and impulsive, and the potential to escape from reality, *shōjo* manifests unreachable beauty, nostalgia for the past (youth), freedom from adult sexuality and family duty, and disconnection of social status for women. Consuming *shōjo*/cute products, such as Hello Kitty goodies and other Sanrio's commodities, brings surplus enjoyments over standard satisfactions because the female subject would never approach the pure qualities *shōjo* manifests.

Although *shōjo* signifies a surplus value by taking advantage of female representation, and the *shōjo* subject is reproduced as a consuming subject herself, scholars pinpoint that *shōjo* has certain subversive potentials that may provide ideological contestation in society. Japanese scholar Susan Napier indicates that the qualities of *shōjo* do not only include ultrafemininity, passive, dreamy, and sometimes even ditzy, but also potentials for change, growth, and compassionate empowerment. She asserts, "Because *shōjo* are not adults, they can perceive things that those in control of society cannot; because they are not young men they see things that those who will someday rule society cannot see."[8] Anthropologist Jennifer Robertson also argues that *shōjo* connotes potentially disruptive sexuality between puberty and marriage. Functioning as an alternative gender among the roles of "daughters," "wives," and "mothers" in patriarchal society, *shōjo* implies heterosexual inexperience and homosexual experience. It is presumably homosexual because the emotional life of *shōjo* is essentially narcissistic, and thus the sexuality of *shōjo* is self-referential and homogenous, employing nonreproductive value.[9]

Unique to Japan, *shōjo* can be considered one important discourse of female subjectivity and male gaze that may affect the global scope of gender politics. Far from being perceived as a political movement or resistance of dominant power, *shōjo* engenders fetishism in Japan's consumer society but paradoxically provides a space for "a quiet, private protest heard only by other girls."[10] The qualities of *shōjo* (the uncertainty, the instability, the potentials for change and growth), the in-between places *shōjo* takes (child and adult, puberty and marriage, homosexual and heterosexual), and the fact that *shōjo* is never about reality, never to be in control, and never to be the ruling group, may empower an imperceptible subversion of gender norms and dominant power.

A *SHŌJO* GENRE: MAGICAL GIRL ANIME

It is fair to say that anime portrays a large number of *shōjo* as an object of fetish eroticism. Largely based on Japan's cute culture and the *shōjo* phenomenon, *shōjo* characters in anime enable both male and female viewers to consume her as a commodity, to maintain the fantasy of *shōjo*, and to reproduce a social reality for *shōjo* subjects. Anime utilizes *shōjo* heroines to attract both female and male audiences. But beyond mere consumption, *shōjo* has a distinctive place in the world of anime since she is outside of the heterosexual economy, privileged by possessing an imagination free from social constrictions. For example, Hayao Miyazaki has mostly *shōjo* heroines to lead the stories of his films. His works in the 1980s, such as *Nausicaä and the Valley of the Wind* (1984), *Castle in the Sky* (1986), *My Neighbor Totoro* (1988), and *Kiki's Delivery Service* (1989), feature cute, sweet, cheerful, bright, and brave *shōjo* heroines. His later works portray a more diverse representation of shōjo heroines: *Princess Mononoke* (1997) has a fearsome wolf *shōjo*; *Spirited Away* (2001) presents a daughter's journey to save her parents (the *shōjo* is no longer free from family obligation); and the *shōjo* heroine is turned into a wrinkled old crone in *Howl's Moving Castle* (2004). Through the lens of Miyazaki's *shōjo* heroines, his *anime* gives viewers the freedom to dream, to be unproductive, to be useless and silly, to indulge in fantasies of flight and adventure, and to explore the potential of change.[11]

Among all *shōjo*-related anime products and practices, this chapter pays attention to a particular anime genre, magical girls (*mahō shōjo*), which always features *shōjo* heroines who have superpowers to fight evil and to protect others. Most anime works of magical girls target a young female audience. *Sally, the Witch* (1966) is the first magical girl anime and is considered the first *shōjo* anime. The story featured a witch princess who left the Land of Magic to live a human life. Her magic power was used to solve various problems in her life, but her identity must be kept secret. It was extremely popular with its target audience, running for 109 episodes, and then the story continued twenty years later, in a sequel run of eighty-eight additional episodes.[12] *Sally, the Witch* developed some notable features to attract female audiences in the 1960s, and these features, being reinforced and reiterated, became common elements in magical girl anime. Plots and thematic settings of magical girl anime include the following:

- The plots are led by and centered on *shōjo* heroines as magical girls.
- Magical girls tend to keep their superpower and identity secret.
- For magical girls to obtain their power, they must undergo a transformation sequence and magical phrases with an enchanted object, such as a pendant, a wand, a compact, or a ribbon.
- Some magical girls transform into a more mature and sexualized female body when they use their power.
- A magical servant, usually a talking catlike animal, always offers advice in combat and helps train magical girls.
- The causes of fights are idealistic, such as love, peace, and hope. Instead of fighting against antagonists as in male-oriented *anime*, the causes of fights often center on friendship, relationships, and well-being for all.
- The stories include both heterosexual romance as well as same-sex love and relationships.
- Narratives are generally emotion oriented, upbeat, cheerful, and intensely personal in nature.

In addition to common plots and thematic settings, the visual style of magical girl anime is heavily influenced by *shōjo* manga since both target young females as the ideal audience and readership. Entailing the aesthetic of cuteness, common elements in the visuals of magical girl anime include the following:

- Thin and fragile lines and figures.
- Common depictions of characters with round face, long hair, big eyes, and accessories of ribbons and candy buttons on the outfits.
- Expressive backgrounds, consisting of disoriented flowers, nebulous shapes, and abstract patterns to express emotion and personality.
- Bright and shiny color compositions, jelly red, yellow, pink, and sky blue, to give an imagery of warmth, cheerfulness, and high spirit.

Popular magical girls, for example, *Card Captor Sakura* and *Sailor Moon*, involve learning to harness their superpower, while the nature of the power remains vague and unclear. The magical girl protagonists must use props to obtain their superpower and fight against evil. Both anime were adapted from popular *shōjo* manga in the 1990s, and both put emphasis on emotions of and interpersonal relationships among characters. Featuring cute, bright, cheerful characters and imagery with exciting action scenes, both anime attracted not only young female viewers but also had high crossover popularity in both female and male demographics.[13] For male audiences, these adorable, whimsical, clumsy, early adolescent magical girls represent excessive qualities of cuteness to evoke viewers' affections. Jason Thompson argues that in the first decade of the 2000s, male affections toward magical girls received a commercial interest in manufacturing and animation production.[14] This line of interest shifts anime consumption from the focus of storytelling to fetishizing adorable and cute anime characters. Whereas the stories and plots of magical girl anime target young female viewers, character designs of magical girls are often hypersexualized, costumed with tight shirts and miniskirts. By adding more action and fights with a male audience in mind, and animating magical girls' transformation sequences with a certain level of *shōjo* nudity, magical girls with their excessive cuteness demand notice and adoration from viewers, regardless of their sex or age.

COMPLICATING MAGICAL GIRLS: *PUELLA MAGI MADOKA MAGICA*

Puella Magi Madoka Magica (Mahō Shōjo Madoka Magika) is a twelve-episode television series, directed by Akiyuki Shinbo and written by Gen Urobchi. As with many other popular anime, three series of *manga* adaptations, a novelization, a video game, and feature films were released after the anime aired. The anime series won Animation Kobe awards, Newtype Anime awards, and the grand prize for animation at the Japan Media Arts Festival in 2011. The Blu-ray Discs of all volumes sold over fifty thousand copies during the first week and mostly at the top of the sales record.[15]

The story follows all common elements of magical girl anime at first glance: A small, cute, catlike talking creature, a Messenger of Magic, whose name is Kyubey, offers a deal to chosen *shōjo*. This catlike creature can grant these *shōjo* a wish, but in exchange they must become Magical Girls and use their given power to defeat Witches, mysterious entities that feed upon emotions, hopes, and dreams of normal people. The story centers on five *shōjo* heroines whom Kyubey chooses to be Magical Girls: Madoka Kaname, Homura Akemi, Sayaka Miki, Mami Tomoe, and Kyoko Sakura. Each has a symbolic color (Madoka is pink, Homura is dark purple, Sayaka is sky blue, Mami is yellow, and Kyoko is jelly red) and a Soul Gem of her color through which she obtains her magical power to fight Witches. Character designs are extremely cute: each *shōjo* has a different style of long hair, round face, big eyes, shiny accessories, ribbons, and candy buttons on her outfit based on her symbolic color.

However, given adorable *shōjo* characters with the aesthetic of cuteness, *Puella Magi Madoka Magica* paradoxically posits an antimagical girl anime. Beyond cute characters and candy-colored costumes, the story of *Puella Magi Madoka Magica* portrays the dark side of life rather than providing an upbeat and cheerful entertainment. In most magical girl anime, *shōjo* heroines transform with sparkles and happiness, fighting back evil forces, but the evil is never actually "evil." Viewers rarely, if ever, are exposed to criminal instances; rather, they are given abstract ideas of evilness against which *shōjo* heroines fight. However, in *Puella Magi Madoka Magica*, plots of poverty, murder, suicide, and violence are not sugarcoated by flowers and metaphors, and hopes and dreams are harshly destroyed. It delves into the mechanics of magical girl anime and reconstitutes them by throwing in dark twists and revelations systematically. In the following sections, three important motifs are examined in *Puella Magi Madoka Magica* through the lens of (anti)magical girl anime and within the *shōjo* phenomenon.

Becoming Magical Girls

First, unlike other *shōjo* heroines who fight against evil due to their heroic and cheerful nature, the *shōjo* characters in *Puella Magi Madoka Magica* become Magical Girls because they contract with Kyubey in exchange for a wish. The deals with Kyubey suggest reference to Goethe's famous tragic hero, Faust, making an arrangement with the devil, implicitly revealed in random texts, direct quotes, appearances and symbols of Withes, and music from the opera of *Faust*. Their wishes involve solving real problems in life, such as poverty, death, and recovery from injuries. Contrary to conventional magical girl anime, in which protagonists happily accept their superpower, *shōjo* heroines are reluctant to become Magical Girls in *Puella Magi Madoka Magica*. Beyond the sugarcoated visual elements, cute character designs, and candy-colored costumes, exchanging a wish by serving as Magical Girls brings certain consequences and ethical dilemmas. One of the consequences is that while granting the *shōjo*'s wishes and power, Kyubey takes control over their souls and places them into Soul Gems. The ethical dilemmas vary depending on each *shōjo*'s circumstance, but revolve around whether one should use her wish for a selfish purpose or for most people's well-being, and if she uses her wish to benefit someone, whether she should expect a reciprocal return from that person.

The protagonist Madoka is an ordinary high school girl, appearing shy, naïve, and insecure. Madoka has a gentle heart but low self-confidence. Becoming a Magical Girl is appealing for her because she may have power to help others. Audiences of magical girl anime would assume that soon she would acquire her magical power to defeat evil. Yet the question is brought to Madoka's attention throughout the entire course of the series: to be a Magical Girl, or not to be a Magical Girl? This question is essentially the core of the story. Just for that one wish, she would be a Magical Girl with superpower, but Madoka cannot make up her mind about that one wish. According to Jonathan Dalton, "[*Puella Magi*] *Madoka Magica* is not about Madoka's life as a magical girl, but rather her journey of understanding what it means to be one, and her discovering whether or not there is a wish that she is willing to risk her life for."[16]

Shōjo heroines must *become* Magical Girls in order to have power and to battle Witches. Madoka is *not* a Magical Girl, but she is *becoming* one. The term *becoming* is critical in this case. Becoming someone implies uncertainty, changing, and a moment that entails a virtuality of future and redirects the past. It involves acknowledgment of the self as a subject as well as reconstitutes it. It also enacts a splitting self, proliferating one's identity and putting the very idea of "I" into question. Because the protagonist Madoka never settles her wish (and thus does not transform into a Magical Girl toward the end), she must constantly question her subject self and reconstitute it. Thus viewers can no longer project a singular subject position for Madoka, but only a temporal mobility that allows Madoka to be seen as a stray of magical girls, giving her subversive potentials to destabilize the *shōjo* subject in magical girl anime.

Witches Are Magical Girls

Second, *Puella Magi Madoka Magica* challenges animation representation of women by positioning ambiguous relationships between Magical Girls (*mahō shōjo*) and Witches (*majo*).[17] Animation representation of women has been reproduced and reinforced into two contradictory roles by Disney: the beautiful princess and the evil witch, such as Snow White and the evil queen, Cinderella and her stepmother and stepsisters, and Sleeping Beauty and the evil fairy. Sleeping Beauty, Cinderella, and Snow White, pretty and young, have very limited mobility. The female's happiness is based on being loved, and to be loved she must possess sublime beauty. She needs to be saved, and she awaits love's coming. On the contrary, the evil witch, who often has an aged face and furious expression, uses magic or superpowers to transform herself in order to obtain her will against the princess. She is certainly independent (presented by the absence of friends, family, or spouse), vibrant (sometimes presented by her hysteric expression), and powerful (she defeats the prince). She is active to pursue what she wants, although this is usually what the princess has: beauty, youth, and happiness.

However, such a clear-cut distinction between Magical Girls (*mahō shōjo*) and Witches (*majo*) does not exist in *Puella Magi Madoka Magica*. The literal translation of *mahō shōjo* is "magical young women," whereas the literal translation of *majo* is "magical women." Witches, the evil forces in *Puella Magi Madoka Magica*, are not represented as old and furious women as in Disney animation. They appear in abstract forms of collage, consisting of words, symbols, photos, and drawings, relying on heavy use of stop-motion and cutout animation styles to create unsettling and otherworldly imagery. By using nonrepresentational collages and surrealist styles of animation, *Puella Magi adoka Magica* defies the binary representation of princesses and witches that takes representation of women for granted, breaking

the signifying chain of animation representations of women: princesses versus witches, good versus evil, young versus old, pretty versus ugly, and
sweet versus furious.

Later this series reveals that Witches are actually past Magical Girls.
Kyubey seeks out overly emotional *shōjo* and offers to grant any one wish in
exchange for servitude. As Magical Girls perform their power, despair con-
taminates their souls gradually, and eventually despair corrupts Magical
Girls and turns them into Witches. Kyubey, who constantly manipulates and
persuades *shōjo* to make a deal with him, asserts in episode 8, "Since this
country [Japan] calls women who are still growing up *shōjo*, for girls who are
on the way to becoming *majo* [magical women, or Witches], it is logical to
call them *mahō shōjo* [Magical Girls]."[18] In *Puella Magi Madoka Magica*,
each Witch symbolizes one common female frustration, presumably more
young females' frustration: distrust, delusion, tenacity, covetousness, ignorance, liberality, self-righteousness, craving, falling in love, vanity, being an
onlooker, and rage. Presented in abstract visual forms, this metaphor of
"Witches are Magical Girls filled with despair" may entail a feminist consciousness of *shōjo* consumption, in which the *shōjo* subject cries for a
reform of *shōjo* representation bound with the qualities of innocence, sweetness, adorable imperfection, and bright and cheerful spirits.

Magical Power Is Something in Her More than Herself

Lastly, "magical power" represents a kind of freedom through which female
viewers feel free from adult responsibility and submission, permitting a tem-
porality and possibility in magical girl anime. Whereas *shōjo* are granted
magic power as a form of female empowerment, the symbolic system of
anime posits magical girls as the Other for consumption. For a *shōjo* heroine
in magical girl anime, magical power is that something in her more than
herself on account of which she perceives herself as worthy of others' desire.
The magical power is the *objet petit a* from Žižek's perspective: it is nothing
but the Thing at the center of the magical girls' world; it is something essential that motivates *shōjo* heroines but the true form of magical power, whether or not there is one, never matters to shōjo heroines and audience; and it is
the Thing that makes consumers desire *shōjo* heroines as magical girls. In
other words, the magical power is the symbolic materialization that fills the
empty core of *shōjo* consumption and masks the fact that magical girls are
empty signs being seen through a distorted gaze in the masculine order.

Except Madoka, four other *shōjo* heroines make deals with Kyubey to
solve their problems in life or ease their tragic circumstance, are forced to
serve as Magical Girls and defeat Witches. They fight against Witches because they are told to, and they are unclear about the consequences and
reasons. For these *shōjo*, being a Magical Girl entails "something in her more

than herself" on account of which she perceives herself as worthy of others' desire. Although these *shōjo* heroines are granted magical power as a symbol of empowerment, it is given by a cute catlike creature, Kyubey. Embodying the aesthetic of cuteness, Kyubey deceives *shōjo* heroines into acquiring something in her more than herself—magical power—in exchange for his control over her soul. In other words, the aesthetic of cuteness (Kyubey) takes over control of the *shōjo*'s agency (Magical Girls' souls). Magical power is precisely the distorted gaze to render magical girls visible. For a *shōjo* subject to perceive herself worthy, she must acquire that "something in her more than herself."

Despite being the titular character, Madoka remains powerless throughout most of the story, acting more as a spectator in the series. All *shōjo* heroines have strong willpower—they want to change something terrible in their lives through their wishes, except the protagonist Madoka. Madoka is indecisive about what wish she is going to make. She does not grow and develop into a courageous heroine, and she constantly cries and mourns. She is never granted the magical power, and she is powerless in fights, needing protection from other Magical Girls. As powerless as she seems to be, Madoka does not acquire magical power—something in her more than herself—in order to perceive herself worthy. She doesn't have a prince (the story has no male protagonist), she doesn't undergo a transformation into a magical girl, and she doesn't fight Witches with her magic power. When she finally makes a deal with Kyubey, she wishes a change of the rules of the universe: a world without Witches and Magical Girls' despair. Kyubey yells, "That wish . . . if you realize this wish, then it's greater in magnitude than tampering with time! It's a violation of the principle of cause and effect itself! Do you really want to become a god?"[19] Her magical power, instead of being used in fights and functioning as an empowerment, is used to strike down the existing order and violate the principles of the universe. Madoka, a nonthreatening, cute, and shy schoolgirl, is an (anti)*shōjo* heroine who has all the qualities to be an object of male desire but directly challenges Kyubey, the embodiment of male distorted gaze masked by its excessive cuteness. Her magical power indeed reveals the masked fact—magical power is not a form of female empowerment, but materialization of the distorted male gaze that makes *shōjo* perceive herself worthy to be desired because she has "something in her more than herself."

THE SELF-REFLECTIVE SUBJECT OF *SHŌJO* HEROINES

This chapter attempts to complicate the idea that *shōjo* heroines are de facto female empowerment in magical girl anime. While this direction of argument is accurate to a certain extent, it may bypass the complexities of magical girls who function as empowerment and yet are a product for consumption. The excessive qualities of cuteness that *shōjo* and the girl ambassadors manifest permit the reinforcement of sexual differences as naturalized, inviting global consumption. Whereas magical girls with the ability of transformation imply a kind of freedom and potential through which female audiences feel free from adult responsibility and submission, the viability and commercial success of this anime genre depend upon the aesthetic of cuteness and sexually appealing *shōjo* characters.

It is precisely this contextual conflict that sets *Puella Magi Madoka Magica* apart from most magical girl anime. Positing the core theme of "to be or not to be a Magical Girl," *Puella Magi Madoka Magica* enacts reconstitution and proliferation of the *shōjo* subject, revisits animation representation between Magical Girls and Witches, and challenges the magical power as the symbolic materialization that fills the empty core of *shōjo* consumption.

Throughout examples of the dark, twisted *shōjo* heroines in *Puella Magi Madoka Magica*, we see this striking and constant quest, which is self-reflective, about who am I to others, as an understanding of subject self as an object to others. For Žižek, the subject that sees objects in the world cannot see himself or herself seeing. However, a subject can reflectively see itself, seeing itself not as a subject but as one more represented object in the world, which Žižek calls the self (versus the subject), a substance who is able to look at itself, and sees itself as alien to itself. The example of *shōjo* heroines in *Puella Magi Madoka Magica* shows us a way in which the female subject sees the self reflectively as an object and constantly speaks quietly *with* and *for* herself/itself, persistently inquiring into her/its relation with others as an imperceptible subversion of the masculine order.

NOTES

1. Takahara Eiri, "The Consciousness of the Girl: Freedom and Arrogance," in *Woman Critiqued: Translated Essays on Japanese Women's Writing*, ed. Rebecca Copeland (Honolulu: University of Hawai'i Press, 2006), 189, 193.

2. Reuters, "Japan Appoints Cute *Anime* Ambassadors," ABC News, 2009, http://www.abc.net.au/news/2009-03-12/japan-appoints-cute-anime-ambassadors/1617308 (accessed June 30, 2013).

3. "Aoki Miasako: Baby, the Stars Shine Bright's Report," YouTube video, 5:20, posted by KawaiiGirlJapan, September 23, 2010, http://www.youtube.com/watch?v=B8w-KQ6X5qI.

4. Christine Yano, "Kitty Litter: Japanese Cute at Home and Abroad," in *Toys, Games, and Media*, ed. Jeffrey Goldstein, David Buckingham, and Gilles Brougere (Mahwah, NJ: Erlbaum, 2004), 55–71.

5. Susan J, Napier, "Confronting Master Narratives: History as Vision in Miyazaki Hayao's Cinema of De-Assurance," *Positions: East Asia Cultures Critique* 9, no. 2 (2001): 467–93; Susan J. Napier, "When the Machines Stop: Fantasy, Reality, and Terminal Identity in *Neon Genesis Evangelion* and *Serial Experiments Lain*," *Science Fiction Studies* 29, no. 3 (2002): 418–35; Susan J. Napier, *Anime from* Akira *to* Howl's Moving Castle*: Experiencing Contemporary Japanese Animation* (New York: Palgrave Macmillan 2005); Susan Napier, "'Excuse Me, Who Are You?': Performance, the Gaze, and the Female in the Works of Kon

Satoshi," in *Cinema Anime: Critical Engagements with Japanese Animation*, ed. Steven Brown (New York: Palgrave Macmillan, 2006), 23–42; Montserrat Rifà-Valls, "Postwar Princesses, Young, Apprentices, and a Little Fish-Girl: Reading Subjectivities in Hayao Miyazaki's Tales of Fantasy," *Visual Arts Research* 37, no. 2 (2011): 88–100, argue that anime representation of *shōjo* heroines empowers female viewers to challenge social norms. Fusami Ogi, "Female Subjectivity and Shoujo (Girls) Manga (Japanese Comics): Shoujo in Ladies' Comics and Young Ladies' Comics," *The Journal of Popular Culture* 36, no. 4 (2003): 780–803, shows the subversive potentials of *shōjo* manga through its readers and writers.

6. John Whittier Treat, "Yoshimoto Banana Writes Home: Shojo Culture and the Nostalgic Subject," *Society of Japanese Studies* 19, no. 2 (1993): 353–87.

7. Emily Wakeling, "'Girls Are Dancin': Shojo Culture and Feminism in Contemporary Japanese Art," *New Voice* 5 (2011): 130–46.

8. Susan J. Napier, *Anime from Akira to Howl's Moving Castle: Experiencing Contemporary Japanese Animation* (New York: Palgrave Macmillan, 2005), 158.

9. Jennifer Robertson, *Takarazuka: Sexual Politics and Popular Culture in Modern Japan* (Berkeley: University of California Press, 1998).

10. Wakeling, "'Girls Are Dancin,'" 142.

11. Freda Freiberg, "Miyazaki's Heroines," *Senses of Cinema*, no. 40 (2006), http://sensesofcinema.com/2006/feature-articles/miyazaki-heroines/#1 (accessed June 30, 2013).

12. Patricia Duffield, "Witches in Anime," *Animerica Extra* 3, no. 11 (2000), http://www.mindspring.com/~theduffields/resume/articles/features/witches.htm (accessed June 30, 2013).

13. *Anime and Manga: Brought to You by Wikiproject Anime and Manga*, ed. Wikipedians (Mainz, Germany: Pedia Press, n.d.).

14. Jason Thompson, "Moe: The Cult of the Child," 2009, http://pulllist.comixology.com/articles/265/Moe-The-Cult-of-the-Child (accessed July 14, 2013).

15. Source from Anime News Network, "Madoka Magica 5 Is 5th BD Volume to Sell 50,000+," *Mantan Web*, 2011 (accessed July 20, 2013).

16. Jonathan Dalton, "Puella Magi Madoka Magica," in *Nerd. Writer. Game Developer*, 2013, http://blog.jonathan-dalton.com/wordpress/review-puella-magi-madoka-magica (accessed July 15, 2013).

17. In the English version, "Puella Magi" is used to translate *Mahō shōjo* to distinguish *Magical Girls* from normal usage *magical girls*. Protagonists must become "Puella Magi" in order to obtain magical power. However, "Magical Girl" is the literal translation for *mahō shōjo* and is more appropriate for the context of Magical Girls in magical girl anime.

18. *Puella Magi Madoka Magica*, episode 8, 2011.

19. *Puella Magi Madoka Magica*, episode 12, 2011.

Part IV

Heroines across Media

Chapter Fourteen

Women on the Quarterdeck

The Female Captain as Adventure Hero, 1994–2009

A. Bowdoin Van Riper

The ship's captain was the original adventure-story hero. Homer sang about Odysseus' twenty-year tour of the Mediterranean, Scheherazade regaled the Sultan with stories of Sinbad's seven voyages, and Irish priests told the story of how St. Brendan the Navigator sailed with fourteen (or seventeen, or sixty) pilgrims to the Isle of the Blessed. The men who sailed to Thule with Hanno of Carthage, or Vinland with Bjarni Herjulfson, doubtless told their own tales—long since lost—of adventures with their old skipper, just as later generations of sailors would court their listeners' interest and respect by declaring, "*I* sailed with Shackleton to Elephant Island . . . with Vanderbilt on *Ranger* . . . with Kinkaid at Leyte Gulf." The pulp science fiction stories of the 1920s and 1930s (and the more serious efforts that followed them at midcentury) traded windjammers for starships, but transposed the genre from sea to space otherwise intact. Gene Roddenberry, in the pitch that sold *Star Trek* to NBC, described the commander of the starship *Enterprise* (then named Robert T. April) as "a space age Captain Horatio Hornblower."[1]

Women commanded ships in the real world,[2] but from Homer's seventh century BCE to roughly 1990, women captains rarely walked the quarter-decks of fictional ships. The handful of exceptions were, almost exclusively, pirates: Bêlit in Robert E. Howard's pulp fantasy "Queen of the Black Coast" (1934), the eponymous Chinese pirate queen in Arthur Ransome's juvenile adventure novel *Missee Lee* (1941), and Blackbeard's (fictional) protégé Anne Providence in Jacques Tourneur's film *Anne of the Indies* (1951). "Tugboat Annie" Brennan, featured in a popular series of short stories written by Norman Reilly Raine for the *Saturday Evening Post* in the 1920s and 1930s, was a rare law-abiding exception.[3] The boisterous, sharp-tongued

Annie was primarily a comic figure, however, and Bêlit—described by Howard as "a goddess: at once lithe and voluptuous," with "white ivory limbs" and hair that "fell in rippling, burnished clusters down her supple back"— existed primarily to add exotic sexuality to the story.[4] Women captains played straight, as adventurers boldly going (like their male counterparts) where no one had gone before, simply did not exist in print or on-screen until a quarter century ago.

The emergence of women ship's captains as adventure heroes in the 1990s was notable both for its suddenness and its speed. Female commanders were, by the end of the decade, striding the quarterdecks of pirate ships, warships, and starships in force. Their ranks included Geena Davis as pirate Morgan Adams in *Cutthroat Island* (1995), the voice of Emma Thompson as Captain Amelia in Disney's animated adventure *Treasure Planet* (2002), and Kate Mulgrew as starship captain Kathryn Janeway—a gender-swapped version of Odysseus—in *Star Trek: Voyager* (1995–2001). David Weber's own "Hornblower in Space" series of science fiction novels, featuring space navy officer Honor Harrington, began with *On Basilisk Station* in 1992. Carmen Ibanez, a minor character in the novel *Starship Troopers* (1959), ends the film version (1997) as the captain of an assault transport. Back on Earth, time-warped female captains crisscrossed the seas of the late Bronze Age in S. M. Stirling's Nantucket Trilogy and helped the Allies win the Second World War in John Birmingham's Axis of Time trilogy, while Captain Amanda Lee Garrett commanded a high-tech destroyer in James H. Cobb's near-future techno-thriller *Choosers of the Slain*, and three sequels. Once vanishingly rare, women captains were suddenly abundant.

The women captains of the 1990s and the 2000s were part of a larger renaissance of female action heroes. It was in the decades bracketing the turn of the millennium, after all, that Buffy Summers slew her first vampire, Lara Croft raided her first tomb, and Sarah Connor traded her pink polyester waitress uniform for combat boots, a black tank top, and an automatic rifle. Captains Adams, Garrett, and Janeway, and their sea- and spacefaring counterparts, are, in that respect, the spiritual sisters of Zoe Washburne (*Firefly*), Evelyn Salt (*Salt*), and scores of similar characters.[5] The women captains also, however, represent a very different model of female heroism: one that grants heroines unprecedented degrees of authority, autonomy, and agency while tying them, in unexpected ways, to traditional gender roles. What follows is an attempt to move this group of fictional heroines out of the scholarly shadow of the turn-of-the-millennium female action hero and consider how their status as "master and commander" of an autonomous world is simultaneously freeing and limiting.

CAPTAINCY AND AGENCY

The female action heroes of the 1990s came from a long line of strong women characters distinguished by their mental and emotional toughness. What set them apart and made them appealing fantasy figures for audiences was an exuberant physicality that women heroes had rarely, if ever, displayed before. Rather than resort to traditional "womanly" strategies of subterfuge, misdirection, and indirect attacks, they confronted their enemies head on, confident in their ability to absorb punishment, shrug off pain, and, whether with bare hands or weapons, decisively defeat whoever stood against them. They were not merely capable of violence when their lives, or those of a loved one, were at stake—like Jill Lawrence in *The Man Who Knew Too Much* (1934),[6] Amy Fowler Kane in *High Noon* (1952), or Laurie Strode in *Halloween* (1978)—but treated it as an integral part of their jobs and, indeed, their identity. Women heroes who could confidently hold their own in a fight had been part of popular culture since the 1960s,[7] but it was in the 1990s that they began to dominate those fights—to confidently and unapologetically kick ass.

Women ship captains did their share of one-on-one ass kicking: Morgan Adams expertly wielded cutlass and flintlock, Marian Alston of the Nantucket Trilogy slew Bronze Age barbarians by the score with her samurai sword,[8] and Kathryn Janeway once stalked a gelatinous alien "macrovirus" through *Voyager*'s corridors with a phaser rifle.[9] They were not, however, defined by their skill with weapons or their physical bravery. Their agency (which was undisputed) and their power (which was considerable) rested instead on their status as "master and commander" of a vessel and its crew. The power they thus wielded was thus an extension of, not a retreat from, the single-combat skills exhibited by more familiar female heroes such as Buffy, Xena, and Nikita. The women captains carried weapons, but they commanded weapon *systems* of immeasurably greater power. They were masters not merely of themselves, but of dozens, scores, or even hundreds of capable and disciplined followers.

The power of oceangoing ships is, as Theodore Roosevelt knew when he sent the "Great White Fleet" on its world cruise, symbolic as well as actual. The presence of such a ship and its crew in waters distant from its home port is a declaration, by those whose flag flutters at the masthead, of their ability to influence events there. Commanders thus speak and act, simultaneously, for themselves, their ships, and their distant masters (whether commercial, military, or political), the roles blending insensibly into one another.[10] James H. Cobb illustrates this early in the Amanda Garrett series, in a scene where Garrett confronts a Brazilian naval officer who has just attempted to pump contaminated fuel aboard her ship. After showing the would-be saboteur a beaker filled with the evidence of his attempted crime, she pours it, slowly and deliberately, down the front of his spotless uniform, declaring, "An official protest will be filed, but until then you may inform your superiors of this. You do not ass around in this fashion with the United States Navy. You do not ass around in this fashion with the USS *Cunningham*, and you most definitely do not ass around in this fashion with *me*!"[11]

Ships' captains, as masters of both ship and crew, hold the reins of that considerable power firmly in their hands, and thus are in a unique position to influence events. Garrett, commanding first the destroyer *Cunningham* and then a squadron of inshore hovercraft, prevents an Argentine land grab in the Antarctic in *Choosers of the Slain* (1996), a nuclear attack by the Chinese government on domestic rebels in *Sea Strike* (1998), and a Rwandan-style bloodbath in West Africa in *Sea Fighter* (2000). Royal Navy destroyer captain Karen Halabi and her ship, HMS *Trident*—part of a multinational naval task force accidentally transported from 2021 to 1942 in John Birmingham's Axis of Time Trilogy—play a pivotal role in turning back an attempted Nazi invasion of Britain in 1944. In another thread from the same story, Captain Jane Willett of the Royal Australian Navy harries Japanese strongholds in the South Pacific aboard her attack submarine HMAS *Havoc*. Female starship captains play on even broader political fields: Captain Honor Harrington holds the fate of the Star Kingdom of Manticore—an interplanetary empire of the early forty-first century—in her hands in virtually every one of David Weber's novels about her. All four have the ability to change the destinies of nations with their decisions, and live with the knowledge that they can (as Winston Churchill said of Admiral John Jellicoe during World War I) "lose the war in an afternoon."

Captain Marian Alston of the Nantucket Trilogy acts on a still larger stage, making decisions that will rewrite four thousand years of human history from the ground up. Commanding officer of the USCG *Eagle*, a steel-hulled windjammer maintained by the U.S. Coast Guard as a cadet training ship, she is cruising near Nantucket when the island is transported, in situ, from the 1990s AD to the 1250s BC by an unexplained natural catastrophe known as the Event. Nantucket, now an outpost of advanced technology and representative democracy in a world of bronze swords and hereditary kingship, becomes the center of a burgeoning empire, wielding—as Portugal, Holland, and Britain did in their imperial heydays—global influence far out of proportion to its size. The *Eagle* becomes both an instrument and a symbol of Nantucket's power, and Alston, as her commander, becomes the face and voice of the Nantucketers (and their Connecticut Yankee–like dreams of improvement) throughout the Atlantic world. She speaks and acts, however, not merely for Nantucket, but for the better, brighter world—free of poverty, disease, hunger, and oppression—that it strives to bring into being.

No ship's captain, however, can match the power and influence of *Star Trek: Voyager*'s redoubtable Kathryn Janeway.[12] Marooned on the far side of the galaxy—seventy thousand light-years and a lifetime of warp-speed travel from Earth—she operated, for seven television seasons (1995–2001), far beyond the reach of her nominal superiors, making decisions whose results she knew they would never see. Janeway thus had extraordinary latitude to ignore the United Federation of Planets' canonical "Prime Directive" of noninterference in the name of a (self-determined) greater good. Beginning with the pilot episode, "Caretaker," in which she acts to prevent the conquest of the peaceful Ocampa by the bellicose Kazon, she regularly intervenes in both intra- and interspecies conflicts on behalf of the defenseless and the oppressed.[13] These interventions reach a peak in the two-part episode "Scorpion," when Janeway forms an alliance with the Borg—the *Trek* universe's gold standard for vicious aliens—in order to defeat the only species in the galaxy that scares even *them*.[14]

GENDERED SPACES AND FEMININITY

Ships are, in Western maritime culture, strongly gendered spaces. Ships themselves might be thought of as female,[15] but the crews that sailed them were, until the last decades of the twentieth century, almost exclusively male. Women who boarded ships in harbor did so in roles (visitors, prostitutes, or peddlers) that emphasized the transient nature of their presence. Women who went to sea did so under circumstances (as cargo, passengers, or guests of the captain) that tightly regulated their interactions with the ship's officers and ensured their complete social isolation from "the men."[16] Paradoxically, as a result of this rigid gender segregation, ships are worlds within which traditional gender roles are blurred. The same self-contained world is the setting for both relaxation and labor—the crews of sailing warships literally ate and slept among the great guns—and male sailors "keep" the ship (by cooking, cleaning, weaving, and sewing) as well as "work" it. The ship's officers are, likewise, obliged to maintain the ship as a "home"—attending to traditional "womanly" duties ranging from provisioning to education, religious guidance, and (in the absence of a ship's doctor) medical care, as well as to the ship's official role(s) as a vessel of commerce, exploration, or war.

Tales of female ship captains routinely use the dual nature of shipboard life as an opportunity that underscores the main character's femininity. Amanda Garrett has access to the USS *Cunningham*'s well-equipped shipboard gymnasium, but even with a full panoply of weights and exercise equipment at her disposal, her preferred workout is a series of dance routines to music that ranges from selections from Rimsky-Korsakov's *Scheherazade* and Richard Rogers' score for *Victory at Sea* to electronic jazz by Japanese composer Ryuichi Sakamoto and a performance of "Valentine" by Belinda Carlisle, onetime lead vocalist of the Go-Gos.[17] Author James H. Cobb takes pains to emphasize Garrett's athleticism, but also her artistry, her preservice history of dance classes, and the fact that she dances in a leotard rather than more conventional workout clothes. Marian Alston of the *Eagle* gets *her* workouts practicing *kenjutsu*—traditional Japanese swordsmanship—but relaxes afterward by cooking, a skill she learned from her mother in the South Carolina home she left hundreds of miles and thousands of years behind.[18]

Kathryn Janeway, like other Starfleet officers, escapes from the pressure of command on her ship's holodeck, a virtual-reality device capable of simulating any environment, real or fictional, the user desires. Male officers' holodeck fantasies cast them as lone adventurers: private detectives, secret agents, World War II fighter pilots, Old West gunslingers, and literary characters ranging from Sherlock Holmes to the Three Musketeers. *Voyager*'s own helmsman, Lieutenant Tom Paris, plays the dashing space explorer Captain Proton in a sharply observed parody of 1950s television serials like *Space Patrol* and *Rocky Jones, Space Ranger*. Janeway, on the other hand, immerses herself in a holonovel set in ancient (that is, early nineteenth-century) England, where she plays Lucille Davenport, governess to the young children of a widower, the handsome-but-brooding Lord Burleigh.[19] The story has mysterious elements—music from a seemingly empty room, a locked fourth-floor door that Davenport/Janeway is forbidden to enter—but its plot arc is more romantic than gothic, seemingly destined to end in Lucille's marriage to Burleigh.[20] The original plot for the holonovel, in fact, would have cast Janeway as a pioneer wife and mother, struggling to raise her family on the nineteenth-century North American frontier.[21] Janeway is thus unique in the *Trek* universe: the only woman whose *own* holodeck programs are shown, and the only Starfleet officer whose fantasies are of home, hearth, and children.

Fictional women captains are also far more likely than their fictional male counterparts to recreate home and hearth on the high seas by forming (or maintaining) committed romantic relationships. Janeway, in the early seasons of *Voyager*, keeps a picture of "Mark," the partner she left behind on Earth, on the desk in her cabin, making her the only spacegoing captain in the *Trek* universe—and virtually the only Starfleet officer of any rank—who has "someone back home." He remains in her thoughts throughout the series, even after she learns that he (believing Janeway lost) has married someone else. Marian Alston of the Nantucket Trilogy—who quietly gives up her first marriage and family before the Event, after coming out as a lesbian—forms a second, less conventional family in 1250 BC. On the *Eagle*'s first visit to the British Isles, she meets, and frees from slavery, a young Celtic woman named Swindapa, who becomes first her protégé and then her lover. The two eventually, in between adventures on the high seas, settle down in a same-sex, mixed-race, mixed-millennium domestic partnership on Nantucket, eventually adopting a pair of young daughters. Amanda Garrett is drawn to

Lieutenant Vince Arkady in the first pages of *Choosers of the Slain*—not yet aware that the handsome aviator has just been assigned to her ship—and remains with him until their career paths diverge, in the third book of the series.

Morgan Adams initially seems to be an exception to the pattern. In the opening scene of *Cutthroat Island*, it is she who, at daybreak, rises from her bed and prepares to leave her lover of the night before with no intention of ever seeing him again, and he who petulantly declares, "I thought we would last forever." When he reveals himself to be a pirate hunter, produces a flintlock from beneath the sheets, and demands her surrender, she turns the tables a second time. She knew his identity all along, she reveals, just as he knew hers, but kept the knowledge secret so that she could bed him for her own amusement. "By the way," she continues, her glance taking in his plan, pistol, and (implicitly) penis, "that won't work." Holding out the ammunition she removed from his guns the night before, she delivers her verbal coup de grace: "I took your balls."[22]

The brash, exuberantly self-confident sexuality that Morgan exhibits in the first scene quickly disappears, however, as she falls into a conventional romantic-comedy liaison with con man, thief, and self-declared "physician" William Shaw. Her original interest in Shaw is purely as a means to an end—she needs his expertise to help her locate a legendary treasure—but by the midway point of the film she has, evidently, forgotten the willingness to use and discard men that she exhibited at the outset. Her courtship with the cowardly, ineffectual Shaw is so out of character—both with her initial appearance in the film and with her reputation as a pirate—that it plays like a scriptwriter's contrivance. It seems driven by an external need for her to end the film sailing into the sunset with Shaw rather than by the character's need for him, or, indeed, for any romantic partner. It falls neatly, however, into a pattern noted by Inness and illustrated by Alston's home cooking and Janeway's romance novel: the relentless feminization of tough women heroes, seemingly designed to reassure audiences that they are "real women" after all.[23]

FAMILY AND COMMAND

A ship's captain, in traditional maritime culture, is the ultimate patriarch. His authority is absolute, his expectations stringent, his judgment final, and his wrath (on the rare occasions it is unleashed) terrible to behold. His pride in, and affection for, his crew runs deep, but they are expressed rarely and parsimoniously. "The Old Man," a sobriquet applied to captains without regard to actual age, evokes the gray-bearded prophets and tribal chieftains of a younger world: Moses at the edge of the Red Sea, or King Arthur at

Badon Hill. The absence of a similar term for female captains suggests a larger truth: patriarchs and matriarchs occupy different spaces in Western culture and cannot be readily interchanged. The standard image of (fictional) male captains as stern but loving fathers and demanding but visionary leaders gives way, in their (fictional) female counterparts, to something more complex.

Patriarchy has multiple dimensions, not all parental, but matriarchy—as embodied by the women captains of the 1990s and 2000s—is specifically and explicitly maternal. They are mothers to their crews not just because of their sex, but because of their style of leadership. Where Captain Kirk of *Star Trek* or Captain Picard of *Star Trek: The Next Generation* might use "my ship" to refer to their command, Captain Janeway was far more likely to use "my people"—acknowledging the crew as individual beings rather than integrating them with the vessel. It's a small step from "my people" to "my family," and although Janeway never took that step, her relationships with her subordinates had a distinctly parent–child quality.

Disciplining Lieutenant Tuvok in an early episode of *Star Trek: Voyager*, she speaks to the Vulcan security officer—who is well over two hundred years old, and her closest friend on the ship—as a mother to an eldest child who has failed to carry out her wishes. "It is vital that you understand me here," she tells him. "I need you. But I also need to know I can count on you. . . . I realize you made a sacrifice for me. But it's not one I would have allowed you to make."[24] Her preferred response to misbehavior is not anger, but sorrow and withheld approval: "I don't have the luxury of throwing you in the brig for the rest of the voyage," she says to an engineering team that has undermined her authority and endangered the ship, "but I want you to know how deeply you have disappointed me."[25] The crew, for their part, embrace the idea. Eulogizing Janeway when the captain is missing and presumed dead, chief engineer B'Elanna Torres declares,

> [W]hen she died, the first thing I thought was that I couldn't do this without her, that I needed her too badly—her strength and her compassion. But then I realized that the gift that she gave me, and gave a lot of us here, was the knowledge that we are better and stronger than we think.

Ensign Harry Kim, the "baby" of the *Voyager* family, continues the theme of adult children mourning the loss of their mother, by recounting his own memory of picking berries with Janeway on a lush alien world.[26]

Amanda Garrett's quasi-familial style of leadership is less pronounced than Janeway's, but shares key features with it. Like Janeway, she holds planning conferences with her senior officers that—though linked by Cobb to techniques pioneered by Britain's elite Special Air Service regiment in the 1970s—have the flavor of family meetings conducted around the ship's equivalent of a kitchen table. "Never having been the kind of officer who believed that a captaincy conferred omnipotence," she solicits input and discussion from trusted subordinates, taking advantage of the opportunity to "discuss and brainstorm" while reserving the right to make the final decision.[27] Her relationship with her intelligence officer, Lieutenant Christine Rendino, is even more conspicuously informal. Rendino's petite frame, blond hair, and Valley Girl speech patterns reinforce the impression. When Garrett bristles at Rendino's teasing suggestion that the captain arranged Arkady's transfer to the ship because he is "sweet to look upon," Rendino responds with a snicker, "I knew that'd be good for a small explosion. Don't get fussed, boss ma'am. I know you're so straight they could use you as a test standard for pool cues."[28] The tone of their private conversation, which continues for several more paragraphs before it is interrupted by an Argentine air raid, is that of a serious-minded older sister and a fun-loving younger one.

A third, more complicated version of maternal leadership is evident in Marian Alston. It is clearly rooted in the fact that the *Eagle* is a cadet training ship—meaning that she is old enough to *be* the mother of many of the young sailors under her command—and reinforced by the fact that they function as surrogates for her own daughters, lost to her in the aftermath of her divorce. Alston also, however, plays the matriarch even when not on the quarterdeck. Obliged at one point to face down a pistol-wielding Nantucketer while she herself is armed only with her sword, she slips into the Gullah patois she heard spoken as a child growing up in an African American farming community in the Sea Islands of South Carolina. "You'd better put that there down, white boy. Y'might hurt yoselfs wit it." Warned to put down her own weapon, she replies, "No, doan think I'll do that thing," before slicing off his gun hand with her *katana*.[29] In another scene, before disabusing a young African American cadet of his fantasies about Bronze Age Africa, she says, "All right, Cadet, just this once I'm going to take off my captain's cap and speak to you as sister to brother." Leaning forward, she continues, "You ever heard the saying, 'Free your mind and your ass will follow?'"[30] In both instances she channels, consciously and for effect, the black matriarchs of her rural childhood: women with soft voices and iron wills who kept, and dispensed, the wisdom of generations.

These images of female leadership echo the established cultural norms for womanly behavior: favoring—to an extent—collaboration and discussion over hierarchy and dominance. They are, in this respect, consistent with the pattern, noted by Sharon Ross, of female action heroes working in tightly bonded partnerships or small, socially cohesive groups.[31] The qualifier "to an extent" is critical, however, since—for all their collaborative, quasi-familial leadership style—female captains remain the unquestioned masters of their ships. "Look, Dix," she says to her weapons officer about an unproven type of antisubmarine missile, "I know that you and General Dynamics think that those things are the antisubmarine wonder of the age, but this is a potential combat deployment and I'm not going to waste cell space on iffy ordnance. Swap them with the *Boone* for whatever you think we can use, just so long as it works."[32] The missile expert acknowledges defeat with an "aye, aye" and a grin, acknowledging in the process a fundamental truth of shipboard life: that the captain's authority transcends gender or leadership style, and is inviolate. Captains, in the end, possess neither partners, nor mentors, nor immediate superiors: only subordinates and—in the event of armed conflict—targets.

CONCLUSION

No single cause adequately explains the sudden surge of stories about female ship captains that appeared in the last decade of the twentieth century, nor their precipitous decline in the first decade of the twenty-first. The rise of women captains in fiction paralleled, and lagged slightly behind, their rise in the real world, but—with the possible exception of fishing-boat captain Linda Greenlaw—no women captains from the real world achieved general notoriety. The popularity of the techno-thriller subgenre at the turn of the millennium, and authors' needs to ring new changes on familiar formulas and situations, can account for Amanda Garrett and the women of the Axis of Time Trilogy, but not for the simultaneous appearance of similar characters in genres ranging from historical drama (*Cutthroat Island*) and alternate history (the Nantucket Trilogy) to space opera (*Star Trek: Voyager*) and animated children's adventure (*Treasure Planet*). The 1990s vogue for female action heroes is, likewise, a superficially plausible explanation but not a comprehensive one. The story of a ship's captain taking her (or his) vessel and crew into unknown space or enemy territory differs—at a fundamental dramatic level—from the story of a lone, heavily armed adventurer on a similar journey.

The real reason is, likely, less concrete, and thus less readily identified. Indeed, it may be rooted in the tension—present in all the stories, resolved in none—between the twin, competing demands of a captain's job. A captain, regardless of gender, is charged with maintaining a parent's level of concern for the well-being of the crew, while at the same time standing ready to place any or all of them in mortal danger if the safety of the ship, or the completion of its mission, demands it. The dilemmas born of that tension—the hard work of learning to strike a balance, and the catastrophic results of failing at it—have been the stuff of maritime storytelling, in print and on-screen, for generations. That they weigh particularly heavily on women (subject to additional cultural expectations and constraints not faced by men) creates fresh dramatic potential. Recognition of that potential, reacting with some yet-unidentified element of the 1990s zeitgeist, may well account for the sudden rise of the woman ship's captain as an archetypal adventure-story character. The nature of command at sea enables writers and directors to frame them as reassuringly, conventionally feminine, while still giving them the freedom to roam, and change, the world.

NOTES

1. Stephen E. Whitfield, *The Making of* Star Trek (New York: Ballantine, 1968), 28. Hornblower, the hero of eleven novels by C. S. Forester, rises from midshipman to admiral during Britain's wars with revolutionary France. Sea stories transposed into space also figured prominently in the work of midcentury science fiction writers such as Robert Heinlein (the Future History series), Poul Anderson (the Polesotechnic League series), A. Bertram Chandler (the John Grimes series), and Andre Norton (the Solar Queen series).

2. See, for example, Joan Druett, *She Captains: Heroines and Hellions of the Sea* (New York: Simon & Schuster, 2000); Ulrike Klausman, Marian Meinzerin, and Gabriel Kuhn, eds., *Women Pirates and the Politics of the Jolly Roger* (Montreal: Black Rose Books, 1997); and Anne Chambers, *Granuaile: Grace O'Malley—Ireland's Pirate Queen* (London: Gill and Macmillan, 2009).

3. A selection of the stories is collected in Norman Reilly Raine, *Tugboat Annie: Great Stories from the* Saturday Evening Post (Indianapolis, IN: Curtis, 1987). The popularity of the stories inspired three films—*Tugboat Annie* (1933), *Tugboat Annie Sails Again* (1940), and *Captain Tugboat Annie* (1945)—and a short-lived Canadian television series, *The Adventures of Tugboat Annie* (1957).

4. Robert E. Howard, "Queen of the Black Coast," *Weird Tales*, May 1934, http://www.gutenberg.org/ebooks/42183.

5. The renaissance of women action heroes in the 1990s and beyond is analyzed at length in Sherrie A. Inness, *Tough Girls: Women Warriors and Wonder Women in Popular Culture* (Philadelphia: University of Pennsylvania Press); Sherrie A. Inness, ed., *Action Chicks: New Images of Tough Women in Popular Culture* (New York: Palgrave Macmillan, 2004); Rikke Schubart, *Super Bitches and Action Babes: The Female Hero in Popular Cinema, 1970–2006* (Jefferson, NC: McFarland, 2007); and Jennifer K. Stuller, *Ink-Stained Amazons and Cinematic Warriors: Superwomen in Modern Mythology* (London: I. B. Tauris, 2010).

6. Jill is established, early in the film, as a champion target shooter. She saves her kidnapped daughter, in the climactic scene, by borrowing a policeman's rifle and killing the criminal gang leader who is using the girl as a human shield.

7. Stuller, *Ink-Stained Amazons*, 13–52; Inness, *Tough Girls*, 31–49; Schubart, *Super Bitches*, 41–64.

8. For an extended example, see S. M. Stirling, *Island in the Sea of Time* (New York: Roc/New American Library, 1998), 350–70.

9. "Macrocosm," *Star Trek: Voyager*, season 3, episode 12, written by Brannon Braga, directed by Alexander Singer, aired December 11, 1996.

10. Useful overviews of this phenomenon include Peter Padfield, *Maritime Supremacy and the Opening of the Western Mind* (New York: Overlook Press, 2000); Kenneth Wimmel, *Theodore Roosevelt and the Great White Fleet: The Birth of American Sea Power* (Dulles, VA: Brassey's, 1998); and Paul M. Kennedy, *The Rise and Fall of British Naval Mastery*, 2nd ed. (Amherst, NY: Humanity Books, 1982).

11. James H. Cobb, *Choosers of the Slain* (1996; New York: Berkley, 1997), 60–61.

12. Robin A. Roberts, "Science, Race, and Gender in *Star Trek: Voyager*," in *Fantasy Girls: Gender in the New Universe of Science Fiction and Fantasy*, ed. Elyce Rae Hedford (Lanham, MD: Rowman & Littlefield, 2000), 203–21.

13. "Caretaker," *Star Trek: Voyager*, season 1, episodes 1 and 2, written by Michael Piller and Jeri Taylor, directed by Winrich Kolbe, aired January 16, 1995.

14. "Scorpion, Parts 1 and 2," *Star Trek: Voyager*, season 3, episode 26, and season 4, episode 1, written by Brannon Braga and Joe Menosky, directed by David Livingston (part 1) and Winrich Kolbe (part 2), aired May 21 (part 1) and September 3 (part 2), 1997.

15. Ships are, by tradition, the only inanimate objects for which English systematically uses a gendered pronoun.

16. Narrative histories of women at sea in the age of sail include David Cordingly, *Women Sailors and Sailors' Women: An Untold Maritime History* (New York: Random House, 2001); Joan Druett, *Hen Frigates: Wives of Merchant Captains under Sail* (New York: Simon & Schuster, 1998); and Joan Druett, *Petticoat Whalers: Whaling Wives at Sea, 1820–1920* (Lebanon, NH: University Press of New England, 2001). See also, however, Margaret S. Creighton and Lisa Norling, *Iron Men and Wooden Women: Gender and Seafaring in the Atlantic World, 1700–1920* (Baltimore, MD: Johns Hopkins University Press, 1996).

17. Cobb, *Choosers of the Slain*, 91–93.

18. Stirling, *Island in the Sea of Time*, 201, 229–31.

19. "Cathexis," *Star Trek: Voyager*, season 1, episode 13, written by Brannon Braga, directed by Kim Friedman, aired May 1, 1995.

20. In "Scorpion, Part 1" (the third-season finale) and several fourth-season episodes, Janeway's holodeck fantasies cast her in a noticeably less gender-determined role: an apprentice sculptor in the workshop of Leonardo da Vinci.

21. Stephen Edward Poe, *Star Trek: Voyager—A Vision of the Future* (New York: Pocket Books, 1998), 11.

22. *Cutthroat Island*, written by Robert King and Mark Norman, directed by Renny Harlin, 1995.

23. Inness, *Tough Girls*, 57–60, 149–50.

24. "Prime Factors," *Star Trek: Voyager*, season 1, episode 10, written by Michael Perricone and George Elliot, directed by Les Landau, aired March 20, 1995.

25. "Prime Factors," *Star Trek: Voyager*.

26. "Coda," *Star Trek: Voyager*, season 3, episode 15, written by Jeri Taylor, directed by Nancy Malone, aired January 29, 1997.

27. Cobb, *Choosers of the Slain*, 32–33.

28. Ibid., 76.

29. Stirling, *Island in the Sea of Time*, 285.

30. Ibid., 254–55.

31. Sharon Ross, "'Tough Enough': Female Friendship and Heroism in *Xena* and *Buffy*," in *Action Chicks: New Images of Tough Women in Popular Culture*, ed. Sherrie A. Inness (New York: Palgrave Macmillan, 2007), 231–55.

32. Cobb, *Choosers of the Slain*, 35.

Chapter Fifteen

The Girl Who Lived

Reading Harry Potter as a Sacrificial and Loving Heroine

Norma Jones

To suggest that *Harry Potter* is popular around the world is an immense understatement. According to the publisher's website, Scholastic.com, *Harry Potter* books have sold over four hundred million copies and are translated into sixty-eight languages across the world. As of 2006, over 57 percent of young adult readers (between the ages of five and seventeen) have read at least one of the *Harry Potter* books.[1] In addition to the popularity of the books, the Internet Movie Database reported that the eight *Harry Potter* films have grossed over $7.7 billion worldwide. In 2010, Harry's story world further crossed into ours when the Universal Orlando Resort in Florida opened their twenty-acre Wizarding World of Harry Potter theme park.

With this in mind, I am interested in further examining *Harry Potter* because the franchise has "become so widely popular that it is critically significant and should be taken quite seriously."[2] While Harry's story was originally published for the young adult audience, his heroic narrative is also impactful on wider audiences. His story creates a space for fan-based social movements that could have a meaningful impact on the real world. With this in mind, I will discuss how Harry might be characterized as a heroine and how that characterization may be extremely helpful in mobilizing fandom-based social change. But first, let me tell you a bit more about Harry and his story.

ABOUT THE HARRY POTTER FRANCHISE

Joanne Rowling's seven books were published between 1998 and 2007. In the series, Rowling tells the story of a young wizard through seven years of his magical education. While I cannot adequately recount Harry's tale, which spans over four thousand pages across the seven books and almost twenty hours of film in eight feature-length movies, I will initially provide a brief introduction of Harry's character and map out a background of his story world.

Harry is orphaned as an infant and grows up to save humanity from subjugation by an evil wizard, Lord Voldemort. We are introduced to the baby Harry as he is flown, in the dead of night, by a giant wizard riding a flying motorcycle. He is left on the doorstep of the Dursleys' (Harry's aunt and uncle) English suburban tract home. We next see young Harry almost ten years later. He is unloved and neglected by the Dursleys. Harry sleeps in a small, cramped cupboard under the stairs, while his cousin, Dudley, occupies two bedrooms upstairs. Dudley has one bedroom to sleep in and the second to store all of his toys. The young Harry is also forced to cook, clean, and serve while his aunt and uncle spoil Dudley.

On his eleventh birthday, Harry is surprised by a very large and strange visitor. Harry learns that he is a famous wizard that is descended from a great wizarding family. Harry has also been accepted into Hogwarts School of Witchcraft and Wizardry. Albus Dumbledore is the headmaster at Hogwarts and becomes Harry's father figure. As the story unfolds we learn, along with Harry, more about the parallel wizarding world that exists next to, but also hidden from, our own. While the borders are permeable, the magical community takes great pains to hide themselves from nonmagical folk, or us, as muggles. Even though the two worlds exist simultaneously and share some similar characteristics, the magical community has their own set of institutions, laws, currency, customs, norms, and terminology. For example, the wizarding community has mail service, but their letters are delivered by owls.

Witches and wizards are born with their magical talents from both wizarding and muggle parents. Children of wizarding and nonmagical parents are integrated in schools, but sometimes, similar to our world, they are subject to prejudice. Some "pure-blooded" wizarding families disparage those of mixed parentage as "half-bloods" and children of nonmagical parents as having dirty blood, or "mudbloods." In the series, Voldemort exploits these prejudices to ignite a race war to subjugate mudbloods, as well as other people in the nonmagical community, and to institutionalize rule of racial supremacy by pure-blood witches and wizards. This war is put on long-term hold—after Voldemort fails to kill the infant Harry—because the evil wizard is presumed dead. Voldemort returns to power about halfway through the series and reignites the war. The war ends in a duel between Voldemort and Harry, in which Voldemort is destroyed, permanently this time, by his own rebounded killing spell.[3]

In the series, Harry could be considered a hero because he completes Campbell's heroic journey in which he "ventures forth from the world of common day into a region of supernatural wonder: fabulous forces are there encountered and a decisive victory is won: the hero comes back from this mysterious adventure with the power to bestow boons on his fellow man."[4] In each book and film of the series, Harry fulfills some parts of the heroic (departure–initiation–return) journey, and completes the journey in the concluding volume as he returns from the dead to defeat Voldemort.[5] Furthermore, as a coming-of-age hero, Harry might be especially influential because the franchise is extremely popular and his character becomes a paradigm or role model for boys and girls as their desired possible selves."[6] By this, I do not imply that young readers will start waving around wands to cast spells or try to fly on broomsticks. Instead, young readers might base their decisions and perceptions about their own worlds based on what they see and read. However, despite being written as a male hero, I read Harry as a heroine because his redemptive power is based on a trope often associated with female heroes: love. With that in mind, I will detail Harry as a loving and sacrificial heroine.

READING HARRY AS A HEROINE

In some instances, and despite Harry's assigned male gender, the young wizard has been read as a female hero. For example, Harry is orphaned, is treated badly by his stepfamily, and is made to cook and clean for them.[7] Beyond that of a simple male Cinder(f)ella, portrayals of Harry also fit two other prominent tropes associated with female heroes: a loving Heidi Redeemer and a dying sacrificial heroine.

Harry as a Loving Heidi Redeemer

A Heidi Redeemer is "often a mere child—who solves problems by selfless love . . . seeking nothing for herself, while loving others in a generous but sexually chaste manner."[8] As such, evil is conquered and societies are redeemed by that selfless love. Characteristics of the Heidi Redeemer are notable in *Heidi's Song*, Maria in *The Sound of Music*, and Dorothy in *The Wizard of Oz*.[9] This love is inexorably linked to female heroes, and the trope of a living heroine breaks from male heroic characteristics based on hypermasculinity.[10] For example, William Marston created Wonder Woman as a force of altruistic love to build loving bonds in opposition to male heroic narratives of violence and destruction.

In the story world, Harry was often not the best, or most capable wizard. Time and time again, Hermione Granger, a muggle-born witch, saves Harry with her knowledge and daring. In fact, Hermione is framed as the greatest witch of her generation. In both the books and films, Harry is often (a damsel) in distress, and females step up to protect him. Thus, instead of being a great wizard or strong fighter, Harry's power is love as well as the bonds created from his love. The powerfulness of love is evidenced in a dialogue between Harry and Dumbledore (as they discuss how to defeat Voldemort):

> "But I haven't got uncommon skill and power," said Harry, before he could stop himself.
>
> "Yes, you have," said Dumbledore firmly. "You have a power that Voldemort has never had. You can—"
>
> "I know!" said Harry impatiently. "I can love!" It was only with difficulty that he stopped himself adding, "Big deal!"
>
> "Yes, Harry, you can love," said Dumbledore, who looked as though he knew perfectly well what Harry had just refrained from saying. "Which, given everything that has happened to you, is a great and remarkable thing. You are still too young to understand how unusual you are, Harry."
>
> "So, when the prophecy says that I'll have 'power the Dark Lord knows not,' it just means—love?" asked Harry, feeling a little let down.
>
> "Yes—just love," said Dumbledore. [11]

In this passage, we can see Harry's recognition that he does not have characteristics often associated with strong heroes. He does not have uncommon magical skill, strength, or power; instead, his power is love. In contrast, Voldemort cannot love, and because of that inability to love, he was doomed to fail. Before the war, and in a flashback conversation with Dumbledore, Voldemort speaks of how he is becoming extremely powerful as a wizard.

> "Certainly," said Voldemort, and his eyes seemed to burn red. "I have experimented; I have pushed the boundaries of magic further, perhaps, than they have ever been pushed—"
>
> "Of some kinds of magic," Dumbledore corrected him quietly. "Of some. Of others, you remain . . . forgive me . . . woefully ignorant."
>
> For the first time, Voldemort smiled. It was a taut leer, an evil thing, more threatening than a look of rage.
>
> "The old argument," he said softly. "But nothing I have seen in the world has supported your famous pronouncements that love is more powerful than my kind of magic, Dumbledore."
>
> "Perhaps you have been looking in the wrong places," suggested Dumbledore. [12]

In other words, the love Harry has is more powerful than Voldemort's magic. However, Heidi, Maria, and Dorothy did not have to die. Whereas, Harry must sacrifice himself to redeem his community, so, I next discuss how Harry is also a sacrificial heroine.

HARRY AS A SACRIFICIAL HEROINE

The trope of the sacrificial heroine traces back to antiquity in mythologies and folktales. When discussing Greek heroine cults, Larson writes that "probably the most famous role of the heroine is the sacrificial victim."[13] The trope is also relevant in the United States as Hume names the self-sacrificial heroine as one of the characteristics of an ideal woman in literature.[14] In the series, Harry almost dies twice and is sacrificed in the concluding book/film of the series. In a series of flashbacks, we see that Harry's mentor and father figure, Dumbledore, has been preparing Harry as a sacrifice since infancy. In a flashback conversation with another teacher, Severus Snape, Dumbledore reveals his plans:

> "So the boy . . . the boy must die?" asked Snape quite calmly.
> "And Voldemort himself must do it, Severus, that is essential."
> Another long silence. Then Snape said, "I thought . . . all these years . . . that we were protecting him for her. For Lily."
> "We have protected him because it was essential to teach him, to raise him, to try his strength," said Dumbledore, his eyes still tight shut. "If I know him [Harry], he will have arranged matters so that when he sets out to meet his death, it will truly mean the end of Voldemort."
> Dumbledore opened his eyes. Snape looked horrified.
> "You kept him alive so that he can die at the right moment? . . . Everything was supposed to keep Lily Potter's son safe. Now you tell me you have been raising him like a pig for slaughter?"[15]

Harry had to die because Voldemort secreted parts of his soul into magical objects called horcruxes. Dumbledore and Harry methodically found and destroyed them until Harry himself became one of the last horcruxes. In this sense, Harry was objectified as a magical object and he had to die as that object so that Voldemort could be destroyed. When Harry realized that he was raised as a sacrifice, he thought,

> How neat, how elegant, not to waste any more lives, but to give the dangerous task to the boy who had already been marked for slaughter, and whose death would not be a calamity, but another blow against Voldemort.
> And Dumbledore had known that Harry would not duck out, that he would keep going to the end, even though it was *his* end. . . . Dumbledore knew, as Voldemort knew, that Harry would not let anyone else die for him now that he discovered it was in his power to stop it.[16]

Even though Harry was terrified of dying, his unselfish love for others compelled him to obey his mentor/father's plan and sacrifice himself.

However, unlike some other sacrificial heroine stories, Harry's story did not end with his death. Instead, Harry was resurrected to defeat Voldemort. The resurrection narrative subverts the sacrificial heroine one because she comes back and shakes free of the binds of patriarchy.[17] For example, Buffy returns to defeat evil and save her community, and "her resurrection suggests possibilities for a feminist democratic social order."[18] Harry's sacrifice subverts Voldemort's domination and allows him to cast off that ideology for a more democratic social order. In other words, instead of death being the end of the story, the resurrection trope provides space to transgress against those ideologies of domination that killed the heroines in the first place. However, Harry also transcends tropes associated with heroines, because his power comes from his mother, Lily. Dumbledore explains:

> Your mother died to save you. If there is one thing Voldemort cannot understand, it is love. He didn't realize that love as powerful as your mother's for you leaves its own mark. Not a scar, no visible sign . . . to have been loved so deeply, even though the person who loved us is gone, will give us some protection forever.[19]

In the film, Lily Potter's dying words to her son were, "Harry. Harry, you are so loved, so loved. Harry, your mama loves you, dada loves you."[20] This marks a further departure from most representations of heroic characters in that many heroes' and heroines' powers originate from fathers.[21] For example, Wonder Woman and Hercules were descended from Zeus, and their powers originate from their divine father. Thus, I next discuss how Harry's heroic narrative allows for spaces of resistance.

HARRY AS TRANSGRESSIVE HERO/INE WITH FANS THAT ARE UP TO NO GOOD

Despite efforts to empower some heroines, these heroic women exist in a contradictory stance in which a "double bind constructs emerging roles for women as both heroic subject and sexual object."[22] With this in mind, I continue my reading of Harry as a hero/ine in order to understand some changing cultural norms and perhaps allow for an understanding of Harry as a metaphor to potentially reimagine spaces of agency in power and change. Before I start, let me first review the role of women in the heroic journey.

From Campbell's perspective, women in a hero's journey are sources of helpfulness, temptation, and conquest, but never the hero herself. Women "represent the totality of what can be known. The hero is the one who comes to know. . . . She lures, she guides. . . . The hero who can take her as she is, without undue commotion but with the kindness and assurance she requires, is potentially the king, the incarnate god, of her created world.[23] Since then, some new heroines have emerged, but their characterizations are bound by significant gendered restrictions. These restrictions are in place because heroines are easily rejected as heroic figures.[24] Some gendered female characteristics are not valued in heroic forms, and heroines are more valued when they behave as men. Thus, by imbuing Harry, a male hero, with characteristics of a female one, and perhaps hiding a heroine as Harry, Rowling allows for a greater stretching of heroine narratives to reimagine spaces of un/gendered agency. Let me build this argument by reviewing a short history of Rowling hiding.

It is well known that Scholastic editors encouraged Rowling to hide her female identity when the *Harry Potter* series was first released. On her website, Rowling writes that "use of a pen name was suggested by her publisher, Barry Cunningham. He thought that young boys might be wary of a book written by a woman, so Joanne chose 'K,' for 'Kathleen,' the name of her paternal grandmother." In other words, Rowling hides her female identity to remove some of the restrictions binding (not only fictional heroines but also real life) women. In 2013, Rowling published an adult crime fiction under the male pseudonym of Robert Galbraith. She once again concealed her female identity. Ironically, that new series earned better critics' reviews when the books were authored by the male Galbraith instead of the female Rowling.[25] Inside of Harry's story world, Rowling also hides traits that may bind perceptions of her characters.

During a book tour stop at New York's Carnegie Hall, Rowling revealed that Harry's mentor, Dumbledore, was in love with, and in a homosexual relationship with, another wizard, Gellert Grindelwald. In the books, this homosexual relationship was never outed. However, during a promotional appearance in New York, she addressed the audience, "I would have told you earlier if I knew it would make you so happy."[26] With this in mind, I believe that Rowling has shown a pattern for hiding: (1) J. K. Rowling was more acceptable than Joanne Rowling, (2) Robert Galbraith was more praiseworthy than J. K. Rowling, and (3) Dumbledore was more acceptable as a heterosexual mentor to a young male hero than as a gay one.

By hiding and then revealing after mass acceptance, Rowling creates an "illegitimate extra-curricular culture."[27] This allows a space as the beginnings for fandom-based social revolutions because the popularity surrounding Harry Potter creates "emotional energy that unites the group."[28] It is not just the mass popularity but the relationship between the story world and ours. Pugh and Wallace explain that Harry's story world (similar to the fans' realities) is bound and limited by dominant ideologies. The massive success of the franchise and Rowling's revelations in New York unbind the characters and narrative from the books. Harry's story is not finished, and the characters (along with their narratives) reach beyond the written pages (and films) and continue in fandom.[29]

As the stories continue in fandom, one of the more overt ways that fans have unchained the characters from the pages bound in a book and borders of the screen is via online fan fiction. Instead of reading, rereading, watching, and rewatching the fixed narratives, fans have taken the popular and fictional characters to weave their own stories. We see that in fan fiction, "the *Harry Potter* saga lives on . . . just not written by J. K. Rowling. Others are taking over her characters out of love, respect, and inspiration."[30] In the popular press, *Time* magazine reports that in the early days "it was apparent that fan fiction was not just an homage to the glory of the original but also a reaction to it. It was about finding the boundaries that the original couldn't or wouldn't break, and breaking them."[31] As of the time of the writing of this chapter, fans have written over 659,000 fan-fiction stories based on the Harry Potter story world.[32]

This massive continuation of the characters in fandom-created narratives allows a heterotopian space that is separate but also connected to Harry's story world/our reality, and it "can be powerful means of opposing the abuses that permeate the spaces in our own world."[33] In the story world, Harry uses a magical map to find physical spaces inside of Hogwarts to help train and plan for the fight against Voldemort. This magical Marauder's Map also shows the location of everyone in the mapped spaces so that Harry can avoid detection. To activate the map, wizards incant, "I solemnly swear that I am up to no good." Cantrell argues that this conception of being up to no good carries into fandom as a way to exercise agency to subvert domination in order to positively "transform the spaces and places in the world at large."[34] An example is also found in fan fiction after Rowling revealed Dumbledore's homosexuality.

> Fans celebrate Dumbledore's sexuality by depicting his youthful passion in all its glory and his dignity and integrity even in loneliness. Dissatisfaction with the source text is an equally compelling motivation to write fanfiction, and fans examine his isolation and heartbreak, explore the possibilities of other lovers . . . for him, and invent alternate universes where he can be happily in love. In slash fandom, Dumbledore's sexuality can achieve expression beyond what Rowling was willing or able to put on the page, and fan responses are an invaluable resource for assessing the ultimate implications of his outing.[35]

Thus, instead of simply relying on narratives provided by others, in some fan fiction writers have reappropriated characters in order to express, reimagine, and perhaps even reclaim agency in order to oppose ideological abuses their own realities. These new narratives "offer new metaphors, alternate designs for the fictional heroine's life" that may allow for growth and perhaps lessen some of the bindings that restrict heroines (and, by extension, women).[36] I have used overt examples from fan fiction, but these themes of liberation extend beyond writing stories about characters in and inspired by *Harry Potter*.

Outside of fan fiction, popular press writers have also found feminist messages in *Harry Potter*. For example, Wilson explains important feminist lessons she found in the last film and encourages readers "to wield our own personal wands."[37] These takeaway lessons include that (1) patriarchy (symbolized as Voldemort's quest for domination) is evil, and it can be destroyed; (2) the personal is political in that oppressive power should always be denounced (when Harry chooses to destroy or not keep a powerful weapon, the Elder Wand); and (3) oppression and emancipation are both participatory (as Harry had a choice, and he chooses to fight instead of participating in his own oppression). Thus Harry's story provides some useful models for feminist action. Next, let me conclude with a few reflections about Harry's power of love.

This sense of selfless love is a commitment to shared bonds in which loyalty overrides selfishness.[38] Although love is most associated with heroines today, selfless love and sacrifice for love are not strictly female tropes. In fact, this love may be traced back to the Bible. In the first epistle to the Corinthians, we are told about this selfless type of love:

> Love is patient; love is kind; love is not envious or boastful or arrogant or rude. It does not insist on its own way; it is not irritable or resentful; it does not rejoice in wrongdoing, but rejoices in the truth. It bears all things, believes all things, hopes all things, endures all things. . . . And now faith, hope, and love abide, these three; and the greatest of these is love.[39]

Also, in the Bible, Jesus, because of his selfless love, willingly sacrificed himself to save/redeem those he loved,

> For this reason the Father loves me, because I lay down my life in order to take it up again. No one takes it from me, but I lay it down of my own accord. I have power to lay it down, and I have power to take it up again. I have received this command from my Father.[40]

Harry follows a similar script as he willingly sacrifices himself based on faith in his father figure's design. Harry is narrativized as a Christlike figure in that he is written as a loving and sacrificial hero. Thus, redemption based on love is not a new male heroic trope, nor is it one that is strictly associated with female heroes. So, by reaching back into this well-known and moral story, Rowling further relaxes the binds of gendered agency as humans (not based on binaries of perceived gender) have the potential to cause change.

Some might suggest that despite feminist readings, Harry Potter ultimately supports patriarchy. For example, in the films, Hermione is considerably more attractive as compared to the book.[41] Also, Rowling indicted that falling in love with another male wizard was Dumbledore's "great tragedy,"[42] thus indicating that his gay relationship was punishable or disciplined. However, and as Brown indicated, these heroines exist as both subjects with agency and objects of domination. To simply ignore these potential spaces of change and agency might be, as Wilson puts it, making a choice to not fight oppression. So, instead of insisting that concepts of loving heroines limit women's agency, love could be considered a legitimate source of change. bell hooks writes, "All great movements for social justice in our society have strongly emphasized a love ethic."[43] Thus, I do not suggest that acting out of love is a passive enterprise.

Instead of a passive act, Stuller writes that "love, when motivated by a spiritual interdependency, can show us how an act of compassion—regardless of who acts and who receives—can change lives, heal past wounds, and even save the world."[44] Instead of simply uncovering sites of domination, feminists and the greater community of humanists might help promote social change by also supporting un/gendered agency in heroic narratives. These heroines may also promote a positive imaginary along with their potentially transgressive heroic narratives. These loving heroines might also help to provide positive images that influence identities and may have the potential to cross traditional boundaries of gender, race, class, and sexuality.[45] In conclusion, I return to hooks to articulate my hopes for the future with loving hero/ines; she urges that "to speak of love is not 'preaching,' for the simple reason that it means to speak of the ultimate and real need in every human being. . . . We can collectively regain our faith in the transformative power of love by cultivating courage, the strength to stand up for what we believe in, to be accountable in both word and deed."[46]

NOTES

1. "New Study Finds That the Harry Potter Series Has a Positive Impact on Kids' Reading and Their School Work," Scholastic.com: About Scholastic, http://www.scholastic.com/aboutscholastic/news/press_07252006_CP.htm (accessed July 17, 2013).

2. Giselle Liza Anatol, introduction to *Reading Harry Potter*, ed. Giselle Liza Anatol (Westport, CT: Praeger, 2003), xiv.

3. J. K. Rowling, *Harry Potter and the Deathly Hallows* (New York: Scholastic, 2007), 743.

4. Joseph Campbell, *The Hero with a Thousand Faces* (New York: MJF, 1949), 30.

5. Julia Boll, "Harry Potter's Archetypical Journey," in *Heroism in the Harry Potter Series*, ed. Katrin Berndt and Lena Steveker (Burlington, VT: Ashgate, 2011), 93. Catherine Tosenberger, "'Oh My God, the Fanfiction!': Dumbledore's Outing and the Online Harry Potter Fandom," *Children's Literature Association Quarterly* 33 (2008): 203, doi: 10.1353/chq.0.0015 (accessed June 22, 2013).

6. Hugh Gash and Paul Conway, "Images of Heroes and Heroines: How Stable?" *Journal of Applied Developmental Psychology* 18 (1997): 351, doi: 10.1016/S0193-3973(97)80005-6 (accessed June 23, 2013).

7. Ximena Gallardo-C. and C. Jason Smith, "Cinderfella: J. K. Rowling's Wily Web of Gender," in *Reading Harry Potter*, ed. Giselle Liza Anatol (Westport, CT: Praeger, 2003), 195.

8. John Shelton Lawrence and Robert Jewett, *The Myth of the American Superhero* (Grand Rapids, MI: Eerdmans, 2002), 69. This might be also identified as agape, or selfless altruistic love.

9. Lawrence and Jewett, *Myth of the American Superhero*, 65–85.

10. Jennifer K. Stuller, *Ink-Stained Amazons and Cinematic Warriors: Superwomen in Modern Mythology* (New York: Palgrave Macmillan, 2010), 87.

11. J. K. Rowling, *Harry Potter and the Half-Blood Prince* (New York: Scholastic, 2005), 509.

12. Rowling, *Half-Blood Prince*, 443–44.

13. Jennifer Lynn Larson, *Greek Heroine Cults* (Madison: University of Wisconsin Press, 1995), 101.

14. Janice Hume, "Defining the Historic American Heroine: Changing Characteristics of Heroic Women in Nineteenth-Century Media," *Journal of Popular Culture* 31 (1997): 4, doi: 10.1111/j.0022-3840.1997.3101;1.x (accessed June 24, 2013).

15. Rowling, *Deathly Hallows*, 686–87.

16. J. K. Rowling, *Harry Potter and the Order of the Phoenix* (New York: Scholastic, 2003), 693.

17. Sara Crosby, "The Cruelest Season: Female Heroes Snapped into Sacrificial Heroines," in *Action Chicks*, ed. Sherrie A. Inness (New York: Palgrave Macmillan, 2004), 174.

18. Ibid., 176.

19. J. K. Rowling, *Harry Potter and the Sorcerer's Stone* (New York: Scholastic, 1998), 299.

20. *Harry Potter and the Deathly Hallows: Part 2*, directed by David Yates (2011; Burbank, CA: Warner Home Video, 2011), DVD.

21. Stuller, *Ink-Stained Amazons*, 105.

22. Jeffrey A. Brown, *Dangerous Curves: Action Heroines, Gender, Fetishism, and Popular Culture* (Jackson: University Press of Mississippi, 2011), 7.

23. Campbell, *Hero with a Thousand Faces*, 116.

24. Jack Balswick and Bron Ingoldsby, "Heroes and Heroines among American Adolescents," *Sex Roles* (1982): 249, doi: 10.1007/BF00287308 (accessed June 23, 2013). Rachel D. Bromnick and Brian L. Swallow, "I Like Being Who I Am: A Study of Young People's Ideals," *Educational Studies* 25 (1999): 127, doi: 10.1080/03055699997855 (accessed June 23, 2013).

25. Ben Steelman, "The Secret's out about J. K. Rowling," *StarNews: Bookmarks*, July 15, 2013, http://books.blogs.starnewsonline.com/17827/the-secrets-out-about-j-k-rowling (accessed July 17, 2013); Alex Moore, "JK Rowling Better Received When She Hides Her Identity as a Man," *DeathandTaxes: News*, July 15, 2013, http://www.deathandtaxesmag.com/202089/jk-rowling-better-received-when-she-hides-her-identity-as-a-man (accessed July 17, 2013).

26. Hanna Siegel, "Rowling Lets Dumbledore out of the Closet," ABC News: Entertainment, 2007, October 20, http://abcnews.go.com/Entertainment/story?id=3755544&page=1 (accessed June 23, 2013).

27. Dustin Kidd, "Harry Potter and the Functions of Popular Culture," *Journal of Popular Culture* 40 (2007): 83, doi: 10.1111/j.1540-5931.2007.00354.x (accessed June 23, 2013).

28. Ibid., 85.

29. Tison Pugh and David L. Wallace, "A Postscript to 'Heteronormative Heroism and Queering the School Story in J. K. Rowling's Harry Potter Series,'" *Children's Literature Association Quarterly* 33 (2008): 192, doi: 10.1353/chq.0.0009 (accessed March 22, 2013).

30. Katherine Batchelor, "In a Flash: The Digital Age's Influence over Literacy," in *Cult Pop Culture: How the Fringe Became Mainstream*, vol. 2, ed. Bob Batchelor (Santa Barbara, CA: ABC-CLIO, 2012), 81.

31. Lev Grossman, "The Boy Who Lived Forever," *Time: Entertainment*, July 7, 2011, http://content.time.com/time/arts/article/0,8599,2081784,00.html#ixzz2ZzMbd7X0 (accessed July 7, 2011).

32. Retrieved from FanFiction.net. Harry Potter has the most entries, and Twilight follows with over 213,000 fan-fiction stories.

33. Sarah K. Cantrell, "'I Solemnly Swear I Am up to No Good': Foucault's Heterotopias and Deleuze's Any-Spaces-Whatever in J. K. Rowling's Harry Potter Series," *Children's Literature* 39 (2011): 195, doi: 10.1353/chl.2011.0012 (accessed June 22, 2013).

34. Cantrell, "I Solemnly Swear," 207.

35. Tosenberger, "Oh My God, the Fanfiction," 204.

36. Ruth Yeazell, "Fictional Heroines and Feminist Critics," *NOVEL: A Forum on Fiction* 8 (1974): 38, doi: 10.2307/1345195 (accessed June 23, 2013).

37. Natalie Wilson, "7 Feminist Take-Aways from the Final Harry Potter Movie," *Ms. Magazine Blog: Arts*, July 16, 2011, http://msmagazine.com/blog/2011/07/16/seven-feminist-take-aways-from-the-final-potter-movie (accessed July 21, 2013).

38. Without delving too much into different styles of love, this type of love might best be described as agape.

39. 1 Cor. 13:4–7, 13:13.

40. John 10:17–18.

41. Unlike the books, in the films she also runs across hilly forests in skintight jeans and gives away her location while in hiding because she is wearing perfume.

42. Siegel, "Rowling Lets Dumbledore Out."

43. bell hooks, *All about Love: New Visions* (New York: Morrow, 2000), xix.

44. Stuller, *Ink-Stained Amazons*, 104.

45. Gash and Conway, "Images of Heroes and Heroines," 369; Bob Batchelor and Josef Benson, "Who Gets to Wear the Cape: The Rise of the Black Superman in Martin Delany, Fredrick Douglass and Beyond," in *Black and White Masculinity in the American South, 1800–2000*, ed. Lydia Plath and Sergio Lussana (Newcastle upon Tyne, UK: Cambridge Scholars Publishing, 2009), 108–9.

46. hooks, *All About Love*, 92.

Chapter Sixteen

"It's about Power and It's about Women"

Gender and the Political Economy of Superheroes in
Wonder Woman *and* Buffy the Vampire Slayer

Carolyn Cocca

Earth girls can stop men's power for evil when they refuse to be dominated by evil men. —Diana (Wonder Woman), in *Wonder Woman* Vol. 1 #5, by creator William Moulton Marston, 1943

It's about power and it's about women, and you just hate those two words in the same sentence, don't you? —Buffy (the Vampire Slayer), in *Buffy Season 8* #4, by creator Joss Whedon, 2007

POWER AND WOMEN

Wonder Woman debuted seventy years ago, and Buffy, twenty years ago.[1] Their male creators intended the two characters to build male acceptance of female power.[2] As strong community-minded "woman warriors" who consult, protect, and rely on friends, both of these superheroes present an alternative to a hierarchical, individualistic, patriarchal society. But at the same time, both conform to some gender stereotypes, as they are white, heterosexual, and middle (to upper) class, battling their enemies while managing to keep their long hair, beautiful faces, and attractive bodies unharmed. That the characters embody these seeming contradictions broadens their potential audiences as well as widening the possibilities for different receptions by those audiences.

In this chapter, I analyze the transgressive possibilities of and the constraints on the portrayals of gender and power in *Wonder Woman* comics (1941–2012) and the *Buffy* television show and comics (1997–2012). To do so, I approach comics as interactive public spheres in which editorial boards, writers and artists, parent companies, and competing constituent audiences empower and constrain each other as to how articulations of gender are produced and how they are received.[3]

I find that moments of more fluid representations of gender in most of *Wonder Woman*'s history were followed by periods of backlash and containment, that the similarities between the two characters illuminate how female heroes are produced for maximum resonance (and maximum profit) across different audiences, and that the differences between the two characters are related to their bodies and their sexuality. I conclude with reflections on how the Third Wave feminist sensibilities and aesthetics of *Buffy*, and of *Wonder Woman* in the 2000s, may serve to moderate those cyclical swings and those differences by simultaneously embodying, parodying, and subverting traditional articulations of gender.

WONDER WOMAN FROM THE 1940s TO THE 1990s: TRANSGRESSION AND CONTAINMENT

William Moulton Marston created *Wonder Woman* in 1941. His Princess Diana of the Amazons was "a woman with the eternal beauty of Aphrodite and the wisdom of Athena, yet whose lovely form hides the agility of Mercury and the steely sinews of Hercules." Her mission was to subdue Axis spies, common criminals, and mythical characters, as well as to teach "Man's World" the peaceful and equal ways of the Amazons.[4] She and her female friends often had to rescue her boyfriend Steve Trevor as well. Diana loved Steve, but refused his proposals: "If I married you, Steve, I'd have to pretend that I'm weaker than you are to make you happy—and that, no woman should do."[5] Space for such subversion of gendered binaries was created through the wartime flux of gender roles.[6]

After the war, all of this changed. Comics were among the many sites that materially articulated multiple Cold War ideologies that worked to construct an American national consensus, reconfiguring order in the face of numerous challenges.[7] Femininity and marriage became central in *Wonder Woman*. A backup feature called "Wonder Women of History" that profiled prominent (mostly white) women was replaced in 1950 by "Marriage a la Mode," which documented marriage customs around the world; similar romance supplements continued for twenty years.[8] Diana's costume covered less, her boots were replaced with laced sandals, and her hair grew longer and her eyes larger. Steve's (and others') marriage proposals became constant. Instead of fighting fascism and crime with other women, she fought fantastic monsters alone, sometimes infantilized as herself at younger ages, "Wonder Girl" and "Wonder Tot." These changes cast her more as object than subject; it became more difficult to read the character as presenting challenges to traditional hierarchies.

"I'll lose him forever if I don't do something to keep him interested in me!" lamented Diana in 1968, as she gave up her powers to be with Steve.[9] While the creative team saw this big change as feminist in that she would have to rely on her wits and not her superpowers,[10] some fans and some feminists didn't see it that way.[11] After lobbying by these groups, her powers were restored in 1973. But under the next editor, who said he "never cared for Wonder Woman," many of the 1970s and early 1980s stories showed Diana in a smaller costume and more suggestive poses as she fought similarly curvy women.[12] Gender-neutral public service announcements and romance supplements were replaced by ads for BB guns and bodybuilding, and letter authors were more often male and adult.[13] From 1974 to 1983, only a handful of letters referred to her as a feminist icon.[14] The portrayals were often campy, sometimes with "battle of the sexes" stories that negatively stereotyped feminism as antimale rather than proequality,[15] indicative of misunderstandings of and backlash against the civil rights movements of the previous decades.

But this would change in the late 1980s when DC Comics relaunched its superhero titles in order to increase profits. The question was whether the crosscutting pressures of the times would push those titles toward the increasingly homogenous fan market and the conservatism that could be inferred by its demographics (male, white, and older)[16] or toward a more inclusive readership and authorship represented by the underground comix movement, identity politics activism, and the growing diversity of writers and artists in mainstream comics.

Wonder Woman's reboot was shepherded by writer and artist George Pérez, who represented the latter trend. His Amazons were created by Greek goddesses from the souls of women who'd been murdered by their male partners. As in the 1940s, Diana forged a new circle of female friends who worked with her to bring "lessons of peace and equality" to Man's World.[17] Pérez drew the Amazons as a more diverse group and implied they might be in relationships with one another. He drew Diana as looking more "ethnic," saying, "I picture her with a deep tan and a foreign accent."[18] She had a strong, fit body with a costume that covered her, wore flat instead of heeled boots, and battled Greek mythological foes.

This portrayal was out of step with most superhero comics at the time, as others had begun to feature hypersexualized, violent "Bad Girls." Why *Wonder Woman* was not pushed in this direction (yet) seems to be because Pérez's vision was supported by three female DC editors, including the title's first female editor, Karen Berger.[19] She wrote, "The overwhelming majority of comics [are] geared to and read by males. . . . [This] new Wonder Woman comic . . . serves as a great role model to young women, but also contains many elements that appeal to males as well. Wonder Woman crosses the gender line."[20] Fan letters were very positive. "You can't keep a good feminist down! WW is back and looking better than ever!"[21] "I fully agree with your perception of Wonder Woman as a positive and strong model for girls/women. It also, hopefully, will take some of the chauvinism out of the male readers brought up on macho men and weak women."[22] Pérez's run sold quite well and remains a touchstone for fans and creators alike.

But by the mid-1990s, the superhero comics market crashed, reduced to the base noted above: about 90 percent male, predominantly white, heterosexual, and young adult.[23] In contrast to Pérez's run, Diana's look was changed drastically as DC Comics played to the presumed wishes of the base fans, "emphasizing her sexuality and downplaying her feminism."[24] This recalls the way in which the 1950s and 1960s hyperfeminized Diana followed the more hybridized gender portrayals of the 1940s. Written by William Messner-Loebs and drawn by Mike Deodato Jr., Diana was often portrayed fighting in a hyperviolent manner, and was often posed in sexually objectified ways.[25] Deodato noted that he asked to draw *Wonder Woman*, even though, as he said, "I hate drawing women. I prefer drawing monsters and stuff like that." But he also noted the sales success of the run: "In three months, the sales doubled and tripled or something like that. . . . Every time the bikini was smaller, the sales got higher."[26]

Letters from several issues praise Deodato's art: "Mike Deodato, Jr. is brilliant!"[27] "Mr. Deodato drew at once a beautiful princess and a fierce warrior."[28] Others were not thrilled with the objectification: "That thong-back thing is not flattering. . . . Through the entire comic, every woman's cheeks are out flapping in the breeze. Give them some rear coverage and some dignity." Another wrote, "Personally, it's a little heavy on the T&A for me, but then, I'm female and that's to be expected. . . . [P]lease get Diana out of that slutty new outfit."[29] There was criticism of the content, too: "The stereotype that men are stronger than women is affirmed."[30] Editor Paul Kupperberg responded that male superheroes were also drawn as "idealized versions of men" and said, bristling with annoyance, "I am, both by temperament and by politics, a feminist."[31]

As with the portrayals of the late 1960s and early 1970s, when Diana lost her powers, the writer and editor in the mid-1990s felt they were presenting a feminist character and comic. But in both time periods, the way in which the character was often drawn as object rather than subject skewed toward the presumed base audience of young adult white males in a way that undercut a feminist reading of the material for others.

BUFFY THE VAMPIRE SLAYER ENTERS THE DARK ALLEY IN
THE DARK AGE OF COMICS: THE LATE 1990s AND EARLY 2000s

As this time period in comics was described by writer Grant Morrison, "the gender confusions and reorganizations of masculine-feminine boundaries that marked the eighties had outgrown their welcome, so men became lads and women were babes."[32] *Wonder Woman* fell squarely into this area. Further, wrote Morrison, "no story could pass without at least one sequence during which an unlikely innocent would find herself alone and vulnerable in some completely inappropriate inner-city back alley setting . . . a skimpily attired naïf penetrating the seedy underbelly of the urban nightmare." Threatened, she would always be rescued at the last minute by a superhero.[33] Joss Whedon thought the hero should be the skimpily attired naïf: "There's the girl in the alley . . . and then the monster attacks her and *she* kills *it*."[34] Whedon both subverted the genre and made a political point: the petite Valley girl cheerleader, societally dismissed as frivolous, has superstrength and is critical to the world's safety.[35] Enter Buffy.

The *Buffy the Vampire Slayer* film ran in theaters in 1992; the television series, darker in tone and much closer to its creator's vision, premiered in 1997. This was at a time during which the Third Wave of feminism became more prominent, grounded as it was by young women organizing in reaction to the conservative politics of the 1980s and 1990s. It retains the Second Wave's emphasis on equality but extends it by building on critiques by feminists of color who saw the Second Wave as having a predominantly white, heterosexual standpoint. The Third Wave sensibility is antiessentialist and nonjudgmental, embracing not only a variety of identities among people but also within people. This includes not only openness to a continuum of race and sexuality but also the reclamation of signs of femininity as empowering. While the slogan "girl power" was used by some Third Wavers early on, it rather quickly became depoliticized and commodified, a slogan on T-shirts to be purchased rather than a description of a collective movement by young women. However, capitalizing on the marketization of the term probably enabled shows such as *Buffy* to get on the air.[36] Pop culture and mass media are important in the Third Wave, not just for deconstruction but also for production, which foregrounds personal narrative and tonally is often playful, campy, and ironic—using humor rather than preachiness to move people toward feminist ideals. Such a frame easily encompasses a female superhero who is comfortably strong in her body and sexuality *and* is also vulnerable in love, who uses humor *and* fights injustice, who is inclusive and compassionate *and* decisive and deadly.

Although they appear quite different at first glance, Diana and Buffy share a number of commonalities. Both superheroes have an origin and mission that stresses their uniqueness; both are referred to as "the chosen."[37]

Both repeatedly show transgressors compassion and allow them a path of redemption. Both have a relationship with a military man that shows a traditional view of opposite-sex relationships and how our heroes do not fit so neatly into such gendered binaries. But at the same time, both characters have a number of "others" that serve to construct them, in their white, heterosexual, middle-class-ness, as "normal" females.

Both, before and after the deaths of their (single) mothers, surround themselves with, love, and rely on others. The ways in which they encourage these chosen families to work with them makes them unlike most other superheroes, male or female.[38] For both characters, these families include their foils: for Diana, this is Artemis; for Buffy, it is Faith.[39] The characterizations of Artemis and Faith can be read as shoring up the main characters as "proper" female warriors, but can also be read as challenging what it means to be a "good" superheroine. Readers and viewers were clear that they wanted both the hero *and* the dark doppelganger. Writers listened and had both Faith and Artemis eventually embraced by other characters, fighting alongside them.[40]

Both Diana and Buffy were constructed to unsettle gender boundaries and especially to push males to embrace strong females. Just as *Wonder Woman* creator William Moulton Marston sought to engender "male acceptance of female love power," *Buffy* creator Joss Whedon said, "The one thing I had hoped to take part in was a shift in popular culture in the sense of people accepting the idea of the female hero."[41] As "others" among us, they live in a liminal space in which they embody gender norms while also questioning and subverting them. In this way the characters can open up more of a "range of gender possibilities" that "baffles the binary" and "create a new gender system in which [they] can enact 'woman' in nontraditional ways."[42]

CONVERGENCE IN THE 2000s: FEMINISM WITH IRONY AND HUMOR

The way in which both characters house great strength in female bodies destabilizes traditional gender norms. But the bodies themselves are quite different. In contrast to Diana's six-foot, solidly muscled, curvy, womanly frame, Buffy is nearer to five feet, slim, and blond. One is a commanding, stunningly beautiful presence; the other is seemingly unthreatening and girlishly cute.[43]

Buffy embodies the attractive female warrior while parodying it through her body and speech, criticizing the superhero and horror genres and gendered inequalities with humor. This complicates the show's politics. Was this show feminist in its strong female characters, or was it reinscribing patriarchy through a cast of pretty, white, stylish girls?[44] Can we reconcile the strong female agency, the friendship and community building, with the commercialized violence and the emphasis on individual consumer power through merchandizing? Do viewers and readers see the big picture about gender and power if the story focuses on the individual hero and delivers its message through irony?[45]

Joss Whedon basically answers yes to all of these questions: "If I can make teenage boys comfortable with a girl who takes charge of a situation without their knowing that's what's happening, it's better than sitting down and selling them on feminism." He also said, "[If I made] a series of lectures on PBS on why there should be feminism, no one would be coming to the party, and it would be boring. The idea of changing culture is important to me, and it can only be done in a popular medium."[46] Pender sums up the problem with those who would criticize *Buffy*'s adherence to traditional forms while delivering a powerfully threatening message about those forms: "If you say Buffy's form and her content are incompatible, then you have to conclude she can't be feminist because she has cleavage."[47]

Buffy and other shows and comics like it created a space for a different *Wonder Woman*, one that would take the character back to the visions of Marston and Pérez while also incorporating more of Whedon's sensibility. By the mid-2000s, *Buffy* became more overt about its feminism and its messages about empowerment, and *Wonder Woman* became more self-conscious and self-referentially humorous. *Buffy* could afford to do the former after having done it gently with its viewers for the previous five years; *Wonder Woman* could leverage increasing audience comfort with a postmodern ironic sensibility to broaden its base beyond the core fans who were already on board with its feminism.

"Diana is an inherently political character—she's about feminist politics, humanist politics, sex politics, the politics of war, etc.," summed up writer/artist Phil Jimenez.[48] He made Diana's mission explicit through her founding of the Wonder Woman Foundation: to promote "the liberation of men, women, and children from the terrible problems that stem from antiquated religious philosophies and patriarchal fear—by educating them about alternatives."[49] The Foundation ideas received mostly positive fan responses; a few were negative, such as, "Gentlemen, your soapbox is showing."[50] Another fan disliked hints that some Amazons might have same-sex relationships: "Lemme get this straight—you'll slight the Christians, but encourage and empower homosexuality? It is clear that homosexuality is *not* normal."[51] In response, the editor wrote, "For the record, Phil is working on giving Diana a boyfriend. . . . Letters like yours make it easy to use the word 'intolerant.'"

Phil Jimenez created Trevor Barnes, a dark-skinned, dark-haired, and dark-eyed man who worked with Diana at the UN. With some Buffy-esque humor not often displayed previously in *Wonder Woman*, she approaches him and asks him out, and he turns her down. After a panel depicting her shocked face, a male friend of Diana's consoles her, "For god's sakes, even

I'd sleep with you! Honey, if he said no to you, he's gay!"[52] The spoiler leaked that Diana might have sex with him. Jimenez commented at the time, "Empowering her when it comes to sexual choices is important. If it's still allowed to happen and all goes well [it] will be done in a respectful and peaceful manner." There was largely positive fan feedback to the idea, recalled Jimenez later, but also very "negative and often racist reactions," as well, that "undermined my goals."[53] What appeared was one panel in which Trevor's parents find them lying on a couch, mostly clothed—a polysemic image.

At the same time, there was more *Wonder Woman*–ness in the *Buffy* universe. In its last television season, 2002–2003, Buffy increasingly made speeches about power, about the strength to be found within each of us, about teamwork and compassion. "I say *my* power should be *our* power. . . . Slayers, every one of us. Make your choice. Are you ready to be strong?"[54] These somewhat more earnest moments in *Buffy*, in and around its usual humor and irony, are a device more identified with *Wonder Woman*: "Girls, there's nothing to it. All you have to do is have confidence in your own strength!"[55] particularly as written by Marston, Pérez, and Jimenez.

The convergence of the two universes occurred in other ways as well. *Buffy* creator Joss Whedon became attached to write a *Wonder Woman* live-action feature film, later canceled by DC/Warner Bros.[56] At the same time, writer Greg Rucka had penned a short story for a *Buffy* project in 2001, called *Tales of the Slayer*. The following year, he began writing *Wonder Woman*, having Diana work at the UN with a strong supporting cast, battling gods, and teaching nonviolent conflict resolution to kids.[57]

Rucka's highly praised run was grounded in the real world, portraying those for and against Diana's ideals as explicated in a book she wrote. The character nixes the first book cover suggested by the publisher, which showed her lying sexily on her stomach with a small pink drape covering very little of her—a meta-image that plays on the readers' savvy in recognizing the objectification of women and its use as a marketing ploy, as well as its inappropriateness for capturing the essence of Diana.[58] Rucka had some characters frame her and her book as "nontraditional": Greek, pagan, probably lesbian, vegetarian. One says of Diana, "I have no problem with her heroics, but the moment that woman gets in front of children to promote a life style and a belief system that right-thinking Americans find, frankly, disgusting, well, enough is enough. . . . She flies in the face of core family values. . . . She needs to remember her place." "As a woman?" he is asked.[59]

The *Buffy Season 8* comic, launched in 2007, contained a similar plot point about the "Americanness" of the main character, grounded in sexism. Says a military general of the slayers, "They got power, they got resources, and they got a hard-line ideology that does not jibe with American interests. Worst of all, they got a leader: charismatic, uncompromising, and completely destructive."[60] It is to this general that Buffy says the epigraph that opens this chapter, "It's about power and it's about women and you just hate those two words in the same sentence, don't you?" *Buffy Season 8* also stated its ideals more directly than had the first several years of the series: "Once upon a time, I did something good. . . . I found a way to share my power. Girls all over the world were given power—not just strength, though that does come in handy—but purpose, meaning, connection."[61] Along with this stating and restating of her mission, Buffy's adventures became increasingly fantastical, with more monsters and demons, alternate dimensions, and large-scale battles—in other words, more akin to *Wonder Woman.*

Wonder Woman writer Gail Simone has noted that her style of writing has often been compared to Joss Whedon's.[62] Like Pérez, Jimenez, and Rucka, she portrayed Diana in the late 2000s as a feminist icon who related well to our world but remained enough of an outsider to comment on its norms, often with humor. In one issue, Diana and the Black Canary team up. The latter informs her that they have to go undercover, and "the sexier the outfit, the fewer questions asked." Once dressed, she comments, "Ah, we look like high-end trashy hookers in a Tarantino nightmare. Perfect!" Diana looks down at herself, uncharacteristically awkward in expression and posture, and asks, "Do we need to expose quite so much of . . . [my breasts]? And these [high-heeled] boots seem completely impractical in a combat situation! I can't believe women are expected to wear these every day."[63] This simultaneous display of and parody of their usual costumes and those of other women may strike more of a chord with some readers than would a lengthy speech about the objectification of female superheroes. The next arc portrayed two kids being saved from a giant serpent by Diana. The girl says, "You're so pretty. I got your lunchbox," and the boy next to her says, "Who cares about that? She's tough!"[64] She is both, destabilizing our gendered expectations.

This mixing of genres, juxtaposing a fantastic monster with talk of merchandising and kids' traditionally gendered comments, along with the importance of protecting the vulnerable, isn't what earns *Wonder Woman* mainstream attention, though. Rather, a short run in summer 2010 was covered broadly in mainstream media because she was wearing pants. In an example of life imitating Rucka's story about the divided reactions to Diana's book, the *Huffington Post* wrote, "It's about time [she] got a pair of pants! Crimefighting pants!"[65] Fox News was less enthused because the pants were black, rather than blue with white stars: "Has she been stripped of her patriotism?"[66]

That outfit looks almost exactly like what Buffy is wearing in the first *Season 8* comic: dark red and gold tank top, tight shiny black pants, and black boots. But by this point in 2010, *Buffy Season 8* was winding down. In its last issue in January 2011, Joss Whedon noted that the comic had diverged somewhat from the series, "We've learned what you like, what you don't. . . . [In *Season 9*, we'll go] back, a bit, to the everyday trials that made Buffy more than a superhero. That made her us. I was so excited to finally have an unlimited budget that I wanted to make the [*Season 8*] book an epic, but I realized along the way that the things I loved the best were the things you loved the best . . . the down-to-earth, recognizable people."

DIVERGENCE IN THE COMICS, CONVERGENCE FOR TELEVISION IN THE 2010s

From this point, the preachiness and the fantastical content would decline in *Buffy*, and the self-referential commentary about gender and power would decline in *Wonder Woman*. For *Buffy* this seemed to be a response to fans by the creative team, as described by Whedon above. For *Wonder Woman*, this was due to DC Comics rebooting all of its superhero books in 2011, as it had in 1987, to improve profits. Mainstream news outlets covered DC's initiative, and sales of all of their titles initially skyrocketed.

This "New 52" *Wonder Woman* has been praised for its writing, its focus on the Greek gods, its story about Diana's protection of a young woman, and its art. It has also been criticized for its revision of her origin story and its level of violence. After seventy years, Diana is no longer born of clay and given life by goddesses; rather, she is the product of her mother's secret affair with king of the gods Zeus. The Amazons are no longer immortal and peace loving. Instead, they seduce, have sex with, and then kill passing sailors. They keep the female babies and sell the males into slavery in exchange for weapons. No longer is the god of war Ares Diana's nemesis; rather, he is her mentor. Writer Brian Azzarello has described this work as "a horror story." Never before would *Wonder Woman* have been described that way, but *Buffy* often has been.

The new backstory gives our hero some family angst to deal with and a hero's journey to take as she rises above her heritage; it also hews more closely to Greek myths. And the portrayal of Diana is far from sexually objectifying. Artist Cliff Chiang has noted that at conventions, the split is almost half and half between women and men who say they love the comic.[67] Writer Brian Azzarello has said, "We've definitely de-sexualized her," and "we've made her a very powerful woman."[68]

However, she also sticks a broken bottle in a demigod's hand when that demigod goads her. She grabs another irritating character's testicles, tells him to respect her or she'll rip them off, and then punches him when he reacts by calling her "cute." She puts a sword through Ares, becoming the goddess of war in his place.[69] This stands in sharp contrast to the character who, for decades, called all women "sister" instead of stabbing them, opened her hand to those who disagreed with her rather than using a closed fist, and avoided war at all costs. She seems less proactive and more reactive, less a leader and more part of a secondary player in an ensemble.

The question is whether these story elements, coupled with the desexualization and physical strength, still serve to enable new gender possibilities in a female body. I would like to say yes, but rather I agree with Phil Jimenez, who once said that this kind of portrayal makes it easy for people who "prefer to see her as just 'one of the guys' so they aren't confronted with the very deep issues she was created to contend with."[70] Her unique, antinormative mission to both embody and teach Amazonian principles of peace and love and equality, always intimately bound with her origin and her upbringing and her woman-ness, seem to have fallen away in this incarnation.

Fans are similarly torn. Podcasters on ten comic-book-centered podcasts initially loved the new comic; seven stayed with it after the first several issues. A few noted that they had never before devoted time to even talk about previous *Wonder Woman* comics on their podcasts. Some who were displeased with her rebooted origin were willing to go with it due to the other assets of the book.[71] On three of the ten, the podcasters liked the first issue. But it was downhill after that, particularly after the new origin of Diana and backstory of the Amazons appeared and the violence increased. Some have said that while it's a good story, it does not read like a *Wonder Woman* story.[72] Postings to message boards reflect the same divide. Unlike the last few writers, and unlike *Buffy*'s writers, the current *Wonder Woman* writer has said that he doesn't go on any message boards or blogs or look at reader comments.

At the same time, in the new *Justice League* comic, which has triple the sales of *Wonder Woman*, Diana's face is drawn younger and sexier. She has the same new outfit, but it's smaller—she spills out of her top and bottom. It made news, as DC intended, that Diana and Superman were portrayed kissing on the cover of the September 2012 issue of *Justice League*. *Good Morning America* showed the cover with the headline, "Superman! New sexy sidekick!" and referred to Diana as a "homewrecker."[73] Both are more traditional views of gender—the *Justice League* portrayal clearly objectifies her, and the mainstream media coverage sees the female character as an accessory to the male, tempting him away from his wife, Lois Lane.

These two new portrayals of Diana constitute yet another cycle in her history. Marston's empowering creation in the 1940s was followed by the more traditionally gendered narratives of the 1950s through 1970s. Pérez's antipatriarchal, propeace mission of the late 1980s was followed by the sexualized bad girl of the 1990s. The overt and playful Third Wave feminism of the 2000s has been followed by a violent portrayal in her own title alongside a more sexualized portrayal in *Justice League*.

Former *Wonder Woman* writer Greg Rucka has observed that portrayals of women and people of color improved in the mid-2000s but have gotten worse in the last few years. He noted that comic book readership has diversified somewhat, but "[the editors and publishers of mainstream superhero comics] reject the presence of a female audience, and a broader readership, and instead embrace a belief in a much smaller readership that is apparently this theoretical 18–34 year old white male who likes his beer cold and his tits big and his superheroes bloody." But statistics show, he and the podcasters continued, that more women go to movies and buy books than men, and that women are more likely to control household spending than men, so the decision to focus on what that audience may want is not economically sound. "In the main, it's a bunch of guys who don't get it. It's very, very gendered with [*Wonder Woman*]."[74] More recently, he said that the publisher hasn't allowed the character "to have a voice that is a political voice, because they're afraid of controversy, because they're afraid that controversy will cost them money."[75] Phil Jimenez, too, has cited "corporate involvement" and "trepidation with labeling anything overly feminist for fear of economic and social backlash" as contributing to *Wonder Woman*'s swings in portrayal.[76]

Buffy, which as a TV show had an audience in the millions, has gone back to its roots in the comic as promised by Whedon in 2011. *Season 9* has backed away from the large-scale otherwordly action and is more focused on Buffy, her friends, and the dark-alley slaying of vampires. She works in a coffee shop and briefly as a bodyguard. When her client asks if her company has anyone bigger to guard him, she replies, "I only come in Buffy size. And it's kind of the point. No one will ever think I'm a bodyguard."[77] Her body is a disguise for her strength. She reaches out to new allies, such as the teen Billy, who wants to slay vampires in part to offset the bullying he has endured for identifying as gay. He worries, "I'm not a real slayer. . . . They're special. They're called. They're strong. . . . They're always girls." His friend assures him, in a compliment that subverts the usually insulting use of the phrase, "I think you can punch like a girl," and Buffy welcomes him to the team.[78]

So in 2013 in their comics, Diana and Buffy remain powerful women fighting dark forces, but the Third Wave similarities, in the mixing of fantastic plot and social commentary and humor, in having a family of friends and foils, in the sharing of power, have faded. There is, however, a potential area of convergence for the two characters on the horizon. A new TV show, *Amazon*, is being cast at the CW network. It is to take place in Diana's pre–Wonder Woman teen years, placing Wonder Woman in a girl-power "box." The producers may be trying to recapture the *Smallville* and *Buffy* audiences through a strong yet vulnerable female character who is younger, prettier, quippier, and more palatable and less threatening than a grown woman—at least to those whose dollars advertisers want to reach whom Rucka mentions above. Jeffrey A. Brown describes the girl-power genre and its limits as follows: "It can depict challenging images of powerful girls without challenging cultural expectations of women."[79] This can certainly be the case, but it may also be pessimistic—couldn't the girls who felt empowered watching the young female hero bring that empowerment into their adulthood? Couldn't the boys who respected that hero bring that respect into adulthood?

What some may see as apolitical, postfeminist, commodified girl power can be someone else's thoroughly political and thoroughly feminist activism, so the potential is still there for innovative, intersectional, and inclusive reworkings of gender and power in this new TV show. As *Buffy* has shown in that medium, the boundaries of a gendered box can certainly be rattled, bent, and pushed through while in some ways relying on the traditional boundaries. Indeed, familiarity can help smooth the path to change. As Anne Marie Smith notes about gender, "the effectiveness of new articulations depends on two basic factors: the extent to which traditional articulations have become increasingly weakened . . . and the extent to which new articulations borrow from and rework various traditional frameworks so that they already appear somewhat familiar."[80]

CONCLUSION: THE POLITICS OF NEGOTIATING THE FEMALE SUPERHERO

Superhero stories don't just reflect elite narratives of gender, or race, or class, or sexuality that are then accepted by passive readers. There is always room for queering the text and for forging spaces for empowerment that may or may not have been intended by writers or editors or corporate owners. But neither are dominant cultural narratives always resisted by consumers actively reading against a hegemonic grain, and producers, mindful of profit and of broadening their characters' appeal, are clearly mindful that different audiences have different levels of power. In the end, *Wonder Woman* and *Buffy* and other titles like them are "read, reworked, or reinvented in quite unpredictable ways"[81] by a variety of constituencies.

Our task is to interrogate the "articulation of larger social and political struggles" that occurs through the site of comics.[82] Why this can and should be done through the genre of the superhero in particular is summarized well by Grant Morrison: "Superhero stories . . . contain at their hearts all the dreams and fears of generations in vivid miniature. . . . They tell us where we've been, what we feared, and what we desired, and today they are more popular, more all-pervasive than ever because they still speak to us about what we really want to be."[83]

NOTES

1. *Buffy the Vampire Slayer* debuted as a live-action theatrically released movie in 1992 and ran as a live-action television show from 1997 to 2003. A comic book series with the same title, from Dark Horse Comics, ran from 1998 to 2004; not all parts of it are considered canon. The current comic book series, also from Dark Horse, has run from 2007 to the present and is canonical and continuous. Picking up directly after the end of the seven-season TV show, its volumes are titled *Season 8* and *Season 9*. There was a pilot for an animated series that wasn't picked up.

Wonder Woman debuted in the comics in 1941 and as part of the team of superheroes in *Justice League of America* in 1960. These were produced by DC Comics. She appeared in a live-action television show from 1975 to 1979. There was a pilot for a new live-action television show in 2011 that wasn't picked up; a second television pilot is currently being cast, tentatively titled *Amazon*. A *Wonder Woman* movie, written by Joss Whedon (the creator of *Buffy the Vampire Slayer*) in 2005–2006, languished in development and was canceled. Wonder Woman could be seen in animated form in the 1973–1986 *Superfriends* and its updated version from 2001 to 2006, *Justice League*, as well as in the direct-to-DVD animated film *Wonder Woman* (2009) and four other Justice League films: *The New Frontier* (2008), *Crisis on Two Earths* (2010), *Doom* (2012), and *Flashpoint Paradox* (2013). There are also two comics for young kids, *DC Superfriends* and *The Justice League Adventures*, that have more simplistic and nonviolent story lines and portray all of the characters smiling and with nonsexualized bodies.

The consumers of these various media—and of widely available merchandise—extend well beyond the stereotypical comic book–reading audience (eighteen- to thirty-four-year-old white males) to other demographic groups.

2. Wonder Woman's creator, William Moulton Marston, sought to create a "feminine character with all the strength of Superman plus all the allure of a good and beautiful woman." W. M. Marston, "Why 100,000,000 Americans Read Comics," *American Scholar* 13, no. 1 (1943): 42. He opined that war would not end "until women control men," but he was optimistic that this would occur because "Wonder Woman, and the trend toward male acceptance of female love power which she represents, indicates that the first psychological step has actually been taken." Quoted in Olive Richard, "Our Women Are Our Future," *Family Circle*, August 14, 1942, http://www.castlekeys.com/Pages/wonder.html (accessed January 1, 2013). Marston's editor at DC Comics, Sheldon Mayer, commented that Marston "was writing a feminist book but not for women. He was dealing with a male audience." Quoted in Les Daniels, *Wonder Woman: The Complete History* (New York: DC Comics, 2009), 33.

Buffy's creator, Joss Whedon, said in 2001, "I always wanted the character to be an icon. I wanted her to be a hero that existed in people's minds the way Wonder Woman or Spider Man does." That same year he stated, "If I can make teenage boys comfortable with a girl who takes charge of a situation without their knowing that's what's happening, it's better than sitting down and selling them on feminism." These quotes are from two interviews with Whedon, respectively, Shawna Ervin-Gore, "Interview with Joss Whedon," Dark Horse News, 2001, http://web.archive.org/web/20080211141837/http://www.darkhorse.com/news/interviews.php?id=737 (accessed January 1, 2013); and Ginia Bellafante, "Bewitching Teen Heroines," *Time*, June 24, 2001, http://content.time.com/time/magazine/article/0,9171,137626,00.html (accessed June 24, 2013).

3. In using the phrase "interactive public spheres," I am drawing from Lisa Duggan's analysis of mass circulation newspapers in *Sapphic Slashers: Sex, Violence, and American Modernity* (Durham, NC: Duke University Press, 2000). In speaking of the production/reception binary as more of a collaboration and negotiation, I am drawing from Jeffrey A. Brown's analysis in *Black Superheroes, Milestone Comics, and Their Fans* (Jackson: University Press of Mississippi, 2000). I am not asserting that producers and consumers are equal in this space. I am asserting that there is a mutually productive relationship between producers and consumers and that each constrains the other in different ways. See Will Brooker, *Batman Unmasked: Analyzing a Cultural Icon* (London: Continuum, 2000); Duggan, *Sapphic Slashers*; and Anna Marie Smith, *New Right Discourses on Race and Sexuality: Britain, 1968–1990* (New York:

Cambridge University Press, 1994), on reception, resistance, and constraints. Jennifer Reed uses the phrase "competing constituent audiences" in her 2009 article "Reading Gender Politics on *The L Word*: The Moira/Max Transitions," *Journal of Popular Film and Television* 37. See also Carolyn Cocca, "Negotiating the Third Wave of Feminism in Wonder Woman," *PS: Political Science and Politics* 47 (January 2014).

I am speaking here of how active comic readers engage with authors, artists, editors, and publishers, traditionally through letter columns (letters from fans, chosen by editors, appearing in the back of new comics) and through comic book conventions. Today, this also occurs through websites sponsored by the publishers, editors, writers, or artists themselves, as well as in reader-sponsored blogs and podcasts. A number of prominent writers sign in to such websites and blogs anonymously to read posts; others do so openly and engage with readers. On the many podcasts geared toward the medium of comics, podcasters discuss particular issues, or story arcs, or characters; a number of them read e-mails, blog posts, or tweets from listeners so as to engage with their concerns. Some of them interview writers, editors, and artists as well.

4. William Moulton Marston (w) and Harry Peter (a), *Sensation Comics* #1, 1942; and William Moulton Marston (w) and Harry Peter (a), *Wonder Woman* [hereafter, *WW*] Vol. 1 #1, 1942.

5. William Moulton Marston (w) and Harry Peter (a), *WW* Vol. 1 #13, 1945.

6. Subversions of narratives of gender and power are not just about women, as a few works on superhero comics note when they write about their appeal to queer youth, particularly in terms of the resonance of a secret identity, for example, Roz Kaveney, *Superheroes: Capes and Crusaders in Comics and Films* (London: I. B. Tauris, 2008); and Brian Mitchell Peters, "Qu(e)erying Comic Book Culture and Representations of Sexuality in *Wonder Woman*," *Comparative Literature and Culture* 5 (2003), http://docs.lib.purdue.edu/clcweb/vol5/iss3/6 (accessed January 10, 2013). A number of gay male *Wonder Woman* fans have expressed that they found in her a strong role model without her strength being linked to being macho, that she was accepting of everyone, that she was true to herself regardless of gendered expectations, and that she didn't bow to cultural stereotypes; Trina Robbins, "Wonder Woman: Queer Appeal," *International Journal of Comic Art* 10 (2008): 89–94; Gail Simone, "Five Questions with Phil Jimenez," 2008, http://fivequestionswith.wordpress.com/phil-j (accessed January 1, 2013); Comic Book Queers podcasts #49, 2007, and #125, 2010; see also Kaveney, *Superheroes*; and Peters, "Qu(e)erying Comic Book Culture" on the resonance of a secret identity for closeted gay youth).

7. For historical overviews of comics and the comics industry particularly grounded in this time period, see Matthew Costello, *Secret Identity Crisis: Comic Books and the Unmasking of Cold War America* (New York: Continuum, 2009); Marc DiPaolo, *War, Politics, and Superheroes: Ethics and Propaganda in Comics and Film* (Jefferson, NC: McFarland, 2011); Jean-Paul Gabilliet, *Of Comics and Men: A Cultural History of Comic Books*, trans. Bart Beaty and Nick Nguyen (Jackson: University Press of Mississippi, 2010); David Hajdu, *The Ten-Cent Plague: The Great Comic Book Scare and How It Changed America* (New York: Macmillan, 2008); Stephen Krensky, *Comic Book Century: The History of American Comic Books* (Minneapolis, MN: Twenty-First Century Books, 2008); and Bradford Wright, *Comic Book Nation: The Transformation of Youth Culture in America* (Baltimore, MD: Johns Hopkins University Press, 2001). None of these addresses gender at any length. Paul Lopes, *Demanding Respect: The Evolution of the American Comic Book* (Philadelphia: Temple University Press, 2009), and Mike Madrid, *The Supergirls: Fashion, Feminism, Fantasy, and the History of Comic Book Heroines* (Minneapolis, MN: Exterminating Angel Press, 2009), are exceptions.

8. Marina Hollon, "Superheroine History, 1959–1984: Wonder Woman and Supergirl" (master's thesis, CSU San Marcos, December 2012), 89, https://csusm-dspace.calstate.edu/handle/10211.8/261 (accessed January 1, 2013). Such supplements appeared in twenty-seven out of thirty-one issues from 1962 to 1971.

9. Dennis O'Neil (w) and Mike Sekowsky (a), *Diana Prince: Wonder Woman*, vol. 1 [collecting *Wonder Woman* Vol. 1, #178–184, 1968] (New York: DC Comics, 2008), #178–179.

10. Quoted in Daniels, *Wonder Woman*, 126. O'Neil spoke about it in this way at the Denver Comic-Con on May 31, 2013, as well. He also admitted that while he was coming from the left

politically, and thought he was serving the cause of feminism, he looks back now and sees that his ideas about gender politics were not as advanced as he thought they were. See also Hollon, "Superheroine History," 102.

11. *Ms.* and DC Comics co-published a collection of Wonder Woman stories with a heartfelt introduction by Gloria Steinem on what the character's strength, compassion, and sense of justice meant to her and other young women. Gloria Steinem, *Wonder Woman* (New York: Holt, Rinehart, and Winston and Warner Books, 1972). Also, *Ms.* magazine debuted in the summer of 1972 with classic Wonder Woman on the cover, hailing her as a feminist icon.

12. Editor Julius Schwartz quoted in Daniels, *Wonder Woman*, 134. Note the change in the Comics Code in 1971 as it amended the Code of 1954 that enabled such portrayals. The deleted material from the old code is in strikethrough and new additions are in italics: "Nudity in any form is prohibited. Suggestive and salacious illustration is unacceptable. Females shall be drawn realistically without *undue emphasis on* any physical qualities." Quoted in Gabilliet, *Of Comics and Men*, 316–20.

13. Hollon, "Superheroine History," 93, 96.

14. Hollon, "Superheroine History," 106, 113, 119, 120, 123. While six letters from 1974 to 1983 referred to Wonder Woman as feminist, twenty-six letters from 1968 to 1983 requested that Steve Trevor be empowered.

15. See, for example, *WW* #219, 1975; #230, 1977; #250–253, 1978–1979; #263–264, 1980; #275, 1981; #288–290, 1982; and #318, 1984; see also Lillian Robinson, *Wonder Women: Feminisms and Superheroes* (New York: Routledge, 2004), and Madrid, *The Supergirls.*

16. In short, higher fuel and paper costs and increasing comic sticker prices, darker and increasingly hypermasculinized stories, the growth of speculation and of comic shops followed by the decline of both, distributor wars, and a royalty system that led to a focus on high sales of superhero comics, as well as other causes, were leading to this more concentrated comic fan base for mainstream superhero stories. See Brooker, *Batman Unmasked*; Gabilliet, *Of Comics and Men*; Krensky, *Comic Book Century*; Lopes, *Demanding Respect*; and Wright, *Comic Book Nation.*

17. Pérez, *WW* Vol. 2 #17, 1987. His run consisted of *WW* Vol. 2 #1–62, 1987–1992. Madrid, *The Supergirls*; see also Brown, *Black Superheroes*; DiPaolo, *War, Politics, and Superheroes*; Gabilliet, *Of Comics and Men*; and Kaveney, *Superheroes.*

18. Interview, Supernova Pop Culture Expo, April 9, 2010.

19. George Pérez, *WW* Vol. 2 #1, 1987, wrote in the first issue that no one else wanted the comic, so he volunteered to take it on. But what he said in later interviews shows something else at work as well. "'They didn't like the way the story was going to go; they didn't like the artist involved,' Perez recounts. 'They were just going to put it out there, settle for what they could get.' Barbara Kesel, then a DC editor, remembers she 'strongly disliked' [the original writer's] take on the character. 'His WW was a nasty uber-bitch, rather than a hero,' Kesel says. 'To me, it was an embarrassing version of the character.' [The] plot had been rewritten several times in an effort to tone down elements some felt were misogynistic, but the revisions, though more tolerable, were still far from satisfactory. Perez observed the apprehension among the staff and realized WW was a book 'no one had any hope for.' He found his challenge. 'I asked Janice if I could come in and draw the first six issues,' he recalls. 'It was my first kiss from an editor.'" Chris Lawrence, *George Perez: Storyteller* (Dynamite Entertainment, 2006), 77.

20. Karen Berger, in George Pérez, *WW* Vol. 2 #2, 1987.

21. Neil Roberts, in *WW* Vol. 2 #4.

22. Malcolm Bourne, in *WW* Vol. 2 #5. Other examples include, "You have Wonder Woman going in the best direction in which the title can be taken . . . emphasizing its Greek myths and feminism" (Paul Carbonaro, in *WW* Vol. 2 #4). "She is a strong and interesting woman" (Norman Ore, in *WW* Vol. 2 #5). "She is a tribute to her sex, a genuine wonder of a woman" (Tonya Falls, in *WW* Vol. 2 #8).

23. Gabilliet, *Of Comics and Men*; Lopes, *Demanding Respect*, 122; Mitra Emad, "Reading Wonder Woman's Body: Mythologies of Gender and Nation," *Journal of Popular Culture* 39 (2006): 969. See also note 16 above.

24. DiPaolo, *War, Politics, and Superheroes*, 83.

25. See also Brown, *Black Superheroes*; Daniels, *Wonder Woman*; Madrid, *The Supergirls*; Grant Morrison, *Supergods: What Masked Vigilantes, Miraculous Mutants, and a Sun God from Smallville Can Teach Us about Being Human* (New York: Spiegel and Grau, 2011); and Kelli Stanley, "'Suffering Sappho!': Wonder Woman and the (Re)invention of the Feminine Ideal," *Helios* 32 (2005). Loebs wrote almost forty issues (*WW* Vol. 2 #63–100, 1992–1995), and Deodato drew only the last ten, but those ten grew sales and drew great attention. The next writer/artist, John Byrne, would draw Diana with curves as well as bulging muscles and a grimace; she was not so objectified and looked almost exactly like his She-Hulk from 1992 (*WW* Vol. 2 #101–36, 1995–1998). Male superheroes' muscles were supersized by this point as well. But also note that male superheroes were never, and still are never, posed in the sexualized, objectified poses often used for female superheroes.

The trend toward these types of portrayals of women in comics was echoed in the wider availability of pornography on the Internet and of role-playing video games with higher levels of violence and sexual content.

26. Interview by Newsarama staff, 2006, archived at http://www.comicbloc.com/forums/archive/index.php?t-29878.html. Generally, sales of a run tend to decline as it goes on. But Deodato is correct—sales during his time on *Wonder Woman* almost quadrupled (http://forums.comicbookresources.com/showthread.php?301596-Wonder-Woman-Sales-Figures-Now-to-1942&p=10238789#post10238789).

27. Henry King, in *WW* Vol. 2 #93.

28. Eric Gerbershagen, in *WW* Vol. 2 #104.

29. The first is Kate Payne, in *WW* Vol. 2 #95; the second is Joanna Sandsmark in the same issue. Joanna seems to undercut her own argument, implying that all women are oversensitive to nudity rather than calling attention to the politics of objectification.

30. Robert Baytan, in *WW* Vol. 2 #91.

31. The first of these was in response to Kate Payne in #95; the second in response to Robert Baytan in #91.

32. Morrison, *Supergods*, 235.

33. Morrison, *Supergods*, 251.

34. Tasha Robinson, "Interview: Joss Whedon," *AV Club*, August 8, 2007, http://www.avclub.com/article/joss-whedon-14136(accessed January 11, 2013).

35. As Fuchs writes, "part of *Buffy*'s genius lies in its ironic undermining of the status quo it appears to epitomize," and Buffy's body is central to that (Cynthia Fuchs, "'Did Anyone Ever Explain to You What Secret Identity Means?': Race and Displacement in Buffy and Dark Angel," in *Undead TV: Essays on Buffy the Vampire Slayer*, ed. Elana Levine and Lisa Parks, 96–115 [Durham, NC: Duke University Press, 2007], 102). But Brown writes that "the overall girlishness of the contemporary action heroine allows these characters to be sexually appealing to male viewers without implicitly challenging patriarchal standards" (Brown, *Dangerous Curves*, 166). Both can be true and so can broaden the appeal of the character. For some readers, patriarchal standards will be subverted; for others, they will be reinscribed.

36. In music, the term was exemplified in the 1990s by riot grrrl bands like Bikini Kill (who used the girl-power slogan on an early one of their zines), Bratmobile, and Sleater-Kinney. They were specifically grounded in protest against the Reagan and Bush policies of the 1980s and 1990s, particularly about reproductive rights. More commercially, the phrase has been associated (in varying degrees of accuracy) with the Spice Girls and Madonna, and with TV shows such as *Buffy, Xena: Warrior Princess, Alias, Dark Angel, La Femme Nikita,* and *Charmed.* The Third Wave has often been conflated, inaccurately, not only with "girl power" but also with "postfeminism"—the latter being the idea that feminism isn't necessary because equality is here.

37. George Pérez, *WW* Vol. 2 #19, 1988. The voice-over introduction of each episode of *Buffy the Vampire Slayer* states that she is the "chosen one."

38. Kevin Durand, *Buffy Meets the Academy: Essays on the Episodes and Scripts as Text* (Jefferson, NC: McFarland, 2000); Frances Early, "Staking Her Claim: Buffy the Vampire Slayer as Transgressive Woman Warrior," *Journal of Popular Culture* 35 (2001); Susan Payne-Mulliken and Valerie Renegar, "Buffy Never Goes It Alone: The Rhetorical Construction of Sisterhood in the Final Season," in *Buffy Meets the Academy: Essays on the Episodes and*

Scripts as Text, ed. Kevin Durand (Jefferson, NC: McFarland, 2009), 57–77; Jowett, *Sex and the Slayer*; Jennifer K. Stuller, *Ink-Stained Amazons and Cinematic Warriors: Superwomen in Modern Mythology* (London: I. B. Tauris, 2010); Sharon Ross, "'Tough Enough': Female Friendship and Heroism in Xena and Buffy," in *Action Chicks: New Images of Tough Women in Popular Culture*, ed. Sherrie Inness (Gordonsville, VA: Palgrave Macmillan, 2004), 231–55; Gladys L. Knight, *Female Action Heroes: A Guide to Women in Comics, Video Games, Film, and Television* (Santa Barbara, CA: ABC-CLIO/Greenwood, 2010); Robinson, *Wonder Women*.

39. William Messner-Loebs (w) and Mike Deodato Jr. (a), "The Contest," *Wonder Woman* Vol. 2 #90–93 (New York: DC Comics, 1995); William Messner-Loebs (w) and Mike Deodato Jr. (a), "The Challenge of Artemis," *Wonder Woman* Vol. 2 #94–100 (New York: DC Comics, 1996); William Messner-Loebs (w) and Ed Benes (a), "Requiem," *Artemis* (New York: DC Comics, 1996).

A number of Buffy scholars have written about Faith in varying levels of detail: see, for example, Early, "Staking Her Claim"; Elyce Rae Helford, "My Emotions Give Me Power: The Containment of Girls' Anger in Buffy," in *Fighting the Forces: What's at Stake in* Buffy the Vampire Slayer, ed. Rhonda Wilcox and David Lavery (Lanham, MD: Rowman & Littlefield, 2002), 18–34; Roz Kaveney, *Reading the Vampire Slayer: An Unofficial Critical Companion to Buffy and Angel* (New York: Tauris Park, 2001); Rhonda Wilcox, "'Who Died and Made Her the Boss?' Patterns of Mortality in *Buffy the Vampire Slayer*," in *Fighting the Forces: What's at Stake in* Buffy the Vampire Slayer, ed. Rhonda Wilcox and David Lavery (Lanham, MD: Rowman & Littlefield, 2002), 3–17.

40. *Buffy Season 7* #18–22 and *Season 8*; Jimenez, *WW* Vol. 2; Rucka, *WW* Vol. 2; Simone, *WW* Vol. 3.

41. "The Last Sundown" featurette, *Buffy the Vampire Slayer*, season 7, disc 6. See also note 2 above.

42. Quotes from Gwyn Symonds, "'Solving Problems with Sharp Objects': Female Empowerment, Sex, and Violence in *Buffy the Vampire Slayer*," *Journal of the Whedon Studies Association* 3 (2004), http://slayageonline.com/PDF/symonds.pdf; Patricia Pender, "'I'm Buffy, and You're History,'" and Sherrie A. Inness, "Introduction: Boxing Gloves and Bustiers: New Images of Tough Women," in *Action Chicks: New Images of Tough Women in Popular Culture*, ed. Sherrie Inness (Gordonsville, VA: Palgrave Macmillan, 2004), respectively. See also Brown, "Gender, Sexuality, and Toughness," and Marc Camron, "The Importance of Being the Zeppo: Xander, Gender Identity, and Hybridity in *Buffy the Vampire Slayer*," *Slayage: The Journal of the Whedon Studies Association* 6 (2007), http://slayageonline.com/PDF/Camron.pdf; Lorna Jowett, *Sex and the Slayer: A Gender Studies Primer for the Buffy Fan* (Middletown, CT: Wesleyan University Press, 2005); Philip Mikosz and Dana Och, "Previously on *Buffy the Vampire Slayer*," *Slayage: The Journal of the Whedon Studies Association* 2 (2002), http://slayageonline.com/PDF/mikosz_och.pdf; Peters, "Qu(e)erying Comic Book Culture"; Zoe-Jane Playden, "'What You Are, What's to Come': Feminisms, Citizenship and the Divine," in *Reading the Vampire Slayer: An Unofficial Critical Companion to Buffy and Angel*, ed. Roz Kaveney (New York: Tauris Park, 2001), 120–47; Arwen Spicer, "'Love's Bitch but Man Enough to Admit It': Spike's Hybridized Gender," *Slayage: The Journal of the Whedon Studies Association* 2 (2002), http://slayageonline.com/PDF/spicer.pdf; and Rhonda Wilcox and David Lavery, eds., *Fighting the Forces: What's at Stake in* Buffy the Vampire Slayer (Lanham, MD: Rowman & Littlefield, 2002).

43. While Diana's body has been more objectified, more often drawn with overt sex appeal for a male gaze than has Buffy's, Diana's sexuality has been far more constrained. In seventy-plus years we have seen Diana kiss a few people a few times, and that's it. This speaks to a discomfort with Diana's sexuality that I would attribute to a Victorian view of a proper woman as being chaste, virtuous, and nonsexual—an object not to be touched, on a pedestal that also serves as a cage. As one *Wonder Woman* writer said of the character, "She'd concretized over the years, had turned into this really cool Porsche that people kept in the garage. . . . One podcaster said that Wonder Woman had become like his grandmother, and he didn't want to see his grandmother being flirty. . . . She became the mom of the girl next door you wanted to date" (J. Michael Straczynski [w] et al., *WW* #600 [New York: DC Comics, 2010]). That girl

was apparently Buffy. While her girlish body has always been more subject than object, her love life and her sex life—in which she is portrayed as an active agent—are integral parts of her stories. None of her relationships is idealized; none is portrayed as being between a dominant male and passive female; rather, they are all messy disruptions of a traditional narrative of heterosexuality.

44. Similarly, Mike Madrid writes of Wonder Woman, "Sex appeal was the spoonful of sugar that helped the medicine of feminism go down" (*The Supergirls*, 155). Also Brown, "Gender, Sexuality, and Toughness"; Madrid, *The Supergirls*; Pender, "'I'm Buffy, and You're History'"; Peters, "Qu(e)erying Comic Book Culture"; and Taylor, "'He's Gotta Be Strong'"; note the performative aspects of being a female superhero: that femininity can be put on, can be camp or burlesque, can distract villains from a superhero's true powers, and can disrupt gendered assumptions.

45. On these questions, see, for example, Brown, "Gender, Sexuality, and Toughness"; Early, "Staking Her Claim"; Frances Early and Kathleen Kennedy, introduction to *Athena's Daughters: Television's New Warrior Women*, ed. Frances Early and Kathleen Kennedy (New York: Syracuse University Press, 2003); Helford, "My Emotions Give Me Power"; Inness, "Introduction"; Jowett, *Sex and the Slayer*; Robinson, *Wonder Women*; Charlene Tung, "Gender, Race, and Sexuality in *La Femme Nikita*," in *Action Chicks: New Images of Tough Women in Popular Culture*, ed. Sherrie Inness (Gordonsville, VA: Palgrave Macmillan, 2004), 95–121; Mary Magoulick, "Frustrating Female Heroism: Mixed Messages in *Xena*, *Nikita*, and *Buffy*," *Journal of Popular Culture* 39 (2006).

46. Quoted in Bellafante, "Bewitching Teen Heroines," and Nussbaum, "Must-See Metaphysics," *New York Times*, September 22, 2002, respectively.

47. Pender, "'I'm Buffy, and You're History,'" 43.

48. Jimenez wrote from 2000 to 2002, *WW* Vol. 2 #164–88. Quoted in DiPaolo, *War, Politics, and Superheroes*, 86.

49. Phil Jimenez, *WW* Vol. 2 #170, 2001.

50. Chris Jackson, in *WW* Vol. 2 #173, 2001.

51. Seth Richard, in *WW* Vol. 2 #177, 2002.

52. Phil Jimenez, *WW* Vol. 2 #170, 2001. The next writer killed off Trevor. The death of Trevor was written by Walt Simonson in 2003 (*WW* Vol. 2 #194). It can be interpreted as a response to the criticism, or as a capitulation to the idea that the way to build tolerance is to have the "noble" minority figure make a sacrifice and earn respect, or it may have been a way to force the character back to her roots of forming new circles of allies around herself.

In another humorous turn, Wonder Girl Cassie Sandsmark appears to say that she has just returned from a trip to Hollywood, where she got to "totally hang out on the set of 'Wendy the Werewolf Stalker'!" The accompanying panel shows a petite blond girl holding a stake in her hand, with three other teens behind her and a werewolf looming over them, an undeniable reference to *Buffy*. Phil Jimenez, *WW* Vol. 2 #171, 2001.

53. "Wonder Man: Phil Jimenez talks Wonder Woman," January 23, 2002, http://www.comicbookresources.com/?page=article&id=796.

54. Joss Whedon, "Chosen," *Buffy the Vampire Slayer*, season 7, episode 22 (20th Century Fox, 2003), DVD.

55. William Moulton Marston (w) and Harry Peter (a), *WW* Vol.1 #13, 1945.

56. Whedon did not base Buffy on Wonder Woman; indeed, he says he had never been a real fan of the comic. Rather, he says Buffy is closest to Kitty Pryde of the *X-Men*. Lev Grossman, "Interview with Neil Gaiman and Joss Whedon," *Time*, September 25, 2005.

57. Greg Rucka (w) and J. G. Jones (a), *Wonder Woman: The Hiketeia* (New York: DC Comics, 2002), and *WW* Vol. 2 #195–226 (New York: DC Comics, 2003–2005).

In 2006, in an acceptance speech to an award given him by the group Equality Now, Joss Whedon recounted that he is constantly asked why he writes strong female characters. He gave many different renditions of his various answers over the years but then said that he always in the end replies, "Because you're still asking me that question" (May 15, http://www.equalitynow.org/media/joss_whedon_accepts_equality_now_award). In 2012, Greg Rucka posted a lengthy essay on the website *i09* titled, "Why I Write Strong Female Characters," because, he too is constantly asked this question. The short answer, he says, is that he writes "strong characters, and some of them are female" (May 22, http://io9.com/5912366/why-i-write-strong-female-characters).

58. Greg Rucka, *WW* Vol. 2 #195, 2003.

59. Greg Rucka, *WW* Vol. 2 #198, 2003.

60. Joss Whedon (w) and Georges Jeanty (a), *Buffy* Vol. 8 #1 (Milwaukie, OR: Dark Horse Comics, 2007). In another parallel, Rucka's run ended with Diana killing a human being, Maxwell Lord, who was controlling Superman and forcing him into destructive actions. This was in keeping with the trend in the 2000s in comics of portrayals of lack of trust in governments as well as in superheroes. See Costello, *Secret Identity*; Kaveney, *Superheroes*; A. David Lewis, "The Militarism of American Superheroes after 9/11," in *Comic Books and American Cultural History: An Anthology*, ed. Matthew Pustz (New York: Continuum); and Morrison, *Supergods*, on this point. Similarly, in *Buffy* Vol. 8 #8 in 2007, Buffy says, in contrast to the seven years of the TV series, that she—like Diana—would consider killing a human being if necessary (Brian K. Vaughan [w] and Georges Jeanty [a]).

61. Joss Whedon (w) and Georges Jeanty (a), *Buffy* Vol. 8 #11, 2008.

62. Gail Simone, December 20, 2010, comment on "Your Favorite Comics Character," at JinxWorld Forums, http://www.606studios.com/bendisboard/showthread.php?201442-Your-Favorite-Comics-Character!&p=7399945#post7399945; and Gail Simone, January 12, 2011, comment on "Your Favorite Comics Character," at JinxWorld Forums,http://www.606studios.com/bendisboard/showthread.php?202271-Gail-asked-to-write-Buffy-season-9-!-!-!&p=7465009#post7465009. She wrote *WW* Vol. 3 #14–44—the first ongoing female writer of the comic. At the end of her *Wonder Woman* run, Simone was asked to write for the *Buffy* comic, although she declined. She also noted at the time that she never read or watched *Buffy*.

Two women had worked on writing *Wonder Woman* in the 1980s before the 1987 relaunch, Mindy Newell (*WW* #326–28, 1985) and Trina Robbins (*Legends of Wonder Woman*, 1986). Robbins also illustrated the series. Newell collaborated with George Pérez after the relaunch as well (*WW* Vol. 2 #36–46, 49 [1989–1990]). Jill Thompson illustrated a number of issues in 1989–1991. In 2007, after yet another relaunch, best-selling novelist Jodi Picoult wrote a few issues (*WW* Vol. 3 #6–10).

Note that there were no letter columns during this run, but that Simone launched a thread on the Comic Book Resources site for fans to post comments and questions (some of which were negative, although most were quite positive), and she quite often responded to them directly. She does the same at gailsimone.tumblr.com.

63. Gail Simone, *WW* Vol. 3 #34, 2009.

64. Gail Simone, *WW* Vol. 3 #40, 2010.

65. Jen Wang and Diana Nguyen, "Wonder Woman Finally Gets a Pair of Pants," *Huffington Post*, June 30, 2010, http://www.huffingtonpost.com/disgrasian/wonder-woman-finally-gets_b_630771.html (accessed January 11, 2013).

66. Jo Piazza, "New Wonder Woman Loses Patriotic Costume in Favor of 'Globalized' Duds," *Fox News*, July 1, 2010, http://www.foxnews.com/entertainment/2010/07/01/new-wonder-woman-loses-patriotic-costume/#ixzz2HK9xqNBO (accessed January 1, 2013). Sales of that issue were almost double those before and after it. J. Michael Straczynski (w) et al., *Wonder Woman* #600 (2010). The costume was designed by Jim Lee. For an example of mainstream media coverage, see George Gene Gustines, "Makeover for Wonder Woman at 69," *New York Times*, June 29, 2010, http://www.nytimes.com/2010/06/30/books/30wonder.html?_r=0.

67. *IFanboy* podcast #272, November 13, 2012.

68. *Fredcast* podcast, February 1, 2013.

69. Brian Azzarello (w) and Cliff Chiang (a), *WW* Vol. 4 #1 (2011), #19 (2013), and #23 (2013), respectively.

70. Quoted in DiPaolo, *War, Politics, and Superheroes*, 86.

71. Among the podcasts I listened to for this article were (N = 20) *Chosen: A Buffyverse Podcast, Comic Book Queers, Comic Conversations, Comic Geek Speak, Comicast, Crazy Sexy Geeks, Fatman on Batman, Fredcast, IFanboy, Invisible Jet Podcast, Matt and Brett Love Comics, Modern Myth Media, Nerdist Writers Panel, The Stack, Supanova, Talking Comics, Talking Toons, Three Chicks Review Comics, War Rocket Ajax*, and *The Word Balloon*. Com-

mentary about the New 52 *Wonder Woman* was on twenty-six episodes (with eighteen men and seven women) of seven of these podcasts: *Comic Geek Speak*, *Crazy Sexy Geeks*, *IFanboy*, *Matt and Brett Love Comics*, *Modern Myth Media*, *Talking Comics*, and *The Word Balloon*. Only one person on these seven shows expressed early and repeated disappointment with the New 52 *Wonder Woman*, Bob Reyer of the *Talking Comics* podcast, who is a lifelong *Wonder Woman* fan. He remarked, "It's using the tools and the settings of what came before, but without quite getting it. It can be its own enjoyable thing; it's just not what it was and doesn't quite grasp the old concept" (*Talking Comics* podcast #50, September 26, 2012). I also listened to interviews with writers, artists, and publishers on an additional fifteen episodes of the eighteen podcasts listed above.

72. These three podcasts were *Comic Book Queers*, *Comicast*, and *Three Chicks Review Comics*. Listen to, for instance, *Comic Book Queers* podcast #179, April 8, 2012. Later, others on the *Talking Comics* podcast noted above became more negative about the New 52 *Wonder Woman*; for example, on August 28 and 29, 2013, during their "Women in Comics" week.

73. Superman and Diana had done this once before in 1988, *Action Comics* #600, John Byrne w/a, which crossed over with Pérez's run. *Good Morning America*, http://abcnews.go.com/GMA/video/dc-comics-rewrite-superman-ditches-lois-lane-woman-17056228. Note that in the new *Justice League*, alongside Wonder Woman's more sexualized portrayal, all of the male superheroes are drawn with huge, chiseled biceps, chests, and thighs.

74. Interviewed on the *Three Chicks Review Comics* podcast #43, September 9, 2012. See, for example, Brown, *Black Superheroes*, on the diversity of readership.

75. *Talking Comics* podcast, "Wonder Woman Panel," August 29, 2013 (the panel included this author).

76. Gail Simone, "Five Questions with Phil Jimenez," 2008, http://fivequestionswith.wordpress.com/phil-j (accessed January 1, 2013).

77. Andrew Chambliss (w) and Georges Jeanty (a), *Buffy* Vol. 9 #11, 2012.

78. Jane Espenson (w) and Karl Moline (a), *Buffy* Vol. 9 #14, 2012.

79. Brown, *Dangerous Curves*, 167.

80. Smith, *New Right Discourses on Race and Sexuality*, 6.

81. Duggan, *Sapphic Slashers*, 155.

82. Lopes, *Demanding Respect*, xxi.

83. Morrison, *Supergods*, 417.

Index

About the Editors

Norma Jones is a David B. Smith Fellowship recipient and doctoral candidate in the College of Communication and Information at Kent State University. Her research interests include popular culture, identity, and narrative. Specifically, she is interested in critically examining heroic narratives as related to cultural identities and representations of various groups in society. Additionally, she has contributed to the *Asian and Pacific Islander Americans* edition in the Great Lives from History series, *American History through American Sports* volumes, as well as popular press books regarding business management strategies and nontraditional student experiences. Recently, she was named as an associate editor *The Popular Culture Studies Journal*, the official journal of the Midwest Popular Culture Association. Earlier in her career, Norma spent over a decade working in the media as well as consulting for international companies in a variety of fields, including public relations, marketing, sales, high-end jewelry, and international telecommunications. Jones received her master's degree from the University of North Texas in communication studies, focusing on gender, race, and the mass media. Her bachelor's degree is also in communication studies, from the University of California, Santa Barbara.

Maja Bajac-Carter is a doctoral student in the College of Communication and Information at Kent State University. She is interested in gender, identity, and media studies. Her research is focused on cultural studies and mass media regarding circulation of gender, racial, and stereotype images and their co-creation between the media and viewers/society at large. Furthermore, Maja is interested in critically examining how portrayals of female characters in popular media influence individual and collective identities within a culture. She has contributed to *We Are What We Sell: How Advertising Shapes*

American Life . . . and Always Has. She serves on the editorial board for a journal in the field of popular-culture studies, the *Popular Culture Studies Journal.* Bajac-Carter received her master's degree from the University of North Texas in communication studies with a focus on constitutive rhetoric and social movements in Serbia. She has received her bachelor's degree in fine arts, also from the University of North Texas.

Bob Batchelor is James Pedas Professor of Communication and executive director of the James Pedas Communication Center at Thiel College. A noted cultural historian and biographer, Bob is the author or editor of twenty-four books, including *John Updike: A Critical Biography* and *Gatsby: A Cultural History of the Great American Novel.* He edits the Contemporary American Literature book series for Rowman & Littlefield. Bob is the founding editor of the *Popular Culture Studies Journal,* published by the Midwest Popular Culture/American Culture Association. He is a member of the editorial advisory boards of the *Journal of Popular Culture* and the *International Journal for the Scholarship of Teaching & Learning.* Bob also serves as director of marketing and media for the John Updike Childhood Home Museum in Reading, Pennsylvania. Visit him on the web at http://www.bobbatchelor.com.

About the Contributors

Catherine Bailey Kyle is pursuing her PhD in English at Western Michigan University, where she teaches contemporary American literature and first-year writing. She has a master's degree in English and a graduate certificate in gender and women's studies from the University of Rochester and a bachelor's degree from the University of Washington. She also studied at Franklin College Switzerland and Temple University Japan; conducted research at the Kinsey Institute for Research in Sex, Gender, and Reproduction; and worked with several nonprofits, including Teen Talking Circles. She has given talks on feminist narratology and popular culture in the United States, England, and Australia. More of her writing on feminist, bisexual, lesbian, and trans* superheroes can also be found in *Colloquy: Text Theory Critique*. Additional articles and reviews can be found in *Yes!* magazine, *Afterimage: The Journal of Media Arts and Cultural Criticism*, *Worldchanging*, *Three Percent*, *The Hilltop Review*, and *The Oxford Encyclopedia of American Cultural and Intellectual History*. Also a creative writer, Catherine's poetry, fiction, and graphic narratives can be found in *Superstition Review*, *The Rumpus*, *Involution* (2013), and numerous other publications.

Cassandra Bausman is a PhD candidate in English at the University of Iowa where she teaches literature and composition classes and serves as an administrative coordinator and tutor in the university's writing center. She is currently at work on her dissertation, which deals with intersections between feminist revisionism and metafiction in a consideration of fantasy literature and its heroines. She was the International Association for the Fantastic in the Art's 2013 graduate student award recipient, and her literary criticism can be found in the *Iowa Journal of Cultural Studies* and the *Journal of the Fantastic in the Arts*.

Jeffrey A. Brown received his doctorate in anthropology from the University of Toronto. He is an associate professor with the Department of Popular Culture at Bowling Green State University in Ohio. Dr. Brown is the author of two books, *Black Superheroes: Milestone Comics and Their Fans* and *Dangerous Curves: Gender, Fetishism and the Modern Action Heroine*. He is also the author of numerous academic articles about gender, ethnicity, and sexuality in contemporary media that have appeared in journals such as *Screen, Cinema Journal, African American Review, Feminist Review, Differences, Men and Masculinities*, and the *Journal of Popular Film and Television*.

Patrice M. Buzzanell is professor of communication in the Brian Lamb School of Communication (and professor of engineering education by courtesy) at Purdue University. Author of three edited books and over 130 articles and chapters, her research centers on the everyday negotiations and structures that produce and are produced by the intersections of career, gender, work-family, and communication such that people construct resilience and occupational aspirations, particularly in STEM (science, technology, engineering, and math). Her work has been published in journals including *Communication Monographs, Human Communication Research, Communication Theory, Journal of Applied Communication Research*, and *Human Relations* as well as in handbooks on organizational, professional, family, conflict, ethics, and gender communication and proceedings in engineering education. She has served as president of the International Communication Association (ICA), the Council of Communication Associations (CCA), and the Organization for the Study of Communication, Language & Gender (OSCLG). She was named ICA Fellow in 2011 and had the honor of delivering the 2010 Carroll C. Arnold Distinguished Lecture, "Seduction and Sustainability: The Politics of Feminist Communication and Career Scholarship," to the National Communication Association (NCA).

Ryan Castillo (MA, California State University, Long Beach) is a doctoral candidate at the University of Denver who is pursuing a degree in communication and popular culture. His scholarship draws on critical theory and masculinity studies to interrogate the relationship between discursive and visual representations of identity and power in commercial entertainment. His previous work examining gender identity in the Hollywood bromance is featured in the collection *Challenging Gender Norms and Gender Marginalization in a Transitional Era*.

Carolyn Cocca is associate professor and chair of the Department of Politics, Economics, and Law at the State University of New York, College at

Old Westbury. She is the author of *Jailbait: The Politics of Statutory Rape Laws in the United States* and the editor of *Adolescent Sexuality*. She has also written about *Buffy the Vampire Slayer* for *Slayage: The Journal of the Whedon Studies Association*. Her current research has two tracks: (1) gender and power in comics and other pop culture media, and (2) teaching critical literacy and political efficacy in our schools, empowering young people to combat educational inequities. Her most recent publication is "Youth Voices for Change: Building Political Efficacy and Civic Engagement through Digital Media Literacy" (*Journal of Digital and Media Literacy*, February 2013).

Robin R. Means Coleman is an associate professor in the Department of Communication Studies, and in the Department of Afroamerican and African Studies at the University of Michigan. She is the author of *Horror Noire: Blacks in American Horror Films, 1890s to Present* (2011) and of *African-American Viewers and the Black Situation Comedy: Situating Racial Humor* (2000). She is the editor of *Say It Loud! African American Audiences, Media, and Identity* (2002), and co-editor of *Fight the Power! The Spike Lee Reader* (2009).

Suzy D'Enbeau is assistant professor in the School of Communication Studies at Kent State University. Her research uses feminisms and critical organizational communication theories as analytic lenses for analysis and explication of organizational processes, structures, and policies. Her research has considered how feminist organizations navigate competing goals around ideology and sustainability, how individuals negotiate work–life intersections and organizational policies, and how popular-cultural representations of gendered workplace practices can both constrain and transform everyday workplace interactions. In addition to numerous book chapters, her work has been published in journals including *Communication Monographs*, *Human Relations*, the *Journal of Applied Communication Research*, *Women's Studies in Communication*, the *Journal of Communication Inquiry*, *Women & Language*, and *Qualitative Inquiry*.

Katie Gibson (PhD, Pennsylvania State University) is an associate professor of communication studies at Colorado State University. Her scholarship focuses on the politics of representation in legal discourse, political communication, and popular culture. Titles of her recent publications include "In Defense of Women's Rights: A Rhetorical Analysis of Judicial Dissent," "Judicial Rhetoric and Women's 'Place': The United States Supreme Court's Darwinian Defense of Separate Spheres," and "Undermining Katie Couric: The Discipline Function of the Press." Katie is also published in *Women's Studies in Communication*, the *Western Journal of Communication*, *Communication Quarterly*, *Women & Language*, and the *Southern Communication*

Journal. She is currently the vice president of the Organization for Research on Women and Communication.

Dr. Maura Grady is an assistant professor of English at Ashland University in Ashland, Ohio. She earned a doctorate in English with emphases in film studies and gender theory at the University of California at Davis, where she worked with film historian Scott Simmon. Dr. Grady was then assistant director of core writing at the University of Nevada, Reno, for three years before joining the faculty of Ashland University. Dr. Grady's research areas include film and television studies, fan culture, gender studies, popular-culture studies, and composition and pedagogy. Her current research is focused on the intersection between fan culture and film-induced tourism. She has previously published articles on the television series *Mad Men* and *Doctor Who.*

Cynthia J. Miller is a cultural anthropologist, specializing in popular culture and visual media. Her writing and photography have appeared in edited volumes and journals across the disciplines. She is the editor of *Too Bold for the Box Office: The Mockumentary from Big Screen to Small* (2012) and co-editor of *Cadets, Rangers, and Junior Space Men: Televised "Rocketman" Series of the 1950s and Their Fans* (with A. Bowdoin Van Riper, 2012); *Undead in the West: Vampires, Zombies, Mummies and Ghosts on the Cinematic Frontier* (with A. Bowdoin Van Riper, 2012); the award-winning *Steaming into a Victorian Future: A Steampunk Anthology* (with Julie Anne Taddeo, 2012); and *Border Visions: Identity and Diaspora on Film* (with Jakub Kazecki and Karen A. Ritzenhoff, 2013). She is also the co-editor (with A. Bowdoin Van Riper) of the forthcoming *Undead in the West II: They Just Keep Coming* (2013) and *International Westerns: Re-Locating the Frontier* (2013). Cynthia serves as series editor for Rowman & Littlefield's Film and History series, as well as on the editorial board of the *Journal of Popular Television.*

Pedro Ponce is a fiction writer and critic. His novella *Homeland: A Panorama in 50 States* was published recently. He is also the author of *Superstitions of Apartment Life*, a hybrid work of fiction and nonfiction about the history of tenement culture. His essays on experimental literature have appeared in the *Los Angeles Review*, the *Review of Contemporary Fiction*, and the anthology *Narratives of Community*. He was awarded a 2012 creative writing fellowship from the National Endowment for the Arts, and he teaches writing and literary theory at St. Lawrence University.

Carol A. Savery (ABD) is a doctoral candidate in the School of Communication Studies at Kent State University. Her recent publications have addressed the role of hospice volunteers as patient advocates, nonverbal communication in political contexts, a transdisciplinary perspective of health communication, and storytelling as an instructional technique. She has also authored a book on diffusion of innovations by public relations practitioners. As an instructor, she has introduced students to concepts and theories regarding gender in communication.

Rekha Sharma (MA, MS, Kent State University) is a doctoral candidate in the School of Communication Studies at Kent State University. Her research interests include political messages in news and popular culture in a variety of contexts. Some of her recent publications have addressed the influence of the Hollywood film industry on news agendas and the impact of diasporic cinema in the articulation of hybridized ethnic identity among South Asian immigrants. Additionally, she has published work regarding YouTube use in U.S. presidential elections, messages about war in animated cartoons, the functions of infotainment in the news environment and on the political process, and the development and implementation of viral marketing campaigns.

Lien Fan Shen is assistant Professor in the Department of Film and Media Arts at the University of Utah. Shen earned a PhD in art education at The Ohio State University and an MFA in computer art from the School of Visual Arts in New York City. Her creative work includes manga, animation, and digital arts. Shen published five series of *shōjo* manga in Taiwan. Her animation and digital arts have been screened and exhibited in Singapore, Japan, Taiwan, and the United States. Her research pays attention to how anime provides alternative politics to empower viewers through their persistent practice.

Katie Snyder is a PhD student in the Rhetoric and Technical Communication Program at Michigan Technological University. Her research interests include feminist theory, gender and sport, and communication studies.

Jennifer K. Stuller is a professional writer, critic, scholar, pop-culture historian, and public speaker. Stuller is the author of *Ink-Stained Amazons and Cinematic Warriors: Superwomen in Modern Mythology*; the editor of *Fan Phenomena: Buffy the Vampire Slayer*; and a contributor to multiple collections, including *What Is a Superhero?* and *Critical Approaches to Comics: Theories and Methods*. As a feminist, historian, and media literacy advocate, her particular interests focus on what popular culture reveals about social mores, particularly regarding gender, race, sexuality, ability, religion, and class in a given time or place—as well as how representations have evolved over time. A regular contributor to national publications and organizations, including *Bitch Media*, Ms. Stuller has been invited to speak at conferences in the United States and internationally, and provided expert opinion and interviews for radio, newspapers, and documentaries, including *Wonder Women! The Untold Story of American Superheroines*. She is a charter associate member of the Whedon Studies Association, and a co-founder of, and the programming director for, GeekGirlCon—an organization dedicated to the recognition, encouragement, and support of women's accomplishments, interests, and contributions to geek culture, including pop-culture industries and STEM professions. She lives in Seattle with her husband and their two Maltese, Giles and Wesley—who protect them from the forces of darkness. She can be found at http://www.ink-stainedamazon.com.

A. Bowdoin Van Riper is a historian who specializes in depictions of science and technology in popular culture. He received his PhD in the history of science from the University of Wisconsin–Madison and is currently web coordinator for the Center for the Study of Film & History and editor of the Scarecrow Press Science Fiction Television series. He is the author or editor of ten books, including *A Biographical Encyclopedia of Scientists and Inventors in American Film and Television* (2011); *Cadets, Rangers, and Junior Space Men: Televised "Rocketman" Series of the 1950s and Their Fans* (2012, co-edited with Cynthia J. Miller); and *International Westerns: Re-Locating the Frontier* (2013, co-edited with Cynthia J. Miller).

CHAPTER ONE

Kendra McAllis took a moment to compose herself as she waited in the hall that would lead her to the children's ward of the hospital. Drawing in a calming breath, she "centered" herself, as she had been taught at the North Carolina School of the Arts where she had studied to be a professional clown.

Speckles, the small black-and-white mutt who accompanied her, waited patiently by Kendra's side as she had been trained to do. They had performed at parties, at benefits, in circuses all over the world, on television and in the movies, but this was different—hospital work required a special performance.

Kendra adjusted her costume—her version of the Tramp, Charlie Chaplin's famous little clown —and smoothed the too small tuxedo top down over the baggy pants, which didn't quite reach her oversize shoes. She straightened her necktie, then partially tucked in her red-and-black-checkered shirt. With a perfunctory tug of her oversize black derby she checked her wig, then wiggled

the hairy black brows and small mustache to make sure that everything was in working order.

When she felt sufficiently in character and ready to interact with her young audience, Kendra wreathed her face, done in white makeup, in smiles, clasped Speckles's leash in her gloved hand, and issued a soft command.

"Come, Speckles."

Expressive eyes alert, ears up, Speckles instantly moved by her mistress's side. Kendra knocked softly on the door of the first room, then opened it slowly and poked her head inside.

In the private room a young boy about six years old lay very still against the stark white sheets of the hospital bed. He was staring vacantly at the ceiling. Kendra had been told that the child had been burned from the waist down. He would still need therapy, but after three months in the hospital he was almost ready to go home. Physically he had progressed well. Mentally he was locked in his own world.

Holding her breath for a moment, Kendra fought for the courage to continue. Her sympathetic brown eyes surveyed the entire scene: the child; the toys; the flowers; and the tall man who sat by the bed, his head resting on his folded arms, his face down on his knees so that Kendra couldn't see his features. His posture told her of his weariness, his helplessness, and his frustration.

When she looked back at the child, she saw only the faintest flicker of curiosity as he gazed at her. She motioned to a red flower in her button-

hole, and when the child looked at it, Kendra squeezed the water-filled bulb in her pants pocket, shooting a thin stream of water toward him.

She saw the hint of laughter in his eyes. Smiling broadly, she held her finger to her lips as she glanced at the dozing man. Then she made a big circle with her hand, signing hello to the boy.

She was rewarded with a shadow of a smile and a small wave that emulated hers. She sensed that the child would enjoy the conspiracy of clown and boy while the man slept. Silently stepping farther into the room, she bent and produced Speckles from behind her with a flourish that made it seem as if the animal had appeared magically.

The boy's eyes glowed with an inner light. Putting his hands to his mouth, he fought back a silent giggle as Kendra held the agreeable Speckles nearer so that she could be petted.

Kendra was delighted by the communion between child and animal. Only a few hospitals were letting her take Speckles into the wards, and then generally only to select patients. She had been told that this child lay listlessly on his bed with no interests and that any sign of his willingness to return to the world would be welcome.

She had seen the magic between clown, dog, and child many times. The good-natured animal wagged her tail and willingly submitted to the overeager caresses of the child. Then Kendra set Speckles on the floor where she waited obediently and patiently, until she was needed again.

11

Kendra reached inside her coat, then extended her hand to the boy. As he shook it she left a balloon in his palm. He grinned as she plucked it from his hand and began to pretend to blow it up but with no success.

When he held out his hand, Kendra shrugged her shoulders, looked wistfully at the balloon, then gave it to him. She watched as he blew with all the determination he had, and after he had succeeded he smiled as he saw that the red ball had the image of Kendra's clown face on it.

She patted him on the head and made a V for victory. Taking the balloon back, she tied it with a blue ribbon, then secured it to the boy's bed.

She turned abruptly when she heard the man groan. She watched as he rubbed his stiff neck and straightened in the chair. Her heart stopped beating when she saw his face for the first time. His was a riveting handsomeness, and there was something moving and vulnerable about him as he slowly opened his compelling blue eyes.

For a moment Kendra couldn't seem to look away as the man glanced anxiously at the boy first, then curiously at her.

Kendra watched him, seeing an entire spectrum of emotions on his angular face as he struggled to compose himself. Running a hand through the straight black hair that fell recklessly across his broad forehead, he made the transition from dozing guardian of the boy to suave stranger to the intruder.

As she gazed from the child to the man Ken-

dra was certain that the boy was the man's son. They looked too much alike not to be related.

"Hello. I wasn't aware anyone else had come in," he said in a thick, cultured Southern voice that still held traces of sleep. He was barely awake as he stood to his six-foot two-inch height.

Kendra didn't know if she could make her fingers move to pantomime. She was used to meeting all kinds of people, and she was reasonably sure that she could cast this one in the proper mold with nothing more to go on than what she had seen and heard.

He was Southern aristocracy. Old money in the South had a certain look, a certain air that no new money could ever buy. Kendra knew, for she had been on the poor side of the fence. However, she was not impressed by either his money or his position; she knew that neither of these things was the true reflection of a man's worth.

His momentary vulnerability had touched her, and she could not shake the picture. She was tempted to tell him that he and the child would survive this misfortune.

Instead she gave him a small wave, and to her gentle amusement he copied it. It always amazed her to see adults respond to clowns in much the same way that children did. She had run into only a few people who didn't brighten at the mere sight of a clown, and it made her chosen career extremely rewarding.

He held out his hand to her, and when she put her gloved one in it briefly, she wasn't surprised to find his handshake firm and warm.

13

"I'm Gable Hunt," he said.

With a broad grin and a flourish Kendra produced an oversize black-and-white card from her coat pocket.

Gable read the bold letters aloud: "Happy, Professional Clown." The only number listed was that of her New York agent.

With penetrating blue eyes Gable assessed her, a slight smile on his full mouth. But then he frowned as he gave his attention back to the boy, and the brooding lines slightly marred his handsome face.

Kendra noted his immediate relief when he saw that the child was smiling, his eyes bright and glowing. "Well, Brian, it seems that you made a friend while I was sleeping," he commented.

Brian nodded but he didn't say anything, and the smile soon slipped from his lips. Kendra looked at him curiously. He seemed to be withdrawing again, and she was disappointed. He had been so animated with her.

Her eyes met Gable's as he went over to the bed and lightly tapped the red balloon, making it dance on its string.

"Did the clown give you this?" he asked.

When Brian didn't answer, Gable patted the child's hand, then turned back to Kendra. Despite her five-foot seven-inch height, she was dwarfed by the towering man.

"You've done very well with him," Gable said in a low voice. "I haven't seen Brian smile in many weeks. Thank you."

14

Kendra could feel herself flush. She didn't need any accolades for what she had done. Brian's smile had been praise enough. She hung her head in a shy, exaggerated pose, staring at her shoes, and shrugged to indicate that she had done very little. Then she pulled two wilted flowers from her coat and handed one to the child and one to Gable.

"I don't think you know just what you've done here," he said. "This is the first breakthrough we've had with Brian since he was burned, and you're responsible. I'd certainly appreciate it if you would come again. I'll pay you whatever you wish."

Kendra frowned. No one could buy what she had given freely from her heart. Her donated time was born out of love for the children and the joy she found in her craft.

Drawing in a steadying breath, she nodded, her derby bobbing on her head. Then she produced another card from her pocket. She had long ago made it a rule never to speak in front of the children she entertained. The pantomime was part of the act and part of the magic.

"My fee is the smile on someone's face," Gable read aloud. He couldn't help but smile himself. "Thank you. I won't forget this, mister."

Kendra grinned. All strangers assumed that she was a man. She liked the anonymity and the freedom of the guise. She turned back to the boy. Delighting a healthy, ordinary child was easy enough, but the special ones held the biggest challenge—and the biggest reward.

Gable extended his hand again, jarring her from her thoughts. Kendra shook his hand, then she waved to Brian, tugged on Speckles's leash, and left. Out in the corridor she drew in a steadying breath. She had other children to see, and she was determined to give them no less than her best.

"You did a fine job, Speckles. Good girl," she murmured, bending down to stroke the dog affectionately.

Suppressing thoughts of Gable and Brian, she walked to the next room, put her big smile on her face, and entered to greet a nine-year-old girl in a body cast. The wonder in the child's eyes was worth more than anything all the money in the world could buy.

"A clown!" she whispered in awe. "A real clown."

Kendra's heart soared. This was what she loved about her work; she wanted to hug the child to her and smother her with kisses. In that moment she truly forgot about everything else as she devoted all her skills and her attention to the child before her.

After Gable had watched the clown walk away he smiled at Brian. "How about him, Brian? Wasn't he silly?"

Brian nodded, but he had already slipped back into his shell. Gable sighed wearily. The trauma of the child's ordeal had been too much, and now he had stopped talking. Psychologists had been

consulted—to no avail. Everyone had tried to help, but he remained mute.

Gable closed his eyes and massaged his neck. The clown had been tremendously encouraging. And the dog. He had seen the way Brian's eyes had followed the mutt.

He smiled again. A clown and a dog. Who would have imagined it? He had never given much thought to clowns. After all, he had never considered them as anything other than the most frivolous of entertainers.

Unconsciously he sighed. He didn't find much in life frivolous these days. His had taken some unfortunate turns. Oh, he knew that in the eyes of the world he had more than most. He *was* successful and satisfied, but it had taken some time to deal with the disappointment of his divorce from Sandy.

He looked back at Brian. And now this. The child who had been a substitute for the baby Gable had wanted was hurt, and there was nothing he could do.

Kendra was worn-out by the time she started out of the hospital that afternoon. She loved to see the smiles on the sick children's faces, but she was always so drained afterward. She wanted to be able to do more.

As she passed Brian's room she couldn't resist peeking in. Gable stood by the bedside with his arm around an elegant woman. He looked back in time to catch sight of Kendra.

"Come on in," he said, motioning broadly.

17

Kendra put a smile on her face and did a bit of clowning as she entered, pretending to capture an imaginary butterfly, clearly delighting both Brian and the couple.

"This is the clown I told you about, Genna," Gable said, turning to the blond.

Kendra noted that the woman had a pale, old-fashioned beauty that was enhanced by lace and frills and upswept curls. She was charmingly appealing in the feminine dress, which set off her fair complexion.

Genna touched Gable's hand, then smiled gently at Kendra. "Thank you so much for being nice to our boy," she said in a sweet, softly accented voice. Her big blue eyes glowed with genuine appreciation. "You are so kind to take your time to entertain a sick child."

The smile remained fully in place on Kendra's lips, but she felt an unexpected twinge of disappointment as she looked at the almost too perfect picture of the man and woman before her. Yet she *had* thought that Brian was Gable's son, and that meant that there must be a mother somewhere. She had no idea why the confirmation mattered to her one way or the other.

Besides, she liked the gracious and beautiful Genna already. The woman seemed warm and sincere. Kendra signed a broad hello, then tipped her hat.

Genna looked back up at Gable. "He's delightful. No wonder Brian was enchanted."

"I told you," Gable said. "Isn't it wonderful that someone in this world can create a little hap-

piness by dressing in a funny costume and doing a silly little jig? Oh, that all of life were that simple."

Kendra could feel herself withdrawing. She was a professional clown, and she was proud of what she had achieved in the entertainment world. She had studied her trade long and hard, and she carefully and tediously worked out her comedy routines.

Her accomplishments had taken years and no small degree of natural talent. There was nothing simple about being a clown, and she had always resented the implication that it was something anyone could do with a costume and makeup. She had met other people—too many—with Gable Hunt's attitude, and she had not appreciated them.

Genna smoothly directed the focus back to the injured child, and Kendra was grateful. "Did you thank Happy for coming, Brian?"

The boy toyed with his fingernails, then looked up shyly at Kendra. In an effort to recapture some of the magic they had shared earlier, she pretended to search for something in her pockets, then suddenly flung out a string full of paper ducks that had been folded accordion-style.

Brian smiled and tried to grab them. Kendra purposely danced an intricate little jig that required skill and dexterity in the huge shoes as she left the paper cutouts on the boy's bed. Then she tipped her derby to Gable and Genna and backed out of the room.

When she was in the hall, she held Speckles to

her breast and sighed. She didn't know why she was so touchy today; she shouldn't have let Gable Hunt's comment upset her. Heaven knew she had heard it before. Anyway, she didn't really care what the man thought, did she?

But the fact remained that Gable Hunt had hurt her feelings. She had liked him, felt empathy for him—and his remark had been thoughtless and careless. It had reminded her of her ex-fiancé, Wyatt, and her aborted marriage plans.

Consciously suppressing her agitation, she returned to the rooms she had rented in a private home in the North Carolina town. She was only an hour from where she had been reared, but it seemed like a lifetime away now. She had left college after the first year, then spent her time on the road until she became engaged. She was a stranger in North Carolina now, having no relatives and no ties.

It seemed ironic that her home state was getting into the moviemaking business and that she was here for a few weeks to play the part of a clown in a film being made in one of several studios springing up in the area.

She smiled as old Mrs. Bogart, who sat in a white porch swing swaying back and forth lazily, called out to her. "How did it go?"

"Very well," Kendra said, beaming at the old lady. The two of them had quickly become friends in the few days Kendra had been here, and she and Speckles felt right at home.

"I've got some soup cooking. You and Speckles come on down after you change. We'll have a big

RECKLESS
ABANDON

To Our Readers:

We are pleased and excited by your overwhelmingly positive response to our Candlelight Supremes. Unlike all the other series, the Supremes are filled with more passion, adventure, and intrigue, and are obviously the stories you like best.

In months to come we will continue to publish books by many of your favorite authors as well as the very finest work from new authors of romantic fiction. As always, we are striving to present unique, absorbing love stories —the very best love has to offer.

Breathtaking and unforgettable, Supremes follow in the great romantic tradition you've come to expect *only* from Candlelight Romances.

Your suggestions and comments are always welcome. Please let us hear from you.

Sincerely,

The Editors
Candlelight Romances
1 Dag Hammarskjold Plaza
New York, New York 10017

Published by
Dell Publishing Co., Inc.
1 Dag Hammarskjold Plaza
New York, New York 10017

*For my sister Carmen, whose delightful paintings add
such warmth and beauty to the world; for my sister Ellen,
the poet in the family.*

*For Patsy and Buddy A., who always have a warm smile
for me when I go into their bookstore.*

And for S.A. and Aunt Peg, who are special people.

Dell ® TM 681510, Dell Publishing Co., Inc.

Candlelight Supreme is a trademark
of Dell Publishing Co., Inc.

Candlelight Ecstasy Romance®, 1,203,540, is a registered
trademark of Dell Publishing Co., Inc., New York, New York.

ISBN: 0-440-17496-1

Printed in the United States of America

September 1986

10 9 8 7 6 5 4 3 2 1

WFH

RECKLESS ABANDON

Megan Lane

A CANDLELIGHT SUPREME

CANDLELIGHT SUPREMES

CANDLELIGHT

Supreme

"I'M NOT INTO ONE-NIGHT STANDS," GABLE SAID ANGRILY.

"Making love means something to me."

"But you know we have no future," Kendra whispered. "We're very different people. Making love doesn't change that."

"Everything *has* changed for me. I've found what I've been searching for, and I'm not going to let you go that easily."

"You *haven't* found what you've been looking for," she cried passionately. "I'm the farthest thing from what you want!"

Grabbing her in his arms, he held her tightly. "No—you're just too stubborn to see it. You and I belong together. You know it in your heart—and someday I know I'll hear you say it!"

bowl and a nice chat," Mrs. Bogart said. "And I won't be taking no for an answer."

Kendra grinned. "You won't be hearing it. I'm starved, thank you."

She skipped up the steps to her rooms, Speckles running happily at her heels. Even though she was a stranger here now, she felt at home in this part of the country. It was good to be back.

When she had stripped off her clown costume, she carefully cleaned her face. After she finished, she changed into jeans and a T-shirt that emphasized her slender figure, making her look more like eighteen than twenty-five. She put on a little lipstick and powder, then brushed her rich, thick mane of brown hair.

She tossed her head back, letting the natural waves fall into place. She had always thought her hair was one of her best features, and she found it ironic that it was hidden under a wig and derby most of the time. As she studied her reflection Gable Hunt's face flashed in her mind. She shoved it aside. There was no reason for her to be thinking about *him*.

Bending down to scratch Speckles's head, she murmured, "You're such a good, sweet girl. Let's go downstairs and visit."

With another toss of her hair she walked down the steps, but as absurd as it was, she found that she was having difficulty leaving the image of Gable Hunt behind.

CHAPTER TWO

"Come on in," Mrs. Bogart said, pulling the living room door open as Kendra reached it.

"Thank you, Mrs. Bogart."

"No need to be so formal," the woman said. "I call you Kendra, and you must call me Darcy."

Kendra grinned at the old woman, who wore a flaming red blouse, blue jeans, and white tennis shoes. Her blue-tinted gray hair was a jumble of curls, and her green eyes twinkled mischievously. At least seventy years old, she was independent and ornery and fighting a good battle with Father Time.

Kendra loved her for it. She savored Darcy's bright and positive attitude, and she enjoyed the homey comfort of the house, which had stood against time and fate since the Civil War.

"So, tell me about the little ones," Darcy said. "Did you cheer them up much?"

Kendra grinned. "I did my best."

"Who did you see today?" Darcy asked eagerly as she scooped up a bowlful of vegetable soup for each of them and joined Kendra at a table where fresh fruit and glasses of cold milk were waiting.

Oddly, Gable Hunt's face surged persistently into Kendra's mind, but she ignored it and told Darcy about the children she had entertained.

"You really love the young ones, don't you?" Darcy asked perceptively, her green eyes dancing. "Haven't you ever wanted to get married and have some of your own?"

Kendra nodded eagerly. "Oh, yes."

Darcy studied Kendra's face. "Then why haven't you?"

Kendra laughed at the frank question. "I'm afraid I discovered that it's not that simple. I was engaged once, but it didn't work out. I realized that I could have either a career or marriage."

She leaned forward in her chair. "You see, all my life I've had this burning desire to be a clown." She laughed again. "Oh, I know it sounds like a foolish obsession for a woman, but I can't recall a time when I didn't want to do it." She leaned back. "I learned my lesson. Husbands don't want wives who run off to the circus in greasepaint and trousers."

Darcy gave a deep, delighted laugh. "Nope, I suppose they don't, at that. But then, you can't lump all husbands together, any more than you can all wives. I'm sure there are circus people who are happily married."

Kendra smiled. "Yes, to other circus people." She leaned forward again and touched Darcy's arm. "You know, Darcy, there aren't many circuses left, but most of the people in them are truly fine. They've always treated me like family. They're all that way—like one big family."

"But what of your family?" Darcy asked. "What do they think about your being a performer?"

Kendra's eyes glowed. "I grew up in a children's home not far from here. My family was all the children and the house parents who lived there."

"Well, I'll be. And isn't it something, you coming back here to play the part of a clown in a movie? We locals are just thrilled to have a new movie studio in town," she confessed. "It's very exciting."

"It *is* exciting," Kendra agreed. "I was elated when my agent told me I'd been selected for the part. I've done a couple of minor roles, but this one is quite substantial."

"I know you'll do real well," the older woman said.

"I hope so. I think the world needs a lot more laughter, and that's what our film is all about."

Darcy smiled. "My father—may he rest in peace—always said the world needed more laughter."

"Has there been a man in your life?" Kendra asked.

Darcy laughed. "No! I'm too mean, too independent. I lived here with Papa until his death. He spoiled me rotten, gave me a generous allowance, and let me live my life just as I pleased. What would I have wanted with a man?"

"Love," Kendra said without thought. "What is life without it?"

She was surprised to hear herself say that. After she and Wyatt had parted, she had been determined to be satisfied without the love of a man. After all, in her profession she felt that she received and gave enough love to keep her going.

But it wasn't the same. No matter what she told herself, she knew all too well that the love of the crowd couldn't compensate for the intimate love of a single man. Still, Wyatt had taught her the hard way that she was married to her career. She put her heart into her clowning now; she would not give it to a man again.

Darcy nodded thoughtfully. "Yes, child. At your age I dreamed of love, too, but it didn't happen." She looked down at her bowl. "Eat your soup before it gets cold, then we'll take an evening stroll. It's good for your constitution."

Later the young woman and the old one were walking briskly down the street when a Cadillac whizzed past them. "There goes Gable Hunt, one of the richest men in North Carolina," Darcy said.

"Oh?" Kendra murmured, brushing at her hair, which danced wildly in the spring breeze.

"Yep. He's something else, that one. Like his daddy and his granddaddy before him, he's president of one of the biggest manufacturing firms in North Carolina. He's into everything—politics, community affairs, national events. You name it, Gable Hunt's in it. People know him from one end of this state to the other, and they respect him. He's not even thirty yet, I believe."

Darcy looked at the young woman. "But a rich man gets heartaches, same as a poor one, you know. If you saw a little boy named Brian at the hospital today, you know what Gable Hunt's heartache is."

"I saw him," Kendra said. She wanted to ask Darcy about Gable and Brian and Genna, but the other woman changed the subject. Kendra concentrated on Darcy's lively chatter as they continued their walk.

Kendra smiled at the other members of the cast as they finished the first takes on the movie set the next day. She was feeling extraordinarily exuberant about her fledgling acting career. She thrived on the energy of a live audience, but she had savored every moment of performing in front of the camera. It was a heady experience. Besides, she was being paid a ridiculously large amount of money to do what she enjoyed most in the world.

Grinning to herself, trying not to let anyone else see how thrilled she was with the day's work, she stared at her oversize black shoes with their bright orange laces as she turned the corner leading from the studio cafeteria. Suddenly she crashed into someone.

An apology was on the tip of her tongue when she looked up into Gable Hunt's blue eyes. Relaxed, he stood before her, laughing easily in contrast to Kendra's tense stance.

"Looks like you've got a little too much shoe there," he commented affably. "Or is it just your happiness that's getting in your way? I saw the smile on your face a mile away."

Nodding, Kendra smiled more broadly, but

she could only wonder what on earth he was doing on the lot. "Can I buy you a cup of coffee?" he asked. "I'd like to talk to you."

"All right," she agreed.

Gable's eyes widened in surprise. Then he laughed aloud. "My word! A *woman!* I thought —I automatically assumed that you were a man because you were dressed as one."

"An honest mistake," Kendra assured him, thinking again how handsome he was standing there before her in a navy suit and light blue shirt that set off his incredible eyes. "It happens all the time."

"Well, it won't happen with me again. I'm delighted to find out that you're female," Gable said with a smile. "Somehow it makes you more approachable."

"Perhaps," she agreed lightly, wondering how much more approachable he wanted her to be and why. When Gable pulled out a chair for her, she settled down warily.

He ordered coffee, then leaned his elbows on the table and locked his fingers together. "I want to thank you again for coming to see Brian."

He looked down at his clasped hands. "Trouble is, he hasn't smiled again since you left." His eyes met hers again, and Kendra tried to keep her sympathy from showing. "I phoned your agency and was told I could find you here at the studio. I know the president of the studio, so I asked if I might come on the lot and look you up."

"I see."

"I wonder if I could hire you to perform at a

party for Brian—sort of a homecoming party."
He grinned. "I saw the way he looked at your
dog, and I've decided that a pet of his own might
do him good. I'd like for you to be the one to give
him a new puppy, if you would."

"I'll be glad to," she answered immediately.
"And you won't need to pay me. I'd consider it a
pleasure."

"I wouldn't dream of taking up your time for
free," he insisted, gazing steadily at her.

"And I wouldn't dream of doing it for pay,"
she retorted.

Gable laughed. "Uh-oh, we've reached an im-
passe—and so early in our relationship. Tell you
what," he said, "will dinner with me one evening
be a satisfactory trade for a couple of hours of
your talent?"

"Oh, really, that won't be necessary," Kendra
insisted quickly. "I can't accept."

Gable gazed thoughtfully at her for a moment.
"Do you have a name besides Happy?" he finally
asked.

"Kendra McAllis."

"I see," he murmured. He seemed to be trying
to look right through her makeup to the woman
beneath. "Well, you are stubborn, aren't you,
Kendra McAllis?"

Kendra laughed softly as she shook her head.
"I'm not really stubborn. I just can't place mone-
tary value on putting a smile on a sick child's
face."

Gable slowly nodded. "All right. I won't look
a gift horse in the mouth, but we'll work out

something later. Can you come to my house at six tomorrow evening? You will be through here by then, won't you?"

"Yes, I think so."

"Good. Here's the address. If you have any trouble, just ask where the old Hunt house is. The place has been in my family for generations, and just about everyone knows where it is." He reached across the table to take her gloved hands in his. "And thanks."

Kendra was quite excited about giving the dog to Brian, and she could hardly keep her mind on her work the next day. She firmly believed that a pet could do wonders to draw the child back into life. She was already anticipating the smile on his face, and she hoped she wouldn't be disappointed. To her surprise she found that Gable was waiting for her when she reached the studio parking lot at the end of the day's shoot.

"Good evening," he said warmly. "How did your day go?"

Kendra couldn't help but smile. "Wonderful. I have all the easy parts."

"Your part may be easy, but it's quite entertaining," he commented. "I watched some of your performance."

"You did?" she murmured. She knew that he was wealthy and could make his own hours, but she was still surprised that he had come to the studio two days in a row.

"Yes, I thought I'd see if I could bring Brian on the set. I believe he would enjoy seeing the movie being filmed. I know he'd enjoy watching you. Also," he added, his blue eyes glowing, "I want to show you the puppy I bought for him if you have time."

"Of course," she agreed.

He led her over to his car, where a chauffeur was holding a wiggling, fat, black-and-white puppy.

"Why, she looks a little like Speckles," Kendra exclaimed.

"I thought so, too," Gable commented. "She's a beauty, isn't she?"

"Yes, indeed." Kendra reached out to take the squirming bundle. "I know Brian will love her."

Gable's tone was solemn. "I hope so. We've got to reach him somehow, to get him to communicate with the world again. You're our first real hope."

Kendra felt uncomfortable under the burden. "I'll do what I can, Mr. Hunt. Children have remarkable resiliency. I'm amazed by them time and time again, especially the troubled ones. I'm sure Brian will be fine eventually."

Gable forced a smile to his lips. "Please call me Gable, if you will. Mr. Hunt makes me feel old and tired."

"We can't have that, can we?" she retorted, thinking that he looked anything but old and tired. "Gable it is."

"Good. Would you like to ride with me in my car?"

Kendra shook her head. "Thanks, but I'd better drive. I need to stop at home to pick up Speckles."

"All right, Happy. Then I'll see you at six." He smiled again, and Kendra watched as he got into the car, looking oddly vulnerable with that lively bundle of fur in his arms.

When Kendra greeted Darcy and Speckles at the Bogart house, she found that Darcy had already fed the dog, which was terrific, since she only had time for a quick sandwich and a cup of coffee.

Darcy laughed gaily as Kendra the clown took huge bites and pretended to wipe her face with the back of her hand in an exaggerated sweep. After her clown's supper she took Speckles in hand and got in her car.

The Hunt house sat on five acres of land on the outskirts of town. As Kendra rounded the bend in the road she saw the majestic building perched on a grassy hill. Magnificently ornate, it appeared like a magical castle with the last rays of the sun highlighting the stained-glass windows that lined the front door and upper doors, which led out onto a veranda.

When she parked in the driveway, she noticed the perfectly manicured lawn, divided by a wide sidewalk and accented by juniper bushes. The picture was an idyllic one. A beautiful home. A handsome father. A pretty mother. The only flaw was the child—the son who had been wounded and must be made whole again.

The late spring evening was still bright, and

31

Kendra couldn't help but smile as she saw all the activity in the house through the windows. Children were scampering around everywhere; she was amazed by their number. She had expected just a few youngsters.

With Speckles in her arms she walked up the long, winding walk to the front door and rang the bell. A maid dressed in a stiffly starched black uniform with a white apron and matching white cap came to the door. Kendra thought the outfit looked like something out of a thirties movie, and she decided that the woman could use a little fun in her correct and proper position. She couldn't resist hamming it up just a little.

She set Speckles on the ground and pulled a crepe-paper rose from her oversize pants' pocket. When she handed it to the maid, the woman's eyes lit up and she smiled so winningly that Kendra produced a bottle of perfume and sprayed the flower with it.

The maid giggled aloud as she held the flower to her nose, sniffing the overpowering scent.

"Janice?"

Another woman appeared at the door, and the maid promptly wiped the smile from her face.

"Yes, ma'am?"

The woman spied the clown and held out her hand. "Good evening. We've been expecting you. I'm Sarah Washington, Mr. Hunt's housekeeper. Come in."

Kendra shook the housekeeper's hand vigorously as she raised her bushy brows and wiggled her mustache. Then she pretended to wipe her feet thoroughly before she picked up Speckles and brushed madly at the little dog's feet.

The housekeeper, almost as proper as the maid, fought back a throaty laugh as Kendra followed her into the hall.

"Good evening," Gable said, coming to meet her. He directed her into a massive room where all the children were now sitting quietly in chairs at three separate tables.

Pandemonium broke loose again when they spied her and Speckles; there were excited shouts and cries. When Kendra looked at Gable, she found him smiling.

"Children! Children!" he said firmly, getting their attention. "This is Happy the clown, and Speckles. Calm down a minute until I can make the introductions. All right?"

Although they had abated to some degree, the whispers and giggles continued. Gable looked at Genna, and she smiled her sweet smile. Going over to the children, she announced in her charming, soft voice, "Let's show Happy and Speckles how good and quiet we can be. Then maybe they will do some tricks for us."

The excitement remained at a fever pitch, but the children smothered their giggles while Gable introduced Kendra to all fourteen of them. Then he turned to three women and a man, who were standing together, watching the commotion with glowing eyes.

"Happy, you remember my friend Genna Lawson."

Kendra was so taken aback to find that Genna

was his friend that she didn't see the way the blond woman was looking at Gable.

"I thought Genna was your wife," she admitted.

Gable's eyes were curious and intense as they met Kendra's. "I'm divorced."

Was it her imagination, or did he stare at her for a moment too long before she dragged her gaze away?

"I see," she murmured. "But Brian is your son?"

"No, my nephew." There seemed to be the slightest pause before Gable introduced her to the other adults.

"I'll let you do your thing, then the children will have cake and ice cream before we produce the surprise," he murmured low.

It took Kendra a moment to remember that the surprise was the puppy.

"Fine," she said.

Falling back on her automatic responses, she began to entertain the children with her routine, pulling a miniature trumpet from her pocket and pretending to try to do a duet with Speckles.

She was rewarded with laughter and giggles from everyone but Brian, who seemed to have withdrawn further into his shell in the midst of all the hubbub. Kendra returned to him repeatedly, trying to elicit his laughter. While she did succeed in getting a few shy smiles, she couldn't reach him as she had in the hospital.

She and the other adults sat at another table and had refreshments when the children did, and although everyone congratulated Kendra on her fine performance, she was disappointed that she hadn't made Brian laugh. She placed her hopes on the puppy, right along with Gable. When the time came, she prayed that Brian would respond.

As if he had read her mind, Gable leaned over and whispered to her. "All right, let's present the surprise now."

Kendra nodded, and Gable stood up.

"Boys and girls, I want you all to close your eyes. Happy has a surprise for the birthday boy, but you must be quiet and keep your eyes closed if you want to see it."

Despite a few peeks and some giggles, most of the children hid their eyes behind their hands, eagerly getting into the spirit of the game.

Leaving a capable Speckles with the children, Kendra went into the hall where Genna held the puppy. She and Genna looked at each other, and Kendra saw how desperately the other woman was hoping the puppy would be the key to free Brian from his silent world.

"I've known Gable almost all my life," Genna said quietly. "He and I grew up together. I still live next door in my family home. I've seen the pain Gable's been through in the past two years. And now this. We love Brian so very much. We've been frantic about him. We were at our wit's end until you came to the hospital." Her big blue eyes filled with gratitude. "I can't tell you how much your help means to us all."

"I'm glad to be of any help I can," Kendra whispered. "I know Brian will be fine in time."

She took the rambunctious puppy in her arms. When she stepped back into the room, several of the impatient children were already watching. Kendra walked over to Brian and stood before him.

"Now, everybody, open your eyes," Gable said.

Kendra held the chubby little dog out to the boy, watching his eyes grow big and round. Brian didn't speak a word, but he clutched the animal to him, letting it kiss and lick him. When his blue eyes met Kendra's again, they were full of tears.

To lighten the moment she suddenly tossed handfuls of confetti into the air and began to dance in the ridiculously large shoes. The children were squealing and begging for more, and she took her bow while the moment was at its height.

Gable caught up with her before she could go out the front door. "Just a minute," he insisted, catching her by her shoulder to turn her around. "Must you hurry off?"

"It's time," she said. "Even a clown can lose its magic if it stays too long."

She was sure that she could feel the warmth of his fingers, even through the topcoat and her shirt. She needed to get away from him, and soon.

Gable smiled at her. "We couldn't let that happen, could we? The world needs all the magic it can get." His eyes met hers. "I really do want to thank you in some way. Say you'll have dinner with me tomorrow night."

Kendra's heart began to pound. She shook her head. "I don't think so."

Gable studied her for a moment, then frowned. "Don't be so difficult. I want to let you know how much I appreciate what you've done tonight."

"It really isn't necessary," she insisted.

He put both his hands on her shoulders, forcing her to look at him. "I know it isn't necessary," he said. "I *want* to do it."

Initially he had considered the dinner only to repay her kindness to Brian and because he wanted to show her, in some small way, what a difference she had made in their lives. But as he looked into her brown eyes, he realized that he wanted to see her again. He had no idea what she looked like, and he was curious, but more than that, he liked her already. She was bright and sensitive, and he admired her dedication to sick children. He could spend thousands of his dollars on charity, but this woman was clearly giving of her heart. He wanted to know her better.

Kendra could feel her pulse race. Staring over Gable's shoulder into the cool, still night, she tried to make herself calm down. She didn't know why she was making such a big deal out of a dinner. It seemed silly to refuse. After all, as he had said, it was only a meal to show her how grateful he was.

When his eyes met hers for the second time that night, she knew she couldn't say no again. She really wanted to see him. She had been attracted to him from the first time she saw him. And even though she knew *that* was the real problem, why deny herself one evening with him? After all, she was the girl who had resolved to live one day at a time.

"All right," she said over the roar of the blood pulsing in her head. "I'll have dinner with you."

Then she opened the door and skipped down the steps. She didn't look back at the house again. If she had, she would have seen Genna staring out the window, tears in her blue eyes.

CHAPTER THREE

Darcy was like a mother hen, clucking and cackling around Kendra as she dressed for her date with Gable.

"Oh, you don't know what a lucky girl you are," the old woman kept saying excitedly. "Gable Hunt! Why, child, do you know—I mean, do you really know who he is? Not only is he handsome, he's incredibly wealthy. Not that it really matters, I know, but it doesn't hurt any, either, if you know what I mean."

Kendra laughed. "Darcy, if you keep on, I'm going to let you go out with him instead of me. You're much more excited about the evening."

It was a lie, of course. Her heart was pounding, her head was spinning, and her mind was overloaded with confusing thoughts. She found herself suddenly concerned about her looks. She was attractive and had never considered herself vain, but tonight she peered into the mirror far too often.

"Oh, pooh," Darcy said disdainfully. "Gable Hunt doesn't want to go anywhere with an old bag like me. He can have any pretty young woman he wants."

It took Kendra a moment to realize what Darcy was saying, then she frowned. "Yes, I'm sure he can. And does," she added almost beneath her breath.

Darcy laughed. "I heard that. He isn't a playboy. Not Gable Hunt. That's why I'm telling you how special this evening is."

"Gable only asked me out to repay me for helping with Brian," Kendra said, reminding herself as well as Darcy.

"Ah, Brian," Darcy murmured. "Isn't it such a tragedy that he lost—"

The door bell rang, and Darcy's hands flew to her face. "Oh, there he is!" she exclaimed. "Gable Hunt is here."

Kendra grinned at the flustered woman. "Yes, I imagine that is him. Will you please go see?"

"Yes, of course," Darcy cried, rushing out of the room.

Speckles began to run back and forth, barking energetically. Kendra glanced in the mirror once more, seeing the way the rose silk dress clung to her slender curves and set off her long dark hair. Her makeup was subtle but enhancing. She spun away from the image, annoyed with herself for caring so much what Gable Hunt would think of her.

"Shh," she told Speckles. "It's okay. Be quiet."

The small dog obeyed immediately, but she tramped down the stairs with her mistress to make sure everything really was all right.

Darcy had already opened the door by the time Kendra got downstairs. The older woman was standing there beaming at Gable. "I'm Darcy Bogart," she said, "and I know who you are. Mr. Gable Hunt. Now you come right on in. Don't stand out there all night."

Kendra smiled and shook her head. Darcy sure was making a big thing about this evening.

But then she, herself, was putting too much emphasis on it too. A simple lamp lit the hall. Kendra knew the light was soft and flattering; Gable still hadn't really seen her.

He stepped inside just as she walked down the hall. Their eyes met, and Kendra found herself holding her breath like a foolish young girl.

"Good evening," Gable said, his voice slightly husky. He seemed to forget that Darcy was standing there, fluttering around like a butterfly. "I had no idea you were concealing such an attractive young woman behind that Charlie Chaplin makeup," he commented, unable to take his eyes away from her.

"Hello," she said brightly. "How are you this evening?"

He laughed. "I had a rough day, but I'm feeling better already. You are a pleasant surprise."

His eyes swiftly appraised her. He was filled with a million questions about this woman, and he was surprised that she interested him so. Although he had a penchant for redheads and blonds, he couldn't deny that she *was* a pleasant surprise for a clown he had originally thought was a man. She had lush brown hair, lovely dark eyes, and the man in him couldn't help but notice the slender curves beneath the clingy dress. She had long legs, too, and tonight they were enhanced by the heels she wore.

With his assets, his social position, and his looks, he could have just about any woman he wanted, but he was oddly drawn to this one. He really couldn't say why. Surely he was only attracted to her because of the overwhelming gratitude he felt.

"Ready to go?" he asked.

"Yes," she said. She smiled at the glowing Darcy. "Good night, Darcy."

"Good night, dear. Have a good time," Darcy said, waving.

Gable glanced at Kendra again as they walked out to his car. "You intrigue me," he admitted. "Maybe it's because I don't usually go out with clowns," he added lightly.

I gathered as much, Kendra wanted to say, but she held her tongue, remembering his insulting remark about her career could serve no good purpose now. Perhaps he hadn't realized how thoughtless he had been. "How does Brian like the puppy?" she asked as Gable started the car.

"He and the puppy have been inseparable since you handed her to him. I had a good idea, and it's all because of you. I'm afraid I'm even deeper in your debt now."

"Please think nothing of it," she insisted. She didn't want him being indebted to her. "I would have done it for anyone who asked," she felt compelled to add.

He smiled at her. "I'm sure you would have, and I admire you for it." All of a sudden he wanted to ask her a million questions, but he forced himself to go slowly.

"Has Brian spoken?" she asked.

Gable shook his head. It was still hard to talk much about the boy, so they drove for a few minutes in silence.

"I hope you like lobster," he said as they reached the restaurant.

Kendra laughed. "It's my favorite."

He smiled again. "Good. I think you and I are going to get along just fine. They have excellent drinks here too. We can unwind." He ran his hands through his thick black hair. "I sure could use a break."

He walked around to her side of the car and opened the door. When he took her hand to help her out, Kendra felt a shiver of delight at his intimate touch.

Gable winked at her. "Maybe you don't suffer the little traumas of everyday life that the rest of us experience. With a name like Happy and a disposition like yours, maybe you're immune."

Kendra smiled vaguely. He was implying again that her life was made up of nothing more than a costume and makeup. "It's all a state of mind, isn't it?"

"Hell, no," Gable said with a laugh. "It's a state of reality for me. I'm sure you deal in illusions, but I can't afford the luxury."

Kendra was pensive for a moment as Gable led her inside the elegant building. She didn't like his implication. But she told herself that she was being overly sensitive.

When they had been directed to a lovely table in a secluded corner, she told Gable, "I've heard all about you from Darcy. I'm told you're extremely wealthy. I suspect you can buy whatever you want, even illusions."

Gable laughed good-naturedly. "You've got a quick mind and a good sense of humor, but you listen to rumor, young lady."

"You aren't rich?" she asked boldly after they had ordered a bottle of wine. "Didn't you inherit a fortune from your family, or was that an old woman's fantasy?"

Gable nodded. "I think rich is relative," he said thoughtfully. "Yes, I have money, but you know the old saying that money can't buy everything."

"I wouldn't know," Kendra retorted. "I haven't had enough to find out, but it's never mattered."

His blue eyes penetrating, Gable studied her as the waiter served the wine. He could believe that money had never mattered to her. She seemed content and fulfilled. She appeared to enjoy every aspect of her life.

Kendra grew uncomfortable under his close scrutiny; when the waiter walked away, she picked up her wine to sample it. Gable continued to watch her, and she was surprised when he reached across the table to grasp her hands in his as she set her glass down.

"Something tells me that you're richer than I'll

ever be, Happy. I see something in your eyes. I sense something in you that I probably would give my fortune to have. I think I'm still searching for something you've found. The hell of it is that I don't quite know what it is I'm looking for."

Even as he said the words he knew they didn't ring true. He did know what he was searching for: He, too, wanted contentment and fulfillment, and for him that meant a wife and family. Both had proved elusive.

Taken aback, Kendra didn't know what to say. She was both flattered and unsettled. He was unconsciously stroking her hands with his thumbs, and she felt a burning inside that frightened her with its intensity.

Suddenly she withdrew her hands and clasped them in her lap. The movement seemed to surprise Gable, causing him to shake his head.

"I'm sorry. I didn't bring you here to make a confession about my life." He laughed uncomfortably. "I really have few complaints. I know how fortunate I am."

He met her eyes again. "I do apologize. I'm afraid you're having a strange effect on me." She *was,* indeed. He could not deny that he found this woman across from him sexually attractive, and he had never anticipated that.

Since the fire he had reevaluated his priorities. Brian had absorbed most of his energy and thoughts. He hadn't had the time or the inclination to develop a romantic involvement, and in truth, he hadn't wanted one. He had been hurt

45

before; he would proceed more cautiously next time. He was aware that he had some old-fashioned ideas, but there had to be a woman somewhere who thought as he did.

Kendra broke into his thoughts. "Don't apologize. Clowns do have an odd effect on most people."

Gable took a sip of his wine. "Tell me about yourself, Kendra," he said. "Where are you from? How did you become a clown? Did you just run off with a circus one day?"

Kendra laughed. Did he really think it was so simple to become a clown? Well, she had no intention of making a confession about her life, either. What did it matter to him who she was?

"I was born in Boston," she told him. That was the truth. She had been brought to North Carolina when she was four and left at the children's home by her unwed mother, who found that she simply couldn't keep her.

"What?" he joked. "A Bostonian with no hidden fortune? No wealth of your own? No blue blood?"

Kendra shook her head and laughed. "All red."

He grinned at her. "How did you become a clown? Better yet, *why* did you become a clown, of all things?"

"Nothing to it," she said casually. "I just ran off and joined the circus."

Gable laughed at her repetition of his words. "I was joking. Did you really do that?"

"Yes, when I became good enough."

"When you became good enough?"

She sighed in exasperation. "I worked very hard to get where I am today. I've succeeded because I wanted it very much. I studied, then auditioned. I got lucky, I suppose. I was accepted by a large circus."

She smiled reminiscently. "When I was growing up, Emmett Kelly was my hero. I wanted to be just like him. He acted the part of a clown in a movie," she confided. "Now I'm doing that too. I've been very fortunate in my choice of career."

Gable was surprised that she was so serious about her work and that she clearly considered it quite an accomplishment. He had no idea that she had gone through so much preparation.

"Then you won't remain in the area?"

Kendra shook her head. "When the movie is finished, I'll spend the summer traveling with a circus, as I always do."

Gable was amazed, and he didn't know why he should be. Of course, that was what he supposed most clowns did, but he couldn't envision this young woman with a traveling circus.

"You're very good at what you do," he said finally. "And I admire your willingness to share your talent so freely with the children."

Kendra's brown eyes sparkled. "Clowns are for children, and I can't tell you how happy it makes me to see them laugh and smile," she said, her voice rising with excitement. "And their parents too. If I never do anything else in life, I know that I've brightened my little corner of the world."

Gable smiled at her. "You've brightened mine too. I'm very glad you came into it. You've done a world of good for Brian, and you've given me the first hope I've had in weeks."

He was gazing at her intently, and Kendra averted her eyes. She was deeply pleased because she had been of some benefit to Brian, but she had foolishly hoped that this attractive man liked her for herself as well. She didn't want him to see her disappointment, and she was relieved when the food arrived.

As they ate, they talked about her travels and his business, and Kendra was glad to focus on general topics.

"Do you really move around most of the time?" Gable asked.

"Much of it," she confessed. "And I love it. The circus is such a wonderful place." Her dark eyes danced, and she gestured animatedly with her hands. "You have to be part of it to understand the magic, the energy, the rewards," she exclaimed.

She spoke faster and faster, her enthusiasm for the subject carrying her along. "There's an excitement, an atmosphere, a *feeling* that can't be explained. I love the thrill of packing up and moving on to a new town where I know people will come with their smiles and joy, wanting us to make them happy, wanting to like us, to be entertained by us."

Gable was studying her again in that way that made her extremely nervous. He was trying to picture this vibrant, vital woman in a circus arena with vagabonds and wild animals, and he couldn't do it. He didn't know why. Perhaps because he didn't want to, he admitted to himself.

Kendra was suddenly embarrassed to be rattling on so. "And how is it being rich?" she asked abruptly, switching the subject back to him. "Do you rich people really live a better life than us peons?"

Gable laughed. "Yes, we wear gold pajamas and eat with silver spoons. I can't tell you what a thrill it is."

Kendra smiled. Gable seemed to take his wealth in stride. "Are your parents dead, Gable?"

"Yes. They've been dead for over three years now. And yours?"

"Yes," she said without elaborating.

"So you're alone?" he asked. "No boyfriend?" He was surprised that he had asked the question; even more surprised to realize that the answer mattered to him.

She shrugged carelessly. "No one in particular. This career doesn't lend itself well to marriage."

"No," Gable agreed. "I don't suppose it would, at that." His eyes met hers again. "You've clearly chosen the single path, haven't you? I don't imagine you're concerned with home and hearth and all that in your line of work. You just pack up and take your possessions with you."

Before Kendra could speak, he lowered his gaze and toyed with his drink. "I'm afraid I'm much too traditional in my thinking. Home and family have always been very important to me. I was raised by two loving parents, and I've always thought that someday I would have a marriage like theirs."

As Kendra listened, she heard an echo of Wyatt's voice. He had said more or less the same thing. Maybe her ex-fiancé had been right. Maybe she didn't have a right to expect to keep her unique career and be a wife and mother too. Perhaps she thought the way she did because she had never had a conventional family life of her own.

"Apparently I was wrong," Gable said, breaking into her thoughts. "Either in my choice of a wife or in my thinking. I believed my wife would be content to raise my children and find enough interests outside the work force to be happy."

He shrugged with a carelessness he didn't feel. "Oh, I know I must sound hopelessly chauvinistic to someone like you, but I had this old-fashioned notion that most women want to have children, and that most would like to be well-off enough to stay home and raise them, at least until school age. I believe in milk, cookies, and a mother's love—a father's, too, of course. In my wife's case I was wrong."

His fingers tightened around his glass. "She loved the social whirl and the freedom of not working. But unfortunately she viewed pregnancy as a physical and social handicap."

Kendra looked into his eyes, and she was surprised to see his vulnerability a second time.

"Where are Brian's parents?" she asked, remembering how she had thought the boy was Gable's child.

"My brother and his wife were killed in the fire," he said.

"Oh, I'm so sorry!" Kendra cried.

"Brian was the only one to escape," Gable explained. "That's why he won't speak. His psychologists believe that he feels guilty because he lived and his parents died."

"How awful for him," Kendra whispered.

"I'm all he has now," Gable said. "It's a big responsibility," he added thoughtfully.

"I wonder if you know just what a treasure you have in your friend Genna," Kendra murmured, remembering the picture of the woman by Gable's side at the hospital.

"Yes, I do. She's been a wonderful friend. She's practically turned her antique store over to her manager so that she can help care for Brian."

He had known Genna all her life; she was loving, serene, patient, and wonderful with people, particularly children. He didn't know how he would have gotten through this time without her.

He gazed thoughtfully at Kendra for a moment as he considered the similarities and contrasts between her and Genna. He took a long drink of his wine, then abruptly asked, "Are you ready to go?"

Kendra hastily wiped her mouth with her linen napkin. "Yes, anytime you are."

With a minimum of movement Gable paid the bill, took her elbow, and escorted her to the door. Well, she told herself, the obligatory dinner was over. She wouldn't be seeing Gable Hunt again. She knew it was all for the best, but strangely, she

51

couldn't deny the disappointment she felt at the thought.

He seemed tense as they made their way back to the car, but she didn't miss the way he brought himself back under control. When he opened the car door for her, he was smiling once again.

"I hope you'll agree to see Brian again," he said as he drove her back to Darcy's. "He's really taken with you."

A vision of the child surfaced in Kendra's mind. What a terrible experience he had endured. How tragic to lose both of his parents.

"Of course I'll see him," she said as Gable parked the car in front of Darcy's house.

"And me too?" Gable asked unexpectedly, a little too lightly. "Can I talk you into seeing me again?"

Before she could reply, he pulled her toward him, and his mouth descended to claim hers. The kiss was gentle, sweet, and filled with soft longing. The moment was exquisitely tender; Kendra would no more have dreamed of drawing away than she would try to fly.

Gable was the one to pull back. He didn't know what had prompted him to kiss her. He certainly hadn't planned it, but he couldn't say he hadn't relished it. Like everything else about this woman, it had had a magical quality—so pure and so sweet.

"Mmm," he said thickly, one hand entwined in her long hair. "I didn't know what I was missing by not going to the circus."

Kendra managed a trembling smile. She had

thought she could take anything in stride these days, but she had not expected a man like Gable Hunt to step into her life.

"We try to please," she murmured with much less lightness than she had hoped.

"You've succeeded," he told her as he drew her against him again.

The first kiss had been unexpected, and while she had found it very pleasurable, she knew that she shouldn't let Gable kiss her again. It was one thing to help Brian but quite another to become involved with Gable Hunt.

He had made his opinion of her and her career all too clear. What he needed was a woman like Genna Lawson, all lady and lace and devoted to home and hearth, as he had put it. In fact, the woman fit his description so well that she seemed to have been molded just for Gable Hunt.

"I really must go in," she whispered. "I have to work tomorrow."

"Are you too busy to see Brian on Saturday?" he asked.

She looked at him with wide eyes, wanting to say yes. But how could she refuse this poor child? Brian already had her heart. The trick would be to make sure that she didn't give it to Gable.

She tossed back her hair. "I'd be delighted."

"Why don't we go on a picnic?" he asked impulsively. "About one o'clock?"

"All right. See you then."

"Good night, Kendra."

"Good night."

As Gable watched her walk away he frowned.

Kendra was fun and fascinating, and he was counting on her help with Brian.

"Hell," he said aloud. Who was he kidding? He wanted to see her again for himself as well as for Brian. She wasn't what he wanted in a lifetime partner by the wildest stretch of the imagination, but then, she didn't want that kind of commitment, either. She had made her position very plain. When the movie ended, she would travel on.

He shook his head in disbelief. A circus clown, of all things! It wouldn't do either him or Brian any good to become too attached to her. Kendra was their big hope for now, but one day she would be gone.

But maybe, just maybe, he and Brian both could claim a little of her magic before then.

CHAPTER FOUR

Kendra spent the week in a flurry of activity, shooting on the movie and making hospital visits. But no matter how swiftly the days passed, she still had time to think of Brian—and of Gable. Saturday arrived before she was ready for it.

By one o'clock she was dressed in her jeans, a long-sleeved blue shirt, and loafers. Her long dark hair was loosely flowing down around her shoulders, as she liked to wear it.

She jumped when the door bell rang, and Speckles started barking. Before Kendra could get down the steps to the front door, she heard Darcy talking.

"Well, well, well, Mr. Hunt, and young Master Hunt. Come on in."

Kendra smiled a little as she listened. Darcy was doing her best to play Cupid, and she had no idea that it was a futile exercise. Kendra knew it, but even she was prone to forget. Gable's kiss had been achingly sweet, and it had lingered in her mind, tormenting her throughout the week. She constantly had to remind herself that she had agreed on this outing only because of Brian. She hurried down the steps to meet the two guests, Speckles at her feet.

"Hello," she said merrily. Brian was clutching his puppy tightly to his chest.

"He insisted on bringing the animal," Gable explained. "He won't let her out of his sight, and I didn't see that it mattered on a picnic."

"That's fine," Kendra said brightly. "We'll take Speckles along to keep the puppy company. How's that, Brian?"

Kendra smiled at him, but to her dismay he looked at her with pained blue eyes. He seemed unable to believe what he was seeing as he gazed at her, then turned to look accusingly at Gable, as if his uncle had betrayed him.

His eyes glistened brightly, and Kendra thought he was going to cry. Hanging his head, he looked down at his hands as he petted the puppy.

Kendra walked over to him. "Hello, Brian," she said gently. "How are you today?"

His lower lip trembled, and he looked up at her with huge eyes. His features crumpled into a pained mask. Then he lowered his long lashes again.

"Brian," Gable murmured, his voice deep and concerned. "What's wrong? This is Kendra. You know her as Happy the Clown. I told you she was joining us for a picnic today."

Brian shook his head as he stared once more at Kendra, his eyes naked with disbelief and unhappiness. He shook his head again in denial, then sniffled, trying mightily to fight back his tears.

But it was no use. His disappointment spilled down his cheeks in the form of two big tears.

Gable glanced at Kendra in dismay. "I don't understand," he said. "Brian was thrilled at the thought of seeing you again. He could hardly wait for today. He was looking forward to it all week, I know. He kept drawing pictures of clowns who looked like you and giving them to his tutor."

Kendra looked at the handsome boy, his dark hair so much like Gable's, the tears trailing pitifully down his unhappy face.

"I think I know just what the trouble is," she said. "Wait right here and I'll be back in a few minutes."

Gable gazed after her in surprise as she vanished, Speckles at her feet. Sitting down in the chair by his nephew, Gable drew him into his arms and held him while the boy wept silently.

Darcy, all concern, fluttered around the two of them, trying to think of some way to bring the happiness back to Brian's little face. She turned around, her eyes wide with surprise when Kendra appeared again, dressed in her clown costume.

"What the devil?" Gable exclaimed. Surely Kendra didn't think she was going on the picnic dressed as a clown.

But apparently she knew what she was doing. Brian slowly looked up, and when he saw the Happy he knew, his face brightened. Flinging himself from the couch, he ran across the room and wrapped his arms around Kendra's baggy pant legs.

Kendra smoothed his hair back as he held tightly to her. She glanced at Gable over the child's head. She was all smiles when she saw the chagrin on his face. He clearly couldn't believe he was taking her out dressed like this. She laughed softly at his dismay. She wouldn't have taken a million dollars for the look on either his face or Brian's.

Abruptly she produced a horn and tooted it near Brian's ear. He looked up at her and smiled. Then she took his hand and led him from the room.

Shaking his head from side to side, Gable glanced at a smiling Darcy, then followed the others. After all, he told himself, this outing was for Brian. Kendra had saved the day by dressing as Happy, and he could hardly object to that.

But Gable was anything but happy, himself, about the turn of events. He had looked forward to spending a near normal day with her and Brian. The kind of day a family might spend together, he mused. The thought troubled him.

He gazed after the clown, boy, and dogs, and smiled slowly to himself. The picnic was going to be an unusual one with this little group.

Kendra smiled at him and dipped her head in acknowledgment as he opened her door, and Gable wondered if she was going to spend the whole day pantomiming. She had already told him that she didn't talk in front of the children because it took away the magic. It was certainly going to take away from his day if she didn't speak.

He was driving his station wagon, and when

Brian's dog, which had been named Puppy until Brian decided on a permanent name, spied Speckles, she began to run around in the back exuberantly. Speckles barked energetically at the puppy. Gable drew in a deep breath. Yes, sir, this was going to be some outing.

"We'll go up into the mountains," he commented when they had all gotten into the car. "There are many lovely spots for a picnic."

Kendra pulled out her horn and tooted it twice to show her approval.

Gable groaned. "Oh, God." He looked at the beaming Brian, who sat between the two of them, then glanced in the mirror at the two dogs frolicking in the back. And suddenly he laughed aloud at the hilarity of it all.

When they had driven for about an hour and a half, they reached the spot Gable had been looking for. Tall trees shaded half a dozen picnic tables that had been placed near a meandering stream.

"How's this?" he asked.

Brian nodded, and Kendra tooted her horn.

The dogs burst from the car the minute he opened the door, scrambling madly across the seats and him. Before Gable could get out of the car, Kendra had tumbled out after the dogs. Motioning to Brian, who was still inside, Kendra coaxed him forward.

While Gable, Brian, and the dogs watched, looking at the clown curiously, she began to clap her hands and spin around in her huge shoes as if celebrating nature and being out in the open. She really did seem to possess some secret to life that Gable didn't know about. Unexpectedly he recalled how automatically she had accepted his kiss and how her lips had lingered so sweetly against his without hesitation.

He shook his head, partly in amusement and partly in amazement, as Speckles stood up on her back legs to join Kendra in the carefree dance.

Gable was taken with the woman's joyous abandon. She projected an innocence, a genuineness that touched him. Of course, she was a clown, skilled in such performances, and no doubt her intention was to entertain Brian, but she genuinely seemed to delight in the pleasures of her profession.

She held out her hands, and Brian shyly joined her and the dog, a big smile on his face. As Gable stared at the trio in disbelief Kendra beckoned to him. He glanced over his shoulder, certain that someone would think he was totally insane, and when he discovered no one around, he became part of the circle. They held hands and frolicked to the music of the wind in the trees. Even Puppy bounded about madly, as if caught up in the impromptu dance.

As Gable moved around and around in the circle he was acutely aware of how Kendra's gloved hand felt in his, and he was sure that he could feel her warmth even through the cloth.

Finally she ended the dance, shooing Brian and the dogs away with a motion of her hands. Speckles took the hint, leading the boy and the puppy on a mad chase.

Gable stared after his nephew, then glanced back at the clown. He had the strangest urge to draw her to him, clown costume and all, and dance with her there in the woods.

Kendra, misreading his thoughts, whispered, "Think of it this way, Mr. Hunt: It will be a day to remember."

"No doubt about it," Gable agreed. "No doubt about it."

"Look at your nephew," she murmured. "He's already having the time of his life."

Gable's thoughts returned to the young boy, and he became pensive as he watched Brian running awkwardly after the two small dogs. The child's legs were still healing. Gable had tried in vain to get him to be active; clearly he would have no problems in that area today.

"Yes," he said thoughtfully. "Brian seems to be his happiest around you."

"Oh, it's not me," Kendra murmured. "It's the clown, don't you see?"

Gable looked at her and grinned. "How can I help it? What I'd like to know is if you really can dance," he said, his teasing eyes holding hers. "I don't think you can without those big shoes to steady you."

Kendra laughed. "Clearly you don't know who you're talking to, mister. They don't call me Twinkle Toes for nothing. Believe me, if I can dance in these shoes, I can *dance.*"

They fell silent as Brian made his way back to them. The boy watched quietly as Kendra and

Gable emptied the car and arranged the picnic lunch on a bright blue blanket on the ground.

"Are you ready to eat?" Gable asked him.

Brian's eyes glowed and he smiled. For one hopeful moment Gable actually thought the child was going to speak. But it was not to be. He reached for Kendra's horn, and when she gave it to him, he tooted twice.

"Oh, God." Gable groaned again. "Not you too."

When he saw the stricken look in his nephew's eyes as the child handed the horn back to Kendra, he playfully ruffled the boy's hair. "I was just teasing. I like the horn," he said gently.

Kendra caught his eye, and he shrugged his shoulders. He supposed that if the horn was good enough for Kendra, it was good enough for the mute boy too. The thought made him grin as the whole group, the two dogs included, settled down on the blanket to eat.

The lunch consisted of fried chicken, biscuits, apples, and soda. Everyone had their fair share, including Speckles and Puppy, and Gable couldn't recall when he had spent a more riotous —or enjoyable—afternoon. He deliberately made leading comments to Kendra, knowing that she would do nothing but toot at him.

"Bet you can't cook a meal like this," he teased.

Kendra tooted her horn and nodded.

"Oh, come now," Gable taunted, "my fifty-year-old housekeeper cooked the chicken and biscuits. Don't tell me a circus clown can do it too."

Kendra tooted her horn twice.

"Is that a yes or a no?" he asked. "I never have gotten the language of horn tooting down."

Instead of answering, she threw a chicken bone at him.

Brian took the horn from Kendra and tooted twice to show his approval. Gable caught the bone with ease and dropped it in the trash sack, but he grinned wickedly at the clown across from him. When he looked back at Brian, he saw that the little boy had stretched out near Kendra. His eyelids were drooping.

"I'm afraid the picnic is over for Brian," Gable said softly. "He doesn't sleep well at night—too many nightmares—and now the outing has worn him out."

Kendra placed a finger to her lips to quiet Gable as she bent down over the boy and brushed the crumbs from his mouth. Gently, softly, she smoothed back the dark hair that fell carelessly across his forehead.

Gable watched in silence, lured by the gentle way Kendra stroked the boy's furrowed brow until all the creases had eased. He found the sight of the woman and her magic compelling. In seconds Brian had fallen soundly asleep, the horn still firmly in his hands. The dogs, taking their cue from him, soon succumbed to the drowsy spring afternoon too.

"Ah, peace and quiet," Gable joked. "Two sleeping dogs, a sleeping boy, and a mute clown."

Kendra made a face at him, sticking out her

tongue and thumbing her clown nose. Caught by surprise, Gable laughed aloud.

Kendra placed her finger to her lips, indicating that he should be quiet so that the boy could sleep. She stood up and motioned for him to follow her. A smile still on his face, he shook his head as he watched her walk toward the gurgling stream.

When they were some distance from Brian, but still near enough to see him, she announced, "Too bad, Mr. Hunt, but I can talk now that I won't ruin the magic for Brian."

"You do create magic, don't you?" he asked, looking down into her eyes.

"I try," she said modestly.

"And you succeed," he told her, his gaze holding hers.

Kendra felt her pulse race. "Do you come here often?" she asked, watching the water tumble over the smooth stones in the streambed.

"Not often enough. When I was a child, my parents brought me here. Those were such happy, innocent days, those boyhood days," he said pensively. "And how about you?" he asked. "Did you go on picnics?"

Kendra became thoughtful for a moment, then she turned back to him, her eyes laughing with some fond remembrance. "I went on picnics like you wouldn't believe," she said. "There were kids of all ages and descriptions, and we did wonderful things—like cook hot dogs and marshmallows over roaring fires."

"It sounds like quite a family reunion," he said, grinning at her.

"It was," she agreed, recalling the children she had grown up with, and she laughed at the memory of the pandemonium of those all too rare picnics.

Gable caught her hands in his. "And were you the clown then too?" he asked.

Laughter still on her lips, Kendra nodded; she found that her voice had been stolen away by the warmth of his touch. He was only inches from her, and she could feel the excitement building in her veins.

"I thought so," he murmured, drawing her closer. For a brief time they seemed to be suspended in a never-never land. Then Gable lowered his head.

"I've never kissed a woman with a mustache before," he teased, but his voice was thick and husky, his eyes all too serious. The touch of her stirred him, and ignoring her makeup, he kissed her.

Kendra's derby tumbled off, and the laughter died on her mouth as Gable's warm lips claimed hers. She had told herself that she could avoid his touch today with Brian nearby, but the little boy slept soundly. Kendra realized that she was at Gable's mercy—and her own. She loved the feel of his mouth against hers, his tongue teasing hers so boldly.

After Wyatt she hadn't let her guard down. She was happy with her world and her work. She felt that she contributed something to life, and that made her total devotion to clowning worth-while.

But here in this exciting man's arms she found it difficult to remember that she had promised to give her heart only to her career. The kiss Gable gave her now was nothing like the sweet kiss he had given her before.

His lips moved powerfully and persuasively against hers, coaxing a response from deep within her. His touch was masterful and stirring, and Kendra felt herself succumbing to the magic of his caresses. Without conscious thought she met the fire in his kiss.

He drew back for only a moment, to look into her eyes before he kissed her again. Kendra felt the warmth of him through the thickness of her clothes, and she wrapped her arms around his neck, wanting more and still more of his touch.

Gable's heady touch stirred the embers of passion that Kendra had so carefully smothered months ago. He was vital and masculine and breathtakingly disturbing. She automatically slid her fingers down his back, longing to know him more intimately.

A sweet, drugging hunger surged within her, and she moaned softly against Gable's lips, instinctively drawing him nearer so that she might savor the thrill of him.

Gable molded himself more tightly to her, his body hard and warm as it met hers. Kendra arched herself against him. She had missed being touched, being held, being loved. Now that Gable had slipped into her life, she couldn't seem to remember all the reasons why she had put up barriers around her heart.

She only knew that she was lost in the moment, lost in the joy flooding swiftly through her with each caress. She drew in her breath sharply when his fingers slipped inside the baggy shirt she wore, and she felt the heat of his hands on her bare skin. Shivers ran up and down her spine as his fingers skimmed lightly over her back, then slipped around her waist.

In breathless anticipation she stood before Gable, trembling as he touched her breasts lightly, which caused the throbbing tips to harden beneath their flimsy cover of lace. Kendra felt the waves of desire building deep inside her.

Suddenly Brian emitted a frightened cry. Kendra and Gable jerked apart to see the child huddled on the blanket, tears streaming down his face.

The two dogs began to whimper. Wagging her tail anxiously, Speckles raced to Kendra's side.

Kendra closed the distance between her and Brian before his uncle could reach him. She sank down on the blanket and drew the child to her bosom, crooning softly as she began to rock him back and forth.

Brian never awakened. He gradually relaxed and soon became still in Kendra's arms. The tears turned into sniffles, then subsided. In minutes only the dampness on his face told of his torment.

Gable didn't realize that he had been breathing harshly until the rasping sound began to dissipate. His eyes had never left the woman and the boy on the blanket. He had lived through too many of Brian's nightmares, and he had been relieved to have someone share the pain.

Now the vision of the Charlie Chaplin clown and the small, sleeping boy with the tear-streaked face finally penetrated his conscious mind. He didn't think he had ever seen a more touching sight. Part of Kendra's makeup was missing, and her mustache was askew. But he was sure that he had never seen a more beautiful woman.

He yearned to draw her back into his arms and hold her as she was holding the child, but he watched, barely breathing, as Kendra held Brian long after his weeping had ceased. She couldn't seem to let him go.

Kendra continued to hold the child who had stirred her so deeply. She had reached out to other children and tried to touch them with her magic. With some she had succeeded. And with some perhaps she hadn't.

But this little boy seemed especially needy. How lonely he was. How hurt and lost. She had seen children like him in the orphanage where she had grown up.

She had been like him. She had lost her mother too. Not in the violent way he had, of course. But it had been a wrenching loss all the same, and it had produced its own share of nightmares.

Funny, but until now she hadn't even remembered them. She had been four years old. And she had finally understood that her mother was never coming back.

"Kendra."

She drew in her breath as she looked up at Gable. Tears danced on her long lashes. Embarrassed, she looked back down at Brian.

"He's asleep now," she whispered thickly.

Gable nodded and helped her ease the boy back down onto the blanket. Then he tilted her chin with his finger.

Trembling, Kendra looked into his eyes. A slow smile spread over her lips, and she began to laugh gently, shattering the tense moment.

"What's funny?" he murmured.

She brushed his hand away and reached out to stroke his face. "You're wearing my makeup," she said. "Lord, but we two must look a sight."

Gable grinned and resisted the urge to tell her that she was the most beautiful sight he had ever seen. "I'm sure we do," he murmured.

He looked levelly at her. "You should have half a dozen children of your own. You'd make a wonderful mother. You know that, don't you?"

She glanced at Brian. "I wouldn't want half a dozen children," she said. She had always dreamed of one boy and one girl. She had been confident that there was enough of her to give to her husband, two children, and still have her career. But those dreams had been abandoned with Wyatt.

"Every woman isn't cut out to be a mother," she added, remembering her own mother as she looked up at Gable. He had implied at dinner that he thought all women should want to be mothers.

Gable was watching her intently, his mouth taut and his eyes hooded. "Yes, I do know."

Kendra recalled another comment Gable had made. She longed to question him about it.

"Why didn't you ever have a child, Gable? You said your wife felt that pregnancy interfered with her social life."

Now it was Gable's turn to avert his eyes. How he had yearned for a child. How he had planned for one. What hopes and dreams he had placed on it.

"After we were married, Sandy decided that she didn't want children. She refused to have them."

"I'm sorry," Kendra murmured.

"Not as sorry as I was," he said. "It was an issue we couldn't compromise on. It caused a lot of anguish and eventually destroyed our marriage. I won't make that mistake again." He looked at Brian. "When I find a mother for him, I'll make sure she wants to be a mother."

A frown darkened Kendra's happy clown face as she considered what he had said.

When Gable saw it, he exhaled wearily and ran his hands through his hair in a frustrated way. Why was he telling her all this?

"I'm sorry," he said. "I don't know what makes me think I can burden you with the details and disappointments of my life."

"We keep apologizing to each other," Kendra said lightly. "We should make a recording and save time."

He strove to find the same light tone she had

used. "Speaking of time, I believe we should call it a day. Don't you?"

She nodded. They should have called it a day much, much sooner: before he had told her he wanted a mother for Brian; before she had let him hold her. Thank God they had been interrupted. She didn't know what would have happened if they hadn't been.

She went back to the stream to retrieve her derby, then quickly began to gather up the picnic supplies. She would be more careful next time. If there was a next time.

CHAPTER FIVE

Kendra watched as Gable gently picked up the sleeping Brian, who still held fast to the horn, and laid him on the backseat of the station wagon. She couldn't help but think what a good father figure he was and how lucky the small boy was to have such an uncle.

As she thought about Gable wanting a mother for the boy, she worked faster to fold the blanket. *She* was not the mother Brian needed, nor the wife Gable Hunt wanted. When she saw Speckles at her feet, she reached down for the small dog. Holding the animal to her bosom like a shield, she walked to the car with the blanket under her arm.

Gable smiled when he saw the two of them. "Did anybody ever tell you how cute you are?" he whispered as he walked over to her.

Kendra tried not to smile, but she hadn't expected the compliment, and she grinned.

Gable leaned forward to touch her mouth with his, and Speckles barked once in annoyance. Kendra laughed nervously, glad for the distraction.

"Selfish!" Gable said, chastising Speckles playfully. Then he glanced around. "Where's Puppy?"

Kendra felt a surge of alarm. Puppy! She should have kept an eye on the young dog, but it hadn't occurred to her that the pet would run off. She had been too distracted by her thoughts of Gable to think of much else. Brian would be inconsolable if something happened to Puppy.

"She can't be far away," she insisted. "She was here just a second ago with Speckles."

"Oh, Lord, we can't lose her," Gable said, turning back toward the woods.

Kendra put Speckles in the back of the station wagon, quickly placed the blanket under Brian's head, and went in the opposite direction from Gable.

"Here, Puppy," she called softly. "Here, Puppy."

Unexpectedly the little animal came bounding out from beneath some bushes, her tongue hanging out.

Kendra scooped her up. "You stinker, you had us worried silly." She glanced back in time to see a small rabbit running for its life. "Aha," she said to Puppy, "you were terrorizing the natives—and us too," she added.

Slipping the squirming animal inside her coat jacket, she strode in the direction Gable had taken. "Gable," she called. "Gable."

When he stepped into the clearing, Kendra produced the puppy as if she had used magic to make her appear. "Ta-da!" she cried, holding out the dog. "One lost puppy!"

The relief on his face was instantaneous. "Oh, thank God," he said with a groan. "I don't know how I would have explained to Brian that she was gone too."

He closed the distance between them and wrapped his arm around Kendra's shoulders. "You always save the day, don't you?" he murmured, looking down at her.

She shrugged with a playfulness she didn't feel. When Gable touched her, she forgot all the things she wanted to remember.

"We'd better get back to Brian before he wakes up," she said softly. "He'll be frightened if he finds himself alone."

Nodding, Gable walked back to the station wagon, his arm still around Kendra's shoulders. She breathed a sigh of relief when he freed her to put the puppy in back with Speckles. Kendra checked on Brian, saw that he was still soundly asleep, then climbed into the vehicle.

When Gable got in, Kendra glanced at him, thinking again how handsome he was and how much his touch thrilled her. His very presence was intoxicating. She gazed out at the woods as Gable started the car. She would not think such things again.

The ride back seemed endless for Kendra. What Gable had said at dinner the first night was true. She was happy, content. Her life was all mapped out, and she liked it the way it was. She didn't know why she was letting this man invade her world.

Kendra reached for the door handle when Gable parked the car in front of her house. She instinctively knew she shouldn't linger; she couldn't forget how easily and totally he had stirred her senses earlier, how recklessly she had abandoned herself to his seduction. But before she could get the door open, Gable caught both her hands in his.

"Go dancing with me tonight," he murmured, his eyes holding hers.

She shook her head. "I don't think that's such a good idea," she whispered. She tried to pull her hands from his, but Gable drew her across the seat. He kissed her lightly again before Kendra could protest.

"I think it is," he retorted. "Eight o'clock, and be sure to wear your best dancing shoes."

"No, really, I don't think so," Kendra said breathlessly. His kisses had only emphasized why she shouldn't see him again. She reached for the door handle, and in her frustration she couldn't seem to get the door open. Gable leaned across her to pull the lock up.

"Eight o'clock," he repeated firmly.

Kendra hadn't even realized she had locked the door. She flung it open, and as fast as her legs would carry her, she raced up the steps.

Suddenly Speckles howled unhappily.

Kendra stopped on the porch and fought to gain some control. Oh, damn! She had forgotten Speckles. She had never done that in her life!

Speckles let out another bereft cry, and Kendra pressed her lips tightly together. This wasn't fair. It really wasn't fair. She drew in a steadying breath, and when she turned to face the station wagon, she saw that Brian had awakened and was sitting up in the backseat. He had seen her, and he tooted the horn twice.

The child's eyes were glowing as Kendra slowly returned. He held up the horn so that she could see it and tooted again. She grinned at him and did a brief clown routine, pretending to bounce an imaginary ball on the sidewalk before she went to the back of the station wagon to retrieve Speckles.

Gable was already there, unlocking the door. Kendra met his eyes only once, then held out her arms to the dog. The little mutt leapt up, and Kendra held her close as she walked away a second time.

She was determined that she wouldn't look back again as she went up the steps. She listened as the door closed, and she heard Gable start the station wagon. But try as she might, she couldn't keep from turning around as the vehicle headed up the street. She looked just in time to see Brian waving at her frantically, the horn held high above his head.

Sighing wearily, Kendra went into the house. When Darcy appeared in the hall, the clown forced a smile to her lips.

"Well, tell me all about it," the old woman insisted, her eyes twinkling brightly. "How was your picnic? I almost died when you went out of here with that costume on, and I don't mind telling you that Gable Hunt did too."

Kendra giggled at the memory of Gable's face when she had walked in with the Charlie Chaplin outfit on. Sitting down on the couch, she pulled off her derby and wig and shook her own hair free.

"He was surprised, wasn't he?"

"Surprised?" Darcy said, laughing lustily. "He was downright dismayed. No doubt he's grateful for what you're doing for Brian, but he's not interested just for Brian's sake. Don't you see that he's got eyes for you, girl?"

Kendra pulled off her mustache and eyebrows and stared down at the wisps of black hair. She couldn't help recalling how Gable's lips had caressed hers or how his touch had aroused her.

"He wants a mother for Brian," she said firmly.

"Well, sure he does," Darcy agreed. "But that doesn't mean he's going to pick just any woman to be his wife."

Kendra stood up as quickly as she had sat down. Both she and Gable knew the kind of woman he wanted—and needed. It wasn't her, and that thought inexplicably saddened her.

"I must go and change," she said quickly. "Look at me! I'm a mess."

Darcy stood up too. "Come on back down when you're ready. I'm fixing some lasagna."

Kendra smiled affectionately at the old woman. "My rooms don't include meals. I don't want you cooking for me every night."

"Nonsense! I enjoy your company."

"You're a dear," Kendra murmured, "but I have other plans for this evening."

Before Darcy could say anything more, the young woman turned on her heel and disappeared up the steps. She would see Gable Hunt once more. To talk. She would tell him that she could only see him to help Brian.

But right now she didn't want to think about it anymore. The mere thought of Gable caused excitement to race through her, reminding her of how foolish she was to see him again for any reason.

"Now, where are you going done up so pretty?" Darcy asked, her eyes glowing when Kendra came downstairs in a full navy satin skirt, a white scoop-necked lace blouse, and patent-leather ballet-type shoes.

"Dancing," she answered.

"With Gable!" Darcy exclaimed, as if it were a coup.

Kendra nodded.

"Oh, you lucky, lucky girl," the old woman cried.

Kendra looked away. Somehow she didn't feel lucky—she didn't feel lucky at all. The door bell rang at one minute past eight. As usual, before Kendra could get to her feet, Darcy had answered the door. Predictably Gable looked quite dashing, and Kendra couldn't stop the foolish beating of her heart when she saw him.

He grinned when he saw her. "You *do* look like a girl who knows how to dance," he teased, his blue eyes lingering briefly on the enticing swell of her breasts above the low-cut blouse.

Kendra blushed. Maybe she had overdone the outfit just a little, but he had invited her to go dancing, and she could dance to her heart's content in the cool blouse, the swish of the full skirt playing about her legs, and nothing between her feet and the dance floor but the thin soles of her shoes.

"Are you ready?" he asked.

"Yes, don't I look like it?" she quipped.

Gable used the question as an excuse to boldly peruse her. "Yes," he murmured at length. "Yes, you look quite lovely."

Kendra felt the color surge to her cheeks for the second time. She couldn't deny how pleased she was that he thought her lovely.

Gable laughed as he reached for her hand. She tried to avoid his warm fingers, but with Darcy standing there, beaming like a Cheshire cat, she had no choice but to let Gable take her hand in his.

"I hope you'll like the night spot I've chosen," he said as he led her to the car. "They have a live band, although I suspect it's a little sedate for you."

"I'm sure I'll enjoy it," Kendra told him. "I love live music."

She was, however, a little surprised by the elegance of the club they entered a short time later. But, she told herself, she should have known that nothing but the best would do for Gable Hunt.

In contrast to her own outfit, the other women

were dressed in their finest. It seemed that Gable knew absolutely everyone in the room, and he stopped en route to their table to introduce Kendra to a succession of people whose names soon blended.

Kendra murmured pleasantries, feeling distinctly out of place by Gable's side. Someone asked about Genna, and Kendra couldn't help but think that Genna was the woman who should be here with him.

She lifted her chin a little as a hostess led them to an intimate table in the all red-and-black room. This was just another reminder of precisely why she wouldn't see Gable again. This setting would only make it easier to explain it to him. Funny how easily she had been distracted from her primary purpose in coming here with Gable tonight when he complimented her.

"What will you have to drink?" he asked, his eyes meeting hers over the hypnotic flame of a single black candle in the middle of the table.

"Vodka and tonic," she said, needing something bracing. She was feeling more and more uncomfortable in her simple skirt and shoes, and she was sorry that she hadn't dressed up more.

She raised her head a little higher. No, she wasn't sorry. She and Gable were in two different worlds. Before it was too late, it was time that they both acknowledged that their only tie was Brian.

She lowered her eyes. Too late for what, she wasn't quite sure. But deep in her heart she knew there was a danger.

The band began to play before Gable and Kendra had been served, and Gable held out his hands to her. "All right. Let's see if you can live up to your boast."

Kendra shook her head. She dare not let him touch her, hold her. Not before she had explained why she had come with him. "Let's talk first," she said. "Then we'll dance."

Gable settled back warily in his chair, as if he had been anticipating this. And, indeed, he had. No one had to tell him how rashly he was behaving with this woman.

He didn't know what drove him to pursue her so recklessly. Surely it wasn't the challenge, her elusiveness; he was above that kind of thing. He wasn't out to prove anything to himself or her. Nor was it that she insisted upon being sane and sensible while he was dancing on the brink of insanity.

She was all the things he swore he didn't want. She was a traveling circus clown. She had clearly indicated that she didn't want children. It seemed a contradiction when she was so wonderful with them. He could only conclude that she didn't want them to interfere with her career.

But that didn't stop him from wanting her. It didn't stop his heart from pounding madly when he was near her; it didn't stop the wild rush of desire that flooded through him when he touched her. It didn't stop the ache that filled him when she wasn't near.

"I don't think we should see each other again, unless it's in the context of my helping Brian,"

Kendra said hurriedly, her words running together as though she couldn't say them fast enough.

Gable could feel the tension crackle between them. There was an odd sensation in his stomach, but he would not let her know it. He put his elbows on the table in a casual manner, idly locked his fingers together, and gazed across at her, his eyes bright in the candlelight.

"There you go again," he murmured after a lengthy pause, as he attempted not to betray his agitation. "I'm not asking you for a lifetime commitment. So far it's just been dinner and dancing."

But he wanted more, so much more, from this woman than a couple of evenings out, and he suspected that they both knew it.

Her voice was ragged when she spoke. "Including a few kisses and caresses? Sorry, I'm not looking for a temporary involvement."

She lowered her long dark lashes. She would like nothing more than an involvement with him, she realized all too well. But she couldn't afford it emotionally. She was already too caught up in this man's life.

"I'm very concerned about Brian, and I want to do all I can to help him while I'm here, but I won't see you like this again. If the kisses and caresses and dinner and dancing are part of your gratitude, I have to say no thanks."

Gable reached across to capture her hands in his before she could move them. "I'm deeply grateful for what you're doing for Brian. You know that." His thumbs stroked her fingers tantalizingly. "But does that mean you can't spare a little concern for me too?"

"Yes, it does," she replied tensely. "I can't afford it."

He freed her hands. He didn't want to hear what she was saying. "Why?" he asked bluntly. "Because you're afraid the kisses will lead to more? Because you know you're attracted to me just as much as I'm attracted to you?"

"No," she lied. "Because we both know there's no point. Because you're looking for a wife and a mother. I'm neither. I'm a performer. I'm leaving in a few weeks. You don't want or need someone like me in your life. You need someone like Genna."

She looked down at her hands. "Frankly I don't know what you're waiting for. Why are you even out with me tonight? Why not with Genna?"

She was surprised to hear herself say that. She wasn't in the business of matchmaking, but every time she thought of Gable and Genna, she thought of how perfect they seemed for each other. She couldn't help it.

"I need your help with Brian, not in finding a wife," Gable said sharply, with a swiftness that startled them both.

Then he sat back in his chair and sighed tiredly, surprised that she had so thoroughly provoked him. He was irritated with her because he knew that she was being sensible. And he didn't want that. He wanted her magic and her fun. He wanted to laugh with her and hold her. He wanted—hell, he didn't know what he wanted anymore.

Their drinks were served, and Gable took a long swallow of his. Then he held out his hands again. He didn't want to talk. He didn't want to think. That much he did know.

"Dance with me," he said.

It was not a plea, and it was not a command. It was a need that Kendra recognized all too clearly. Without a word she let him take her hands and lead her out onto the floor.

Gable sighed raggedly when he drew her against his long body, and the anger he had felt seconds ago dissipated. This was what he wanted, what he had wanted since this afternoon when he had kissed her by the stream.

He wanted to smell the sweet fragrance of her long hair, to feel the warmth of her slender curves beneath his fingertips, to burn with an aching need that he hadn't felt in far too long, to lose himself in the wonder of the woman melding so intimately against him.

His breath was warm against her cheek, and Kendra involuntarily locked her fingers in the thick hair at the nape of Gable's neck. She forgot that they were in an elegant night spot, crowded with rich and finely dressed people. She forgot that she had just told this man that she wouldn't see him again. She wanted—no, needed—this moment for her own sanity. She needed to feel the heat of his body against hers. She needed to know that she could stir a man and be stirred by him—especially *this* man.

Her sigh mingled with Gable's. She wanted him to hold her, to want her, no matter how dangerous the desire was. When he touched her, she forgot to be reasonable.

The room was dimly lit, and Gable and Kendra's dance went unnoticed by the others, but in their own little world they moved against each other hungrily, achingly. Kendra told herself that she would enjoy just this one crazy moment in this man's arms, and then she would never let him touch her like this again.

But the magic enveloped her, and the music played on, as if it had been orchestrated only for them. Caught in the spell of the song, Kendra forgot to be logical. She closed her eyes and locked her arms around Gable's neck, letting him guide her ever so surely in their passionate dance, her body burning against his, her heartbeat echoing his.

Kendra didn't know when one song ended and another began. She was only aware of Gable and the heady sensations that spiraled up inside her each time he drew her closer. His fingers were playing on the bare skin above her blouse, and she could feel the warmth wherever he touched her.

He drew her even more tightly to his strong body, as if he couldn't hold her close enough, and Kendra felt a shiver go through him.

"Let's get out of here," he whispered hoarsely near her ear.

As though she were incapable of fighting back her own passion, much less his, she let him lead her by the hand out of the room. She didn't see anyone else. She didn't hear anyone else.

They stepped outside. Rain had begun to fall, and the night air smelled crisp and fresh. It swiftly and irrevocably cleared Kendra's foggy mind, and she realized that she was doing the very thing she had promised herself she would not do. She pulled her hand from Gable's.

"Please take me home," she said quietly.

He turned around and gazed at her, his eyes feverish with desire. "You don't mean that."

"I do," she insisted. "This is foolish. I'll be gone in a matter of weeks."

His fingers bit into her shoulders, and he forced her to look at him. "Maybe you won't want to go," he murmured thickly.

Her eyes met his searchingly. He really thought it would be simple for her to turn her back on her life. She shook her head.

"I'll want to go," she said with conviction.

Her career was the most important thing in her world. She would not let Gable turn her life around in a matter of days. She would not permit him to threaten all that she held dear. She would not fall in love with him. It was too dangerous.

"I don't want to see you again," she whispered emotionally. "I *won't* see you again."

CHAPTER SIX

Kendra was weary when she awakened the next morning. She was scheduled as one of the entertainers for a big charity benefit at two o'clock, and she was glad to have something to do. It would help to keep her mind off Gable and Brian.

When she had eaten a leisurely late breakfast prepared by Darcy, she lingered over coffee and the Sunday paper. Then she put on her costume, gathered Speckles in her arms, and set out for the affair.

The place was already like a madhouse when she arrived, and she had difficulty finding a parking spot. Held at the civic auditorium, it appeared to be one of the bigger social affairs of the year. Most of the town and much of the local media had turned up.

Kendra naturally attracted attention as she hurried from her car. Some of the youngsters spied her and began to run in her direction.

"Look at the clown! Look at the clown!" they called out.

She never passed the children by, no matter how much of a hurry she was in. When she had pantomimed hello, she pretended to rummage madly in her oversize pockets. She produced two whistles and gave them to two boys. As she turned to hand a paper flower to a little girl, Brian walked up with his shy, sweet smile and his hand held out.

Kendra felt both elated and sad at the sight of the child she had grown to care for so deeply. She gave the little girl the red flower and searched in her pockets until she found a blue one for Brian. Then she bent down low and handed it to him. When she had squirted it with cheap perfume, she sniffed it with pretended delight before tucking the stem into his shirt pocket.

Brian smiled sweetly and ran away with his treasure. Kendra's gaze followed him. She was sure that Gable couldn't be far behind. He wasn't. He was waiting on the sidelines with Genna.

She drew in her breath as her eyes skimmed over the tall man in the maroon suit and gray shirt. He seemed more handsome than ever today, but perhaps that was only because he was with the beautiful, blond Genna.

"Hello," Genna called out pleasantly, daintily waving a hand in recognition.

"Hello, Happy," Gable said as he strode toward her. She was surprised by the sound of her professional name on his lips after he had called her Kendra so often. Her pulse pounded at her temples as he reached out to her, and for a second she was shocked to realize that his only intention was to pet Speckles.

"How are you, girl?" he asked, playfully rubbing the dog's head.

Kendra felt his fingers brush lightly and maddeningly against her breast where she held Speckles, and she was sure that the warmth burned right through to her skin. It was all she could do to stand there and endure his provocative touch.

When he looked into her eyes, she felt faint. With a strength born of desperation she finally had sense enough to extricate herself from his uncomfortable nearness by unexpectedly tooting her horn.

Gable arched his brows in surprise, and Kendra quickly gave Brian an extravagant wave before hurrying on toward the auditorium. She couldn't seem to move fast enough to satisfy herself. A swift pain rose up inside her, and she told herself that she was walking too fast. But she wasn't sure that was the problem at all.

It was something much more severe. It was Gable Hunt. And she didn't understand why she was feeling this way.

When her turn came, Kendra rushed on stage, trying to outrun her disturbing thoughts. She had a crowd to entertain. She was a clown. This was her life, what she loved. Professionally, painfully, she put thoughts of Gable, Genna, and Brian in the back of her mind.

And she thrilled the crowd. She couldn't recall when she had been better. Today she wanted more than ever to give to the people and to be loved by them. She achieved what she wanted; she knew it in the way a performer does.

She was feeling high when she left the stage. She smiled broadly, pleased by all the applause she had received. Abruptly she stopped in her tracks at the back of the curtain as a swift realization overtook her. She had performed so well because she wanted Gable Hunt to see that this was what she was best at, that she didn't need him, and that he and Brian had no place in her life.

Tears began to build in her eyes, and to her utter dismay they spilled down her cheeks, making deep inroads into her white makeup, dripping down on her jacket before she could contain them.

She closed her lids against them, caught in the storm of her unhappiness. She cursed the day she had come back to North Carolina. She was sorry she had accepted the role in the film. For the first time in a very long time she felt confused and out of control.

She sniffled and tried to contain her unhappiness when she felt small fingers tug at her costume. Oh, Lord, it wouldn't do to have a child see the clown crying.

Quickly patting her face dry with a bandanna, she sneezed loudly and wiggled her nose as if she had an awful cold, then put on a broad smile and looked down. It was Brian! He had seen her unhappiness, and his own eyes were full of tears. He was gingerly holding out the paper flower she had given him earlier.

Kendra pressed her lips together and tried to

hold back burning tears. She wanted nothing but happiness for this child. She didn't want to be part of his pain.

She took the flower, then shot a burst of confetti at him from a concealed bulb. He was totally unprepared for the shower of colored paper. When Kendra saw the instant smile on his mouth, she waved to him and walked away.

She knew that Gable and Genna couldn't be far behind, and she didn't want them to know she had been crying.

When Monday morning finally came, Kendra was glad to get up and get ready for work. The night had been another long one, and she didn't feel very rested. She wanted to get to the studio and experience the excitement of the performance, the joy of the other actors, the thrill of working in front of the camera.

Just the thought of the day ahead put her in a better mood. By the time she arrived on the set, she was eager to work. She pantomimed outrageously for all she encountered, smiling when her clowning drew laughter.

Her part today included an act with another clown in which they tried to play on a seesaw by balancing Speckles in the middle. Kendra was in rare form as she and Speckles went onto the set. The scene went off without a hitch on the first take, and she hugged Speckles as she listened to the director.

"Cut and wrap!" he called out. "Excellent,

Happy! You're a natural, sweetheart. Your comedic timing is instinctive and superb."

Kendra was grinning from ear to ear, feeling pleased about her work as she walked away. Then she happened to look across the room.

Standing off to one side were Gable and Brian. Brian tooted his horn twice, then came racing toward her at full speed on his weak limbs.

"Oh, no," Kendra whispered despairingly. "Oh, no."

The boy flung himself around Kendra's legs and hugged her as he had done before. When he looked up into her face, she smiled at him tenderly.

When she looked up, she saw that Gable was crossing the room. Her heart began to beat more rapidly, and she tried desperately to still her insides as the handsome man walked over to her.

"He wanted to see you," Gable said simply. "I know how you feel, but please don't punish the child because of me. He needs you. All morning long he drew pictures of crying clowns and tooted his horn. He would not be consoled."

She closed her eyes briefly. She knew that Brian was enamored of her, and God knew she wanted to help him, but couldn't Gable see—didn't he realize—that the more dependent Brian became upon her, the harder it would be for him when she left? And leave she would. There was no doubt in her mind about that.

"Kendra."

She opened her eyes to look into Gable's.

"Just for a while. That's all I'm asking for the boy."

Kendra pressed her lips together. Why, oh why, couldn't she commit herself just for a while, as Gable asked? Why did she feel that she was putting herself in jeopardy instead of feeling the uplifting thrill of helping a needy child?

She stared at the man before her. He was part of the reason, of course. Then she squeezed Brian's shoulders and gently pushed him away from her. Brian was the other part. She didn't want to become intimately involved with him, then travel on.

Already she was too fond of him. He mirrored some part of her that was still raw. Brian and Gable had intruded into her orderly world, and deliberately or not, they were doing their best to rearrange it.

But she couldn't say no.

"Can we talk about it over dinner?" Gable asked, causing Kendra's head to snap up. He saw the doubt on her face and quickly added, "Just a hamburger somewhere, and the topic will be the boy only. I promise."

She sighed inwardly. Yes, the topic would be the boy, but the man would be there with her, stirring her up inside. Against all her better instincts and judgment, she nodded.

"Seven o'clock tonight?"

She nodded again, then ruffled Brian's hair and turned away toward the dressing room she shared with several other minor actors. She didn't need to change clothes. She always wore her costume

93

home, but she did need to get away from the child and the man. Feeling oddly awkward in the huge shoes she had long ago mastered, she made her way out of the room. She did not look back.

For the rest of the afternoon Kendra was in a dither. She remembered the way her heart had beat so furiously at the sight of Gable, and she recalled how her insides had quivered when he approached her. She tried to convince herself that she could deal with Brian without becoming further involved with his uncle. But she was hard put to believe it.

When she reached home that night, Kendra found Darcy in her usual good humor as she busied herself in the kitchen.

"I've got a chicken baking," she called out. "Change and come on to dinner."

Stepping into the kitchen, Kendra shook her head. "Not tonight, thanks. I've made other plans."

Darcy turned away from the oven where she was basting the already golden-brown bird. Her green eyes were curious. "With Gable?"

"Only because of Brian," Kendra said, hastening to assure the woman. "He needs my help."

"I see," Darcy said, grinning broadly.

It was all too plain to Kendra that the woman didn't see at all. And Kendra wasn't sure she did herself. Without any further conversation she went upstairs to change clothes.

Darcy had already let Gable in by the time Kendra returned, and she couldn't miss the way he was looking at her. To her chagrin her heart once again took up its fierce beat, and she tried to calm herself down as she walked down the hall.

"Good evening," Gable said warmly.

"Hello."

He winked at Darcy. "Something you're cooking smells wonderful."

"It's chicken. I'd be happy to have you two stay here and have dinner with me," Darcy offered.

Gable looked at Kendra, then shook his head. "We're having hamburgers."

Darcy arched her white brows a little, but she didn't say anything as she looked at the grinning Gable. When she glanced at Kendra, she saw the frown on her face. Darcy went back to her chicken.

"Ready?" Gable asked.

Kendra wasn't ready, she realized. She had agreed to this for Brian's sake, and she tried to hold that thought in mind as she moved toward the front door.

"Did Brian enjoy being on the set today?" she asked much too brightly, wanting to stick with the topic for the evening.

Gable smiled as he walked out to the car and opened the door. "His eyes lit up and he began tooting his horn the moment he saw you."

Kendra frowned a little as Gable started the car and drove off. "I wonder if I've made a mistake by giving him the horn. Perhaps he'll keep using it as a substitute for talking instead of trying to speak."

"I asked the psychologist about it, and he said

95

he thought it was a wonderful idea," Gable said. "It gets Brian in the habit of communicating in some manner, and at this point the doctor feels that it's better than nothing. Besides, Brian is having fun with the horn, and the doctor believes that's very important." He glanced over at her. "Instinctively you do the right thing."

She looked away. Her instincts told her not to be here with him tonight. "I didn't plan that, you know," she quickly assured him. "I used the horn in several of my routines, and I randomly took it along that day."

It wasn't quite the truth. Kendra hadn't missed the fact that perhaps Brian related to her not only because she was a clown but also because she was mute when she performed. Maybe he was able to identify with her because of it, to see her as a friend, an equal. She had subconsciously thought that Brian might try to communicate in his own way when he saw her use the horn. She just hadn't expected him to copy her so completely.

"For whatever reasons," Gable said, breaking into her thoughts, "you've been our salvation."

Kendra ignored that. "Doesn't that toot-tooting drive you bananas?" she asked, trying to inject a light tone into her voice.

Gable laughed. "I'm used to it now. It lets me know where Brian is. You've no idea how upset the housekeeper, Genna, and I would get when we couldn't find him. He's so still and silent most of the time, and we would get frantic when we called and got no response. Now he toots."

Kendra knew this had been a trying time for

96

them all: the boy, the man, the housekeeper—and Genna. She fell silent as Gable turned into the parking lot of a little hamburger joint in the middle of town. Several teenagers were lolling around outside, joking and elbowing each other.

"Here we are," Gable said, his voice reflecting his less than favorable opinion of the place. "I don't know why we can't discuss Brian over a more substantial meal. Why don't we make the most of the evening?"

Kendra opened her car door. "Why not take Genna for your more substantial meal?" she suggested. "She would appreciate it much more than I, I'm sure. For me a hamburger *is* a substantial meal."

Gable sighed. The evening was going to be trying and difficult. He knew that Genna was right for him in all the ways he believed counted, but he didn't want to take her to dinner.

Night and day this woman—this clown—stayed in his mind, tormenting him. *She* was the one he wanted.

"Have you changed your mind about coming with me?" Kendra asked, leaning down to look into the car.

Gable shook his head. No, he hadn't changed his mind. Now the trick would be to see that she changed hers—not just about the meal but also about the entire situation.

Kendra found that even sitting across from Gable in the crowded hamburger stand was intoxicating. He had managed to find a table for two in a corner, and in spite of all the noise surrounding them, as she looked into his eyes she found herself believing that they were the only two people in the room.

She shivered as she remembered having that same feeling in the middle of the dance floor with Gable's body much too close to hers.

"Cold?"

She blinked her eyes and looked at the handsome man across from her. "I beg your pardon?"

"You shivered," he said, gazing evenly at her. "I wondered if you were cold."

Her laughter betrayed her nervousness. "No, not really."

He seemed to be able to look right into her soul, and Kendra was afraid that he would be able to read her mind. She picked up her burger and bit into it, managing to keep the pickle and tomato slices from falling off.

"I had no idea one could look so good on a diet like this," Gable said jokingly as he watched her eat. "But junk food has served you well. I find you quite appealing."

Kendra blushed a little as she swallowed, then washed the burger down with a sip of her Coke.

"Now about Brian," she said, plowing right into the only safe topic. "Perhaps I could arrange to see him three times a week while I'm here. That should give me a good deal of time to spend with him."

Gable smiled at her, and she prayed that her silly heart would stop beating so wildly. "You're very generous, and Brian and I both are grateful.

I think it's a splendid idea. Shall we set up the days now?"

She agreed, even though she hadn't planned the schedule in advance. She wasn't sure she knew what she was doing; for days she hadn't been able to think clearly.

"Monday, Wednesday, and Friday sound good," she answered quickly, believing those the safest days. Both she and Gable had to work, so she wouldn't spend more than an hour or two with the boy each evening. As much as she wanted to help Brian, she wanted to avoid his uncle equally as much.

He frowned in disappointment. "Couldn't you spare a Saturday or Sunday? You surely won't have much time during the weekday evenings. I know that sometimes movie days are incredibly long. How about Saturdays?" he said coaxingly.

Kendra sighed. Why not? After all, she wouldn't be here much longer, anyway.

"All right," she heard herself murmur, against her better judgment. "I'll pick Brian up around two o'clock on Saturdays. Weekdays, it will probably be around seven."

"I could save you time by bringing him over," Gable suggested.

"No," she said, shaking her head. "That won't be necessary. I'd prefer to pick him up."

"Whatever you say." Gable reached for his hamburger and took a large bite. His pickle and tomato slices fell from the sandwich and splattered on the table and his shirt.

Kendra couldn't help but grin. He really wasn't the junk-food type.

"A little messy, don't you think?" he asked, not the least bit perturbed as he wiped at the stain on his shirt with a napkin.

She marveled at his good humor. "That's part of the fun," she joked. "This is finger food."

"If you can hang on to it," he said wryly. "I'd much prefer lobster and shrimp. Now *that's* finger food."

"I suppose," she agreed, looking at his hands. She recalled the way the long, tanned fingers had burned against her skin on the day of the picnic. Her gaze traveled up the length of his muscled arms, and she remembered how tightly they had held her. When she looked at his face, she couldn't forget the thrill of his kisses.

Across from her, Gable's gaze strayed to the lush, dark hair that carelessly tumbled around Kendra's shoulders. He studied the long, delicate column of her neck, then saw how her face, free of makeup now, was slightly flushed. He seemed briefly mesmerized by the tantalizing shape of her mouth before he looked at her eyes. How could he keep his mind on Brian when Kendra was so deliciously appealing?

When their eyes met, Kendra was embarrassed to have him catch her staring. She wondered what he would think at the moment if he could read her mind and know how much he excited her.

She averted her eyes. "Now about Brian," she said, determinedly directing the subject back to the boy, "I can't run all over town with him while I'm in my clown costume, so I think I'll take him to Darcy's and spend time with him there."

"Why not spend your time with him at the house? He'll be more comfortable there around things and people he knows."

"But I won't," Kendra wanted to cry. However, once again, she couldn't refute his logic. "Where will you be?" she blurted. She could have bitten her tongue, but it was too late.

Gable studied her for a moment. "I don't know. Does it matter?"

"No, of course not," she retorted, hoping he wouldn't recognize the flicker of doubt in her voice. "But I believe I can establish a better rapport—a better bond—if it's just Brian and I." She only hoped she wasn't lying to herself.

Again Gable seemed thoughtful as he dipped his head to take a drink of Coke. "It's your game plan," he murmured at last. "We play by your rules." They looked at each other for a long moment, neither of them able to break the spell that bound them.

Suddenly a slow and sensual song began to play on the jukebox. Several teenage couples slipped out onto the floor as though irresistibly drawn by the sensuous music and suggestive words of the contemporary song.

Gable and Kendra watched as the young people went into each other's arms, their supple bodies moving rhythmically to the throbbing beat.

Kendra experienced a sudden, fierce desire to

have Gable draw her possessively to his hard body and move her around the floor with the uninhibited abandon of the dancers. As she watched a girl boldly run her hands up and down her partner's back, she wished she could let go of her fears and freely savor the excitement of Gable. When she glanced back at him, he was watching her, and when she imagined that she saw the longing she felt reflected in his eyes, she hastily took the last bite of her food.

"I'm ready when you are," she said.

"You're in quite a rush," he commented.

She shrugged with pretended nonchalance. "We've finished our business."

His blue eyes were bold and intense when they met her brown ones. "Have we?"

She stared at the paper wrappings on the table. "Is there something more you wanted to add about Brian?" she asked over the pounding of her heart, unable to meet Gable's penetrating gaze.

When he didn't speak, she was forced to look at him. Only then did he comment. "No. Not about Brian."

"Then that's settled, isn't it?" she asked with a relieved sigh. "Well, I'd better run. I have a new routine to do tomorrow, and I need to work out the details."

It was another lie, but she couldn't help it. She couldn't force herself to keep her mind on Brian when Gable looked at her the way he did, and she dared not let herself weaken. She wasn't sure what she wanted anymore.

"Ready?" she repeated again.

Gable stood up. "Anytime you are."

She was much too aware of his towering body as he walked beside her. When he opened the door, she tried to slip past without touching him, but the tips of her breasts brushed provocatively against his arm. Hoping that Gable hadn't felt the rush of desire she had, Kendra hurried out the door. He easily caught up with her before she had gone very far.

Suddenly a carful of youths sped across the parking lot to the drive-through lane of the restaurant. Kendra had almost plunged out in front of the vehicle when Gable appeared behind her. He pulled her toward him, wrapping his arms around her as he crushed her against his chest.

Kendra trembled as she automatically braced herself with her hands on his shoulders. She looked up into his eyes, and she could feel her pulse pound at her temples. Her legs were weak. For a moment they stayed just as they were; Kendra was aware of every burning line of Gable's body where it met hers.

"You're all right," he murmured eventually.

She managed a quivering smile and abruptly freed herself. She wasn't all right. He couldn't know, of course, that it was his touch that had shaken her to the core. She had hardly noticed the speeding car, even less so once Gable drew her into his arms.

"Thanks," she whispered, moving away from him. "That was terribly careless of me." She couldn't meet his eyes as she walked rapidly across the parking lot, Gable striding beside her.

"It was the junk food," he said teasingly. "It might wear well on the body, but it's not good for the brain."

Kendra laughed too enthusiastically, glad that he was making light of the incident. If she hadn't been thinking so intensely about him, she would have seen the car. And even now she struggled to forget how good he had felt when he held her.

She made an attempt at light chatter as Gable drove her home, but she proved a failure at it. She gave up and peered out the car window as if she were fascinated by the scenery. She was grateful when he finally pulled up in front of Darcy's house.

"Good night," she said with forced cheer, facing him at last. "Thanks for the burger. I'll see Brian Wednesday around seven."

She turned to open the door, but Gable stopped her by touching her shoulder. As their eyes met, she prayed that he wouldn't do or say anything to complicate matters further.

"Thank you."

"I'm happy I can help," she repeated, the words sounding bright and rote. Then she reached for the door handle, shoved the door open, and made herself leave Gable and the car behind.

But try as she might, she couldn't forget the burning, almost despairing look in Gable's eyes as he watched her go.

CHAPTER SEVEN

Wednesday evening came much too soon. Neither Gable nor Brian had been out of Kendra's thoughts since she had agreed to see the child again. She would, of course, go dressed as Happy, and that in itself gave her a barrier, a protection from Gable, should she see him.

With a tired shake of her head she set Speckles in the front passenger seat and climbed in for the drive to Gable's house. The trip seemed endless, and when Kendra reached the grounds, she realized again how beautiful it all was.

She found herself looking at the house differently this time. She no longer saw it as Genna and Gable's house but as Gable's alone, and suddenly she wanted to peep into every room, to see if she could learn more about the man who attracted her so imprudently.

She brushed aside the foolish thoughts. Putting a happy smile on her lips, she carried Speckles up the walk. Then she rang the bell and stood in nervous anticipation, wondering who would answer. The housekeeper, Sarah Washington, opened the door and grinned broadly at her.

"Oh, how delightful! Happy the clown. Mr. Hunt told me you would be coming." She motioned broadly for Kendra to enter. "Brian will be so excited. He's in his room."

Kendra fought down the urge to ask if Gable were home while she quietly followed Mrs. Washington down the long hall and up the steps to Brian's room.

The housekeeper smiled sadly as she indicated the boy lying on the navy corduroy spread of a double bed. He looked lost and lonely against the bookcase headboard, which was filled with books. Puppy lay snuggled up near him, sleeping. Brian was stroking the little animal, his small hands moving in patterns over the soft fur. The horn Kendra had given him lay at his side.

She quickly surveyed the room. It was a wonderful room, full of furniture and objects that would interest a boy, from a richly detailed and compartmented desk to a heavy trunk spilling over with toys and gadgets. But Brian lay very still and silent, staring vacantly out the window while he petted his dog as though they were the only two souls in the whole world.

Kendra's heart melted as she looked at the handsome, forlorn lad. She ached to run to him and hold him close, to make him laugh, and, most of all, to make him talk. She knew it wasn't that simple. She was beginning to fear that Brian never would speak.

"Brian," Mrs. Washington said softly. "Brian, there's someone here to see you."

Listlessly Brian turned toward the woman,

looking at her questioningly. Kendra set Speckles down on the floor and waited for the boy to notice her and the little dog. His gaze fell first on Speckles, who eagerly wagged her tail, anticipating recognition.

Briefly Brian appeared puzzled, but Kendra could see the excitement building in his small body. He glanced at her and couldn't seem to believe his eyes.

She held her breath, silently praying that he would call out her name in his exuberance. But it wasn't to be. He reached for the horn and tooted wildly.

Then he burst from the bed and raced to embrace Kendra, his thin little arms clinging tightly around her waist, his head pressed against her. Puppy bounded after the boy, barking loudly, caught up in the child's unexpected explosion of energy. Kendra held Brian while she smoothed his dark hair back from his pale face.

"Just let me know if you want or need anything," Mrs. Washington said warmly.

Kendra nodded, watching as the housekeeper left. Then she turned to Brian. Making a grand motion with her hand, she widened her eyes, as if in amazement, and gestured around the room. Brian grinned shyly, but he was clearly pleased because she liked his room. Clasping her hand tightly in his, he guided her over to the toy box, evidently his favorite place.

He tugged at her until she sat down on the floor beside him. Then he paused for a moment, waiting for Puppy to slump down near him. Solemnly he began to empty out the toy box, feverishly taking out trucks, soldiers, spaceships, puzzles, and blocks. At last he came to a worn book with a ragged hard-back cover.

He held it tightly in his hands, as if it were a treasure too precious to risk damaging. He gazed at it for a long moment, then sat back down beside Kendra and opened it. The story was about a traveling circus, and the first page had been inscribed.

Brian pointed to the lavish, flowing penmanship. "To Brian," it read. "With love from Mama."

Her heart skipped a beat, but Kendra smiled brightly at Brian as he began to turn the pages until he came to a picture of a clown.

Kendra made a face that expressed delight and surprise as she looked at the clown. Then she touched the picture with her glove, tracing the image.

Brian's face lit up as he pointed to her, then to the picture. Kendra nodded vigorously and tooted her horn. She looked up abruptly when she sensed someone watching them. Her eyes met Gable's, and her heart took up an erratic beat.

"His mother gave him that book," Gable said.

Brian looked back over his shoulder at his uncle, then ran to grab Gable's hand. Gable let himself be tugged into the room and coaxed into sitting down beside Kendra. Their shoulders touched briefly and his leg grazed hers. She could feel her face color under the clown makeup. She had hoped she could avoid Gable, but even now Brian was working against her.

The boy held the book out to his uncle as he nodded his head eagerly and pointed to himself and Kendra. A mischievous twinkle flashed in Gable's eyes only briefly as he crossed his long legs Indian-style, pulled Brian down between them, and laid the book on his lap. He began to read each page to the smiling boy and the clown who were his audience.

Kendra listened as his smooth, deep voice told the story of a clown who had run away with the circus so that he could make all the children laugh. Gable's eyes met Kendra's over the top of Brian's dark head, and Kendra arched her brows as if to say, "You see, there are others who feel as I do that laughter is the best cure for unhappiness." Then she pretended to concentrate on the tale, looking at the pictures as Gable read the text.

To her chagrin she found herself thinking about how wonderful he was with the child, how much she admired him, and how charming and handsome she found him. He really should have a houseful of children. He would make a loving and good father. She had never seen Gable so playful, and his teasing nature with the child made him even harder to resist. She didn't realize that he had finished the brief book until Brian tooted his horn twice in appreciation, startling Kendra from her reverie.

"Did you like it?" Gable asked, searching the boy's face.

Kendra knew how anxiously he waited each time for a spoken response from Brian. She waited, too, caught up in the moment of drama, praying fervently that this would be the time that the boy would open up. But it did not happen.

Brian tooted again, then reached for Kendra's horn and held it up for her, indicating that she should let his uncle know that she had enjoyed it too. Obligingly she tooted twice. This time her eyes met Gable's, and she couldn't help but smile.

His return smile was sweet and stirring. His gaze lingered on her face for a moment. Then he helped Brian up and stood, himself, before reaching down to pull Kendra up. Their eyes and hands lingered briefly before Gable turned away to put the book back in the toy box. He stayed a moment longer to watch as Brian sought another treasure from those lying around the floor. He glanced at Kendra a final time before turning toward the door.

Kendra stared after him, drinking up the sight as he walked away. Brian impatiently tugged on her hand once more, his spirits high as he held up another treasure for her to see. It was a wooden puzzle of a sleek tiger in a lush green jungle, and Kendra pretended to give her attention to it as Brian dumped the pieces out on the floor so that they might work it. But her thoughts remained on the man who had walked out the door. And she wondered how she would ever endure until the movie was finished and she could leave North Carolina.

She stayed an hour, and when she was ready to

110

leave, Brian began to cry. Kendra tried several of her favorite tricks, but the boy would not be placated. She didn't know what to do when Gable appeared unexpectedly at the child's side, bending down so that he was at eye level.

"You want Happy to come again, don't you?" he asked softly.

The little boy's bottom lip quivered uncontrollably, and big tears spilled from his eyes. He nodded his head up and down and gave a tiny double toot on his horn.

"Then you mustn't make the clown unhappy by crying," Gable said gently. "Clowns come to make people laugh. They don't like tears."

Sniffling loudly, Brian brushed valiantly at his tears. Then he put his trembling little hand into Kendra's gloved one. Stoically he smiled up at her. But the tears still glistened in his eyes.

Kendra wiped her eyes, too, then painted big, imaginary smiles on both their faces. She squeezed his hand firmly, then tipped her derby. When she had given him a big wave, she gathered Speckles in her arms, did a silly somersault, and started for the front door.

She didn't realize until she looked back that Gable was right behind her. Her pulse began to pound again.

"I'll see you to your car," he said, his voice much too near.

She turned to flash him a big smile, shaking her head to indicate that he needn't bother. She had had enough of his tantalizing presence, of his warmth and smile and scent. But Gable paid no

111

attention. Without another word he followed her out to the driveway.

"Your hour with Brian seemed to go well," he commented, opening Kendra's car door before she could. "You've certainly gained his confidence. He's crazy about you."

"But he's so dependent on me," Kendra murmured. "I don't think that's good."

"For now it's all we've got," Gable said, his voice suddenly very strained. "At least he relates to you. He obeys me, but I can't seem to reach him."

He ran his hands through his thick hair, and Kendra felt a rush of empathy. Impulsively she reached out and squeezed his shoulder consolingly. The feel of his hard muscles beneath her gloved fingers caused her to withdraw her hand instantly.

"It will work out eventually," she assured him. "I'm certain of it. Brian will speak again."

But she had no way of knowing for sure. She was wishing just like Gable, and she wanted to give him all the hope she could, whether she believed it would happen or not.

"Good night," she said softly. "I'll be back on Friday."

Gable's gaze lingered on her face, but he shoved his hands into his pockets and nodded brusquely. Kendra was sure he had something else he wanted to say to her, but he didn't speak again. An awkward silence hung between them for a moment, then Kendra slipped into her car.

She gave Gable a brief wave before she started the engine and drove off down the road.

The familiar sight of Darcy swinging idly in the porch swing reassured her as she parked her car in front of the house.

" 'Evening," Darcy called out as Kendra made her way toward the porch, pulling off her derby and wig en route. She stripped off her brows and mustache and dropped them in her hat.

"Good evening," she said warmly. She couldn't think of anyone she would rather see.

Darcy slowed the swing long enough for Kendra to join her, then she resumed the lazy back-and-forth movements. "You're working late tonight, aren't you?"

Kendra shook her head. "No," she admitted, knowing that Darcy would start speculating about the possibility of a romance if she confessed where she had been.

When Kendra didn't explain, the other woman said, "I haven't had dinner. Have you?"

"No, I haven't."

"Why don't we go out?" Darcy suggested.

"Wonderful!" Kendra exclaimed. "Just give me a few minutes to get out of this costume."

"I need to change out of these jeans," Darcy said.

"Don't do that. I'm going to wear jeans. We'll find a casual place. I feel like letting my hair down."

Darcy's eyes twinkled. "That's even better. I'll wait here."

Minutes later Kendra strolled down the steps.

She had changed into jeans, a white shirt with the sleeves rolled up to the elbows, and the familiar worn loafers. Her hair hung long and free. She had on just the faintest hint of lipstick and powder, and she felt better already. The blue feeling that had hovered over her all the way home was rapidly evaporating.

A casual night out sounded like just the thing to take her mind off her troubles. She would laugh and drink and dream of new places and new people. She would not think of Gable or Brian Hunt and the special places they had already made for themselves in her heart.

She and Darcy found a little Italian place that boasted the best pizza in town, and the older woman agreed that it was indeed good. After they had settled down in a padded red booth, they ordered a medium cheese-and-green-pepper pizza and a pitcher of beer. They were drinking the brew from frosted mugs and laughing delightedly when Kendra heard a commotion near the door. She looked up to see who had caused it.

She felt herself stiffen, and she drew in her breath sharply when she saw Gable and Genna talking to several people at a big table. Self-consciously she set down her mug and brushed at her hair.

Genna was impeccably dressed in a white-and-gold flowered confection that looked very feminine. She wore pretty high-heeled shoes and carried a neat little bag in her hand. Her hair was softly curled around her face, and her makeup was done with just the right touch.

114

Gable, in his suit, stood with his feet slightly apart, looking appealingly masculine, his right hand resting lightly on Genna's waist.

Kendra didn't want to give a name to the emotion she was feeling as she watched the attractive couple. This was the first time she had seen Gable and Genna without Brian. She recalled how she had felt when she first thought that Genna was Gable's wife.

She had been disappointed then, even before the man had held her in his arms and kissed her. And no matter how much she insisted to herself that this was what was best for all concerned, she couldn't deny that she found that the sight of them together disturbing.

She watched as they exchanged cheerful greetings with people at several tables. She, herself, had advised Gable to develop more than a friendship with Genna; again she told herself that they seemed so right together.

And she didn't know why she felt so wrong inside when she thought it. All too soon, the couple was standing before her. Kendra affixed one of her brightest smiles to her lips.

"Good evening, Kendra, Darcy," Gable said. "I don't know if you know Genna Lawson, Darcy."

Darcy smiled. "Yes, of course. I go to her antique store. How are you, Genna?"

Genna smiled sweetly. "I'm fine, Darcy. And you?"

"Just fine. And do you know my boarder, Kendra McAllis?"

115

"Oh, is she staying with you? How lovely. Yes, I do know her. She's our wonderful clown. She's doing so much to help Brian." Genna held out both her hands to Kendra and warmly clasped the other woman's. "It's good to see you again."

"Thank you." Kendra knew that Genna was honestly being nice; she liked and respected the other woman, and she shoved back the disappointment of seeing her with Gable.

"Won't you join us?" she invited politely, though she hoped they would decline.

"We'd love to, wouldn't we, Genna?" Gable said, glancing at the pretty blond.

"Of course," she agreed.

Kendra moved nearer to Darcy so that the couple would have room to sit in the booth. She swallowed and cleared her throat. "We've already ordered a pizza. We'll have more than enough if you'd like to share."

"Thank you," Genna said, taking her place by Kendra, leaving Gable to sit at the end. The blond looked at him. "I think I'll just have a salad and iced tea. You probably want shrimp scampi and wine, don't you, Gable?"

Kendra felt her smile fade a little. Of course Genna would have tea. No beer for her. She was too much of a lady, too much of a Southern belle. Too much of what Gable Hunt needed.

Kendra's eyes met Gable's, and she drew in her breath as he smiled at her for a long moment. "I don't think so tonight," he finally said. "The pizza sounds fine, and I believe I will have a beer."

Genna looked at Gable oddly, then glanced at Kendra with a faint smile. Kendra's throat felt so constricted that she didn't think she could ever speak again. She nodded and looked away.

A stiff silence began to settle over the table that even Genna and Darcy couldn't shatter. Kendra felt like she was suffocating in the small restaurant with Gable so near. She thought frantically for a moment. She was the entertainer, the maker of merriment and magic.

Abruptly she began to regale the foursome with some of the tales of circus life. "Let me tell you about the time one of the tigers began to attack the wild animal trainer at a circus where I was working," she said, her eyes suddenly bright with the memory.

"I was so scared that I didn't think I could stand it, but everybody else seemed momentarily paralyzed, and I couldn't let James—the animal trainer—get hurt. I marched into the cage, as big as you please, shaking right down to the tips of my size thirteen shoes, and I squirted my water pistol at the tiger—right in his eyes."

She grinned. "You should have seen him. He was as surprised as I was, but it gave James the single second that he needed to gain control again."

She laughed. "People have told me what a crazy chance I took, but that's just the way things are in the circus. We work together. We look out for each other. James would have done it for me."

Genna and Darcy exclaimed about how brave

117

Kendra had been, but Gable, gazing steadily at her, felt like shaking her after the fact. "You could have been killed," he said sharply. "It was a foolish thing to do."

Kendra met his blue eyes. "It's circus life," she repeated, wanting him to understand and knowing that he never would. She realized that she was doing everything she could to make him realize how different their lives were.

Neither one of them saw the way Genna looked from one to the other as the tension grew. Gable looked away coolly, then took a long swallow of his beer. He didn't look at Kendra again, but he did get the message. She was reiterating how absurd it was for the two of them to become involved.

And all he could think of was that she could have been injured, maybe killed, and he never would have known her. Brian never would have known her. She wouldn't be laughing and dancing and entertaining those who needed her so much.

Kendra told several other amusing tales while they ate. As she expected, Darcy and Genna laughed, and she laughed with them. Only Gable was restrained in his merriment.

Kendra glanced over to see him studying her pensively. Then she looked down at her watch and exclaimed, "I'd better get home! I didn't realize it was so late."

"It's only nine-thirty," Darcy protested.

"Only nine-thirty for you," Kendra joked.

118

"But I've got to work tomorrow. I need my beauty sleep."

"Oh, pooh," Darcy said. "Your face is covered in makeup when you perform."

"Let's not quibble," Kendra teased. "I still need to be at my best. It's time I went home."

It was way past time, she added to herself. She gave Genna and Gable a bright smile and excused herself.

"Good night."

Then she walked with Darcy out into the night air. She inhaled deeply. She couldn't explain the constriction in her chest. It felt oddly like heartache, yet that was absurd. She hardly knew Gable Hunt, and from what she did know of him she knew that she didn't belong with him.

She jumped when Darcy touched her arm as they made their way to the car. "You *are* interested in Gable," Darcy exclaimed jubilantly. "I could see it."

Kendra forced a smile to her lips. "I've explained to you that I only help him with Brian. That's where I was tonight before I came home. I'm going there on Mondays, Wednesdays, Fridays, and Saturdays until I leave North Carolina."

"I don't care what you say," Darcy murmured. "That man is interested in you as a woman. If you two don't know what's happening, you're just fooling yourselves, but you're not fooling me."

Kendra shrugged and smiled patiently at the older woman. "I'll finish the movie in a matter of

119

weeks. Then I'm joining a traveling circus for the summer months. I don't think Gable would look good on an elephant or working with tigers, do you?"

Darcy was clearly taken aback. "Why, no!" she cried. "Not Gable Hunt, of all people. Why, he's not the circus type. I've got nothing at all against circus people, but Gable would never fit in."

"And can you see me sipping tea from a china cup with a bunch of society matrons while we discuss the Literary Guild's selection of the month?"

"You?" Darcy shook her head. "Well, no, not really. You wouldn't fit in with that group."

Kendra's smile was slow and sad. "Now do you begin to understand what I've been trying to tell you?"

Darcy blinked twice as the words sank in. "Oh, dear, I do begin to understand," she murmured, her voice filled with disappointment.

Kendra made herself laugh lightly. "And that, I'm afraid, is that on the matter."

But her own sense of disappointment lingered all the way home, and long after she had gone to bed. It all sounded so right, so logical. She didn't know why her heart insisted on rebelling at the practicality of it all, or why her body insisted upon remembering the way Gable's fingers had felt on her skin and how his lips had caressed hers.

CHAPTER EIGHT

Kendra seemed to be in a fog at work on Thursday. She couldn't stop thinking about Brian. She had to find some way to get him to speak, but she had so little time. The thought of him shut up in his lonely world ate at her; she was determined to find the key to unlock the door that closed him off from others.

She was glad when the day ended, for it meant that she would get to see Brian soon. It also meant that there was a chance she would see Gable. But she wouldn't let herself think about that.

Friday dawned brilliant and sunny, and Kendra set out for work with a light heart. Her part in the movie had been expanded twice, and she was thrilled because the producer and director found her performance so satisfactory. Their enthusiasm and encouragement made her work that much harder, and she eagerly anticipated each day.

The hours fled by, and before Kendra knew it, it was time to see Brian. Her mind was full of ideas for getting the child to open up to her. She could hardly wait to finish the ride out to the house that evening.

When Mrs. Washington had shown her in, Kendra, with Speckles in her arms, made her way down the hall toward the child's room. She paused, her heart pounding, when she saw Gable working at a desk in the library.

She wanted to rush on by, but she was mesmerized by the sight of him. His brow was furrowed in concentration, his fingers tapping on the desktop. For the moment he seemed totally oblivious to anything but the papers in front of him.

The sight touched Kendra in a way she couldn't explain. She felt as though she were an intimate part of his life, even though she was an outsider. She had a foolish longing to make him a cup of coffee and silently slip into his room with it so that he might have some comfort while he worked. She shook her head at the silly thought.

As though Gable had sensed her there, he looked over his shoulder. Their eyes met, and he smiled broadly, the frown instantly leaving his brow.

"Good evening. How are you?"

"Fine," she murmured shyly, embarrassed because he had caught her staring and because his smile made her heart beat faster.

"Good." He gazed at her for a minute, then said, "Brian is expecting you. He's waiting in his room."

"All right." She lingered by the door a few seconds longer before turning away. She didn't know what else to say.

Brian was grinning from ear to ear when Kendra reached his door. He gave her a big wave and motioned for her to come in.

She waved in return, danced a little jig to show how happy she was to be here, then set Speckles on the floor. Taking the clown's hand, Brian led her to the toy box.

Kendra breathed a sigh of relief as the boy began to rummage around in the box. She touched his hand lightly, then pointed to herself, indicating that she wanted to find a toy.

Brian tooted his horn and nodded agreeably. Her heart pounding, Kendra searched through the box until she found the storybook again. Her hands trembled as she put a huge smile on her lips, hugged the book to her chest, and sat down on the floor with an ecstatic expression on her face.

Brian watched her curiously for a moment, then he smiled. He seemed pleased that Kendra had liked the book. She patted a place by her on the floor and motioned for him to join her.

When he did, she held out the book to him, pointing at him, then at her lips. She hoped he would understand that she was trying to tell him to read or tell her the story. She was sure he knew it by heart and could recite it from the pictures, even if he couldn't read it all.

He took the book in both hands and gazed down at it forlornly. Kendra could feel the perspiration moisten her gloves as she clasped her hands together in a pleading gesture and again made an indication that she wanted him to read to her.

Brian seemed to be in quite a dilemma; clearly he didn't want to disappoint her, but he couldn't do what she was asking of him. His blue eyes wide, he looked unhappily at her. He pointed to her lips and shook his head. Then he pointed to his own mouth and shook his head.

Kendra felt her heart turn over, but she did her best to look appropriately crushed. Again she gestured for him to read the story to her.

Brian's frown grew. He wanted to please her, but he obviously thought she was asking the impossible. Suddenly he laid the book down and motioned for Kendra to follow him. The dogs stirred at the boy's movement, eager to go on whatever adventure he offered. They ran out of the room with him.

Kendra gazed disappointedly after the boy. He hadn't fallen for her ploy. She didn't know what to try next. She had hoped that he treasured her friendship and the book so much that he would try to speak.

When Brian looked back over his shoulder and motioned to her again, she glanced at the book a final time, then left the room. The child led her down the hall to a sprawling den. His eyes gleaming, he took Kendra over to a big television set. When he had skillfully set up a video game, he gave her one set of controls and sat down on the floor, eager to try his hand against her.

Kendra had never played the game, and Brian tooted his horn repeatedly as he knocked more spaceships from the sky than she did. But at last she got the hang of the game, and she managed to get her gloved fingers to work with some degree of dexterity.

The first time she beat Brian, she laughed aloud in delight. When she turned to him, she saw that he was watching her cautiously. She realized that he hadn't heard her voice as the clown before. She had spoken, as Kendra on the day of the picnic, but he had not been pleased.

Their eyes met, and Kendra kept a smile on her face, determined that Brian would think that there was nothing unusual about the clown laughing. It worked.

The next time Brian beat her, he, too, laughed aloud. Kendra tooted her horn wildly, feeling that there was some real hope that this child was finally going to speak.

She was so ecstatic that she wanted to race down the hall and tell Gable, but she knew it was too soon for such confidence. Again she beat Brian, and again she laughed. When he won, he did the same.

In her burst of enthusiasm she pushed her luck. "I won!" she cried the next time. "I won!"

Brian looked at her in dismay. Evidently he could accept laughter from the clown, but he could not accept speech. He had that betrayed look in his eyes, and Kendra wasn't sure what her next move should be.

"I can talk when I want to, Brian," she said gently but emphatically. She didn't want to alienate him by moving too rapidly. "I just choose not to when I'm a clown entertaining people. You can talk, too, when you want to, can't you?"

He seemed distressed by the question. Slowly he shook his head. Then he reached out to touch Kendra's lips with his fingers, wanting her to be quiet too. His whole body was shaking.

She held her breath, disappointment flooding through her. Maybe she had gone too far, too fast, though she had tried to be cautious. Perhaps she should have been happy with laughter for today. She had gotten too excited, too ambitious.

Now she didn't know what to say, how to react. She didn't want to hurt the boy, when all she had to do was keep quiet and entertain him to make him happy. And he clearly found so little happiness in his young life. But she was afraid that he would never make any progress if she didn't experiment to the limits of her ability.

Instinctively she hugged him to her, holding him in her arms for a long time, wanting him to know that she was still his friend, his equal. It was the right thing to do.

At last his trembling subsided, and he met her eyes. She smiled. His blue blue eyes searched her face for what seemed an eternity. Eventually a small smile played on his lips

Kendra sat very still, willing the child to say something—anything, any kind of breakthrough —so that he would start talking, no matter how painful the experience was for both of them.

He looked all around him, seemingly confused for a moment. Then his blue eyes brightened. In his anxiety he had dropped his horn. Now he spied it. He picked it up and tentatively tooted it twice.

Although Kendra's spirits were sinking, she responded with two toots of her own horn, signaling that everything was still all right.

Brian reached out for her hand, and she let him lead her back to his room. Clearly he felt more secure there, and Kendra felt her spirits sink further. She knew this was going to be a difficult and trying time for them both, but she hadn't anticipated being in the position of having to hurt Brian more before she could help him. Now she realized that that was going to be the case.

Her mind was reeling when he reached for the clown book again. He gave it to Kendra, then hurried out of the room. She gazed after him, puzzled. Clearly some of his sense of security also lay in the clown book. In minutes he returned with his uncle.

Gable's eyes glowed, and he was grinning. He was pleased to be invited into the room by Brian, but when he looked down at the child, he was suddenly aware of his agitation. When Gable glanced back at Kendra, she gave him a small shrug. Brian pointed to a place on the floor by the clown and held out the book to the tall man.

"You want me to read the book again?" Gable questioned, his brows raised. Usually Brian relished the reading of the book, but this time there was no smile on his lips, no anticipation in his eyes.

Brian nodded determinedly and pointed again

127

to himself and Kendra. Once Gable began to read, Kendra realized why Brian had wanted him to tell the story again.

The clown in the book didn't talk, either. He pantomimed just like she did. And Brian wanted her to know that that was what he needed from her. He had felt threatened when she spoke, and he wanted the security of his room, his book, his uncle reading, and his silent clown.

She became lost in deep thought as Gable finished the story. He glanced at his watch. "Uh-oh," he murmured, looking down at the little boy who had begun to yawn. "I think it's past your bedtime."

Brian sleepily reached out for Kendra's hand, but Gable shook his head.

"The clown has to go home and go to bed too. Change into your pajamas, and Mrs. Washington and I will come to tuck you in. All right, partner?"

Reluctantly Brian tooted.

Kendra and Gable left the room as Brian went in search of his nightclothes.

"Come, Speckles," Kendra called. The little dog bounded after her out into the hall. Kendra picked her up and stroked her.

"What was that all about?" Gable asked when he had shut Brian's door. "Why did Brian have me read the book again?"

Kendra sighed. She knew that she needed to talk to Gable about her plans for tomorrow. She was going to come to the house as Kendra, and she needed Gable's support.

Brian's uncle was intimately involved in this matter, and she couldn't keep avoiding him. It was foolish and impractical. She simply would have to be mature about it and control her emotions, which even at the moment threatened to get out of hand merely because she was walking beside this man.

"Could you spare a cup of coffee?" she asked brightly.

Gable smiled. "I thought you'd never ask. I'd be delighted. I'll even fix it myself while Mrs. Washington gets Brian ready for bed."

He led her downstairs to the kitchen and pulled out a chair from under the small table. In seconds he had returned with a steaming mug of hot coffee and a spoon. "There's milk in the refrigerator and sugar there in the sugar bowl. I'll be back shortly."

Before he could leave, Kendra called over her shoulder. "Will Brian be coming into the kitchen? I'd like to take off my wig and makeup if you don't mind."

Gable grinned in such a way that Kendra's heart skipped a beat. "This is sounding better all the time," he murmured, causing her to wonder if she shouldn't remain hidden behind her makeup. He pointed across the hall. "That's a small bathroom. Please make yourself right at home. Use anything you need."

Kendra nodded, suddenly too breathless to speak. She walked over to the refrigerator and helped herself to some milk before generously adding a spoonful of sugar to her coffee. Glancing down at her watch, she saw that it was nine-thirty, and she was surprised that it was so late.

Carrying her coffee with her, she crossed the hall. When she opened the bathroom door, she gazed around in amazement. A small bathroom, indeed! There was a shower, a claw-footed tub, a commode, and double sinks and dressing tables. She couldn't imagine what he considered a big bath. She wondered what his private bath was like.

Firmly discouraging herself from such thoughts, she pulled off her mustache and brows and eagerly reached for her wig. Her own masses of dark hair were soon freed. She shook them out with relief. She had left the bathroom door open, and when Gable walked down the hall, he paused.

"You're looking better all the time," he murmured in a low voice.

Kendra shook her head at him and quickly shut the door. When she looked back in the mirror, she could see the color creeping up her neck beneath the white makeup. She took off her jacket and rolled up her sleeves so that she might wash her face.

Several minutes later she had put on lipstick, which she carried in her pocket, and combed her hair with a prop comb she had. She assessed her image. Her hair was still disheveled and her face was scrubbed clean, but there was a glow in her eyes and a kind of innocent carelessness about her. She was alarmed by the mad beating of her heart. She kept repeating over and over that she was only going to talk about Brian, but her heart kept telling her otherwise.

"Ah, that's much better," Gable said as she returned to the kitchen. "I always can relate to you more easily when I see you as a woman. You're adorable as a clown, but that male image is disconcerting."

"About Brian," she said firmly, sitting down, "I need to ask your advice."

"What happened?" Gable questioned, all concern, the teasing gone from his voice. "Did he speak?"

Kendra held up her hands. "No. I did, and Brian got upset about it. That's why he wanted you to read the book again. I had tried to get him to read it to me. He wanted me to realize that he liked me better as a silent clown, like the one in the book."

"I see," Gable said, clearly disappointed.

"He did laugh," Kendra offered hopefully. "Aloud."

Gable's blue gaze met hers. "Aloud?" he repeated.

She nodded. "I laughed unthinkingly when I beat him at the video game, and Brian later did the same when he beat me. But when I tried to explain that I could talk when I wanted to, just as he could, he retreated. He got very upset."

Her brown eyes were dark and solemn. "Tomorrow I want to come dressed as Kendra. I know Brian's going to be unhappy, but my plan is to make us both up like clowns so that he can see

131

me as the clown and as Kendra—and speaking both times."

For a moment Gable was pensive, then he clapped his hands, startling Kendra with the sudden noise. "By heavens, I think it might work! He identifies with you. If he sees you in both roles, it just might work. What a clever idea!"

In his enthusiasm he reached across to clasp her hands in his. Kendra allowed herself the luxury of his touch only briefly. She could feel the slow burning begin deep inside her as his warm fingers gripped hers.

Slipping her hands from his, she took a big drink of her coffee, then kept her hands wrapped around the cup. "I just stumbled onto the idea," she said. "And it might not work at all. We have to be prepared to be disappointed."

Gable became momentarily grave again. "Yes, I know." When he looked back at her, his face was animated. "But I do believe you're making progress. You might not see it because you don't live with the boy. But Mrs. Washington, Genna, and I have noticed. He's more alert, more interested in the world around him, more lively in the past two days since your last visit than in weeks. My goal is to have him well enough to go to school in the fall."

"I think he'll be well enough," Kendra said, trying not to remember that he had mentioned Genna, yet wanting to know if their friendship had begun to deepen into anything else.

"You have eaten dinner tonight, haven't you?" Gable asked unexpectedly.

132

To Kendra's own surprise she realized that she hadn't. "I'm not hungry, but I do have to get home and get some sleep." In truth she was hungry, but she had spent enough time with Gable.

"I'd love to take you out to eat. Even for a hamburger," he added, smiling teasingly.

Kendra shook her head. "No, really, I have to get home." She stood up. "But I'll be here tomorrow at two."

"I wish you wouldn't run away," he said, standing up as she did.

She laughed. "Look at me." She indicated her tousled hair and clown costume. "Any girl who looks like this *should* run away and hide."

"I think you look beautiful."

His softly spoken compliment was so unexpected and so solemn that Kendra didn't know whether to laugh or cry.

"You should get glasses," she finally managed over the pounding of her heart. She couldn't deny how thrilled she was.

All the way home Gable's words echoed in her head, and she was touched and warmed by them.

CHAPTER NINE

Kendra hardly slept at all, so full of plans was she for Brian on Saturday. A lot hinged on how well she carried off her dual identity and how well she could get Brian to relate to Kendra, the woman. She couldn't forget how unhappy he had been the day of the picnic, but she was ready this time and was determined to get him to understand that the clown and the pantomime were only for fun. In the real world of day-to-day existence, one needed to talk, to communicate, to make people happy.

Kendra knew just what she had in mind, and Saturday morning went by in a blur as she searched through the secondhand stores for a costume that would be similar to hers. The baggy shirt and pants were no problem, but finding a tuxedo and derby for a six-year-old boy proved quite another story.

"Hello there."

Kendra looked up in surprise to see Genna Lawson standing before her, an old canister in her hands. Even in the dusty surroundings with junk piled all around her, the woman managed to look perfect. Dressed in a lacy yellow outfit with matching yellow shoes, she was like a ray of bright sunshine in the crowded and cavernous room.

"Hello, Genna," she said. "I didn't expect to meet you here."

Genna laughed in her warm, genteel way. "But, Kendra," she said, "this is what I do for a living. I rummage around in old stores and places, looking for discarded treasures for my antique store."

Kendra blushed charmingly. "Yes, of course. I keep forgetting that you run a store. I usually see you with Gable and Brian and—" Her voice trailed off in embarrassment.

"And what?" Genna persisted gently. "And you think of us as a family?" She shook her head slowly. "I'm afraid you couldn't be more wrong, Kendra," she said quietly.

Kendra didn't know what to say. That was what she had been thinking. Was she the only one playing Cupid with Gable's and Genna's lives?

The two women looked into each other's eyes, and for a moment there was an awkward silence. Then Genna laughed lightly. "What are you doing here is the real question. You can't claim my excuse."

Kendra grinned. "I'm trying to find an old Charlie Chaplin look-alike coat for Brian. I also need a derby." Her smile softened as she told Genna her plan.

"I love the idea!" Genna said, her blue eyes sparkling at the thought. She reached out and touched Kendra's arm with her free hand. "You're so good to help, Kendra. I never think of you without thinking about your generosity."

Again Kendra blushed, wishing she were as noble as Genna believed. In truth, as desperately as she wanted to help Brian, she couldn't deny that part of the desire was also to make Gable happy. She wished she were as noble and self-sacrificing as Genna apparently was.

"I'll be leaving in such a short time," Kendra murmured inadequately. "I only hope that some way, somehow he will speak before then. It means so much to me—to all of us, of course."

Genna was quiet for a moment, then she said, "Yes, Gable told me you'll be joining a circus for the summer." There seemed to be more she wanted to say, but she held back.

"Yes," Kendra repeated awkwardly. She was a little surprised that Gable had spoken to Genna about her.

Abruptly Genna exclaimed, "Say, I think I have a coat and a derby that might serve your purposes in my store. Why don't you follow me over? I'd love to give them to you." Her eyes met Kendra's again. "I have such an emotional investment in that child, Kendra. He *has* to speak."

Kendra nodded again. There were underlying currents here that she didn't quite understand. It all seemed like a normal conversation between two women with the same cause and desire, but something wasn't quite right.

"Perhaps we could have lunch," Genna added brightly. "Do you have time?"

Kendra nodded again, a little reluctant and wondering why. Finally she smiled. "I'd love to have lunch with you."

"Good. If you're finished here, you can follow me over to the store. It's not far, and I know a wonderful little place for lunch. Gable and I—" She stopped in mid-sentence, then smiled and continued. "Gable and I eat there often."

"All right." Before she knew it, Kendra found herself parking in front of an intriguing, fanciful store in the heart of town.

Her eyes lit up the minute she stepped out of her car. "Oh, Genna!" she cried, "what a wonderful, wonderful place! I had no idea."

The front of the building was lavishly and ingeniously designed as a magnificent gold circus tent. Two revolving glass doors were painted with pictures of gaily adorned and beribboned carousel horses that actually seemed to move up and down as the doors turned to let people enter and leave the store.

"It's a universal theme," Genna said modestly. "I, too, loved the circus as a child. I suppose all children do."

She looked back at Kendra. "But I never had the daring that you have. I never had the ambition to explore the world. I wanted my circus, my daydreams, to come true right here at home." Her eyes held a faraway look. "Money," she said pensively as she gazed at her fantasy store. "It can buy almost anything, can't it? Something to occupy a woman's time—until she fulfills her real desires, her real destiny, her family's hopes for her."

Kendra thought she heard a bitter note in Genna's voice, but surely she was mistaken. It would be totally out of character.

"Well, come on in and take a look," Genna invited warmly, making Kendra suspect that she had imagined the bitterness. "There are those who believe I've made a success of some of my daydreams."

"Many, I'm sure," Kendra insisted as she went through the revolving door. People were hustling about as if they were on an endless shopping spree.

Genna's eyes were bright as she showed Kendra around. "You see," she said, "this store really is like a circus. I have all types of costumes. It's madness at its best"—she grinned like a shy little girl—"and very fashionable to shop here, I might add. The city's elite flock here for costume balls."

"It's incredible," Kendra breathed. This was certainly the crème de la crème of the antique stores. What money could buy was right!

A tall, attractive, fair-haired man strode toward them, a smile on his face. "Genna, how nice of you to drop in," he murmured. "I didn't even know you were in town."

Genna blushed sweetly as she turned to introduce Kendra. "Kendra McAllis, this is my store manager, Alexander Harrington. Everyone calls him Zan." Her eyes twinkled mischievously. "He's had control of the store so long now that apparently he thinks it's his."

Zan laughed easily. "Just a gentle reminder, dear," he whispered, "that the proprietor's appearance is always appreciated."

He then gave his total attention to Kendra. "I'm pleased to meet you," he said warmly. "Is there anything I can show you?"

Genna smiled. "See how well trained he is? He gets right to the point—business. He's definitely part of the reason we're a success. His talent and my money."

"Don't be modest," Zan insisted. "Olden Golden Gifts was already well established when I joined you."

"Yes, but not doing nearly as well as it is now," Genna said.

Zan grinned at her wickedly. "One has to *work* when one owns a store, dear. You refused to travel. You closed at four."

Lowering golden lashes, Genna murmured, "My family didn't consider it proper for me to traipse all over, gathering up other people's discards. And they didn't like the idea of me keeping the store open after dark. They didn't consider it safe or necessary."

Zan smiled winningly. "Mine never had such worries." He winked at Kendra. "They had lovely connections, just like Genna's family, but no cash. Connections don't put bread on the table. Selling the family heirlooms to Genna did."

Genna blushed. "Zan, you don't need to tell such things."

He laughed good-naturedly and joked, "Why not? I don't want Kendra to think I'm without a pedigree. I'm the impoverished elite. I fell at this woman's knees, and she took me in—that is, she gave me a job."

"Zan!" Genna scolded. "You're being silly. I couldn't have succeeded without you, and you know it."

Zan laughed. "Regardless of who did what, we made the store work, didn't we?"

Genna laughed. "We did that."

Kendra was impressed by their camaraderie and their devotion to the business venture. She sensed a strong tie between them, and she marveled that Genna had such good rapport with two men in her life. This man was clearly no less her friend than Gable was.

"Excuse us, Zan," Genna said, breaking into Kendra's thoughts. "I want to show Kendra a coat."

"It was lovely to meet you," Zan said. "I hope I'll see you again."

"Thank you," Kendra returned. "The pleasure was mine." Then she went with Genna up some spiraling steps to a top room that housed organized collectibles from an earlier period.

"This is it," Genna said, walking over to a boy mannequin with a coat draped on it. "Won't this do?"

"Perfectly!" Kendra exclaimed. "You're an angel, Genna."

Genna smiled. "No, not by a long shot, but I am pleased I can do something to help. I love that little boy so much, but I've been able to do nothing to reach him."

Genna began to take the coat off the mannequin. "I wish I could be there to see you make
him up," she said.

Kendra knew it was going to be a touchy time;
she truly didn't want anyone there but Brian and
her—and maybe Gable. But she couldn't refuse
Genna.

"Do come if you want," she offered.

Genna seemed to consider for a moment, then
she smiled her sweet smile. "Thank you, but I
believe it will be best if I stay at the store today."

"All right," Kendra said, but she found herself
wondering for whom it would be best, and why.
She accepted the coat and derby Genna handed
her and went over to look at a trunk.

"This is like Brian's toy chest!" she said. "Just
like it."

"Yes, I gave his to him. Now *that* he does seem
to appreciate."

Kendra quickly spun around. "He appreciates
you too. Surely you must know, Genna. This is
just such a difficult time for him."

Genna smiled. "Yes, for all of us. A very difficult and uncertain time," she murmured. "And
who would have thought a clown—an illusion—
would come into our lives to turn them all
around?"

Before Kendra could ask just what the other
woman meant, Genna quickly asked, "Are you
ready for lunch? I'm absolutely famished."

"So am I. In the morning's excitement I ate
very little."

141

"Then come along. I think you'll love this restaurant."

Kendra found that she did love the restaurant. Colorful and enchanting, it catered to a business clientele and specialized in quick, but good, food. She and Genna had vegetarian sandwiches on pita bread and coffee.

Kendra found Genna to be a delightful and interesting lunch companion as they shared their mutual fascination with costumes, but she was unable to learn anything of a personal nature about the other woman. She was thwarted and disappointed time and again when she tried to talk about Gable.

"I thought you two were married the first time I saw you in Brian's hospital room," she confided.

Genna smiled. "What made you think that?"

"You made such a perfect pair, for one thing," Kendra said. "And the three of you seemed like a family. The way you and Gable related to each other was so warm and intimate, and I believe you referred to Brian as *our* boy."

Laughing lightly, Genna agreed. "Yes, I probably did. That's how I think of him. Of course, I've known Brian since the day he was born, and Gable since *I* was born." She laughed. "The two sets of parents showed me to him the day I was brought home from the hospital. He was less than two years old, and the only child between the old friends. They were so afraid he would resent me."

It was all information Kendra had already

heard, and she realized that she was probing, trying to learn more.

"You two just seem unusually compatible," she
said.

Genna lowered her gaze, revealing lovely, long
golden lashes as she gingerly placed some of the
stray lettuce back into the pocket of her bread.
"We should, shouldn't we? After all, we've been
friends and neighbors for all of my twenty-eight
years. I've seen Gable through his childhood, his
teen years, his bad marriage"—she looked at
Kendra—"and I'll probably see him through his
remarriage."

Kendra's eyes widened in alarm. "Is Gable serious about some woman?" she asked, unable to
keep the tremor from her voice.

Genna gazed thoughtfully at the dark-haired
woman across from her for a long moment while
Kendra's heart beat in double time. "Gable will
marry again," she responded evasively.

"Is there someone he's considering now?"
Kendra asked anxiously, unable to stop herself.

Genna frowned slightly, marring her pretty
face with faint lines. "If there is, perhaps he
hasn't discovered it yet, but he's not a man to
remain single for long."

Kendra couldn't keep from sighing in relief,
even though it made her feel absurd. "You mean
because he wants a mother for Brian?"

"Oh, that he does," Genna agreed. "But that
won't be the only reason he marries."

Finding that she was no longer hungry, Kendra toyed with the food on her plate. Darcy had

said the same thing. A mother for Brian wouldn't be the *sole* reason he married, but it would be a big part of it.

"Have you been married, Genna?" Kendra couldn't resist asking.

Again Genna frowned, then shook her head. "No."

"May I ask why?"

"Oh, I don't know. Perhaps I set my standards too high. And you, Kendra?" she asked, turning the tables.

Kendra could feel herself blush. She didn't want to talk about Wyatt. She looked away. "I was engaged to be married. I'm afraid my fiancé decided he didn't want a clown for a wife."

She was surprised to see the firm set of Genna's pretty mouth. "Don't give up your dreams, Kendra. Don't give up your identity. You *are* a clown. Besides, men don't know what they want. Believe me, I know."

Kendra glanced curiously at the blond. Abruptly Genna looked down at her watch. "It's almost two. I've got to run." She put money down on the table and stood up. "Lunch is on me. Good luck with Brian."

Genna was gone before Kendra could say a word. For a long time she stared after the other woman, puzzling over what she had said. Then she realized that she would be late, herself, if she didn't hurry.

She tossed her napkin down on the table and rushed out to her car. But all the way to Gable's house she pondered Genna's warning—for that's what it seemed to be.

She sighed as she parked her car. She now realized that there wasn't anything between Genna and Gable, she couldn't decide if she was pleased or sorry.

CHAPTER TEN

Kendra was nervous and excited as she walked up to Gable's front door, her makeup case in one hand, Brian's costume and her own in a bag in the other. She had decided to leave Speckles at home today. She rang the bell and waited for Mrs. Washington to come to the door, but to her surprise, Gable answered. Kendra immediately felt that old, familiar weakness in her knees.

"Hello," he said, smiling warmly.

"Hello," she returned. "I expected Mrs. Washington."

"She's off on weekends," he explained, a teasing note in his voice. "Won't I do?"

Her face was flushed, and she was determined not to fall into his trap. "Yes, of course."

His gaze roved over her, taking in her slim figure in the blue jeans and a blue shirt. He felt like a young boy standing there. He wanted to drag her into his arms and smother her with kisses. He wanted to hold her to him until his heart slowed and his senses returned to normal. Instead he tried to concentrate on why she was here.

"Let me help you," he insisted, taking her

makeup case. His fingers brushed against hers, and he looked into her eyes. "It appears that you're ready for serious business today."

She released her breath in a ragged sigh. "I'm so hopeful that this will work, and so nervous that it won't," she admitted. "I'm afraid it's a little bit like killing the Easter bunny. Where is Brian?"

"He didn't know you were coming today, and when the bell rang, I told him to wait for me in his room. If he's as unhappy today as he was on the day of the picnic, we're in for trouble."

"I know," she agreed with a sigh, "but it's a chance we'll have to take. He's just got to start talking."

Gable nodded soberly as he opened the door for her to enter. "I'm at my wit's end," he admitted. "I would have very little hope if it wasn't for you."

"I don't even know how to start," she confessed as she and Gable went up the steps.

"Any way you can," he murmured, rapping lightly on Brian's door before opening it.

Sitting in the middle of the bed with Puppy, Brian stared at them. It only took a moment for him to register what was happening as he looked from his uncle to the woman. His face twisted into a mask of unhappiness.

"Here we go again," Gable murmured to Kendra as he set down the case and walked over to the boy's bed. "Look who's here, Brian. You know your friend, Kendra. She's the same person as Happy the Clown. Now give her a big smile

147

and show her how much you appreciate her entertaining you as the clown."

Sadly, slowly, Brian shook his head. Then he covered Puppy's eyes as if to protect her from viewing something terrible. Finally he rolled them both over so that they were facing the wall next to the bed.

Gable sat down on his nephew's bed and touched the boy's shoulder. "Brian, turn around and look at me," he said firmly. "I won't have you being rude to our guest, not after all the time Kendra has shared with you. Now, come on, turn over."

Tears slipping from his eyes, the dark-haired lad dragged himself over on his back, the puppy still in his arms.

Kendra joined Gable on the bed, gently patting the child's hand. "I have fun things planned for today, Brian," she said with pretended cheerfulness. "You're going to like what I have to show you. Come on, take a look at what I've brought with me."

Again he shook his head, the tears still falling. Kendra felt a well of panic building inside, and for a moment she truly didn't know what to do. She couldn't *make* the child let her dress him as a clown. She felt like breaking down and weeping herself.

Maybe that wasn't such a bad idea, she decided. The actress in her came to her rescue. It was easy enough to cry when she saw the child's misery, and that's just what she did. Looking right at Brian, Kendra let tears spill from her big brown eyes.

Gable realized immediately what Kendra was doing. "Brian," he murmured, "look how unhappy Kendra is because you won't play with her today."

Brian's face crumpled. Gable could see that he was weakening. He was a sensitive child and did not want to make Kendra unhappy.

He looked at her for a long time as he put Puppy aside and sat up in bed. He patted her face with a quivering hand and shook his head, silently pleading with her not to cry. Then he solemnly slid off the bed and walked over to stand before her makeup case.

Gable's face was filled with concern as he squeezed Kendra's hand briefly and wiped away her tears with his index finger. "I think Brian wants to see what you've brought," he said quietly.

Kendra nodded as she went over to stand beside the child. First she opened the bag to show Brian her own costume. His solemn expression never wavered; clearly he was not pleased at having the magic of the clown laid out so vividly before him. Then Kendra pulled out the replica costume she had gotten for him. For the first time she saw a flicker of interest in his eyes.

"This is for you," she said. "It's a costume just like Happy's. Do you want to try it on?"

He nodded his head and softly tooted his horn. When she saw that she had captured his interest and piqued his curiosity, she breathed a sigh of relief.

"Will you help us, Gable?" she asked, turning to him.

"I'd love to. I'm sure Brian will make a wonderful clown," he said, crossing the floor. He looked at his nephew as he bent down before him. "Won't this be fun, Brian?"

Again the child nodded, but he did not speak or toot his horn. With Gable's help Kendra soon had the little boy dressed like a miniature copy of her clown self, right down to the oversize shoes with orange laces.

Taking Brian by the hand, she walked with him over to the mirror. "Look," she said. "You're almost a clown."

He was trying his best not to seem too enthusiastic, but a small smile danced on his lips, and his eyes sparkled.

"What do you think, Brian?" she asked, beaming. "Do you like it?"

He nodded again.

"Now I need to get dressed," she said, trying to keep up a happy patter. She turned to Gable. "Where shall I change?"

"Why not in the master bedroom?" he suggested. "Then you and Brian can make up in the master bath. It has excellent lighting."

"Fine," she said. "Lead the way."

As he picked up the makeup case and bag Kendra took Brian by the hand for the trip down the hall. Gable's room was at the end of the hall on the opposite side, next to the library.

When they entered, Kendra gazed around the lavish room. Massive and beautifully appointed, it was decorated in deep grays and blues, well suited to the aristocratic Gable Hunt.

"Brian and I will wait next door. Let us know when you've changed," Gable said.

"All right."

She watched as they left, Gable closing the door behind them, and for a moment she gazed around the room, noting the kingsize bed with its navy blue spread, the two Colonial wardrobes, and the gray-and-blue-striped settee.

"Stop daydreaming, Kendra," she said aloud, admonishing herself sharply. "Get changed."

In minutes she was dressed like Brian, from her shoes to her tie. She peered out into the hall. "I'm ready," she called out.

When Gable and Brian came back into the room, Kendra smiled as she watched the child walking in the large shoes, placing his steps very carefully. He looked adorable in the clown costume, and she could see that he was very proud of it.

Gable caught her eye and smiled at her. He made a circle of success with his thumb and forefinger as he directed her to the bath. Once again she was struck by the beauty of the room, also done in blues and grays. Clearly the Colonial house had been renovated to have all the modern conveniences while still keeping its historical charm. The huge navy bathtub was equipped with a Jacuzzi.

"Shall I put the makeup case on the counter?" Gable asked.

Kendra nodded, directing her mind back to the events at hand. Brian was looking from her to himself curiously. Kendra was delighted to see that he was pleased to be a copy of Happy.

"Do you like your costume, Brian?" she asked again.

He lowered his eyes and smiled shyly.

"Wait until you see what happens next," she told him. She turned to Gable. "We need a tall chair."

"How about a kitchen stool?"

"Great."

While he went to get it Kendra laid out some of her makeup on the dressing table. By the time Gable came back, she was ready to begin.

Gable helped Brian up on the stool, and Kendra could sense the boy's excitement as she began to make him up. His eyes fixed on his image in the mirror, he watched as Kendra went step by step with the makeup, doing first him and then herself, slowly transforming them into carbon-copy clowns, from the whiteface right down to the matching eyebrows.

Kendra was having a wonderful time. She loved working with the makeup, creating a funny face; transforming Brian into a clown was a special treat. She could sense the excitement course through his body with every stroke of her brush, and she knew he was eager to see the results. Every once in a while he caught a glimpse of himself and squirmed restlessly, trying his best not to show how thrilled he was. Kendra smiled to herself, lost in the pleasure of seeing his little face become a magical mask.

As Gable watched her work, he found himself entranced by her uniqueness. She had a sweetness and a radiance that showed through the makeup as the skilled touch of her fingers on her face and Brian's made them figures of fun. He could see the pride she took in her trade and the love she had for what she did. He couldn't help but appreciate her talent.

"See," she said proudly to the boy. "Now you're a clown, and I'm a clown, but we're also Brian and Kendra." She stepped aside so that he could look in the mirror when she had finished.

"Well, what do you think? How do you like the clown?" She held her breath, hoping that in his excitement Brian would speak.

For a moment he gazed at the mirror in disbelief. He tentatively touched the bushy brows and the mustache, as if to assure himself that they were not a mirage. Then he giggled aloud and hunched up his shoulders. When the reflection moved, he laughed happily.

He was ecstatic. He was bursting with pride. He had forgotten all about Kendra not coming as Happy as he scrambled down off the stool and hugged her baggy pant legs, being careful not to muss his makeup or knock off his derby.

Proudly he walked over to stand in front of his uncle so that Gable could get a better look at him. He was smiling broadly, and with his clown smile on, his whole face smiled.

"You look terrific!" Gable exclaimed. "What a wonderful clown you make. Can you tell Kendra thank you for making you look so marvelous?"

Brian's face seemed to droop a little, even behind the clown makeup. He obviously hadn't anticipated anyone expecting him to talk as a clown.

"It's all right to talk," Kendra said gently. "I talk as Kendra, and I can talk as Happy, as I showed you last night. Won't you tell me how much you like yourself as a clown?"

She bent down in front of the little clown, pleading with her eyes, waiting expectantly. He hung his head forlornly for a second. Then abruptly he flung his arms around her and kissed her mouth very hard and quickly before backing away.

Kendra looked up at Gable. She was disappointed because the boy hadn't spoken, but she was moved and touched by the kiss. Her eyes met Gable's as she straightened.

Brian tugged at her hand and pointed to Gable. Kendra looked from him to his uncle, not sure what he wanted. "Yes?" she said. "What about your uncle, Brian? Tell me."

The boy tooted his horn and nodded his head, but Kendra still didn't know what he wanted. Impatiently he pointed to her, himself, and then Gable.

"Oh," she said. "Do you want me to make Uncle Gable a clown too? Tell me."

He nodded vigorously.

Kendra looked at Gable, a big smile playing on

her painted mouth. He shook his head. "Uh, uh, not me. I'm not the clown type."

"Ask him to be a clown with us, Brian," Kendra coaxed, still trying desperately to get the boy to speak.

Brian walked over to his uncle and clasped both his hands as he nodded eagerly, trying every way he could to get Gable to agree but not asking him verbally.

"Oh, all right," Gable said, but Kendra could tell that he wasn't the least bit enthusiastic about it. She chuckled softly as she indicated that he should sit on the stool Brian had vacated.

She grinned as she set about making one of the best-known men in North Carolina into a figure of fun and merriment. Gable watched his reflection in the mirror almost as interestedly as Brian had.

Kendra hoped he wouldn't notice how her fingers trembled as she traced the shape of his mouth, smoothed makeup on his handsome face, and adhered the false brows to his own heavy ones. She knew she was being ridiculous, but touching him seemed too intimate, too provocative, even in this situation.

Gable told himself that it was almost worth being made to look absurd to have her touch him. She was so close, so dangerously close, that he ached to draw her to him and trace the curves hidden beneath the baggy costume. He looked up into her eyes, and when they met, Kendra quickly glanced away. Did she feel it, too, or was he only hoping she did?

"Do I look that bad?" Gable asked, joking to ease the tension he was feeling.

"Look in the mirror."

They both broke into laughter when he saw what she had done. She had turned him into an orange-haired, bulb-nosed, white-faced clown, and he looked ridiculous sitting there in his black slacks and white shirt.

Brian loved his uncle's new look. Unable to contain his jubilation, he bounced around eagerly, tugging on Kendra's and Gable's hands while Puppy barked excitedly at the threesome.

Brian was pulling them toward the stairs when Gable asked, "What do you want, Brian?"

The boy kept trying to drag them along. Gable gently disengaged his hand from his young nephew's. "Tell me what you want," he encouraged. "I don't know."

But all his hopes and efforts to get Brian to talk were in vain. Bubbling over with happiness, Brian motioned with his hand for his uncle to come with him. Gable met Kendra's eyes over the boy's head and gave a resigned sigh. Brian was not going to speak today, despite all their attempts.

Disappointed and silent, they followed the youngster out onto the porch. "Oh," Gable said, "you want to show Genna how you look. Well, you two go ahead. I think I'll wait inside."

Brian shook his head, and his blue eyes pleaded with Gable to go with them.

"I can't believe this," Gable said, moaning in mock misery. "I can't go out in public looking like this."

156

"Take heart, Mr. Hunt," Kendra teased. "Nobody but *nobody* will know who you are. Genna might not be home, anyway. I met her at a secondhand store today, then she and I went to her antique shop. That's where I got Brian's coat and derby. When I left, she was still at the shop."

To Brian's glee Genna answered the door. He gave her a big wave in perfect imitation of Happy.

Immediately she got into the spirit of the thing. "Why, what have we here?" she asked, blue eyes wide. "Three clowns?" She grinned in amazement when she glanced at Gable. "And who are you?"

"Happy!" Kendra exclaimed.

"Dopey," Gable chimed in, feeling it.

"And you?" Genna prompted. "Who are you, little clown?"

Brian seemed stuck for a moment, but he was a sharp little boy. He tooted his horn—once.

Genna noticed the disappointment on Kendra's and Gable's faces. "Is that your name? Toot?" she asked Brian.

He nodded happily and pushed past her into the house.

"Well, come on in," she said to Kendra and Gable.

For the next two hours Kendra and her clown friends carried on merrily as they did tricks for Genna. Gable obligingly accommodated Kendra when she showed him how to operate her concealed gadgets, but Brian was the real trooper. He was thrilled by each and every new tactic,

157

each and every concealed treasure, from the confetti to the paper roses, and he was an apt and quick pupil.

Still, he never said a word. They all took heart in the fact that he did laugh, as he had last night, and they held on to the hope that it was a start in the right direction. Laughter filled the house, and Kendra was especially impressed by Gable's willingness to behave in such a silly and frivolous manner. It seemed so out of character for him.

Kendra sent Brian to the bathroom to fill up her water bulb. A little later the three adults noticed that he failed to return. "Maybe you'd better go see about him," she suggested to Gable.

"Yes," Genna added. "Perhaps the whole bathroom is under water by now."

Grinning at the thought, Gable went off in search of the boy. Seconds later he walked quietly back into the room. "Come and see where the littlest clown is," he said.

The women followed him back down the hall. Brian had climbed up on a bed in the guest bedroom and was sound asleep, his clown face grinning, even in sleep.

"How precious," Genna whispered.

Gable grinned. "I think he's had too much of a big day. I'd better carry him home." He started to run a hand through his hair, then laughed softly. "I want to get out of this getup, anyway."

"Don't move him," Genna whispered. "Let him sleep here. When he wakes up, I'll bring him home."

"I don't want to put you to that trouble," Gable insisted.

Genna made a face at him. "Gable Hunt, shame on you. Since when is Brian any trouble? He's almost as much my child as he is yours."

Gable looked sheepish. "Yes, he is, isn't he? Thank you, Genna. You've really been wonderful with him." He turned to Kendra. "And so have you. I just pray that we're on the verge of ending this nightmare now."

"Me too," Kendra murmured softly as she looked at the sleeping child. "Me too."

"Well, come on, clown," Gable said. "I'm all for getting cleaned up."

"Thanks for being our audience, Genna," Kendra told the other woman.

Genna smiled. "I wouldn't have missed it. I'll bring Brian over when he wakes up."

Gable thanked her again, and then he and Kendra walked back to his house. "Well, Brian definitely loves being a clown."

"Yes, but he still didn't speak."

Gable wrapped his arm around Kendra. "Not yet, but I believe that things are looking better. I'm beginning to think it's only a matter of time until this entire situation works itself out."

Kendra felt a slight shiver race over her skin. Gable was talking only about Brian, wasn't he?

159

CHAPTER ELEVEN

When she and Gable entered the house, Kendra was acutely aware that she was now alone with him. The housekeeper wasn't there, and neither was Brian. She smiled at the memory of the little clown curled up asleep on Genna's bed.

"Brian made a wonderful clown, didn't he?" she asked, spinning around as Gable closed the door behind them.

He was much nearer than she had thought, and she bumped his feet with her big shoes. She tottered uncertainly until he braced her with his strong hands.

Their eyes locked; neither spoke for what seemed an eternity. "Yes," Gable drawled softly at last. "And so do you. Oh, Kendra," he said, suddenly hoarse.

He drew her forward until his lips lightly brushed hers. Kendra instinctively started to pull away, but Gable held her firmly against his body. She could feel the fire in him right through her costume.

"I've ached to hold you again, Kendra. You've made wonderful magic for Brian today. Now I need some of it. Don't turn away from me," he said thickly. "I want you."

His words made her tremble, and when she looked into his eyes, she forgot everything, even the fact that he was made up like a clown.

His mouth sought hers again. His kisses were hot and demanding. She felt a rush of warmth as his tongue slipped between her lips to tease and probe the tender insides of her mouth. She told herself that she must pull away, now, while there was still time.

But she knew that it was already too late. It had been too late the very first time Gable Hunt had touched her. She had only been fooling herself. She wanted him as much as he wanted her, perhaps even more.

His kiss was deep and passionate, instantly sending flames of desire raging through her body. This time she met the fire in his kiss, holding nothing back as she locked her fingers at the back of his neck. It had been much too long since she had responded fully to the needs of her body.

She was a passionate woman with all the desires and yearnings of a woman, no matter how she tried to submerge them. Gable had aroused her sleeping passion, and she needed him.

When she touched his hair, she was startled by the coarse feel of the curly orange wig and drew back in surprise. Their mustaches clung stubbornly together, making Kendra laugh nervously. Gently she pulled hers away from his.

"Let's get out of this mess," he said thickly, lifting her up in his arms in his impatience. Her derby tumbled to the floor as Gable strode down the hall and up the steps to his bedroom.

Locking her arms around his neck, she closed her eyes and reveled in the hard feel of his muscular body as he easily carried her. She promised herself then and there that she would not think of anything but this moment, this single day in her life.

After all, she was the one who had vowed to live every day to the fullest and maybe—just maybe—she would finally stop trembling and dreaming and wondering, if she let Gable cool the fires that flamed so hotly in her blood. Maybe she could get on with her life if she let Gable love her.

He stood her on her feet in the blue-and-gray bathroom. "How do we get this stuff off?" he asked raggedly.

Kendra smiled at his eagerness. "I have some cream to take it off more easily," she said, surprised by the huskiness of her own voice.

"Well, dammit, let's do it," he said.

Kendra smiled again as she directed him to the stool and began to remove his makeup with quaking fingers. Then she swiftly cleansed her own face.

"That's better," Gable said, cupping her face in both his hands. "I want the woman, not the clown."

Kendra knew that all too well, and it frightened her. But not enough to make her draw away again.

Lightly, lovingly, he traced her features with

his thumbs and fingertips while Kendra stood before him, hardly daring to breathe. It was all she could do not to throw herself into his arms as he outlined her features with his gentle caresses. His fingers strayed to her throat as he kissed her eyelids, the tip of her nose, the corners of her mouth.

Hungrily he claimed her mouth, moaning softly in satisfaction as she returned his kiss. He drew her back into his arms, aching for the feel of her. He had suppressed his desire for her for far too long, and he would not be denied now. His fingers swift and sure, he stripped off her coat and unbuttoned the baggy trousers. Then he slowly slid the heavy britches down Kendra's long, lean legs.

"Lovely, so lovely," he whispered huskily as he followed the length with his eyes. Bending down on his knees, he removed the huge shoes from her feet and took off her socks while she held on to his shoulder.

Gable then unbuttoned the oversize shirt and slipped it from her shoulders. His hands were suddenly unsteady, and his blue eyes burned with fire as they roved over the tempting woman in the lacy white bra and bikini panties.

"You are so very beautiful," he said thickly, his eyes meeting hers, causing Kendra to feel shy. "You can't imagine how much I've wanted you, how I've longed to make you mine."

"I believe I can," she whispered. She reached out to remove his shirt and found herself trembling. She could barely get the buttons undone, and she was grateful when Gable slipped his pants down his lean hips and long, muscled legs.

For a moment they stood there almost naked, feasting on the sight of each other. Kendra ached to draw the hairy, muscled man to her body and press her sensitive breasts against him. She longed to feel his warmth and his need. In the navy briefs he wore he was potently masculine and provocative.

Gable's blue eyes were feverish with desire; he had wanted her so long that he was determined to savor her loveliness, to glory in the beauty of her body, to satiate himself with the sight of her.

He picked Kendra up and gently laid her down on the bed. "I've dreamed of making love to you for so many nights," he murmured, his breath warm on her face.

"Then I hope I won't disappoint you," she whispered.

"Never," he murmured swiftly. "Never. You are so beautiful, so exquisite, even more so than I dreamed."

"And so are you," she said softly.

Looking surprised, he whispered, "Have you dreamed about me? Tell me."

She looked away, suddenly shy.

"Don't be shy with me," he coaxed as he removed the last barriers to their loving. "Look at me, Kendra."

She wasn't really gorgeous, and she knew it, but when she gazed into his flaming blue eyes, she felt gorgeous. He was looking at her so intently, so adoringly, that she thought at that moment that she was the most special woman in the world.

"Did you dream about my kisses like I did yours? Did you go home after you had been with me and ache to hold me again? Did I come to you in the night full of promises and love?" he asked passionately.

She nodded, lowering her eyelashes. "Yes, all of those things."

Gable tipped her chin up with his forefinger. "Look at me, Kendra. Look at how ready I am to love you, to make all those dreams come true for both of us. Don't be shy with me. I want this to be a time to remember."

Trembling, she gazed at him, and she wondered how he thought she could ever forget this moment.

He lay before her like a Greek god, muscled and well defined, from his head to his toes. He was virile and beautiful, and he was ready to make love to her. As she looked at him, so bold and eager and powerful, she could hardly wait to know him intimately.

He smiled at her as her feverish brown eyes met his blazing blue ones. Slowly he began to kiss her again, his lips placing fiery little kisses along the corners of hers, then claiming them possessively. His mouth left hers to scatter kisses along the length of her throat. Her hands sought the defined muscles of his back as she relished his skilled lovemaking.

When his lips closed down over one nipple, Kendra shivered with desire. It had been so long since she had known such tormentingly delicious sensations, so long since she had been caressed. Gable's fingers stroked and touched both her breasts while his lips and tongue teased and tasted the pointed nipples, which throbbed at his slightest contact.

Locking her fingers in Gable's hair, she tugged gently as he trailed his tongue down her long, slender body, savoring her sweetness. He traced her navel with his tongue before dipping into the slight indentation. Then he kissed the rich smoothness of her abdomen before trailing his tongue lower.

On fire, Kendra lay back against the pillows and arched her hips. She was burning with desire for this man, her body throbbing and aching from his caresses. A spasm of delight went through her, followed by ripples that set her mind and body spinning. Her fingers bit into his shoulders, and she held on for dear life as her body rocked in passionate response to Gable's loving.

When she thought she could stand no more without exploding, Gable let his weight rest lightly on her, his potent manhood pressing provocatively against her. In her eagerness to know him she let her hands skim down his back to his muscled buttocks, drawing him to her, encouraging him to become one with her.

But Gable took his time, again kissing and stirring her to new peaks of passion. His mouth found hers again and again, and she met his fire and his thrusting tongue hungrily. At last he slid his hands under her hips and eased his body into hers.

Kendra drew in her breath in surprise at the thrilling feel of him inside her. She was quivering with passion, lost in a world of sensuous satisfaction as Gable met the eager arching of her body with slow, powerful thrusts that gradually increased in tempo.

As he moved against her, his arms on either side of her, Gable gazed down at Kendra's flushed and eager face. It seemed to her like a wonderful, intoxicating eternity, but it took only moments for them to reach unparalleled heights of passion and touch the stars in each other's eyes.

"Oh, Gable, Gable!" she cried, expressing her delight. "Oh, Gable, you're wonderful."

His deep laugh was husky and passionate. "And you're delicious, absolutely delicious, my gorgeous Kendra," he murmured, punctuating each word with a kiss.

When the fires of their desire had cooled, they lay in each other's arms, marveling that such splendor had been theirs. "You have so much to give a man, Kendra."

She smoothed back her hair and laughed teasingly, her shyness gone in the afterglow of their loving. "And you, Gable, you have so much to give a woman. I had no idea that so much could be so good."

For a moment Gable seemed taken aback by her slightly naughty teasing. Then he laughed deeply. "Well, well, well. What a wicked little siren you've been hiding behind that colorful clown makeup," he said jokingly.

He slapped her playfully on her fanny. "We'd better get up and get presentable before Genna brings Brian home. It's been quite some time now, and he doesn't usually sleep for long periods at one stretch."

Kendra sighed, unwilling to go back to the real world. "Can't we stay and play just a little longer?"

Gable drew her closer. "Don't tempt me, sexy woman. I've been starved for your love, and one time with you certainly won't keep me satisfied, but right now we have to get out of this bed. We'll have lots of time to play later."

Later, she thought unhappily. Didn't Gable understand that there really was no later? The movie was nearly finished. She was going away. But she didn't want to think about that now. Not with this wonderfully appealing man at her side.

She was surprised when he whisked her up in his arms and strode to the bathroom with her. And there she found that later was sooner than she had thought. When Gable had adjusted the water, he led her into the shower and began to make sweet love to her again.

Kendra was with him every step of the way, savoring his skilled loving, glorying in his tender caresses, climbing to the stars with his fierce claiming of her. The fires of their desire didn't die down until the shower water began to run cold and they gradually became aware of the world around them.

"I'll never be able to get enough of you," Gable murmured huskily while he dried her. "I was afraid of that before we made love. Now I'm sure of it."

Unexpectedly Genna's voice shattered their cocoon of love.

"Gable! Gable! It's me, Genna. I knocked but got no answer."

Kendra looked at Gable wide-eyed as he handed her the towel to wrap around herself and quickly grabbed for his robe on the back of the door.

"Just a minute," he called out, but it was already too late.

Holding Brian's hand, Genna walked into the bedroom. She looked at Gable as he slipped out of the bathroom, his hair and body still dripping water. Genna looked behind him, her face white as she watched him hurriedly close the door to protect Kendra.

But he hadn't closed the door quickly enough. In a moment all too clear, Kendra had seen the shock, the disappointment—the love Genna had for Gable—in her eyes.

Oh, no, Kendra thought unhappily. *I should have had better sense. I should have realized that Genna was in love with him!*

Although both Genna and Gable had denied it, Kendra had suspected it all along but had not wanted to believe it. She remembered what Genna had implied about the antique store being something to occupy a woman's time until she fulfilled her real desires, her real destiny, her family's hopes for her: Gable. Gable Hunt.

"Oh, no," Kendra whispered. She had shattered the woman's dreams, and no doubt for a second time. How Genna must have been hurt when Gable married the first time, and then she had thought she had a second chance. Now a clown had taken the place she wanted. A clown to destroy the illusions.

And the real shame of it was that she and Gable could share only a brief time of love. He and Genna could have had forever. As Kendra had felt they should. Now it was too late.

She briskly towel-dried her hair as she listened to Gable talking to Brian. Then she stood perfectly still as Gable opened the door.

"Genna's gone and Brian's in his room," he said. "You can feel free to come out now."

Kendra shook her head. "Oh, Gable, how can you be so cavalier about it?"

He walked across the bathroom floor and drew her up against his body. "Cavalier? Who's cavalier? About what? Making love to you? It was too wonderful to deny to anyone."

Kendra frowned. "Don't you know what we just did to Genna?"

He shook his head, his hair now jet-black with water. "I'm sorry if she was embarrassed, but she's a grown woman. She won't be so surprised when she thinks about it."

"Oh, Gable, don't you know? Can't you see how Genna feels about you? She's in love with you!"

Now it was Gable's turn to frown. "Genna? No. You're mistaken, Kendra. You're embarrassed because she knew we had been intimate. That's all."

Kendra slowly shook her head from side to side as she clutched at the towel, which threatened to fall. "You're wrong, Gable. She's in love with you. She probably has been all her life. Don't tell me you've never considered the possibility."

Gable released her instantly. "Yes, of course I've considered the possibility. It was what both sets of parents hoped for, but it never happened. Nobody can make someone love someone else, no matter how well they're suited. I'm the first to admit that Genna seems to be everything I want, everything I need. You've said it to me. I've even said it to myself. But there's a crucial element missing in our relationship. I don't love her—not in the way a man loves a woman he wants to share his life with."

Do you love me that way? she wanted to ask, but she bit back the question. Even if he did— and she doubted that—nothing had changed regarding how he felt about her career. Or how she felt about it. She had to remain independent. Her survival depended upon it. She would not let herself be subjugated, no matter what the reason. But right now what mattered was that they had hurt Genna.

"She's in love with you, Gable," she repeated.

"I'm sure you're mistaken," he said, running a

171

hand over his chin, "but I'll get dressed and go talk to her if you'll put Brian to bed for me."

"All right."

His eyes roved over her once more. "I have to be crazy to walk away from you when you look like that," he murmured, then turned on his heel.

Kendra reluctantly watched as he slipped off his robe and pulled on a pair of slacks and a shirt. When he had slid his feet into some loafers, he told her, "I won't be long." He blew her a kiss and then he was gone.

Kendra finished drying and quickly slipped into her jeans and shirt. Then she walked barefoot down the hall to Brian's room. He had curled up on his own bed, Puppy at his side, and was drifting off again.

As Kendra looked at him all her maternal instincts took over. He looked so adorable lying there, a small replica of her own clown self, his derby in his hand, his wig and mustache askew. She crossed the room and gently awakened him.

"Let's get you out of your clown suit and into your pajamas," she said softly.

Sleepily Brian shook his head, but he was too tired by his exciting day to do much protesting. Kendra managed to get him out of his costume, carefully laying it on a chair. Then she helped him into his pajamas and wiped his face free of the clown makeup.

"Are you hungry?" she asked.

He nodded yes, then no. She realized that he was too tired to know, but he would be hungry by morning.

"You get under the sheet. I'll be back in a few minutes." She smiled at him and watched as he obediently slid beneath the covers before she went down to the kitchen. She hastily made a cheese sandwich and poured milk into a glass. When she returned, Brian was nearly asleep. She gently coaxed him into having a few bites of the sandwich and most of the milk.

"You're very good at that," Gable said from the doorway.

Kendra looked up at him, seeing the big smile on his face. She put her fingers to her lips, indicating that the boy was nearly asleep, and Gable nodded. In seconds Brian was sleeping soundly.

Kendra tiptoed out of his room, and Gable caught her as she started down the hall. His fingers slid under her shirt and up to her breasts, which responded immediately to his touch.

"Mmm, no bra. I like that," he said huskily. He drew her back to him, crushing her against his hard body.

"What about Genna?" she whispered against his lips.

He shook his head. "She seemed to be fine. I'm sure you're mistaken."

"I don't believe it," Kendra insisted.

Gable put his finger against her lips. "Shh, I don't want you to wake my nephew. The boy might be crazy about you, but so am I, and I want more than a cheese sandwich and milk."

"Oh, Gable," she murmured, "I—I—"

"You what?" he asked, leading her back down the hall to the bedroom. "Feel my heart pound when I touch you," he murmured, holding her hand to his chest. He let her fingers slide down the front of him. "I told you I'd never be able to get enough of you."

As she blushed, he grinned. "Don't be embarrassed. The way I feel about you is beautiful, special."

She didn't doubt that. She felt that he was beautiful and special, and she did want to make love with him again. Suppressing the nagging thoughts of Genna, not quite reassured by Gable, she went with him into his bedroom.

When Gable had shut the door behind them, he unzipped her jeans and eagerly eased them down her legs.

He kissed her lips as he lay her down on the bed. "Have I told you what beautiful legs you have?" he asked against her mouth, nibbling at her lips in between words. His hands slid down over her hips to her thighs, where he parted them and provocatively stroked the sensitive skin.

"Oh, Gable," she whispered tremblingly. "You make me want you shamelessly."

"Good," he breathed against her lips. "Then you know how I want you." He raised her shirt without unbuttoning it and pulled it over her head.

"No fair," she murmured. "You're still dressed."

"I can take care of that," he said, taking off his clothes. He grinned at her. "This is a lot easier without underwear, isn't it?"

She nodded as she watched him through passion-glazed eyes. He was the most magnificent man she had ever seen, and her body felt flushed and eager when she looked at him. She was afraid that *she* would never get enough of *him*. And there was so little time. She wanted to make this moment count. Opening her arms, she welcomed him as he moved onto the bed.

CHAPTER TWELVE

Kendra had every intention of getting up and slipping out of the house before either Brian or Gable awakened, but she couldn't make herself leave the warmth and security of Gable's arms.

As she lay cuddled against Gable, his arms wrapped around her, she felt a light tug on her hand. She sleepily opened one eye, trying her best to rouse herself, but she was still lost in the magic of the night and Gable's loving.

At last she managed to open both eyes. Suddenly she gasped and pulled at the sheets. Brian was standing at her side of the bed, his milk glass in one hand and his horn in the other.

He was grinning happily at her, and despite her embarrassment, Kendra couldn't help but smile at him. He looked so sweet standing there in his pajamas, a little carbon copy of Gable.

"Good morning," she whispered.

Gable stirred when she spoke, drawing her back against his body. She could feel his instant desire for her. "Gable," she murmured, "Brian's here."

Gable lazily raised up on one elbow to look at

the child standing at Kendra's side of the bed. "Good morning, partner," he said with much affection. "Aren't you up awfully early?" He glanced at the clock. "Good heavens. It's only six o'clock."

Brian glanced at his uncle, then adamantly tugged on Kendra's hand again, trying to pull her up. He held out the milk glass again. It seemed that the two of them in bed didn't bother him at all. He had other things on his mind.

"I hate to tell you," Gable murmured, "but I think you've been elected to cook breakfast this morning."

Gazing at Brian, Kendra asked, "Are you hungry? Do you want breakfast?"

He smiled sheepishly, then tooted his horn.

She glanced back over her shoulder at Gable. "I don't think I'm dressed for this part."

He laughed, and the husky sound warmed her. "I can see the problem—and just between you and me, it looks really good."

"Gable!" she admonished. "The child's hungry."

"Mmm," he said, giving her neck a fleeting kiss. "So am I. But, alas, I've had you all night, haven't I?"

He reached down to the foot of the bed where he had tossed his robe. When he had it in hand, he said to Brian, "Go on to the kitchen and we'll be right there."

Brian tooted his horn and left the room as he had been told to do. When he had shut the door, Kendra blushed. "I'm so embarrassed."

"Why?" he said. "Brian wasn't. You spend too much time worryng about what other people think. Brian was used to seeing his parents in bed together—especially on Sunday mornings. My brother said the boy always woke them early and asked his mother to cook him pancakes. He didn't think anything about us being here together."

Gable's comments drew her thoughts back to him and Brian. "Does that mean I'm supposed to cook pancakes at this hour of the morning?"

Gable laughed. "Don't tell me you really can't cook."

"I can," she insisted, "and very well."

He handed her the robe. "I'm from Missouri. Show me."

Kendra grinned at him as she started to slip from the bed, but before she could, Gable drew her back to him again. "What a shame I didn't wake up before Brian," he murmured against her neck as he brushed aside her long hair. "I want to make love to you."

Kendra laughingly pulled away from him, but there was no denying to herself that she *wanted* him to make love to her. He was a wonderful lover, and she had never felt so fulfilled as she had in Gable's arms.

"Brian's waiting. He might come back in," she said.

Gable gave her a lingering kiss, then freed her. "I know it, dammit! What lousy timing that boy has."

Kendra stood up and pulled on the robe, which

almost swallowed her. Gable's eyes roved over her hungrily. "I like you better without clothes," he said thickly. "Mmm, you are a sexy woman."

His words sent a shiver over her skin, and she looked away as he stood up. Gable walked over to stand in front of her, his naked body well defined and so appealing.

"I don't like you looking away from me," he said firmly. "This is a sight I want you to get used to seeing."

Kendra slid her arms around his waist and rested her head on his shoulder for a moment. "It's a sight I find incredibly attractive," she admitted.

"Could you look at it every day for the rest of your life?"

She raised her head to gaze into his eyes. They were very serious. She laughed nervously. "What are you suggesting, Mr. Hunt?" she asked, trying to keep her tone light.

"I'm not sure," he said pensively. He was in love with her, but it was much too soon to tell her. And what would he say when he did? When would he start offering life-style and goal compromises, and how far would he go in his desire to have her for his wife?

Kendra laughed lightly and moved away from him. "Well, don't give it too much thought. It's early in the morning and you're not thinking clearly."

He drew her back to him, forcing her to meet his eyes. "Perhaps I'm thinking clearly for the first time in a long while."

179

She trembled at the depth of emotion she saw in his eyes. She wasn't ready for this. She pulled his hands away. "I doubt it. I know I'm sure not. It's too early in the day."

Then she tightened the belt to his robe and left the room. Gable stared after her in frustration, wondering where it all would end.

Brian was waiting for Kendra when she reached the kitchen. To her amusement he had three different boxes of pancake mix sitting out on the table. He was standing protectively beside them.

"Do I gather you want pancakes?" she teased.

He tooted his horn twice and gave her an irresistible grin.

"Good," she said. "I'm going to make you some of the best pancakes you've ever tasted." But not from a box. She searched through the cabinets until she found all the ingredients. Then she looked in the freezer. She was in luck. There was a package of frozen blueberries there.

"All right," she told Brian, "we're going to make pancakes. Will you help me?"

He shook his head.

"No?" she murmured. "Why not?"

He backed away from the table, his eyes widened, and he looked terrified.

"Brian," she coaxed, "it's all right. You don't have to. I thought you might like to."

She looked up as Gable walked into the room, wearing another robe. Brian ran to him and wrapped his arms around Gable's legs, burying his face against Gable's thighs.

Kendra watched in dismay as Gable soothed the boy. When he looked at her over Brian's head, she was sure she saw tears in his eyes.

"Did you ask him to help you cook?" he wanted to know.

Kendra nodded, not understanding.

"He's afraid of the stove, the fire," Gable explained.

Kendra felt like a fool! Of course, that explained it. "I'm sorry," she murmured, feeling inadequate.

"It's not your fault," he said gently. He glanced at all the pancake ingredients on the counter. "It looks like you want to work hard," he said with a smile, then he bent down before Brian and put his hands on the boy's shoulders.

"Listen, partner, all Kendra wants you to do is help her mix the pancake batter. Maybe she'll let you put those blueberries in. What do you say to that?"

Glancing up from beneath lowered lashes, Brian looked at the preparations Kendra was making and nodded.

"Good," she said, breathing a sigh of relief. She had almost ruined breakfast. When she had placed the berries in the microwave to thaw, she returned to the counter. Gable set Brian on a tall kitchen stool, and Kendra instructed the child on how to help her, letting him stir in some of the ingredients while Gable got out a griddle and set it on the stove.

After Brian had dumped the blueberries in the mixture, Kendra carefully folded them in. When grease began to sizzle on the griddle, she poured out the batter in the shape of bunny rabbits.

She scooped up the first rabbit when it was done and placed it on a plate for Brian. He grinned at her when he saw the animal shape, and his eyes lit up. He tooted his horn to show his approval.

"Do you like the rabbit?" she asked.

He nodded again.

"I'll bet you can make one," she said, wondering why she was pushing her luck and knowing that she wanted him to get over his fear of fire.

He looked at her interestedly.

"Come and watch me," she urged. "I'll show you how."

Gable helped the boy down, then took the stool over to the griddle. At first Brian hesitated, but Kendra went about her business, pouring the batter on the hot griddle as if nothing in the world was awry. Brian watched, and when the bunny took shape, he laughed aloud.

Kendra let him hold the pitcher and guided his hand, pretending nothing was wrong when he jerked back as he felt the heat rise from the griddle. They managed to pour out a reasonably good rabbit, and again Brian laughed.

He and Kendra made all the pancakes in the shape of bunnies, and by the time they had finished, Gable had set the table and put out syrup, juice, and milk.

Brian climbed into his accustomed chair at the

side of the table, and Gable pulled out a chair for Kendra. As he seated her he whispered, "You're very good in this role. Couldn't you give up clowning for it?"

Kendra's eyes were unreadable when she looked back at him. "No," she said coolly. She couldn't believe that he could so easily dismiss such a big part of her life.

Saying nothing, he settled at the head of the table. They ate in silence, although both adults managed to smile at the child. Brian was having a great time with the bunnies, eating the ears, then the tail, then the head, then the body. To Kendra and Gable's surprise he ate five pancakes.

"You're eating very well this morning," Gable commented. "I'm pleased."

Brian grinned at him, then nodded to Kendra and tooted his horn.

After Brian had finished his breakfast, Gable asked, "Which do you want to do? Help Brian with bathing and dressing, or do the cleanup here?"

She knew that he was hoping she could be lured into helping Brian. He knew that the more time she spent with the child, the more irresistible she found him.

"I made this mess. I'll clean it up," she said.

If he was disappointed, he didn't show it. "Fine. I'll be back in a little while."

When he returned, both he and Brian were dressed, and Gable was freshly shaved. Kendra had just finished cleaning the kitchen.

"Now I'd better get dressed," she said, turning away. "It's time I went home."

Gable and Brian both looked like disappointed little boys. "Why do you have to leave?" Gable asked.

Kendra felt her cheeks turn pink. "I've been here since yesterday afternoon. I need to change clothes and I have things to do at home. Darcy has been baby-sitting Speckles, and I'm sure she wonders what's happened to me."

"Give her a call and spend the day with us," Gable urged.

Kendra shook her head. "No, I can't really." She started down the hall while Gable followed her up to his bedroom.

He shut the door behind them. "When am I going to see you again?" he demanded.

Kendra averted her eyes as she sought her underwear, jeans, and shirt. "I'll be here Monday evening, just as I said, to help with Brian."

Gable whirled her around to face him. "No," he said emphatically. "I did not ask about Brian. I asked when *I* was going to see you again."

She lowered her lashes, avoiding his penetrating blue eyes. "I don't know."

This time he roughly cupped her chin in his thumb and forefinger. "What do you mean you don't know? If you don't know, then who the hell does?"

There were tears in her brown eyes when they met his. "Don't do this, Gable," she said softly, her lips trembling. "You knew that we had no future. That hasn't changed. I'm leaving when the movie is finished."

"Still? After last night?" he asked incredulously.

She pulled his hand away. "Last night didn't change the circumstances of our lives," she told him. "I am still a clown, and you are still Gable Hunt of North Carolina. We represent two sides of the coin. You know that. I know it."

"Then why did you let me make love to you?" he asked, his voice tight and angry.

"I let you make love to me because I wanted you too much to say no," she returned just as tightly. "Why did you do it? To persuade me with your body to see things your way when your words didn't work?"

For a moment Gable looked stunned, then he wearily shook his head. "No. I did it because I wanted you so badly that I ached for you. I told you that yesterday. Yet you say it changes nothing."

She shook her head. "I didn't say that. I said it didn't change the circumstances of our lives."

His fingers bit into her shoulders as he forced her to look at him. "I'm not into one-night stands. Making love means something to me. Everything has changed for me, Kendra," he said fervently. "I've found what I've been searching for, and I'm not going to let you go easily. You should know that right now."

"You haven't found what you're looking for," she countered with equal passion. "I'm the farthest thing from what you want."

He shook his head. "No—only you're too stubborn to see. You and I belong together."

"You're the stubborn one!" she said, flaring. "You're not listening at all. You're not trying to understand. You wouldn't fit into the circus way of life, and that's where I belong."

His eyes searched her face. "Tell me that you don't want to stay with me, Kendra. Tell me that. Tell me that you can just pack your bags and run away to the circus when the movie is finished as if I'd never touched you—loved you."

Her eyes met his, and he saw the pain revealed in their brown depths. "I'd like to stay, Gable, but it just won't work. What you and I want are too different. You've said it over and over. I won't give up my career, and I won't be tied down to one spot. I've tried to tell you all along that I don't fit into your life. I told you that you needed someone like Genna."

She looked away, recalling the pain on the other woman's face, but Gable's voice brought her attention back to him.

"Try, Kendra. Try to fit into my life. That's all I ask of you. Before you join the circus for the summer, sample my life and see if you couldn't be happy with Brian and me. Let time decide."

Kendra drew in a deep breath, then released it in a ragged sigh. She longed to hear him say that he loved her, and to what purpose? Just to know it? Because she loved him? She didn't know. She only knew it would mean a lot to her.

"I'm not a wife or mother type, Gable," she

said unhappily. "I am a circus clown. I follow the big tents."

"But you're also an actress," Gable said. "That's a more stable career. One you certainly could pursue."

"There aren't too many clown movies being made," she retorted quickly.

"All I'm asking is that you try to fit into our lives," Gable repeated. "Is that asking too much?"

Gable's request weakened her. She knew she was a fool. She knew this would only create more pain, but she had already made a grave error. She had given her heart to Gable Hunt; she had fallen in love with him. And she just couldn't say no.

She looked away from him and forced the words from her lips. "I'll try," she said tersely.

Gable freed her. "That's all I ask," he repeated. "I don't want you to be unhappy, Kendra, but can you honestly tell me that you can turn your back on me and never think about what we might have had? Do you care so little? Last night I had a different impression."

She reached for her jeans and shirt. "I care a lot, Gable," she admitted tightly. She almost confessed that she was in love with him, but she was already vulnerable enough.

Gable spun her around again, to draw her against his body. As his mouth sought hers, Kendra met his eager lips. She was shaking when she finally drew back from him.

"I'd better get dressed," she said.

"When will *I* see you again?" he repeated.

"Next weekend. There's a circus coming to town. Why don't we all go? You can see what I really do for a living. You can see what my life's all about."

Gable nodded. After all, this had been his idea. If he was going to try to fit her into his life, he had to explore hers as well.

"All right," he agreed. "Sunday there's a big charity dinner. Will you attend it with me?"

She nodded. If he was willing to make the effort, then so must she. "Let me know what time."

She put her clothes on, gathered up her clown gear, and started for the door. Before she reached it, Gable caught her in his arms and kissed her lingeringly, reminding her again that no matter how wise and cautious her thoughts, her heart listened only to her growing need.

CHAPTER THIRTEEN

Kendra left Gable standing in the front doorway as she drove off. When she passed Genna's stately home, she peered at the windows to see if anyone was there. She didn't see any signs of life, but that didn't dissuade her. She drove down the street and waited long enough for Gable to close his door before making a U-turn and heading back to Genna's.

When she rang the bell, there was no answer. She knocked and called Genna's name softly. For a few minutes longer there was still no answer, then, just as Kendra decided to leave, the blonde opened the door.

Kendra's gaze roved swiftly over Genna. The night had taken its toll on her. She had dark circles beneath her eyes, and her skin seemed paler than usual. Kendra had never seen her look so unkempt. The blue robe she wore was exquisitely feminine and set off the pretty color of her eyes, but her hair was disheveled.

"May I come in?" Kendra asked quietly.

Genna avoided looking at the other woman again. "It's early," she murmured, hiding partly behind the huge white door. "I sleep late on Sundays."

Glancing down at her watch, Kendra conceded that it was early. It was not even eight yet, but she had a feeling that it would never be late enough for Genna to see her.

"I'm sorry if I awakened you, but I really need to talk to you. Please."

Although clearly reluctant, Genna finally opened the door without further ado. Kendra entered the lovely home and waited for Genna to direct her.

"Coffee?" she asked politely. Kendra watched as Genna pulled herself together with some effort and became the smiling hostess.

"Yes, please," Kendra said, realizing that she hadn't had her first cup yet today.

"Lorraine, my maid, is still sleeping, but I think I can manage coffee," Genna said, leading the way down to a huge country kitchen.

"Please," she said, indicating a big captain's chair at the oak table in the kitchen, "sit down and make yourself comfortable. I'll only be a minute."

Kendra watched tensely as the other woman efficiently made the coffee and poured it into a graceful china pot. When she had put the pot, cups, spoons, milk, and sugar on a tray, she brought it to the kitchen table.

"We can go into the living room if you'll be more comfortable," she suggested.

Kendra shrugged her shoulders and shook her

head. "This is fine with me, if it is with you. It's more cozy."

Genna nodded, slipping into a chair across from Kendra. "Now what did you want to talk about? Brian?"

Kendra stirred milk and sugar into her steaming coffee while she tried to think of how to begin. She took a sip of the hot brew, then deliberately set the cup down. There was no point in beating around the bush.

"No, I've come to talk about you and Gable."

Kendra saw the rush of red seep up Genna's pale neck to stain her ivory cheeks. The blonde avoided looking at Kendra as she took a drink of her coffee, then smiled.

"I'm afraid there's nothing to say, then. I've already told you how Gable and I feel about each other. We're very old friends."

Kendra didn't miss the way Genna's smile trembled. "You're in love with him, aren't you?" she asked softly.

Genna's eyes widened in alarm, and the rush of color that had tainted her cheeks so brightly ebbed away, leaving them paler than before. "Why have you come here? What do you want from me?" she asked, her sweet and silvery voice tinged with the strain she was experiencing. "Do you want me to say that I'm in love with him? Is that what you want? Are you playing some kind of game with me?"

Now it was Kendra's turn to look shocked. "No, I wouldn't do that. I'm sorry if I've handled this badly. I came here because at first I believed you and Gable when you said there was nothing between you. Then I saw the pain in your eyes last night when you walked into his bedroom." She lowered her gaze, embarrassed. "I don't want to hurt you. I admire you. I've told Gable repeatedly that he's looking for someone like you, not me."

Genna stood up suddenly. *"You don't even know me!"* she cried. "I'm a facade! A shell! A creation that I molded precisely to fit Gable Hunt's needs and stated specifications. And still he didn't want me! He wanted you!"

The words shook Kendra to the core, and the implications of what Genna said sobered her. She reached out to take Genna's trembling hands in hers. "Please sit down," she said consolingly. "He doesn't want me, either. He doesn't want a clown. He wants a wife and mother."

Genna slowly sank back down. She toyed with her coffee cup for a few minutes, then suddenly burst into tears. Covering her mouth with her hands, she sobbed.

"Oh, please don't cry," Kendra murmured, walking behind the other woman and putting her arms around her, tears in her own eyes. Genna sobbed for some time, her head down on the table. Kendra found some tissues and gave them to her, but there was nothing else to do but let her cry out her bitter disappointment.

At last Genna opened her tear-drenched eyes and dabbed at her face with the tissues. "I'm sorry," she murmured contritely, "but I'm afraid that's been building for heaven only knows how many years."

She smiled tremulously. "Would it surprise you to know that I've planned to marry Gable since I was fifteen years old?" She looked away. "Or at least our parents planned for Gable and me to marry." She laughed self-mockingly as her eyes met Kendra's again. "Only Gable wasn't willing."

"I'm sorry," Kendra whispered. "I wouldn't have been the one to hurt you for all the world."

Genna reached out and clasped Kendra's hand in both of hers. "I believe you wouldn't, Kendra. It's not your fault. It's no one's fault. Gable said repeatedly that he wanted a woman like his mother, so I strove for that goal. After all, I had the model right next door to me, and I had both Gable's mother and mine instructing me in the best behavior, the most ladylike behavior, the old South behavior. You can't imagine all the years I wasted being what I thought Gable would want."

Genna laughed without mirth. *"Gable* doesn't know what he wants. I was crushed when he married, and I sadly admit to you that I was pleased when that marriage fell apart. I thought I still had a chance, that he would see that I was what he wanted. It looked like it might happen when he suddenly needed a mother for Brian, and then you walked into our lives."

"I'm sorry," Kendra murmured again.

Genna freed her hand. "Don't be. Don't you see—if it hadn't been you, it would have been someone else. Gable doesn't want me." She looked into Kendra's eyes. "I'm just glad that last night finally made me see it. I don't know how much more of my life I would have wasted waiting for him, trying to be what he wanted."

"But what now?" Kendra asked.

Genna stood up again and firmly retied the belt to her robe. "I'll live!" she announced. "That's what now for me. I thought about it most of the night. I'll step out from this image created to please Gable Hunt and I'll live my own life. Zan was right. I really am a very good businesswoman. I'll do the traveling myself. I'll be a career woman. I'll have a string of antique shops. I can afford them, and I know I can make them work."

"Please don't live your life bitter and alone," Kendra said with sudden passion. "You're young and lovely. Go out and find love."

Again her own words troubled her; she gave that advice, but she didn't follow it herself. She was in love with Gable but terrified. Part of her wished it had never happened; part wished it could be a dream come true.

Genna seemed a little taken aback, and she sat down again. "I want love," she said, half to herself, "but I won't ever look for it again. Next time it can look for me."

A fever was burning in her eyes again when she looked at Kendra. "Gable has talked to me about you, Kendra. I should have guessed days ago that he's in love with you."

Kendra bit at her lower lip. "He's never told me," she confessed. Dare she dream that Genna

194

was right? And what if Gable did love her? What then?

"Well, for heaven's sake, don't change for him!" Genna said fervently. "Not if you love him. Remember what I told you. Gable Hunt doesn't know what he wants. He probably does love you —but the way you are now. If you let him change you, then it won't be you he loves."

A shaft of fear shot through Kendra's heart at Genna's words, for they had a ring of truth to them. And there was no denying that Genna had tried to be the epitome of what Gable *said* he wanted and that he hadn't wanted her. But then, he hadn't *loved* Genna, Kendra's heart cried.

She had come here out of her concern for Genna, and now suddenly she was concerned for herself, for her own heart. She was in love with Gable, and she knew now that she was willing to compromise, if she saw that their lives were at all compatible. Oh, she wasn't willing to give up her career, but she was willing to make adjustments to fit Gable and Brian's life.

It was all so confusing. A definite surge of panic was building inside her. As much as she believed in love, as much as she wanted it, any love that had so far touched her life had been very unkind. She simply couldn't stand any more rejection. Like Genna, she had carefully built up her life so that it suited her needs.

But unlike Genna, she loved her career, her clown self, who she was. The magnitude of the impossibility of a future between her and Gable was frightening. She would see Gable's plan through, but she saw no hope at all for them. She glanced at Genna when the woman spoke softly.

"Please don't ever tell Gable what a fool I was," she asked.

Kendra patted her hand. "I promise you I won't say a word to him. He'll never know we talked. I want you to be happy, Genna. Please believe me."

Genna smiled. "If you ever marry Gable, I hope we can be friends, Kendra. He is still a big part of my life and he always will be. I can get on with my life, but I can't shut out what's been a part of it. Gable and I will remain friends, and I will always have a fond place in my heart for him." She smiled sadly. "And I will always love Brian. He's been my little boy for all practical purposes for months now."

"I'd consider it a privilege to have you for a friend," she said. "I think both Brian and Gable are fortunate to know you."

"You're not so bad yourself," Genna said in a light voice. "Not many women would give of themselves so freely to so many in need."

"It's my life," Kendra said truthfully. "I love doing it."

"Then think about what I said and don't let Gable take it from you," Genna repeated.

"I'll think about it," Kendra said. She stood up. "Thank you for talking to me, Genna. I'd better go now."

Genna walked with her to the door. "It's I who should thank you, Kendra. You didn't have to be concerned about my feelings or care what went on—or didn't go on, as the case happened to be—between Gable and me."

Kendra just smiled and said, "I hope I'll see you again, Genna."

"Yes," the blonde said gently, and then she shut the door.

Kendra was filled with anxiety as she made her way back to the house. She was relieved to see Darcy's smiling face when she pulled up in front. The old woman was in her accustomed place in the swing, gazing out curiously at Kendra.

"Get lost, did you?" she asked simply, her words dry.

Kendra smiled. "I hope you didn't worry about me, Darcy. I would have called and said I wouldn't be coming home if I had known it."

"I'm not your keeper, and I suspected you were at Gable Hunt's house," Darcy said, trying to keep the excitement out of her voice. "Speckles and I made out just fine."

"I'm going to have to pay you for baby-sitting," Kendra said.

Darcy laughed. "Don't bother. I'm pretending she's my grandchild—the only one I have. I had some of the girls over to play cards last night, and we made a lot of jokes about how hairy my poor grandchild was—and of questionable birth."

Kendra grinned. "Thanks, Darcy." She knew that Darcy was bursting to know *something* about her time with Gable, but Kendra didn't know what to say.

"Well," Darcy asked at last, "is it serious?"

Kendra felt flushed. Wasn't love always serious? "I love him," she said simply, "but it's still the clown and the millionaire."

"Uh-huh," Darcy said pensively. "Well, have you had breakfast? I've got some fresh hot apple muffins."

Kendra looked at Darcy fondly. Food. Darcy thought it would solve any problem. Especially when there was no other solution.

"I'm starved," she lied. Muffins did sound appetizing, and she followed Darcy to the kitchen, glad to think about something besides Gable.

The day passed quickly, and Kendra thoroughly enjoyed the time she spent with Darcy. The old woman was remarkably upbeat and optimistic, and she kept Kendra laughing as she told tales about her old cronies who had played cards with her the previous night.

But even as Kendra laughed at the stories she longed to talk to the other woman about the situation with Gable, though she knew there was no use. She had resolved to go along with Gable's plan, however futile. She would have to let time determine the future, just as Gable had said.

By bedtime, Kendra was glad to escape to the isolation of her room. She had things on her mind, and she wanted time to explore them.

Yet as she dressed for bed she found herself thinking of how Gable had touched her, held her, and loved her. She wanted nothing more than to slip into bed beside him and have him create all the magic once again, to have him take her away from the here and now and her worries about the future. And she wouldn't mind at all if she awakened to the feel of his body next to hers.

She wouldn't even mind waking up to the sight of Brian tugging on her hand, wanting her to make his breakfast. But what then? What would happen after the newness wore off? What would her life be? What would happen to the very essence of her, her clowning talents? And what would Gable Hunt think of her if he managed to convince her to be a housewife and a mother?

She shook her head, unconsciously rebelling at the image. It wasn't her. It would never be her. Her mind filled with troublesome thoughts, and her body yearning for Gable's caresses and the fulfillment of being in his arms, Kendra lay down on the bed and tried to sleep.

Tossing and turning, she was so restless that Speckles finally hopped off the bed to sleep on the floor. Kendra listened as the little dog settled down with a weary sigh. With a sigh of her own she closed her eyes and breathed deeply, hoping to find some method of inducing sleep.

But when she closed her eyes, Gable was there, laughing, teasing, loving. She relived her time with him, feeling the touch of his fingers on her skin, the way her body thrilled to the union with his.

She opened her eyes again. It was impossible to sleep with tormenting thoughts of Gable.

She tried desperately to think of something else —anything else. Tomorrow was a workday. It was also a day to see Brian. She smiled a little as she thought of the delightful clown the young boy had made. He had loved learning her clown secrets, and he had finally seemed to accept the fact that she was both Happy and Kendra. Now, if only he would talk.

Her thoughts became just as turbulent as she considered ways to get Brian to speak, as they had been what she thought about Gable. But as she focused on the child her body began to settle down somewhat, and at last she was able to sleep.

Only then did she really rest, for in her dreams Gable claimed her time and again. There she achieved the freedom she couldn't find in her real life.

CHAPTER FOURTEEN

Kendra was distressed when she went to work the next day, but she had only been on the set a matter of minutes when her mood improved tremendously. Generally she spent much of her time waiting around while other scenes were filmed, until her turn came, but today the producer announced that she was on first. He was expanding her part yet again, and she couldn't help the thrill that went through her.

"Can you do something more with the playground scene?" he asked. "We loved the seesaw thing. How about something with a merry-go-round or the slides?"

"Yes!" Kendra cried, scooping up Speckles and carrying her to the improvised playground. In minutes they were the center of attention as Speckles, hastily dressed like a baby, dutifully slid down the slide while Kendra waited at the bottom to catch her. Then, to everyone's amusement, Kendra slid down the slide while Speckles waited at the bottom, standing up on her hind legs, her front paws out as though she could really catch Kendra.

They were the hit of the day, and Kendra was in a fantastic mood as she left the studio and drove toward Gable's house. When she turned onto his street, her heart began its crazy rhythm and her legs felt suddenly weak. She didn't know how she would react when she saw him again, but she was grateful that at least she was in costume. She could feel her face turn red at the mere thought of looking at the man who had made love to her so thoroughly and so thrillingly.

She was relieved when Mrs. Washington answered the door. She almost hoped that Gable was out for the evening. Almost. For in her heart of hearts she wanted very badly to see him, to know that he wanted to see her. That he still wanted her.

Mrs. Washington's face was beaming brightly when she spoke to Kendra. "Come in, Happy."

Kendra tipped her hat as she entered the house. She gasped in surprise when Brian suddenly burst out from behind Mrs. Washington's ample skirts. He was dressed in his clown costume, and he giggled mischievously because he had surprised his guest.

"Well, what have we here?" Kendra asked.

His blue eyes sparkling, Brian tooted one time.

"And what does that mean?" she asked, her heart beating faster as she tried to get him to speak.

He tooted once again and smiled happily as he gestured first to her and then to him.

"Are you a clown?" she asked.

He nodded vigorously.

"But where is your makeup?"

Cleverly he pointed to the makeup kit she was carrying. Kendra laughed openly, and she was happy to hear Brian copy her laughter.

"Well, come on, then. Let's go to the bedroom and get you made up."

Her heart pounding madly, she walked down the hall with Brian. Her feet slowed as they went up the steps to the second floor. Perhaps she shouldn't use Gable's bathroom, even though he had said it had the best lighting. She could make Brian up downstairs. She looked down the hall hesitantly, and before she could turn back, Gable walked out of his bedroom.

"Good evening," he said warmly, leaning back against the door frame, his arms crossed.

"Hello," she said softly. Her eyes skimmed over him, noting the navy slacks he wore and the white of his tailored shirt across his muscled chest.

"Come on in," he invited, his eyes dancing.

"I thought we might put Brian's—" She looked down at the boy when he tugged on her hand. He shook his head firmly, tooted once, and pointed to himself. "Excuse me," she whispered. She looked back at Gable, a smile playing on her mouth. "I thought we might put Toot's makeup on in your bathroom, but I'm sure the one downstairs will work just fine."

"No, come on in. I insist. I do have the best and biggest of everything in here—the lighting, I mean," he said with a playful smile.

Kendra couldn't seem to keep a civil thought

in her head as she glanced at the bed when she and Brian walked through the room. She felt breathless, and her insides trembled as she recalled the way Gable had made love to her on that big bed. Fighting to keep her mind on the child, she set him on the stool that had been left in the bathroom.

"Who helped you get dressed, Toot?" she asked, encouraging him to speak.

"I did. It's one of the things I do well, dressing and undressing people." Gable spoke behind her so that his warm, teasing voice sent a shiver over her skin. She didn't know how she would get through this hour with Brian. She had such a heightened awareness of Gable that her nipples tightened against the lacy bra beneath the baggy shirt she wore.

She started when Mrs. Washington unexpectedly rapped at the door. "I'll be leaving now, Mr. Hunt. I'll come back at seven in the morning."

"Fine, Sarah. Enjoy yourself."

Kendra looked back at him when the woman had gone. "I thought Mrs. Washington lived here during the week."

Gable nodded. "She does, but tonight she's going to see her new granddaughter."

"I see," Kendra murmured, but she could only think that she and Gable would again be alone when Brian went to bed. She forced the thought from her mind. She was going to spend her time with the boy, then go directly home. She wasn't going to spend any time with Gable until Saturday. She had to stick to that resolution to protect herself. Everything was happening too fast, and she needed time to adjust to her new place in Gable's life.

As though reading her mind again, he smiled at her. "I'll leave you two clowns to your tricks," he said. "If you need me, I'll be in the library."

Kendra nodded, then asked, "How's Genna? Have you seen her since—since—"

"Yes, briefly. She came to see Brian for a while, but she told me she's spending more time at the store now that she knows you're here with the boy."

"I see." Kendra glanced at Brian, and when she looked back, Gable had gone. For the first time since arriving, she allowed herself to breathe normally. "Now, Brian," she said as she made up his face, "tonight we're going to do things as a team. Do you know what that means?"

He shook his head.

"It means that I need you to help me with my clown tricks or I won't be able to do them."

His blue eyes grew big and wide; he seemed thrilled at the idea of being needed. But abruptly his happy face drooped, and he pointed to Speckles, who lay on the bathroom floor with Puppy.

"What about Speckles?" Kendra prompted.

Brian pointed to the dog, then to Kendra, as he held up two fingers.

She laughed at his ingenuity. "Yes, we are a twosome, but I need a human clown for these tricks. Will you help me?"

He nodded vigorously.

Her heart began to beat faster. "To help me tonight, Brian, you will need to speak. Can you do that?"

He looked up at her as if she had struck him, his eyes seeming much larger with the whiteface around them. For a moment she thought he was going to cry. He struggled to get control of himself, and she sighed unhappily as he slowly shook his head.

"Why not?" she asked with pretended calm. "I speak to you. Why won't you speak to me?"

He seemed to ponder the question, his dark brows meeting in a frown, his lips drooping exaggeratedly beneath the red mouth she had painted on his face. His whole body seemed to sag at once. He lowered his head to stare down at his legs concealed in the baggy pants.

Kendra thought her heart would break as she watched the small child struggling with his problem. She couldn't stand it. He was trying so hard, and she really believed that he was making some progress. He had been happy and laughing when she arrived.

"Well," she said with forced nonchalance, "if you don't want to speak tonight, we'll have to put it off until Wednesday. We'll work on the tricks that only require hand signals between us as a team tonight. How's that?"

He raised his head to nod halfheartedly. Kendra wanted desperately to see his happy smile again. She tooted her horn twice, startling him, and a slow smile spread over his face. Then she lifted him up in her arms and held him in front of the mirror.

"Look, Brian," she said cheerfully. "We're twins! A big clown and a little clown!"

As he studied their reflections in the mirror his good humor was soon restored.

"Are you ready for those tricks now?" she asked.

He tooted his horn twice, and she stood him on his feet. Then they went down to the den where there was lots of space. Kendra took an assortment of props from her pockets and laid them out on the floor. Brian watched interestedly as she unfolded a long red rope. He eagerly took one end when she handed it to him.

"Now, what we do is make it look like you're pulling against me," she said, tugging lightly on the rope. "Then, after what seems to be a struggle, I loosen my grip and it appears that you have pulled me down. Understand?"

He nodded, eager to try the trick, but before he could, Speckles suddenly jumped up and grabbed the rope from his hand. This was her trick, and she wasn't about to be cheated out of it. Brian tried to take it back, but Speckles was a jealous partner. Suddenly she grabbed it from Kendra's hand, too, and raced down the hall with it.

Squealing with delight, Brian chased after her, Puppy at his heels. Kendra could have retrieved the rope easily. Speckles was well trained and would return when she was called, but Kendra felt that the boy was having too much fun. She went into the hall to watch the child and dogs having a tug-of-war with the rope.

"What's going on?" Gable asked, joining her.

"Oh, I hope we're not disturbing you," Kendra said. Then she pointed down the hall. Brian was on the floor, laughing with abandon as he tried to seize the end of the rope that dangled from Speckles's mouth.

Gable smiled, then he moved closer to Kendra. "You always disturb me," he murmured low. "You always have, don't you know that? I couldn't sleep last night, and I couldn't work today for thinking about you." He reached out to let his fingers brush teasingly down her chest.

"Gable!" she admonished, afraid Brian would see, but she couldn't stop the shiver that raced over her skin at Gable's slightest touch. "Don't."

"You don't mean that," he murmured, looking at her thoughtfully. For a frightening moment he was afraid that she might have decided not to let him make love to her again.

"This is my evening with Brian," she whispered, but her words didn't have the conviction she meant for them to have. "You know the rules."

"But don't you want to break them just once?" he whispered, his eyes perusing her face.

"I've broken them too often already," she said.

He grinned wickedly. "And you'll do it again, you know."

Her smile was vivid for only an instant. "Perhaps." She turned back to the dog. "Speckles!"

The little dog came running with the rope, and

Brian wasn't far behind. Kendra glanced at Gable once more before giving all her attention to the child. "Tell you what we'll do," she said to Brian. "We'll include Speckles, then she won't steal the rope."

When Brian nodded agreeably, she led him and the two dogs back into the den. She didn't look back at Gable again. She didn't have the nerve; she was afraid she would weaken.

Many tricks later Kendra was amazed to see what a natural Brian was. She ruffled his hair. "You are very good! You're the best little clown I've ever worked with."

His blue eyes glowing, Brian suddenly hurried away. Kendra shook her head. She knew where he was going. He wanted his uncle to see his clowning.

Minutes later Gable entered the room. "I think he has something he wants me to do," he explained to Kendra.

She shook her head. "He has something he wants to show you. Watch."

Gable stood by interestedly as the trio worked out the routine they had been practicing. "Oh, no," Gable groaned in mock despair, "not *two* clowns," but he laughed delightedly when Speckles supposedly helped Brian tumble Kendra to the floor.

All smiles, Brian ran over to his uncle.

"Very good," Gable said. "I'm really impressed." He looked at Kendra. "Is it my imagination or is my boy a quick learner?"

"A very quick learner," she said. Then she

couldn't help adding impishly, "And a natural clown. It is a *talent,* you know, Mr. Hunt."

Gable's brows rose. "Do you really think he's talented?"

"Indeed I do. Watch the trick again. Brian has been practicing about an hour. Notice the timing with Speckles on his end of the rope." She smiled at Brian. "Come on, let's show this disbeliever—and for free, yet!"

Gable laughed and clapped when the routine had been completed. Brian looked like he might burst with pride. "Well, partner, how do you like being a clown?" his uncle asked.

He held his breath, as did Kendra. Brian was so excited that they both just *knew* he was going to talk. But once more they were disappointed. This time he raced over to Gable, drew him down, and planted a big kiss on his uncle's mouth.

Kendra was moved by the scene, and to cover her tender emotions she told Brian, "I'm jealous. Where's my kiss?"

His face all smiles, he raced over to give her a hard, brief kiss. Then he stood between the two adults, full of self-importance. They watched him and smiled at each other. Kendra squealed in delight as Brian suddenly bent down and kissed Speckles on the nose.

"Good heavens, Brian," Gable said, joking, "I think it's time we unclowned you and put you to bed before you start kissing the rope."

The smile instantly evaporated from Brian's mouth, but Gable was firm. "Your tutor will be here in the morning. It's time for you to go to bed. Now don't make Kendra think she shouldn't have come at all. You know how she feels when you cry."

His head lowered, his mouth trembling, Brian looked at her from beneath long lashes. "Good night, Toot," she said softly. "I'll see you on Wednesday."

He nodded solemnly, then plodded slowly from the room, Puppy at his heels.

"You've spoiled him," Gable said, "but I love you for it." He wanted to say much more, but he thought it was still too soon. They had to go step by step, for both their sakes.

Still, as he looked at Kendra's clown face, he knew that he loved her. He reached out to take her hand, and Kendra let hers linger there only briefly.

"I have to get home too," she murmured, afraid of the fire in his touch.

"Stay the night with me," he coaxed.

Kendra wanted to, but she was determined that she wouldn't. There was no way she could be logical when she was in his arms.

"I've had a long day," she said. "I need to go home."

"Are you sure?" he whispered, reaching out to touch her chin with his forefinger.

When she nodded, he lowered his head and gently kissed her red mouth, smearing her makeup on him and her. She let her mouth caress his, but she dare not put her arms around him.

211

Their lips clung sweetly together, neither Kendra nor Gable wanting to be the one to end the kiss.

"Good night," she murmured when he reluctantly freed her. "I'll see you on Wednesday."

Then she retrieved Speckles, the rope, and her makeup kit. When she was ready to leave, Gable followed her down to the front door, then watched as she went to her car. He could feel his body tighten with need for her. And he wondered where it would all lead. What would Saturday bring? What would be the outcome of Sunday?

Shaking his head, he went back upstairs to see that Brian had gone to bed. But his heart was as heavy as his leaden steps.

Kendra was shaking when she climbed into the car. She wanted so much to lie next to Gable, to feel his warmth and his love, to let him take her away to that special place.

For several minutes she sat there, wavering between going home and returning to Gable's arms. This time she was weak, too weak to leave. She would let him make love to her, against all her better judgment and determination.

On swift feet she ran back to the door, Speckles in her arms. Gable had just left Brian's room when he heard a faint knock on the front door. His legs shaking, he hurried back down the stairs to fling the door open.

"Oh, Kendra," he murmured, drawing her back inside and holding her to his body.

"I couldn't remember the way home suddenly. I guess I'll have to stay here. That is, if you don't mind."

212

He held her a little way from him. "You know I don't," he said. "I was trying to get ready for a long and lonely night. I promise you won't be sorry you're staying."

"We both will if you don't let me take a shower," she said with a lightness she didn't feel. Her voice sounded funny and breathless, and she was shivering.

His eyes glowed instantly. "Let you take a shower? I have a better idea. I'll help you. I much prefer kissing you without that mustache."

She was about to protest when he lifted her into his arms and marched up the steps with her. Kendra took off her brows and mustache as he carried her up to his bedroom. Gable kissed her again before he put her down, and she laughed at the sight of him with whiteface on his nose and cheek.

"You'll need a shower if you keep that up," she said.

"Any excuse," he joked, already taking off his clothes.

For a moment she stood silently watching him, again thinking he was perhaps the most handsome man she had ever seen.

"Are you waiting for me to undress you too?" he asked. "Or are you only enjoying the view?"

As her cheeks began to turn pink beneath the makeup, Gable drew her into his arms again. "I'm glad you like the view," he murmured, letting his hands run down her body. Abruptly he pushed her from him. "But let's get you out of

213

this getup so I'll have something beautiful to see."

Adroitly he began to undress her. Kendra shivered as he lingered over the task, his fingers teasing and exploring the satiny skin he exposed. At last she was standing before him nude. He grinned at her, and she glanced in the tall bureau mirror. She had taken off her derby to put her mustache and brows in, but she still wore her wig and whiteface.

Abruptly she pulled the wig off and shook her hair loose. Then she turned toward the shower before Gable could catch her again. Seconds later she was standing beneath the warm water, watching her makeup run down her body in white rivers. Gable stepped into the shower behind her and closed the door.

"I want to bathe you," he said huskily.

Kendra could only nod in agreement as he soaped his hands and ran them over her skin, down her back to her shapely derriere, and around her slim thighs to the thick, curling hair between her legs. She drew in her breath sharply as Gable touched her with the gentlest of caresses, sending swift spirals of warmth curling up deep inside her.

When he slid his hands up over her stomach to her breasts, she felt her nipples tighten as he made circles around them. The circles grew smaller and smaller until he was teasing the peaks with only his forefingers. When he bent his head, claiming one throbbing tip with his lips, Kendra moaned and reached out to him.

While the warm water cascaded down over them her fingers played with the hair on his chest, then trailed down his stomach and abdomen. Gable sucked in his breath sharply when her fingers tentatively touched his potent masculinity. His sweet groan of desire was lost inside her mouth when he raised his head to caress her lips possessively, his tongue seeking hers.

He had already tasted Kendra's treasures, and tonight, because she had almost walked away from him, he was even more eager to claim her. He drew away from her long enough to turn off the shower. Kendra watched as he closed off the tub and it began to fill.

In minutes the warm water was swirling around in the huge navy tub, the Jacuzzi having been activated. Gable sat down on one of the built-in seats, then drew her on top of him. Kendra cried out in pleasure as he eased into her trembling body, filling her.

She braced her hands on each side of Gable and closed her eyes, abandoning herself to the thrills inside her as he slowly eased her up and down. She was shaking with desire, crying out her delight time and time again as ecstasy exploded inside her with each delicious, erotic movement.

"Now," she murmured excitedly. "Oh, now, Gable. I can't wait."

His husky laughter washed over her. "You don't have to. I'm ready," he said thickly as he increased the rhythmic pace of their loving, thrusting deeply inside her as he brought her down on him again and again.

Kendra was lost to all but the thrill of their exquisite desire as she and Gable crested love's wildest waves. The water whirled madly around them, heightening their passion.

Gable stayed inside her, holding her body to his as the fires inside them cooled. They could hear the water gurgling and rushing all around them, and Kendra relaxed against him as he stroked her breasts and thighs with gentle caresses.

When he withdrew moments later, she slipped down beside him on the contoured seat and rested her head on his shoulder. "We'd better get out of here before we turn into prunes," she murmured reluctantly.

Gable smiled at her as he nodded. Her hand in his, he shut off the water. When he had taken two thick towels off the bath racks, he dried first himself, then her.

"I'm pleased you stayed," he whispered as he lightly kissed her mouth.

She smiled softly. "Mmm, me too."

"You look exhausted," he commented.

"Yes, but a nice exhausted."

"Ready for bed?"

Kendra nodded. The invitation sounded too tempting to resist. She let Gable take her in his arms, and she shivered again as she slipped beneath the gray sheets. She suspected that the loving was far from over.

CHAPTER FIFTEEN

Kendra eased out of Gable's arms before daylight. He didn't awaken as she silently slid from beneath the sheet and pulled on her baggy pants and shirt. In minutes she had donned her big shoes, found Speckles, and slipped out the door.

The morning was crisp and fresh; she smiled a little as she made her way back to Darcy's. She knew she had no reason to feel so good—if anything her situation was all the more impossible because she had fallen in love with Gable—but she felt satiated in the way only a woman who's been well loved can.

Darcy was baking bread and frying apples when Kendra went into the house. She tried to make her way quietly down the hall, but it wasn't easy to sneak around on the hardwood floors at Darcy's house.

"Breakfast will be ready in about fifteen minutes. Fried apples, bacon, eggs, and hot biscuits," Darcy called out.

Kendra was grateful for the old woman's thoughtfulness and discretion. "Thanks, Darcy. I'll be down in a few minutes."

She took a quick shower, put her costume back on, and hurried back downstairs. The food was already on the table.

"It looks wonderful, Darcy," she said as she went to the cupboard for some dog food.

"She's already eaten," Darcy said, pointing to the dog.

"Thanks, Darcy. Are you keeping a running total on what I owe you?"

"No problem," Darcy said dryly. "I'll just keep that dog when you move on."

Kendra looked at the other woman with a startled expression, and Darcy laughed heartily. "Don't looked so shocked. I'm only fooling. I know that not only do you love that animal, but also she's your bread and butter."

"We have a new partner now," Kendra informed her as she scooped up a forkful of apples. "You should see Brian do the rope trick with us."

"Really?" Darcy asked interestedly. "How is he? Has he said anything yet?"

Kendra shook her head, disappointment evident on her face. "Not a word, but he's certainly in good humor these days. Oh, Darcy, you'd love that little boy. He thoroughly enjoys being a clown. You should see him puff up when he's in costume."

"I'd like to," the older woman said.

"Maybe on Wednesday I'll bring him over." Kendra thought it a good idea. That way she could stay out of Gable's tempting arms, because, as much as she savored his loving, she knew it would only make parting more painful when the time came.

"I'd love that." Darcy looked at the clock. "You'd better get a wiggle on. Shouldn't you be at the studio?"

Glancing at the clock, Kendra was surprised at how rapidly the time was passing. She took a couple more bites of food, washed it down with coffee, and stood up.

"Come on, Speckles," she said. She smiled at Darcy over her shoulder as she headed out the door. "Thanks, Darcy. You're a real friend."

Darcy waved and went back to her food.

The producer was waiting for Kendra when she reached the studio. She glanced at her watch, wondering if she was late, in spite of all her hurrying.

"Kendra, just the gal I'm looking for," the robust man said. "How would you like to do me a tremendous favor?"

"If I can," Kendra said cautiously.

"Oh, you can. This is right up your alley. My wife told me to get some entertainment for our granddaughter's eighth birthday party tomorrow night, and I forgot all about it until she cornered me this morning. What are my chances of hiring you for a couple of hours tomorrow evening? You can leave work early."

"Gee, I'm sorry," Kendra said. "Tomorrow's my night with—" She paused, then continued. "Tomorrow's my night to spend with a little boy who's a friend of mine, but I'd love to do the party if I can bring him. He's an aspiring clown," she added.

"That'll be great," he boomed. "Just great. You just set the price and I'll give you a check."

"No fee," she said. "This is on me. I love my work."

"I can't let you do it for free," he said, frowning.

"Free or not at all."

For a moment he looked exasperated, then he smiled. "Then I'll take it, with thanks." He handed her a business card and gave her directions to his home. "Will six be all right?"

"Fine," she said, walking with him to the set. "We won't disappoint you."

He smiled. "I know you won't. You're really quite good, as I'm sure you know. That's why you were selected for the film role. By the way, have you done anything besides the clown act in front of the camera?"

"Not really. The commercials I did were as a clown too."

He was pensive for a moment, then he slapped her on the back. "Guess you and I had better get to work. Thanks again for tomorrow night."

"My pleasure," she assured him, grinning.

The day passed quickly, and Kendra could hardly wait to get home. She was full of plans for the birthday party. She was excited about having Brian work with her.

When she pulled up in front of Darcy's, she remembered that she had told the woman she would bring Brian by on Wednesday. She shrugged her shoulders. "Oh, well, Darcy can see our act another night."

She explained the change of plans to Darcy and then called Gable. He was delighted and thought it would do wonders for Brian's self-esteem. Kendra felt truly excited when she hung up the phone.

Gable had Brian dressed in the clown costume when Kendra parked in front of the Hunt house the following day. The air was fairly crackling with excitement as Gable watched Kendra make up the boy. When he was ready, they went to the car, Brian marching down the sidewalk like he was the most important person in the world.

Kendra smiled at Gable over the boy's head. "I don't know how long we'll be. Probably only a couple of hours," she said. "But I'll return him to you." She could see by the look in Gable's eyes that he would like to go to the party, too, but she couldn't invite him.

The producer's house was modern and even more palatial than Gable's, Kendra observed as she drove up the long, winding driveway. A young man came forward to park the car. He smiled when he saw the little and big clowns.

"Come on, partner," Kendra said, adopting Gable's term for the boy as she helped him from the car.

Swelling with pride, Brian swaggered up the walk. It was all Kendra could do not to laugh aloud at the child. He was in his element in the clown costume, and Kendra was thrilled that he was so cocky. Now, if only he would begin to talk again . . .

The entire basement of the massive house had been turned into an entertainment center. After a butler led them downstairs Kendra found that all the children were already there. The room was filled with noisy chatter, which only increased when they entered the room.

Cries of "Look, clowns! Clowns!" went up, and Kendra smiled at Brian.

For just a moment she saw his hesitation as he surveyed all the children, then he straightened his shoulders, pulled his derby down farther on his forehead, and smiled broadly.

Kendra did several routines first, then worked with Speckles, before the three of them did the rope trick. She had to admit that she was more nervous than Brian. She wanted so badly for this first time to go well.

She tugged. Brian and Speckles tugged. She appeared to tug harder, pulling them far forward. They tugged, and so the performance went for several minutes, until at last she pretended that they had bested her, tumbling end over end in a well-practiced fall until she lay on her back. The children howled with laughter. Kendra glanced at Brian, watching him savor the satisfaction of the love of the audience and the thrill of a performance well given.

To her amazement he gave an improvised little routine of his own, tooting his horn and tossing the rope down disdainfully at the big clown's feet. Then he took his derby off, and bowing with it in his hand, he and Speckles walked around the circle of children.

The little ham's trying to steal the show, Kendra thought, and laughed.

Suddenly Brian lost his composure. In his exuberance and excitement he raced back over to Kendra and wrapped his arms around her legs. She lifted him up in her arms and accepted his hard kiss to the children's delight, and when Speckles howled in jealousy, she held Brian down so that the little dog could be picked up in his arms.

Speckles, apparently not wanting to miss out on her share of the act, suddenly licked Brian's nose. The children laughed and shrieked, and Kendra found herself thinking that she could never duplicate this performance. Then she nodded slowly to herself. She *could,* and she and Brian couldn't miss! He would be wonderful for the morale of other children in the hospitals.

She put the boy and dog down, and the three of them took another bow. Both she and Brian pulled wilted flowers from their big pockets to toss to the eager children and they left while they were at the height of their glory.

Back out in the car, Kendra hugged the boy to her side. "Well, partner, we did it! They loved you! What did you think about that?"

Brian tooted his horn twice and bobbed his head up and down.

"Can you tell me what you felt when those children clapped and laughed for you?" she coaxed.

He nodded again, still relishing that moment.

"But how did it feel?" Kendra asked again, trying to get him to speak.

Brian just nodded again and tooted.

Kendra sighed in defeat as she started the car. She would not ruin the child's first special day by pushing him too hard.

"You were simply wonderful," she said. Then she drove them back to Gable's house.

He was waiting eagerly for their return. Brian raced up the sidewalk to the front door, greeting him triumphantly. "Well, how did it go, partner?"

Brian tooted his horn and rushed inside, motioning madly to show that the children had clapped and laughed at him. Then he magnanimously gestured over his shoulder to include Kendra and Speckles.

Gable bent down on his knees, and Kendra could see the hope in his eyes. "Tell me about it, Brian," he said encouragingly. "I want to hear all about it."

Brian went through all the gestures again while Kendra watched the disappointment mar Gable's handsome features. She wanted to hold him and tell him to be patient, but she, herself, was just as frustrated in her attempts to get the child to speak.

"Come on in," Gable invited. "I'll get some coffee for you."

"Thank you, but I believe I'll go on home," Kendra said, suddenly tired now that the performance was over.

"Are you sure?" Gable asked, closing the door after him.

Kendra nodded. "I'll see you and Brian on Friday."

As Gable walked with her to the car he asked, "How was he?"

"He was wonderful!"

"That good?" Gable asked.

"Excellent timing. The little ham even tried to steal the show," Kendra murmured.

Gable seemed amused and surprised. "But he didn't say anything?" he asked.

"Be patient," Kendra urged. "He's come a long way from the miserable little boy who lay so still in bed when I saw him such a short time ago."

"Yes," Gable agreed, looking at her meaningfully. "And you know how grateful I am."

Kendra nodded. "Good night, Gable. I'll be back Friday."

He looked at her longingly, then took her in his arms for the sweetest kiss before murmuring, "Good night."

The following day at work, Kendra was forced to face the fact that the movie was almost completed. The producer began planning cast parties and discussing the final takes with the actors and actresses. Then he walked over to Kendra and invited her to meet him in the cafeteria for lunch. She knew that he was grateful for her and Brian's performance at his granddaughter's birthday party, and she accepted the invitation.

She met him there at one, smiling when she saw him sitting at a table with the prettiest woman in the room. As she walked over she pantomimed, indicating that she wouldn't interfere if he wanted to woo the beauty with him. Everyone around them began to laugh, and the producer smiled good-naturedly at Kendra. Then he shooed the woman away, blowing her a kiss when she pouted prettily. That, too, elicited laughter, and Kendra was in a good mood as she sat down at the table.

"The special today is a cheeseburger and fries. I've taken the liberty of ordering for us," he said. "Is that all right?"

"Fine. My favorite."

"Good." He pulled out the chair next to his and helped Kendra into it, laughing as she bumped her shoes against the table legs. When he had settled his ample frame down again, he peered at her thoughtfully. "What will you do when the movie's finished next week, Kendra?"

She smiled. "I'm joining a traveling circus for the summer. It's time I moved on. I'm getting restless."

"Oh?"

She nodded. "I've loved working on the picture, but I love the circus too."

"Would you be interested in doing more movie work?"

"Yes, of course," she answered spontaneously. "This has been wonderful, but I doubt that you make very many clown movies."

He shook his head. "No, but I come across an

occasional funny script that might be right for you. You've a fine comedic talent."

"Do you mean a part that's not for a clown?"

"That's what I mean. You're a natural."

"Thank you," she said, truly flattered.

Their food arrived, and as they ate, the producer talked about one of the scripts he was considering. "Nothing firm yet, but I was just curious if you'd be interested."

"What girl wouldn't?" she asked a little breathlessly.

He laughed. "I want to thank you again for coming to entertain at Sherry's birthday party. You and that kid were marvelous."

Kendra grinned. "That was his first time performing before an audience."

"No kidding? Is he any kin to you? Maybe he gets his talent honestly."

"He's no kin," she said quickly. "He's just a special friend."

The producer took a final bite of his burger. "Well, I've got to get back. Don't forget what I said."

"No."

She watched as he walked away. Did he really think she could forget such a thing? Even if nothing came of it, she was excited just because he had mentioned it.

CHAPTER SIXTEEN

Friday night Kendra experienced the same sense of expectation she always felt when she went to Gable's house.

Brian and Mrs. Washington answered the door together. Although Kendra was disappointed not to see Gable, she tried not to let it show. Brian eagerly tugged on her hand, leading her to Gable's bathroom so that she could do his makeup.

Kendra was nervous as she knocked on the door. She half expected Gable to step out of the room and draw her into his arms. Instead Mrs. Washington came down the hall.

"Go on in. Mr. Hunt's not home. Some business matter. Oh, yes," she said, pulling a note from her pocket. "He left this for you."

Her fingers shaking, Kendra opened the piece of blue paper. "Will see you tomorrow at two," it read. "I believe it's circus day for us."

Kendra managed a trembling smile. This was better. She wouldn't be tempted to spend the night with him this way. A rush of disappointment shot through her, and she tried to ignore it. She knew she had wanted to stay with him. She had missed him in the past two days, and she kept remembering the way he had looked when she left Wednesday night.

She glanced down at the little boy who waited so expectantly for her to complete his clown look. "Come on, partner," she said, ruffling his dark hair. "Let's get to work."

While making up Brian her thoughts turned inward. She had been planning on calling the orphanage where she grew up and setting up a time to entertain the children. She did want to do that before she left, but oddly, the thought was causing her a certain amount of trauma. She didn't know how she would react. She hadn't been back since she left when she was eighteen, and there were many memories, some good and some not, connected to the home.

"How would you like to go with me to entertain some children?" she asked Brian impulsively. "I think you'd have fun."

He nodded and grinned. Then he tooted his horn for emphasis.

"Good," she said pensively. She would feel better having him with her, as if she had some family of her own, even if it was a temporary one. "Good," she repeated. "Let's get you ready and work on some new tricks."

The evening passed quickly as Kendra and Brian got down the specifics of a second routine. The boy was an amazingly quick study, and Kendra applauded him time and again. She also encouraged him to speak with the usual disappointing results.

When he began to tire, she realized that it was late. Guiltily she gave him over to Mrs. Washington and left. Unconsciously she had been staying much too long, hoping that Gable would return before she went home.

She slept poorly that night, her dreams distorted and confused: dreams of Gable and Brian and her years in the children's home. Years that included sporadic stays in other people's homes: a family who wanted a baby-sitter for their own six children; a man who wanted a companion for his invalid mother; a foster family who let her sample real family life but who kept no one child longer than a short time. Each time was a bitter disappointment and another rejection. Kendra had been too old to be considered a premium adoptable child, even if her mother had consented.

She woke up in a sweat. She couldn't wait to dress and get downstairs, where Darcy was busy cooking breakfast. Maybe she'd made a mistake coming back to her home state, regardless of the reason. Maybe she would be making a mistake to remain. This wasn't her life. These weren't her people. The circus was her home.

"Good morning," Darcy said cheerfully. "You're up early."

Kendra nodded, still trying to shake off her nightmares.

Darcy frowned at her. "Is anything wrong? Are you all right?"

Drawing in a ragged breath, Kendra picked up Speckles and hugged the little dog to her chest.

"I'm fine," she lied. "I just didn't get to sleep until late."

Darcy's frown grew. "Are you sure there's not something more? Anything you want to talk about?"

Kendra shook her head again, then impulsively put Speckles on the floor, went over to the old woman, and wrapped her arms around her. "You've been so good to me, Darcy. I won't forget you."

Darcy returned her hug. "Nor I you. You've been like family to me, Kendra. You come back anytime and see me. You'll always be welcome here—you and my dog grandchild."

The women laughed, then Kendra set the table while Darcy served up the food. The rest of the morning, they sat around talking, enjoying coffee and the warmth of each other's company.

Before Kendra realized it, it was time for her to dress for the day with Brian and Gable at the circus. Her heart began to beat faster at the thought, and she wasn't sure why. Was it because she'd be seeing Gable again, or because she was going back to the circus? She knew most of the performers traveling with the show, and she was looking forward to seeing them. The performance wouldn't begin until four today, so she, Gable, and Brian would have an hour or so to spend with her friends.

The thought thrilled her as she made her way up the stairs to put on familiar jeans, her white shirt, and loafers. She left Speckles with Darcy and headed to Gable's house.

Gable answered the door. Kendra drew in her breath when she saw him casually dressed in form-fitting blue jeans that outlined his lean hips and muscular legs. He wore a navy-blue pullover shirt and brown boots. He looked even more virile than usual, and Kendra ached in some way she couldn't quite define.

"How are you?" he asked, not missing the way her gaze skimmed over him. "Will I pass for a day at the circus?"

She smiled. "You'll do fine. Just fine."

Her smile broadened when Brian stepped out from behind Gable, hanging on to his uncle's leg. He was in cords, a blue shirt, and boots.

"Don't you look great!" Kendra said, thinking that the adjective applied equally to both of them.

"I'm glad we pass muster," Gable said in a low voice. "You don't look so bad yourself. But then, you've always been able to make me think that, no matter what you wear. Or don't wear," he added playfully, causing Kendra to blush as she looked at Brian.

She cleared her throat. "I guess you two fellas are ready to go."

Brian nodded and tooted his horn.

"What do you say we leave that here at the house," Gable suggested gently to the boy. "Kendra isn't taking her horn, and I'll bet you won't need yours."

"That's a good idea," she agreed. "We don't want to scare any of the circus animals."

Brian's forming frown quickly vanished at the mention of the animals. A sparkle glittered in his blue eyes as he looked up at Kendra. He let Gable take the horn, then put a hand in each of the adults', and prodded them to leave.

Kendra and Gable smiled at each other as they walked out the door, letting Brian pull them down the sidewalk to the car.

The circus was still setting up in the fairgrounds at the far end of town when Kendra, Gable, and Brian arrived. The first show was to be at four o'clock, and everyone was in the midst of preparing for it.

"Let's go see Ruthie first," Kendra called out merrily. "She oversees the elephants."

Gable nodded, and Brian looked ecstatic as Kendra worked her way around behind the area where the circus was set up.

"Hey, you there!" someone called out. The three of them stopped as a brawny, bald man came running toward them. "We're not open yet, and you got to pay around front."

The tall, weathered man wore a T-shirt, worn blue jeans with a chain belt, and old boots with spurs. Gable looked at the burly bum, wondering what he would do if there was trouble, but Kendra turned around to face the man.

Suddenly she squealed a greeting. "Bad Bill! It's me, Kendra—Happy the Clown!"

A frown creased the man's face, making him appear even more menacing. Then abruptly he stepped forward and swung Kendra up in his arms to spin her around while she laughed happily.

"Baby," he bellowed. "Honey girl, how are you?"

Gable was relieved when the man set Kendra on her feet. "I'm fine, wonderful. And you?"

He shrugged broad shoulders. "Same as always. Doing all right. Back's a little achy now and then. I miss your massages."

When he glanced warily at Gable and Brian, Kendra happily introduced them. "These are my friends Gable and Brian Hunt."

Bad Bill extended his huge hand. "Any friend of Happy's is a friend of mine. Nice to meet ya."

"Thank you," Gable said with cool politeness. The man was friendly enough, but Gable simply couldn't see Kendra traveling with these people, living this life, giving this ruffian a massage, and he suspected that this day would only confirm his suspicions about the circus life. The gulf between his life and hers was already evident, and they had been here for only five minutes.

"Ya'll come on in," Bad Bill said. "Everyone will want to see you, Happy." Suddenly he turned to look at her again. "You still making that movie?"

She nodded.

"How's it going?"

Kendra began to talk animatedly about the movie as they made their way across the grass to a row of small trailers hidden on the other side of the main circus tent. Gable's sensitive nostrils contracted at the unfamiliar smell of the animals in their enclosures.

Suddenly a bleached blonde in heavy makeup

and a brief, spangled costume came running to-ward them.

"Happy! Happy! Honey, it's Darlene!"

Kendra whirled around to embrace the woman, who flung herself forward. "Darlene, how wonderful to see you!"

"You look gorgeous!" Darlene cried. "Are you signing on with us here?"

Kendra shook her head. "I'll be along in a couple of weeks. The movie is wrapping up."

"Good. We miss you. Things aren't the same without you."

Kendra kissed the woman's cheek. "I've missed you too. Oh, Darlene, let me introduce you to my new friends. This is Gable Hunt and his nephew Brian."

Darlene's eyes twinkled. "Happy, honey, how good a friend is he? He's so handsome! Is he taken?"

Kendra blushed. "Not yet."

"Well, welcome to the circus, big boy," Darlene cooed.

"Knock that stuff off, Darlene," Bad Bill said, glancing at the straight-faced Gable.

"Where's Ruthie?" Kendra asked.

"She's over with Talula. Some boys threw rocks at her in the last town, the dirty little bas-tards."

"Watch the mouth, Darlene," Bad Bill mut-tered. "The kid's got ears."

"Sorry," Darlene cooed, bending down in front of Brian. "Will you excuse me?"

When Brian nodded, she patted his head.

"Shy, huh?" she said. Without waiting for confirmation she told Kendra, "We're having an opening-night dinner in the mess tent after the eight o'clock show. You all will come, won't you?"

Gable had already started to shake his head when Kendra agreed. "Darlene, that would be great. Thanks. We'll be there. I'll get to see everyone that way."

"Okay, sweetie. See you then. Bye, Gable. Bye, Brian." She blew them kisses, then sashayed off in the direction of the costume trailer.

"We'll see you at dinner, Bad Bill," Kendra announced, eager to find Ruthie. Then she clasped Gable's and Brian's hands and hurried toward the elephants. "Ruthie's my mentor," she said excitedly. "This is the circus I started with, and I was scared to death. Ruthie showed me the ropes and eased me into circus life. I traveled with her in her tent, and I even rode an elephant sometimes in my beginning acts. You'll love her."

A silent Gable had his doubts, but he went with Kendra toward the animal pens just the same. There were half a dozen elephants of varying sizes, and Brian was so excited by the sight that he could hardly contain himself. As they neared, he hurried faster and faster.

Sensing company, an old woman in baggy pants, a man's shirt, and boots rose up from where she was bathing an elephant's leg. "What do you want—" she asked, then she spied Kendra and promptly worked her way through the tons of elephant flesh to the edge of the enclosure. "Happy! What a wonderful surprise!"

Gable had never seen a big woman move so rapidly. He stood silently by, watching a reenactment of the warm greeting the other two circus workers had given Kendra. He wondered if everyone loved her this much. At last he understood why she considered these people her family. They welcomed her like a much missed relative—or, he thought pensively, a fairy princess.

"Hello, Ruthie," Kendra said, leaning forward for the woman's kiss. "How are you?"

"Crusty as ever," Ruthie said. "Somebody hit Talula with a rock, and I'd like to break his neck. I've been worried silly about her. She's leading in the show tonight, but she's got a nasty cut on her leg. But how've you been, honey? I got your card in D.C., but I haven't had time to write. You know how it is on the road."

Kendra smiled understandingly. "Yes. I'd like you to meet my friends."

Ruthie warmly clasped Gable's hand in both of hers when Kendra introduced them. "I'm so pleased to meet you, Mr. Hunt. And you, too, Brian," she said, ruffling his hair. "Father and son, are you?"

"Uncle and nephew," Gable explained.

"Looks like a fine boy," Ruthie said. She looked at Kendra. "This one's like my own daughter. She was not quite twenty when she joined us, and I watched out for her like she was a babe in the woods. Never a sweeter girl lived."

Kendra blushed. "Ruthie, don't overdo it."

"It's the truth," the old woman said. "She would help me wash down my elephants and feed them. She'd help anybody who needed it."

Gable nodded. She had helped him. She had helped Brian. She had helped at the hospital. She was a rare treasure. Clearly he wasn't the only one who thought so. It sounded as if a whole circus of people thought so too. Inexplicably he felt his heart sinking. Kendra loved the circus and the circus people. They loved her. She didn't want to give this up. He was afraid she *wouldn't* give it up.

He walked along beside Kendra, trying to seem interested as they went to inspect Talula's wound and sympathize with Ruthie; however, he was feeling too sorry for himself to empathize much with the aging elephant.

After a few minutes Kendra was off in search of James, the wild-animal trainer. Gable remembered the story she had told in the Italian restaurant about James, and he was certain she would be greeted with warmth and love by this man. He was correct.

James was a young, handsome man of talent and charm. He had a polish that the others hadn't had. Gable felt an unreasonable surge of jealousy when the trainer kissed Kendra fully on the lips.

Her face flushed, her arms still around the other man, she introduced Gable and Brian. Although Gable did his best to seem friendly, he was becoming increasingly tense. He felt a desperation that he hadn't known in a long time. These people, this place, were a part of Kendra.

He was vastly relieved when it was almost time for the show to start and the ringmaster showed the three of them to some of the better seats in the house.

Gable hadn't seen a circus since he was a child, and he had to admit that once the show started, he was captured by the magic just like the rest of the crowd. There were three rings, and they were full of activity for two hours, with everything from acrobats to performing bears.

"I'm glad we came," he told Kendra.

"I'm delighted to hear that," she said, smiling a little shyly at him before looking back at the dancing bears.

When Gable glanced at Brian, he smiled tenderly to himself. The child was in his element, his eyes glued to the rings, trying to see everything at once, especially each and every clown who came out to entertain them.

As he looked at Kendra, Gable saw the same expression of rapture on her face. He watched as she squeezed Brian's hand repeatedly, pointing first one way, then the other, trying to make sure that he didn't miss a thing. Gable gave his attention back to the show. He didn't think he could bear to think about Kendra now. He was afraid. She was slipping slowly but surely out of his grasp.

When the show ended, it was decided then and there that they would return for the eight o'clock show too. In the interim they strolled around the grounds, eating cotton candy and hot dogs and sitting in the circus manager's trailer, talking with him. Gable wasn't surprised when the man asked Kendra to catch up with the show as soon as possible.

After they had sat through the second show they went to the mess tent, where there was more hugging and kissing as Kendra met old friends she hadn't yet talked with and introduced Gable and Brian to all kinds of people. For the most part Gable found that what Kendra had said about them being honest and open was quite true.

As he ate with them, listening to their tales and stories, he thought how basic and different they were from the society crowd he knew. The thought sent a chill over him. Tomorrow Kendra would have dinner with him at a senator's house. He wondered if she would receive the genial acceptance from his friends that he had received from hers. The answer that echoed in his head didn't please him.

He looked over at the dark-haired beauty as she talked amiably with a midget couple, giving them advice on a car commercial they were going to try out for. He looked down the long table full of circus people, seeing every conceivable kind of individual, except the kind he knew best—the upper crust—and he wondered if they were as happy as they seemed. They had put on a good show, and they were high with the thrill of success.

His gaze fell on Kendra again. Oddly she seemed to be the happiest of them all, and she hadn't even performed in the show. She was positively radiant under all the attention she was receiving. Gable couldn't recall ever seeing her more ecstatic—unless it was when she was making love with him.

Holding that thought close to his heart, he prayed that it would be some comfort when Kendra made her decision about leaving North Carolina—if she hadn't already.

Brian had fallen asleep before dinner began, and Ruthie had put him in her trailer. Gable could hardly wait to have Kendra all to himself, and he couldn't resist using Brian as an excuse to go. He saw a brief reluctance in Kendra's eyes, then she readily excused herself.

There was more embracing and kissing, then finally she, Brian, and Gable were alone in the car, returning to his house. Only then did he begin to feel secure again, though he didn't know if he had any cause. He just knew that he wanted to hold her in his arms again and dream that she would be part of his future.

If it was an impossible dream, as he suspected, he didn't want to think about that.

"Stay the night with me," he whispered. When she softly told him yes, he was more relieved than he could possibly say.

CHAPTER SEVENTEEN

The sense of desperation Gable felt carried over into his lovemaking. When he and Kendra had gotten Brian into bed, Gable couldn't wait to take her in his arms. Lifting her up, he carried her down the hall to his bedroom.

"I'm not that tired," she joked playfully.

"You'd better not be tired at all," he tried to say teasingly, but the words came out thick and urgent.

He needed her tonight. He wanted to show her all the love and tenderness he had in his heart. He wanted her to know that he loved her as much—more—than all those circus people loved her, but his pride wouldn't let him say it. He was afraid that his words would be diminished by the many proclamations of love she had heard at the circus. He could only show her how much he cared.

Slowly, lovingly, he undressed her. After he had taken off his own clothes, he lay down on the bed beside her. He gently drew her into his arms and began to kiss her, his lips clinging warmly to hers.

Kendra wrapped her arms around his neck,

sighing contentedly as she molded her body to his, entwining her long legs with his muscled ones. She could feel the fire in her blood at the intimate contact with the man she loved, and she forgot all about the circus and her excitement at seeing her friends.

Gable had the power to make her concentrate on only the splendor of the moment as he caressed her willing body with a tender touch. His lips and hands were warmly persuasive as they stroked and loved her.

Kendra was touched and stirred by his unusually gentle and sweet ministrations. She smiled at him as he kissed her eyelids, her nose, the corners of her mouth, then gently sucked her lower lip in between his and teased it with his tongue. She was simmering with desire as he continued to love her, his hands tracing the shape of her body as though he might someday forget and have to rely on his memories.

The room was dark, but she knew each detail of his magnificent body and how his blue eyes glowed and his dark hair glistened. She opened her mouth in pleasure as his tongue trailed down the crest of her breast and erotically circled it. She shivered as he moved lower, tasting her body with his lips and tongue, sending thrills through her. He parted her legs and kissed the sensitive inside of her thighs until she quivered from the sensual sensations that seemed to center deep inside her.

Her fingers bit into his muscled shoulders as she urged him to complete the union with her.

She wanted to hold him to her heart and feel his heartbeat echo her own. She wanted to travel higher and higher with him on a trip that only two could take.

Gable had meant to love her leisurely tonight, but he found himself responding to her needs, and he could tell that she was ready for him. He rolled over on his back and pulled Kendra down on top of him, letting her know that he was as ready for love as she.

He drew her legs up on each side of his body and guided her into position to receive him. Kendra gasped at the sensations that shook her when Gable slowly filled her with his love. This time she controlled the rhythm of their loving, slowly, sensually moving her body up and down on his while Gable caressed her breasts and hips, his fingers finding their way down to the sensitive spots where the two of them were joined.

"Oh, Gable," she whispered, trying to make out his outline in the dark. "You feel so good, so very good," she said thickly.

His own passionate response was muffled when she leaned down over him and sought the sweetness of his mouth. Her tongue slipped inside to tease his before she resumed the erotic movements that sent them both spiraling toward the peak of passion. She continued to move faster and faster, suddenly caught in a whirlwind of desire.

"Now, love. Now," Gable said raggedly.

Kendra gasped as he put his hands on her hips and helped lead them both to the highest pinnacle of love. Gable's expressions of delight mingled with her own as they touched each other in the most intimate and rewarding way.

For a long time they lay locked in each other's arms, Kendra resting on Gable and listening to the slowing of his heart. He wanted more than anything in the world to tell her now, at this moment, that he loved her. But he didn't want to pressure her.

Neither of them said anything when Kendra lay down at his side. He held her close and kissed her damp forehead as he brushed her dark hair aside. She had given him total pleasure, and he hoped he had done the same for her. Tomorrow night she would walk in his world. And then— then they must decide what to do from there.

As he closed his eyes he prayed that some way, somehow they could overcome the impossible. That somehow they could compromise. He would tell her that he loved her. And if she loved him, too, as he dared to hope, wasn't that love enough to see them through?

Kendra awakened slowly, still drowsy from a night in Gable's arms. She wasn't quite sure what had disturbed her, but when she wearily opened one eye, she saw that Brian had lain down in front of her on top of the spread. She glanced over at Gable, who was snuggled up to her back.

Then she smiled tenderly at the little boy, who had already closed his eyes. She wrapped an arm around him and drew him nearer. Gable shifted slightly in his sleep, and Kendra listened for a moment before drifting back off herself.

When she awakened the next time, it was to the tug of Brian's hand. She pulled the sheet and spread around her and struggled to sit up in bed. She saw that both Brian and Gable were dressed.

They also had made her breakfast. She laughed delightedly when she saw the gourmet meal—a Spanish omelet, hash browns, juice, coffee, and cinnamon toast covered with melted butter.

"How wonderful!" she cried. "You must have made this, Brian."

She looked at Gable with teasing eyes.

Brian shook his head and pointed to Gable.

Kendra looked at the man again. "Not you? You didn't cook this. Is Mrs. Washington staying over this weekend?"

Gable laughed heartily, remembering how he had teased her on the picnic. "I'll have you know that I'm an excellent cook. I don't expect my women to do anything I can't do."

"Oh?" she murmured, the teasing tone somewhat subdued. "Your women?"

"Woman," he corrected. His blue eyes were serious when they gazed into hers. "Are you my woman, Kendra?"

Her eyes held his for a moment. She didn't know what to say. Did he want to know that she loved him? She laughed nervously.

Then she looked down at the tray of food. "I'm starving. This looks wonderful."

Gable tried to keep his heart from sinking as he handed her the tray and sat down on the bed. Brian scrambled up in the center of the bed and clapped his hands, encouraging her to eat.

246

"Have you had breakfast?" she asked him.

He had retrieved his horn, which he tooted twice, then proceeded to take half a piece of her toast.

"Brian," Gable said, "that's Kendra's breakfast."

"I have more than enough," she insisted. "Let him have whatever he wants. And how about you? Do you want anything?"

He grinned at her. "Yes. Lots of things. Are you interested in listening to my list?"

She pretended total absorption in the contents of the tray. She was afraid she knew his list, but she nodded, anyway.

His smile wavered. "Later," he said. "I'm going to clean up the kitchen while you eat." He dropped a kiss on her forehead and left the room.

Kendra gazed after him for a moment, then laughed when Brian reached over to take the other half of her toast. He grinned at her as if he had done something sneaky, and she laughed aloud.

When Kendra looked at the clock, she was surprised to see that it was almost nine. She and Brian shared the rest of her food before she sent him down to help Gable. After he had gone, she took a quick shower and put on her clothes. By the time Gable returned, she was dressed.

"Going somewhere?"

"Yes, in fact," she said cheerfully. "I'm shopping for a dinner dress. I don't want you to be ashamed of me. I'm sure it's a very dressy kind of to-do tonight."

He laughed and drew her into his arms. "I'd never be ashamed of you. You know that, don't you?"

"Maybe," she said, lowering her lashes as she toyed with his shirt collar. But she wasn't so sure. She was afraid the dinner would be filled with people who would look down on her, and she didn't think she could stand it if Gable were embarrassed because of her.

"It *is* a dressy affair," he murmured. "May I take you shopping? I'd love to buy you something pretty."

She shook her head. "No thanks. I pay my own way." She raised her lashes. "Unless you want to be sure that I select something proper."

"No, that's not why I wanted to go," he told her firmly. "You have excellent taste." He tried to smile. "You want me, don't you?"

"Yes," she said with an honesty that left him unprepared. "I want you, but I've learned that I can't have everything I want in life." She stood up on her toes to lightly kiss his lips. "Got to run," she said. "What time are you picking me up?"

"Seven. Dinner's at seven-thirty."

She picked up her breakfast tray, but Gable took it from her hands. "I'll take it down."

"Thanks. See you later." She smiled at him and walked ahead of him down the hall.

She returned to the house to find Darcy cleaning it from end to end. "My, but you're ambitious," she said. "Do you need my help?"

Darcy shook her head. "Just doing my spring cleaning. What are you up to?"

Kendra's smile fell a little. "I'm going shopping for a dress—an extra special dress. Gable is taking me to dinner at a senator's house tonight. There are thirty people invited."

Darcy's eyes glowed brightly. "Oh? That sounds downright exciting. I was just up in the attic going through a trunk." She frowned a little. "Did you just want to buy a new dress?"

Kendra laughed. "Good heavens, no! I need one. I'm not even sure what to wear. Gable said it will be dressy."

"You might not like this idea at all," Darcy said, "but I wonder if you would take a look at some of these dresses I've had put away. They're in bags and look and smell as fresh as a daisy. Most of them have never been worn. They're a size ten." She waved a hand. "Never mind. Of course you don't want to wear them. They're old dresses and they're not you."

"Don't say no after you've told me something so fascinating," Kendra insisted, really pleased. "Of course I want to see them. Do you think you have something fancy enough and current enough for this dinner?"

Darcy nodded. "I know about those dinners. My family was very prominent in this town at one time." She laughed deeply. "Before I flaunted tradition and ruined Mama's image as a society matron with my willful ways." She shook her head at some long-ago memory. "Mama bought these things for me to wear. They're the best that money could buy, and I tell you, they look just as lovely now as then." She shook her head. "Mama had such hopes for me but she died, and Daddy let me live just as I pleased."

"Oh, do let me see the dresses," Kendra coaxed.

Darcy motioned for her to follow, and the two women went upstairs, Speckles at their heels. Kendra was amazed by all the lovely, delicate pieces of furniture stored in the attic. There were heirloom lamps and vases and dishes.

"Why, Darcy, these look like items from Genna's shop," Kendra cried.

Darcy's green eyes sparkled. "You know why? Periodically I sell off some of the stuff to her." She made a grand gesture with her hand. "All Mama's. All absolutely beautiful, and some of it worth a fortune. But it was never me, Kendra. I couldn't bear to part with some of it, so I put it up here. Well, enough about that. Come look."

She opened an ornate chiffarobe and revealed a veritable treasure of beautiful clothes. "Now you tell me if you're not interested. Don't humor me," Darcy insisted. "It's probably a silly notion."

Kendra draped her arm around the other woman and squeezed her shoulder. "You're a silly notion," she said affectionately. "This is one of the nicest things anyone has done for me. I can see that the clothes are gorgeous, and they've meant something to you for you to have kept them all this time. I'm honored you're willing to let me wear one of your dresses."

Darcy began to uncover the lovely garments. "You can see that they're not me," she said with a sigh. "Poor Mama. She had such hopes. She shopped so carefully."

Kendra gently touched the first dress. "They're not me, either," she said. "They're more like Genna." She looked back at Darcy. "Oh, but they're beautiful. Maybe I don't know what 'me' is in a situation like this. I've never been invited to a senator's house."

"Now, don't you feel you should try these things on to please me," Darcy said.

"Darcy, these clothes are the most exquisite, the most beautiful I've ever seen. You couldn't make me leave now."

Darcy smiled and began to remove the dresses from their covers. She hung ten of them on the back of the door.

"Oh, Darcy!" Kendra squealed as they appeared, each one more beautiful than the other. "Don't take out any more. The decision already will be too difficult."

Darcy laughed. "Let's take them one at a time and see what we've got."

Kendra's fingers were trembling as she tried on the one that she considered the loveliest. It was a midnight-blue velvet bodice bustier with a lace skirt and matching lace jacket. The heart-shaped bodice clung enticingly to her high breasts, and the tiny waist fit perfectly before the skirt flared out into a middie length.

"You look beautiful," Darcy murmured. "This is you."

Kendra laughed nervously. "I don't know about that, but, oh, Darcy, I feel beautiful. No wonder Genna loves these lacy confections. I feel like such a lady. No, a princess, a fairy princess going to my first ball."

"It truly is beautiful on you, but do you like it?"

Kendra looked at Darcy as if she had lost her mind. "Can you seriously ask me that, Darcy? I'm a sane woman. I've got eyes. I never looked so good. Of course I like it." She admired herself in the cheval mirror standing in the corner. "If I eat dinner, however, I may come apart at the seams. What a tiny little waist this has."

Darcy laughed. "Let's see how the others fit. Perhaps you'll like one of the others better."

"I don't believe that's possible. I love this one!"

"Come on," Darcy said, eager to see the others on Kendra.

They were equally beautiful, but the young woman had her heart set on the first one, and she couldn't be persuaded to change her mind, not even for a black lace-edged middie with a gored hem that set off her dark hair and eyes.

Kendra tried them all on with a reverence that caused Darcy to laugh. "Good heavens, girl. They're only dresses, and they've been hanging there for forty years. They won't fall apart."

Kendra laughed. "I hope not! Gable would be so embarrassed."

Darcy frowned when she saw that Kendra was really concerned about what Gable would think. "He's just a man, Kendra," she advised. "Oh, he's Gable Hunt, all right. He's rich and he's powerful in this state, and his rich and powerful friends will be there showing off, but you're a very special girl. That's why he's invited you. You aren't nervous about this evening, are you?"

Kendra's dark eyes met Darcy's glittering green ones. This night was more than just a dinner with a lot of rich and powerful people. Kendra didn't know how to explain to Darcy that she and Gable were sampling each other's lives while they savored a bittersweet love that had no future.

"I want him to be proud of me," she said, telling the truth.

"Don't you worry," Darcy said fiercely. "He'll be proud of you. You just go and be yourself and have a good time."

Kendra smiled. "Thank you, Darcy. Thank you so much for sharing your life and your treasures with me. I'll be very careful with the dress."

"Don't you give it a thought! It's only a dress, and I'm sure it's damned glad to be getting out of that chiffarobe. If something happens to it, we have plenty more."

Kendra laughed delightedly. "Darcy, you're priceless." She bent over and kissed the old woman on the cheek. "Come with me to the circus tomorrow. I want you to meet my friends. You'd love them, and they would love you."

A little twinge of disappointment went through Kendra as she recalled her day with Gable and Brian at the circus. Gable had been tense and silent. But she had expected that. She had known that Gable Hunt wouldn't fit in with circus people. Just as she knew that she couldn't fit in with his rich and powerful friends.

"What a great idea!" Darcy cried. "Thank you, Kendra. I'd really love that. I don't know anybody who doesn't like a circus. Why, when I was a child, the real big ones used to come here and Daddy would take me."

Kendra smiled as the woman launched into her reminiscences of her circus days. Everyone loved the circus. Everyone but Gable.

The day passed in a whirl of activity as Kendra and Darcy prepared for the evening's event. Darcy found more treasures, from the shoes that matched the dress, to real teardrop diamond earrings she insisted that Kendra wear.

Kendra soaked in the tub for an hour, then did her nails while Darcy touched up the dress with a warm steam iron. Kendra was all aflutter by the time Darcy had used a curling iron that left Kendra's hair in charming ringlets. They brushed the loose curls away from her face and secured them with lovely old combs.

When Kendra was finally ready, she really did feel like a fairy princess. She knew she looked beautiful, but her thoughts kept returning to Genna. This was the kind of outfit Genna would wear, but Genna didn't have the bold attractiveness Kendra had. On Kendra, with her height and dark looks, the lovely old dress had a touch of sultry beauty that Genna could never have achieved with her fair looks.

Kendra was dressed thirty minutes before it

was time for Gable to arrive, and she nervously paced the floor, despite Darcy's compliments. Kendra did want Gable's friends to accept her, though she didn't know why it was so important.

When the bell rang, she hurried to answer it, for once beating Darcy to the punch. Gable, dressed in a slate-gray suit and white shirt with a silver and navy tie, looked very handsome. For a moment Kendra stared at him, thinking he was simply too appealing.

Standing silently at the door, Gable gazed at the beautiful woman before him. He had never seen anyone who appealed to him more. She was looking at him shyly, expectantly, but he couldn't seem to find the right words to tell her how lovely he found her.

He cleared his throat and tried to laugh. "You certainly found a dress that suits you."

His compliment broke the spell that had bound them, and Kendra laughed sweetly. "This is Darcy's dress. It really is beautiful, isn't it?"

"Isn't that my line?" he asked, entering the house while she held the door open for him. He took her hand. "Or am I only to tell you how very beautiful you look?"

"I accept any and all compliments," she said, smiling at him. She looked down at the dress again. "But isn't this wonderful? It's been hanging up in the attic for forty years. Darcy never wore it." She held out one navy shoe. "These are hers, too, and the diamond earrings."

When she gestured toward her ear, Gable pretended to move closer to see the earring, then he lightly kissed her neck. "My heart is pounding," he murmured against her neck. "I want to rush home with you and make love to you until you promise—"

Darcy stepped out into the hall, her green eyes glowing. "Isn't she beautiful, Gable?" she asked proudly. "Isn't she the most beautiful creature you've ever laid eyes on?"

Gable straightened and winked at the woman. "She is, without a doubt," he said. "I had no idea you were hiding such beautiful clothes upstairs, Darcy. If you had worn them forty years ago, some man would have carried you straight to the altar."

Darcy smiled. "Didn't want to go to the altar," she said good-naturedly. "I liked my life just the way it was. I still do," she added. "It's just a little lonely sometimes now, but whose isn't?"

"You can say that again," he agreed. "Whose isn't?" He looked back at Kendra. She, like Darcy, liked her life just the way it was, and he was deeply afraid that he could never convince her that she would be happy as his wife and Brian's mother.

"Are you ready to leave, my beautiful dinner companion?"

"Whenever you are," she said, wondering what he had wanted her to promise when Darcy suddenly came into the hall. She mentally shrugged off the thought.

They both fell silent as they walked to the car. Gable could feel that now familiar sinking sensation in the pit of his stomach. Kendra withdrew into herself, wondering why tonight mattered so much to her. She was an imposter in these clothes. She didn't belong with Gable.

CHAPTER EIGHTEEN

Many of the other guests were already there when Kendra and Gable arrived at the senator's sleekly manicured residence in one of the wealthier neighborhoods in town. Kendra could feel a slight dampness on her palms as she and Gable walked up the cobbled walk to the front door.

A butler greeted them, and immediately they were thrust into the midst of many gorgeously dressed men and women, most of whom stood around chatting with wineglasses in their hands.

"Gable, how nice to see you," a distinguished, gray-haired man announced, extending his hand. Gable shook hands with him and kissed the cheek of the woman at his side. "And who is this lovely young woman?" the man asked, looking at Kendra.

"Mrs. Washburn, Senator Jackson Washburn, I'd like you to meet Kendra McAllis."

"To what do we owe the honor of your company?" the senator asked, giving Kendra a charming smile. "I don't think I've heard Gable mention you before."

"Kendra's new to the area. She has a part in

the new movie being filmed at the studio," Gable explained.

"Ah, an actress. No wonder you're such a beauty," the senator said.

"I'm really a clown," Kendra told him. "I'm a professional clown who plays the part of a clown in the movie."

With one brow arched the senator looked at Gable.

Gable smiled. "It's true. I'll vouch for it. Yesterday we went to the circus and met her circus friends."

Kendra knew she wasn't imagining that Mrs. Washburn was looking at her differently. "How interesting," she said. "Shall I take her around and introduce her to the others, Gable, or do you want that pleasure?"

"Go ahead, dear," the senator said. "I need to speak with Gable for just a moment, if you two will excuse us."

Kendra had only a moment to wonder what the two men would talk about as Mrs. Washburn led her off. When she was introduced to each person, the other woman faithfully added that Kendra was a professional clown. Kendra was already growing weary of the surprised looks when Mrs. Washburn touched the arm of a sleek blonde who had her back to them. Kendra let her gaze skim down the daring red dress the blonde wore to the four-inch backless heels.

When the woman turned around, Kendra gasped in surprise. "Genna!" she cried. "Is that you, Genna?"

Genna frowned for a moment, then laughed with the tinkling laughter Kendra considered so feminine. "Kendra! I didn't recognize you." Genna held Kendra's hand and openly appraised the dark beauty. "You look exquisite, perfect."

"Thank you," Kendra said, resisting the urge to explain that the dress was Darcy's. "And you —I didn't recognize you, either. My goodness, how you've changed in the days since I saw you last."

"Do you like it?" Genna asked. "I feel so—so free!" She gestured to the cap of blond hair, which had been cut in a short, pixyish style and gave her a contemporary look. Her lipstick was as dark and bold as her off-the-shoulder dress.

"I think you look wonderful," Kendra said sincerely. "So very different."

"So do you," Genna said with a sweet smile. "My heavens, we've traded costumes. Do you realize that? You look like me and I look like you."

The thought sent a shudder through Kendra. She didn't want Genna to think that she was dressing to please Gable as Genna had done. Of course, she told herself, in a way she had, but only because she had had the use of clothes styled in such a manner that they were what Genna had always worn.

"Where's Gable?" Genna asked.

Kendra looked back over her shoulder. "He's talking with the senator."

"Zan's over there." Genna indicated a circle of men. "Let me take you over."

"Oh, would you take her around?" Mrs. Washburn asked. "I'll see to my other guests."

"My pleasure," Genna said sweetly. When they had walked a short distance from the others, Genna squeezed Kendra's hand. "It's so good to see you, Kendra. I've wanted to talk with you. I owe you much more than you'll ever know."

Kendra looked at Genna, her expression puzzled.

"I feel great!" Genna whispered. "Zan and I went to San Francisco last week to buy antiques. I had such a marvelous time!"

"You and Zan?" Kendra murmured, wondering if she was reading something into Genna's sentence.

The blonde nodded happily. "He was there for me all the time," Genna said, "and I didn't know it. I mean, I did know that he was there—but not for *me*. Oh, I sound ridiculous. Do you know what I'm saying?"

Kendra smiled. "Yes."

"Once I let go of the idea—the compulsion— that I must have Gable Hunt regardless of the sacrifices, I opened my eyes and saw a whole world I could love and explore. But how are things with you and Gable?" Genna asked, only a trace of discomfort in her voice.

Kendra sighed as they walked over to Zan. "The same, I'm afraid."

Zan spied them and stepped free of the circle of men. "Hello, Kendra," he said pleasantly. "What are you and I doing with these people?" he whispered behind his hands. *"Stuffy!"*

Kendra laughed as he drew Genna up to his side. "Except for this one. She has seen the light. Thank God," he said, rolling his eyes heavenward. "She's finally seen *me!* After years of wasted time!"

Kendra grinned at the couple. She really believed that Genna had seen the light. She and Zan were smiling at each other in that way new lovers have. Kendra felt a heaviness lift from her heart.

"I'm happy for you both," she said. She turned when a large woman came up behind her.

"Are you the clown?" the woman asked.

Kendra nodded as Genna made the introductions.

"Are you going to do some tricks of some sort for us tonight?" the newcomer asked.

Kendra glanced at Genna, who gave the woman her sweetest smile. "Ida, of course Kendra isn't going to do tricks, any more than I'm going to sell antiques or you're going to lecture on wildlife. You *aren't* going to lecture tonight, are you?" she asked with the same sweet smile and even voice.

The woman made a *tsk*-ing sound with her mouth. "Of course not! I'm here for dinner."

Genna nodded. "Of course you are, and so is Kendra."

With an angry look the woman walked away.

"Please don't make enemies on my behalf," Kendra whispered. "It isn't worth it. I would have dealt with her."

Genna giggled. "I enjoyed it. That pompous duck has intimidated me all my life."

Gable came up behind them, placing his hand on Kendra's waist. "Who intimidated you?" he asked Genna, drawing their attention to him. He forgot his question as he looked at her. "Why, Genna! What on earth have you done to yourself?"

"You make it sound like I just came out of a cat fight," Genna joked lightly. "Don't you like my new look?"

Gable boldly assessed her. "Yes, in fact I do. It really becomes you. It's just such a contrast from the pretty little Genna I'm used to seeing." He glanced down at her tall heels. "You look so chic and contemporary. You even look like you've grown in the past week."

Genna gazed at him pensively for a moment, and Kendra held her breath, wondering what the woman who had loved him for so long would way. "I finally grew up, Gable," she said softly. "I finally gained some height in my own eyes." They all laughed when Genna held out a four-inch red heel.

But Kendra knew there was double meaning in the woman's words, and she wondered if Gable caught it.

"It takes a good man to bring out the best in a woman, don't you think, Gable?" Zan asked smoothly. "Genna is the best." He smiled playfully at her. "I'm thinking of marrying her for that antique shop."

Gable laughed. "There are more reasons than a shop to marry this woman, Zan. She's a treasure herself. I'm surprised you've never noticed before."

Zan smiled. "I noticed. I just couldn't seem to open her eyes to the fact that I was a treasure too. She had to find that out in her own good time."

They all laughed again, and suddenly Genna's eyes became solemn. "What about you, Gable? Do you know when you have a treasure? Or are you too busy looking for what you think you want, to see what you really have?"

Senator and Mrs. Washburn announced that dinner was served, and the conversation ended as they went into the massive dining room. All through the meal Genna's question echoed in Gable's mind. He could hardly concentrate on the conversations being conducted with him as he pondered his long-time friend's question. He gazed at Kendra, watching as she easily talked with the people around her, and he wondered if she was telling tales about the circus.

For the first time he let himself admit that he had been worried that Kendra wouldn't fare well with these people. Yet as he watched her she seemed at ease and confident. And she looked so ravishingly beautiful. He didn't see another woman at the table. His eyes were only for Kendra. His heart was only for her. Yes, he knew what a treasure he had. Tonight he was going to tell her he loved her. And pray.

The dinner seemed endless to Gable, but finally it was over. He politely excused himself and Kendra and said good night. He wanted to get on with his plans.

As they drove, Kendra found herself thinking that Gable's friends weren't so bad. Oh, some of them had felt their importance, but that was true of all kinds of people from all walks of life. She had seen prima donnas in the circus too. She glanced at Gable, noticing how distracted he seemed.

He drove her back to his house in silence, and Kendra wondered how this evening would end. She still felt like a fairy princess in Darcy's dress. She had received many compliments on it, and she knew that Gable had been proud of her. She saw it in his eyes.

But what about now? She needed to tell him tonight that she would be leaving soon. She *needed* to, but she didn't know if she could. She felt like she had left so many things unfinished in this town. She wondered if she would come back again—ever—if the producer found another script for her. She wondered if Brian would ever talk. And she wondered if Gable loved her.

He parked in front of the house. "You did want to come back with me, didn't you?" he asked.

"Yes," she said softly. She felt beautiful tonight. She would feel more beautiful in Gable's arms.

"Good," he said. "I had no intention of letting you get away tonight."

Hand in hand they walked to the house. "Who's staying with Brian?" Kendra asked.

"He went over to Mrs. Washington's daughter's house to see the new granddaughter. She'll bring him home in the morning. He wasn't very happy about it. I think he suspected I'd bring you home with me, and he didn't want to miss seeing you. He loves you," Gable said as he unlocked the door and led her inside.

He directed her to the living room where he suddenly pulled her against him. "I love you, too, Kendra. You must know that. I want you to stay here with Brian and me. I want you to marry me."

Kendra closed her eyes. She told herself that she should have been prepared for something like this, but she wasn't. She was sure that the evening would make Gable see more clearly how unsuited they were, how impossible their love was. But it hadn't worked that way.

Her lips trembled as she tried to formulate an answer. "I love you, too, Gable. And I love Brian." She searched his face. "But I can't stay."

He made her look at him. "Was my world so bad? You seemed to fit into it rather well."

"But what about my world?" she asked tiredly. "What about my career?"

Gable exhaled wearily as he drew her down on the couch with him. "I'd hoped that you loved me enough to give up clowning," he answered honestly, knowing that he was asking the impossible. He had meant to talk of compromises, but he only knew that he never wanted her to go away again.

Kendra felt an unreasonable surge of temper. After all this time nothing had changed. No, she thought, correcting herself, that wasn't quite the

266

truth. A lot had changed. She loved Gable and he loved her.

But he had seen her world and how much she loved it, and tonight he could still suggest that she simply abandon that world. How could he claim to love her and still expect her to give up what was such a vital part of her life?

He tipped her chin up with his finger and saw the tears shimmering in her eyes. "I love you. I don't want to lose you," he said thickly. "I meant to talk of compromises. I *need* to talk of compromises. I'll give up my dreams of children of my own—beautiful children that I want with you —if you can give up your career, or at least compromise on it."

Kendra's brows drew together as she looked at his face. "You'll give up your dream of children? Why?" She had never expected to hear him say that. His first marriage had fallen apart over his desire to have children. Was it because of Brian? Because of her work? She didn't understand.

She saw the muscle twitch in his jaw and knew how much this was costing him. "Some women don't want children. I can accept that. But I know you love Brian. We'll be a family with him as our child."

"But *I* want children!" she cried.

He frowned. "You do? I thought you said— I believed, when you said some women weren't cut out to be mothers, that you were talking about yourself."

She drew his hands into hers and smiled at him. "You misunderstood, Gable," she said gently. "I wasn't talking about me. I was talking about—about someone else I knew. I want a boy and a girl."

He couldn't deny the relief that rushed through him, but before he could speak, she continued. "But I won't give up my career. Don't you know, Gable, that you wouldn't want me if I wasn't who and what I am? Don't you see?" She looked beyond him. "I need the circus. I need my people. I will not abandon them."

"*I* need you, Kendra," he said fiercely. "*Brian* needs you. How can you give us what we need if you're traveling all over the country with a circus? Don't you see how impossible, how *totally* impossible it is?"

She did see. She always had. She had told him that right from the start. She nodded. "Yes." Her eyes met his. "I'm sorry I couldn't be of more help to Brian," she said, her voice full of regret. "I know he'll speak someday. Please be patient with him."

"What are you telling me?" he demanded, feeling his throat tighten painfully.

"The movie will be finished next week. I'll join the circus the following week. I won't see Brian again after next Sunday. I'm taking him to the orphanage with me to entertain the children there, if you don't mind. He and I have been working on a new routine."

"Kendra, don't do this," Gable said tightly. "Don't walk out of our lives. Stay. We can make you happy. I know it."

Kendra began to withdraw as a method of self-protection. "I love you, Gable," she said softly, "but this isn't my life. I can't stay here." She stood up. "I think I'd better go. Will you take me home?"

"Kendra, please," he said sharply. "Don't behave rashly. We've got something beautiful, something rare. Don't turn me down now. Think about it. Think about our lives, our future."

"Please take me home," she repeated.

Gable tried to draw her back to him, but she had already retreated. With a ragged sigh he stood up. He had failed. He couldn't *force* her to stay in his life. And how could he say that he could accept her career as a clown? What kind of life would that be for any of them?

His face set in a tight mask, he drove her back to Darcy's house. Neither spoke when she got out of the car. Darcy was peering from the window and saw Kendra's tears start to fall before she reached the front door. Gable drove off without looking back. Darcy sighed as she let Kendra into the house.

"It didn't go well, did it?"

Kendra was already sobbing. "I'm sorry, Darcy. Excuse me," she said, rushing past the older woman, the navy heels tapping as she went down the hall and up the steps.

Darcy didn't know whether to go after her or not. Kendra seemed to want her privacy. With an unhappy sigh Darcy picked up Speckles and went into the living room.

Somehow Kendra got through the week. There was very little left to do at the studio, and the producer hadn't mentioned any more about a new script. There was a huge going-away party planned for the cast on Sunday night; Kendra was saving her good-byes until then.

She had lived through the most painful good-bye already, and she dreaded going to Gable's house Monday evening to spend time with Brian. She had to talk herself into keeping her promise to be there. But she didn't know if she would be able to carry on.

She anticipated falling apart right in front of Gable and Brian when she went to the front door of the house, but her fears proved unfounded. Gable wasn't home. Kendra found that she was happy to lose herself in the joy of clowning with Brian.

Wednesday was a repeat, and Kendra spent her time with the boy, working on the routine for the orphanage. But every time she saw the child, her heart cracked a little more. She hated to leave him as much as she hated to leave Gable.

Friday eventually came, then Saturday, and finally Sunday. Kendra had gone to the circus with Darcy Saturday, and she had promised the woman that she could go to the orphanage the following day. She was glad to have Darcy's company when she parked in front of Gable's house. His car was in the driveway, and Kendra didn't know how she would get through seeing him again. It seemed like weeks, instead of days, had dragged by.

He opened the door for them. "Hello, Kendra, Darcy," he said quietly. "Brian's ready, except for his makeup." His eyes met Kendra's as she entered the house. "I'd like to go with you if you don't mind."

"No, of course not," she murmured. She could hardly refuse. Brian was his nephew, and after all, Darcy was going. But she *did* mind. She didn't know how she would get through this final day. Not with both Gable and Brian to tug at her heartstrings.

CHAPTER NINETEEN

When Kendra had completed Brian's makeup, she led their little group out to her car. She was unusually tense today, and having Gable with them didn't help any. She could sense Brian's excitement and anticipation, but all she felt was extreme nervousness.

She hadn't been back to the home since that day when she had walked away at eighteen. She wondered if she would see anyone she knew besides the woman who ran the home. Her stomach felt so agitated that it hurt. She had awakened several times in the night with terrible nightmares still vivid in her mind.

Darcy tried to keep up light chatter, but Gable and Kendra sat tensely side by side in the front seat of the car. Occasionally he glanced at her, or she at him, but no other words passed between them.

Kendra's hands were shaking when she parked in front of the home. Bits and pieces of her past flashed through her mind. Once again she recalled how her own mother had walked away and left her, never to send so much as a single word inquiring about her welfare after that.

"Kendra," Darcy prompted.

Kendra visibly drew in a deep breath, trying to center herself as she had done so many times before a performance. But she couldn't seem to find herself today. She kept thinking about that young girl who had lived here for so many years, hoping that someone would love her. Tears rushed to her eyes, and she prayed that Gable wouldn't see. Somehow she found the strength to get herself in hand.

When she reached for her car door, she realized that Gable had already opened it and was gazing at her curiously. Embarrassed, she climbed out of the car and took Speckles from Darcy. The little dog gave her the measure of security she needed to keep walking until she reached the front door.

She rang the bell, then looked down at Brian as he slipped his little gloved hand into her free one. He smiled up at her, making Kendra wonder if he knew how much she needed him today. Instead of returning triumphantly and joyously, as she had intended, she felt lost and alone.

Then Mrs. Zennacoff opened the door. Just the sight of the woman brought back the good memories, the memories of times when Kendra had sat in this woman's homey office and had hot chocolate and oatmeal cookies while she talked about her hopes and dreams and disappointments. Kendra felt a warmth spread from her heart, which soothed her fears.

"Kendra!" the graying woman cried excitedly. "Girl, is that you?"

"Yes, Mrs. Zennacoff. It's me," Kendra said proudly, knowing that this woman shared in whatever success had come to the clown. She turned back to her companions. "This is Darcy Bogart, Gable Hunt, and Brian Hunt."

Smiling happily, Mrs. Zennacoff shook Darcy's hand. "So nice of you to come," she said pleasantly. "And don't you look adorable?" she asked Brian, leaning down. Then she straightened to grin broadly at Gable. "Mr. Hunt, you dear, dear man. Did you get the notes from the children thanking you for their Valentine presents? They were so thrilled with the hearts full of candy and the personal letters. I can't begin to tell you how much your time and care means to them."

Gable looked a bit embarrassed, and Kendra glanced at him in surprise. She hadn't considered the possibility of him supporting the orphanage, but of course he would, being such a prominent citizen.

"Thank you, Mrs. Zennacoff. It was my pleasure, I assure you."

Beaming, Mrs. Zennacoff indicated Kendra. "This is what becomes of some of our children, Mr. Hunt. Kendra lived with us from the time she was four years old."

Gable was taken aback, but he tried not to show it. Kendra had said she had lived in Boston. He remembered the conversation clearly.

"Well, come on in. The children are eagerly awaiting you," Mrs. Zennacoff announced.

"They're beside themselves with joy. Everybody loves a clown."

The line echoed in Gable's head. Everybody did love a clown, or at least the clown image. But he loved the woman. Desperately.

"As you can see, Brian is my clown partner," Kendra said. "He's very good, and children love him. As I told you on the phone, he wants to be introduced as Toot."

Kendra smiled broadly as Mrs. Zennacoff led them down to the recreational room where about forty children of all ages, from toddlers to teenagers, were gathered. There were shouts and cries of welcome as the clowns entered the room. When Mrs. Zennacoff introduced them, the children clapped loudly. Darcy and Gable grinned at each other, then took their seats so that Kendra, Speckles, and Brian could make their magic.

All eyes were on Kendra, Brian, and Speckles as they did their routines. In the spirit and feeling right at home now that she had broken through her fear, Kendra entertained the audience royally.

Brian's timing, once again, was incredible, and twice he stole the show from her. Kendra glanced at Gable to see him smiling proudly at his young nephew. She smiled to herself, wondering if Gable knew that he could never stifle the clown in the boy now. Once in a while she saw him talking with Mrs. Zennacoff, a frown marring his handsome features. But she tried not to wonder about the topic of conversation. She had a show to give.

"I'm so proud of Kendra," Mrs. Zennacoff

murmured. "It would have broken your heart, Gable, if you had seen that little girl sobbing in her bed night after night when she realized that her mother was never coming back for her. The mother dumped her off like a sack of potatoes one day when Kendra was four years old. Oh, it was a sad thing, but not an unusual one," she murmured behind the constant smile she wore for the children.

Gable could feel the ache begin in his heart for the woman he loved. No wonder life with the circus was so appealing to her. She had never had a real home. Oh, he was sure they had been good to her here, but it was an orphanage; it had to be something like circus life, with all the children and the workers pulling together to make a success of it.

"Was there no time in her life when she knew a normal family relationship?" he asked, his voice tinged with pain.

"She loved one foster family she stayed with, but it was only temporary, and Kendra begged not to be sent anywhere else again. She was so unhappy that we didn't force her. She concentrated all her attention on becoming a clown. She wanted to be like Emmett Kelly because she said everyone loved him."

As Gable watched the big clown and little clown work so smoothly with the dog, he began to put the pieces of the puzzle together. Slowly, enlighteningly, he began to see why Kendra had become a clown, aside from the obvious talent required, and why she was so adamant about not giving up the world she had found for herself where everyone loved her.

She no doubt helped the children because she knew how it was to hurt, and she had a heart full of love to give. He watched her working with Brian and wondered again how either of them would face the future without her.

The clowns finished their act to loud laughter and applause, and there were many happy children clutching faded flowers, balloons, and an assortment of gadgets Kendra and Brian had pulled from their oversize pockets.

"We're having refreshments in the dining room," Mrs. Zennacoff announced. "The children made them. Please join us."

She led the way to the dining room, and Gable marveled at the orderly fashion in which forty children marched behind them. A man greeted Kendra as she entered.

"Hello, Happy," he said in a warm voice. "I watched from the sidelines. You were great."

She tooted her horn and smiled broadly at the man. Then she impulsively gave him a kiss on the cheek, leaving a red smear.

"I've known her since I came to the home when she was ten," the man shyly explained to Gable and Darcy. "We're real pleased at how well she's turned out."

"You have a right to be pleased," Gable said, and Darcy agreed. "This is a fine place here, and she's a wonderful and loving woman." And he didn't want to let her get away.

Gable tried his best to keep his mind on the

events at hand, knowing that the children needed his attention and affection, but he could barely think of anything but the revelations about Kendra. He felt that he understood her now, and while he realized that she truly loved being a clown, perhaps he could be a part of her work and world now that he understood her better.

It was still early afternoon when they left. All Gable could think about was how much he wanted to be alone with Kendra so that he could talk to her. He watched as she told Brian how wonderfully he had performed, then he waited until the boy had gone inside. "I have to talk to you, Kendra."

"I'm sorry, Gable," she murmured. "I don't have time. I have to get home and get ready for a cast party at six-thirty."

He reached for her hand. "Surely you can spare me ten minutes. Darcy will excuse us."

"Of course," the other woman said.

Kendra shook her head again. She didn't want to be alone with him. There was no point. She was leaving in the morning.

"Kendra, don't throw our relationship away," Gable said. "I still think we can work this out."

Kendra didn't. They had tried and failed, as she had known they must.

"Good-bye, Gable."

"That's it?" he asked in an anguished voice. "You're going to walk away just like that without a backward glance?"

"I'm sorry," she whispered, her heart breaking. "We both knew it wouldn't work."

278

Gable gazed at her for a moment. He didn't know what else to say. He had told her he loved her. He had asked her to marry him. He had pleaded with her to talk to him. Now it really was up to her. He couldn't hold her against her will—and he wouldn't want her if he could. Without another word he got out of the car and went into the house.

Darcy looked at Kendra, but she, too, realized that it was useless to speak. The two women traveled home in silence. An hour later Kendra left for the cast party.

Her head was aching when she returned to the house three hours later. Not only had she eaten and drunk too much, she had pondered the producer's offer that she stay and do a part in a comedy he planned to produce. It wasn't the big part that he had promised, for this wasn't the film he had had in mind for her, but it was a chance for her to play Kendra McAllis instead of Happy the Clown. With much regret she had finally turned the part down.

She didn't want to stay in North Carolina, and she had promised Tom that she would travel with the circus that summer. But she had told the producer that she would be interested later if he had anything.

Now she wanted only to finish her packing, say her good-byes to Darcy, and leave town. But she couldn't seem to make herself carry out her plans in just that order. She owed it to Gable and Brian to see them one more time. She felt that she had to say good-bye. She could not take the coward's way out. They both deserved better.

She was already an emotional wreck after she said good-bye to a tearful Darcy and loaded her few belongings into her car. Then she climbed behind the wheel and headed out to Gable's house, praying that he would be home. Or maybe she was praying that he wouldn't be. She couldn't be sure.

It took her several minutes to summon her courage so that she could walk up to the front door. She stood there another moment before she managed to ring the bell. Gable answered.

"Kendra!" he cried, causing her to feel guilty about the hope she heard in his voice.

"I'm only here to say good-bye to you and Brian," she said softly. "May I come in?"

"Yes, of course," he said stepping back. No matter what she said, he couldn't stop the surge of hope that filled his heart. "We have to talk. There are things I have to know."

"What?"

"Why didn't you tell me you were raised in an orphanage in this area?" he asked her gently.

She looked at him, her dark eyes solemn. "Why? What difference would it have made?"

"A lot, I think," he answered. "I believe I understand you now, Kendra," he said, leading her into the living room. "I realize that you love the circus so much because it's your home and those people are your family—a home and a family you never had." He clasped both her hands in his and looked into her eyes. "Give Brian and me a chance to be your family, Kendra. Just a chance. Stay and let us give you the love you need. I think you'll be happy."

She shook her head, her heart beating rapidly. The night had been too much for her. She didn't want to hear this. "I can't give up my career," she insisted.

"I'm not asking you to," Gable said. "Let's talk compromise. Travel in the summer with the circus. Live with Brian and me nine months of the year. Just don't walk away from us. Please." He didn't want to pressure her; the decision had to be hers, but he couldn't let her leave forever without trying some way to keep her.

She shook her head. "No, it wouldn't work. You don't want a clown for a wife. And if I changed, you wouldn't love me. Don't you know that?"

The words Genna had said at the dinner echoed in his head. But he no longer wanted to change this treasure he had found. "I know that I would love you, no matter what, Kendra. You're not just a clown. You're a beautiful, sensitive, and caring woman with so much to give. Give your love to the world. Make people laugh. Make children happy. But give your heart and part of your time to me. That's all I'm asking."

"It just wouldn't work, Gable. You said so yourself. What kind of wife would a clown make? And I wouldn't be happy sitting at home for nine months."

A smile played on his lips. "I don't believe that, Kendra. I believe you want a home and a family. I believe you want something more than the distant crowds adoring you or the circus family welcoming you home. I'd give you something to keep you busy—that boy and girl you say you want. And you and Brian could perform your act close to home. Besides, I still think you have a chance at a movie career here. I know how good the producer thought your work was."

She nodded. "He offered me another small part—as myself, not Happy—but I turned it down." She stood up, suddenly feeling panicky. If she stayed, how long would it be before Gable regretted his compromises? She couldn't forget how quickly her plans with Wyatt had ended when he realized that she would not give up her career.

"I can't stay, Gable. It wouldn't work," she reiterated.

"Let me get Brian, then," Gable said quickly. "He wouldn't understand if you left without saying good-bye."

Kendra knew it was true, but she dreaded telling the boy that she was going away. She chewed on her lower lip nervously as she waited for Gable to bring him down.

He grinned like he'd been given a big surprise when he saw her, and Kendra's heart sank. She held out her arms to him, and when he ran across the room and climbed up into her lap, she looked up at Gable unhappily.

She cleared her throat. "I want to say good-bye, Brian," she managed. "This is the last time I'll come to visit, but I'll call and write," she added quickly.

Brian looked up at her as if she had struck him physically. He shook his head in disbelief, but she only held him closer.

"I have to go away," she said. "I came here to make the movie, and now it's time for me to join the circus again."

His eyes lit up as he gestured madly for her to take him with her. Kendra could feel her heart pound. This was much too difficult.

"I can't, Brian," she said. "You have to stay here with Uncle Gable."

Brian gestured furiously, frantically indicating that Gable could go with them, but Kendra solemnly shook her head.

"You be a good boy and keep practicing your clown tricks. One day I'll come back and see you. All right?"

She could feel the boy's desperation. His body was growing tense in her arms, and he shook his head again, fighting not to cry. Then the tears came. He clung to her neck and sobbed.

Kendra pressed her lips together and blinked her eyes, trying to hold back her own tears. "I love you," she whispered. Then she quickly stood the boy on his feet and fled from the room. She looked back over her shoulder once and silently whispered that she loved Gable too. Then she closed the door behind her.

Before she could get to her car, the front door of the house flew open. Brian raced down the sidewalk after her, his little legs pumping desperately. Gable was right behind him.

"Please don't leave me!" Brian cried, flinging

his arms around her legs to hold her there. "Please don't leave me. I love you."

Tears streamed down Kendra's face as she lifted the child up in her arms. She remembered how she had felt when her mother walked away. Brian had reminded her of that day so many times. He had made her face it at last.

Now he was feeling some of what she had felt when her mother left her. And this was the second time he would lose a woman he loved. How could she leave this child?

She looked back at Gable. She loved them both with all her heart. She did want something more than the circus and the crowds. She had told Darcy that the love of a single man was what really counted in this world. But she was just so afraid of giving up the security she had found with the circus.

Genna's words about Gable being a compulsion she had to leave behind to get on with her life echoed in Kendra's head. The circus had been her compulsion, her world. Perhaps it was time she let it go. There were other worlds open to her now—and this one came complete with a man and a child who loved her.

Several minutes passed before she realized that the miracle they had all prayed for had taken place. Brian had spoken! The realization swept over her all at once. She went over to Gable and put her free arm around his neck.

"He spoke, Gable!" she cried excitedly. "Brian spoke!"

"And did you listen to what he said?" Gable asked in a thick voice.

Their eyes met as Kendra set Brian on his feet. "Do we have a chance, Gable?" she whispered. "I do love you, and I love Brian." She looked back over his shoulder at the big, sprawling house. "Could we make it a home? Could we be happy? I mean forever, Gable. I don't want to taste heaven only to lose it."

Gable pulled her into his arms and spun her around. "I promise you we'll be happy—forever —as long as we live. I can say that with no doubts, Kendra," he said. "You love me and I love you. All we need is that chance to be happy, to let our love grow. We haven't even begun to taste heaven."

She locked her arms around his neck and looked into his eyes. "I believe you, Gable," she whispered. "I do believe you."

His lips closed down over hers in a sweet kiss that sealed his promise of happiness. Brian flung himself against their legs and laughed. They were a family, a happy family. There would be more laughter than tears through the years.

Rekindle your secret
yearnings for
romance and passion
with the splendid
historical novels
of

Vanessa Royall

___ FIRES OF DELIGHT 12538-3-15 $3.95
___ FLAMES OF DESIRE 14637-2-29 2.95
___ FIREBRAND'S WOMAN 12597-9-05 2.95
___ THE PASSIONATE AND THE PROUD . . 16814-7-11 3.50

M